HOLLYWOOD VAMPIRE

An Expanded and Updated Unofficial
and Unauthorised Guide to *Angel*

Keith Topping

This edition first published in 2004 by
Virgin Books Ltd
Thames Wharf Studios
Rainville Road
London
W6 9HA

First published in Great Britain in 2000, updated in 2001

ISBN 0 7535 0807 9

Typeset by TW Typesetting, Plymouth, Devon
Printed and bound in Great Britain by
Mackays of Chatham PLC

Hollywood Vampire is, yet again, dedicated to

Rob Francis

and

Paul Simpson

and

Susannah Tiller

Once more, with feeling.

Acknowledgements

The author wishes to thank numerous colleagues and friends for their encouragement and contributions to three editions of *Hollywood Vampire*. Specifically: Ian and Janet Abrahams, Holly Aird, Roger Anderson, Greg Bakun, Sean Brady, Jo Brooks, Matt Broughton, Steve Brown, Mike Burton, Will Cameron, Suze Campagna, Mark Clapham, Wendy Comeau, Paul Condon, Jeff Cooper, Paul and Caroline Cornell, Allison Costa, Karen Cox, Michael Cule, Peter Darvill-Evans, Tony Dryer, Jonn Elledge, Irene Finn, Simon Guerrier, The Godlike Genius of Jeff Hart, Claire Hennessy, David Howe, Mike Lee, Jennifer Lowden, Christian Lukas, Scott Matthewman, David and Lesley McIntee, David Miller, John Molyneux, The Legendary Ian Mond, Ingrid Oliansky, Tara O'Shea, Eva Palmerton, Alex Popple, Melanie Pratt, David Protheroe-Bynon, Leslie Remencus, Bruce Rux, Jim Sangster, Jill Sherwin, Dan Smiczek, Tom Spilsbury, Paul Steib and Wendy Wiseman, Jim Swallow and Mandy Mills, Yochanan and Veda Urias, Deb Walsh, the *real* Maggie Walsh and Bill and Jacque Watson.

Also, the Fat Dragon Ladies, everyone at Gallifrey One and CONvergence, notably Jody Wurl, Windy Merill and Stephanie Lindorff and Anna Bliss, my companions in the Campaign for a Tasteful-Lesbian-Shower-Scene. Thanks to all my friends on the *Outpost Gallifrey* forum and the *Buffywatchers* mailing list, Steve Purcell and Chris Cornwell, who provided several desperately needed business lunches during the course of this book. And to numerous website custodians who spared the time to answer my, no doubt annoying, emails.

Special thanks go to the ever reliable *Scooby Gang*: my editor at Virgin Kirstie Addis, Martin Day (*my* Watcher), Diana Dougherty, Clay Eichelberger, Robert Franks,

Tony and Jane Kenealy, Shaun Lyon, Graeme Topping, Jason Tucker, Deb Williams and Mark Wyman, all of whom, once again, loaned me their talent and enthusiasm for the duration. Plus, the remarkable Kathy Sullivan, without whom, *as ever*, there would have been no book.

Hollywood Vampire was written on location in Newcastle-upon-Tyne, North Hollywood, Van Nuys, Minneapolis, London and Madeira. And various airports and hotels in between.

Contents

Preface

'You're vampire detective now? What next? Vampire cowboy? Vampire fireman? Vampire ballerina?'

– 'In the Dark'

It's one of the fallacies of the TV age that there's no such thing as a genuinely great spin-off from an already successful show. There haven't been many, it's true, but there *are* a few.

Angel is one of the best.

Crawling from the apocalyptic emotional wreckage of *Buffy the Vampire Slayer*'s extraordinary third season, *Angel* was a chance for creators Joss Whedon and David Greenwalt to escape the teenage-and-growing world that Whedon had fashioned in Sunnydale and step into the adult morass of Los Angeles. If one element defines the fundamental differences between the two series, it's *Angel*'s ability to get down into the gutter of the Big City while *Buffy* is still stuck within the confines of small-town America. 'Because *Angel* is set in Los Angeles,' notes *Science Fiction World*, 'a degree of reality creeps in. We're talking about an existing city and the speculation of its seamy underside.' Producer Marti Noxon adds: 'Los Angeles was the place that Joss picked for very specific reasons . . . There's a lot of preconceptions about what the city is, but there's also a lot of truths. It's a pretty competitive, intense town where a lot of lonely, isolated and desperate people end up. It's a good place for monsters.' When he was directing *Chinatown*, Roman Polanski spent many nights in Jack Nicholson's house on Mulholland Drive and remarked about L.A., 'there's no more beautiful city in the world . . . Provided it's seen at night and *from a distance*.' For this reason *Angel*'s shape was drawn in many people's minds before the show even began. It would be 'darker' than *Buffy*, most fans decided. More graphic. More visceral.

'*Buffy* is definitely aimed at a younger audience,' Marti Noxon insists. *Angel*, on the other hand, has an audience including: 'People who are potentially out of college and making their way in the big city. We noticed in our premiere episode we had a much stronger male audience.' In reality, *Angel* treads a contextually similar path to its predecessor featuring a near identical mixture of soundbite friendly dialogue and eye-bulging set pieces. When Associated Press's Ted Anthony called *Buffy* 'a vivid piece of hip TV-splatterpunk, a hybrid of *Fast Times at Ridgemont High*, Gothic romance and one of the video games you might think was favoured by Columbine's "Trench Coat Mafia",' he could equally have been describing *Angel*. But *Angel* did, quickly, establish an identity of its own, together with themes that it intended to explore. And, like those in *Buffy*, these were both universal and timeless. Another quality that the two series share is an ability to avoid being constrained by aesthetics. *Angel* might look like *The Matrix* but the story is pure *King Lear*.

Hollywood Vampire, then, is a book about where *Angel* came from, how it reached the screen and what it looked like when it got there. It concerns the creation and development of a major television series as it became hugely successful across the world. Strap yourselves in for a few surprises along the way.

Headings

Dreaming (As *Buffy* Often Proves) is Free: Lots of series do cool dream sequences. *Angel* (and *Buffy*) do *magnificent*, surreal, scary, funny ones. You'll find them listed here.

Dudes and Babes: A meditation on all of the pretty girls and boys that flit across our screens. Even more than Sunnydale, Los Angeles is full of beautiful people. Most have a story to tell.

It's a Designer Label!: In the first episode of *Buffy*, Cordelia Chase is envious of the new girl who has arrived from Los Angeles. 'I'd kill to be that close to *that many shoes,*' she notes. Now she is and her clothing budget runs to a few expensive items. We check out the quality *and* feel the width.

References: Joss Whedon's shows take delight in slipping pop-culture and Generation X references into both the dialogue and the visuals. Whether it's the recurring *Batman* motif, Cordelia's habit of name-dropping movie stars, or the subsequent fascination with karaoke, this category tries to catch all of them.

'West Hollywood?': The debate in fandom about whether Angel is gay or not continues to be a fierce one. The *Angel* writers are not oblivious to this and, after many fans misheard Doyle's question 'Are you game?' in the pilot as 'Are you gay?', they seem to have used several scripts to indulge us with a few 'slash-fiction' fantasies.

The Charisma Show: For many, even before the cameras started rolling, the main centre of attention wasn't Angel himself, David Boreanaz, but rather his female co-star. Charisma Carpenter, who plays Cordelia, is often the best reason for watching *Angel*. 'There aren't many people who are that funny *and* that beautiful,' David Greenwalt told *TV Guide*. 'She can do every colour of the rainbow.'

L.A.-Speak: S'up, homie? 'From the netherworld known as the 818 area code,' this category lists as much *valley-slang* as requires an explanation. *Totally*.

Sex and Drugs and Rock'n'Roll: In L.A. *all* are rife, even in TV shows. The city may have, as Raymond Chandler once noted, 'the personality of a paper cup', but it's a place where literally *anything* goes.

There's A Ghost In My House: An occasional category listing the activities of Cordelia's less-than-substantial housemate, Phantom Dennis.

Logic, Let Me Introduce You to This Window: An acknowledgement that even in the best shows there are sometimes logic flaws, bits of bad continuity or plain foul-ups. Part of the job of being a fan is looking for these, laughing at them

when they occur and then aggressively defending them to
your non-fan friends.

I Just *Love* Your Accent: *Angel*'s perceptions of Britain and
the British.

Quote/Unquote: Dialogue that's worth stopping the video
for.

Other categories appear occasionally, including a few old
friends and some new to this edition. Most should be
self-explanatory. **Critique** details what the press thought
whilst **Comments** from the cast and crew have been added
where appropriate. **Soundtrack** highlights *Angel*'s excellent
use of music. Each episode will conclude with a review and
copious notes on continuity and other general trivia that
doesn't fit in anywhere else.

Preface to the Third Edition

'You were always so good with your books. Made it look so easy.'

– 'Epiphany'

It started out as a ten-words-or-fewer idea for a spin-off series. *Vampire with soul seeks redemption and fights demons in L.A.* Who would have predicted just how far *Angel* has come? Set up during *Buffy the Vampire Slayer*'s critically acclaimed third season, and debuting a year later, *Angel* had rather schizophrenic beginnings, seemingly unable to decide what sort of show it wanted to be. Whereas with *Buffy* it had been quickly established that the main reasons that viewers were watching was the ensemble cast and the soaplike story-arcs, on *Angel* it was initially felt that the series could work best as an anthology, in which guest characters would often be the central focus. That theory lasted for about half a dozen episodes before the producers got the dichotomy right and started telling more personal tales from the underground. In doing so, *Angel* has become, over the subsequent years, an even more consistent show than *Buffy*. It may never quite hit the dramatic heights of *Buffy* episodes like 'The Body', 'Doppelgängland', 'Hush' or 'Once More, With Feeling' (though 57, 'Waiting in the Wings' comes pretty close), but *Angel* seldom produces a duff note. In its own quiet way, *Angel* is building a stunning back catalogue for syndication and the DVD age.

Since the last edition of *Hollywood Vampire*, published in December 2001, many things have changed, in both the *Buffy* universe and in the real world. But some universal constants remain and one of them is that *Angel* will be adored by its fans and, generally, unappreciated by much of the media. This is especially true of its terrestrial broadcasts in the UK where it has remained hidden in a graveyard slot. Hopefully the move to Channel 5 in the summer of 2003 will help to erase the bitter memories of Channel 4's dreadful misreading of what the show was all about.

But *we* know its true worth, right? It's one of the best television series in the world.

Keith Topping
Escaping By Canoe
Merrie Albion
October 2003

Previously on *Buffy the Vampire Slayer* . . .

*'A vampire in love with a Slayer. It's rather poetic.
In a maudlin sort of way.'*

– 'Out of Sight, Out of Mind'

Born in Galway, Ireland in the eighteenth century, Angel was, according to Margaret (one of his victims): 'A drunken, whoring layabout and a terrible disappointment to [his] parents.' Though, as he told his vampire sire Darla: 'With the exception of an honest day's work, there's no challenge I'm not prepared to face.' Asking her to 'show me your world', Angel became a vampire in 1753. Angel is the nickname of his possessing demon, *Angelus* ('the one with the angelic face'). He created havoc and terror across Europe for decades and was, according to the elite vampire The Master: 'The most vicious creature I ever met'. His *modus operandi* involved sending his victims insane firstly by killing their family and friends before finally murdering them without mercy or pity. However, all bad things come to an end and in 1898, after he murdered a Romanian gypsy from the Kalderash Clan, Angelus was cursed by her people to regain his soul and have knowledge of the dreadful crimes he committed against humanity.

> *'I know what it's like to take a life. To feel a future, a world of possibilities, snuffed out by your own hand. I know the power in it. The exhilaration. It was like a drug for me.'*
>
> – 'Consequences'

Damned to walk the Earth, Angel ('the vampire with a soul') spent most of the following century in misery over his past deeds, shunning other vampires, coming to America and living in the gutter. Rescued by a friendly demon, Whistler, in New York in 1996 and shown a path of hope in the shape of the Vampire Slayer, Buffy Summers, Angel accepted that he had a destiny and travelled to Sunnydale and the Hellmouth.

> *'Things used to be pretty simple. A hundred years, just hanging out, feeling guilty . . . I really honed my brooding skills. Then she comes along.'*

– 'Lie To Me'

Once there, he spent almost two years helping the Slayer and her friends Willow Rosenberg, Xander Harris, Cordelia Chase, Daniel Osborne and Rupert Giles fight vampires, demons and the forces of darkness. He killed his sire and nemesis, Darla, and helped Buffy to defeat The Master and prevent the opening of the Hellmouth and the end of the world. Briefly, he lost his soul again after enjoying a single moment of happiness with Buffy, and returned to his evil ways, killing Giles's friend Jenny Calendar and stalking Buffy with the aid of his 'offspring', the English vampire couple Spike and Drusilla. He was eventually cured by a reversal spell performed by Willow and sent to Hell by Buffy to save the world from the coming of the demon Acathla.

On his return, Angel slowly regained his humanity and resumed his relationship with Buffy. But he spent much time questioning the reason why he was allowed to escape from Hell by The Powers That Be.

> *'I'm trying to think with my head instead of my heart.'*

– 'The Prom'

Realising that there could be no future in a lasting relationship with Buffy, and after helping her to defeat the apocalyptic schemes of Mayor Wilkins and the rogue Slayer, Faith, Angel left Sunnydale for Los Angeles. Here, he continues to fight demons and monsters whilst searching for the reason why he returned to this dimension and trying to forget the girl he left behind.

> *'Angel, you have the power to do real good, to make amends. But if you die now, then all that you ever were was a monster.'*
>
>   – 'Amends'

> *'If you hang with me and mine, you'll be accepted in no time. Of course, we do have to test your coolness factor. You're from L.A., so you can skip the written . . .'*
>
>   – 'Welcome to the Hellmouth'

Cordelia Chase was born into a wealthy Sunnydale family and spent most of her formative years developing a wilfully narcissistic view of herself at the centre of the universe (simultaneously inspiring the existence of the 'We Hate Cordelia' club: Founder member and treasurer, Alexander Harris).

In school, she was at the centre of a group of similarly minded girls known as 'The Cordettes', who spent their time avoiding learning anything remotely educational, wearing fashionable clothes and dating rock musicians and football jocks.

However, beneath Cordelia's bitchy and selfish exterior was a very different person, someone who realised that she was a magnet for people who just wanted to be 'in the popular zone,' and had little interest in the *real* Cordelia (albeit she preferred being alone in a crowd to 'being lonely all by yourself').

> *'What, I can't have layers?'*
>
>   – 'Band Candy'

Once Cordelia's life had been saved by Buffy when attacked by the demented invisible girl, Marcie Ross, she became a reluctant, if occasionally vital, member of the

Scooby Gang and even dated Xander before discovering his attraction to Willow. After surviving a near fatal injury shortly after this trauma, Cordelia was further horrified to discover that her family had lost all of their money due to tax evasion and that she had to work for the first time in her life. Consumed by bitterness over her break-up with Xander, she briefly wished Sunnydale into an alternative reality. Now Cordelia, her dreams of college shattered by financial considerations, has come to L.A. to begin an aspiring acting career and forget all about Sunnydale.

> *'I should leave you in there, but I'm a great humanitarian. You'll just have to think of a way to pay me back sometime.'*

> – 'Doppelgängland'

Into the City of Angel

'A lot of people who worked on Buffy including David and Charisma, obviously, are on Angel . . . We check the ratings to see if they came out a little ahead or a little behind but it's really one big family.'

– Joss Whedon

Creators of cult shows often fail to strike lucky with their second projects (*Crusade* and *Millennium* are two recent examples). In a revealing interview with Rob Francis, Joss Whedon was asked the secret of creating a spin-off whilst simultaneously maintaining the standards on the parent show: 'We were very careful to learn while we were doing *Angel* not to set a formula until we had seen the results. I was determined not to have a second show that brought down the quality of the first.' It was during the *Buffy* episode 'I Only Have Eyes For You' that Whedon began thinking about a spin-off: 'Seeing David open himself up to playing this really emotional female role and doing it excellently – without overdoing it or being silly, without shying away from it as a lot of male action stars might have – was extraordinary. That was when I thought "This guy could carry his own show".'

As *Angel* entered production David Boreanaz explained to *TV Guide* that his character 'goes to L.A. and fights for humanity. A lot of people from *Buffy* will come visit me and I'll come back and visit them.' Though Sarah Michelle Gellar told *Sci-Fi TV Magazine*: 'I probably won't be making crossovers', in the event, links between the two shows *did* become a major part of the schedules for the next two years.

Angel initially co-starred Glenn Quinn as Doyle, Angel's half-demon spiritual mentor. Joss Whedon told

Entertainment Weekly: 'The higher powers have called Doyle to be Angel's guide. He's the last person in the world who wants to – or should – be doing this. He just wants to play the ponies and drink a lot. But he has unexpected wisdom in the midst of his extreme foibles.'

Whedon, having succeeded in getting *Buffy* and *Angel* scheduled back-to-back on the WB was keen, at first, to stress the differences between the series, noting that *Angel* 'is more of an anthology show than *Buffy*. There's not a soap opera at the centre of it.' We also saw a more humorous side to Angel, but good old Cordelia was still reliably 'self-involved and in her Cordelia-bubble, which is her charm,' according to Whedon. Boreanaz also revealed that the plan was to 'explore Angel's past, [and the] period when he was wandering the streets in abject misery, cursed by the gypsies.' This element took a while to manifest itself and it's not until **11**, 'Somnambulist', that Angel's history is delved into in any significant way.

In the event, *Angel* quickly became a hit, achieving respectable ratings on the back of *Buffy* (it was the top-rated new WB show of the year) and impressive critical backing. Fans immediately took to the central trio of characters and there was a huge outcry at the first change in the regular cast (see **9**, 'Hero'). In Britain, Sky quickly bought the series and opted to follow US scheduling, showing *Buffy* and *Angel* back-to-back on Friday nights. These proved to be popular, gaining the satellite company some of its highest ratings. Sadly, as with their purchase of *Buffy* two years previously, the BBC dithered over *Angel*, unsure whether they could find a suitable timeslot for a series with such adult content. This allowed another terrestrial company, Channel 4, to buy *Angel*. But Channel 4, frankly, didn't have a clue what to do with the series either and their treatment of *Angel* was roundly criticised not only by fans but also by the ITC who objected to the adult content of the series. This was a predictable reaction, given that Channel 4 chose to show the episodes, including scenes of graphic torture and serial stalkers, at 6 p.m. (see **3**, 'In the Dark').

The *Angel Demo Reel*: 'I figured life didn't have any more surprises . . . I thought I'd seen everything. Then I came to L.A.' In May 1999, as an advertising tool for the forthcoming series, Whedon and Greenwalt prepared a six-minute promotional video of specially shot sequences (and clips from *Buffy*). It begins with Angel on a rooftop doing the 'Who I Am And How I Came To Be'-bit. 'I was born 244 years ago in Ireland,' he notes. 'Life as a vampire was a constant thrill. The power. The danger. The outfits. *Good* outfits. Never getting old was also a plus.' The flashbacks include clips from 'Becoming' Part 2, 'Amends', 'Passion', 'Anne', 'Graduation Day' Part 2, 'I Only Have Eyes For You', 'Reptile Boy', 'Doppelgängland', 'Beauty and the Beasts' and the memorable bit from 'The Wish' of Cordelia getting out of her car wearing *that* leather skirt. Over a pounding rock soundtrack (three songs by Vast: 'Here', 'Dirty Hole' and 'I'm Dying'), Angel and Doyle share a scene that almost mirrors the street sequences in 1, 'City Of' ('hell of a city,' notes Doyle. 'Buckets of fun if you're a nasty creature.'), while Cordelia tells Angel (uniquely wearing a white T-shirt) that they should 'charge the helpless.' There's also some great dialogue exchanges like Doyle telling Angel that there are dangerous people in town. Angel: 'They're not gonna like me stirring up the water.' Doyle: 'You're *afraid* of that?' Angel: 'I'm *counting* on it.' Doyle: 'Quite the masculine fellah, aren't you?'

Extracts from the demo were put to good use in the subsequent *Angel* title sequence along with several of the travelogue scene-breaks of Los Angeles at night.

Did You Know?: Despite the disparity in their ages on the series, Charisma Carpenter is actually nine months *older* than David Boreanaz.

List of Episodes

*'The idea of a vampire in a white hat
probably seems a little "gimme a break-y".'*

– 'War Zone'

'After centuries of terror, redemption has a price . . .'

Angel – Season One
(1999–2000)

**Mutant Enemy Inc/Greenwolf Corp[1]/Kuzui Enterprises/Sandollar
Television/20th Century Fox**

Created by Joss Whedon and David Greenwalt
Consulting Producers: Marti Noxon, Howard Gordon (1–16),
Jim Kouf (18–22)
Producers: Tracey Stern (1–7), Tim Minear (1–13),
Kelly A Manners, Gareth Davies (1)
Supervising Producer: Tim Minear (14–22)
Co-Producers: Skip Schoolnik, James A Contner (2–6, 10, 18)
Associate Producer: RD Price
Executive Producers: Sandy Gallin, Gail Berman, Fran Rubel Kuzui,
Kaz Kuzui, Joss Whedon, David Greenwalt

Regular Cast:
David Boreanaz (Angel/Angelus)
Charisma Carpenter (Cordelia Chase)
Glenn Quinn (Allen Francis Doyle, 1–9[2], 14[3])
Sarah Michelle Gellar (Buffy Summers, 1[4], 7[5], 8, 19)
Michael Mantell (Oliver Simon, 1[6], 17)
Christian Kane (Lindsey McDonald, 1, 18–19, 21–22)
Elisabeth Rohm (Detective Kate Lockley, 2, 4, 6, 11, 14–15, 19, 22)
John Mahon (Trevor Lockley, 6, 15)
Thomas Barr (Lee Mercer, 6, 18–19, 21)
Carry Cannon (Female Oracle, 8, 10, 22)
Randall Slavin (Male Oracle, 8, 10, 22)

---

[1] Except **1**, 'City Of' which does not carry the 'Greenwolf Corp' logo.
[2] Although Glenn Quinn appears in the title sequence of **10**, 'Parting Gifts' (and in the 'previously on *Angel*' scene repeated from **9**, 'Hero'), he is not present in the episode itself.
[3] Uncredited, voice only in **14**, 'I've Got You Under My Skin'.
[4] Uncredited, voice heard on the telephone and seen in flashbacks in **1**, 'City Of'.
[5] Uncredited, seen in flashback in **7**, 'The Bachelor Party'.
[6] Uncredited in **1**, 'City Of'.

Alexis Denisof (Wesley Wyndam-Pryce, 10–22)
Julie Benz (Darla, 15, 18, 22)
Stephanie Romanov (Lilah Morgan, 16, 18–19, 21–22)
Eliza Dushku (Faith, 18–19)
J August Richards (Charles Gunn, 20[7], 21–22)
David Herman (David Nabbit, 20, 22)
Sam Anderson (Holland Manners, 21–22)

1
City Of

US Transmission Date: 5 October 1999
UK Transmission Date: 7 January 2000 (Sky),
15 September 2000 (Channel 4)

Writers: David Greenwalt, Joss Whedon
Director: Joss Whedon
Cast: Tracy Middendorf (Tina), Vyto Ruginis (Russell Winters),
Jon Ingrassia (Stacy), Renee Ridgeley (Margo), Sam Pancake (Manager),
Josh Wolloway (Good-Looking Guy), Gina McClain (Janice)
French title: *La Cité des Anges*
German title: *Licht und Schatten*

Angel is living in Los Angeles, trying to forget all about
Sunnydale and Buffy. He is contacted by a half-human
demon, Doyle, who tells Angel that 'The Powers That Be'
have chosen him for a special mission. Angel tries to save
a coffee waitress called Tina who is being stalked by
industrialist Russell Winters. He fails, but does manage to
rescue Cordelia Chase, Buffy's former friend, from Winters's vampiric intentions. Killing his nemesis, Angel makes
an enemy of Winters's legal representatives, the sinister
firm of Wolfram & Hart.

What Might Have Been: The first-draft script (entitled
'Angel Pilot') followed the basic plot of **1**, 'City Of', but
included some elements not taken forward. It confirmed
what many fans suspected: the role of Angel's mentor was
originally written with the character of Whistler (see *Buffy*:

---

[7] Uncredited in **20**, 'War Zone' on the original US transmission. This was corrected
in subsequent overseas broadcasts and on the Fox video release of the episode.

'Becoming') in mind. 'You know what I don't need?' Angel asks when meeting his old friend. 'A wacky sidekick from Hell.'

The opening scene has Angel bitter over Buffy, commenting: 'Women, they're just ... So round and comfy and then they say, "Oh, could you pass me that fork, honey? And your heart, too, come on." [Pounds pretend fork into a heart on the bar.] I'm not bitter.' After this, with the exception of the odd line of dialogue and Stacy being spelled 'Stacey' throughout, the script proceeds much as per **1**, 'City Of'. However ...

What A Shame They Dropped ...: The following gem. Tina: 'You kinda remind me of the cowboys back home. 'Cept you're not drunk.' Angel: [deadpan] 'I'm high on life.'

Dudes and Babes: Much low-cut cleavage on display at Margo's party, via the hostess, Tina's and (especially) Cordelia's dresses. Plus a girl wearing a *very* tight black PVC skirt. Also, the scene when Angel first meets Doyle and David Boreanaz gets to show off his rippling biceps.

It's a Designer Label!: Cordelia's red dress is a Neiman-Marcus. Angel pulls the 'wearing a Hawaiian shirt to convince the villain that he's a tourist' trick for the first time (see **6**, 'Sense and Sensitivity').

References: Apart from the general Gotham City look of twilight Los Angeles and Angel walking down the alley at the end of both the tag sequence and the titles with his coat billowing behind him like a cape, there's the first of many *Batman* references, Doyle noting that Angel's home 'has a nice Bat-cave sort of an air to it.'

Doyle being half-human 'on my mother's side,' is a characteristic he shares not only with Mr Spock in *Star Trek* and the Doctor in *Doctor Who*, but also with Jesus, the mythical Hercules of *Legendary Journeys* and many literary and comic-book characters. The plot is similar to an animated movie, *Vampire Hunter D*, in which a brooding half-vampire helps a woman stalked by an ancient vampire. 'I'm parched from all this yakkin', man. Let's go treat me to a Billy Dee,' refers to Colt .45 beer and

actor Billy Dee Williams (*The Empire Strikes Back*,
Batman) who did commercials for the brand. Also references to the notorious L.A. nightclub The Lido, Grand-
master Flash and the Furious Five's 'The Message' and the
Minnesota Vikings football team.

The Charisma Show: Charisma steals the episode from her
first appearance at the party asking Angel: 'Are you still
. . . *GRRR*?' Plus the memorable exchange with Russell at
his mansion. 'I finally get invited to a nice place with no
mirrors and lots of curtains. Hey, you're a *vampire*.'
Russell: 'What? No, I'm not.' Cordelia: '*Are too* . . . I'm
from Sunnydale. We had our own Hellmouth. I think I
know a vampire when I'm alone with him in his fortress-
like home.'

'West Hollywood?': Readers without Internet access may
be astonished at the number of *Angel* fans who *totally*
misheard Doyle and Angel's closing 'Are you game?', 'I'm
game,' as 'Are you gay?', 'I'm gay.' Oliver tells Angel he is
a 'beautiful man', but denies that he is coming on to him,
noting that he [Oliver] is in a serious relationship with a
landscape architect.

**'You May Remember Me From Such Films and TV Series
As . . .':** Born in Buffalo and raised in Philadelphia, where
his father is a TV weatherman, David Boreanaz had done
little acting before landing the role of Angel. Aside from a
couple of low budget movies, his only claim to fame was a
guest slot on *Married . . . With Children*. Recently he
starred in the horror movie *Valentine*.

A former cheerleader with the San Diego Chargers,
Charisma Carpenter began her acting career in the
Baywatch episode 'Air Buchanon', playing Hobie's girlfriend, Wendie. Aaron Spelling auditioned her for the
deliciously saucy 'über-vixen-bitch' Ashley Green in NBC's
Malibu Shores, a performance described by *TV Guide* as,
'The Shannen Doherty bad-girl role is taken by *sultry
stunner*, Charisma Carpenter, who comes across as the
most beguiling and fleshed-out character on-screen.' She
also landed another role in a short-lived series, Beth
Sullivan in the *Josh Kirby: Time Warrior* TV movies, plus

a legendary advert for Spree sweets ('It's a kick in the mouth!'). Glenn Quinn spent seven years playing Mark Healy, Becky's husband, on *Roseanne* (where he worked with Joss Whedon). He was Hal Evans in *Stick & Stones* and appears in *Live Nude Girls*.

Tracy Middendorf played Risa Holmes in *Ally McBeal*, Laura Kingman in *Beverly Hills 90210* and Carrie Brady on *Days of Our Lives*. Her guest appearances include most of the important US series of the 90s: *The X-Files*, *Millennium*, *Chicago Hope*, *Star Trek: Deep Space Nine*, *Murder She Wrote* and *The Practice*, as well as *24*. 'It seems like I always get cast as emotional women in crisis,' she complained to *TV Guide* in 1999. Still, it's a living, isn't it? Renee Ridgeley appeared in *The Computer Wore Tennis Shoes*.

Vyto Ruginis has also been a guest star on *Ally McBeal*, along with *Star Trek: The Next Generation* and *NYPD Blue*. His movies include a memorable cameo in *The Devil's Advocate*, *Phenomenon*, *Descending Angel* and *Jumpin' Jack Flash*. Christian Kane played Wick Lobo on *Rescue 77* and Flyboy Leggat on *Fame L.A.* He also fronts his own country-rock band, Kane, who recently played Johnny Depp's legendary L.A. club, the Viper Room (see **40**, 'Dead End'). Michael Mantell has been in movies such as *The Velocity of Gary*, *Dead Funny*, *Quiz Show*, *Passion Fish* and *The Brother from Another Planet* and on TV series as diverse as *Charmed*, *ER*, *Party of Five*, *When Billie Beat Bobby*, *The X-Files* and *Matlock*. Readers may recognise him as Howard Sewell in *Space: Above and Beyond*.

The Men Behind The Camera: When asked how much like *Buffy*'s Xander Harris he was as a teenager, Joss Whedon noted: 'Less and less as he gets laid more and more.' Whedon is a third-generation Hollywood scriptwriter (his grandfather wrote for *Leave It To Beaver*, his father worked on *The Golden Girls*). His education included a period at Winchester public school in England ('my mother was a teacher,' he told Rob Francis. 'She was on sabbatical in England so I had to go somewhere'.) After writing many speculative scripts in his teens, he landed a job on the

popular sitcom *Roseanne* (he also produced the TV version
of *Parenthood*). 'My life was completely about film,' he
told *teen movieline* magazine. '[I] learned about filmmaking
by analysing the Western *Johnny Guitar* and the melo-
drama *The Naked Kiss*.' However with an encyclopaedic
knowledge of the horror genre Whedon had always wanted
to write for that market (his favourite film remains
Kubrick's *The Shining*). 'I watched a lot of horror movies,'
he admitted to *The Big Breakfast*. 'I saw all these blonde
women going down alleys and getting killed and I felt bad
for them. I wanted one of them to kill a monster for a
change so I came up with *Buffy*.' His movie script for *Buffy
the Vampire Slayer* suffered years of rejection before being
produced in 1992. Subsequently, Joss became one of
Hollywood's hottest properties, Oscar-nominated for his
script for *Toy Story*, writing *Alien: Resurrection* and
contributing (often uncredited) script-doctoring to *Twister*,
Speed and *Waterworld*. Although his *X-Men* script was one
of several not used on the summer 2000 blockbuster, he *did*
write *Titan A.E.* and produce the SF Western *Firefly*.

One of David Greenwalt's first industry jobs was as Jeff
Bridges's body-double before he became a director on *The
Wonder Years*, preceding a period as writer/producer on
The X-Files, *Doogie Howser MD* and, in 1997, *Buffy the
Vampire Slayer*. His film scripts include *Class*, *American
Dreamer* and *Secret Admirer* (which he also directed) and
one acting role as 'Uniformed Cop' in a 1981 horror spoof
called *Wacko* (see **18**, 'Five By Five'). Producer Skip
Schoolnik was the regular editor on *Buffy* along with over
30 films and TV movies.

An explanation of the role of the various producers is
provided by Tim Minear: 'The title "producer" on a TV
show can mean anything from writer to line-producer (the
man or woman in the trenches running the day-to-day
operations of the set) to someone billed as an "executive
producer" who might have some stake in the property but
wouldn't be let through the gate by the security guard for
lack of recognition. On our show, most of the producers
you see are writers. Kelly Manners is our on-set producer.

He has the thankless task of making sure the show gets made on schedule. RD Price, our associate producer, is a catch-all producing entity. He babysits the set when one of us can't be there, shoots second-unit material and directed **14**, 'I've Got You Under My Skin'. Skip Schoolnik, runs our post-production department. So far as my involvement, I've had the chance to get my hands dirty in all aspects of the production. I'm in the early concept meetings with the writers as we pitch story ideas. When one of my scripts is in prep, I work with the director and the production department heads going over all the elements. This includes casting, wardrobe, sets, locations. I "tone" with directors, meaning going over the script scene by scene trying to get across what we want the tone of [the] episode to be. After it's shot and the director has had his cut, I sit with the editors, sometimes redesigning sequences which don't work and deciding what additional material is needed. I work with post-sound on the sound design and talking to the composer about music. Then, when it's ready to put in the oven, we mix the sound and sometimes I'm on the dubbing stage for that.' Don't these guys ever sleep?

L.A.-Speak: Tina: 'I'm sort-of having relationship issues.'
Cordelia: 'Wow, what a nice place. Love your curtains. Not afraid to emphasise the curtains.' And, as Doyle extracts bullets from Angel's chest: 'Finally. I thought I was going to faint while *barfing*.' And: 'You're not exactly rolling in it Mister I-was-alive-for-200-years-and-never-developed-an-investment-portfolio.'

Classic *Double Entendre*: Angel, on Cordelia: 'You think she's a Hottie?' Doyle: 'She's a stiffener all right, I can't lie about that. But, you know, she could use a hand.'

Sex and Drugs and Rock'n'Roll: There are wholly unsubtle hints from Tina and Cordelia that 'helping' someone in L.A. usually means that you get to have sex with them. Tina is astonished when she is ready to give herself to Angel only for him to turn down the offer – she notes: 'Boy, are you ever in the wrong town.' In addition to being a vampire, there are hints to a dark side to Russell's sexuality, Tina alleging that he 'likes pain'. Margo takes some pills while on the phone to Cordelia. She's also drinking what looks like tomato juice, but could be blood. Is she a junkie, or a vampire, or both?

Logic, Let Me Introduce You to This Window: As with various *Buffy* episodes (for instance, 'What's My Line?') Angel can be seen on videotape, despite video cameras using mirrors as part of their focusing mechanism (see **24**, 'Are You Now or Have You Ever Been?'). When Angel pretends to be drunk in the bar his sleeves don't have the retractable stakes that he wears one scene later. Doyle uses the fact that he walked uninvited into Angel's home as proof he [Doyle] isn't a vampire, but it's later established that vampires' homes are not protected from other vampires entering, since the owner is dead. (This also explains how Angel can get into both Tina's apartment after she's been killed and Russell's mansion. Russell's ability to enter Tina's apartment is specifically explained by the fact that he owns the building.)

In the coffee shop, Angel's reflection is visible on a table top. The bomb Angel sets says '30' when he triggers it. Although it ticks quickly, the numbers don't change. When Angel is handed Oliver's business card, he holds it between a finger and his thumb. Next shot, it's between two fingers. When Angel picks up Cordelia to escape Russell's guards she is wearing different shoes to those seen when they jump to the floor. The fight between Angel and Russell features a pair of stuntmen who look *nothing whatsoever* like David Boreanaz and Vyto Ruginis. As Russell falls and bursts into flames his reflection is visible in the building's windows. Angel dials seven numbers when calling Buffy. Sunnydale should not be a local call from L.A.

I Just *Love* Your Accent: Contrary to popular belief, Glenn Quinn *was* Irish and used his natural accent in his appearances on *Angel*.

Asked about a perceived British influence in his writing and whether his time in England during the early 1980s and exposure to British Telefantasy had scarred him for life, Joss Whedon noted: 'I saw *Blake's 7*, *Sapphire and Steel* and *Doctor Who* but not a great deal. I was at boarding school and didn't have much opportunity. What we watched were our heroes like *Starsky and Hutch* but I watched a huge amount of British TV while I lived in America. That's one of the reasons I was anxious to come. I was an entire PBS kid. *Masterpiece Theatre, Monty Python,* BBC Shakespeare.' Asked if he believed his time in Britain had helped to get characters like Giles and Wesley 'right', Joss confirmed: 'You want the contrast between Giles and Buffy but at the same time I hope he's been a little more human than just stuffy. Of course, the great thing is there are dirty words that the American audience don't know.'

Motors: Angel drives a black 1968 Plymouth Belvedere GTX convertible. Stacy's car is a 'grey '87 black Mercedes 300E [which is] going to need some serious work on the bumper.'

Quote/Unquote: Doyle: 'I've been sent. By The Powers That Be.' Angel: 'The powers that be *what?*'

Doyle, when Angel asks why The Powers That Be are using him as their instrument: 'We've all got *something* to atone for.'

Angel: 'I don't want to share my feelings, I don't want to open up. I want to find Russell and I want to look him in the eye.' Doyle: 'Then what?' Angel: '*Then* I'm going to share my feelings.'

Cordelia: 'A cockroach. In the corner. I think its a bantamweight.'

Notes: 'Los Angeles. You see it at night and it shines. Like a beacon. People are drawn to it. People and other things. They come for all sorts of reasons. My reason? No surprise there. It started with a girl.' A cracking beginning, setting up all of the elements that *Angel* will focus on – guilt and redemption, the quest for happiness, the cheapness of life in Los Angeles and the hollowness of 'status', the cost of 'fighting the good fight' – and yet still having time to tell a story. Nicely paced and with a rather appealing sense of irony. The visuals are tremendous, particularly the recurring shots of the sun rising and setting in speed-motion above the L.A. skyline that crop up throughout the series (see *The Angel Demo Reel*; this trick had been used to great effect in the vampire movie *Blade* which came out while *Angel* was in pre-production). Not as dark (in several senses) as was expected by many but perhaps more interesting for exactly that reason.

While Doyle tells Angel's past history for anyone who's never watched *Buffy*, we see flashbacks to 'Amends', 'Innocence', 'Becoming' Part 1, 'Anne' and 'Graduation Day' Part 2. Cordelia summarises her own history from 'Lover's Walk' and 'The Prom': 'I grew up in a nice home. It wasn't like this, but we did have a room or two that we didn't even know what they were for. Until the IRS got all huffy about my folks not paying taxes for, well, ever. They took it all.' There's a subtle crossover to 'The Freshman' episode of *Buffy* which was shown immediately prior to 1, 'City Of', when Angel calls Buffy and then hangs up when she answers. Doyle indicates that Angel drinks exclusively pig's blood. Angel confirms that the last human blood he tasted was Buffy's (see *Buffy*: 'Graduation Day' Part 2). Angel has seen fourteen wars in his lifetime, not including Vietnam (which was never officially declared). He has tea in his apartment but not milk or sugar. He can differentiate between humans and demons by smell. He has good reflexes and admits to Tina that he is lonely.

Cordelia says she lives in 'Malibu. A small condo on the beach.' When we actually see her apartment, however, it's neither a beach-condo *nor* in Malibu. Her agent is called Joe and she seems to have had plenty of auditions with the networks to such an extent that they've seen enough of her. She tells Russell that she's had 'a lot of opportunities. The hands in the liquid-gel commercial were almost mine, bar one or two girls.' She practises yoga and is reading a book called *Meditation for a Successful Life*. Doyle notes: 'I get visions. Which is to say great splitting migraines that come with pictures. A name, a face. I just know whoever sends them is more powerful than me or you and they're trying to make things right.' Tina comes from Missoula, Montana. Angel says he was there 'during the Depression'.

The episode was rated 'TV 14'. The subject matter probably would have justified it anyway, but including a 'piss off' and a 'bastard' in the opening scenes made it certain. Some filming took place in the basement car park of the prestigious Sunset Strip hotel, the Argyle.

Soundtrack: The theme is by Darling Violetta (accompanying the stunning title sequence designed by Regis Kimble). Also 'Right of Left Field' by Wellwater Conspiracy and 'Maybe I Belong' by Howie Beck. The two songs used during Margo's party are 'Ladyshave' and 'Teenage Sensation', both by Gus Gus.

Most of the music on *Angel* is performed by Robert J Kral (whose previous work included soundtracks for *The Legend of Billy the Kid, Cyberkidz* and *Sliders*). He told Rob Francis: 'I owe my break into the TV industry to Chris Beck. He hired me as an assistant on a show called *TWO* [then] for assistance on several HBO and TV movies. He recommended me to Danny Lux, so I ended up writing for 41 episodes of *Sliders*. Chris was offered *Angel*, but knew he wanted to turn more energy toward feature films. He took up the offer, but had explained to the producers that I would be coming on board.'

Explaining in detail the equipment he uses, Robert noted: 'A G3 Macintosh computer running Digital Performer which is the command centre for the rest of the studio, comprised of Roland and Emu samplers and the Gigasampler. I spent an entire session recording the insides of a grand piano: scraping the strings etc. There are some truly terrifying sounds lurking under the hood of that. The most unusual thing might be my three-year-old daughter's toy that when you press a button a trap door opens and it has this hilarious "boing" sound from a spring being released. Play it down about four octaves and its scary. That's the fun thing about samplers: it's "open season" on anything that makes a sound.'

Critique: *TV Guide* trailed *Angel* as: 'One of the best new shows'. Noted critic Matt Roush said *Angel* 'best preserves the virtues of the original – the wit and danger of *Buffy* are here – while giving us an entirely new experience . . . *Angel* is grimmer than *Buffy* which is why Cordelia is so welcome, still unflappably spouting such lines as, "I've known a lot

of demons and, slime aside, not a lot goin' on there."
Gotta love her!'

Less Accurate Critique: Channel 4 prepared a synopsis of
this episode for the first UK terrestrial broadcast which
appeared verbatim in *Radio Times* amongst other publications: 'The first in a new supernatural spin-off series from
Buffy the Vampire Slayer, starring David Boreanaz. *City of
Angels*. Teenage vampire Angel leaves Sunnydale for Los
Angeles, where he meets his old friend Cordelia, a struggling actress, and a mysterious spiritual mentor named
Doyle who has visions of those in need.' So, two factual
errors in four lines *and* they got the title wrong. *That*'s a
promising beginning (see **3**, 'In the Dark').

The Novelisation: Nancy Holder's novel of **1**, 'City Of'
(Pocket Pulse Books, December 1999) is a classic TV tie-in
(in the best traditions of this underrated literary sub-genre)
taking the script and fleshing it out with pop culture
references (*Beverly Hills Cop*, *Gone With the Wind*). Holder
used the opportunity to tell Angel's back-story in inter-
ludes set in Galway in 1753 (see *Buffy*: 'Becoming' Part 1,
although much of Holder's Angelus-origin speculation is
contradicted in **15**, 'The Prodigal'), Manhattan in 1996 (see
Buffy: 'Becoming' Part 1), the death of Jenny (see *Buffy*:
'Passion'), Dublin in 1838 (see *Buffy*: 'Amends'), London
in 1860 (see *Buffy*: 'Becoming' Part 1), a marvellous Spike
and Drusilla fragment set in Hungary during the 1956
Russian invasion, Romania in 1898 (see *Buffy*: 'Becoming'
Part 1, **19**, 'Sanctuary') and the collapse of Buffy and
Angel's relationship (see *Buffy*: 'The Prom').

Did You Know?: The sequence in which Angel is approached by an agent at the party was, as Marti Noxon
told *Science Fiction World*: 'Something very similar [to
what] happened to David. His manager saw him walking
his dog and went up and said' "I'm going to represent
you." Although Boreanaz was already an actor, his
discovery was very much like that.'

David Boreanaz's Comments: Asked by *DreamWatch* what
his first reaction was when he heard about the spin-off,
David replied: 'We were just finishing up the second season

of *Buffy* and Joss called me into his office and said, 'I have this great idea for this character. I want to put him in Los Angeles [to] be the defender of evil in a city of lost souls.' At the time my mind wasn't really into it, I was focused on the season finale we were shooting, so I remember saying, 'Oh that's great.' It didn't really hit me until we went to the WB Event for the show in New York. They did a presentation and I realised this could really happen.'

What Might Have Been . . .: Writer David Fury, speaking in April 2000 at the Canadian Film Centre, responded to an audience question about whether any of his scripts had been spiked: 'The one script I've written that was never produced was the second episode of *Angel* . . . [It] was going to be a much darker show. An example is in the first episode, when he finds a girl he's protecting is dead, he has her blood on his hands; he was going to start licking the blood off his fingers like he can't control himself. Then, being repulsed, he goes to the bathroom and scrubs his hands. It was about recovering alcoholics, that was the allegory. We were going to [have] him struggling to remain good. Along those lines the second episode which I'd written was called "Corrupt". It was about junkie prostitutes, not usually what you see on the WB. Kate was an undercover cop who was addicted to cocaine and was sleeping with men because she got a bit too far into her work. About two days before shooting, the network got a hold of the script and went, "WOAH. This is the WB." They said "Corrupt" was far too dark and disturbing, we'd like something nice and friendly and with pretty people in it. So, I had to very quickly turn over a new script.'

Tim Minear revealed: 'It's true that the initial first episode after the pilot was scrubbed. The network wasn't really asking for anything Joss didn't agree with. It really wasn't a big drama, we were still in the formative stages. So far as the "dark" episodes, before the network ever approached us with their concerns, each *Angel* writer was developing their first script. Mine happened to be 11, "Somnambulist" [which was] conceived and first-draft written before we started shooting. We always understood that *Angel* had its dark side and never shrinked from that. I don't think you'll find the main character on any other WB show, or any other show for that matter, eating his family any time soon!'

2
Lonely Heart[8]

US Transmission Date: 12 October 1999
UK Transmission Date: 14 January 2000 (Sky),
22 September 2000 (Channel 4)

Writer: David Fury
Director: James A Contner
Cast: Lillian Birdsell (Sharon Richler), Obi Ndefo (Bartender),
Derek Hughs (Neil), Johnny Messner (Kevin),
Jennifer Tung (Neil's Pick-up Girl), Tracy Stone (Pretty Girl),
David Nisic (Slick Guy), Ken Rush (Guy), Connor Kelly (Regular)
French Title: *Cœurs Solitaires*
German Title: *Einsame Herzen*

Investigating one of Doyle's visions at a singles bar, Angel becomes attracted to Kate Lockley, failing to realise she is an off-duty cop searching for a serial-killer who uses the bar as a base. Kate, naturally, suspects her new friend . . .
Dudes and Babes: A bar full of them. Most are good-looking, lonely, vacuous and shallow. L.A. in a micro-cosm.
Denial, Thy Name is Kate: Angel quickly works out that his newest ally has problems trusting people, particularly men. We find out why in **6**, 'Sense and Sensitivity'.
It's a Designer Label!: Cordelia namechecks Calvin Klein. Doyle's huge-collared shirts are a focus of this (and subsequent) episodes and clash violently with his tan leather jacket. Cordy wears a *very* revealing red boob-tube

---

[8] Often mistakenly called 'Lonely Hearts'. Notably in the first edition of this book. This confusion extended to Fox's video release, which has the correct title on the video itself, but the plural version on the packaging!

in the opening scenes and a similar blue one later. Also, Kate's desperately obvious 'take-me-now' flowery dress and Sharon's bright red top and slit-skirt. As a seeming comment upon the hedonistic, yet hollow L.A. club scene, the bar is overflowing short skirts, curves, big chests and pretty faces.

References: The plot is reminiscent of *The Hidden*, in which a body-swopping, sex-seeking alien mollusc causes mayhem in L.A. while chased by a police detective and a rival alien. More *Batman* references, like Doyle's: 'It's not like you have a signal folks can shine in the sky whenever they need help.' The scene where Angel pulls out his grappling hook and Kate asks 'who are you?' closely parallels Batman's first meeting with Vicki Vale in Tim Burton's 1989 film. The demon that bursts out of people's chests may have been influenced by *Alien*.

'The International House of Posers' refers to the restaurant chain International House of Pancakes (IHOP), they of the award-winning pancakes, omelettes and other breakfast specialities. Also *Mission: Impossible* ('Your visions are kind of lame. They should send you one of those self-destructing tapes that come with a dossier'), *Cagney and Lacey*, classic 50s cop show *Naked City*, *Peter Pan*, Patricia McLachlin's novel, 'Sarah, Plain and Tall' (or the Glenn Close movie version), Ken and Barbie dolls and Screech, a character from *Saved by the Bell*. Geographical locations mentioned include Barstow, a town in the Mojave Desert.

The Charisma Show: Cordelia's incompetently drawn cards for Angel Investigations don't look much like an angel but, despite Kate's assertion at the end, they aren't a lobster either (see **34**, 'Blood Money'). Cordelia's reaction to Doyle picking up her bra in the apartment is great: 'That is *so* high school. Cordelia wears bras. *Ooo*, she has *girlie-parts*.'

L.A.-Speak: Cordelia: 'See *jazz-hands* over there? Mama's boy. Peter-Pan complex? Self-absorbed closet-dud, with a big "the-world-owes-me" chip on her shoulder. Check out Sarah, plain and tall? Has, or comes from, big money.'

Troublemaker: 'Nobody's talking to you, *wipe*.'

Kate: 'Way-to-come-off like a drunken slut. Slut's better then a hypocrite, right?' Angel: 'Kind of hard on yourself.' Kate: 'That's me. *Self-flagellating-hypocrite-slut*.'

Guy: 'I was pretty much a *spaz* in high school. A real 'something is out there' geek, with the gang of geek toy minions.'

Cordelia: 'It moves from body to body. And when it leaves one for the next, not going to *gag* here, the first one goes *kaplooey* pretty fast.' Doyle: 'Curdles like cream on a hot day.' Cordy: 'I believe I covered that with non-dairy *kaplooey*?'

Not Exactly A Haven For The Bruthas: The only black face with a line of dialogue is working behind the bar.

Cigarettes and Alcohol: Kate refers to a daiquiri, a cocktail of rum, lime and sugar. Sharon seems to be drinking red wine. Angel, inevitably, orders a Coke.

Sex and Drugs and Rock'n'Roll: Cordelia suggests that Doyle learned his computer skills 'downloading pictures of naked women'. Doyle agrees this is 'more or less accurate.'

Angel says the demon eviscerates its victims and that it may only be able to do so after some kind of a sex act, 'exchange of fluids kind-of-thing.' The entire episode is marbled with impotence metaphors.

'You May Remember Me From Such Films and TV Series As . . .': German-born Elisabeth Rohm is best known as Dorothy Hayes in *One Life to Live* and Alison Jeffers in *Bull*. She's also in *Law & Order* and *Eureka Street*. Obi Ndefo was Bodie in *Dawson's Creek* and has appeared in both *Star Trek: Deep Space Nine* and *Voyager* as well as *3rd Rock From the Sun*. Johnny Messner was Rob Layne in *The Guiding Light*. Jennifer Tung played an Ensign in *Star Trek: Insurrection*, appeared in *What Lies Beneath* and was on the stunt team on *Armageddon*. Tracy Stone was in *Malibu Shores*, *Dead Man on Campus* and *The Sky is Falling*. Ken Rush's movies include *Life of a Gigolo*, *Paradise Cove* and *The Midnight Hour*.

Don't Give Up The Day Job: Director James A Contner's work includes *Midnight Caller*, *21 Jump Street*, *Wiseguy*,

The Equalizer, Miami Vice, The Flash, SeaQuest DSV, Lois & Clark: The New Adventures of Superman, Roswell, Hercules: The Legendary Journeys, Dark Skies, American Gothic, The X-Files and *Charmed*. He was a cinematographer on movies like *Heat, Monkey Shines, Jaws 3-D, The Wiz, Superman* and *Times Square*. It's his camerawork on the concert footage in *Rock Show: Wings Over the World* (1976) – there's a *Six-Degrees-of-Kevin-Bacon* question: Paul McCartney to David Boreanaz. In *one*.

Logic, Let Me Introduce You to This Window: Angel and Kate run past a mirror in which Angel's face is visible. Similarly, as Angel walks away from Kate at the end, he passes a car and his reflection is seen in the window. Kate says she searched Angel's apartment (and notes he has 'some pretty weird stuff'). She certainly opens his fridge, so presumably she found the blood in it? Once again, we have stuntmen who look nothing like the actors they're supposed to be replacing during the climactic alley brawl.

I Just *Love* Your Accent: Doyle uses the *very* European insult 'git'.

Quote/Unquote: Angel: 'This socialising thing is brutal. I was young once, I used to go to bars. It wasn't anything like this.' Doyle: 'You used to go to *taverns*. Small towns, where everybody knew each other.' Cordelia: 'Yeah, like high school. It was easy to date there. We all had so much in common. Being monster food every other week, for instance.'

Kate: 'You can go to *Hell*.' Angel: 'Been there, done that.'

Notes: 'Are you maybe in need of some rescuing?' Considering how well David Fury writes comedy on *Buffy*, 'Lonely Heart' spends a lot of time getting surprisingly few laughs. Fundamentally flawed, it shows much evidence of last minute rewriting, while the payoff is a long time coming and we go down a lot of blind alleys (literal *and* metaphorical) before we get there.

Angel Investigation's telephone number is 555-0162 (the reason 555 is used as a phone prefix in many US TV shows is that it's one of the few three-figure numbers that isn't a real area code. See, also *The X-Files*, *Roswell*). The two newspapers Doyle finds details of the murders in are the *West Hollywood Courier* and the *Los Angeles Globe Register*. Doyle explains that the invitation rule for vampires only stays in effect while the owner of the home is alive (see **1**, 'City Of', **5**, 'Rm W/a Vu', **15**, 'The Prodigal'). Cordelia's apartment is half-painted and sparsely furnished.

Doyle mentions Piasca, a flesh-eating Indian demon that enters victims through the mouth and eviscerates from within. Kate lives close to the D'Oblique, where she is a regular. She has a hard time trusting people, particularly 'male people' (see **6**, 'Sense and Sensitivity').

Soundtrack: A vast array of rave and techno is heard including: Ian Fletcher's 'Deadside', Ultra-Electronic's 'Dissonance', 'Girlfish' by THC, 'Do You Want Me?' by Kelly Soce, Sapien's 'Neo-Climactic', Chucho Merchan's 'Ballad of Amave', Mark Cherrie and Ian McKenzie's 'Lady Daze', 'Emily Says' by Chainsuck, 'Touched' by Vast, Adam Hamilton's 'For You' and 'Quango' by Helix.

Did You Know?: When it comes to the stunts on *Angel*, David Boreanaz told *The Big Breakfast*: 'I do as many as I possibly can. Of course the producers don't want me to . . . My stuntperson Mike Massa does [about] 80 per cent.'

Joss Whedon Comments: Joss told the *BtVS* posting-board: 'Re: *Angel* [and] sunlight. That's been a problem. It's hard to light the show and avoid it entirely. Tonight there was a shot that was colourtimed so that what was supposed to be pre-dawn came out like post-dawn. Bear with us, we know it's not all there yet.'

Previously on *Buffy the Vampire Slayer*: 'The Harsh Light of Day': Spike returns to Sunnydale to locate the Gem of Amara, a vampire holy grail which renders its wearer indestructible. After finding the gem, Spike attacks Buffy but she manages to wrestle the ring from his finger. Buffy tells her friends that she wants Angel to have it. Oz has a gig in L.A. and will deliver her gift.

3
In The Dark

US Transmission Date: 19 October 1999
UK Transmission Date: 21 January 2000 (Sky),
29 September 2000 (Channel 4)

Writer: Douglas Petrie
Director: Bruce Seth Green
Cast: James Marsters (Spike), Seth Green (Daniel 'Oz' Osborne),
Kevin West (Marcus), Malia Mathis (Rachel), Machael Yayweli (Lenny),
Ric Sarabia (Vendor), Tom Rosales (Manny the Pig),
Gil Combs (Bouncer), Buck McDancer (Dealer),
Jenni Blong (Young Woman)
French Title: *Et Pour Toujours La Nuit . . .*
German Title: *Der Ring von Amara*

Oz gives Angel the Gem, but Spike, together with a vampire torturer, Marcus, kidnaps Angel demanding the ring as a ransom for his life. Angel is eventually rescued by Doyle, Cordelia and Oz but not before Marcus has double-crossed Spike to obtain the ring. Angel kills Marcus and enjoys his first daylight in over two hundred years. Then he destroys the ring so that it cannot fall into the wrong hands again.

Dudes and Babes: Rippling bicep-alert. Again. (See **1**, 'City Of'.)

It's a Designer Label!: Cordelia mentions the late fashion designer Gianni Versace. We'll pass quickly over Rachel's *Urban Tramp* look and on to Cordelia's jogging pants. Also, Oz's purple sunglasses.

References: 'The Angel-mobile' is yet another *Batman* reference (the fifth in three episodes for those keeping count; and that's ignoring visual stuff). 'I think the trick is laying off the ale before you start quoting *Angela's Ashes* and weeping like a baby-man,' concerns Frank McCourt's novel about a family living in America and Ireland. There are namechecks for Matthew McConaughey (*A Time to Kill*, *Amistad*, *Dazed and Confused*), Barney, Betty and Bam-Bam Rubble from *The Flintstones* and Johnny Storm the Human Torch (of *The Fantastic Four*). 'The Johnny

Depp once-over' refers to the hotel-wrecking antics of this author's favourite actor, celebrity *Fast Show* fan and occasional Oasis slide-guitarist, star of *21 Jump Street*, *Cry-Baby*, *Edward Scissorhands*, *Ed Wood*, *Donnie Brasco*, *Sleepy Hollow* and *From Hell*.

Spike's 'Lucy, I'm home!' was Desi Arnaz's catchphrase in *I Love Lucy*. Cordelia's 'See girl in distress. See Angel save girl from druggy-stalker-boyfriend' speech follows the format of the *Dick and Jane* books. Spike preferring Mozart's 'older, funnier symphonies' is an allusion to Woody Allen's *Stardust Memories*. Marcus quotes *Hamlet*: 'There is nothing either bad or good but thinking makes it so.' When searching for the ring Cordelia notes: 'It's not in the freezer and it's not in the toilet tank. In the movies it's always in one of those places.'

Oz's van interior includes posters for US grunge act Filter and the seminal Nick Cave and the Bad Seeds LP *The Good Son*. The two movies showing at the Orpheum (a splendid downtown cinema with a mix of French Renaissance and Baroque decor, see **57**, 'Waiting in the Wings') that Oz's van passes are *The Sixth Sense* and *Deep Blue Sea*. Many of the shots of Oz driving around L.A. were filmed on the Ventura Freeway near the Warner Brothers studios in Burbank and at the Red Line Subway Terminus on Lankershim Blvd in North Hollywood. Geographical references include a nod to Los Angeles's most legendary street, Sunset Boulevard ('that freaky church on Sunset'). Also, 'a joint on Third called the Orbit Room', and 'Peterson's Fishery between Seward and Westminster'.

Bitch!: Spike's miaow-moment when he tells Cordelia, 'you look smashing. Did you lose weight?' Cordy confirms that she's been using the gym before realising that she's being patronised.

Cordelia, on Doyle's apartment: 'I couldn't get comfortable in here if the floor was lined with mink. How can you live like this?' Doyle: 'I didn't until last week. Then I saw what *you* did with *your* place and I just had to call my decorator.' (See **2**, 'Lonely Heart'.)

Spike: 'It's called addiction, Angel. We all have it. I believe yours is named *Slutty the Vampire Slayer*.'

'West Hollywood?': 'Nancy boy hair gel', 'magnificent *pouf*', Rachel understanding Angel because she has a 'nephew who is gay'. Does anyone get the impression that the subtext is rapidly becoming the text?

The Charisma Show: Cordelia's realisation that Frankie Tripod isn't a three-legged demon, but rather a nickname for a man with a large penis.

L.A.-Speak: Cordelia, on Doyle: 'He "air quotes" works here.' And: '*No way*. My apartment is nowhere near this *yucky*.'

Doyle: 'Can we concentrate on the *motherlode* Angel just hit?' And: 'Think of it, man. Poolside tanning, bargain matinées, plus I know a couple of strip-clubs that have a fabulous luncheon buffet . . . I've heard.' And: 'What, a C note? I absolutely paid that back.' And: 'I bet he's out *hangin'*-ten right about now, out on the sandy shore at Malibu. Wind in his hair, bikini babes a-whistlin'.'

Rachel: 'I just start to *jones* for him. The way he *jones's* for *rock*.'

Spike: 'Caught me fair and square, white hat. I guess there is nothing to do now but go quietly and pay my debt to society.' And: 'To coin a popular Sunnydale phrase: "*Duh*".'

Cigarettes and Alcohol: Rachel stubs out her cigarette on a used dinner plate. Disgusting.

Sex and Drugs and Rock'n'Roll: Rachel refers to rock (the street name for crack-cocaine). Oz listens to KLA-Rock, 'L.A.'s only modern alternative' radio station.

'You May Remember Me From Such Films and TV Series As . . .': Seth Green's movies include *Stephen King's It*, *Radio Days*, *Can't Hardly Wait* (as Kenny Fisher), *Idle Hands*, *Enemy of the State*, *Knockabout Guys*, *Josie and the Pussycats* (as Travis), *Austin Powers: International Man of Mystery* and *Austin Powers: The Spy Who Shagged Me* (as Scott Evil) and *My Stepmother is an Alien* (as Alyson Hannigan's boyfriend). He played a very Oz-like character in *The X-Files* episode 'Deep Throat' and provides the voice for Chris Griffin in *Family Guy*. Seth is a *great* actor and his (usually understated) contributions to *Buffy* can't be praised highly enough. 'He can *own* a scene he has no lines in,' notes Joss Whedon.

James Marsters isn't from London, though the accent is good enough to fool the most discriminating UK fans. He's actually from Greendale, California and, aside from *Buffy*, he can also be seen (using his "real" voice) in *Millennium* and, briefly, the movie *House on Haunted Hill*. Kevin West's movie CV includes *Super Mario Bros*, *Indecent Proposal* and *Killer Tomatoes Eat France!* Jenni Blong has roles in *Cry-Baby* and *200 Cigarettes*.

Don't Give Up The Day Job: Doug Petrie wrote the 1996 movie *Harriet The Spy* along with episodes of *Clarissa Explains It All*. No relation to his actor near-namesake, director Bruce Seth Green's TV work includes series such as *Knight Rider*, *Airwolf*, *MacGyver*, *She-Wolf of London*, *V*, *SeaQuest DSV*, *Xena: Warrior Princess*, *Roswell*, *TJ Hooker*, *Hercules: The Legendary Journeys*, *American Gothic* and *Jack & Jill* as well as numerous episodes of *Buffy*.

Despite a noted appearance as Richard Nixon in *Hot Shots: Part Deux*, Buck 'Dallas' McDancer's usual role is that of stuntman, having worked on films including *Scarface*, *Legal Eagles*, *In the Line of Fire*, *Airheads*, *Vampire in Brooklyn* and *Star Trek: Insurrection*. Gil Combs is also a stuntman on *Hollow Man*, *Very Bad Things*, *Speed* and *Die Hard*. Aside from acting (in movies as diverse as *8 Heads in a Duffel Bag* and *Short Circuit 2*), Ric Sarabia is the frontman of L.A.-based funk-rap band Tastes Like Chicken.

Logic, Let Me Introduce You to This Window: When Cordelia prints an invoice, the printer has paper in it for front-shots, but from the back the tray seems empty. As Angel and Spike fight around Angel's car, reflections of both can be seen in the windows.

I Just *Love* Your Accent: *Yer man* Doyle conforms to 'drunken Oyrishmen' stereotypes by 'going to celebrate with a drink down the pub'. Cordelia helpfully adds that he'd celebrate the opening of a mailbox with a drink at the pub. Guinness, no doubt? *Begorrah*.

Spike notes: '*Ooh*, the Mick's got spine. Maybe I'll snap it in two.' Cordelia refers to Spike as 'little cockney'.

Quote/Unquote: Spike's opening commentary. The funniest thing on TV in *years*: [Rachel voice] 'How can I thank you, you mysterious black-clad hunk of a night-thing? [Angel voice] No need, little lady, your tears of gratitude are enough for me. You see, I was once a badass vampire, but love and a pesky curse defanged me. Now I'm just a big, fluffy puppy with bad teeth. No, not the hair! Never the hair! [Rachel voice] But there must be some way I can show my appreciation. [Angel voice] No, helping those in need's my job, and working up a load of sexual tension and prancing away like a magnificent *pouf* is truly thanks enough. [Rachel voice] I understand. I have a nephew who is gay, so . . . [Angel voice] Say no more. Evil's still afoot. And I'm almost out of that nancy-boy hair-gel I like so much. Quickly, to the Angel-mobile, away.'

Oz asks if 'Detective' Angel has a hat and a gun. Cordelia: 'Just fangs.'

Spike, as Marcus sticks a skewer into Angel: 'Someone's having shish-kebab.'

Cordelia: 'This isn't a needle in a haystack, this is a needle in Kansas.'

Notes: 'I don't know about you, but I had a nice day. Except for the bulk of it where I was nearly tortured to death.' An episode that is, by turns, hilarious (Spike's opening narration) and extremely graphic. Those without *very* strong stomachs might want to avoid some of the Marcus/Angel torture sequences. Truly wonderful final scenes, however, and it's conceptually a cornerstone of the series with Angel facing his darkest corner and emerging triumphant.

Angel performs t'ai-chi exercises (see *Buffy*: 'Band Candy', 'Revelations'). He refers to Doyle's mother and indicates that they have met, or at least spoken (see 7, 'The Bachelor Party'). Doyle, in demon form, has the ability to smell the location of inanimate objects (or super-powerful rings, anyway). Oz knows basic sixth-grade first aid.

When Oz arrives, Cordelia's 'catching up' involves asking how the Bronze is ('the same') and the Scooby Gang ('they're good'). She later asks about Buffy and if she's 'still the brave little Slayer or is she moping around in the dark like nobody around here.' Oz sums up the plot of 'The Harsh Light of Day' thus: 'Your buddy Spike dug up Sunnydale looking for [the Gem]. He got a fistful of Buffy and left it behind.' Spike's version is somewhat different: 'Speaking of little Buff, I ran into her recently. Your name didn't come up. Although she has been awful busy jumping the bones of the first lunkhead that came along. Good-looking fellah. Used her shamelessly. She *is* cute when she's hurting.'

Cordelia tells Doyle that Spike has 'nearly done Buffy in a few times', and mentions that he claimed to have killed two Slayers (see *Buffy*: 'School Hard', 'Fool for Love' and **29** 'Darla'). She condenses the complex plot of the *Buffy* episodes 'Surprise' and 'Innocence' into: 'One time he and Dru raised this demon that burned people from the inside. It was this whole weird thing with an arm in a box.' This *is* accurate.

The Gem of Amara 'renders its wearer one hundred per cent unkillable if he's a vampire'. Doyle notes that this includes fire and sunlight. Spike says Marcus is 'a bloody king of torture ... Beneath the cool exterior, you'll find he's rather shy. Except with kids ... [He] likes to eat. And other nasty things.' Spike confirms that Angel sired him (see *Buffy*: 'School Hard') which is flatly contradicted in *Buffy*: 'Fool for Love' (and **29**, 'Darla').

Soundtrack: Mozart's *Symphony No. 41*. Unfortunately, Spike can't tell his Mozart from his Brahms. The song on the radio in Oz's van is 'Smoker's Revenge'. The artist is unknown.

Jane Espenson's Comments: Asked on the *BtVS* Posting Board about the writing process, Jane Espenson fascinatingly spelled out what happens to an average script: 'Joss and the staff work out the story for each episode together and in detail. In theory. In actuality, we all sit and pretend we're being helpful while Joss works out the story. Then the writer for that episode writes a "beat sheet", then a "full outline", based on that work. An outline is usually fourteen pages of single-spaced text in which each scene is described [as per] what Joss worked out. What the writer has added at this point is an indication of the shape of the scene – the order the information comes out in, some more specifics about what each character thinks and expresses during the scene, how it transitions into the next scenes, a few sample jokes. Joss gives the writer notes on the outline. He nixes bad things, adds good things, makes sure it's on track. Then the writer writes the first draft. From fourteen pages you go to approximately 50–55 pages of fun-filled description and dialogue. It may sound like this doesn't leave much room for individual creativity, after all, the writer knows exactly what will happen in each scene, but in fact, there are many ways to write each scene and the writer has to pick the best way. Then Joss gives notes on the first draft. These can be minor or enormously detailed, or "This scene? Make it better." There may be further drafts after that, time-permitting. Eventually, Joss takes the script away from the writer, into his lair of genius and does his own rewrite. Again, [it can be] minor or enormous. Then it gets filmed. So I laugh when people say that one of us has better "plotting" than another or that Joss wouldn't have let a character say that if he'd written the episode. It *all* goes through the big guy and it's all better for it . . . When Joss writes an episode, Joss writes an episode *himself*. It's a beautiful process of aloneness. Actually quite inspiring.'

Channel Swore: Channel 4's decision to broadcast *Angel* at 6 p.m. finally came unstuck with this episode which, despite their editing over five minutes from the running time, still aroused the ire of the ITC, British television's independent watchdog. This upheld 86 viewer complaints against *Angel* in breach of sections 1.2 (i) and 1.6 (i) of 'The Programme Code' concerning taste and decency. In their subsequent report, the ITC noted that 'viewers were concerned about the violence and the generally adult tone of the series shown at a time when young children could be watching television on their own. Some viewers were also dismayed at the amount of editing that had been carried out by Channel 4. They, too, believed that this series should have been shown later.' Channel 4 defended its transmission of the series on the grounds that *Angel* is 'enjoyed by a wide audience'. After viewing the series, the ITC was concerned about the dark tone of Angel's world. Even with editing, the ITC considered that three episodes were unsuitable for this early evening slot; 3, 'In the Dark' ('scenes of torture and paedophile references'), 4, 'I Fall to Pieces' ('the theme of a stalker had an underlying sexual tone and images reminiscent of a late-night horror film') and 5, 'Rm W/a Vu' ('poltergeist attributes of a ghost along with the harrowing storyline of a mother bricking up her son alive'). Seemingly they didn't look much beyond those episodes. Wonder what they'd have made of something like 16, 'The Ring'? Overall, the ITC was concerned about the scheduling 'which clearly even substantial editing could not always address'. When Channel 4 became aware of the ITC's concern, it discontinued the scheduling of episodes starting even earlier at 5.25 p.m. and dropped stronger episodes altogether (for instance, 12, 'Expecting'). Channel 4 also informed the ITC that *Angel* 'would be rescheduled from late November after the 9 p.m. watershed.' Where it should have been all along.

4
I Fall To Pieces

US Transmission Date: 26 October 1999
UK Transmission Date: 28 January 2000 (Sky),
6 October 2000 (Channel 4)

Writers: Joss Whedon, David Greenwalt
Director: Vern Gillum
Cast: Tushka Bergen (Melissa Burns),
Andy Umberger (Dr Ronald Meltzer),
Carlos Carrasco (Vinpur Narpudan), Brent Sexton (Dead Cop),
Garikayi Mutambarawa (Intern), Kent Davis (John),

Jan Bartlett (Penny), Patricia Gillum (Woman Patient)
French Title: *Jeu De Mains, Jeu De Vilain!*
German Title: *Die Maschen des Dr Meltzer*

A woman hires Angel Investigations to guard her from the attentions of the doctor who is stalking her. Angel discovers that the man, through a form of Eastern mysticism, can dismember himself and use his body parts to spy on the object of his desire and kill those who get in his way.

Dudes and Babes: Cordelia, on men: 'Either you like them and they don't like you. Or you can't stand them, which just guarantees that they're gonna hover around and never go away.' Doyle [trying not to hover]: 'I hate guys like that.'

It's a Designer Label!: Cordelia notes that she has certain needs. For 'designer . . . things.' She wears a white T-shirt and a fetching purple dress. Angel asks: 'Am I intimidating?' Cordelia: 'As vampires go, you're pretty cuddly. Maybe you might want to think about mixing up the black-on-black look.' Next scene, he's changed into a cream sweater.

References: The title comes from Patsy Cline's 1962 hit (it's the song a heartbroken Xander listens to after Buffy rejects him in 'Prophecy Girl'). Influences on a story about a detached hand with a life of its own include *The Addams Family*, *Dr Terror's House of Horror*, *The Hands of Orlac*, *The Beast With Five Fingers*, *The Hand* and *Evil Dead 2*. Kate notes that Wolfram & Hart are 'the law firm that Johnny Cochran is too ethical to join'. Also, a quote from Walter Scott's poem 'Flodden Field' ('what a tangled web'), references to escapologist Harry Houdini, and OJ Simpson. Doyle hilariously quotes Barbara Streisand's 'People' (from *Funny Girl*).

Bitch!: Cordelia's in sympathetic mode, but she does tell Doyle: 'You're a lot smarter than you look. Of course you look like a retard.'

'West Hollywood?': Doyle on Angel: 'He likes playing the hero. Walking off into the dark, long coat flowing behind him in that mysterious and attractive way.' Cordelia: 'Is this a private moment?' Doyle: 'I'm not saying *I'm* attracted . . .' Then, later, after Angel leaves in exactly this fashion: 'Okay, maybe I'm a *little* attracted.'

The Charisma Show: Cordelia's assessment of Meltzer: 'Here's this poor girl, she hooks up with a doctor. That's supposed to be a good thing. You should be able to call home and say: "Hey mom, guess what? I've met a doctor." Not, "guess what? I met a psycho and he's stalking me and oh, by the way, his hands and feet come off and he's not even in the circus".' Plus her triumphant: 'See, you *can* save damsel *and* make decent money. Is this a great country or what?'

L.A.-Speak: Doyle: 'Protect and serve. It's *entirely* my bag.'

Cordelia: 'Just between us what's the real dish on this guy?'

Cordelia: 'You *so* don't want this guy fixated on you. What is stalking nowadays, the third most popular sport among men?' Angel: '*Fourth*, after luge.'

Cigarettes and Alcohol: Doyle asks for a single malt scotch after his vision. Whatever Angel gives him, it tastes more like 'polymalt'. Doyle puts whisky in Melissa's tea to help her sleep.

Sex and Drugs and Rock'n'Roll: Melissa is taking the tranquilliser Xanitab. Meltzer prescribed a Calcium-Selenium supplement for her.

Meltzer describes Angel as a 'vacuous L.A. pretty boy.'

'You May Remember Me From Such Films and TV Series As . . .': Tushka Bergen played Alice Hastings in *Journey to the Centre of the Earth*. Her films include *Culture*, *Voices* and *Barcelona*. On TV she appeared in *The Others*, *Fantasy Island* and the fantastically weird 'The Dig' episode of *Bergerac*. Andy Umberger is well known to *Buffy* fans as the vengeance demon D'Hoffryn in 'Doppelgängland' and 'Something Blue'. He's also been in *The West Wing* and *NYPD Blue*. Carlos Carrasco's movies include *The Fisher King*, *Speed*, *Crocodile Dundee II* and *Across the Line*. He appeared in several episodes of *Star Trek: Deep Space Nine*.

Don't Give Up The Day Job: Vern Gillum has worked on *Baywatch*, *Space: Above and Beyond*, *Sliders* and *Brimstone*. The 'part' of the doctor's dismembered hands was played by Christopher Hart who did a similar job for Thing in *The Addams Family*.

Logic, Let Me Introduce You to This Window: In the opening scene, Cordelia has the invoice in her left hand. The camera switches angle and it moves to the right. When Angel spies on Ronald in his office, he walks past a chrome light-switch cover on which his reflection is seen. Angel drinks coffee, despite the fact that in *Buffy*: 'The Prom' he told Joyce Summers that he didn't because it makes him jittery. When Angel goes to see Kate, he leaves wearing the cream sweater, but arrives wearing the black one he had on earlier.

As Meltzer catches Angel in his office, Angel is holding a book. Yet when he turns the book is gone. If Angel has no heart, why does the poison affect him? How is Ronald able to change Melissa's bank PIN number? Cordelia asks Doyle if he's ever had a relationship and he replies 'Not me personally. But I've read . . .' Three episodes later we find out that this simply isn't true (see 7, 'The Bachelor Party').

I Just *Love* Your Accent: Doyle tells Melissa 'drink up, love, it's all over'. Say 'love' to the average American and they either think you're coming on to them, or that you're a hippy. He also calls Cordelia 'princess' without getting his nose broken, which is an achievement.

Quote/Unquote: Cordelia's slogan for Angel Investigations: 'We help the hopeless.'

Doyle: 'Protecting young women such as yourself? Yeah, there've been . . . four. And *three* of them are very much alive!'

Kate: 'This guy could go to jail tomorrow and still kill her in her dreams every night. I've put a few of these creeps away and the hardest thing is to know that he's still winning.'

Notes: 'Flesh, anytime you want to stop crawling is okay with me.' A study of voyeurism that just about manages to avoid being, itself, voyeuristic by focusing on empowerment. A *lot* of old horror clichés are thrown about with abandon and much of the acting and dialogue are indifferent. However, the 'False-Teeth-of-Death' raise the episode to the level of high camp. And *what* an opening shot of the sun rising over Los Angeles.

Cordelia, on Doyle's visions: 'Last time [they] led to a sex-changing, body-switching, tear-your-innards-out-demon, right? I guess they don't call you for their everyday cases,' refers to **2**, 'Lonely Heart'. Doyle mentions an Aunt Tudy who seems rather a large woman. Angel uses the alias Brian Jensen when visiting Meltzer. The book that Angel steals from Meltzer's office is *Anything's Possible* by Vinpur Natpudan. The inscription reads: 'To Ronald. Thanks for having the "nerve" to believe. Fondly, Vin.' The magazine in the hospital cafeteria is *The Journal of Diagnostic Orthopedic Neuropathy*.

Did You Know?: The Angel Investigations building used in season one was located on a soundstage at Paramount Studios on Melrose Avenue in Hollywood, not too far from the *Star Trek: Voyager* bridge. Both are close to the CrashDown Café set from *Roswell*. Paramount was also where legendary sitcoms like *Happy Days* and *Mork & Mindy* were filmed.

Joss Whedon's Comments: Joss has confirmed that 'I Fall to Pieces' started life as a *Buffy* story idea: 'The fellow whose limbs came apart I originally thought [of] as a *Buffy* thing but . . . when we talked about a story on stalking it made perfect sense to have it on *Angel*.'

Changes: As Tim Minear told *The Watcher's Web*: 'Initially, *Angel* was conceived as more of an anthology show, with the emotional emphasis on the 'guest' characters' problems. You can see this in stories like the woman being stalked in **4**, 'I Fall To Pieces.' As we found our legs, we discovered that our core of regular characters seemed to be where our, and in turn the audience's, interest was. I think this is clear by the time we got to **17**, 'Eternity.' Watching the core group interact is where the real emotional action is. I think that will shape the future.'

5
Rm W/a Vu

US Transmission Date: 2 November 1999
UK Transmission Date: 4 February 2000 (Sky),
13 October 2000 (Channel 4)

Teleplay: Jane Espenson
Story: David Greenwalt, Jane Espenson
Director: Scott McGillis
Cast: Beth Grant (Maude Pearson), Marcus Redmond (Griff),
Denney Pierce (Vic), Greg Collins (Keith), Corey Klemow (Young Man),
Lara McGrath (Manager), BJ Porter (Dennis Pearson),
Lyle Kanouse (Disgusting Man[9])
French Title: *Jeune Femme Cherche Appartement* – less a title, more a plot
description
German Title: *Zimmer mit Aussicht*

Cordelia finds a beautiful apartment for a very reasonable price. The only snag is that it has a ghost who doesn't like sharing its living space. Doyle, meanwhile, is having problems of his own with a demonic debt collector.

Dreaming (As *Buffy* Often Proves) is Free: The flashback to Maude walling up her son is one of the scariest moments in the series because the dialogue is so bland and casual.

Dudes and Babes: Boreanaz appears almost naked (covered only by a small towel). *Very* popular with people of all sexualities, interestingly.

Denial, Thy Name is Maude: Spending 40 years chasing off every female in the vicinity isn't the most balanced of actions, even for a ghost.

It's a Designer Label!: Cordelia's suitcases are from Louis Vuitton's collection. She wears Nike trainers. Even Angel's Calvin Klein boxers are black. Cordelia confirms what we've all suspected for some time, Angel wears mousse.

References: The episode title is written in the style of a classified newspaper advert for an apartment. *A Room With a View*, from which this is a shortened form, is a Merchant-Ivory film adapted from EM Forster's novel.

---

[9] Uncredited.

There's another *Batman* reference (Cordelia says her rival for an acting job looked like Catwoman). The credit card commercial Doyle talks about seems to be a Mastercard ad: these usually end with something that cannot be defined by money. Also, *Casper The Friendly Ghost*, *Poltergeist* ('You see a light? Go towards it.'), Patrick Swayze and his performance in *Ghost*, Elton John's 'The Bitch is Back' and the acting brothers Dave Paymer (*Get Shorty*, *City Slickers*, *Murphy Brown*) and Steve Paymer (*Mad About You*).

Bitch!: Maude calls Cordelia a 'stupid little bitch'. Cordelia replies: 'I'm not a snivelling whiny little cry-Buffy. I'm the nastiest girl in Sunnydale history. I take crap from no one ... Get ready to haul your wrinkly translucent ass outta this place, because lady, *the bitch is back*.'

The Charisma Show: *The* episode for Charisma fans. She insists that she is *not* giving up the apartment because, despite its being haunted, it's also 'rent controlled.' And, best of all: 'I'm a girl from The Projects!'

L.A.-Speak: Demon: '*Screw you.*'

Doyle, on the story of his life: 'Quite a tale it is, too. Full of ribald adventure and beautiful damsels with loose morals ...'

Cigarettes and Diet Root Beer: Cordelia drinks diet root beer judging from the can that Dennis moves around her coffee table.

Sex and Drugs and Rock'n'Roll: Since Angel doesn't eat (see **8**, 'I Will Remember You', **40**, 'Dead End') it *must* have been Cordelia who got the peanut butter on the bedclothes.

'You May Remember Me From Such Films and TV Series As ...': Beth Grant was Helen in *Speed* and Sissy Hickey in *Sordid Lives*, while her other movies include *Doctor Doolittle*, *Dance With Me*, *A Time to Kill*, *Too Wong Foo, Thanks For Everything, Julie Newmar*, *The Dark Half*, *Flatliners*, *Child's Play 2* and *Rain Man*. On TV, she's been in *Malcolm in the Middle*, *Friends* and provided voices for *King of the Hill*. Marcus Redmond played Detective Kevin in *Fight Club* and Raymond Alexander in *Doogie Howser*

MD. Greg Collins gets lots of roles in big budget movies, normally playing cops. He's in *Enemy of the State*, *Gone in Sixty Seconds*, *Armageddon*, *Godzilla*, *Con Air*, *Independence Day*, *The Rock* and *Police Academy 6: City Under Siege*. Corey Klemow was Joe Martindale in *Spiders*, Benson in *Family Audit* and Ross in *Rubbernecking*. Lyle Kanouse appeared in *Kate's Addiction*, *Whipped* and *The Nanny*.

Don't Give Up The Day Job: Award-winning *Buffy* writer/producer Jane Espenson ('Band Candy', 'Earshot', 'The Harsh Light of Day', 'Pangs', 'A New Man', 'Superstar', 'Triangle', 'The Replacement', 'I Was Made to Love You' amongst others) has also written for *Ellen*, *Dinosaurs*, *Nowhere Man* and *Star Trek: Deep Space Nine*. Scott McGillis, before becoming a director, was an actor on *Star Trek III: The Search for Spock*, *Sky Bandits*, *You Can't Hurry Love* and *Operation Petticoat*. Though he acted in *Lawnmower Man* and *Terminator 2: Judgment Day*, Denney Pierce is primarily a stuntman with credits on *The Cider House Rules*, *American History X*, *Anaconda*, *Primal Fear*, *Last Man Standing*, *Village of the Damned*, *Sneakers*, *The Abyss* and *1969*.

There's A Ghost In My House (or Two ...): Dennis Pearson, walled up by his insane mother to stop him eloping, so his spirit is bound to the apartment. He is able to manifest his face by pressing into surfaces and can also move objects and change TV channels. He seems relatively harmless and Cordelia takes something of a shine to him. His mom, on the other hand ...

Logic, Let Me Introduce You to This Window: When Doyle enters the offices, he puts his key in the lock and opens the door, but we never see the lock turn. The second hand on his watch isn't moving when he looks at it. When Cordelia and Doyle are in Angel's apartment, the can of Chock Full O' Nuts is facing in different directions from one shot to the next. There are two different models of Philco refrigerators used in Angel's apartment. The one in this episode is squarish with the maker's name across the door. The other model (seen in other first season episodes) is rounded, with the name near the handle. When Angel rings the office from the police station, not only doesn't he wait for the coin to drop, but he dials too many numbers. The noose used to hang Cordelia disappears and reappears several times.

When Cordelia is giving her audition to Doyle she brushes her hair behind her ears. During an angle switch it moves back to its original position. When the ghost face peers through the wall there is a lamp on the table to one side which disappears in subsequent shots. As Angel and Doyle arrive at the apartment, it's obviously afternoon. How did Angel get there without bursting into flames, especially as Doyle walks in and closes the drapes? One of the Kailiff demons shoots a tile on the fireplace, but later, the tile is intact. Angel is hit in the head with a flying book during the cleansing scene (that could have been deliberate, though it looks rather painful for David). There is no chain lock on Cordy's old apartment door, yet there was one in 2, 'Lonely Heart'. When Angel tells Doyle about the Cordettes, he is reading a book. From one angle, his hand is on the desk, but in another, it's resting on his leg. There's a red neon sign flashing and a fire escape outside the window of Doyle's apartment. The front shot of the building shows a fire escape, but no neon sign. Footsteps can be heard within the office when Doyle shows Angel and Cordelia what he's found on the computer. When Cordelia walks into the bedroom in the new apartment, there is one large picture over the bed; that night, there are two small pictures. Vampires can, seemingly, be invited into a home even if they are nowhere near the home at the time (and it isn't even yet purchased). As Cordelia notes, the rules are 'getting all screwed up.'

I Just *Love* Your Accent: Doyle asks Cordelia if anybody rang asking about him. 'Your cousin called, with one of those names from your part of England.'

Quote/Unquote: Angel, on Aura: 'I think she's one of Cordelia's group. People called them *The Cordettes*. A bunch of girls from wealthy families. They ruled high school. Decided what was in, who was popular. It was like the Soviet Secret Police. If they cared a lot about shoes.'

Cordelia: 'My urination just hasn't been public enough lately.'

Doyle: 'What about friendship and family and all those things that are priceless like they say in that credit card commercial?'

Notes: 'You're gonna pack your little ghost bags and *get the hell out of my house.*' Jane Espenson again proves she's one of the best writers of comedy *and* character-based drama on TV. Often at the same time. This *House That Bled to Death* variant is brilliantly assembled, with a great line of dialogue every 30 seconds and some genuine scares amid the Cordelia-induced hilarity. The series' standard themes of guilt and redemption continue with Cordy the focus this time (see **1**, 'City Of', **3**, 'In the Dark', **9**, 'Hero'). Unsurprisingly, it's Charisma's favourite episode and *Angel*'s first 24-carat classic.

There's a painting by the sliding door in Angel's apartment of a woman playing a flute. Angel says that Cordelia can't type or file, which we knew anyway. The stations that appear on Cordelia's 'haunted radio' are 107.9FM and 1400AM. Cordelia's latest audition is for trash bags. The names in her phone book under 'D' are: Tom D, Doyle, Danielle, and two entries for David (one crossed out). Doyle's phone number is 555-0189. Doyle notes that Cordelia's high school diploma is 'all burned' – 'It was a rough ceremony,' notes Cordy, referring to the events of *Buffy*: 'Graduation Day'. One of her five trophies 'with some of the shiny worn off' is Queen of the Winter Ball. Cordelia's new address is #212 Pearson Arms (see **23**, 'Judgment'). Doyle claims to play badminton; he always meant to learn Latin but never did.

Presumably Aura is the same girl who found the 'totally dead' guy in her locker in *Buffy*: 'Welcome To The Hellmouth'. When Cordy is discussing 'who's wearing what in Sunnydale', and hears about a girl who 'never did have any taste . . . She is *so* nasty', Aura *could* be telling her about their old friend Harmony Kendall and which vampire she's dating in *Buffy*: 'The Harsh Light of Day', 'The Initiative' and 'Pangs' (see **39**, Disharmony).

The three suicides mentioned as occurring in apartment 212 were: Margo Dressner, 3 October 1959, Jenny Kim, 18 October 1965 and Natalie Davis, 7 March 1994. Doyle finds the report of the death of Maude Pearson in the *Los Angeles Globe Register*, one of the newspapers seen in **2**, 'Lonely Heart' (see **11**, 'Somnambulist').

Soundtrack: The Mills Brothers' 1940s classic 'You Always Hurt the One You Love' is heard along with Beethoven's 9th Symphony (the 'Ode to Joy'). This seems to be a favourite of Angel's as he hummed it in *Buffy*: 'Killed By Death'. Maybe he's a fan of *A Clockwork Orange* which also uses it prominently. Tommy Henriksen's 'Everyday' and the instrumental 'Big Band Era' from OGM Production Music. Also worthy of praise is the excellent soundtrack: dramatic in places and funny in others and, as such, a perfect metaphor for the episode.

Did You Know?: As the ghost says, 'this is my house,' and Cordelia gets up and runs away from camera, the tattoo on Charisma Carpenter's back can be briefly glimpsed. Readers can see it in much greater detail on the cover of the October 1999 edition of *FHM* magazine.

Jane Espenson's Comments: On how scripts are assigned: 'Usually it kind of rotates. Whoever has had the longest break writes the next one. But if one person pitched a specific idea, they usually get to write it (like my 'Band Candy'). Or if a specific story calls for a specific kind of writing strength – Marti [Noxon] tends to get the big love relationship stories. And then sometimes a writer's personal schedule will dictate which episodes they're available for . . . As for Angel dripping wet in a towel, actually, first I wrote the scene with him reading a book, fully clothed. Then I thought, hey, not particularly cinematic choice. What might work better? Dripping wet and naked just suggested itself . . . I think it's a little better than the whole book thing. But America didn't get to hear all the funny lines I wrote about *Wuthering Heights*.'

6
Sense And Sensitivity

US Transmission Date: 9 November 1999
UK Transmission Date: 11 February 2000 (Sky),
20 October 2000 (Channel 4)

Writer: Tim Minear
Director: James A Contner
Cast: John Capodice (Little Tony Papazian), Ron Marasco (Allen Lloyd),
Alex Skuby (Harlan), Kevin Will (Heath), Ken Abraham (Spivey),
Jimmy Shubert (Johnny Red), Ken Grantham (Lieutenant),
Adam Donshik (Uniform Cop #1), Kevin E West (Uniform Cop #2),
Wilson Bell (Uniform Cop #3), Colin Patrick Lynch (Beat Cop),
Steve Schirripa (Henchman), Christopher Paul Hart (Traffic Cop),
Michael Beardsley (Accident Onlooker)[10]
French Title: *Raison et Sensibilité*
German Title: *Verwirrung der Gefühle*

Kate enlists Angel's aid in arresting notorious gangster
Tony Papazian which is successful. However, Kate's rough
treatment of the prisoner leads to her department having
to bring in a sensitivity consultant. And it couldn't happen
at a worse time, with the retirement of her father from the
police force bringing long-suppressed emotions to the
surface.

Dudes and Babes: Judging from Harlan's comment, Kate
must have a strong bladder as she never 'needs to pee'
during interrogation. Kate's uninhibited view of Doyle and
Cordelia's relationship: 'Where's the truth? He's hiding
behind Mr Humour. Look at Doyle, what do you see?'
Cordelia: 'A bad double-poly blend?' Kate: 'That's defence. Maybe you should open your heart to a new
possibility.' Kate wants to picture Angel in his underwear.

Denial, Thy Name is Kate: 'I'm hearing a *lot* of denial' – as
Lloyd very perceptively notes, genuine emotion makes
Kate uncomfortable. Her 'inappropriate sarcasm' masks
anger. She's been hurt before, and she's afraid of being
hurt again.

---

[10] Uncredited.

Denial, Thy Name is Trevor: 'In my day we didn't need any damn sensitivity,' says Trevor and that becomes clearer as Kate tells her colleagues about her childhood. Trevor forgot how to be anything but a cop a long time ago and she reflects that perhaps that's why she became one too. 'After mom died, you stopped,' she tells Trevor. 'It was like you couldn't stand the sight of me. Her face, her eyes looking up at you. But big girls don't cry, right? You said, *gone's gone* and there is no use wallowing. Worms and dirt and nothing, forever. Not one word about a better place. You couldn't even tell a scared little girl a beautiful lie.' Kate continues that she wanted to drink with her father, and laugh with him in the way he laughed with Frank and Jimmy. 'My best friend, Joanne, her mom was soft and she smelled like macaroni and cheese and she'd pick me up on her lap and she would rock me. She said that she wanted to keep [me] to herself. She said that I was good and sweet. Everybody said I was.' Bitterly she concludes that Trevor never even told her that she was pretty.

His ultimate denial comes at the end: 'You make an idiot out of yourself, embarrass me in front of the guys. You don't bring that up ever again. As far as I'm concerned it didn't happen.'

It's a Designer Label!: Cordelia has a pair of new orange sandals which Angel fails to notice, but Doyle does. Her other clothes include a white and red top and denim skirt, and her panties are briefly visible peeking over the waist of her jeans during some of the station scenes. Must mention the cool end of Angel's wardrobe, that royal blue sweater. Kate's blue dress at the retirement party is gorgeous.

References: The title is a misquotation of Jane Austen's *Sense and Sensibility*. Also, the planet Mongo (Emperor Ming's home in *Flash Gordon*), Jar Jar Binks (from *Star Wars: Episode I – The Phantom Menace*), Frankie Valli and the Four Seasons' 'Big Girls Don't Cry', Conan O'Brien's chatshow *Last Night*, *Armageddon* ('asteroids are hurtling towards the earth'), *Clueless* and Dr Laura Schlessinger (New York author and controversial radio host). 'Mr and Mrs Spock need to mind-meld' refers to

Star Trek, of course. 'Makes Mark Fuhrman look like *Gentle Ben*,' combines the police detective who was accused of racism during the OJ Simpson trial and a sickly 1970s TV series about a bear.

Los Angeles area locations mentioned include: Stockholm, the San Fernando Valley (the area of suburbs including North Hollywood, Sherman Oaks, Van Nuys and Reseda), Burbank (although Hollywood is synonymous with the movie industry, most of the studios relocated over the hills in 'beautiful downtown Burbank', the butt of many a Johnny Carson and *Rowan and Martin's Laugh-In* joke), Long Beach, San Pedro and Carlsbad.

Bitch!: Kate: 'I don't want to come off as insensitive, but if either of you tries to stop me I'm gonna have to blow you the crap away, because I've got to go find my daddy.' She later tells Papazian: 'I am not a bitch. I'm just protected.'

'West Hollywood?': Trevor says he's relieved to see Kate out with a man. He was starting to think she leaned in another direction. Papazian calls Angel 'a nancy boy'.

The Charisma Show: 'Am I wrong in thinking that a "please" and "thank you" is generally considered good form when requesting a dismemberment?' and 'You *do* remember leaving us in the sewer with a giant calamari?'

L.A.-Speak: Spivey: '*Bite me.*'

Cordelia: 'Hey. What's your *damage*?' And 'You stink of *whammy.*'

Angel: 'I wanted to, you know, thank you so much for going through those coroner reports, because I can imagine how not fun it is to read about, you know, coroner stuff.' Cordelia: '*Lame.*'

Angel: 'What've you got?' Cordelia: 'The *weebies*. This guy clearly has anger management issues.'

Papazian: 'Who's the *mook*?' And 'Nobody beats me, baby, especially not a stone-bitch like you.'

Cigarettes and Alcohol: Internal Affairs blame the outbreak of sensitivity on spiked alcohol in the Blue Bar. Kate drinks a beer with her father and a white wine at the retirement party. Trevor Lockley, on the other hand, seems to enjoy shots of neat vodka.

'You May Remember Me From Such Films As . . .': John Capodice has been in *Out of the Black, Hoods, The Misery Brothers, The Doors, Jacob's Ladder* and *Wall Street*. He played Aguado in *Ace Ventura: Pet Detective*. John Mahon was in *Austin Powers: The Spy Who Shagged Me, Armageddon, L.A. Confidential, Sinatra, The People Under the Stairs, The Exorcist* and the 1994 TV movie *Roswell*. Ken Grantham's movies include *Peggy Sue Got Married, Tucker: The Man and His Dream, Sibling Rivalry* and *Class Action*. Colin Patrick Lynch appears in *Hot Shots!* and *Terminator 2: Judgment Day*. Ron Marasco is Mr Casper in *Freaks and Geeks* and plays the Halliwells' neighbour in *Charmed*. Ken Abraham's movies include *Girlfriend from Hell, Vampires on Bikini Beach, Creepzoids* and *Hobgoblins*. Stand-up comedian Jimmy Shubert can be seen in *Coyote Ugly* and *Go*. Steve Schirripa was Bobby 'Bacala' Baccalieri in *The Sopranos* along with *Detroit Rock City, Welcome to Hollywood* and *Casino*. Christopher Paul Hart played Nelson in *Sgt Bilko*. Michael Beardsley played Humphries in *Freaks and Geeks* and was in *Dude, Where's My Car?*

Don't Give Up The Day Job: Writer/producer Tim Minear's previous credits include *The X-Files* (co-scripting the classic 'Kitsunegari' with Vince Gilligan), and *Lois & Clark: The New Adventures of Superman*. 'Chris Carter got a hold of a spec *X-Files* script I'd written,' he told Rob Francis. 'Chris invited me to join the writing staff before my tenure at *Lois & Clark* was up. *The X-Files* was a dream for me. It was the one show I watched religiously. It's very rare that a writer gets a gig on the show he sampled. I was the first in that show's history. Ken Horton's assistant, Kim Metcalf, introduced me to *Buffy*. She told me, 'I want you to work with Joss.' Mutant Enemy always seemed to be lurking around the corner.'

Logic, Let Me Introduce You to This Window: In the scene where Kate is chasing Spivey, he throws his bag on top of the car, but in later shots the bag is gone. During the fight between Kate and Spivey, he opens a car door. When the camera changes angle, it's closed. Why does a vampire need night-vision equipment? Where does Angel get the Hawaiian shirt and hat from – does he carry disguises in the car? When Kate first sees her father at the police station, she is holding books, but when she reaches the counter, they've disappeared. As Kate gives her speech she goes from having no purse and her arms at her side to clutching a purse with one hand on her hip. How did Angel enter Allen Lloyd's house? Yet again, Angel's image is captured on video (see **1**, 'City Of', **19**, 'Sanctuary', **24**, 'Are You Now, or Have You Ever Been?').

Quote/Unquote: Spivey: 'I heard it was suicide.' Kate: 'Supervisor Caffrey shot himself.' Spivey: 'It happens.' Kate: 'In the back of the head. Wrapped himself in plastic and he locked himself in the trunk of his car?' Spivey: 'He'd been depressed.'

Lieutenant: 'Your need for catharsis is not the issue here.'

Angel: 'My parents were great. Tasted a lot like chicken.'

Notes: 'I'd like to apologise for having treated you so shabbily, so I wrote a poem about it. "I saw a leaf and I did cry ..."' Two parts *Goodfellas*, one part absurdist-comedy. This hits all of the wrong notes and yet, somehow, manages to stay on course thanks, largely, to fine performances from the regulars (Boreanaz is on particularly good form). Nice to see the series taking some format risks and, mostly, succeeding.

Angel uses the alias 'Herb Saunders from Baltimore'. He confirms that he doesn't have a pulse. After Cordelia breaks into the police station, there's another shot of Charisma's tattoo as she wipes her hands on her pants (see **5**, 'Rm W/a Vu').

Kate is stationed at the LAPD Metro Precinct. Her badge number is 3747 and her extension is 229. She has been awarded a number of Commendations, including the Medal of Valour. Trevor Lockley, a corporal in the LAPD, is badge number 6873. His retirement party is held at the

Blue Bar. The memo on sensitivity training is dated 9th November 1999.

Soundtrack: The songs heard in the bar are by soul legend Solomon Burke, 'Everybody Needs Somebody to Love' and the much less famous 'Baby'.

Did You Know?: In an extraordinary interview with *FHM*, Charisma Carpenter revealed much detail about her early days in Las Vegas ('the weirdest thing was that we had a normal life. There are school districts, stores, churches. Everyone thinks of The Strip when you say "Vegas", but it's a really normal town,') and her school days ('I was a social butterfly . . . My problem was that I had boys on the brain – my hormones were going wild'). She talked candidly about getting into trouble for taking her father's Corvette without permission ('I took a whuppin' for that'), being 'tortured' by her elder brother and his friend ('on a red-hot day they made us stand barefoot on the asphalt') and about her time as a cheerleader ('I was the best. I took it to the *"Ooomph"* degree. And I can still do the splits.')

7

The Bachelor Party

US Transmission Date: 16 November 1999
UK Transmission Date: 18 February 2000 (Sky),
20 October 2000 (Channel 4)

Writer: Tracey Stern
Director: David Straiton
Cast: Kristin Dattilo (Harry), Carlos Jacott (Richard Howard Straley),
Ted Kairys (Ben), Chris Tallman (Nick), Brad Blaisdell (Uncle John),
Robert Hillis (Pierce), Lauri Johnson (Aunt Martha),
Kristen Lowman (Rachel), David Polcyn (Russ)
French Title: *Comment Enterrer Sa Vie De Garçon*
German Title: *Party mit Biß*

Just as Doyle plucks up the courage to ask Cordelia on a date, a complication arrives in the form of his ex-wife, Harry. She is about to remarry and wants Doyle's blessing, which he reluctantly gives. But at the bachelor partly for Harry's new husband, the need for Doyle's blessing takes on a far more sinister meaning.

Dudes and Babes: After Cordelia compliments Doyle on his bravery: 'You think you could say that again without so much shock in your voice? You're stepping on my moment of manliness here.'

Denial, Thy Name is Doyle: Although she was initially 'freaked' by Doyle's assimilation of his father's genes, Harry learned to accept it and encouraged Doyle to explore his inheritance. It was Doyle himself who couldn't face his demon aspect, and this wrecked the marriage.

It's a Designer Label!: Cordelia calls Pierce 'Mr Armani'. She also mentions Tiffany & Co, one of America's leading jewellery retailers. Cordy's black evening dress and matching shawl are, in Pierce's words: 'Wow'. Also in the *phwoar!* department, Cordy's black jogging vest, the shiny pinky purple pants of the female vampire and the stripper with the blue feather boa. Mark down Doyle's hideous orange shirt as a 'fashion crime' however.

References: The episode shares its name (and some, mostly aesthetic, details) with a Tom Hanks movie. 'They have trivia games on the Internet now,' refers to the NTN game network which provides interactive games for services like AOL. Also, a misquote from *Gone With the Wind* ('tomorrow is another day'), Primal Scream's 'Movin' On Up', the 'Spelling Bee' competition, *Pulp Fiction* ('pumpkin', 'hon bun'), USA For Africa's 'We Are The World', the US Green Card, Pictionary, the sports network ESPN and (obliquely) *A Hard Day's Night* ('A book!'), Kentucky Fried Chicken and Bob Hope's 'Thanks for the Memory'.

Bitch!: Cordelia: 'I swore when I went down that road with Xander Harris, I'd rather be dead then date a fixer-upper again.'

Cordelia, on Pierce: 'All I could think about was if this wimp ever saw a monster he'd probably throw a shoe at it and run like a weasel. Turns out the shoe part was giving him too much credit.'

Doyle, on Richard: 'Tell me again how ugly he is?'

The Charisma Show: She asks: 'Doyle taught third grade? The kind with children? Are you sure he wasn't just held back and used that as his cover story?'

L.A.-Speak: Pierce: 'I'm not really sure about this neighbourhood.' Vampire: 'You're right, it's crappy.'

Doyle: 'That wasn't . . .' Cordelia: ' . . . An incredible *spaz attack*?'

Angel: 'Where are you?' Cordelia: 'In the netherworld known as the 818 area code.'

Not Exactly A Haven For The Demon Bruthas: Once a nomadic tribe with violent leanings, the Ano-movic demons gave up their orthodox teachings and language (Aratuscan) at the turn of the century. They appear to be a peaceful clan that has totally assimilated into human society. However, they still follow some of the ancient ways. When one marries a divorcée, the brains of the newly betrothed woman's former spouse must be eaten during a ritual performed by a family elder. This is said to bring luck to the new union.

Cigarettes and Alcohol: Doyle admits that what Harry used to say was right – the booze does him no good. He even refuses (initially) to drink whisky with Angel, but he does share a toast to Harry with Richard.

Sex and Drugs and Rock'n'Roll: Stripper alert.

'You May Remember Me From Such Pop Videos As . . .': Despite a long TV career on *Parker Lewis Can't Lose*, *21 Jump Street*, *Friends* and *Ally McBeal*, Kristin Dattilo's main claim to fame is the lead in Aerosmith's 1990 video, 'Janie's Got A Gun'. Coincidentally, Rob Hillis appeared in another Aerosmith video, 'Love is Hard on the Knees'.

'You May Remember Me From Such Films and TV Series As . . .': Carlos Jacott was tremendous as the agent in *Being John Malkovich* and also appears in *She's All That*, *It's a Shame about Ray*, *The Last Days of Disco* and *Grosse Pointe Blank*. He was Ramon the Pool Guy in *Seinfeld* whilst *Buffy* fans will remember him as Ken in 'Anne'. Brad Blaisdell played Mike the Bartender in *Three's Company* and was also in *Happy Days*, *ER*, *Caroline in the City*, *Inspector Gadget* and *The Rat Pack*. Kristen Lowman played Mrs Henderson in *Problem Child* and has been in *Frasier*.

Don't Give Up the Day Job: David Straiton's previous work includes *FreakyLinks*, *Legacy* and *Providence*.

Logic, Let Me Introduce You to This Window: When Pierce and Cordelia are having dinner, watch the background – moving from a close up to a long shot, we see the same shot of the waitress approaching the lady behind Cordelia twice. During the party, Angel walks into the kitchen and his reflection can be seen in the window. And also on the glass shutters in his office. If Harry and Doyle have not spoken in four years, how did Harry find Doyle at Angel Investigations? Doyle's cross pops in and out of his T-shirt at regular intervals. Richard's red demon make-up can be spotted ending above his wrists in one scene. If Doyle and Harry married before they were twenty, how could Doyle have been teaching third grade when they met at such a young age?

I Just *Love* Your Accent: When Doyle sees a picture of Buffy, he asks Angel how he thinks she would feel about a man with an Irish accent.

Motors: Cordelia's date, Pierce, along with lots of money, a house in Montecito and a place in the hills with a pool, also possesses a Mercedes CLK 320.

Quote/Unquote: Harry, on Richard: 'He's got a good heart, Francis, just like you.' Doyle: 'Yeah, maybe, but the container? Can I get a side of *bland* with that bland?'

Uncle John reading from the party itinerary: 'First we greet the man of the hour. Then we drink. We bring out the food. Then we drink. Then comes the stripper, darts, then we have the ritual eating of the first husband's brains. And then charades.' Ben: 'Wait. What was that? Charades?' Nick: 'I don't know about that . . .'

Uncle John: 'He's going to eat the guy's brains with a shrimp fork?' Nick: 'Pardon me if our ancient ancestors didn't leave behind any former-husband-brain-eating forks.' Uncle John: 'Get a soup spoon, you moron.'

Harry: 'You know how I feel about these barbaric Ano-movician customs.' Nick: 'You're nothing but a *racist*.'

Notes: 'I'm only going to ask you this once, Richard, and I expect a straight answer. Were you or were you not intending to eat my ex-husband's brains?' An amusing episode which fills in much background detail on Doyle. Nice characterisation and an impressive bar-room brawl at the end, however, can't disguise a *very* thin plot. Good performances all round, though, particularly Charisma and Kristin Dattilo's effective double act.

Doyle married Harriet before he was twenty. The marriage began to go wrong after he reached his 21st birthday and inherited his father's demon aspect. Doyle never met his father and his mother (see 3, 'In The Dark') didn't tell him about his demon side. Doyle wears a Celtic cross. According to Harry, Doyle was a third-grade teacher and a volunteer worker at a food bank which was where they met. The only money in Doyle's family was 'underneath the couch cushions'. He says that the duck served in La Petit Renard is dry, indicating that he's visited this very exclusive restaurant.

Since the break-up, Harry has visited Kiribati, Togo and Uzbekistan. She met Richard while researching North American demon clans. The whiteboard in Angel's office during the opening scene reads: 'Order cards, water, coffee. 818-555-1961. 10:00AM.'

Soundtrack: Four instrumental pieces can be heard: 'Come Correct' (by C Tory/Z Harmon) from *Transition Music Sampler: Urban Songs and Instrumentals*, Paul Trudeau's 'Don't Do It', 'Fab Gear' from *Killer Tracks Music Library* and Diana Terranova's 'Come On 2000'.

Critique: *Xposé*'s Brian Barratt was impressed with this episode noting that 'Writer Stern brilliantly trades off cosy feelings of domestic mundanity: the demons seem unthreatening to the point of being dull. The twist: They can't comprehend anything out of the ordinary in chomping on somebody's frontal lobe.'

Previously On *Buffy The Vampire Slayer*: 'Pangs': Xander accidentally releases Hus, a Chumash Indian spirit, seeking vengeance on settlers who took his people's land. Buffy wants to have a Thanksgiving with her friends, but must try to anticipate who Hus will attack next. Angel, secretly in town after Doyle's vision, tells Willow, Xander and Anya that Hus will target Buffy. They rush into a war between Buffy and a tribe of spirits. With the battle over, everyone sits down to enjoy the meal and Xander reveals Angel's presence.

8
I Will Remember You

US Transmission Date: 23 November 1999
UK Transmission Date: 25 February 2000 (Sky),
27 October 2000 (Channel 4)

Writers: David Greenwalt, Jeannine Renshaw
Director: David Grossman
Cast: David Wald (Maura Demon #1),
Chris Durands (Maura Demon #2)
French Title: *Je Ne T'Oublierai Pas*
German Title: *Liebe auf Zeit*

Buffy follows Angel to L.A. for a confrontation but, as they prepare to go their separate ways, a demon attacks. They pursue the demon and Angel kills it, but a mingling of blood restores Angel's humanity. The Oracles, Doyle's link to The Powers That Be, confirm Angel's new status and he and Buffy share a perfect day together. After hearing that Buffy would perish if he were to remain human, Angel begs the Oracles to fold back time. Despite Buffy's certainty that she will remember what they shared, when time is reversed only Angel has the knowledge of what might have been.

Dreaming (As *Buffy* Often Proves) is Free: The ultimate dream episode; it never happened.

Dudes and Babes: Buffy looks as great as ever. Plus, naked-Angel alert with Buffy licking ice cream off his chest.

It's a Designer Label!: Cordelia: 'That's our Buffy.' Doyle: 'She seemed a little . . .' Cordelia: 'Bulgarian in that outfit?'

She certainly does (particularly the boots). Cordelia's denim skirt puts in another appearance. Angel's red dressing gown puts in its first. And hopefully last.

A Little Learning Is A Dangerous Thing: Buffy knows that Angel's axe is Byzantine. Since when was she an expert on antiques?

References: The title is from a song by Sarah McLachlan. Cordelia mentions 'the director's cut of *Titanic*'. Also, *Teenage Mutant Ninja Turtles*, Orson Welles, the game show *Let's Make a Deal* ('tunnel number one it is') and the contemporaneous Arnold Schwarzenegger movie *End of Days* (which was released in the same week that this episode premiered in the US). Angel's line 'being on the outside, looking in' is very similar to dialogue from the *Forever Knight* episode 'Dying for Fame'.

When Buffy meets Angel outdoors, the scene was filmed against the backdrop of the Santa Monica Pier and Pacific Park.

Bitch!: Cordelia, on Buffy and Angel: 'Let me explain the lore here. They suffer, they fight. That's 'business as usual'. They get groiny with each other, the world as we know it falls apart.'

Cordelia: 'They didn't even have cookie-dough-fudge-mint-chip when you were alive.' Angel: 'I want some. Can you get that?' Cordelia: 'It'll go straight to your thighs.'

Plus a scene of vintage Buffy/Cordelia 'second grade' bitching.

L.A.-Speak: Buffy: 'Oh, boy. I was really *jonesing* for another heartbreaking sewer talk.' And: 'That was *unreal*.'

Cordelia: 'My bad . . .'

Cigarettes and Alcohol: Doyle seems to be drinking a margarita in the bar with Cordelia where a distinctive white bottle of Malibu can be seen behind the bar.

Sex and Food and Rock'n'Roll: Once Angel announces that he's hungry, he eats a PopTart, an apple, a bologna sandwich, a chocolate bar and yogurt (which he doesn't like). He also asks Cordelia to get him cookie-dough-fudge-mint-chip ice cream which he and Buffy eat in bed along with crunchy peanut butter (see 5, 'Rm W/a Vu'). Buffy is also holding a packet of strawberries.

'You May Remember Me From Such Films and TV Series As . . .': Sarah Michelle Gellar was a child star, appearing in Burger King adverts as a four-year-old and starring in *Swans Crossing*. She won a Daytime Emmy for her role as Kendall Hart in *All My Children*. Her movies include *I Know What You Did Last Summer* (as Helen Shivers), *Cruel Intentions* (as Kathryn Merteuil), *Scooby Doo* (as Daphne) and *Scream 2*. She also plays Buffy Summers in . . . Hang on, you all *know* who she is. And if you don't, why are you reading this book?

Randall Slavin has appeared in *Beethoven's 2nd*, *Marshal Law*, *Primal Fear* and *Generation X*. Carry Cannon was in *Cops on the Edge*.

Don't Give Up The Day Job: Jeannine Renshaw was initially an actor playing the teacher in *Hook* and appearing in *Home Improvements* before co-creating *VR.5*. David Grossman has worked on *Roswell*, *Sabrina the Teenage Witch*, *Early Edition*, *Ally McBeal*, *M.A.N.T.I.S.*, *Mad TV* and *Weird Science*. David Wald is a stuntman with credits on *The Glimmer Man*, *Escape From L.A.*, *Blade* and *Beverly Hills Ninja*. As well as acting in *Mighty Morphin Power Rangers* he was also camera assistant on the movie *976–Wish*.

Logic, Let Me Introduce You to This Window: Angel's reflection can be seen in the glass door behind Buffy in the pre-title sequence. Angel is very close to the broken window while fighting the demon in the office, but he visibly flinches from the sunlight streaming into the sewer. Buffy has the time to change her outfit between the scene in Angel's office and chasing the demon into the sewers. Another question asked a few times in *Buffy* (see, for instance, 'Graduation Day' Part 1): how does Angel, whose heart does not beat, bleed?

I Just *Love* Your Accent: 'You have so much to learn little Irishman,' Cordelia tells Doyle.

Quote/Unquote: Buffy, on the demon: 'It was rude. We should go kill it.' Angel: 'I'm free.'

Cordelia: 'I've decided not to feel sorry for myself. I'm taking matters into my own hands, organising a little 'going out of business' sale to subsidise the severance package Angel never bothered setting up for me.'

Male Oracle: 'Temporal folds are not to indulge at the whims of lower beings.'

Notes: 'Batten down the hatches, here comes Hurricane Buffy.' An overtly romantic episode with a very illogical (pure fantasy) sub-plot that gives us our first look at representatives of 'The Powers That Be'. Boreanaz and Gellar are, as ever, highly watchable together, but the story replaces form and substance with sentimentality which is occasionally mawkish. It's thus a triumph of style over content. In other words, it's fan-fiction. Worse, it's slushy *shipper* fan-fic designed to jerk tears and nothing more. Despite the time metaphor, no cigar.

There are allusions to various *Buffy* episodes: Buffy's reference to a 'heartbreaking sewer-talk' concerns 'The Prom', Cordelia asking Angel 'did you *do it* with Buffy?' refers to 'Surprise', whilst the 'It's a long story'/'maybe not *that* long' exchange mirrors a similar line in 'Faith Hope and Trick'. Angel's two gifts to the Oracles are his wristwatch and a Famille rose vase – Ch'ing dynasty, circa 1811. Buffy, ostensibly, came to L.A. to visit her father, Hank (see *Buffy*: 'Welcome to the Hellmouth', 'Nightmares', 'When She Was Bad', 'Spiral', 'Normal Again').

Cordelia tells Doyle that Angel was 'in Sunnydale for three days, tracking her and that *thingumajiggy* you saw in your vision' – a one-line summation of 'Pangs'. She used to have a cat. Doyle reads about the demon from *The Book of Kelsor*. The extract says: 'DEVIL TURN'D. Mohra Demon or ASSASSINS for Darkness. Veins run with the BLOOD of eternity. In what manner, and how zealously he is affected with the moving of the Spirit. With the Holy Sisters desire Copulation (if he would vast quantities of salt to live) . . .' A 'dive on 2nd near Beach' in Santa Monica called the Long Bar is used as a hideout by demons.

Soundtrack: The stock-instrumental 'Moonlight Orchestra' is used in several *Buffy*/*Angel* scenes.

Critique: *TV Guide*'s Matt Roush wrote: 'While *The X-Files* only gets more ponderous in its 'mythology' (the lugubrious season opener), *Buffy* just gets more entertaining, returning to its epic storyline – the tragic Buffy–Angel romance – in a fabulous recent crossover. A newly human Angel, able to smile and fulfil his passion for Buffy (and for post-coital cookie-dough-fudge-mint-chip ice cream), is forced to turn back time, eradicating her memories of their fleeting bliss. "They've got the forbidden love of all time," says Cordelia. No lie.'

Ian Atkins in *Shivers* added: 'The poignant last protests of Buffy, and Angel's resignation, make the most of these two extremely talented actors in a scene of incredible beauty. Some people may have seen it coming ... but for an episode focusing on the value of those special moments in all our lives, it does a marvellous job.'

Kristine Sutherland, who plays Buffy's mother Joyce, was equally impressed, telling Paul Simpson: 'I caught that episode where Buffy goes to visit [Angel] and they have that one day. I loved it ... When you watched their relationship over the years, there was so much that thwarted it and made it impossible. It was an incredible release for me as an audience person to go there at least once. The romantic in us *does* live.'

9
Hero

US Transmission Date: 30 November 1999
UK Transmission Date: 3 March 2000 (Sky),
27 October 2000 (Channel 4)

Writers: Howard Gordon and Tim Minear
Director: Tucker Gates
Cast: Tony Denman (Rieff), Anthony Cistaro (Scourge Commander),
Michelle Horn (Rayna), Lee Arenberg (Tiernan), Sean Gunn (Lucas),
James Henricksen (Elder Lister Demon),
David Bickford (Cargo Inspector),
Christopher Comes (Storm Trooper #2), Paul O'Brien (Captain),
Ashley Taylor (First Mate)
French Title: *Le Héros*
German Title: *Helden Wie Wir*

Doyle's latest vision leads Angel to a terrified group of half-demons hiding from The Scourge, pure-demons who exterminate half-breeds. As Angel tries to arrange safe passage for the group, Doyle reveals his true heritage to Cordelia. However, when their plan is betrayed to The Scourge, Doyle makes the ultimate sacrifice to save his friends.

Making Adverts (According to Cordelia) Can Be Cheap: Cordelia surreally directs, in voice-over, *The Dark Avenger* advert.

It's a Designer Label!: Cordy's blue and red 'tie-around-and-backless' top is abandoned later for a blue-tank-top-and-ponytail look.

References: The narrator for Cordelia's commercial should be: 'That bald *Star Trek* guy or one of the cheaper Baldwins.' Also, *Braveheart*, *The Man With Two Brains*, *Mask*, *Very Bad Things*, *Roots*, *Seinfeld* ('yadda, yadda, yadda'), I Timothy 6:12 ('fight the good fight'), Alfred Lord Tennyson's 'In Memoriam', *The Love Boat*, *End of Days* (see **8**, 'I Will Remember You', presumably these events are what the Oracles were predicting) and, oblique-ly, Randy Newman's 'Short People'.

'West Hollywood?': Cordelia, discussing having Angel in *The Dark Avenger* commercial asks: 'Would it kill him to put on some tights and a cape and garner us a little free publicity?' Doyle: 'I don't see Angel putting on tights . . . Oh, now I do and it's really *disturbing*.'

The harbourmaster's brother is called Big Randy and he's known to Angel who may or may not have bitten him. Enough said.

The Charisma Show: The visualisation of Cordelia's advert. Plus the threat, 'This may look like a popular brand of breath freshener; it's really a cunningly disguised demon repellent.'

L.A.-Speak: Cordelia: 'Buffy blows into town and puts you into a permanent funk. And I'm just supposed to stand by and watch our business go belly-up?'

Doyle, on The Scourge: 'They have a big hate-on for us mixed-heritage types.'

Cordelia: 'I've rejected you way before now. You're half-demon? *Big Whoop*. I can't believe you'd think I care about that. I mean, I work for a vampire, *hello*?'

Doyle: 'That *doohickey* – it's fully armed, isn't it?'

Not Exactly A Haven For The Half-Demons: An allegory of the persecution of the Jews and other ethnic and religious groups by the Nazis, this is not the first time that a Howard Gordon script has explored anti-Semitism. His highly-rated *X-Files* episode 'Kaddish' in 1997 touched on similar themes.

Cigarettes and Alcohol: Doyle used to smoke but seems to have given up.

'You May Remember Me From Such Films and TV Series As . . .': Tony Denman was Ben Smythe in *Good Vs Evil* and appeared in *Fargo, Go* and *Poor White Trash*. Anthony Cistaro will be known to fans of *Cheers* as Henri. He also played Mario in *Alright Already*. Michelle Horn was Saghi in two episodes of *Star Trek: Deep Space Nine* and provided one of the voices for *Lion King II: Simba's Pride*. Lee Arenberg's movie CV includes *Cradle Will Rock, Johnny Skidmarks, The Apocalypse, Mojave Moon, Car 54, Where Are You?, RoboCop 3, Live! From Death Row, Bob Roberts, Whore* and *Meet The Hollowheads*. He's played Ferengi characters in *Star Trek: The Next Generation* and *Star Trek: Deep Space Nine* and was Bobby G in *Action*. Sean Gunn plays Kirk in *Gilmore Girls*. Paul O'Brien was in *Second Sight* and *Soul Man*.

Don't Give Up The Day Job: Howard Gordon was executive producer on *The X-Files*, co-writing 'Synchrony' with David Greenwalt in 1997 (see **35**, 'Happy Anniversary'). Gordon is now a producer on *24*. He is reported to be developing an American version of the UK vampire miniseries *Ultraviolet*. Fans of the original (the best example of British telefantasy since *Doctor Who*) await the outcome with some trepidation. Tucker Gates directed episodes of *The X-Files* along with *Roswell, Space: Above and Beyond, Nash Bridges* and the US version of *Cracker*.

Logic, Let Me Introduce You to This Window: When Angel grabs the motorbike to make his escape from The Scourge, he is wearing one of their uniforms, but when he arrives at the ship he's no longer wearing it. In the Lister hideout, when Cordelia and Doyle are talking, their lips and the sound are not in sync.

Motors: Angel can drive a motorcycle. Cordelia's driving licence seems to include heavy goods vehicles judging by the truck she delivers.

Quote/Unquote: Doyle: 'Angel Investigations is the best. Our rats are low.' Cordelia: 'Rates.' Doyle points to the script: 'It says "rats".'

Doyle: 'Too bad we'll never know if this is a face you could learn to love.'

Notes: 'The good fight, yeah? You never know until you've been tested. I get that now.' Ignore the Nazi-subtext and concentrate instead on a trio of staggering performances by the regulars. A hymn to nobility, heroism and self-sacrifice, Doyle and Angel 'fight the good fight', knowing that it will cost one of them their lives. The fan outrage that followed the episode seemed to miss this point entirely. The dramatic intensity of Doyle's prior rejection of his heritage and his subsequent redemption is breathtaking. A noble death ensures that the character won't be forgotten in a hurry.

Angel has a punch-bag in his apartment. Doyle says that Harry (see **7**, 'The Bachelor Party') has decided to stay in L.A. Brachen demons have a good sense of direction (see **3**, 'In The Dark') and are, according to Doyle, good at basketball.

Soundtrack: Robert Kral, in a fascinating interview with *The Watcher's Web*, noted: 'A woodwind player, Chris Bleth, comes in each week to supply me with the 'human element' to the score. It's really essential in love scenes. Samplers are great, but the soloists bring the music to life. I especially enjoy when we've brought in Elin Carlson for the vocal parts used on **9**, 'Hero' and **15**, 'The Prodigal'. First there's the spotting session. This is where David Greenwalt, myself and the music editor [Fernand Bos] sit together and watch the episode, deciding on where the music should go. The sound guys are also present, so there's discussion about dialogue and sound effects as well, which is very handy because it can often affect the music. I usually write in the order of appearance, which I like because the music develops as it goes along. Sometimes I'll write a theme first that I know will be needed, fully fledged and orchestrated, then I can go backwards and develop it through the episode. In **9**, 'Hero' for example, the theme was orchestrated, but first time you hear it is solo voice with no harmony.'

Did You Know?: Special effects supervisor Loni Peristere told an online webchat: 'Because it's television I wasn't sure [what I could get away with] but David Greenwalt said: "I want [Doyle's] flesh to melt off muscle and then bones." That was the original idea but we thought that would be a bit too graphic so we did it in make-up stages.'

Joss Whedon's Comments: Joss maintains, despite persistent fan rumours, that Doyle was only intended to be on the show for nine episodes. In an interview with *Eon*, Joss bemoaned: 'Our big surprise has been ruined. We were gonna take away [Angel's] mentor – shake up his life a little bit. But, yes, this was our idea from the beginning.' Asked, in another interview, about this ruination and if he would do anything differently in future, Joss noted: 'I honestly don't know how I could because an actor's agent will always start putting him up for stuff. You have an entire crew and extras [who] will sometimes get on the Internet. It's not like the old days, all you need now is one person and everybody in the world can know.' He also told *SFX* that: 'It did cause a lot of fuss. He's a popular guy . . . He wasn't *that* popular before we killed him; something I have to remind people of.'

Real Gone Kid: Tim Minear also confirmed: 'We knew very early that we were going to kill off Doyle. All the character development which led up to that moment was written with [his] impending death in mind. The notion to bring in Wesley came later. We never planned for *Angel* to be the Angel/Cordy show. In fact, by the end of the season you'll see that we've been adding characters all year.'

Around this time, Tim also began to post on to the alt.tv.angel newsgroup. Asked if he was surprised at fan reaction to Doyle's fate, he commented: 'Not a bit. Ever since it was leaked, I've seen the growing trend. We were pretty much expecting this kind of response.' On any possible return for Glenn Quinn, Tim noted: 'Doyle is dead. Glenn Quinn is not. I don't think that doors, particularly on fantasy shows like ours, are ever completely shut. But then, I am not an Oracle.'

Conspiracy Theory: Fuelled by some offhand comments by members of the cast and crew ('the producers felt that his character didn't fit the direction that the show was going in', David Boreanaz noted, while Howard Gordon told *SFX*: 'If the death of Doyle was in Joss's mind from the beginning, I honestly didn't know'), rumours persist about dark goings-on behind the exit of Glenn Quinn. This is particularly awkward for Boreanaz who remained a close friend of Quinn. 'I see him all the time,' he told Sky, and the pair spent New Year's Eve 1999 together at *Playboy*'s millennium party. When appearing on UK MTV David mentioned that he was learning to play the drums. 'My friend Glenn Quinn is teaching me.' According to *Starlog* magazine, 'Quinn departed under rather murky circumstances. The party line states that Doyle was never intended to be a permanent fixture on the show ... [Rumours] however, suggest that Quinn was let go after the producers determined that the character had outlived his usefulness.' 'I don't know which is which and I don't ask,' Charisma Carpenter told the magazine. 'All I know is that I am very sad to see Glenn go. Personally, there was a kinship that forms when you work that many hours. He was very charismatic and jolly and just an all-around fun person to be with. As far as the characters go, Cordelia and Doyle had such a great relationship. There was a lot of chemistry. My mom said, 'I was really sad to see him go because I felt he was going to reach you.' Quinn himself maintained a dignified silence concerning his departure, telling *Starburst*: 'It's a personal matter I have chosen not to discuss. I love Doyle and hope they are able to bring him back some day.'

An article in the *Oakland Tribune* noted: 'Creator Joss Whedon says that was always the plan. *Look me in the eye and say that, buddy.* So [when] Whedon actually goes eyeball-to-eyeball and says "That was always the plan," it's hard to call the guy a fibber. Whedon admits he got hate mail concerning the decision, but thinks that offing a character keeps the viewers on their toes.' According to Christopher Golden: 'Whatever Joss says, as far as I'm concerned, that's Gospel.' Ironically, in the week that *Angel* premiered, *TV Guide*'s 'Hollywood Grapevine' featured a piece on Glenn Quinn noting that: 'If things don't work out [on *Angel*], he's covered having bought a share in a Hollywood nightclub called Goldfingers.' Perhaps the actor really *did* know from day one.

Comic Requiem: Issue six of the popular Dark Horse *Angel* comic included a piece of scripting worthy of the TV series. Written by Christopher Golden and Tom Sniegoski, part two of 'Earthly Possessions' takes place during the period immediately before and after this episode. Doyle is seen fixing a plaque to the wall of the office. The next sequence occurs a week later, in the aftermath of Doyle's death. A grief-stricken Cordelia reads the inscription on the plaque:

'An Irish Blessing'
May you be in Heaven
half an hour before the
Devil knows you're dead

'Oh, Doyle,' Cordelia notes sadly. 'You had to be the hero.'

10
Parting Gifts

US Transmission Date: 14 December 1999
UK Transmission Date: 10 March 2000 (Sky),
3 November 2000 (Channel 4)

Writers: David Fury and Jeannine Renshaw
Director: James A Contner
Cast: Maury Sterling (Barney), Jayson Creek (Producer #1),

Sean Smith (Producer #2), Sarah Devlin (Producer #3),
Jason Kim (Soon), Brett Gilbert (Reptilian Demon),
Henry Kingi (Kungai Demon), Lawrence Turner (Hank),
Cheyenne Wilber (Concierge), Dominique Jennings (Mac),
Kotoko Kawamura (Ancient Korean Woman)
French Title: *Cadeau D'Adieu*
German Title: *Das Abschiedsgeschenk*

A demon named Barney seeks Angel's help, saying that he
is being chased by a killer. However, when Angel investi-
gates, the killer turns out to be Wesley Wyndam-Pryce,
Buffy's former Watcher, and now a (self-styled) 'rogue-
demon hunter', who is on the trail of a creature that steals
the powers of others. He thinks Barney, an empath, will be
its next target. Only later, do the pair realise that Wesley
has been chasing the wrong demon and that Barney is the
real danger. But Barney has a new goal, Cordelia's recently
acquired gift of vision.

Denial, Thy Name is Cordelia: The empath Barney sees
through Cordelia's façade. She knows that she's a terrible
actress and feels a burden of guilt over Doyle's demise,
wondering if things would have been different if she'd been
nicer to him.

It's a Designer Label!: Wesley's biker pants are impressive
('interesting look for you') if not for the wearer. 'They tend
to chafe one's . . . legs.' His lightweight cream suit is much
more *him*. Barney says Cordelia is wearing shoes she can't
afford. The green and white dress and cream blouse she
sports to her audition are rather plain, something that
can't be said for the green woollen top-thing-with-lots-of-
holes that crops up later. Its practicality is questionable
(being so short that it doesn't cover her naked midriff and
gives us *another* look at Charisma's tattoo). But, it's
certainly a talking point.

References: Wesley's middle name is a tribute to the king
of British SF, John Wyndham (1903-1969) author of *The
Day of the Triffids*, *The Midwich Cuckoos*, *The Kraken
Wakes* and *Random Quest*. Also, misquotes from Alexander Graham Bell ('for every door that closes, another
opens'), Isaiah 48:22 ('no rest for the wicked') and *Macbeth*

('what is done cannot be undone'), allusions to the fairytale *The Frog Prince* ('I'll smooch every damn frog in this kingdom'), the Japanese healing art of Shiatsu and *Ace Ventura: Pet Detective* ('allrighty then'). The 'grey blobby thing' from Cordelia's vision is the sculpture *Maiden with Urn* by Van Gieson.

Wesley's 'through storm and rain, heat and famine' is inspired by an inscription on the New York City Post Office which is, in turn, an adaptation of a quote from *The Histories of Herodotus*. Angel Investigations is south of L.A.'s Koreatown.

Bitch!: Cordelia: 'That's one spooky talent you got there. You can just look at me grinding my teeth, sighing, grunting and sense that I'm frustrated? Amazing.'

Barney: 'Why aren't you in your coffin?' Angel: 'I hate that stereotype. You're a demon and you don't know anything about vampires?' Barney: 'Only what I learned from TV.' Angel: 'Vampires don't sleep in coffins. It's a misconception made popular by hack writers and ignorant media. In fact, you know, we can and do move around during the day.'

The Charisma Show: Cordelia, discovering that her 'gift' came via Doyle's kiss, spends the episode snogging anyone within kissing distance in the hope that it will vanish. She gets some great lines too: Barney: 'Can I help?' Cordelia: 'Not unless you can explain to me why I have to suffer skull-splitting migraines, getting visions so vague they require closed captioning.' And: 'I didn't ask for this responsibility, unlike some people, who shall remain lifeless.' Also, the superb comedy as she tries to continue her incompetent, emotion-filled audition for Stain-Be-Gone while having a vision ('*GRASS STAINS!*').

L.A.-Speak: Cordelia: 'Well, thanks for that insight, Mr Emotional Radar.'

Domestic Matters: At some point in his life, Angel learned to cook. After late night sessions stalking evil, he prepares a breakfast of toast and eggs, served with glasses of orange juice. Cordy brews the office's coffee in an old-fashioned pot, using Maxwell House.

Sex and Drugs and Rock'n'Roll: Cordelia is horrified by the gift that Doyle's kiss has given her: 'Why couldn't it have been mono or herpes?'

'You May Remember Me From Such Pop Videos, Films and TV Series As . . .': Alexis Denisof can be seen in the video for George Harrison's 'Got My Mind Set On You'. He played Richard Sharpe's love rival, Johnny Rossendale, in *Sharpe* and appeared in *Rogue Trader*, *First Knight* (as Sir Gaheris) and *True Blue* before landing the role of Wesley on *Buffy*. Recently, he portrayed an American hitman in the Vic Reeves/Bob Mortimer remake of *Randall & Hopkirk (Deceased)*. Maury Sterling was Vaughan Lerner in *Alright Already*. Jayson Creek can be seen in the movie *Domination*. Jason Kim was in *Edtv* whilst Cheyenne Wilbur appears in *Passion's Peak*.

Don't Give Up The Day Job: Henry Kingi has acted in *Vampires*, *Barb Wire* and *Predator 2* but is best known for a 30-year career as a stuntman in movies such as *F/X – Murder By Illusion*, *Die Hard*, *Patriot Games*, *From Dusk Till Dawn*, *Dante's Peak*, *The Lost World: Jurassic Park*, *Batman & Robin*, *US Marshals*, *Armageddon*, *Lethal Weapon 4*, *Blade* and *End of Days*. On TV he was the stunt co-ordinator on *The Bionic Woman*.

Logic, Let Me Introduce You to This Window: The initial shot of Angel in his office with Barney shows his hands in his lap. The shot over his shoulder has his fingers steepled beneath his chin. When Angel hands Cordelia a pencil and pad to sketch her vision, one shot shows the pencil and pad in Angel's left hand. The next has the pencil in his right hand and the pad in his left. David Boreanaz seems to be laughing during the scene where he knocks the crossbow from Wesley's hands. He appears to be prompted from off-screen when he speaks Korean. As Angel is startled by the demon in the bathhouse, he spins around. In the next shot he is still in the process of turning. When Barney slaps Cordelia, you can see his hand doesn't connect with her face.

I Just *Love* Your Accent: It's good to have Wesley back, especially as he's 'on the trail of a particularly nasty bugger'. But, 'butcher an innocent girl, will you? I'm going to thrash you within an inch of your life.' Just as we were starting to think that somebody had finally got the right idea about how we speak in England. As Angel notes, 'Easy tiger.'

Motors: Wesley drives a 'Big Dog' motorcycle (see **25**, 'First Impressions').

Quote/Unquote: Barney's advice to Cordelia on overcoming nerves: 'Little trick; picture everybody . . .' Cordelia: 'In their underwear?' Barney: 'I was gonna say dead. But hey, if that underwear thing works for you . . .'

Wesley: 'A lone wolf such as myself never works with anyone . . . I'm a rogue demon hunter.' Cordelia: 'What's a rogue demon?'

Notes: 'We get at least an extra thousand if the seer's eyes are intact.' Although he doesn't appear anywhere except the credits, Glenn Quinn's presence is all over this episode. A story about loss, redemption and friendship, 'Parting Gifts' moves *Angel* in a new direction without sacrificing the set-up of the previous episodes. The reintroduction of Wesley is well-handled (and *very* funny) and there are some terrific moments like the strange menagerie of creatures at the auction and the marvellous breakfast cameo at the end.

Angel speaks Korean. Wesley speaks a smattering of the oriental language of Kungai demons. He was unaware that his former date Cordelia (see *Buffy*: 'The Prom') is working for Angel. Angel and Cordelia last saw Wesley in 'Graduation Day' Part 2, the episode in which Cordelia and Wesley kissed. Cordelia remembers Doyle: 'He drank too much and his taste in clothing was like a Greek tragedy. And he could be really sweet sometimes. He was half-demon. A secret he kept from me for, like, ever. I guess that's the reason he sometimes smelled weird?'

Wesley mentions that he was sacked by The Watcher's Council after Buffy would no longer take orders from them (in the aftermath of 'Graduation Day' Part 2). Wesley refers to the two Slayers assigned to him. One [Faith] 'turned evil and now vegetates in a coma,' (this is the first definitive statement in either *Buffy* or *Angel* to confirm that

Faith is still alive. See **18**, 'Five By Five', **19**, 'Sanctuary') and the other [Buffy] 'is a renegade'. The Byzantine axe Angel carries is the same one Cordelia wanted to sell in **8**, 'I Will Remember You'.

Popular fan theory: Doyle didn't actually intend to pass his powers to Cordy with the kiss in **9**, 'Hero' – he just snogged her because he knew he was going to die. It was actually The Powers That Be who did the passing. It's less noble, perhaps, but much more human and touching than Doyle giving the object of his affections a gift that she doesn't want.

Alexis Sold: Although born in the US, Alexis Denisof had done most of his work in Britain and, seemingly, has an old friend to thank for the part of Wesley. 'They were looking for somebody "who thinks he's Pierce Brosnan but is actually George Lazenby",' Tony Head told Paul Simpson and Ruth Thomas. Head, the erudite British Watcher Rupert Giles on *Buffy*, suggested Alexis, with whom he had worked in a 1993 theatre production of *Rope* in Chichester. 'He played one of the two guys who did the murder and he was fantastic, as indeed they've found on *Angel*. I'm hoping to get a little guest spot in *Angel* because I'd love to do some more work with Alexis. I had one scene with David [*Buffy*: 'Pangs'] which was really nice. I miss the tension between the characters. It's nice to keep it alive.'

'I have more fun writing Wesley than I did Doyle,' Joss Whedon told *Fangoria*. 'When Wesley came on, we were finding our legs. He was a part of that and Alexis has made it a lot of fun to write. Glenn Quinn's greatest talent was glowering and we already had David doing that. It was a banjo-act and a banjo-act. When we brought Wesley in, the element was there that we needed. Plus, he's a hoot.'

David Fury's Comments: Speaking to the Canadian Film Centre in Toronto, Fury noted: 'I enjoy Wesley. I reintroduced the character with my script **10**, 'Parting Gifts'. There are dimensions to the character that are slowly being introduced. There's more to Wesley than people think.'

11
Somnambulist

US Transmission Date: 18 January 2000
UK Transmission Date: 17 March 2000 (Sky),
7 November 2000 (Channel 4)

Writer: Tim Minear
Director: Rick Kolbe
Cast: Jeremy Renner (Penn), Nick McCallum (Skateboard Kid),
Kimberleigh Aarn (Precinct Clerk), Paul Webster (Uniform #1),
Brian Di Rito (Task Force Member #1)
French Title: *Le Somnambule*
German Title: *Schatten der Vergangenheit*

Angel's dreams seem to be coming true and he faces the possibility that he has reverted to his old ways. However, investigations prove that the vampire on the loose is Penn whom Angel sired in the eighteenth century. Angel tracks down his apt pupil but, in the course of this, reveals his secret to Kate Lockley.

Dreaming (As *Buffy* Often Proves) is Free: Given the subject matter it's remarkable that the episode doesn't make more of Angel's dreams. The ones we see are very literal with none of the surrealism we've come to expect from *Buffy*. The implication that Angel has a psychic link to Penn (and others he has sired) gives a context to this.

Denial, Thy Name is Penn: Angel correctly guesses that Penn has spent the last 200 years recreating the thrill of his first nights as a vampire, re-enacting the killing of his family as serial murders. Penn's search for a father figure to please inevitably leads him back to his sire (Penn: 'You approved of me in ways my mortal father never did. You're my real father, Angelus.' Angel: 'Fine. You're grounded.')

It's a Designer Label!: Cordelia has a mother-of-pearl bracelet. She wears some great gear including a striking red dress, a pink blouse and a white vest-style T-shirt. Angel seems to sleep in his day clothes and we see even his socks are black. Kate's chunky white sweater doesn't do much for her.

References: 'A real *Psycho*-Wan Kenobi' combines the Hitchcock classic with *Star Wars*. 'Gallagher's changed his act more times than this dude has in the last two centuries' concerns an American stand-up comedian famous for his physical comedy often involving watermelons. Also, Stephen King's *Apt Pupil* and Angie Dickinson's *Police Woman*. 'Somnambulist' also features elements of two *Forever Knight* episodes: 'Bad Blood', in which Nick Knight had the chance to stop Jack the Ripper (who was also a product of his sire, LaCroix) and 'Blackwing', in which Nick dreams he is murdering women before the murders take place in real life.

Three L.A. areas are targeted for the manhunt. Compton, Downey and Norwalk, all in South Central.

Bitch!: Kate, to Angel: 'I know what to do. Drive a stake right through the son-of-a-bitch's heart. And when that happens, I suggest you don't be there.'

The Charisma Show: On Wesley's stake: 'Kind of rude coming into a vampire's place of business with one of those. Could be misinterpreted.' And, to Angel: 'My glamorous L.A. life. I get to make the coffee *and* chain the boss to the bed. Gotta join a union.'

L.A.-Speak: Cordelia: 'For a guy who's two hundred plus, you're not usually with-the-bags.' And: 'Compare *skinnies* on the current "evil happenings"?' And: 'The DMV is *totally* stalkerphobic.' And: 'Jeez, Wesley. *Hover much*?' And: 'You're totally pumping me for information, aren't you? . . . Oh crap. You're him. *He*. The guy. *Apt-Pupil-boy*.'

Kid: '*Hey dude.*'

Cigarettes and Alcohol: The skateboard kid wants Penn to buy him beer from a liquor store.

Sex and Drugs and Rock'n'Roll: Wesley: 'While executing my duties as Watcher in Sunnydale I did extensive research. Specifically on Angel, given his uncomfortable proximity to the Slayer.' Cordelia: 'He looked pretty comfortable to me.'

'You May Remember Me From Such Films and TV Series As . . .': Jeremy Renner plays Ted Nida in *The Net*. He was also Jack in the pilot episode of *Zoe, Duncan, Jack & Jane*. Kimberleigh Aarn appeared in *Bonfire of the Vanities* and *Presumed Innocent*.

Don't Give Up The Day Job: Director Rick Kolbe has worked on *Millennium, JAG, Star Trek: Voyager, Tales of the Gold Monkey, Star Trek: The Next Generation* (including the finale 'All Good Things'), *Magnum PI, Battlestar Galactica, CHiPS* and *The Rockford Files*.

Logic, Let Me Introduce You to This Window: As Penn and Angel stand over Penn's sister's body, their breath can be seen (see **15**, 'The Prodigal'). During the first fight between them, Penn grabs Angel by the shirt. The camera angle changes and he's holding Angel's coat instead. When Penn refers to Angel not meeting him in Italy, he says he waited 'until the nineteenth century'. Angel gives his reason as getting held up in Romania, which took place in 1898, so Penn must mean the *twentieth* century. Kate has never worn a cross on-screen, so it's convenient for her to be not only wearing one here, but fiddling with it so prominently. Angel leaves for the police station wearing a grey sweater, but when he arrives it's changed to a black shirt. Kate gets out of the car at the crime scene, without latex gloves. We see her reach the police tape, the camera cuts to a frontal view and she has one glove on.

Angel is wearing his trench coat when he comes through the ceiling at the warehouse; it gets covered in dust and plaster. He's wearing it in the next scene at the offices and it's as clean as a whistle. Do vampires sweat? Penn wipes perspiration from his face as he holds Wesley hostage. Kate tells Angel that she's read about him. In *Buffy*: 'Angel', Giles says that he could find no mention of Angelus in the texts, but he did in *The Watcher's Diaries*. Kate's line, 'a demon with the face of an angel,' is exactly what Giles reads in the *Buffy* episode. With The Council of Watchers' desire for secrecy it seems remiss that they've let this publication into the public domain. When Kate is lying on the floor in the warehouse, her cross is inside her sweater, but when she gets up, it's on the outside. How strong do you have to be to shove a blunted piece of wood through *two people*? How does Angel know Kate's address? Once again, Angel's photograph is taken despite cameras using mirrors as part of their focusing mechanism (see **1**, 'City Of').

I Just *Love* Your Accent: Wesley says, 'You'd be locked up faster than Lady Hamilton's virtue,' referring to Emily Lyon (1765–1815), the wife of Sir William Hamilton and the lover of Admiral Horatio Nelson. The Irish accents in this episode are woeful, though Boreanaz's is *slightly* better than Jeremy Renner's.

Quote/Unquote: Cordelia: 'I don't care how many files you have on all the horrible things he did back in the powdered-wig days. He's good now and he's my friend and nothing you or anyone else can say will make me turn on a friend.' Angel: 'He's right.' Cordelia, to Wesley: 'You stake him, I'll cut his head off.'

Angel: 'People change.' Penn: 'We're not *people*.'

Angel: 'I'm sorry for what I did to you, Penn, for what I turned you into.' Penn: 'First-class killer? An artist? A bold re-interpreter of the form?' Angel: 'Try cheesy hack. Look at you. You've been getting back at your father for over two hundred years. It's pathetic and clichéd. Probably got a killer shrine on your wall, huh? News clippings, magazine articles, maybe a few candles? You are *so* prosaic.'

Cordelia: 'You're not him, Angel. Not any more. The name I got in my vision, the message didn't come for Angelus, it came for you. And you have to trust that whoever that The Powers That Be be ... are ... is ... anyway, they know the difference.'

Notes: 'I believe in Los Angeles. It's the city of dreams, a mystical oasis, built from a desert. But even sunny-blonde-L.A. has its trashy dark roots.' The best episode of *Angel*'s first season, as Angel's past (in the shape of one of the unfortunate wretches that he sired) comes back to haunt him. A multi-layered story, with a great part in it for Elisabeth Rohm and some memorable set-pieces. The Cordelia/Wesley double act continues to delight. The continuity with various *Buffy* episodes is good too (see **15**, 'The Prodigal').

Angel says that he has a link which allows him to see through Penn's eyes while he's sleeping. (Presumably this ability exists for all those he has sired, including Drusilla? Does Darla see through Angel's eyes?) Penn displays superhuman speed and agility, more than any vampire previously seen. Penn's family were Puritans and he was sired by Angelus in the late 1700s. He was in Los Angeles in 1929 and 1963, returning each time to the same spot. In 1929 it was the Regents Gardens Hotel and in 1963 it was the Cloverwood Apartments. He may also have been responsible for deaths in Boston in 1908. In current day L.A., he has been dubbed 'The Pope' by the tabloid press due to his 'signature': a cross carved into the victim's cheek. His victims include Reggie Sparks, a crossing guard; Jinny Markem, tenth grader and Jessica Halpern, 25, a waitress. Kate's profile of the killer is that he is a white male. He will not seem a monster to an observer. His victims do not struggle, so he is probably charming and attractive. But at the core he is a loner, possibly a dual personality who, once the crime is committed, retains no memory of it. He doesn't view his victims as subhuman, rather it's himself that is more than human, a superior species. Unmarried, he may have recently had a long-term relationship end badly. Prior to this there may have been an inactive period when he regarded this as his salvation, but once ended, it resulted in recidivism. 'What's not in question is his experience. He's been doing this for a very long time, and he will do it again.' So, is it Angel she's profiling, or Penn?

Penn: 'What's in Romania?' Angel: 'Gypsies,' refers to the events of 1898 (see *Buffy*: 'Becoming' Part 1, **18**, 'Five By Five', **29**, 'Darla'). Angel's dreams are like those induced by The First Evil in *Buffy*: 'Amends'. Angel tells Penn 'It *has* to end.' He used a similar line to Drusilla in *Buffy*: 'Lie to Me.' It's something of Angel's catchphrase, he also used a variation to the Tahlmer in **2**, 'Lonely Heart'. Angel Investigations is next to the business premises of Dr Folger, a dentist (see **22**, 'To Shanshu in L.A.').

Wesley reads the *Los Angeles Globe*, finding references to Penn in 1929 and 1963 (is it a sister paper of the *Los*

Angeles Globe Register? See **2**, 'Lonely Heart', **5**, 'Rm W/a Vu'). Among the headlines in 1963 are US DELEGATION ATTEND MEET and EUROPE SECRET PACT EXPECTED THIS WEEK. The 1929 paper, deliciously, includes WALL ST CONFIDENT AS STOCKS SURGE. In Wesley's extensive Angel file a briefly glimpsed clipping has a headline involving President Roosevelt. Los Angeles has an occult bookstore called The Ancient Eye (see **24**, 'Are You Now Or Have You Ever Been?') which contains a book on Angel's past, including an illustration of him feeding.

Alexis Denisof is added to the title sequence with this episode, with clips from **10**, 'Parting Gifts', **12**, 'Expecting' and **13**, 'She'.

Soundtrack: 'Leave You Far Behind' by Lunatic Calm.

Did You Know?: Perhaps unsurprisingly, at school, Charisma Carpenter hated her name (inspired by a brand of Avon perfume): 'How can you call yourself Charisma when you go to a [strict private] school and your mom dresses you in pink hot-pants?' she asked *TV Guide*'s Jennifer Graham. 'They looked at me like I was Satan!' To James Brady, of *Parade*, she confessed that she called herself Chrissy for several years: 'It took me until I was thirteen to go by my real name.' After graduating, Charisma worked in her father's San Diego restaurant, did property management and clerked at a video store. During a visit to her boyfriend in L.A. during 1992 she landed a job waitressing at Mirabelle's restaurant on Sunset Boulevard – 'I was the waitress from hell.' There she got a theatrical agent and ultimately landed over twenty commercials including a two-year stint as the 'Secret Antiperspirant' girl. 'Being on commercials is funny because no one ever recognises you. They just come up and say, "Did I go to school with you?"'

Tim Minear's Comments: From *The Watcher's Web*: 'Someone came up with the concept: "A serial killer [using] Angel's old MO. It turns out it's a vampire he created in his heyday". We sit in the writer's room with a big board [and] beat out the story scene by scene, creating the teaser and acts one-through-four. We sharpen and define the elements (at first Angel thinks he's doing the murders in his sleep). Joss is involved in everything from concept to final approved story. The writer of the particular episode will then flesh out the story. He or she will get notes on that outline and make some (hopefully minor) changes. **11**, "Somnambulist" was actually my first script. **6**, "Sense and Sensitivity" was the second I wrote, though the first produced. I like good old-fashioned ripping yarns. And I think "Somnambulist" is very funny, actually.'

12
Expecting

US Transmission Date: 25 January 2000
UK Transmission Date: 24 March 2000 (Sky),
26 March 2001 (Channel 4)

Writer: Howard Gordon
Director: David Semel
Cast: Daphnee Duplaix (Sarina), Ken Marino (Wilson Christopher),
Josh Randall (Bartender), Doug Tompos (Doctor Wasserman),
Louisette Geiss (Emily), Julie Quinn (Pregnant Woman),
Maggie Connelly (Nurse), Steven Roy (Jason)
French Title: *La Semence Du Démon*
German Title: *Teuflische Leidenschaft*

After a night out with friends Cordelia wakes to find herself hugely pregnant. Angel and Wesley discover that a demon is using men to impregnate women to propagate its spawn. Despite a possessed Cordelia's attempts to stop them, they destroy the demon and end the women's nightmare.

Dudes and Babes: Cordelia's friends Emily and Sarina are gorgeous while the bar sequences include lots of girls in short skirts. Wilson and his hunky chums surely don't need demonic help to attract the ladies?

It's a Designer Label!: What on earth is Cordelia wearing in the opening scenes? It looks like a green bra with a triangular dangly bit.

References: Cordelia's nickname for her ghostly flatmate, Phantom Dennis, is a pun on the full title of *Star Wars:*

Episode I. Rosemary's Baby, *I Don't Want To Be Born*, *The Unborn*, *Demon Seed* and *To The Devil . . . A Daughter* are obvious recurring riffs given the subject matter, while aspects of the story bear resemblance to *The Midwich Cuckoos*. Also, the Joker from *Batman*, the film version of *Evita* (and its star, Madonna), *The Dating Game*, KC and the Sunshine Band's 'Shake Your Booty' and the biblical story of David and Goliath.

Bitch!: Wilson: 'This is a private club, featured word, *private*.' Angel: 'You don't talk to me, I'll kick your ass. Featured word, *ass*.'

'West Hollywood?': Cordelia's girlfriends jump to conclusions about Wes and Angel. 'The good ones are always gay.' Wesley notes: 'I didn't mean doxy in a sexually promiscuous sense. You don't think sticking the axe in the wall put them off?' Angel: 'That was charming.' Wesley: 'What about the fact they thought we were gay?' Angel: 'Adds mystery.'

The Charisma Show: Like 5, 'Rm W/a Vu', this is primarily Cordelia's story. Some of her exchanges with Angel are amongst the series' finest: 'Have you talked to Wilson?' Cordelia: 'What would I say to him. I had a really great time and I think you left something at my place?' And: 'You're not alone.' Cordelia: 'That's sort of the problem, isn't it?'

L.A.-Speak: Cordelia: 'You're photographing all these gorgeous, famous people. *Where's the insecure*?'

Sarina: 'Sometimes the guys were like, jumpy. But this town, you know? Everything is fake. Things are weird and you stop asking questions.' And: 'Jase, *moolah*!'

Angel: 'You guys proxy for big-daddy-demon?'

Cigarettes and Alcohol: Sarina drinks (heavily) from a bottle of wine.

Sex and Drugs and Rock'n'Roll: The Hacksaw Beast is described as an inner earth and procrea-parasitic demon. The young are maintained by a telepathic link to their parent in the early stages of development. This influence also extends to the surrogate mothers to control them. Sarina's line 'nice axe' is *loaded* with innuendo. Cordelia assures Angel that the sex she had with Wilson was 'safe'.

This is the first episode to explicitly deal with sexual intercourse.

'You May Remember Me From Such Centrefolds As . . .': Daphnee Dupliax was *Playboy*'s 'Playmate of the Month' for July 1997.

'You May Remember Me From Such Films and TV Series As . . .': Ken Marino played Steve in the US remake of *Men Behaving Badly* and was in *101 Ways (The Things a Girl Will Do To Keep Her Volvo)* and *Carlo's Wake*. Louisette Geises was Sarah in *Cahoots*.

Don't Give Up The Day Job: Away from acting, Josh Randall was a grip on movies including *Pure Danger* and *Skyscraper* while Steven Roy was best boy on *Electra* and an electrician on *Street Law*. Director David Semel was a producer on *Dawson's Creek* and *Beverly Hills 90210* and has directed, among others, *Chicago Hope*, *Malibu Shores*, *7th Heaven*, *Roswell*, *Judging Amy* and *The Love Boat: The Next Wave*.

There's A Ghost In My House: Cordelia: 'Dennis, knock it off. This is the one guy I've actually liked in a long time and if you keep killing the mood, I'll kill you. All right, empty threat, you being a ghost and already dead and all. But I'll do something worse. I'll play *Evita* around the clock. The one with Madonna.'

In one of the most touching moments of the season, a tearful Cordelia sitting in bed is firstly offered a tissue by Phantom Dennis and then tucked in.

Logic, Let Me Introduce You to This Window: When Angel bribes the bartender, the reflection of his hands can be seen on the bar. Sarina's apartment building uses the same hall set as Barney's in **10**, 'Parting Gifts'. When the syringe drops to the floor, it has no writing on it, but another shot shows writing on the tube. The light is visible in the office fridge even after the door is closed. During the gun-club fight, part of the wall comes off; Angel steps on it and you can hear the polyfoam crunch. Where does Cordelia get her maternity denims from?

When Cordelia drinks the blood, some dribbles from her mouth and she wipes it with her sleeve yet there's no blood on her overalls or her sleeve in later scenes. Someone coughs as Angel enters the Lounge LaBrea.

I Just *Love* Your Accent: Wesley is compared to Hugh Grant. He says: 'No one is more fond of Cordelia than I, but if she wants to go *gadabouting* with those *doxies* . . .' Blimey, that's a bit judgemental. Plus he's the only English person to use the phrase 'trendy hot spot' since 1975 (see **38**, 'Epiphany'). Cordelia says that compared to her old apartment the new one is Buckingham Palace. Angel and Wesley breaking into the wrong house is *very* reminiscent of a sequence in the 1978 'Hard Men' episode of the British police series *The Sweeney* but that's most likely a coincidence as few Americans have even heard of it.

Quote/Unquote: Bartender: 'You're the boyfriend?' Angel: 'No. I'm family.'

Angel: 'Why is Mrs Benson filed under "P"?' Cordelia: 'Because she's from France. Remember what a pain she was?' Angel: 'It made me wanna drink a lot.' Cordelia: 'That's the French for ya.'

Wesley's heroic moment: 'I'm here to fight you, sir. To the death. Preferably yours.'

Cordelia: 'I've learned men are evil. Oh, wait, I knew that. I learned that L.A. is full of self-serving phoneys. Nope, had that one down too. Sex is bad?' Angel: 'We all knew that.' Cordelia: 'I learned that I have two people I trust absolutely with my life and that part's new.'

Notes: 'You're afraid of what's inside of me.' Derivative, but a lot of fun, 'Expecting' takes a potentially ludicrous situation and creates an amusing and at times touching story from it.

Angel says that bright light hurts his eyes and that he doesn't hum (although we saw Angelus do so in *Buffy*: 'Killed By Death'). He knows that Wilson is human, probably from his smell (see **1**, 'City Of'). The sword Angel uses to kill the Tahval demon appears to be the one Doyle gave him to kill the sewer beast in **6**, 'Sense and Sensitivity'.

Wesley appears to start crying when Cordelia thanks him and Angel for saving her. He claims to have some allergies, but we don't believe a word of it. Wesley and Cordelia pose as a married couple using the alias Mr and Mrs Penborne when they visit the gynaecologist. Wesley has a new Bavarian hunting axe. Cordelia refers to coming to L.A. as like 'skydiving without a parachute except for the smashing your body to bits part.'

Soundtrack: Splashdown's 'Games You Play' and 'Deeper than a Milkshake' by Shayrna NuDelman.

Joss Whedon's Comments: Asked by *DreamWatch* about the more experimental episodes of *Buffy* and *Angel* and how they compare to those done by other series, Joss confessed: 'I don't want to do things that are just a wink to the audience. I thought the *X-Files/Cops* thing made sense, it actually worked in a weird way. But *Felicity* did *The Twilight Zone*, *Chicago Hope* did a musical show and I don't want to be one of those shows that is self-indulgent.'

13
She

US Transmission Date: 8 February 2000
UK Transmission Date: 31 March 2000 (Sky),
14 November 2000 (Channel 4)

Writers: David Greenwalt, Marti Noxon
Director: David Greenwalt
Cast: Bai Ling (Jhiera), Colby French (Tae),
Heather Stephens (Captured Demon Girl), Sean Gunn (Mars),
Tracy Costello (Laura), Andre L Roberson (Diego),
PJ Marino (Peter Wilkers), Honor Bliss (Girl),
Chris Durand (Demon Henchman #1), Alison Simpson (Demon Girl #1),
Lucas Dudley (Security Guard)
French Title: *Elle*
German Title: *Die Frauen der Oden Tals*

Angel and his friends become caught up in the pan-dimensional battle between Jhiera, a female member of the Vigories, and her male oppressors who remove their women's passion-centre, to subjugate them at an early age.

Dreaming (As *Buffy* Often Proves) is Free: Cordelia says Wesley awoke her from a dream about a Going Out of Business sale at Neiman's. Not so much free, then, as *cheap*.

Dudes and Babes: For the fellahs, Cordelia's party. Check out the *skirt*. The extremely short dress worn by the girl following Jhiera up the steps to the art gallery also deserves a few seconds of your time. Speaking of Jhiera, those leather pants . . .

The ladies, on the other hand, may like to view yet another appearance of Boreanaz topless for no adequate reason. It's worth keeping your finger on the 'pause' button during the first opening of the portal. The wind effects are so strong, they blow David's shirt up and reveal his belly button.

It's a Designer Label!: Orange shirt alert. The fashion store Neiman Marcus is mentioned (see **1**, 'City Of'). Wesley's sweater is the talk of the party. Unfortunately, he doesn't know who knitted it and this loses him the chance of a date. Cordelia's multi-coloured dress is wonderful, while her extremely tight jeans and black boots get lots of screen time.

References: The title is from H Rider Haggard's 1886 novel. In the episode's best scene Angel describes the 1862 painting *La Musique Aux Tuileries* by French Impressionist Edouard Manet (1832–1883). 'On the left one spies the painter himself. In the middle distance is the poet and critic Baudelaire, a friend of the artist. Now, Baudelaire, interesting fellow. In his poem "Le Vampyr" he wrote: "Thou who abruptly as a knife didst come into my heart." He strongly believed that evil forces surrounded mankind and some even speculated that the poem was about a real vampire. Oh, and Baudelaire was actually a little taller and a lot drunker than he is depicted here.' The implication being that Angel knew symbolist poet Charles Baudelaire (1821–1867), author of *Les Fleurs du Mal*, and that 'Le Vampyr' is about Angel himself. Also, *Carrie*, English novelist Nancy Mitford (1904–1973), Steve and David Paymer (see **5**, 'Rm W/a Vu'), a misquote from Depeche

Mode's 'Blasphemous Rumours' and the Sizzler steakhouse restaurant chain.

During the car-tailing sequence, the marquee on the Los Angeles Theater is for the movie *Heartbreaker*. And just as it's starting to look like they'd given up on the obvious visual references to *Batman*, watch Angel jumping off the roof of the security firm.

Bitch!: Cordelia to Wesley: 'Grovelling isn't just a way of life for you, it's an art.'

And, to Jhiera: 'Can I get you something? Knife to our throat so you can run away?'

'West Hollywood': Wesley hugging Angel.

The Charisma Show: On Angel's mood at the party: 'I'm so glad you came. You know how parties are, you're always worried that no one's going to suck the energy out of the room like a giant black hole of boring despair. But, there you were in the clinch.'

L.A.-Speak: Cordelia: 'Gross.' And: 'A *hottie*, huh? I guess she's that all right. What with the *sizzle*?' And: 'Stop kissing butt.'

Mars: '*Excellent*. Just when I need the artistic eye of a Goddess.' And: 'They're *chillin*'. The little sisters are fine.' And: 'Man, that's *lame*.' And: 'My shaman has a place in the desert. He never could turn away scantily clad women in distress, from any dimension.' Can we say 'scene-stealing'?

Not Exactly A Haven For The Sisters: This is a Marti Noxon script, isn't it? Like her *Buffy* episode 'Beauty and the Beast', this story (with its implicit castration metaphor) tries to make big statements but ends up full of stereotypes and dangerously obvious solutions. No one could argue that the enslavement of women is a good thing, but, sadly, some complex issues about empowerment are turned into something not far short of penis-envy here.

Cigarettes and Alcohol: 'Let the consumption of cold things begin.' There's a link between Angel drinking beer at Cordelia's party and the security man at the ice factory also having a can. After Cordelia's vision she holds a glass of something to her throbbing temple. It *could* be iced water, but it may just as easily be neat vodka.

Cordelia: 'Can I get you some blood or anything?'
Angel: 'I'm good.'

Sex and Drugs and Rock'n'Roll: The Vigories are from the Oden Tal dimension. The males are fierce warriors. The females have raised ridges running down either cheek and a row of ridges on their back. These are called the Ko. This area contains their personality and passion. When they come of age, the Ko controls their physical and sexual power and signals when they are aroused. Initially, there is a period where the Ko manifests itself as heat and intense strength. At first the girls cannot control this power and need to be cooled constantly. With practice they can use the power at will. When the Ko is removed they become docile. Females are enslaved by the males who cut off their Ko.

Cordelia: 'Diego, *pants on!*'

Wesley: 'What say a couple of brooding demon hunters start chatting up some of the fillies?' Wesley says the thing he enjoyed most about the party was 'the tiny Reubens and the shrimp puffs'. A man of taste, clearly.

'You May Remember Me From Such Films As . . .': Bai Ling was one of *People* magazine's '50 Most Beautiful People in the World in 1998'. She played Tuptim in *Anna and the King* and Miss East in *Wild Wild West*. She can also be seen in *Nixon* and *The Crow*. Heather Stephens's movies include *Clubland*, *The In Crowd* and *Dante's Peak* while Lucas Dudley appeared in *Solo* and *Letters From a Killer*.

Don't Give Up The Day Job: Alison Simpson is a dancer who can be seen in *The Big Lebowski* and *Man on the Moon*. Chris Durand is best known for playing Michael Meyers in *Halloween H20: Twenty Years Later* but his stuntwork is visible in *Soldier*, *Slappy and the Stinkers*, *Scream 2*, *The Mask* and *Maniac Cop 2* and *3*.

There's A Ghost In My House: Angel: 'Hi Dennis. How are you doing? Still dead? I know the feeling.'

Logic, Let Me Introduce You to This Window: Are vampires pan-dimensional? If not, how does Jhiera know what one is? (see **42**, 'Over the Rainbow'). Angel appears to be in direct sunlight on more than one occasion.

I Just *Love* Your Accent: Wesley: 'I feel rather chipper myself. That was quite a soirée last night.' In **12**, 'Expecting', Wesley blamed the crumbling of his stiff upper lip on allergies. This time it's 'something in my eye'. *Sure*.

Motors: Angel's licence plate is NKD 714. Jhiera drives a red Dodge Durango.

Quote/Unquote: Angel: 'The quiet reserved thing, don't you think it makes me, kinda cool?' Cordelia [points at Wesley]: '*He* was cooler.' Angel: 'Now I'm depressed.'

Notes: 'Call me old-fashioned, but I can't allow tourists to go around torching locals.' A real disappointment. 'She', with its heavy-handed moralising and lack of interesting characters, is paced with all of the tension of a snapped elastic band. And it's *annoyingly* PC. The hole where the rain got in this season, clearly. Wesley's three (count 'em) pratfalls during the episode are an insult to both the character (who is, ironically, just starting to find his feet) and the audience (who are trying hard to like him). Plus, it's difficult to escape a nagging suspicion that this is actually a rejected *Deep Space Nine* script with its 'dimensional portals'. Noxon is a fine writer of human emotion but is occasionally prey to miscalculations like this; bland and gauche beside Jane Espenson's urbane comedy or Tim Minear's smooth character essays, and anaemic in relation to the sophistication of Whedon or Greenwalt.

Angel tells Cordelia about Hell (see *Buffy*: 'Becoming' Part 2, 'Anne', 'Faith Hope and Trick') for the first time. He notes that, 'You tend to know a lot of the people' unlike Cordelia's party. He says he has two modes with people: 'bite' or 'avoid'. The cellphone that Cordelia gave Angel is a Motorola Digital. The date it displays is 12 January 2000. Angel believes that cellphones were invented by a 'bored warlock'. Cordelia thinks that 'a guy who knows how to use an ancient scythian short bow' should be able to figure out how to use a phone. Cordelia uses the *Los Angeles Globe Register* (see **2**, 'Lonely Heart', **5**, 'Rm W/a Vu', **11**, 'Somnambulist') to research four similar killings in the last eleven months. When Angel tells Jhiera that 'gypsies have a strange sense of humour' this is not only a reference to his curse (see *Buffy*: 'Becoming' Part 2 and **18**, 'Five by Five') but also a line from the *Angel Demo Reel*. Angel's grappling hook puts in its first appearance since **2**, 'Lonely Heart'. Wesley officially joins the firm. The invoice lists the number for the ice factory as 555-0197.

Soundtrack: 'Strangelove Addiction' by Supreme Beings of Leisure, 'In Time' by Morphic Field and 'Light Years On' by 60 Channels. The music Angel and Wesley (ahem) 'dance' to is 'Pure Roots' from *Non-Stop Music Library*.

Did You Know?: David Boreanaz has a phobia about chickens. What a *girl*! Charisma, on the other hand, suffers from a phobia of tarantulas. That's much more understandable.

You Dancin'?: Highlight of the episode is the sequence where Wesley dances (love Angel's smirk while watching him) and then Angel imagines what his own efforts at grooving would be like. In case you miss it first time round, the sequence is repeated beneath the closing credits. It's so funny you'll have trouble staying upright and will temporarily forget what a rotten episode this is.

14
I've Got You Under My Skin

US Transmission Date: 15 February 2000
UK Transmission Date: 7 April 2000 (Sky),
9 April 2000 (Channel 4)

Teleplay: Jeannine Renshaw
Story: David Greenwalt, Jeannine Renshaw
Director: Robert David Price
Cast: Will Kempe (Seth Anderson), Katy Boyer (Paige Anderson),
Anthony Cistaro (Ethros Demon), Jesse James (Ryan Anderson),
Ashley Edner (Stephanie Anderson), Patience Cleveland (Nun),
Jerry Lambert (Rick the Clerk)
French Title: *Je T'ai Dans La Peau*
German Title: *Das Böse an Sich*

Cordelia's vision sends Angel to the home of a family just in time to save young Ryan from being run over by a car.

But all is not what it seems and Wesley discovers that someone in the house is possessed by a demon. Angel unmasks Ryan and, to his parents' relief, arranges an exorcism. But, when Wesley confronts the released demon and taunts it about not getting the boy's soul, it replies, 'what soul?'

Denial, Thy Name is Paige: One of the worst cases witnessed since Joyce Summers. Poor Paige just doesn't want to admit that her son is a murdering monster, does she?

It's a Designer Label!: Cordelia suggests that Wesley wears too much cologne. Also, Cordelia's white trainers and pink roll-neck sweater.

References: 'I remember the children's rhyme. How come they're all full of death and cradles falling and mice getting tails cut off?' is Cordy's rant about nursery rhymes (specifically *Rock-A-Bye, Baby* and *Three Blind Mice*). She twice refers to *The Exorcist* ('head spins around?' and 'I wonder if I should put plastic down. Are you expecting any big vomiting here because I saw the movie?' confirming an earlier observation that Cordelia had seen the film in *Buffy*: 'I Only Have Eyes For You'). It's also an obvious influence on the plot. Wesley says he owns two Thighmasters (the second was a free gift accompanying *Buns of Steel*, a popular workout video). Also, *The Bad Seed* and a misquote from Evelyn Waugh's *A Handful of Dust* ('I'll show you *fear*'). The title of the episode is taken from a Cole Porter song made famous by Frank Sinatra. Cordelia's 'kill, kill, kill' is a line from The Doors' 'The End'. The cards that Ryan and Stephanie have look like Pokémon trading cards.

L.A.-Speak: Cordelia: 'You don't have to be *Joe-Stoic* about his dying. I know that you have this unflappable vibe working . . .' Angel: 'I'm not unflappable.' Cordelia: 'Great, so *flap*.'

Cordy: 'No one could have said "demon poo" before I touched it?' And: '*Jeez*, we got it. Circle, angry, kill, kill, kill. Go to church already.'

Cigarettes and Alcohol: Seth Anderson smokes. Angel says that this doesn't bother him.

Sex and Drugs and Chocolate Brownies: Cordelia's recipe for chocolate brownies was handed down to her by her mother (who got it from *her* housekeeper). And she's improvised a little. Wesley is less than enthusiastic about the results. Angel's attempts are more successful, at least in confirming the presence of a demon in the Anderson household.

'You May Remember Me From Such Films and TV Series As . . .': Will Kempe was Rick Von Sloneker in *The Last Days of Disco*, Acid Sid in *Pledge Night* and Legs Diamond in *Hit the Dutchman*. Katy Boyer appears in *The Lost World: Jurassic Park* and, on TV, in *Babylon 5*, *Beauty and the Beast* and *Silk Stalkings*. Jesse James can be seen in *Gods and Monsters*, *Message in a Bottle*, *Slap Her, She's French*, *Pearl Harbor* and the *X-Files* episode 'The Uninvited'. Nine-year-old Ashley Edner has also been in *The X-Files* and plays Kelly in *Malcolm in the Middle*. She's also done voice-work on *Hanging On* and *Lion King II: Simba's Pride*. Patience Cleveland played Miss Hanson in *Green Acres* and appeared in *Psycho II*.

Don't Give Up The Day Job: Jerry Lambert is also a composer, his music being heard in *Texas Chainsaw Massacre 2* and *Hidden Agenda*, though his most famous work is the theme song to *It's Garry Shandling's Show*.

Logic, Let Me Introduce You to This Window: Angel tells Paige: 'I'm not a big bleeder'. As noted previously he shouldn't be a bleeder *at all*, as his heart doesn't beat. Why didn't the car that almost ran over Ryan stop? Angel's reflection is visible on his desk in the opening scene. If holy objects like crosses and holy water burn a vampire, then why is Angel able to hold a copy of the Bible without bursting into flames? (see **24**, 'Are You Now or Have You Ever Been?') There are bars on Stephanie's windows early in the episode, yet when Angel saves her from the fire, they're gone.

I Just *Love* Your Accent: Wesley's scarred relationship with his father is dealt with. It has some parallels with Angel's relationship with *his* father (see **15**, 'The Prodigal', **41**, 'Belonging'). 'A father doesn't have to be possessed to terrorise his children' is a telling statement and explains a lot about Wesley.

Quote/Unquote: Stephanie: 'Angel's funny.' Seth [dryly]: 'He hides it well.'

Nun: 'You would come into a place of worship?' Angel: 'I'm not what you think.'

Ethros: 'Do you know what the most frightening thing in the world is? Nothing. That's what I found in the boy. No conscience, no fear, no humanity, just a black void . . . That boy's mind was the blackest Hell I've ever known. When he slept, I could whisper in him. I tried to get him to end his life, even if it meant ending mine. I had given up hope. I know you bring death. I do not fear it. The only thing I have ever feared is in that house.'

Notes: 'I like to think of myself as possessing . . .' An interesting filler. There's a nice set-up that initially suggests the subject will be child-abuse and then switches to something more supernatural which throws the viewer. *The Exorcist* set-pieces are well-handled and the child actors do a good job, but the whole thing is rather uninvolving.

Angel uses the alias Angel Jones. He tells Cordelia that Rick's Magick-N-Stuff is between a yoghurt shop and the Doggie Dunk on the corner of Melrose and Robertson (in West Hollywood). Although Ethros demons have a physical body, they can possess people. They have a tendency for mass murder and try to corrupt the souls of those they possess. They can scan the surface thoughts of those near them, imitate voices and possess a level of telekinetic power. They secrete a green fluid called plakticine. The possessed have enhanced strength and can manifest a demonic appearance. If the host of an Ethros demon ingests eucalyptus powder they show their demon aspect. When an Ethros demon is cast out it immediately seeks another body. The demon is expelled with such force that the newly inhabited rarely survive. When wounded, an Ethros demon seeks primordial volcanic basalt to aid its regeneration. In order to trap an Ethros demon a special box must be used, an item made of 600 species of virgin woods hand-crafted by blind Tibetan monks. Lizzie Borden (1860–1927) was suspected of murdering her stepmother and father in a sensational trial in Massachusetts in 1892. Despite a wealth of circumstantial evidence, she was acquitted. Wesley suggests that she was possessed by an Ethros demon.

Did You Know?: During Charisma Carpenter's time as a cheerleader in San Diego she and two male friends were at the beach one night when they were attacked by an armed man. He ordered Charisma to tie up her friends with the clear intention that he would then rape her. With astonishing bravery and a gun held to her head, Charisma refused and, in the ensuing commotion, the group were able to fight off the man who fled, shooting and wounding one of Charisma's friends. Their witness statements eventually led to the arrest of the assailant, a police officer and serial rapist. A dramatisation of the incident was filmed by the Discovery Channel's *The Justice Files*, with an interview with Charisma herself.

15
The Prodigal

US Transmission Date: 22 February 2000
UK Transmission Date: 14 April 2000 (Sky),
21 November 2000 (Channel 4)

Writer: Tim Minear
Director: Bruce Seth Green
Cast: J Kenneth Campbell (Angel's Father), Henri Lubatti (Suit #1),
Frank Potter (Uniformed Delivery Man), Eliza Szonert (Chambermaid),
Bob Fimiani (Groundskeeper), Christine Hendricks (Barmaid),
John Maynard (Uniformed Worker),
Glenda Morgan Brown (Angel's Mother),
Mark Ginther (Head Demon Guy),
John Patrick Clerkin (Black Robed Priest), Mike Vendrell (Suit #2)
French Title: *Le Fils Prodigue*
German Title: *Vaterliebe*

A case on which Kate again requires help from Angel dramatically reveals the involvement of her father, Trevor, in the illegal schemes of a drug-dealing demon. This forces Angel to recall some of the issues he had with his own father (see **Denial, Thy Name is Liam's Father**). But he is unable to prevent Trevor's death, distancing him further from Kate.

Denial, Thy Name is Liam's Father: The relationship between father and son is best described as strained. 'It's a son I wished for. Instead, God gave me *you*. A terrible disappointment,' Liam is told. He replies that his father couldn't have asked for a more dutiful son. 'My whole life you've told me . . . what it is you required of me and I've lived down to your every expectations.'

When Angelus tells Darla that by killing his father he has 'won,' his sire tells him that his victory took moments, but that his father's defeat of *him* will last a lifetime. Angelus is horrified: 'He can't defeat me now.' Darla notes: 'Nor can he ever approve of you, in this world or any other. What we once were informs all that we have become. The same love will infect our hearts, even if they no longer beat. Simple death won't change that.' Angelus asks if the death of his family is the work of love? 'Darling boy', says Darla. 'Still so very young.' Compare this with Angel's half-spoken assertion that a vampire's personality after death isn't *so* different from what it was like before in *Buffy*: 'Doppelgängland' (see also *Buffy*: 'Fool for Love').

It's a Designer Label!: Cordelia's 'undercover' get-up (blonde wig, dark glasses, long pink overcoat) is spectacular. Also, her short multicoloured top, and red trousers in the opening scene. Where does she get the money for all of these designer clothes?

References: The title is from the parable of The Prodigal Son told by Christ in Luke 15. There's an allusion to the belief that garlic will repel vampires. Also Alexander Pope's *An Essay on Criticism*, and *The Lord's Prayer*.

Bitch!: Wesley: 'Fools rush in . . .' Cordelia: 'No, he wants you to stay here.'

'West Hollywood?': Trevor, on Angel: 'Must be something wrong with him. "West Hollywood?"' Kate: 'Daddy, no. Angel's just not my type.' During the 70s West Hollywood was known for its progressive social environment and the area attracted a large number of gay residents. It is still regarded as the gay capital of Los Angeles.

The Charisma Show: Cordy crouched over the demon's body waving a hacksaw shouting 'Found it,' just as Wesley comments on how sensitive women can be around the subject of demons is a definite highlight.

L.A.-Speak: Cordelia: 'Maybe it was having a bad *skanky-rag* day.' And: 'No *lurky* minions from Hell will get in here.'

Delivery Man: 'Just your average *Joe-Stink* homeless guy.'

Angel: 'It was an "evil thing" in terms of that word. It just wasn't an *evil* "evil thing".' Kate: 'There are not-evil "evil things"?' Angel: 'Well, yeah.'

Wesley: 'I think that it would be a fair intuitive leap to assume that the Kwaini was *jonesing* to get well.'

Cigarettes and Alcohol: 'Up again all night, is it? Drinking and whoring. I smell the stink of it on you.' Trevor Lockley drinks a glass of scotch.

Sex and Drugs and Rock'n'Roll: Wesley says that the demon drug is very similar to PCP (phencyclidine). 'I did identify "Eye of Newt" as one of the ingredients, but one suspects added chiefly for taste rather than kick.'

'You May Remember Me From Such Films and TV Series As . . .': A former ice-skater, once ranked 12th in the US, Julie Benz auditioned for the role of Buffy Summers in 1997. Although unsuccessful, her consolation prize was becoming Angel's sire, Darla. She played Kate Topolsky in *Roswell* and appeared in *Taken, As Good As It Gets, Jawbreaker, A Fate Totally Worse Than Death, Darkdrive, Shriek if You Know What I Did Last Friday the 13th* and *Satan's School for Girls*. Henri Lubatti plays David Sherman in *Felicity*, Eliza Szonert was Danni Stark on *Neighbours* while Glenda Morgan Brown appeared in *Dreamers*. J. Kenneth Campbell was the Marquis de Sade in *Waxworks*. His other work includes *US Seals, Blue Streak, Bulworth, Mars Attacks!, The Abyss, Crash, China Beach, Wonder Woman* and *Matlock*.

Don't Give Up The Day Job: John Maynard is a Hollywood producer, working on *Loaded, All Men Are Liars* and the classic SF movie *The Navigator*. He was also technical advisor on *Bloodmoon* and, in England, wrote for legendary BBC soap operas *Dr Finlay's Casebook* and *EastEnders*. Mark Ginther played Lord Zedd in *Mighty Morphin Power Rangers: The Movie*, and is a stuntman on movies like *Hoffa, Joe Versus the Volcano* and *Hologram Man*. Michael Vendrell, the series stunt co-ordinator, is a martial-arts expert and served as specialist on *Commando*. He was Sean Connery's stunt double on *The Rock*.

Logic, Let Me Introduce You to This Window: When Angel trails the delivery man the frost on his breath can be seen. This also applies, more obviously, to Angel and Darla in the scene where Angel rises from the grave. There is no dent on the driver's side fender of Angel's car, though one was apparent in 13, 'She'. He must have got it fixed. Darla's wig in the newly filmed scenes is more elaborate and a different colour to the one used in the footage culled from *Buffy*: 'Becoming' Part 1.

I Just *Love* Your Accent: Wesley refers to Kate as 'skittish'. More extremely dodgy Irish accents are to be heard. This is probably Boreanaz's blackest hour, because he's required to carry it off for so much of the episode. There are times when the accent doesn't so much slip as crash to the ground and shatter into a million pieces.

Quote/Unquote: Barmaid, on Liam: '[He's] God's gift all right.' Darla: 'Really? I've never known God to be so generous.' Barmaid: 'His lies sound pretty when the stars are out. But he forgets every promise he's made when the sun comes up again.' Darla: 'That wouldn't really be a problem for me.'

Kate: 'Look, no offence. I think you're probably a pretty decent guy for what you are, but let's keep this strictly business . . . I'm not your girlfriend.'

Cordelia: 'Move your entrails.'

Angelus, about to kill the father he hated: 'Strange. Somehow you seemed taller when I was alive . . . To think I ever let such a tiny, trembling thing make me feel the way you did.'

Notes: 'You're a layabout and a scoundrel and you'll never amount to anything more.' A brilliant reformatting of the series, telling (in more detail than before) Angel's Year One-style origins. The clever juxtaposition of Kate's uncomfortable relationship with her own father (previously glimpsed in **6**, 'Sense and Sensitivity') and Angel's troubled past is neatly handled and the acting from all concerned is excellent (despite the accents).

Angel's Christian name when he was human was Liam. He was born in 1727 and had a younger sister called Kathy whom Angelus killed (along with his mother and father) after he became a vampire in 1753. The family had one servant, a chambermaid called Anna. The scenes of Darla siring Angelus are taken from *Buffy*: 'Becoming' Part 1. Although the date of Liam's death confirms the on-screen information of *Buffy*: 'Becoming' Part 1, it contradicts other dates given in *Buffy* (notably Willow's observation, taken from *The Watcher's Diaries*, in 'Halloween' that Angel was 18 years old in 1775 and still human). It seems that vampires take their 'age' from the time that they actually become a vampire (see, for instance, Spike's age as given in *Buffy*: 'The Initiative') though in Angel's case this is *still* a couple of years away from the dates mentioned in *Buffy* episodes during 1997–98 (that Angel was either 240 or 241) and with the *Angel Demo Reel* where he is 244 in 1999. He should be 246, at least. (It's also worth noting that the *Demo Reel* says that Angel was 27 when he became a vampire; here, the priest says he's 26.) There are approximately eleven people at Liam's funeral, including the priest, his mother, father and sister and several upset-looking ladies. The inscription on his gravestone reads 'beloved son'.

Darla tells the newly revived Angelus: 'Welcome to my world. It hurts, but not for long. Birth is always painful,' echoing similar sentiments expressed by Angel in *Buffy*: 'School Hard'. Angelus's first victim was the graveyard groundsman, followed by his sister, who believed he had returned as an angel (this is possibly where his nickname derives from).

   Cordelia's birthday was a fortnight ago. Angel claims he didn't know. She suggests that they use her birthdate for the office's security code so that he'll have eleven and a half months of typing it in and, therefore, no excuses not to remember next year. When she does input a code, she uses '0522' which many fans have taken as meaning that her birthday is 22nd May, however, there is no confirmation of this. Angel Investigations have purchased a digital camera that Cordelia uses when tailing the delivery man.

   Trevor Lockley (1938–2000) was on the police force for 35 years. Angel tells the vampires attacking Trevor: 'The minute his soul leaves his body, I am through this door to kill you both,' which confirms that a vampire may not enter uninvited a live dwelling.

   The scene with Trevor and Kate eating hot dogs was filmed at the Fisherman's Village in Marina Del Rey.

Did You Know?: The name Liam is Gaelic for 'guardian'.

What Might Have Been: Does Julie Benz wonder how her life may have changed if she'd got the role of Buffy? As she told Paul Simpson and Ruth Thomas in *SFX*: 'No, that would be silly. Everybody makes a big deal of it. When I auditioned for Buffy, it was just one of a thousand auditions I had that pilot season. I was one of a thousand girls they saw for it so it really wasn't a big deal.'

16
The Ring

US Transmission Date: 29 February 2000
UK Transmission Date: 21 April 2000 (Sky),
23 April 2001 (Channel 4)

Writer: Howard Gordon
Director: Nick Marck
Cast: Marcus Redmond (Tom Cribb),
Douglas Roberts (Darin McNamara),
Scott William Winters (Jack McNamara),
Anthony Guidera (Ernie Nellins), Chris Flander (Mr Winslow),
Marc Rose (Mellish), David Kallaway (Doorman),
Juan A Riojas (Val Trepkos), Michael Philip (Announcer),

Mark Ginther (Lasovic)
French Title: *L'Arène*
German Title: *Die Gladiatoren von L.A.*

A man hires Angel to investigate the kidnapping of his brother but, too late, Angel realises that this is a trap to lure him into the horrors of a demon fight club. As Wesley and Cordelia try to formulate a plan to rescue their friend, Angel attempts to persuade his fellow prisoners to rebel. With limited success.

It's a Designer Label!: Cordelia's black evening dress.

References: The bracelets are similar to the restraint devices in *The Running Man*. Also, *Jeopardy*, *Wheel of Fortune* and *Jerry Springer*, Tim Burton's *Beetlejuice*, the Marvel superhero Captain America, *Robin Hood*, Bob Marley's 'Exodus' ('Set the captives free'), Leonard Bernstein and Stephen Sondheim's *West Side Story*, Mahatma Gandhi (1869–1948), Moses and, obliquely, actor Keanu Reeves (*Bill & Ted's Excellent Adventure*, *Speed*, *The Matrix*). Howard Gordon's *The X-Files* episode, 'Firewalker' also featured a character called Daniel Trepkos. Tom Cribb (1781–1848) was an English bare-knuckle boxer. Dare I mention how much like *Spartacus* the whole thing is? Or *Fight Club*? (Not to mention a couple of *Star Trek* episodes, 'Bread and Circuses' and 'The Gamesters of Triskelion').

Bitch!: Cordelia: 'Every night it's *Jeopardy*, followed by *Wheel of Fortune* and a cup of hot cocoa. Look out girls, this one can't be tamed.' Wesley: 'I'll admit, it may not be as intoxicating as a life erected on high-fashioned pumps and a push-up bra.'

The Charisma and Alexis Show: Cordelia and Wesley undercover is one of the highlights of the season (Wesley: 'Something's going down tonight. Something with *the man*!')

L.A.-Speak: Cordelia: 'The bookie, who may get his *jollies* cutting off people's extremities?'

Cribb: 'Bloodsucker is crazier than I thought.'

Cigarettes and Alcohol: Lilah is something of a boozer, drinking red wine in the bar, a whisky when watching one of the bouts and champagne in her office with Angel. Lots of crates of Carlsberg lager are visible in the bookies' office.

Sex and Drugs and Rock'n'Roll: Cordelia thinks there ought to be an inter-demon dating base: 'Archfiend.org, where the lonely and the slimy connect.' Wesley tells Cordelia that he leads a rich and varied social life.

Wesley: 'He wrote "claw-like hands".' Cordelia: 'Could be a mixed breed. Smell?' Wesley: 'Sulphuric.' Cordelia: 'Add a Porsche and hair plugs and I've dated this guy. A lot.'

'You May Remember Me From Such Films and TV Series As . . .': Douglas Roberts was Richard Yzerman in *L.A. Law*. Scott William Winters played Clark in *Good Will Hunting* and also appeared in *The People Vs. Larry Flynt*. Stephanie Romanov began her career as a model aged fifteen, working for *Elle*, *French Vogue* and *Vanity Fair* before moving into acting with the role of Teri Spenser in *Melrose Place* and *Models Inc.* She has also appeared in *Due South*, *Spy Hard*, *Tricks* (as Candy), *Sunset Strip* (as Christine), *Thirteen Days* (as Jackie Kennedy) and *Dark Spiral*. Anthony Guidera was in *Armageddon*, *The Rock*, *Species* and *The Godfather: Part III*. On TV Juan Riojas has appeared in *The West Wing* and *Walker, Texas Ranger* while his movies include *Conspiracy Theory* and *In The Line Of Fire*.

Don't Give Up The Day Job: James E Mitchell, the assistant fight co-ordinator and David Boreanaz's martial-arts trainer has a lucrative sideline as George Clooney's stand-in for *Out of Sight*, *Batman & Robin* and *From Dusk Till Dawn* among others. He also doubled for Mel Gibson in *Payback*. Nice work if you can get it.

Logic, Let Me Introduce You to This Window: How does Angel know which drain in Beechwood Canyon the Howler demons are hiding in? During the bout with Trepkos, Angel's mouth is bleeding as he lies in the dirt. When he rises, most of the blood is gone. The hole in Angel's shirt switches sides several times. Trepkos has the same problem as Angel: his metal cuff and leather cuff switch wrists during their fight. After Angel refuses to make the killing blow on Trepkos, he stands and moves away. Note there is no wound in his side.

I Just *Love* Your Accent: Wesley: 'A name rife with *single entendre.*'

Ernie: 'You're from another country, right? [Wesley pulls a crossbow from behind his back] What are you, Robin Hood?'

Quote/Unquote: Cordelia: 'You'd think people would get enough gratuitous violence watching *Jerry Springer.*'

Wesley: 'These Octavian matches date back to the Roman Empire. I'd heard rumours of a revival.' Cordelia: 'Couldn't they have just done *West Side Story*?'

Notes: 'How does it feel to be a slave?' A very brutal subject handled in an oddly dispassionate manner makes for an episode that's difficult to feel strongly about. 'The Ring' features some nice stuff (Wesley's on good form, particularly his heroic use of a crossbow), but the main story just rambles and, after a while, bores.

Angel speaks Spanish, Russian and Italian. Wesley talks to Kate on the telephone after Angel goes missing. Cordelia owned a Palomino horse called Keanu 'before the IRS took him away' (see **1**, 'City Of'). She still keeps a lock of his hair in her bracelet. Wesley mentions the Vigories of Oden Tal (see **13**, 'She').

There are a dozen species of demons indigenous to L.A. county. Jack and Darin run the illegal sporting venue XXI, which is located under the Parker Bros warehouse. The signs in Nellins's office read: 'Danger Hot Girls' and 'We Have Ice'.

This episode was nominated for an Emmy for 'Outstanding Achievement in Makeup For A Drama Series'. Named in the nomination were the entire *Angel* make-up department: Dayne Johnson, David DeLeon, Louis Lazzara, Steve LaPorte, Rick Stratton, Jill Rockow, Toby Lamm, Jeremy Swan, Stephen Prouty, Earl Ellis, Dalia Dokter and Robert Maverick.

Soundtrack: Morphic Field's 'Consciousness (Aware of You)'.

Did You Know?: Many of the drawings on the *Demons, Demons, Demons* database are sketches by Joss Whedon used to create the monsters for *Buffy* and *Angel*. These include the demons from 'Gingerbread' and 'The Wish', a Kailiff from **5**, 'Rm W/a Vu', a Kawaini from **15**, 'The Prodigal' and a Brachen demon from **9**, 'Hero'.

Lost Angel?: David Boreanaz believes that Angel's character has 'evolved and taken on a totally new lifestyle being in the environment that he's in'. He told *The Big Breakfast* that 'it's refreshing to see him mixing with people and trying to find himself in the human realm. He's [been] closed off from that society and he's finding his place now. It's good to see him smile and be part of the human race.'

17
Eternity

US Transmission Date: 4 April 2000
UK Transmission Date: 28 April 2000 (Sky),
28 November 2000 (Channel 4)

Writer: Tracey Stern
Director: Regis B Kimble
Cast: Tamara Gorski (Rebecca), Robin Meyers (Masseuse)
French Title: *Éternité*
German Title: *Für Immer Jung*

Angel saves actress Rebecca Lowell from a hit-and-run driver, although he subsequently discovers that this, and other threats to her, are part of a publicity stunt devised by her agent. Rebecca, on finding out Angel is a vampire, is desperate for him to sire her so that she can retain her youth and beauty forever.

Dudes and Babes: Rebecca is a beautiful actress best known for the character of Raven who she played on the TV show *On Your Own*, which ran for nine and a half years. Rebecca has been famous since she was fourteen.

It's a Designer Label!: Rebecca's impressive wardrobe includes a series of stunning evening gowns. Her vampy sunglasses seen when she visits Angel are outstanding. She also wears a baseball cap with a Japanese symbol on it but we'll forgive her. Compared to such elegance, Cordelia's white sweater and shiny red pants and Wesley's cream tie stand no chance.

References: Cordelia appears in the play *A Doll's House* by Henrik Ibsen, in the role of Nora Helmer. Also, *ET – The Extra-Terrestrial*, Emma Thompson, *Entertainment Tonight*, *Batman* (again), *The E! True Hollywood Story*, *The National Enquirer*, *Fright Night*, Ernest Borgnine, *The Wizard of Oz* ('What're you going to do? Melt me?'), the *Los Angeles Times*, plus the Emmys and the Oscars. Rebecca: 'Bela Lugosi, Gary Oldman, they're vampires.' Angel: 'Frank Langella was the only performance I believed,' refers to actors who played the Count in *Dracula* (1931), *Bram Stoker's Dracula* (1992) and *Dracula* (1979) respectively. No Christopher Lee? *Philistines*. There's a great bit of TV industry mockery. Cordelia: 'It was a seminal show, cancelled by the idiot network. I was going to picket them but I didn't have any comfortable shoes . . .'

Bitch!: You forget how cutting Angelus is when you haven't seen him for a while. On Cordelia's acting: 'You were really, let me tell you, *bad*.' Cordelia: 'Stop it.' Angelus: 'Why? *You* didn't. I mean, I've been to Hell, but that was *so much* worse!'

Cordelia: 'You *slut!*'

The Charisma Show: Her incompetent eavesdropping as Angel refuses to take Rebecca as a client (*'Are you insane?'*) and her fake vision. Excellent comedy with Boreanaz too. Angel: 'You brought a cross?' Cordelia: 'Along with three double half-caf, non-fat, skinny lattes.' Angel: 'And a cross?' Cordelia: 'Judging by the outfit, I guess it's safe to come in. Evil Angel never would have worn *those pants*.'

As some fans have pointed out, Charisma plays three separate characters here. Her normal role, the bad-actress-Cordelia in the opening scenes and an Oscar-winning-Cordy towards the end. A truly fine bit of acting. Her comic timing remains impressive, that '*Pffft!*' at the end in particular.

L.A.-Speak: Cordelia: 'Angel is the Dark Avenger. Only not too dark. Happy dark.' And: 'Think of the *karma*.'

Oliver: 'This will be all over the tabs come morning, Bec. We might as well just put our own spin on it first.'

Masseuse: 'You have to be proactive with deterioration.'

Cordelia calls Wesley: '*Doofus*.'

Angelus: 'There wasn't a dry eye in the house, everybody was just laughing so hard. Maybe you can get Raven here to coach you, then you'd actually *suck*.'

Cigarettes and Alcohol: Rebecca brings a bottle of Dom Perignon to Angel's apartment.

Sex and Drugs and Rock'n'Roll: Doximall, the drug that Rebecca uses on Angel ('just a little happy pill') is a powerful tranquilliser that induces bliss. 'Remind me to get the number of your dealer before I kill you,' Angelus tells Rebecca.

Wesley is concerned about what sorts of questions Rebecca asks Cordy regarding Angel. 'Where does Angel hail from,' replies Cordelia, 'what's his favourite colour, what kind of aftershave he wears? The exact specific details on how someone could make themselves into a vampire.' Wesley: 'Surely, you don't think . . .?' Cordelia: 'That she'd try to manoeuvre Angel into an exchange of bodily fluids in order to make herself eternally young and beautiful, thus saving her failing career? Gee, now you mention it . . .'

'You May Remember Me From Such Films and TV Series As . . .': Tamara Gorski played Megan Torrance in *Poltergeist: The Legacy*, Alexandra Corliss in *Psi Factors: Chronicles of the Paranormal* and Morrigan on *Hercules: The Legendary Journeys*. She's appeared in *Forever Knight*, *Highlander*, *The Kids in the Hall*, *Earth: Final Conflict* and *To Die For*.

Don't Give Up The Day Job: Regis B Kimble began as an editor (on *Matlock* and *The X-Files*) and it was in that capacity that he worked on *Buffy*, before directing the classic 'Earshot'.

The police officer talking to Angel after the attempted shooting of Rebecca was played by Dan Smiczek, a background extra on many TV series. Dan has a fascinating and humorous website, *The Adventures of Dan: Extra Extraordinaire*, at http://www.adventuresofdan.com/ which details his experiences working on shows as diverse as *Buffy*, *Roswell*, *The X-Files* and *The West Wing*. 'The idea was that they were trying to recreate a Golden Globe awards-type atmosphere at a theatre on Hollywood and Wilcox,' he says. 'They only needed three cops and unfortunately they picked the tallest guy and a girl. They needed one more person to be in the scene talking to David Boreanaz. Translation: screen-time! The best part was the AD looked right at me and said 'he looks the most like a cop'. I'm not sure whether to take that as a compliment or not.' Dan also notes that '[David] seemed like a pretty friendly guy considering they had been doing night shoots lately. One of the PAs came over to give us our meal ticket (a piece of orange tape with a handwritten '2') because only the 8 p.m. people were going to get to eat. David was curious as to what the deal was with the orange tape. He insisted on getting one as well and then plastered it over his suit. So a star with his own show who jokes around with the extras is pretty okay in my book.'

Logic, Let Me Introduce You to This Window: When Angel first looks at the car it has a cloud of exhaust fumes coming out of the tail pipe, the camera is away for less than a second, then returns to show none whatsoever. As Angel opens the door into the alley, his reflection can be seen. When the bookcase is knocked over in Rebecca's house, vases go flying but none of them break, even though there is the sound of breaking glass. Watch closely as Angel goes to change his shirt: you'll notice no sign of his tattoo. Angelus has blood on his hand after force-feeding Rebecca, but in the next shot his hand is clean. When Rebecca arrives at Angel's apartment with the champagne the time is 8.25 p.m. At the scene's completion some moments later, the clock still says 8.25. When Rebecca puts Doximall in Angel's glass it turns cloudy and doesn't seem to be dissipating very fast. But as soon as the camera cuts to Angel walking back into the room, the champagne is clear again.

Confronting Angelus, Wesley is wearing a pair of slacks. When he pushes Angelus down the elevator shaft he has jeans on. In the final scene the slacks are back. The length of Rebecca's hair changes quite dramatically between the opening scene and the next in which she appears. Concerning Angel's appreciation of Frank Langella's *Dracula*: when exactly did Angel *see* this since he's never been known to watch TV (in this episode he specifically says he doesn't possess one) and in *Buffy*: 'Enemies' he noted that it was 'a long time' since he'd been to the cinema. Did Rebecca invite Angel into her home off-screen? There's also discontinuity with *Buffy*: 'Surprise'/'Innocence'. It's established that one moment of perfect happiness will turn Angel into Angelus even if he doesn't feel much happiness after the transformation. Yet here it is implied (and subsequently confirmed) that he will only remain Angelus as long as he is experiencing the effects of the drug and that once he comes down he will revert. If that's the case, why did it take eight episodes and a *spell* to revert him in *Buffy* season two?

I Just *Love* Your Accent: When Cordelia mentions *ET*, Wesley thinks she's talking about actress Emma Thompson. Tasteful. He also says, in response to Cordelia's comment about television seasons: 'And they say there are no seasons in Los Angeles.'

Motors: The car that drove at Rebecca was a 'green, freshly painted '76 Chevy Nova.'

Quote/Unquote: Cordelia: '[Angel] can fight off Donkey Demons who rip people's guts out, but he can't help one defenceless actress from a psycho? What is your *thing*?'

Rebecca: 'You're not a killer?' Angel: 'I gave that up.' Rebecca: 'There's a support group for everything in this town, I guess.'

Wesley: 'Angel's moment of true happiness occurred because he was with Buffy. Do you realise how rare that is? What are the odds he'd find it with an actress?' Cordelia: 'And what's that supposed to mean?' Wesley: 'I meant TV actress.' Cordelia: 'Save it.'

Angel: 'You looked into that mirror and all you saw was yourself. That's all you ever see, Rebecca, and that's what really frightens you. This isn't about the way the studio, the network, or the fans see you. It's about how you see yourself.'

Notes: 'You walk a fine line Angel, I don't envy you.' This one is *really* good. A very clever examination of the pitfalls in the quest for eternal youth that takes an oddly dispassionate view of all the characters (Cordelia is at her most narcissistic and it's difficult even to feel sympathy for Angel when you see Angelus at his worst). Tamara Gorski is excellent and the direction is amongst the series' best. Amazingly, no one dies.

There are references to Angel's trip to Hell in *Buffy*: 'Becoming' Part 2, while Cordelia's: 'You weren't around the last time Angel went mental. I, on the other hand, was on the first wave of the cleanup crew,' refers to the final episodes of *Buffy* Season Two. Angel remembers Oliver giving him his card at the party in **1**, 'City Of'. Angelus suggests Wesley has an inferiority complex (see **14**, 'I've Got You Under My Skin', **41**, 'Belonging'). The name of the movie premiere that Rebecca is going to is *The Venne Diagram* [sic].

When Cordelia notes: 'They close off stores for her. And lunch at Mirabelle's. I had the most to-die-for veal fillet with a light truffle marinade,' she's referring to the exclusive Mirabelle's Restaurant on Sunset Boulevard. Wesley has a pager. The tabloid Rebecca reads is the *Global Snooper*. There are approximately fifteen people in the audience for Cordelia's play which doesn't, indeed, count as a 'crowded theatre'.

Critique: In an article in *TV Guide* as part of a series entitled *What Can I Watch With My Kids?*, Joe Queenan noted: 'I enjoy *Angel* because it is well-written, it addresses the issues of sin and redemption, it doesn't trot out the same story every week and it is far less camp than *Buffy*. My wife enjoys the show because of the eerie lighting and the creepy cello music . . . I have no idea why my kids enjoy the show.'

Previously on *Buffy the Vampire Slayer*: 'This Year's Girl'/ 'Who Are You?': Faith wakes from her coma and seeks vengeance on Buffy and her friends. Meanwhile, three mysterious men arrive in Sunnydale by helicopter. Faith receives a final gift from the Mayor and goes to Buffy's house to attack Joyce. Buffy arrives and the pair fight, but Faith uses the device to switch bodies. As 'Faith' lies unconscious, Joyce asks 'Are you okay?' 'Five by five,' 'Buffy' reassures her.[11] 'Faith' is to be taken by the Watcher's Council back to England. Living as 'Buffy', however, opens Faith's eyes to the realities of Slayerhood and she heroically saves a group of hostages from Adam's vampire protégés. Buffy, meanwhile, uses Willow and Tara's magic to reverse the switch. An anguished Faith skips town.

18
Five by Five

US Transmission Date: 25 April 2000
UK Transmission Date: 5 May 2000 (Sky),
7 May 2001 (Channel 4)

Writer: Jim Kouf
Director: James A Contner
Cast: Tyler Christopher (Wolfram & Hart Lawyer),
Rainbow Borden (Gangbanger[12]), Francis Fallon (Dick),
Adrienne Janic (Attractive Girl), Rodrick Fox (Assistant DA),
Thor Edgell (Romanian Man), Jennifer Slemko (Romanian Woman)
French Title: *Cinq Sur Cinq*
German Title: *Alte Freunde*

Faith arrives in Los Angeles and is immediately recruited by Wolfram & Hart with a view to eliminating Angel. Having alerted Angel to her presence in L.A., she firstly attacks Cordelia, and then kidnaps and tortures Wesley, in an attempt to get Angel interested enough to kill her.

---

[11] The Buffy/Faith body-swop in 'Who Are You?': 'Buffy' refers to Faith inhabiting Buffy's body and 'Faith' refers to Buffy inhabiting Faith's body. Confused? You will be . . .

[12] Although Rainbow Borden's character is named 'Marquez' in the episode, he is credited thus on-screen.

Dudes and Babes: Wesley: 'A fight in a bar ... a woman fitting Faith's description was involved.' Cordelia: 'She charm her way out?' Wesley: 'Apparently she managed to break a policeman's jaw with his own handcuffs.' Cordelia: 'For Faith, that *is* charm.'

Denial, Thy Name is Faith: As previously hinted at in *Buffy*: 'Consequences', 'Enemies' and (especially) 'Who Are You?' Faith suffers severe self-loathing which is why actually *becoming* Buffy had such an attraction for her. Just as the final sequence of 'Who Are You?' shows Faith, in Buffy's body, beating *herself* and screaming how 'evil' she is, so in this episode the poignancy of Faith's battle with Angel is highlighted by her desire that he should kill her to end her horror at what she has become.

It's a Designer Label!: Cordelia's blue top and Faith's red shirt vie for attention though both are trumped by Faith's leather gear in the club. Marquez's hilarious *Boyz 'n' the Hood* threads.

References: The title, Faith's catchphrase, is a radio communications call sign meaning 'loud and clear'. Also, the Dalai Lama, Elvis, Spike Lee's *Do The Right Thing*, *The Game*, the American Bar Association and Spider-Man ('your friendly neighbourhood vampire').

The location of the Wolfram & Hart offices is, in real life, the former MGM-UA building in the Sony Pictures Plaza in Culver City.

Bitch!: Concerning the events of *Buffy*: 'Consequences'. Wesley says Faith is not a demon, 'she's a sick, sick girl. If there's even a chance she can be reasoned with . . .' Angel: 'There was. Last year I had a shot at saving her. I was pulling her back from the brink when some British guy kidnapped her and made damn sure she'd never trust another living soul.' Cordelia: 'It's not Wesley's fault that some British guy ruined your ... Oh wait, that was *you*. Go on.'

Faith is described by the guy she beats up as 'the bitch from Hell' while Lee refers to Lilah as a bitch.

The Charisma Show: Eclipsed by a Tasmanian-Devil performance by Eliza, Charisma nonetheless gets some marvellous moments: 'I knew it when you brought him in last night. Someone with that much body art is gonna have a different definition of civic duty.'

L.A.-Speak: Marquez: 'Yo *ese*. What the hell you burning there man? Yo, you're hangin' in the wrong place man. My boys ain't gonna be too happy when they get here and see what kind of mess you made.'

Cordelia: 'You don't change a guy like that. In fact, generally speaking, you don't change a guy. What you see is what you get. Scratch the surface and what do you find? More surface.' And: 'You can always tell when he's happy. His scowl is slightly less scowly.'

Faith: 'Why do they know me when I don't know *jack* about you?' And: '*Dude*, I'm getting paid. They hate you almost as much as I do.'

Sex and Drugs and Rock'n'Roll: Faith dancing. Pure sex.

'You May Remember Me From Such Films and TV Series As . . .': The great Eliza Dushku made her film debut aged eleven in *That Night*. She went on to play Emma in *Bye Bye Love*, Missy in *Bring it On*, Dana Tasker in *True Lies* and appeared in *Jay and Silent Bob Strike Back* and *Soul Survivor*. Tyler Christopher was Nikolas Cassadine in *General Hospital*. Rainbow Borden has appeared in *Punks*, *Random Acts of Violence*, *The Limey* and, ironically, the 1998 movie *City of Angels*.

Don't Give Up The Day Job: Jim Kouf wrote several movies including *Stakeout*, and was producer of *Con Air* and the cult-favourite *Kalifornia*. His only acting role came in the 1981 film *Wacko* (which he also wrote), something he has in common with fellow producer David Greenwalt (see **1**, 'City Of'). Francis Fallon is guitarist with L.A. rock band Ester. He can also be seen in *Jerks* and *Southside*.

There's A Ghost In My House: Dennis shuts the door in Cordelia's and Wesley's face, trying to warn them that Faith is inside. Wesley: 'Your ghost, I presume?' Cordelia: 'He's jealous. [Loudly] Don't worry, Hell will freeze over before I have sex with *him*.'

Logic, Let Me Introduce You to This Window: At the bus depot when Faith is coming down the steps, there's a pair of sneakered feet with anklets behind her on the pavement. When the shot pans up, the same girl is just coming off the stairs. Cordelia's apartment was 212 in 'Rm W/a Vu'. Here it's number six. She had no neighbours to the left nor across the hall from her door, but now she does. When Faith tells Wesley he has a stake up his 'English Channel', it looks like there was a different bit of dialogue that got overdubbed. In the initial shot of the kitchen counter in Faith's apartment, there are no knives in the cannister. Why doesn't Phantom Dennis physically restrain Faith? It's been established that he can move objects, so what's to stop him clobbering her with a chair?

I Just *Love* Your Accent: Wesley's finest hour: 'I was your Watcher. I know the real you. Even if you kill me there's just one thing I want you to remember.' Faith: 'What's that, love?' Wesley: 'You are a piece of sh . . .' *Nice one*. This, after Faith has told him: 'Face it, Wesley, you really were a jerk. Always walking around like you had some great big stake rammed up your English Channel.' Plus, use of the word 'ruffian' in a non-ironic way. Faith's 'where's that stiff upper lip?', however, *is* dripping with irony.

Motors: Faith arrives in L.A. on a Greyhound bus.

Quote/Unquote: Angel: 'Your name Marquez? Good, I hate saving the wrong guy.'

Angel: 'You'd think with all the people I've maimed and killed, I wouldn't be able to remember every single one.'

Wesley: 'Seems you're taking this personally.' Angel: 'She tried to shoot my own personal back, so yeah.'

Notes: 'Feel young, do ya? You're looking pretty worn out to me.' The astonishing Eliza Dushku brings her many talents to *Angel* with devastating effect. Includes – definitively – the finest moment of *Angel* so far. Wesley dropping the knife that Faith used to torture him in slow motion and Faith collapsing into Angel's arms begging him to kill her. Truly epic.

Faith says she likes black. She left Sunnydale, according to Giles 'about a week ago' (see *Buffy*: 'Who Are You?') Faith dancing wildly at a club is reminiscent of her antics in *Buffy*: 'Bad Girls'. Wesley appears to sleep on Angel's couch. Lindsey says he has the conversation with Angel recorded on Hi-Def tape. His assistant is called Jesse. The three lawyers that we see at Wolfram & Hart have the initials 'LM'. Coincidence? Lilah says that green is her favourite colour, that she looks good in diamonds and loves riding in limousines.

The Romanian street scenes were filmed at Universal Studios' 'Little Europe'. The bus depot set seems to be the same one used for Sunnydale bus station in *Buffy*: 'Inca Mummy Girl'. The alley where Angel and Faith fight had previously been seen in **3**, 'In the Dark'.

Soundtrack: Rob Zombie's 'Living Dead Girl' and the *APM Dance-Indie-Mix* instrumental 'Pressure Cooker'. Robert Kral told Rob Francis: 'For **18**, "Five By Five", there was a scene where there was this strange seagull crying-type sound in the background for a second. I thought David Greenwalt would think it was in my music track and ask me to remove it and I'd have to tell him that I couldn't because it was actually on the production track: recorded during filming. I got the comments back on the score and David said he loved that sound. 'Can I hear more of that?' he asked. I explained [that] I had no idea what it was, however I found a very similar string sound, but spookier, as if the strings are crying one by one, so I added it.'

Did You Know: Christian Kane auditioned for the role of Riley Finn on *Buffy* but was narrowly beaten by his friend Marc Blucas. The pair appear together, along with Freddie Prinze Jr, in the romantic comedy *Summer Catch*.

19
Sanctuary

US Transmission Date: 2 May 2000
UK Transmission Date: 12 May 2000 (Sky),
14 May 2001 (Channel 4)

Writers: Tim Minear, Joss Whedon
Director: Michael Lange

Cast: Alastair Duncan (Collins), Jeff Ricketts (Weatherby),
Kevin Owens (Smith), Adam Vernier (Detective Kendrick)
French Title: *Sanctuaire*
German Title: *Gehetzt*

As Angel tries to rehabilitate Faith, he realises that it won't
be easy with both the Council of Watchers team *and* (a
very upset) Buffy in town looking to stop Faith from doing
any more harm. And it seems that even his own staff don't
agree with his methods.

Dreaming (As *Buffy* Often Proves) is Free: Faith's dream of
killing Angel. That girl really has got some nasty stuff
floating around in her head. She also has a flashback to her
murder of Allan Finch in *Buffy*: 'Bad Girls'.

Denial, Thy Name is Buffy: Buffy is horrified that her
greatest enemy seems to have her claws into her former
lover and this colours her actions for the rest of the
episode.

It's a Designer Label!: Kate's chunky sweater puts in
another appearance.

References: *The X-Files* (Kendrick: 'Everybody knows
you've gone all Scully. Any time one of these weird cases
crosses anyone's desk, you're always there.' Kate: 'Mul-
der's the believer, Scully's the sceptic.' Kendrick: 'Scully's
the chick, right?') When Faith channel-surfs she sees a
fragment of a 1940s *Superman* cartoon. Third & Long, the
bar where Wesley meets the Council, is a real location in
New York on 3rd Avenue, close to the Empire State
Building.

The Charisma Show: She only appears for one scene, but
still has time to tell Wesley: 'If it's any consolation, it really
does look like you were tortured by a much larger woman.'

L.A.-Speak: Cordelia: 'Like I'm gonna stick around here
while psycho-case is roaming around downstairs with three
tons of medieval weaponry. *Not.* Oh, and I'm thinking,
sugar high, maybe not a great idea.'

Lilah: 'It's strictly a handshake deal.' Lindsey: 'Not that
it's necessary for you to have hands for us to do business.'
Lilah: 'That was speciesist of me, I apologise.'

Buffy: 'You hit me.' Angel: 'Not to go all schoolyard on you, but you hit me first.'

Wesley: 'She cleaned your clocks, didn't she?'

Angel: 'For a taciturn shadowy guy, I got a big mouth.'

Cigarettes and Alcohol: Lilah drinks whisky in Lindsey's office (see **16**, 'The Ring'). In the pub, Wesley and the Council team drink, variously, Guinness, lager (or possibly cider) and brown ale. Collins smokes in the bar despite there being a 'No Smoking' sign (as there are in all bars in California).

Sex and Drugs and Rock'n'Roll: The sexual tension in the Angel/Faith/Buffy scenes is something to see: Angel: 'She's not to run.' Buffy: 'Why would she? When she has her brave knight to protect her? Does she cry, pouty lips, heaving bosom?'

Later, Angel tells his former love: 'You found someone new. I'm not allowed to, remember? I see you again, it cuts me up inside and the person I share that with is me. You don't know me any more, so don't come down here with your great new life and expect me to do things your way.'

'You May Remember Me From Such Films and TV Series As . . .': Alastair Duncan has appeared in *Blossom*, *Sabrina the Teenage Witch*, *Babylon 5* and *Highlander*. Kevin Owens was in *Titanic*. Jeff Ricketts's movies include *Spoof! An Insider's Guide to Short Film Success*, *The Prime Gig* and *Psycho for Milk*.

Don't Give Up The Day Job: Michael Lange has worked on *Roswell*, *Snoops*, *Crisis Centre*, *Early Edition*, *American Gothic*, *The X-Files*, *Crazy Like a Fox*, *TJ Hooker* and *Knots Landing*. Adam Vernier is possibly best known for a role he didn't get. As a six-year-old he narrowly lost out to Danny Lloyd for the part of Danny in Kubrick's *The Shining*. He can be seen in *Route 666*.

Logic, Let Me Introduce You to This Window: At the end of 'Previously on *Angel*', we see Faith and Angel in the alley exactly as we left them in **18**, 'Five by Five'. However, Wesley was in the middle of the alley, but here he is standing to the side. Everyone's bruises go through startling changes throughout the episode. Faith's, for instance, vacillate between raw to nearly invisible and back again.

Also, the cut on Buffy's lip from Angel's punch disappears entirely in one scene, only to reappear later. Faith killed the assassin demon. Where did it go? How 'Elite' is the Council team? They have automatic weapons and yet they miss everything in range. So, Angel *does* have a TV, despite what he told Rebecca in 'Eternity'.

I Just *Love* Your Accent: Wesley displays moments of laconic wit, asking Angel: 'Developed a sweet fang, have you?' His anger when he says, 'Don't you dare take the moral high ground with me after what she did' is heartfelt.

We learn about the machinations of the Council of Watchers: Weatherby: 'Wouldn't cough up the dosh for the airfare home?' Smith: 'All those alchemists on the Board of Directors and they still make us fly coach. *Miserly bastards*.' Wesley tells them that he will help, but 'no harm must come to the vampire'. Weatherby replies: 'Don't be a *ponce*!' Presumably Joss Whedon watched a lot of darts while he was in England? Weatherby has a wonderful *Sweeney*-style Jack Regan moment: '*SHUT IT!*'

Quote/Unquote: Angel: 'It wasn't too long ago that you were the one making the case for her rehabilitation.' Wesley: 'It wasn't too long ago that I had full feeling in my right arm.'

Buffy: 'Giles heard that she tried to kill you.' Angel: 'That's true.' Buffy: 'So you decided to punish her with a severe cuddling?'

Lee: 'This is getting ridiculous. The first assassin kills the second assassin, sent to kill the first assassin, who didn't assassinate anyone until we hired the second assassin to assassinate her.' Lindsey: 'This obviously isn't working.' Lilah: 'You *think*?'

Notes: 'What do you want to do? You gonna throw me off the roof, again?' Doesn't quite have the spirit and the dark, nefarious undertones of the previous episode, but this is a superb mini-action movie (including helicopters, machine guns and rooftops) in which Buffy, for once, is the enemy and Faith's redemption is the crux.

The trio of Council soldiers comes to L.A. to recapture Faith and bring her to justice in England having failed to catch her in Sunnydale (see *Buffy*: 'Who Are You?'). They try to entice Wesley into helping them by promising his reinstatement. Sunnydale is said to be north of L.A.

Joss Whedon's Comments: Asked for his favourite episodes of the first season, Joss noted: 'Seventeen, eighteen and nineteen ['Eternity', 'Five By Five', 'Sanctuary']. We get into some very interesting and creepy personal stuff with our characters and the people around them and they made me more excited about the show than I've been yet.'

Tim Minear's Comments: 'Eliza is a force of nature. Just amazing. Faith is a fantastic character who, in my opinion, flourishes in *Angel*. If I have anything to say about it, she'll be back.

Previously on *Buffy the Vampire Slayer*: 'The Yoko Factor': Angel follows Buffy to Sunnydale to apologise, but gets into a fight with Riley Finn before he and Buffy can settle their differences. Meanwhile Spike plays off the Scooby Gang against each other, resulting in a drunk Giles and an argument between Willow, Xander, and Buffy.

20
War Zone

US Transmission Date: 9 May 2000
UK Transmission Date: 19 May 2000 (Sky),
21 May 2001 (Channel 4)

Writer: Garry Campbell
Director: David Straiton
Cast: Michele Kelly (Alonna), Maurice Compte (Chain),
Mick Murray (Knox), Joe Basile (Lenny), Sean Parhm (Bobby),
Sven Holmberg (Ty), Rebecca Klingler (Madame Dorion),
Kimberly James (Lina), Ricky Luna (James)
French Title: *Zone De Guerre*
German Title: *Der Bandenkrieg*

While handling a delicate blackmail case, Angel's path crosses with that of Charles Gunn who leads a street gang of itinerant teenage vampire hunters. Although eventually deciding that Angel poses them no threat, Gunn is contemptuous of the idea of a 'good' vampire.

Dudes and Babes: Lots of babes at millionaire David Nabbit's party. Sadly, he doesn't know any of them, even if one or two appear to know him. More are in evidence at Madam Dorion's, including the alluring Lina who tickles Angel's manhood with her tail.

Knox's vampire gang includes punks, skins and rastas.

It's a Designer Label!: The series' first 'anorak'. Since Gunn's wearing it, however, no sarcastic comments will be made. Gunn wears a 'New York' sweatshirt and various coloured bandanas. Cordelia's party dress is lovely, as is her maroon scarf.

References: *The Naked Truth*. Gunn's gang and their armoury is reminiscent of *Mad Max 2: The Road Warrior*. Angel running the gamut of traps may be a homage to *Raiders of the Lost Ark*. Nabbit mentions playing Dungeons and Dragons and that 'some of us really got into it' which could be an allusion to *Mazes and Monsters*. Alonna quotes from Beck's 'Loser' ('So why don't you kill me?') Variations on 'You expecting someone else?' have been used in *Doctor Who* ('The Caves of Androzani') and trailers for *Austin Powers: The Spy Who Shagged Me*.

Classic *Double Entendre*: Cordelia: 'I like David. It's such a strong, masculine name. It just feels good in your mouth.'

L.A.-Speak: Lina: 'Look, ma, no hands.'

Alonna: 'It shouldn't have gone down the way it did.'

James: 'I suck, okay?'

Knox: 'Stupid human street trash. For seventy years we ruled this neighbourhood. Used to be decent people lived here. Working people. And now? You can't even finish one without wanting to puke.'

Yo, A Haven For The Bruthas, Homeboy: Even if it's in the gutter . . .

Cigarettes and Alcohol: Cordelia drinks what looks like champagne at Nabbit's party.

Sex and Drugs and Rock'n'Roll: Madame Dorion's is a demon brothel in Bel Air. Wesley notes that 'The Watchers Council is *rife* with stories about it.' David Nabbit has been there twelve times: 'I always said that I would make a billion dollars in the software market and learn to talk to girls. Still working on step two.' The conversation between Wesley and Angel over the incriminating black-mail photographs is hilarious. Angel: 'It's upside down.' Wesley: 'Certainly not something you'd want to have framed.'

Cordelia: 'Perspectively speaking, I might want to pros-titute myself to billionaire David Nabbit.'

'You May Remember Me From Such Films and TV Series As . . .': J August Richards played Richard Street in *The Temptations* and appeared in *The West Wing*. David Herman provides voices on both *Futurama* and *King of the Hill* and played Michael Bolton in *Office Space*. He was also in *Born on the Fourth of July*. Rebecca Klingler has appeared in *The Green Mile*, *Titanic*, *L.A. Confidential* and *Copycat*. Kimberly James was Furrier in *Mystery Men*. Maurice Compte appears in *Double Whammy* and *The Substitute*.

Don't Give Up The Day Job: A former Mouseketeer on *The Mickey Mouse Club*, Ricky Luna spent much of his childhood in his family's trapeze circus act, 'The Flying Lunas'.

Logic, Let Me Introduce You to This Window: As Cordelia bandages Angel's ribs there appears to be no correspond-ing hole in his shoulder, although the stake went in through his back. He also has no wound in his hand where he caught the crossbolt. Even though vampires heal fast (as noted on several *Buffy* episodes) Angel still sports bruises.

I Just *Love* Your Accent: Wesley's exclamation 'Good Lord' suggests that somebody has overdosed on *The Avengers*.

Motors: There's a wonderful attack on L.A.'s pollution record. Cordelia: 'There's nothing like riding in a convert-ible with the top down to make you see the sun and sand. Smell that salt air?' Wesley: 'That's not salt.' Cordelia: 'I don't think it's air either.'

Quote/Unquote: Nabbit: 'Are you familiar with "Dungeons and Dragons"?' Angel: 'I've seen a few.' Wesley: 'You mean the role-playing game?' Angel: 'Oh, game? Right.'

Cordelia: 'Did someone find out you were a big nerd?'
Nabbit: 'No, that's actually public record.'

Gunn: 'I don't need advice from some middle-class white dude, that's *dead*.'

Notes: 'You expecting somebody else?' Another *fine* episode, 'War Zone' is about the huge dichotomy of L.A. and includes a star-making performance by J August Richards. The plot is thin in places, but the verve and energy of the (mainly young) cast more than make up for this, particularly in several excellent fight sequences.

When asked what he wants, Angel replies: 'Love, family, a place on this planet I can call my own.' The bridge in the opening sequence has been the backdrop of other episodes, including 11, 'Somnambulist.' As kids, Gunn and Alonna lived in a shelter on Summer Street.

Soundtrack: Gunn's character theme is a variation of Angel's. Also, A Friend of Rio's 'Para Lennon and McCartney' (at Nabbit's party) and 'Hellfire' from the APM Music Library.

Joss Whedon's Comments: On the introduction of another two semi-regular characters Joss told Rob Francis: 'It's becoming clear that *Angel* works in a similar way to *Buffy*. The main characters are the people we're most invested in. We thought of it more as an anthology when we first devised it but clearly it's going to be more *Buffy*-like and we need a reserve of characters who have all different opinions. Wesley and Angel have a lot of similarities and so we wanted some voices that are unique.'

21
Blind Date

US Transmission Date: 16 May 2000
UK Transmission Date: 26 May 2000 (Sky),
28 May 2001 (Channel 4)

Writer: Jeannine Renshaw
Director: Thomas J Wright
Cast: Jennifer Badger Martin (Vanessa Brewer),

Keilana Smith (Mind Reader #1), Dawn Suggs (Mind Reader #2),
Charles Constant (Security Centre Guard), Scott Berman (Vendor),
Derek Anthony (Dying Black Man), Rishi Kumar (Blind Child #1),
Karen Lu (Blind Child #2), Alex Buck (Blind Child #3)
French Title: *A l'aveuglette*

Angel encounters Vanessa Brewer, a blind woman working
as a contract killer for Wolfram & Hart. As he attempts to
infiltrate the law firm to find out who Brewer is meant to
kill, much to his surprise, he gains a new ally, Lindsey
McDonald.

Dudes and Babes: According to Vanessa Brewer's LAPD
profile, she was born 18 July 1967 in San Francisco. Under
'Arrests' the record notes: '1 misdemeanour, (12 July 93 –
Driving w/o a licence); 2 felonies (23 Apr 95 – Aggravated
assault; 6 Oct 99 – Double Homicide).' In her latest case,
defended by Lindsey, she was acquitted. She wasn't born
blind but lost her sight at the age of 21, the loss being
self-inflicted. She spent five years studying in Pajaur with
the Nan Jin (cave-dwelling monks). She reached enlightenment and can now 'see' with her heart and not her mind.

Denial, Thy Name is Lindsey: Suffering a crisis of conscience over the activities of Wolfram & Hart, Angel tells
Lindsey that he has the chance to change. However, his
mentor, Holland Manners, who hand-picked Lindsey when
he was a sophomore because of his potential, offers the
lawyer the one thing he cannot refuse: 'the world'.

It's a Designer Label!: Cordelia's red T-shirt is excellent,
but for garishness, check out Gunn's orange sweatshirt and
the vampire's leather trousers. *Very* 1980s.

References: Cordelia's 'Hellen Kellerus homicidalus' refers
to blind author Helen Keller (1880–1968). Also, *Superman*,
Peggy Lee's 'Is That All There Is?', *Etch-A-Sketch*, the
Rubik's cube and LAPD online (the site Cordelia goes to
for research looks nothing like the real LAPD homepage).
The removal of the disks from Wolfram & Hart is very
Mission: Impossible. Vanessa's eyes are reminiscent of
those of the children in *Village of the Damned*. 'The
righteous shall walk a thorny path' may be an allusion to
Tantra Six of Tirumantiram. Gunn's anti-racist rant could

have been influenced by similar sentiments from a classic
late 1960s issue of the DC comic *Green Lantern/Green
Arrow*, one of the first genuinely socially aware superhero
tales, written by Denny O'Neill.

Bitch!: Lindsey: 'Sorry I'm late. Hope I didn't worry
anyone.' Cordelia: 'We just figured you were dead.'

The Charisma Show: The charming scene of Cordelia
talking to Willow on the telephone.

L.A.-Speak: Cordelia: 'That's not the real *whammy*.' And:
'I thought *born-again guy* was gonna do it.'

Not Exactly A Haven For The Bruthas: Gunn's anti-
Wolfram & Hart rant: 'They told me it was true, but I
didn't believe them. Damn, here it is. Evil white folks really
do have a Mecca. Now girls, don't get all riled up. Did you
just step on my foot? Is that my foot you just stepped on?
Are you *assaulting* me, in this haven of justice? Somebody
get me a lawyer, because my civil rights have seriously been
violated. Oh, I get it. You all can cater to the demon. Cater
to the dead man. But what about the *black man*?'

**'You May Remember Me From Such Films and TV Series
As . . .':** Sam Anderson was Kevin Davis in *The Cape*,
Doctor Keyson in *ER* and the Fonzie-loving doctor who
delivered Phoebe's triplets in *Friends*. He's also appeared
in *Forrest Gump*, *La Bamba*, *The West Wing* and *The
X-Files*.

Don't Give Up The Day Job: Dawn Suggs directed the 1990
movie *Chasing The Moon*. Jennifer Badger Martin is
Charisma Carpenter's stunt-double on *Buffy* and *Angel*,
was one of the stunt team on *Austin Powers: The Spy Who
Shagged Me* and appeared in *Summer of Sam* and *Speed 2:
Cruise Control*.

Logic, Let Me Introduce You to This Window: Lindsey tells
Angel that the secret vault is on sub-level two, but when
Lindsey exits the elevator it warns him that he is entering
sub-level three. Vanessa joined the blind monks in another
country aged 21 and stayed with them for five years, but
her police record says she was arrested for driving without
a licence on July 12 1993, which is only four years after she
would have joined the monks. The credits say Jennifer

Badger Martin plays 'Vanessa Weeks', but she is called Vanessa Brewer throughout.

Quote/Unquote: Angel: 'It's their system and it's one that works ... Because there's no guilt. No torment, no consequences. It's pure. I remember what that was like.'

Wesley: 'There *is* a design, Angel. Hidden in the chaos it may be, but it's true. And you have your place in it.'

Notes: 'Are you telling me self-mutilating, psycho assassin chick reached enlightenment?' This one rambles a bit, though some of the set-pieces are terrific and there's an excellent performance by the dryly sinister Sam Anderson and another smashing little cameo from J August Richards. The main let-down is the unconvincing rationale behind Lindsey's sudden change of character motivation.

In a mini-crossover, Willow Rosenberg helps Cordelia, via the telephone, decrypt the Wolfram & Hart files (see **39**, 'Disharmony'). We learn that Willow has finished decrypting disks stolen from The Initiative placing these events in the middle of *Buffy*: 'Primeval'. Also note that Willow says 'hey' to Wesley. In real life Alyson Hannigan (who plays Willow) and Alexis Denisof had just started dating.

Angel's father (see **15**, 'The Prodigal') was a silk and linen merchant. Lee Mercer held talks with another law firm, Klein & Gabler, his employment with Wolfram & Hart being subsequently terminated. With extreme prejudice. Lindsey went to Hastings Law School. He was poor but ambitious, one of six children from a very deprived background. The Wolfram & Hart lawyers call their clerks 'the amoebas'.

22
To Shanshu in L.A.

US Transmission Date: 23 May 2000
UK Transmission Date: 2 June 2000 (Sky),
4 June 2001 (Channel 4)

Writer: David Greenwalt
Director: David Greenwalt

Cast: Todd Stashwick (Vocah), Louise Claps (Homeless Woman),
Daren Rice (Uniform #1), Jon Ecklund (Uniform #2),
Lia Johnson (Vendor), Robyn Cohen (Nurse), Susan Savage (Doctor),
John Eddins (Monk #1), Gerard O'Donnell (Monk #2),
Brahman Turner (Young Tough Guy)
French Title: *Vivre et Mourir À Los Angeles*
German Title: *Duell mit dem Bösen*

Wolfram & Hart summon a powerful demon, Vocah, with the intention of getting the Scrolls of Aberjian back from Angel. The demon reminds them that the scrolls are needed to raise the very thing that will tear Angel away from his link to The Powers That Be: Darla.

Dreaming (As *Buffy* Often Proves) is Free: Cordelia's terrifying vision-overload ('I saw them all. There is so much pain.')

Denial, Thy Name is Kate: As alluded to by Kendricks in **19**, 'Sanctuary', Kate seems to have become an object of ridicule to her LAPD colleagues (note the conversation between the two officers: 'She listens to the nut-calls on our scanner.' 'Are you sure she doesn't pick up the radio waves on her brain chip?') She tells Angel that she doesn't care about what people think of her. 'What I care about is ridding this city of your kind.' This leads to a major confrontation in the aftermath of the attacks on Cordelia and Wesley. 'I'm glad we are not playing friends anymore,' says Kate. Angel: 'I didn't kill your father. I'm sick and tired of you blaming me for everything you can't handle. You want to be enemies? Try me.'

It's a Designer Label!: Cordelia's fringey-yellow blouse and her lovely red patterned top are obvious highlights, especially alongside Wesley's chunky blue sweater. Watch out for a 'Mayhem' T-shirt on sale when Cordelia goes shopping. Lilah's short black skirt is also worthy of attention.

Reference: 'Shanshu' is a late imperial genre of didactic writing incorporating the teachings of Confucianism, Buddhism and Daoism. Given what 'Shanshu' is said to mean, *To Live and Die in L.A.* takes on a new meaning. Also, the 'Magic eight-ball' toy, Judas Iscariot's betrayal of Jesus to the Pharisees for 30 pieces of silver, ouija boards, *Pinnochio* and the discount store Pennysaver. Geographical references include the Valley towns of Reseda and Tarzana.

Bitch!: A couple of 'Cordelia-Special' moments: 'I just hope skin and bones here can figure out what those lawyers raised *sometime* before the prophecy kicks in and you croak.' And: 'Typical. I hook up with the only person in history who ever came to L.A. to get older.'

Lilah tells Lindsey: 'Remember when Robert Price let the senior partners down and they made him eat his liver?'

The Charisma Show: 'Nobody gets my humour,' bemoans Cordelia after an inappropriate joke has fallen flat. 'I thought it was funny,' replies a straight-faced Angel.

Some of Charisma's best acting of the year, especially in the hospital. Plus, the wonderful scene where she and Wesley discuss Angel's lack of connection to humanity over doughnuts and Cordelia's subsequent suggestion that they get him a puppy.

After Wesley has revealed that the prophecies say Angel will die: 'Is this that opportune time to talk about my raise?' On the prophecy itself: 'Angel faces death all the time, just like a normal guy faces waffles and French fries. It's something he faces every day like lunch. Are you hungry?'

L.A.-Speak: Nabbit: 'That was *awesome*. Can we do it again? . . . I just popped by to hang. I blew off my board of directors because tonight it's my turn to be dungeon master. What do you think of my cape?' Cordy: 'Shiny.'

Cordelia: 'Well, that *sucks*.'

Gunn: 'Lot of hungry people're gonna appreciate this. You're doing God's work here. If God was a busboy he'd look just like you. Toss it up, brother.' And: 'Yo, heads up.'

Gunn: 'I know this *fool*. That was entertaining. What y'got under that hood?' Angel: 'I need your help.' Gunn: 'I figured you didn't roar in here to ask me after my health. Pretty good, by the way. You getting enough iron? You look a little pale. Okay, it's traditional in the human world to humour people who've done favours for you.'

Cigarettes and Alcohol: On discovering that he will eventually become human, but not for a while, Angel tells his friends not to open the champagne yet. Cordelia prepares some blood for Angel and tells him that he shouldn't be embarrassed drinking it in front of her and Wesley because 'we're family'.

Sex and Drugs and Lexicography: Wesley believes 'Shanshu' isn't an Aegean word but instead: 'descends from the ancient Magyar's. Its root is proto-Hungaric.' He later discovers that it 'has roots in so many different languages. The most ancient source is the Proto-Bantu and they consider life and death the same thing, part of a cycle. Only a thing that's not alive never dies. It's saying that you live until you die.'

After Cordelia has her 'scratch'n'sniff' vision, she asks for a painkiller. In hospital, the doctor suggests Ativan to sedate her ('We're trying a number of different drug therapies. Do you know if she has any allergies?' Angel: 'Drugs won't help her.')

'You May Remember Me From Such Films and TV Series As . . .': Todd Stashwick appeared in *Spin City*, *Law and Order* and *Lucid Day in Hell*. John Eddins was in *Rikki the Pig*.

Logic, Let Me Introduce You to This Window: Considering he's just had his hand cut off, there's a surprising lack of blood all over Lindsey as Angel grabs the scroll from him. When Cordelia leaves the art stall she is carrying two shopping bags, which mysteriously disappear after Vocah touches her. During her visions at the outdoor market, Cordelia's bracelets switch from her left wrist to her right and back again. When Angel first opens the weapons locker, the left-hand door has three sais hanging on it. Vocah opens it later and there is only one sai, and a slim dagger. Watch the doughnut that Wes and Cordy share. It's never in the same half-eaten condition two shots running. Though Angel knocks off Vocah's mask, it is mysteriously back in place when Angel kills him. Cordelia opens a bottle, in the next shot she's clapping her hands together and the bottle is on the table in a different spot, with the cap on.

Motors: Unsurprisingly, Wolfram & Hart own the biggest black limo you've probably ever seen, along with a green Isuzu truck used to transport crates containing the Hell-raised.

Quote/Unquote: Cordelia: 'If I ever meet these Powers That Be I'm gonna punch them on the nose. Do you think they *have* a nose?'

Vocah: 'I am summoned for the raising, the very thing that was to bring this creature down to us, tear him from The Powers That Be. And *he* has the scroll?' Lilah: 'We're *not* unaware of the irony.'

Lilah: 'Aren't we going to be late?' Holland: 'You never want to be on time for a ritual, the chanting, the blood rites, they go on forever.' And, on arriving at the ceremony: 'They haven't even gotten to the *Latin* yet!'

Notes: 'Don't believe everything you're foretold.' A turbocharged end to the season with one of the most spectacular bits of pyrotechnics ever seen on US TV, some great Hell-like imagery and a shocking final revelation.

Angel Investigations is room 103 of its building. Room 101 is Casas Manufacturing, 104 is John Folger, DDS (see **11**, 'Somnambulist') and 105 is Herbert Stein. According to the prophecy the beast of Amalfie (a 'razor-toothed six-eyed harbinger of death') is due to arise in 2003 in Reseda. Cordelia buys paints for Angel at a stall called 'Art Attack'.

Lindsey is now a Junior Partner in Wolfram & Hart. The Oracles bleed like humans.

Soundtrack: Grant Langdon performs 'Time of Day' as Cordelia shops in the open market.

Did You Know ...?: While it is every fan's dream to contribute to their favourite show, few actually get the chance. Not so for Tam Cox of North Carolina, who seized an opportunity to showcase her design skills on the Angel Investigations set. Responding to frequent references to the lack of suitable coffee making facilities (particularly the need for a grinder in **13**, 'She'), Tam designed the *Angel Automatic 2000* – a coffee grinder packaged in a stylish box depicting images from the show and a version of Angel's tattoo. The production team (in particular David Greenwalt) were so delighted to receive the *AA2000* that the grinder was given a spot on top of Angel's fridge during filming of **22**, 'To Shanshu in L.A.'

Critique: *Science Fiction World*'s Michael Wright wrote enthusiastically about the season, believing *Angel* 'opted for the traditional route of playing off the season's slow build in fine style, giving us a final confrontation with the forces behind Wolfram & Hart and a slam-bang head-to-head with the agents of evil. This is a series which really established itself, putting down strong roots for future seasons and using the occasional crossovers with *Buffy* to excellent effect. The characters of Angel and Cordelia have developed strongly and in some unexpected directions now they've moved to centre stage instead of being part of an ensemble cast, and Boreanaz and Carpenter were ably supported by Glenn Quinn as Doyle and Alexis Denisoff [sic] as Wesley, who both brought depth and subtlety to what could so easily have been one-note "side-kick" roles.'

John Mosby, in *DreamWatch*, found the season: 'hugely enjoyable [with] oodles of dark potential, some lessons learned about the strengths of an ensemble cast and then a great cliff-hanging ending. What more can we ask?'

Wesley: 'Release her or die!'
Angel: 'Don't I say that?'

– 'Guise Will Be Guise'

Angel – Season Two (2000–2001)

**Mutant Enemy Inc/David Greenwalt Productions/
Kuzui Enterprises/Sandollar Television/20th Century Fox**

Created by Joss Whedon and David Greenwalt
Supervising Producer: Tim Minear (23–31, 33–35)
Co-Executive Producer: Tim Minear (36–44)
Consulting Producers: Marti Noxon, Jim Kouf (23–41)
Producers: Shawn Ryan (23–41), Kelly A Manners
Co-Producers: Skip Schoolnik, James A Contner (25, 32, 40)
Executive Producers: Sandy Gallin, Gail Berman,
Fran Rubel Kuzui, Kaz Kuzui, Joss Whedon,
David Greenwalt

Regular Cast
David Boreanaz (Angel/Angelus)
Charisma Carpenter (Cordelia Chase)
Christian Kane (Lindsey McDonald, 23, 27, 29, 31–34, 37–38, 40)
Elisabeth Rohm (Detective Kate Lockley, 27, 30, 32, 36–38)
James Marsters (Spike, 29)
Alexis Denisof (Wesley Wyndam-Pryce)
Julie Benz (Darla, 23, 25–27, 29, 31–33, 38)
Stephanie Romanov (Lilah Morgan, 23, 26, 32–34, 37, 40)
Eliza Dushku (Faith, 23)
J August Richards (Charles Gunn)
David Herman (David Nabbit, 25)
Sam Anderson (Holland Manners, 26, 29, 31–32, 34, 37)
Andy Hallett (The Host[13], 23, 25, 27–28, 31, 33, 35, 37–44)
Matthew James (Merl, 23[14], 33–34, 36)

---

[13] Finally named as Krevlornswath of the Deathwok Clan (or, Lorne, preferably) in
41, 'Belonging', all prior official press releases had dubbed the character as The
Host. This is also how most fans know him (and how he seems to refer to himself,
see **43**, 'Through the Looking Glass').
[14] Credited as 'Merl Demon' in **23**, 'Judgment'.

Juliet Landau (Drusilla, 27, 29, 31–33)
Brigid Brannagh (Virginia Bryce, 28, 33, 35, 37)
Mark Metcalf (The Master, 29)
Zitto Kazann (Gypsy Man, 29[15])
Julia Lee (Anne Steele, 34, 36)
Gerry Becker (Nathan Reed, 34, 37, 40)
Marie Chambers (Mother, 36–38[16])
Jarrod Crawford (Rondell, 36, 41)
Darris Love (George, 36, 41)
Kevin Fry (Skilosh Demon, 37–38)
Mercedes McNab (Harmony Kendall, 39)
Alyson Hannigan (Willow Rosenberg, 39, 44[17])
Amy Acker (Winifred Burkle, 41–44)
Brody Hutzler (Landokmar, 41, 43–44)
Michael Phenicie (Silas, 42–44)
Brian Tahash (Constable Narwek, 42–43)
Tom McCleister (Lorne's Mother, 43–44)
Mark Lutz (The Groosalugg, 43–44)
Adoni Maropis (Rebel Leader, 43–44)
Dahan Pere (Rebel #1, 43–44[18])
Andrew Parks (Priest #1, 43–44)

23
Judgment

US Transmission Date: 26 September 2000
UK Transmission Date: 5 January 2001 (Sky),
8 June 2002 (Channel 4)

Teleplay: David Greenwalt
Based on a story by: Joss Whedon and David Greenwalt
Director: Michael Lange
Cast: Justina Machado (Jo), Rob Boltin (Johnny Fontaine),
Iris Fields (Acting Teacher), Keith Campbell (Club Manager),
Jason Frasca (White Guy), Andy Kreiss (Lizard Demon),
Glenn David Calloway (Judge), EJ Gage (Mordar the Bentback)

---

[15] There's no finer example of the attention to detail in *Buffy* and *Angel* than the rehiring of Zitto Kazann to recreate, for a one-scene cameo, a role he played (in another one-scene cameo) four years previously in *Buffy*: 'Becoming' Part 1.
[16] The character's name is given as Francine Sharp in dialogue.
[17] Uncredited in **44**, 'There's No Place Like Plrtz Glrb'.
[18] The character's name is given as Sasha in dialogue.

A case of mistaken identity sees Angel kill a demon who is, in reality, protecting a pregnant woman whose unborn daughter will have a key role in the future of mankind. Angel is compelled to become the woman's new champion in an other-dimensional trial (despite her lack of confidence in him). But he is unaware of the return from Hell of his sire, Darla, who is recovering from her resurrection at Wolfram & Hart's offices. Meanwhile, in a karaoke bar downtown, something very odd is singing 'I Will Survive'.

It's a Designer Label!: The Host tells Angel, '*love* the coat'. Also, The Host's own tasteful white jacket, Wesley's yellow shirt, Cordy's red top and Darla's beautiful purple dress.

References: The Bravo Channel, the elegant cinematic style of *film noir* (how apt in a Los Angeles setting. See **24**, 'Are You Now or Have You Ever Been?'), 911 emergency calls, Buddha, Franco–Polish composer Frédéric François Chopin (1810–49), Johannes Brahms (1833–97), the warehouse-shopping club Costco, Joan of Arc (c. 1412–31) and singer/songwriter Barry Manilow (Faith refers to the Manilow song, 'Copacabana'). Also allusions to *The Donny and Marie Show* ('A little bit Country, a little bit Rock and Roll'), Proverbs 16:18 ('what's that thing that goes before a fall?'), actor Curt Jurgens (1915–82) and his performance in Dick Powell's *The Enemy Below*. The Russian composers that Darla doesn't like probably include Mussorgsky, Tchaikovsky and Rimsky-Korsakov. Locations referenced include: 4th and Spring in downtown L.A. (a junction close to the Biddy Mason Park), Boyle Heights (situated east of the Los Angeles river) and Silver Lake. There's a reference in the book that Wesley consults to Pope Gregory IX (Ugolino the Count of Segni, 1148–1241, most famous for his feud with the emperor Frederick II of Germany). The plot is reminiscent of *The Terminator*.

Work In Progress: The whiteboard in Cordelia's apartment features headings: 'Cases', 'Leads', 'Progress' and 'Status'. The first line reads: 'Zaroh, first seen 10/7 killed two police officers, beheaded – reborn – torched, closed.' Also listed are: Vocah (see **22**, 'To Shanshu in L.A.'), Sloth ('NS Varna 565-6123'), Khee Shak ('Book of Santhry vs. 21 pg.

101, death by fire and beheading. Killed when bldg exploded'), Ethros ('possession of child in Alhambra area. Exorcism not successful. Try priest.' See **14**, 'I've Got You Under My Skin'), Vartite ('many eyes, lives underground' and which, Cordelia says, took two days to kill), Konsoo ('likes dark dank places') and Carnyss ('carnivorous, must eat live flesh'). The last named is the creature Angel faces in the gym. Sloth demons don't sacrifice adolescents, according to Cordy.

'West Hollywood': The Host's assessment of Angel: 'Smart *and* cute!' In fact, if it wasn't for the demons, Caritas would be a gay bar, surely?

Awesome!: The opening sequences of Cordelia and Wesley getting on with their lives, then receiving a summons from Angel, like the Bat Signal, and rushing off to the rescue. An absolutely *brilliant* beginning.

'You May Remember Me From Such Films and TV Series As . . .': Justina Machado was America in *Swallows* and Marita in *The Week That Girl Died*. Jason Frasca was in *Silent Men*, Matthew James features in *Tattoo Boy* and Glenn David Calloway can be seen in *True Identity*. EJ Gage (who has also appeared in *Buffy*) was in *My Uncle the Alien*.

Don't Give Up The Day Job: Keith Campbell played Oz as a werewolf in *Buffy*: 'Phases'. He was Tom Cruise's stunt-double in both *Mission: Impossible* movies and doubled for Val Kilmer in *Batman Forever* and *The Saint*. He was on the stunt team for *Supernova*, *Analyze This*, *Blade*, *Wolf*, *Stargate* and *Deep Impact*. As an actor, readers may recognise him as Perp in *Men In Black*. He also appeared in *Fatal Instinct* and *Suburban Commando*.

Andy Hallett began singing when Patti LaBelle invited him on stage at a gig. He first worked as a runner for an agency and then as a property manager. When Joss Whedon and Dave Greenwalt saw Andy singing in a Universal City blues revue, they conceived the character of Lorne there and then. Andy has also appeared in *Chance* and *The Enforcers*.

L.A.-Speak: Cordelia: 'I threw that in myself. She seems so spineless, begging this creep not to dump her.' And: 'Maybe it's time we pay your stoolie a little visit. Make with the chin-music until he canaries.' And, on Gunn: 'He's a great guy with a really *fly street-tag*.'

The Host, on Angel's singing: 'You great big sap, there is not a destroyer of worlds that can argue with Manilow.' And: 'I know you're feeling smooth-in-the-groove.'

Gunn: 'I'll hook up with y'all back at the crib.'

A Haven for Demons (But Only if They Sing): Caritas is a karaoke bar which is a safe haven for demons. It is considered neutral ground and no demon will fight there. The Host is an anagogic demon, a psychic with mystic connections who can see into a person's aura when they bare their soul by singing (see **42**, 'Over the Rainbow'). He is characterised by his green skin, red eyes and horns, and by his cheerful and pleasant disposition, which seems to piss Angel off no end. Among the demons seen in the bar are: Merl, a parasite demon whom Wesley uses as a snitch – he has no tongue and even less spine; A Lizard Demon (it's hatching season and 'Liz' is contemplating eating its young); Mordar the Bentback and Durthock the Childeater, a demon searching for the Gorrishyn Mage who stole his powers. The demon from Cordelia's vision is Kamal, a Prio Motu. They are an ancient Afga-beast, bred to maim and massacre. Although Prio Motus are traditionally evil, this one was, apparently, good.

Cigarettes and Alcohol: The Host always seems to have a glass of whisky in his hand. At Caritas, Wesley drinks beer while Cordelia has what looks like vodka (see **13**, 'She').

Sex and Drugs and Rock'n'Roll: There are three things Angel says he doesn't do. Tan, date and sing in public. 'The vampire with soul,' The Host notes after Angel's massacre of 'Mandy'. Also references to anabolic steroids and how they're not very good for you.

There's a Ghost in My House: Cordelia tells Wesley not to shout as he will scare Dennis who, she notes, is very sensitive. 'He's more a person than a G-H-O-S-T.'

Logic, Let Me Introduce You to This Window: The exterior shot of Faith's jail is Folsom prison (the one Johnny Cash memorably sang about). Isn't that an all-male establishment? So, let's get this straight: a medieval-style joust happens in the middle of downtown L.A. with a tribunal of black-clad judges and two guys on horseback? Without anyone noticing? Some fans have suggested the whole thing is mystical and therefore not noticeable to anyone not involved (obscured behind a Someone's Else's Problem, Joyce Summers-style denial shield no doubt). It's still a hell of a contrivance. Maybe they all thought it was a movie shoot? Angel blows out a match after lighting a candle. It was established in *Buffy*: 'Prophecy Girl' that he has no breath. The handkerchief in The Host's jacket pocket moves from side to side. When Angel writes 'Prio Motu' on the board, Wesley's previously added 'NDUO' is not visible. Anyone notice the tape markings on the street where Angel and the knight fight? When Angel slams into the whiteboard, it's obvious that the wall behind is not real, as everything shakes. It is implied that Cordelia's area code is 368, but the real codes for Silver Lake are 213 and 323. Angel says that 'caritas' is Latin for 'mercy' – it isn't, it's Greek for 'charity'. 'Exorcised' is spelt wrong on the whiteboard. Angel's shield during the joust is obviously plastic.

I Just *Love* Your Accent: Wesley's prowess at darts (see **19**, 'Sanctuary') is again seen. He seems to be making a bit of money on the side as a darts hustler (if such a thing exists). Many British fans have doubted that a US bar would have a dartboard in it, but as this author can confirm, several British-style pubs (complete with dartboard) are popular with the expat community in the L.A. area, particularly Ye Olde King's Head in Santa Monica and Robin Hood's in North Hollywood.

Motors: Gunn asks if the Prio Motu is like a '62 Chevy 'with the really big cam.'

Quote/Unquote: Gunn, on the Prio Motu: 'Did you find the scumbag that killed him?' Angel: 'I *am* the scumbag that killed him.'

Lilah, to a client: 'If you don't sign we'll sue your ass off and kill your children. Just kidding, Donald. No one wants a lawsuit.'

Jo, to Angel: 'Do me a favour? Stop helping!'

Notes: 'In this city you better learn to get along. Because

L.A.'s got it all. The glamour and the grit, the big breaks and the heartaches, the sweet young lovers and the nasty, ugly, hairy fiends that suck out your brain through your face. It's all part of the big wacky variety show we call Los Angeles.' Not quite the reformatting that the season openers in *Buffy* traditionally produce. This is *Angel* at its best, however, with lots of jokes, some wonderful action sequences and a moral dilemma. Gorgeous.

Cordelia is taking acting classes and seems to have improved greatly as an actress since last year. She is playing a scene as Eleanor whose boyfriend, Johnny, is about to leave her. She has been in commercials for a suncare product called *Tan'n'Screen*. From the back of an Angel Investigations business card, Cordelia's full address seems to be 141 Embury St, Apt 212, Silver Lake 90026, and her phone number is 323-555-0175. Perhaps the name 'Pearson's Arm' has been changed since 5, 'Rm W/a Vu'? It's still clearly supposed to be the same apartment since Phantom Dennis is in residence. Gunn's new 'crib' is off 8th Street. Angel picked 'Mandy' to sing because he thought it was pretty and he knew all the words. He says he grew up around horses (see 15, 'The Prodigal'). Faith's prison number is 43100.

Lindsey says that Darla is 400 years old (in *Buffy*: 'Angel', The Master told Collin that Darla had sat at his right hand for 400 years. However, see 29, 'Darla'). Darla tells Lindsey that Angel killed her 'with a soul in his heart,' a variation on Angel telling Buffy that he maimed and killed and he did it with a song in his heart. Angel tells Jo that his office 'kind of blew up' (see 22, 'To Shanshu in L.A.'). When Gunn meets Cordelia and Wesley, he tells them that he once saw them in bed (again, a reference to 22, 'To Shanshu in L.A.' when he watched over them in hospital). There's a further reference to sires being able to sense when their 'offspring' are near, in this case Darla's ability to 'feel' Angel (see 11, 'Somnambulist'). Wesley has a book called *Suliman's Compendium* containing details of demons from Northern Pakistan, the Hindu Kush and Kazakhstan.

Soundtrack: As if the idea of a karaoke bar where demons sing for enlightenment isn't cool enough, it also provides much of the music for this episode, including nice versions of Gloria Gaynor's 'I Will Survive' (by The Host) and the Pointer Sisters' 'I'm So Excited' (by the Lizard Demon). And *terrible* versions of Billy Ray Cyrus's 'Achy Breaky Heart' (by Durthock the Childeater), Marvin Gaye's 'Sexual Healing' (by Mordar the Bentback) and 'Mandy' (by Angel). The latter, so bad it's *brilliant*, is replayed (including various giggly out-takes) over the end credits and includes Boreanaz's allusions to Frank Sinatra ('what's everyone doing in my living room?') and Elvis ('thankyouverymuch'). Darla and Lindsey listen to Chopin's Prelude No. 20 in C Minor. Also 'Last Confession' by Kid Gloves.

Did You Know?: Eliza Dushku was looking forward to what Joss Whedon had planned this season for Faith. 'I always joke with Joss, I've jumped off a building, gone into a coma, been in jail,' she told *The Watcher's Web*. 'If you can find a really witty and great way to bring me back, then I'll come. So far, he's lived up to his end.'

24
Are You Now or Have You Ever Been?

US Transmission Date: 3 October 2000
UK Transmission Date: 12 January 2001 (Sky),
15 June 2002 (Channel 4)

Writer: Tim Minear
Director: David Semel
Cast: Melissa Marsala (Judy Kovacs), John Kapelos (Hotel Manager),
Tommy Hinkley (Mulvihill), Brett Rickaby (Denver),
Scott Thompson Baker (Actor), JP Manoux (Frank Gilnetz),
David Kagen (Salesman), Terrence Beasor (Older Man),
Julie Araskog (Over-the-hill Whore), Tom Beyer (Blacklisted Writer),
Eve Sigall (Old Judy), Tony Amendola (Thesulac Demon[19])

---

[19] Uncredited.

Wesley and Cordelia are assigned to research the violent past of the abandoned Hyperion Hotel. Angel stayed there in 1952 and was involved in a suicide cover-up that involved a paranoia demon. Although Angel tried to help a girl on the run from the police, he ultimately abandoned her and everyone else to their fate.

Denial, Thy Name is Angel: An interesting look at the kind of life that Angel led before Whistler convinced him that humanity was worth saving (see *Buffy*: 'Becoming' Part 1). In 1952, Angel's attitude was to stay as removed from humanity as possible. Ironic, therefore, that he should do so in a seedy Hollywood hotel full of lost souls. As the fake T'ish Magva notes in **28**, 'Guise Will Be Guise', Angel clearly is a contradictory individual.

It's a Designer Label!: Wesley's trampy green sweater and Cordelia's figure-hugging multi-coloured top are the highlights until we get to the stunning period costumes, particularly Angel's blue shirt and Judy's flowery dress.

References: The title was a phrase made famous during the House UnAmerican Committee (HUAC) hearings of 1947 and 1951. HUAC, notably senator Joseph McCarthy, interrogated Americans about alleged leftist connections holding witnesses in contempt if they refused to answer the question 'are you now or have you ever been a communist?' The investigation of Hollywood radicals by HUAC turned into a media circus when some of the first witnesses refused to co-operate and tried to read statements condemning the committee's disregard for freedom of belief. Congress cited ten witnesses (including noted director Edward Dmytryk) for contempt and by mid-1950 most had served one-year terms in prison.

Also, Lana Turner (*The Postman Always Rings Twice*, *Peyton Place*, *The Bad and the Beautiful*, *Dr Jekyll and Mr Hyde*), Lucille Ball ('that zany redhead'), *Dracula* (Angel calls Denver 'Van Helsing junior') and *Blackadder* (a hotel guest called Mrs Miggins). The episode has similarities to *Forever Knight*'s 'Spin Doctor' and *Tower of Terror*. Tim Minear, during an online interview, listed various references that he had intentionally used, some obvious, others very oblique: *The Shining*, *Barton Fink*, *Rebel Without A Cause*, *Chinatown* (the detective's injured nose), *Vertigo*, *L.A. Confidential*, *Psycho* ('68 rooms, 68 vacancies') and *The Hudsucker Proxy*. The manager reads the *Los Angeles Times* with a headline SOVIET SPY RING REVEALED AT HOLLYWOOD RED INQUIRY. This may refer to the real-life trial of atomic spies Ethel and Julius Rosenberg. However, that took place in 1951, though the couple weren't executed until 1953. Angel's 'Maybe it was the wallpaper that drove him to it' could refer to the reputed last words of Oscar Wilde (1854–1900), 'either this wallpaper goes or I do'. Judy's hysterical denouncement of Angel ('it was *him*!') may have been inspired by Arthur Miller's play about the Salem witch trials, *The Crucible* – itself written, in 1953, as a reaction to the HUAC fiasco.

Locations: The Griffith Observatory has been a major L.A. landmark since 1935. A domed Art Deco monument on the southern slope of Mount Hollywood, it commands a stunning view of the Los Angeles basin below and the Hollywood sign to the right. A gift to the city by Griffith J. Griffith (1850–1919), the Observatory's purpose is to provide information on astronomy to the public. It's also a perennial favourite of Hollywood filmmakers, best known as the location for the climax of Nicholas Ray's *Rebel Without a Cause* (a bronze bust of that film's tragic star, James Dean, is one of the site's icons). Angel's red jacket is similar to one worn by Dean in the movie, which also has a female lead called Judy. The site has featured in many movies like *The Terminator* and *Bowfinger*. The premises used for Denver's book shop is the legendary Hollywood Book City store on Hollywood Blvd. A building in the Los Feliz area just south of Griffith Park provides the exterior shots for the Hyperion Hotel.

Bitch!: Actress: 'Who knows what else she's lied about, the little slut!'

When Wesley and Gunn start sniping at each other in the hotel, Angel assumes that it's the influence of the demon until Cordy confirms that they 'were like this all the way over here in the car.'

'West Hollywood?': There's an implicit critique of gay Hollywood in the 50s, with the actor clearly unable to out himself for fear of studio ostracism, despite the obvious presence of his young boyfriend in the hotel. This echoes the real-life dilemma of many gay stars of the era, forced to deny their sexuality in public.

L.A.-Speak: Cordelia: 'Cryptic much?'

Beat-Poet-Speak: Denver: 'No other cat but me. What can I do you for?' Also, deliciously, he called Angel 'daddio'.

Not Exactly A Haven For The Sisters: Judy is of mixed heritage, her mother being black and her father white. She has been passing as white since she was fifteen. In Salina Judy worked as a teller for the City Trust Bank. When the bank found out about her parents, they fired her. Her boyfriend, Peter, also abandoned her. In anger, she stole a satchel of money and ran away to L.A. The hotel manager turns away a 'coloured' family, despite having vacancies.

Cigarettes and Alcohol: Angel smoked in 1952, as did Judy.

Sex and Drugs and Blood: The raising of a Thesulac demon involves an incantation, sacred herbs, binding powder and an orb of Ramjerin. Cordelia gives Angel his blood with cinnamon.

'You May Remember Me From Such Films and TV Series As . . .': One for *Forever Knight* fans, John Kapelos played Nick Knight's partner, Don Schanke. He was also in *The Craft*, *Wiseguy*, *Guilty as Sin*, *Weird Science*, *Sixteen Candles*, *Home Improvements*, *Quantum Leap* and played Carl in *The Breakfast Club*. Brett Rickaby appeared in *New York Cop*, *Handgun* and was Chad in *The Strip*. Julie Araskog's movies include *Our Lips Are Sealed*, *Nixon*, *Se7en* and *Anna to the Infinite Power*. Scott Thompson Baker played Connor Davis on *The Bold and the Beautiful*, Craig Lawson on *All My Children* and Colton Shore on *General Hospital*. Terrence Beasor's CV includes *Days of Our Lives*, *Jaws: The Revenge*, *Police Squad!* and *Please Don't Hit Me Mom*. Tommy Hinkley can be seen in *The Little Vampire*, *Anarchy TV*, *Star Trek: Generations*, *Mad About You*, *That '70s Show*, *ER* and *MacGuyver*. David

Kagen's films include *Hologram Man* and *Conspiracy: The Trial of the Chicago 8*. JP Manoux was Glenn in *Just Shoot Me* and can also be seen in *Galaxy Quest*, *How High?*, *Inspector Gadget*, *The Drew Carey Show* and *Shasta McNasty*. Melissa Marsala was in *Bringing Out the Dead* and *Mickey Blue Eyes*. Eve Sigall was Agnes in *Roswell* and appears in *End of Days* and *The Night Caller*. Tony Amendola, was Bra'tac in *Stargate SG-1*, Sorrel in *Kindred: The Embraced*, Carl Jasper in *Cradle Will Rock* and Sanchez in *Blow*.

There's A Paranoia Demon In My Hotel: The Thesulac whispers to its victims and feeds on their insecurities. This particular Thesulac laid claim to the Hyperion Hotel as it was being erected in 1928, and was the cause of mayhem and paranoia for over 50 years.

Logic, Let Me Introduce You to This Window: 'It's not that vampires don't photograph, it's that they don't photograph *well*.' Since when? As noted, cameras use mirrors as part of their focusing mechanism. If a vampire can have his picture taken, why was Angel so fascinated with his reflection in **8**, 'I Will Remember You'? How long is the statute of limitations on a bank robbery? When the money stolen in 1952 is seen, it's in new $100 bills – with the 'big' Ben Franklin head – which weren't minted until the 1990s. In the Hollywood Blvd bookstore a star from the Walk of Fame can be seen. The first star wasn't placed on the street until February 1960. There's also a 1970s-style telephone on the wall along with a poster for a Flying Circus that appears to be photocopied (something not possible in 1952). The clipping regarding Judy Kovacs says that she worked at the Union National Bank, but Judy tells Angel her employers were the City Trust Bank of Salina. Also, the clipping's fourth paragraph is a repeat of the third. When the elevator stops at the lobby for Angel, the arrow indicator is not at the bottom. Cordy and Wes see Angel in a photo taken after the police arrive at the Hyperion to arrest bell hop, Frank Gilnetz. However, we see Angel tell the demon to take all the souls and then leave the hotel for good, so how could he be in this photo? The photos that

Cordelia has in her hand and then gives to Wesley are
different to the one shown on camera. The demon sounds
like Foghorn Leghorn. Angel is burned by touching the
bible, yet held one to no effect in **14**, 'I've Got You Under
My Skin'. The TV in the hotel lobby is not a 1950s model.
Certainly the screen (it looks about 18 inches) is way too
big for 1952. We've seen in previous episodes that Angel
keeps his blood refrigerated to keep it fresh. However, in
1952 he was, seemingly, drinking it straight from an ice
bucket. Shouldn't it be at body temperature to satisfy a
vampire? How did the Thesulac keep Judy alive since the
hotel closed in 1979? It's implied she's never left her room
since Angel left. What did she eat and drink? Anybody
notice the same three vintage cars are driving up and down
outside the Hyperion in the 1952 sequences? In the
blending shot from the present day photo of the Hyperion
to 1952, although the hotel seems to go from run down to
good condition, the trees and bushes around it are all
exactly the same. The reflection of Angel can be seen on
the silver tray he picks up. When Angel walks down the
stairs after Judy dies, there's a large window in the
background with his reflection on it. Angel doesn't
breathe, so how does he smoke?

Classic *Double Entendre*: Angel: 'Watch his tentacles.'
Cordelia: 'Excuse me?' Wesley: '*Tent-a-cles*!'

I Just *Love* Your Accent: Wesley drinks English breakfast
tea. The demon alludes to Wesley as being especially
paranoid (see **14**, 'I've Got You Under My Skin', **41**,
'Belonging'). Despite some very good Wesley dialogue in
this episode, he still gets some 'nobody-*really*-talks-like-
that' lines, including: 'A storied legacy of murder and
mayhem.'

Quote/Unquote: Angel, to Denver: 'It's been a long time
since I opened a vein but I'll do it if you pull more of that
Van Helsing-junior-crap with me.'

Writer: 'Maybe he saw you with one of your trysts!
Threatened to tell the studio. Expose perhaps your little
peccadilloes to the press?' Actor: 'Don't you dare use
alliteration with me, you hack. You're just mad because

the studio won't take your phone call, *comrade*!' Writer: 'Pansy!' Actor: 'Red!'

Thesulac: 'See what happens when you stick your neck out for them? They throw a rope around it . . . There is an entire hotel here just full of tortured souls that could really use your help. What do you say?' Angel: 'Take 'em all.'

Notes: 'Everyone here's got something to hide.' A magnificent episode that shakes an angry fist at the shameful HUAC fiasco, racism and human weakness while still finding time to explore, again, the key themes of redemption and forgiveness. Minear's script is literate, with many shades of grey instead of the black and white that it would've been easy for him to use.

The Hyperion Hotel was constructed in 1928 (Wesley notes that its architecture is California Spanish with deco influence). Angel says that it's in what used to be the heart of Hollywood. The real estate agent was the Melman Realty & Development group, 555-0157. On 16 December 1979, the hotel officially closed. That morning concierge Roland Meeks made his wake-up calls with a 12-gauge shotgun. Angel was a resident in this hotel, in room 217 in 1952. Angel drank bottled Type O human blood (ironically he's still drinking Type O today; maybe the different groups have different flavours and O's his favourite). Angel refers to Cordelia as 'Cordy' for the first time. This is the hotel into which Angel and Jo emerged from the tunnels, in **23**, 'Judgment'. Gunn has a pager. The exterior of the Hyperion is the same location as that used for Melissa Burns's apartment building in **4**, 'I Fall to Pieces'. Angel tells Denver that he hasn't drunk human blood for a long time. As far as we know, 1900 was the last time (see **29**, 'Darla') until he reverted to Angelus in 1998 (see **Buffy**: 'Innocence'). Angel confirms he was less than 30 when he was sired (see **15**, 'The Prodigal'). If Denver is 'just north of 30' in 1952 then he must be approximately 80 when Angel visits him in **37**, 'Reprise'.

Soundtrack: 'Hoop-De-Doo' a 1950 hit for Perry Como and the Fontane Sisters features prominently.

Did You Know?: It was, according to Tim Minear on the alt.tv.angel newsgroup, producer Kelly Manners who arranged filming at the Griffith Observatory, though 'There was no way in Hell it should ever have fitted into our schedule,' he noted.

25
First Impressions

US Transmission Date: 10 October 2000
UK Transmission Date: 19 January 2001 (Sky),
22 June 2002 (Channel 4)

Writer: Shawn Ryan
Director: James A Contner
Cast: Chris Babers (Henry), Cedrick Terrell (Jamil),
Edwin Hodge (Keenan), Lucas Babin (Joey), Alan Shaw (Deevak),
Angel Parker (Veronica), Ray Campbell (Desmond),
Sarah Brooke (Nurse), Janet Song (Doctor Thomas),
Kelli Kirkland (Young Black Woman)

Gunn enlists Angel's help in fighting the demon Deevak who has moved into his area. Cordelia has a vision of Gunn in trouble and is unable to contact Wesley or Angel, so she goes to save Gunn herself. But she and Gunn fall into a trap set by Deevak, leaving Angel and Wesley to rescue *them*. Meanwhile Angel's recurring dreams about Darla continue.

Dreaming (As *Buffy* Often Proves) is Free: Erotic, much? The climax of the episode reveals that Angel's dreams of Darla are mostly manipulated by her. However, before that we get two wonderfully surreal moments: Angel and Darla dancing in the deserted Caritas and, later, the pair in swimming costumes and sunglasses moonbathing, while, nearby Wesley hammers a nail into a coffin (for Angel?). Angel awakes and finds himself strangling Wesley, screaming 'you made her go away'. Oh dear, he's got it *bad*.

Dudes and Babes: Darla, in red. *Phwoar*!

It's a Designer Label!: Cordelia's black split skirt and leather boots. Also, Gunn's red tracksuit top, The Host's not-very-tasteful threads (note the yellow hankie) and one of the vampires' leather trousers.

References: Cordelia's 'You may wanna be a little more Guy Pearce in *L.A. Confidential* and a little less Michael Madsen in *Reservoir Dogs*,' and Gunn's reply: 'I haven't bothered to see a movie since Denzel was robbed of the Oscar for *Malcolm X*,' refers to three of this author's favourite films. Also, C3PO from *Star Wars*, the Barbie doll and singer Dionne Warwick and her appearances on the *Psychic Friends Network* infomercials. 'Send In The Clowns', written by Stephen Sondheim for the musical *A Little Night Music*, is about the break-up of a relationship. Originally sung on-stage by Glynis Johns, the song has been covered by hundreds of artists including Frank Sinatra and Judy Collins (whose version was a UK hit in 1975). 'Tears of A Clown' was a massive hit for its writer, Smokey Robinson, and his group the Miracles, in 1970.

Locations: Brentwood is an upscale community in West L.A. bordered by the San Diego Freeway to the east and San Vicente Boulevard to the south. The Garment District sprawls over 50 blocks between Broadway and Wall Street and includes CalMart, the Cooper Building and Santee Alley. The sequence in which Cordelia and Gunn bitch at each other while driving was filmed in Burbank and on Magnolia Blvd in North Hollywood (best known as the setting for Paul Anderson's 1999 travelogue in human misery, *Magnolia*). Some of the shots of Wesley and Angel riding on the motorbike were filmed on Ventura Blvd in Sherman Oaks.

Bitch!: Cordelia: 'Can't you, you know, hot-wire it?' Gunn: 'Just because I know some car thieves don't mean I *am* one.' Plus the entire second half of the episode, with the pair sniping wonderfully at each other. Finest moment, however, is when Angel has taken the wind out of Gunn's sails by insisting that Cordy and Wes accompany them to get information about Deevak. As Gunn sulks and heads for the car Wesley childishly shouts, 'shotgun'!

'West Hollywood?': Wesley, with Angel lying on top of him: 'About the naked thing . . .' Angel: 'I'll get dressed.' Wesley: 'Much appreciated.' Love the saucy way that one of the vampires looks at Angel as he removes his pink crash helmet. When Wesley gives him this, Angel is horrified. 'How come I have to wear the ladies' helmet?' 'Stop being such a wanker and put it on,' says Wesley, before adding: 'Looks good. Hop on *gorgeous*!'

Movie Critique: The *great* four-way discussion on Denzel Washington's performance in *Malcolm X*. As Angel notes, 'Who doesn't love Denzel?'

The Charisma Show: 'Are you friends with every criminal in town?' The development of Cordy as a person continues. The episode is built around the resourcefulness and bravery of this young woman who has come so far from her one-dimensional roots in Sunnydale. Her saving of Veronica's life at the party is one of the highlights of *Angel*, brilliantly underplayed, and yet emotionally exact. The moment where Charisma shouts, 'she needs a doctor', and then after a pause, silently mouths 'NOW!' to Gunn will give you a lump in your throat the size of Australia. Her later 'self-destruct' conversation with Gunn is further evidence of what a great actress Charisma has become.

L.A.-Speak: Gunn: 'You wanna jack *beemers* in Brentwood, be my guest. But leave the neighbourhood cars alone.' And, on Cordelia: 'I gotta tell ya, you are one high-maintenance chick.' And: 'Always enhances a guy's rep when some skinny white beauty queen comes to his rescue in front of his crew.' And: 'We're meeting a snitch downtown.' And: 'There you go assuming those brothers are criminals.'

Jamil: 'I'm just here to pay my respects and be off the streets 'fore sundown like my momma taught me.'

Cordelia: 'Jeez, short enough leash or do you just go all warm and tingly on the whole power-trip thing?'

Desmond: 'G-man. Can I get you a brew?'

Not Exactly A Haven For The Bruthas: It isn't once Cordelia arrives, bashing poor Joey's skull on the assumption that he's a demon. The party, however, gives us a good look at *Angel*'s take on South Central (it's never actually stated exactly where Gunn's homeboy turf is, though the next episode suggests it's close to Hollywood and Wilcox). And, mercifully, it's not bad at all; Shawn

Ryan's keen ear for dialogue meaning that at least the characters sound authentic.

Cigarettes and Alcohol: Plenty of brew at the party.

Sex and Drugs and Rock'n'Roll: In Angel's dream as he and Darla dance and kiss at the Caritas, The Host is moved to suggest: 'Somebody get these two love-vamps a *room*!' Later, they share a couch and Darla straddles him, ready for some hot vampire lurve action saying, 'I know how to please you.' Her use of an ice cube is supremely provocative too.

'You May Remember Me From Such Films and TV Series As . . .': Chris Babers played Monroe in *Santa Barbara* and also appeared in *JAG*, *The Faculty* and *Due South*. Kelli Kirkland was Yolanda in *Superhuman Samurai Syber-Squad*, Mary in *Blossom* and Rinna in *Star Trek: Voyager*. Edwin Hodge played Jamaal in *Boston Public* and was in *Big Momma's House* and *Die Hard: With A Vengeance*. Sarah Brooke was Lacey's mom in *Born to be Wild*.

Don't Give Up The Day Job: Shawn Ryan was a producer on *Nash Bridges*, co-wrote the movie *Welcome to Hollywood* and episodes of *Life with Louie*, one of which earned him a 'Humanitas Award' nomination.

There's A Ghost In My House: On entering her apartment Cordelia berates Dennis for the temperature. 'Jeez, it's like a meat locker in here. What is it with ghosts and cold rooms?' Dennis helpfully moves the thermostat up. Cordy then has a vision and Dennis gives her the phone to alert her friends.

Logic, Let Me Introduce You to This Window: When David Nabbit talks about how to buy the hotel with no money down, he mentions 'FHA with PMI to cover the down'. (PMI is Private Mortgage Insurance. When you put down less than 20 per cent on a purchase loan, this insurance covers the lender in case the borrower defaults on payment and the borrower pays the premium monthly.) FHA call their version of this scheme (which must have a down payment of 3 per cent minimum) MIP (Mortgage Insurance Premium), not PMI.

One has to assume that the vampires were able to enter Tito's house because, as Henry tells Gunn, 'everyone was invited'. When Darla pulls Angel's sweater off he has no tattoo, even though it was there in a previous scene. When Angel mounts the motorcycle behind Wesley, his hands are in different positions when the camera switches angles. Police cars blocking traffic so filming can take place are seen as Gunn and Cordelia cruise along Magnolia. Cordelia's extensive knowledge of *film noir* was seen in **23**, 'Judgment'. So how does she get the phrase 'stool pigeon' wrong? Gunn says Angel's car is a ''67 Plymouth convertible'. It isn't, it's a '68 (see **1**, 'City Of').

Motors: Wesley's Big Dog chopper (see **10**, 'Parting Gifts') is seen again. As he rightly tells Angel, California law states that anyone on a motorcycle requires a helmet.

Quote/Unquote: Cordelia, on dusting: 'This isn't mere dust, this is 'son of dust'. The kind of dust that spawns countless generations of little baby dust. I give up.' Wesley: 'Very well, we'll just move our offices back to your living room.' Cordelia: ' . . . And I'm dusting.'

Cordelia: 'Paging Mister Rationalisation.' Gunn: 'Paging Ms About-to-be-thrown-out-of-a-moving-vehicle.'

Gunn: 'I find Deevak, I'm gonna need more than C3P0 and stick-figure-Barbie backin' me up. No offence.' Wesley: 'Very little taken.'

Cordelia, on her vision: 'You were so scared.' Gunn: 'Now I know you're trippin', cos I don't get scared.' Cordelia: 'I do. The things I've seen, sometimes they get downright terrifying. Right now, I am scared for *you*.'

Notes: 'Name's Gunn. He's under the false impression that he runs this town.' The first episode in which Gunn's character doesn't seem to have been grafted on to the plot, but is there by right. This is great, two parts *Shaft*, one part *Vampiros Lesbos*, with fine performances from the regulars and giving lie to the notion that Boreanaz can't do comedy.

Gunn's 'The minute I take it easy somebody like Alonna pays the price,' refers to the death of his sister in **20**, 'War Zone'. Either Gunn genuinely believes that Angel sleeps in a coffin, or he's just being facetious (see **10**, 'Parting Gifts'). Cordelia has mace and a Byzantine axe (see **8**, 'I Will

Remember You') which she uses for self protection. David Nabbit, who has just returned from a hostile takeover in Kuala Lumpur, made his first million by inventing software that allowed blind people to surf the web. He's also involved in a charitable trust. Angel says that he is leasing the hotel for six months with an option to buy (see **42**, 'Over the Rainbow').

Soundtrack: The Host sings a glorious version of Oleta Adams's 'Get Here' in Angel's dream. Also, 'Who Ride Wit Us' by Kurupt (playing at the party).

J August Richards's Comments: 'What's the coolest thing about being on *Angel*?' the series' newest recruit was asked by *E!Online*. 'The fight scenes. I dig kicking those evil booties,' he notes. 'We start at 8 p.m. Vampires can only come out at night, so that's when we do it. I remember when we were doing my first episode, I shot all night. It was, like, four in the morning. I had to do a fight scene, and I was so tired. I was working the graveyard shift.'

Did You Know?: 'It can be very lonely,' David Boreanaz told Jeff Gammage about his life. 'I'm constantly working. The light at the end of the tunnel is you're happy. The workday can stretch fourteen or even sixteen hours, and the pace is fast. *Angel* often shoots eight pages of dialogue a day. A major movie [does] one or two.' The show moulds Boreanaz's life, from what he eats to when he exercises. He doesn't go out much and has no use for Hollywood parties and premieres. Coming from Philadelphia, he says, gives him a different outlook from those raised in L.A. 'Some of the people out here believe their own crap, it's ridiculous.'

26
Untouched

US Transmission Date: 17 October 2000
UK Transmission Date: 26 January 2001 (Sky),
29 June 2002 (Channel 4)

Writer: Mere Smith
Director: Joss Whedon

Cast: Daisy McCrackin (Bethany Chaulk),
Garth Williams (Bethany's Father), David J Miller (Man 1),
Drew Wicks (Uniform Officer), Michael Harte (Detective),
Madison Eginton (Young Bethany)

Angel's attempt to rescue a girl attacked in an alley sadly comes too late. For the men attacking her, that is. The girl, Bethany, who is currently staying with Lilah Morgan is highly telekinetic. Bethany seeks Angel's help and Wesley deduces that she was abused as a child. But as Angel starts to reach Bethany, Lilah sends the girl's father to bring her to Wolfram & Hart.

Dreaming (As *Buffy* Often Proves) is Free: The dream theme continues from the previous episode. When Angel admits that he has been 'sleeping weird', Wesley asks if he has been dreaming. Wes seems to have acquired a sense of foreboding concerning Angel's dreams since the killing spree by Angel's protégé, Penn, in **11**, 'Somnambulist'.

Dudes and Babes: When Darla catches Lilah in Lindsey's office, she notes: 'Exciting, isn't it? Going through their things, all the little pieces of themselves locked away, given you a naughty little thrill of control.' Lilah replies that she likes to keep abreast of his latest project. 'He's probably in my office right now trying to find out about mine. That's how it works at our firm.' This is the first time we see Lilah off-duty, in her apartment (though, of course, *technically* she isn't off-duty at all since Bethany *is* her latest project). She says that folding clothes is a Zen experience.

It's a Designer Label!: Cordelia mentions that she leaves clothes at the hotel so that she can change after her 'forty-five minutes of sleep' (see **34**, 'Blood Money, **39**, 'Disharmony'). Check out Darla's cleavage-bursting red dress and Cordy's tight black skirt.

References: *A Christmas Carol* ('Ebenezer here doesn't want to share the wealth'), the Fox Network ('Go home and watch a high-speed chase on Fox'), *King Lear* ('what *are* you?' and Gunn refers to 'Fair Cordelia'), *On the Waterfront* ('you could have been someone important'), Don Gibson's 'Sweet Dreams' and Mr Bill (a Play-Doh figure created by Walter Williams who appeared on various comedy series including *Saturday Night Live*). Angel's 'You wouldn't like me when I'm happy', is an obvious (and funny) allusion to *The Incredible Hulk*. The plot bears similarities to *The Fury*, *Firestarter*, *The Medusa Touch*, (obliquely) *Charmed*, and more obviously *Friday the 13th, Part VII – The New Blood* and *Carrie*. Locations: the junction of Hollywood and Wilcox and Brentwood are mentioned.

Bitch!: A classic Cordy moment: 'Thing about Angel, he's old-fashioned. *Old* fashioned, like the age of chivalry. He sees you as pretty much the damsel in distress. I think it's a little more complicated than that . . . I think you're kind of dangerous. I'm not being mean, I like you. But, you come on all helpless.' Plus Cordelia calling Wesley 'a sheep' (an insult she previously used on Harmony in *Buffy*: 'Bewitched, Bothered and Bewildered') and telling him 'all evidence to the contrary, but you're not a woman'. Wes, brilliantly, gets his own back when Bethany is told by Cordelia that Angel helps those in need. 'So, what's wrong with *you*?' asks Bethany. 'Where to begin?' chips in Wesley icily. As Wesley tells Angel: 'Our discussions tend to go about three minutes. Then it's strictly name-calling and hair-pulling.'

The Charisma Show: When Angel threatens to sack Cordy, she tells him that he can't because she's 'vision girl' then she sticks her tongue out. Even Angel cracks a smile. Also, her attempts to apply a bandage ('Stop breathing.' Angel: 'I don't breathe.' Cordelia: 'Then stop flexing your manly boob muscles'.)

L.A.-Speak: Angel: 'You're not from L.A., are you? Town kind of attracts loners.'

Cordelia, on Bethany: 'I'm getting a vibe. She's vibey.' And, on the subject of child abuse: 'There's not enough yuck in the world.'

Gunn: 'I'm still dealing with this man's ugly-ass living-room set. Some people just shouldn't have money.' And: 'What kind of scaly puss-monster y'all want me to slay this time?'

Sex and Drugs and Rock'n'Roll: 'Angel, he's strictly a no-bone,' Cordelia tells Bethany, though, as Beth herself notes when finding Angel dreaming about Darla, 'looked like a pretty happy dream. Or maybe the covers were just rumpled?' The extraordinary scene in which Bethany offers herself to Angel for some meaningless sex ('Shocked I'm a great big slut? Everyone thinks I'm so fragile and innocent. Men love it,') is wonderfully played, especially the bit where Angel asks, 'You want to make love, but you don't want to be touched?' Bethany laughs and replies, 'What are you, from the eighteenth century?' When Bethany asks Cordelia: 'Are you and Angel . . .?' Cordy is horrified: '*No*! I like my men less broody and more spendy!' There's a heartfelt rant from Bethany about telekinesis being a disease rather than a gift and her resistance to Angel treating her as a test subject is impressive ('don't start asking me a bunch of stupid questions like when were you potty trained').

Plus the dreams of Angel and Darla in literal bodice-ripping action. Darla is using Calynthia powder (which is purple) to keep Angel asleep when she is with him.

'You May Remember Me From Such Films and TV Series As . . .': Garth Williams was in *Santa Barbara*. Madison Eginton was Captain Picard's imaginary daughter in *Star Trek: Generations*, and also appeared in *Eyes Wide Shut* and *Psycho Beach Party*.

Don't Give Up The Day Job: Mere Smith previously worked as a production assistant on *Strange World*. David J Miller was director of second unit photography on *Sensation* and assistant cameraman on *Krush Groove*. As an actor, he can be seen in *Shriek If You Know What I Did Last Friday the 13th*.

Logic, Let Me Introduce You to This Window: As Angel crosses the police line his reflection can be seen in the bodywork of a car. When Bethany is taken into the van she appears to be at the Burbank Promenade close to Warner Brothers studio, but the subsequent car chase occurs through downtown Los Angeles. When Bethany sees her father her reaction blows out the windows for several floors around them but, when she throws him out, most of the formerly broken windows are intact. Cordelia is hit by a nail in her upper arm, but when she gets up her wound is much lower. The warehouse where Angel first meets Bethany is a recycled set; it was once the home of the vampire gang that Gunn's crew attacked in **20**, 'War Zone'. The exterior shot of Lilah's apartment building looks a very similar to the building used as Faith's hideout in **18**, 'Five by Five'.

I Just *Love* Your Accent: Note that Wesley says he will be at his 'flat', rather than the more American description 'apartment'.

Classic *Double Entendre*: Gunn, on his new home-made axe: 'Thought I might get the chance to stick it in something.' Cordelia: 'Men are all alike.'

Quote/Unquote: Darla: 'There's nothing so lovely as dreams ... Open those chambers and you can truly understand someone, and control them.' Lilah: 'What's hidden in Angel's secret chambers?' Darla: 'Horrors.'

Gunn: 'You still saving my life?' Cordelia: 'Every minute.' Gunn: 'How's that working out?' Cordelia: 'You're alive, aren't you?'

Cordelia: 'You have never had a single opinion you didn't read in a book.' Wesley: 'At least I opened a book.' Cordelia: 'Don't even try with the snooty-woolly-boy. I was top ten per cent of my classs.' Wesley: 'What class? Advanced bosoms?'

Lilah, on Angel: 'He's a vampire, you know?' Bethany: 'Weird.'

Notes: 'The time I've lived, I've seen some horrors, scary behaviour, and a couple of fashion trends I constantly pray to forget.' Good God, what have we here? *Angel* gets properly 'adult' at last. Dark subtext and bawdy humour share prominence in a disturbing and realistic look at the horrors of sexual abuse and the way in which its victims can themselves become trapped into believing such evil is 'normal'. Wesley's provocation of Bethany is one of the best sequences the series has ever done, plus that little bit of silent comedy involving Angel leaning on the door then falling through on his face. An extraordinary episode, too dark to be enjoyable, but never less than impressive. Plus a cool L.A. car chase.

Angel asks, 'Do you know how hard it is to think straight with a rebar through your torso?' Cordy replies 'Actually I do. Benefits of a Sunnydale education,' referring to her own implement in *Buffy*: 'Lover's Walk'. Darla whispers to Angel about a bound and gagged Gypsy girl (see **15**, 'The Prodigal'). Bethany tells Angel, 'I don't want to share,' a line very similar to one that Angel himself used in **1**, 'City Of'. Lilah's apartment number is 102. It is implied that one of her former duties at Wolfram & Hart was to speak at high schools around the country while searching for students with special abilities that the company could use (in Bethany's case, as an assassin). Judging from the business card that Angel gives Bethany, the new ones seem to be based on the design of the old, only with the new address (see **2**, 'Lonely Heart', **27**, 'Dear Boy'). Cordelia and Bethany share a vanilla mocha latte.

Soundtrack: The instrumental 'At the Fairground' (from the Opus Music Library).

Julie Benz's Comments: Asked by Paul Simpson and Ruth Thomas in *SFX* whether she had input into her character, Julie noted that, 'Darla's a collaborative effort and the writing is so good that by the time we get the script, there's never anything that Darla wouldn't say. I think that David Greenwalt, Doug Petrie, Tim Minear, Marti Noxon, Shawn Ryan [bring] these characters to life. By the time it gets to us, it's all there.' However, with regard to the future: 'They don't tell you a thing. On the first episode this season, I bumped into Joss and he [told me] we're thinking of making you human? I said really? So they didn't even *know* at that stage. The scripts are written pretty much a week in advance of shooting. I think they like to keep it exciting. They're flexible and just when you think you know what they're doing, they pull the rug from underneath you.' Julie also believes: 'Darla's greatly misunderstood. When people say that she's evil, I don't view her that way. She loves Angel like no other. She has not made another sire since she kicked him out. There's a reason for that. They were together for 150 years. She was waiting for the perfect specimen to come around. She stalked him for a long time, she followed him to make sure he was the right one. I think it is a great love, a mother/son love. When he tells her that she never made him happy, she simply can't understand why Buffy did. She's the jilted ex-wife.'

Did You Know?: 'I hope I'm different from Wesley, but I would have to admit if you're able to play a character, it means that somewhere that character exists inside you,' Alexis Denisof told an online interview. When asked about the differences between *Buffy* and *Angel*, Alexis noted: '*Angel* shoots at Paramount whereas *Buffy* has its own stages in Santa Monica, so there is a practical difference of being in a big studio, as opposed to a self-contained lot.'

27
Dear Boy

US Transmission Date: 24 October 2000
UK Transmission Date: 2 February 2001 (Sky),
6 July 2002 (Channel 4)

Writer: David Greenwalt
Director: David Greenwalt
Cast: Stewart Skelton (Harold Jeakins), Sal Rendino (Man),
Cheryl White (Claire Jeakins), Matt North (Stephen Cramer),
Derek Anthony (Hotel Security Guy), Darren Kennedy (Cop 1),
Rich Hutchman (Detective Jack Carlson)

While Angel dreams of his first encounter with Drusilla in 1860, he encounters a very real Darla. Wolfram & Hart set up his, now seemingly human, sire with a false identity and Angel follows her into a trap. Kate Lockley tries to capture Angel, but he eludes her and kidnaps Darla himself. Although he is tempted to either love her or kill her he does neither and, knowing that she will soon need his help, allows her to go.

Dudes and Babes: Lindsey tells Darla that Wolfram & Hart don't want Angel dead. 'We want him dark. There's no better way to a man's dark side than to awaken his nastier urges.' When Darla expresses her desire to kill Angel, Lindsey notes: 'Our plans for Angel are a little more long term. But if you can't help yourself then, by all means, be my guest.'

It's a Designer Label!: Three spectacular highlights, Cordelia's almost pornographic waitress outfit, The Host's white jacket and Cordy's purple pants.

References: Wesley says that Angel is eccentric, 'all the greats are. Sherlock Holmes, Philip Marlowe'. Cordelia describes Darla and Angel as 'Bonnie and Clyde if they'd had 150 years to get it right', referring to the infamous American bank-robbers Bonnie Parker (1911–1934) and Clyde Barrow (1909–1934). Angel is called 'the world's oldest teenager', a popular description of US TV host, Dick Clark. While in Lindsey's office, Darla plays with a set of scales, a representation of Diké, the Greek Goddess of Justice and Punishment and a vital part of the Greco-Roman Dionysian sex-cults in the first and second century AD.

Also, daguerreotype, a pre-photographic process invented in 1839 by Louis-Jacques-Mandé Daguerre (1787–1851) which involved sensitising a silver-coated plate with iodine to form an image. *Bring It On*, SWAT (special weapons and tactics) teams, the Actor's Studio (of Sausalito more formerly known as Action-In-Acting) and the Theatre of the Absurd. The work of certain European and American dramatists who agreed with Existentialist philosopher Albert Camus's assessment, in his essay *The Myth of Sisyphus* (1942), that the human situation is essentially devoid of purpose. Though no formal Absurdist movement existed, writers as diverse as Samuel Beckett, Eugène Ionesco, Jean Genet, Arthur Adamov, Harold Pinter and others shared a pessimistic vision of humanity struggling to find a purpose. Claire says she was abducted by aliens to the Triffid Nebula (M20), so named because of the trisecting dark nebulosity in its centre. It's in the constellation of Sagittarius and is 11,000 light years from the Earth.

Locations: The Promenade is in Santa Monica on Third Street, an open-air pedestrian street with restaurants, shops, movie theatres and nightclubs. Fremont Street is nearby, just south of Wilshire Boulevard. The address that Darla and Steven give is 1409 Galloway, Studio City. Sandwiched between North Hollywood, Burbank and the huge Universal Studio site, Studio City was built in the 1920s when Mack Sennett had outgrown his studio facilities in what would later become Silver Lake. He built a new facility near Ventura Boulevard and Laurel Canyon. Today the site is home to the CBS Studio, where such shows as *Hill Street Blues*, *Roseanne* and *Seinfeld* were filmed, and also a thriving residential community.

Bitch!: Wesley: 'Get a vision.' Cordelia: 'It's not like you just hit me in the head and wham it happens.' Wesley: 'What if we test that theory with one of my big old books?'

The Charisma Show: 'See his file? He has Visa, MasterCard and a problem. He's our target audience.' Plus, the delicious: 'That was really fun. The public humiliation, running from the hotel security staff and the nifty little outfit which seemed to tell so many conventioneers, "Pet me, I'm a whore!"' One of the episode highlights sees a confused Angel caressing Cordelia's hair and Cordy, horrified, squawking: 'Personal space!'

L.A.-Speak: The Host: 'You're sending out some family-sized vibes. My fillings are still humming.'

Gunn: 'My uncle Theo always said never buy a dull plough and never get in the middle of a religious war.' Cordelia: 'You really have an Uncle Theo?' Gunn: 'No, but it's still good advice.'

Kate: 'Got any priors?'

Cigarettes and Alcohol: The Host tells his barman, Rico, to 'Top off my Seabreeze, earn my everlasting devotion, huh?' (A Seabreeze is a cocktail of vodka, cranberry juice, grapefruit juice and crushed ice.) Stephen and Darla share some red wine with their linguini. Lindsey drinks whisky while listening to the ensuing set-up of Angel.

Sex and Drugs and Rock'n'Roll: When Angel kidnaps Darla, the final scene between them is packed with sexual tension. 'It's been a long time since I said this to anyone,' Angel tells her, 'but you can scream all you want.' When Darla tries to seduce her sire, Angel shouts, 'That's enough.' 'I'm pretty familiar with the international sign for enough,' Darla replies. Angel tells her that she took him places that 'blew the top of my head off. But you never made me happy.' Darla is incredulous. 'That cheerleader *did*? There was a time, in the early years, when you would have said I was the definition of bliss. Buffy wasn't happiness, she was just new.' When the sunlight forces Angel back into the shadows, Darla mocks him: 'You see, no matter how good a boy you are, God doesn't want you. But *I* still do.'

Wesley tells Angel that he doesn't believe Angel can just sniff a person. 'You had sex last night with a bleached blonde,' Angel replies. Wesley is, understandably im-pressed. So is Cordelia: 'That's unbelievable. I didn't think you *ever* had sex.'

Classic *Double Entendre*: Darla, touching Lindsey's hand: 'You don't feel anything?' Lindsey: 'Not in my hand.'

'You May Remember Me From Such Films and TV Series As . . .': Juliet Landau, despite appearances in films such as *The Grifters*, *Pump Up the Volume*, *Theodore Rex* and *Citizens of Perpetual Indulgence* and TV series such as *Parker Lewis Can't Lose* and *La Femme Nikita* is best known for her performance as Loretta King opposite her father, Martin, in Tim Burton's *Ed Wood*. Stewart Skelton was in *Civil War Diary*. Matt North played Lobb in *Dirty Pictures*. Cheryl White was Mrs Roberts in *Cicadas* and appeared in *Judging Amy*. Sal Rendino's films include *Volcano* and *Renaissance Man*. He played the title role in the video for Weird Al Yankovic's 'John Bobbit'. Darren Kennedy was Nicholas in *The Pretender* and was also in *Clockwork Mice*.

Logic, Let Me Introduce You to This Window: The events of **22**, 'To Shanshu in L.A.' and this episode suggest that when a vampire is staked (as Darla was in *Buffy*: 'Angel'), although their bodies are turned to dust, their 'spirit' goes to Hell and thus, in extreme circumstances (as with Vocah's raising of Darla) can be resurrected, something never hinted at previously. I'm right in assuming that this is a huge contrivance to get Julie Benz back on to the show permanently, yes? Not that most fans, or indeed this author, have *any* problem with that . . .

If cops were stationed around the hotel, how did Angel get inside unseen? Kate did an extensive research on Angelus (see **11**, 'Somnambulist'), so why doesn't she know about Darla? Wesley found a daguerreotype of Darla pretty easily and, since Kate read information that we were led to believe in *Buffy* was only in a Watcher's diary, there is no excuse that Kate wouldn't have access to the same source. The police arrive at the scene of the crime remarkably quickly. Even if Lindsey set the whole thing up and called them ahead of Darla's 911 call, Kate's on the scene within, what, five minutes? Just before Angel refers to Wesley and the bleached blonde, we see Wes loosening his tie. He then claps a hand to Angel's back. But in a different angle he is still working on the tie. There isn't a Galloway in Studio City, although there is one in Pacific Palisades. Also, the house number couldn't be 1409 as the number of the house directly across the street is 729. The area code given for the Hyperion, 213, is a downtown code, not a Hollywood one (it should be 323).

Quote/Unquote: Cordelia: 'What if, every time you identified a demon in one of your big, old books, we give you ten bucks, or a chicken pot pie?' Wesley: 'I have another idea. *NO.*'

Cordelia: 'We have an exciting new case. Could be aliens, could be adultery. It's a corker.'

Angel: 'I saw her. I'm not crazy.' Wesley: 'Where?' Angel: 'Between the clowns and the big talking hot dog!'

Darla: 'We made quite a mess out there. Blood and habits everywhere.'

Drusilla: 'Snake in the woodshed. Snake in the woodshed. *Snake in the woodshed!*'

Notes: 'Woman should have her own series.' Indeed she should. Julie Benz is quite brilliant, moving back and forth between a dangerous animal and a suddenly human, and vulnerable, young woman. It's a great performance and it needs to be because the rest of the episode is a bit limp, with some decidedly sloppy plotting in the early scenes – not the kind of thing you normally expect from a writer as sharp as Greenwalt. The direction, on the other hand, is exceptional, particularly that devastating opening shot of the sun rising above L.A. mixed over Darla's face.

Wesley says Angel staked Darla 'three and a half years ago' (see *Buffy*: 'Angel'), and continues, 'Vampires don't come back from the dead.' '*I* did,' notes Angel. All the broken windows on the Hyperion Hotel from the last episode seem to be repaired. Angel refers to his age as 247 again (see **15**, 'The Prodigal'). Although the flashbacks are undated, we know that Angelus first encountered Drusilla in London in 1860 (see *Buffy*: 'Becoming' Part 1). These events seem to take place shortly before that meeting. Angel mentions he has 'a thing for convents', and the flashback clearly illustrates Angelus's love for draining nuns. Angelus drove Drusilla mad by killing all of her family (see *Buffy*: 'Lie to Me') and she fled to a convent to escape him. There, Angelus sired Drusilla on the night she was to take her Holy Orders. Drusilla's mother and uncle had previously been mentioned, but here it's confirmed that she also had two sisters and a father. It's also confirmed that she had 'the sight' prior to Angel sending her mad (see *Buffy*: 'Becoming' Part 1). When Darla strokes Lindsey's prosthetic hand, she says: 'Angel did that to you' (see **22**, 'To Shanshu in L.A.'). Gunn's rap-sheet includes arrests for disturbing the peace, resisting arrest, and assault. The address of the hotel is 1483 Hyperion Avenue, Los Angeles 90036 and its phone number is 213-555-0062.

The Thrall Demon is a very large, sedentary demon currently being worshipped in the water tank that used to be Saint Bridget's Convent. Gunn splits its skull in two with his axe. St Bridget's was a convent built on native burial grounds. The land was cursed: they had eight murders in two years before the place burned to the ground, which, according to Angel is nothing compared to what happened at Our Lady of Lochenbee. The latest case of Angel Investigations involves Harold and Claire Jeakins. Claire, to cover up her trysts at the Franklin Hotel, claims to be abducted by aliens on a regular basis. Kate, due to her interest in the 'extraordinary', has been transferred away from the Metro Division. Darla takes the assumed name Dietta Kramer.

Soundtrack: David Boreanaz absolutely *massacres* Wang Chung's 1980s disco-party classic 'Everybody Have Fun Tonight' at Caritas. Also, 'Stinky Stinky Ashtray' by Damn!

Did You Know?: It was reported in July 2001 that David Boreanaz had purchased a home in the Sunset Strip area. Built in 1936, the house is Cape Cod-style, measuring 1,700 square feet with two bedrooms and a pool. The asking price was just under $1.3 million. So exactly how does one get invited for a swim chez Boreanaz? Maybe if you hang out at the Viper Room long enough, or just lounge around outside the Hyatt Hotel he'll walk past? Not very likely, is it?

28
Guise Will Be Guise

US Transmission Date: 7 November 2000
UK Transmission Date: 9 February 2001 (Sky),
13 July 2002 (Channel 4)

Writer: Jane Espenson
Director: Krishna Rao
Cast: Art LaFleur (T'ish Magev), Patrick Kilpatrick (Paul Lanier),
Todd Susman (Magnus Bryce), Danica Sheridan (Yeska),
Saul Stein (Benny), Frankie Jay Allison (Thug 1),
Michael Yama (Japanese Business Man 1),
Eiji Inoue (Japanese Business Man 2), Ed Trotta (Man)

Angel makes a sojourn to seek a swami's counsel. While the boss is out of town, a businessman demands Angel's services to protect his daughter, so Wesley poses as the vampire. And both he and Angel get more than they bargained for.

Dudes and Babes: Virginia's great and it's about time a good-looking lad like Wes managed to get himself a girlfriend. In L.A., with that accent, it's virtually impossible *not* to score. All the chicks *love* the accent. Some of the guys too!

Denial, Thy Name is Angel: Despite the fact that the person claiming to be the T'ish Magev isn't actually the swami, he still manages to highlight many of the contradictions inherent in Angel's personality that Angel himself is doing his best to smother.

It's a Designer Label!: 'Why is Wesley wearing my coat?' Wes gets to wear the cool clothes this week. Also, Cordy's beautiful blue top and her business suit, The Host's tasteful cravat and spotty hanky, Virginia's red party dress and Gunn's designer biker jacket.

References: The plot is similar to the 1991 film *To Cast A Deadly Spell*, in which a sorcerer hires a private detective to retrieve a magic book, which he needs to cast a spell that will sacrifice his virgin daughter to a demon and grant him power. The lack of virginity of the heroine is also the denouement. When Angel tells The Host he is feeling 'a little rocky', the reply is: 'You're *Rocky*, *Rocky II* and half of the one with Mr T' referring to Sylvester Stalone's Rocky Balboa movies. Also, Barry Manilow again (see **23**, 'Judgment'), *Live and Let Die* (a reference to 'Fillet Your Soul'), the Buddhist concept of the Chakra (psychic-energy centres of the body, prominent in the occult physiological practices of many forms of Hinduism and Tantric Buddhism. The chakras are conceived of as focal points where psychic forces and bodily functions merge. Also mentioned in **13**, 'She'), Shemp Howard (one of the original Three Stooges), Cher, Yoda (the Jedi Master from the *Star Wars* movies), Joan Armatrading's 'Love and Affection' ('once more with even less feeling') and *Riverdance*.

Locations: The T'ish Magev lives in Ojai, a city two hours north of Los Angeles (and the setting of *The Bionic Woman*).

Bitch!: Angel: 'Maybe my persona *is* a little affected.' T'ish Magev: 'Come on. How many warriors slated for the coming apocalypse do you think are gonna be using hair gel? Don't get me wrong, you're out there fighting the ultimate evil you're gonna want something with hold.'

Angel, on Wesley: 'You're jealous he's getting some attention?' Cordelia: '*Damned skippy*! He's getting famous off this. Reflected glory, that's my thing.'

The Charisma Show: Although it's mainly Alexis Denisof's episode, Charisma does get one glorious line, sarcastically mimicking Angel: 'I can't do anything fun tonight ... I have to count my past sins, then alphabetise them. Oh, by the way, I'm thinking of snapping on Friday.'

L.A.-Speak: Gunn: '*That*'s the plan? Walking real quick was the *plan*?' And: 'How'd I live in L.A. all my life and not notice weird-ass stuff was going on?'

Cigarettes and Alcohol: Wesley and Virginia drink champagne while shopping in the high class store. There's also lots of champagne at the party (and Cordy uses a bottle of it to brain one of the guards during the ensuing fight). Wes, Cordy and Gunn share a beer while Angel talks to The Host.

Sex and Drugs and Rock'n'Roll: Virginia Bryce was deflowered by her chauffeur aged sixteen (she had another chauffeur, literally, at eighteen and also dated Rick, one of the guards) and was rendered impure for sacrifice even before Wesley's attentions (Virginia: 'I was *not* a virgin.' Wesley: '*Thank goodness.*')

'You May Remember Me From Such Films and TV Series As . . .': Frankie Allison was in *Casino*, *Indecent Proposal* and *Why Do Fools Fall in Love?* Brigid Brannagh played Claire in *Hyperion Bay*, Sasha in *Kindred: The Embraced* and Donna in *Dharma & Greg* and has appeared in *The Man in the Iron Mask*, *Sliders* and *The West Wing*. Eiji Inoue's movies include *Samurai Vampire Bikers from Hell*, *Atomic Samurai* and *Impact Zone*. Michael Yama was in *Molly*, *Murder Live!*, *Down and Out in Beverly Hills*, *Indiana Jones and the Temple of Doom*, *The Bad News Bears Go to Japan*, *The X-Files* and *Home Improvements*.

Patrick Kilpatrick was Red Five in *Dark Angel*, and also appeared in *The Toxic Avenger*, *Hijack*, *Free Willy 3: The Rescue*, *Riot*, *3 Ninjas Knuckle Up*, *The Stand*, *Russkies*, *The Lazarus Man*, *Raven*, *Star Trek: Deep Space Nine*, *Charmed* and *Tour of Duty*. Ed Trotter's CV includes *Pump up the Volume*, *Night Club*, *Babylon 5* and *Mac-Guyver*. Art LaFleur's long career includes *The Replacements*, *Hijacking Hollywood*, *In the Army Now*, *Jack the Bear*, *Field of Dreams*, *The Blob*, *Zone Trooper*, *Cobra*, *Rescue from Gilligan's Island*, *M*A*S*H*, *Charlie's Angels* and *Hill Street Blues*. Danica Sheridan was Matilda in *Married . . . With Children*, and can also be seen in *Eating L.A.*, *Isle of Lesbos* and *Black Scorpion*. Saul Stein appeared in *Zoo*, *He Got Game*, *Pink as the Day She Was Born*, *Heaven's Prisoner* and *Law & Order*.

Don't Give Up The Day Job: Aside from a lengthy career in films and TV series as diverse as *The Rat Pack*, *Blast from the Past*, *Coneheads*, *Beverly Hills Cop II*, *Kojak*, *The Waltons*, *Remington Steele*, *St Elsewhere*, *California Dreaming*, *Star Spangled Girl* and as Glen in *Grace Under Fire*, Todd Susman's main claim to fame is as the PA Announcer on *M*A*S*H* as well as playing the Tooth Fairy in a series of commercials for Sonicare. Krishna Rao was the writer/director on *Crossworlds*. Before this, he was a camera operator on films such as *Rock'n'Roll High School*, *Halloween*, *Predator 2*, *Star Trek: Generations* and *Species*.

Logic, Let Me Introduce You to This Window: When Angel approaches the cabin his reflection can be seen in the pond. There's another reflection in the water when Angel and T'ish are fighting, and also the reflection of Angel's hands in the desk's finish when he reads the article about Wesley at the end. Readers may like to visit the LAPD website and see if they can hack into the mugshots as Cordelia manages here. Bet you can't. Since Lanier never spoke to or heard Wesley speak, how did he know he was English? There's now 'official' doubt about what exactly constitutes 'perfect happiness', it seems, given Angel's embarrassed cry that he isn't a eunuch. If there's an easy way into the basement at

Wolfram & Hart like the grate through which Gunn and Angel emerge, then why did Angel have to cut his way in through a sewer tunnel in **21**, 'Blind Date'? The guard's shoe was punctured before Angel stabbed him through it with the stake. A stock shot from the *Angel Demo Reel* is used when Angel is driving to Ojai. The car is burgundy and it isn't even the same model. Shouldn't Angel's coat have a hole in it where Bethany stabbed him with a rebar? (see **26**, 'Untouched'). How did Angel get in the house? Was it a proxy invite through Wesley? Wesley comes around the corner to Virginia's bedroom and has his glasses on. Just before the ensuing fight they're still in place. In the next shot, the glasses are missing.

Motors: T'ish Magev: 'What kind of mileage do you get with that thing?' Angel: 'I don't know. Twelve in the city, maybe.' Magev: 'Gas hog. Still, probably a chick magnet, right?'

Quote/Unquote: T'ish Magev: 'A vampire living in a city known for its sun, driving a convertible. Why do you hate yourself?' Angel: 'I got a deal.' T'ish Magev: 'Why not a personalised licence plate that says "irony"?'

Angel: 'Were you in Virginia?' Wesley: 'That's besides the point!'

Cordelia, on Wesley's sudden found sexiness: 'One day as Angel. One day and he's *getting some*!'

Notes: 'Bodyguard to the stars, yeah right ... There's no 'Wyndam-Pryce Agency'.' *This* is the stuff. It's about time we had a Wesleycentric episode and the lad got some goddamn respect. Alexis pulls out all of the stops in a performance full of comedy touches that perfectly capture the character's charm. It's really hard not to like Wesley. He's a bit useless but he tries his best and, when the chips are down, has a surprising bravery. Just like most of us, in fact.

Angel confirms he doesn't have a body temperature. Among the names of the criminals Cordelia looked at are Albert Grey, George Pollon and Irvin Oliver. The magazine she reads is called *Bio* (headline: RICHARD'S SIDE SALE). Angel tells T'ish Magev that wearing all black makes

co-ordination easier since he has no reflection with which
to check out his outfit.

Magnus Bryce is a wizard who casts custom spells for
the rich, his software company and cable network being
front organisations. His great-grandfather created the
family's first spell in his garage. It is said that there are
several companies in Hollywood who provide this kind of
service, including one run by Paul Lanier ('scary little
euro-creep'), whose firm grants wishes. Also mentioned is
Briggs at 'Consolidated Curses'. Magnus notes that 'the
goddess Yeska does not give with both hands.' Yeska is a
Davrik demon who will only serve a human if they make
a sacrifice of a virgin daughter on their 50th birthday.
Angel has had dealings with Yeska before. Virginia is 24
years old; she wants to have her own apartment and find
work spraying perfumes or selling tyres.

Soundtrack: Two Japanese businessmen sing a hilariously
bad version of Sonny and Cher's 'I Got You, Babe' at
Caritas ('that was Cheriffic, boys!'). Also, Mozart's 'Vedrai
Corine' from *Don Giovanni* and one of Franz Joseph
Haydn's string quartets.

Critique: 'A terrific showcase for the often annoying
Wesley,' Brian Barratt noted in *Xposé*, '[it] gives Denisof
the opportunity to play action hero and romantic lead and,
some might say surprisingly, he fits the bill perfectly.'

Did You Know?: Alexis Denisof's hobbies include scuba
diving, horse riding, skiing. 'I skied all my life,' he told an
Internet interview. 'I had a much more adventurous
childhood than Wesley did. I moved around a lot, going
between the Pacific Northwest and New England. So I had
a lot of different experiences and I lived in England when
I was a teenager.' Asked what he missed most about
England, Alexis replied: 'The newspapers, the tea, the sense
of a city centre, which L.A. lacks. I miss the culture of
theatre, art galleries, music, and every conceivable art
form, industry and business all going on. L.A. is more of
a one-business town in the sense that the engine of
Hollywood is driving the city. London is this extremely
complicated, cosmopolitan mix of so many influences.'

Previously on *Buffy the Vampire Slayer*: 'Fool for Love': When a vampire stabs Buffy she seeks information on the last battles of past Slayers from the only person she knows who has witnessed a Slayer's death: Spike. He not only details why his victims lost their lives, but also his own history as a vampire with Drusilla, Angel and Darla, a gang of four who created havoc and terror across the world.

29
Darla

US Transmission Date: 14 November 2000
UK Transmission Date: 16 February 2001 (Sky),
20 July 2002 (Channel 4)

Writer: Tim Minear
Director: Tim Minear
Cast: Bart Petty (Guard)

As Angel broods about Darla, she begins to feel guilt about her past. Wesley worries that Wolfram & Hart have planned this to keep Angel busy. Darla tries to contact Angel for help and then, with Lindsey's aid, attempts to escape. Lindsey gives Angel information as to where Darla is being kept and Angel saves her. Darla begs her former lover to sire her so she won't be plagued by her soul, but Angel refuses.

Flashbacks (As *Buffy* Often Proves) Are Free: Glimpses of Darla being sired by The Master in 1609 Virginia, Darla introducing Angel to The Master in 1760 London, Drusilla deciding she wants a playmate in 1880 London, Darla killing the gypsy who cursed Angel in 1898 and Angel trying to rejoin Darla in China in 1900.

Dudes and Babes and Horrible Vampires: The Master is an ancient and powerful vampire, so old when he sired Darla that he had lost his human features completely. He is the leader of a vampire cult called the Order of Aurelius, who worship the 'old ones' and plan to bring an end to the plague of humanity (see *Buffy*: 'Welcome to the Hell-mouth', 'The Harvest', 'Prophecy Girl', 'The Wish').

As a human in 1880, William (Spike) was a sensitive (if 'bloody awful' poet) who was intimidated and ridiculed by his peers and Cecily, the woman he cherished (*Buffy*: 'Fool for Love'). 'Darla' means beloved one, an Anglo-Saxon derivation of 'darling' that was a popular girl's name in the eighteenth century. She doesn't remember her real name; it was The Master who named her Darla.

Denial, Thy Name is Angel: It's noticeable that Angel still believes he's searching for atonement on his own even after Cordelia states that he isn't alone.

It's a Designer Label!: Angel wears a brown coat and a striped shirt. Perhaps he took the fake swami's fashion advice in **28**, 'Guise Will Be Guise' to heart. Wesley's pink shirt and tweed jacket are criminal. Also, Cordy's blue top.

References: Part of the story takes place during the Boxer Rebellion (1898–1900), an officially supported peasant uprising to drive foreigners (particularly Christian mission-aries) from China. 'Boxers' was the name foreigners gave to a Chinese society, *I Ho Ch'üan* ('Righteous and Har-monious Fists'). They practised boxing and calisthenic rituals in the belief that this gave them supernatural powers and made them impervious to bullets. Also, Neil Simon's comedy *Out of Towners*, The Master tells Angelus that the Order of Aurelius lives below ground to 'give tribute to those who have gone before', similar to what Armand, whose coven haunt the cemetery, *Les Innocents*, tells Lestat in *The Vampire Lestat*. Darla's soliloquy to Lindsey regarding her body dying was influenced by Peter S Beagle's *The Last Unicorn*. After Angelus regained his soul, he searched for Darla and begged her to take him back. He killed but, Darla notes, only murderers, rapists, thieves and scoundrels. This is reminiscent of Nick Knight in *Forever Knight* who, like Angel, searched for centuries to regain his humanity. When Knight first made the decision not to kill again, he wasn't strong enough to give up blood (his sire, LaCroix, wouldn't allow him to stop killing), so he killed only the guilty. Cordelia mentions Sun Valley, a neigbourhood at the east of the San Fernando Valley. Mostly rural hillside with ranches, it has a bad reputation for crime. Also a reference to Naples, the capital of Campania in Italy.

Bitch!: Cordelia: 'This would be the same woman you didn't notice was in your bedroom every night for like three weeks straight?' Angel: 'That was different.' Cordelia: 'Different in the sitting-right-on-top-of-you sense?'

The Master: 'We stalk the surface to feed and grow our ranks. We do not live amongst the human pestilence.' Angelus: 'I'll be honest, you really couldn't with that face.'

Drusilla: 'His head's too full of you, grandmother.' Darla: 'Stop calling me that.' (Later, Drusilla tells Darla 'I could be your mummy', anticipating the events of **32**, 'Reunion').

'West Hollywood?': Even in 1880 Spike was putting Angelus's backup, calling him a 'poofter' (*Buffy*: 'Fool for Love'). Darla asks Lindsey if he has a girlfriend. Or a boyfriend.

The Charisma Show: A couple of classics. Angel asks why Cordy's still at the office, she replies: 'Unless there's a website called *www.ohbythewaywehaveDarlastashedhere. com* we're pretty much out of luck.' (There is, incidentally, a real website at this address run by an *Angel* fan, not surprisingly.) Her excellent assessment of the Valley ('why go there if you don't have to?'). Plus the wonderful bit where she answers the phone and then tries several times unsuccessfully to cut into Angel and Wesley's conversation about where Darla is before telling the person on the line: 'Hi Darla. He can't talk right now. He'll call you back.'

L.A.-Speak: Angel: 'We investigate things. That's what we're good at.' Cordelia: 'That's what we *suck* at.'

Classic *Double Entendre*: Darla: 'It's not me you wanna screw.'

Sex and Drugs and Rock'n'Roll: Angelus used snuff in the 1760s.

'You May Remember Me From Such Films, TV Series and Heavy Metal Videos As . . .': Mark Metcalf played Doug Neidermeyer in the classic *National Lampoon's Animal*

House and appears in *The Oasis, Rage, Julia* and *Drive Me Crazy* along with the video for Twisted Sister's 'We're Not Gonna Take It'. Zitto Kazann was Henry in *Melrose Place*, and can also be seen in *Waterworld, Thirteen Days, Robin Hood: Men in Tights, Red Dawn, Satan's Triangle* and *Starsky and Hutch*. Bart Petty was in *Kansas*.

Logic, Let Me Introduce You to This Window: Shown fully in *Buffy*: 'Fool for Love', and in less detail here, are the circumstances of Spike's sireing by Drusilla, despite Spike having said on two previous occasions (*Buffy*: 'School Hard', **3**, 'In the Dark') that Angel sired him. To be fair, Joss Whedon has mentioned several times that Dru was actually Spike's sire (on 2 January 1998 he told the *Posting Board*: 'Angel was Dru's sire. *She* made Spike. But sire doesn't just mean [the] guy who made you, it means you come from their line. Angel is like a grandfather to Spike.' When Angel is sitting at his desk there are reflections of him in the finish. In *Buffy*: 'Angel' Angel tells Buffy that after the gypsy girl, he never killed another human being. Here we find that isn't true. Cordelia tells Angel it's 1 p.m., but her desk clock reads 6.45. As many fans have noted regarding the accents, pick one and stick to it. Boreanaz's Irish brogue comes and goes as usual, but Julie Benz's southern-belle lilt suddenly disappears in the middle of her sickbed dialogue. There's no nameplate on Lindsey's office door. Holland's tie is off-centre as he steps into the hall from Lindsey's office, yet it's straight seconds later. Darla cuts Angelus's throat. The next shot shows him with no cut, and the shot after that has the cut much lower on his neck. Also, Angelus's cut left eye comes and goes. Although the costuming is ambitious, some of the styles seem anachronistic. In 1760 Angelus is dressed in the style of a European gentlemen, but his boots are early by a decade at least. Darla's clothes from the same era include a dress with a sacque back and a long train which largely fell out of fashion around 1750. In 1880 London, Angelus is sporting an ascot, though thinner ties were the fashion norm. Angelus, in 1900, reeks of vermin, has filthy hands and wears rags, yet he's clean-shaven. Wesley says that

Darla is 'out there among six million other people'. The population of the L.A. area is closer to fifteen million. David Boreanaz wears different clothes in the 1898 sequence to the view of the same events seen in both *Buffy*: 'Becoming' Part 1 and **18**, 'Five By Five'. What did Angel do with the baby he rescued from Darla in 1900?

Motors: Lindsey drives a silver Mercedes C-class (C55), licence plate 3210879.

I Just *Love* Your Accent: 'I patterned Spike's accent after a guy I was in a play with, but that was three years ago. Now I listen to Tony Head who sounds kind of like Spike in real life,' James Marsters told an online interview. 'His accent is just as fake as mine!'

Quote/Unquote: Angelus: 'Why don't you make yourself a playmate?' Drusilla: 'I could pick the wisest and bravest knight in all the land and make him mine for ever with a kiss.' William, brushing past them: 'Watch where you're going!' Darla: '*Or*, you could just take the first drooling idiot that comes along.' So, she does.

Angelus: 'I could never live in a rat-infested stinkhole like this, pardon me for saying so. But I gotta have meself a proper bed or I'm a terror.'

Darla: 'I can feel this body dying, Lindsey. I can feel it decaying moment by moment. It's being eaten away by this thing inside. It's a cancer, this soul.'

Notes: 'He won't last. I give it a century, tops.' An absolute 24-carat masterpiece which forms, with its Buffy counterpart, 'Fool for Love', a movie-length epic with scope (almost four hundred years) and truly magnificent themes of lust and passion. That shot of Angelus, Darla, Drusilla and Spike, striding amidst the chaos of the Boxer Rebellion as if they owned the world, is TV history in the making. Staggeringly dramatic and chilling.

Wesley tells Angel that 'you yourself wandered for a hundred years without ever seeking redemption', to which Angel replies, 'I sought her.' The first implication that he continued to consort with Darla after he regained his soul (see **18**, 'Five By Five'). Angel tells Darla: 'There is a Hell, a few of them. I've been to one.' (see *Buffy*: 'Becoming'

Part 2). A great bit of continuity confirms what Angel told Darla in *Buffy*: 'Angel', that the last time they met, she was wearing a kimono. It is implied that in Darla's human life she was a prostitute (see **31**, 'The Trial') as well as being an unmarried woman 'of some property'. Angel is an accomplished artist, as previously seen in *Buffy*: 'Passion'. Angel Investigations now owns a smart Panasonic video camera (see **15**, 'The Prodigal'). Sue, the Wolfram & Hart property manager, helped Cordelia identify Darla's location after Cordy spun a cock-and-bull story about her older ('like four hundred years older') sister and her mom and dad being in a coma. Darla is being housed in Unit 319 of a condo under the cover of Annapolis Olive Oil Import and Export. Darla, Angel remembers, always loved a view, as well as the finest silks and linens. Spike got the scar on his left eyebrow from the Chinese Slayer in 1900. Lindsey may be a Catholic; certainly he wears a cross. The extermination area for Wolfram & Hart is at an abandoned bank at Figueroa and Ninth (located in the South Park area of L.A.).

Soundtrack: Excellent dramatic score by Robert Fral.

Did You Know?: 'It's just me and a guitar, so I'm not going to be doing a lot of Smashing Pumpkins,' James Marsters told the press concerning his debut performances as Acoustic-Rock God at 14 Below in Santa Monica on 13 July 2000, opening for Barry Williams (Greg from *The Brady Bunch*). 'I do Tom Waits, Neil Young, Bob Dylan. Songs written for just voice and guitar. I wish I could do Johnny Lee Hooker, but I'm not that good.' James was also a huge hit at the N2K convention in London when he entertained a sizeable audience with a set of covers and original material. He subsequently played some dates supporting Four Star Mary.

Tim Minear's References: Tim views the flashback approach used in this episode and 'Fool for Love' as akin to the one popularised by Quentin Tarantino, as he told *E! Online*: '*Pulp Fiction* starts off in that coffee shop with Tim Roth and Amanda Plummer. And at the end of the movie we're in this coffee shop with John Travolta and Sam

Jackson and we see Tim and Amanda in a booth across the way and they're having the conversation they had at the beginning of the movie. We realise that this is the same time and place. It's a different story happening in the same universe.' On the subject of the romance between Darla and Angel, Tim noted: 'A hundred and fifty years of being with somebody, that's what I call having a history. But at no time was I trying to play this as being Angel's true love. It's like *Who's Afraid of Virginia Woolf*, this troubled, old married couple with secrets.' Tim also pointed out that we've seen this type of split storytelling with twin points of view in Anne Rice's novels *Interview with the Vampire* and *The Vampire Lestat*.

Timeline Revisited: So much information is revealed in this episode (and *Buffy*: 'Fool for Love') that it's worth taking stock *and* giving praise to the writers as, the identity of Spike's sire aside (see **Logic, Let Me Introduce You to This Window**), the continuity is spot on.

Born as Liam in 1725 (**15**, 'The Prodigal'), Angelus was sired by Darla in 1753 (*Buffy*: 'Becoming' Part 1). According to her, '[Angelus's] name would already be legend in his home village, if he had left anyone alive there to tell.' Afterwards the pair travelled. ('We cut a bloody swath through South Wales and Northern England,' notes Darla. 'Yorkshire men, tough as leather,' adds Angelus.) They met Darla's sire, The Master, in London in 1760. Although Angelus insulted The Master and the pair left as enemies, at some stage there must have been a reconciliation as The Master remembers him fondly in *Buffy*: 'Angel'. Thereafter they swept across Europe (they plan to go to Naples) creating mayhem and death wherever they went. On some occasions they operated alone, as when Angelus sired Penn (**11**, 'Somnambulist') in the late 1700s, or when he was in Dublin in 1838 (*Buffy*: 'Amends'). They were together in 1860 in London when Darla found Drusilla, a girl with frightening psychic ability, and Angelus stalked her, killed her family and finally sired her (*Buffy*: 'Lie to Me', *Buffy*: 'Becoming' Part I, **27**, 'Dear Boy') and in the same city in 1880 when the young poet, William, was sired by Drusilla

(*Buffy*: 'Fool for Love'). The gang then hid in Yorkshire, fleeing London barely ahead of an angry mob, largely due to William's outrageous exploits.

In Borsa, Romania in 1898, after killing a Kalderash Romany gypsy, Angelus was cursed to regain his soul (*Buffy*: 'Becoming' Part 1) and, although Darla's initial reaction was to destroy him (**18**, 'Five By Five') Angel, with his soul intact, rejoined them in China during the Boxer Rebellion in 1900 (*Buffy*: 'School Hard', 'Fool for Love') where Spike killed the then-current Vampire Slayer. However, when Angel saved a missionary family from Darla and refused to feed from a baby, she once again rejected him. It's possible they met on at least one further occasion (in *Buffy*: 'Angel' he says that he last saw Darla in Budapest at the turn of the century). Instead he travelled to America and was there during the depression in the 1930s (**1**, 'City Of'). He lived in Los Angeles in 1952 (**24**, 'Are You Now or Have You Ever Been?') and New York in 1996 (*Buffy*: 'Becoming' Part 1) before travelling to Sunnydale.

Critique: 'The real hero of this episode is [Tim] Minear,' wrote Ed Gross in *SFX*. 'Armed with the show's always amazing crew, he manages to present a tremendous sense of scope . . . but never a sense of frugalness.'

30
The Shroud of Rahmon

US Transmission Date: 21 November 2000
UK Transmission Date: 23 February 2001 (Sky),
27 July 2002 (Channel 4)

Writer: Jim Kouf
Director: David Grossman
Cast: W Earl Brown (James Menlo), Dwayne L Barnes (Lester),
R Emery Bright (Detective Turlock),
Tom Kiesche (Detective Broomfield), Tony Todd (Demon),
Robert Dolan (Bob), Michael Hagy (Jay-Don),
Jim Hanna (Surveillance Cop 1), Danny Ricardo (First Cop)

When Gunn's cousin Lester falls in with a group of supernatural thieves who are planning to rob a museum of the Shroud of Rahmon Gunn and Angel infiltrate the gang. Wesley discovers that the shroud is reputed to hold the power of a demon who could cause madness, and fears that Angel could be affected by it.

It's a Designer Label!: Cordelia got her new, short (Courtney Cox style) haircut ten days ago. Neither Wesley nor Angel noticed. Gunn's '555 Soul Brooklyn' sweatshirt. Wesley spilled shrimp and cocktail sauce down Cordy's top at the 'shallow soul-sucking Hollywood party' he took her to. Wesley knows of Jay-Don's reputation for being loud and extravagantly flashy. Presumably it's he that comes up with the awful clothes that Angel wears: a lime-green shirt and electric-blue trousers. Kate's blood-red leather jacket, Wesley's drawstring pants.

References: Jay-Don is said to have been part of the 'Sinatra Rat Pack-thing,' referring to the showbusinesses partnership of Frank Sinatra, Dean Martin, Peter Lawford, Sammy Davis Jr and Joey Bishop. The group originally sprang up around Humphrey Bogart, whose wife Lauren Bacall christened them. Angel uses Joey Tribbiani's catchphrase from *Friends*, 'How *you* doin'?' Also Altoids breath mints, Elvis Presley, Hong Kong action star Chow Yun-Fat (*Crouching Tiger, Hidden Dragon*), Jimmy Webb's 'MacArthur Park', the University of New Mexico, the Los Angeles County Museum of Art, the Museum of Contemporary Art, the Gene Autry Museum of Western History and the Southern California Museum of Natural History. The shroud itself is obviously influenced by the Shroud of Turin which for centuries was purported to be the burial garment of Christ. Preserved since 1578 in the Cathedral of San Giovanni Battista in Turin, it features two faint images of a gaunt, sunken-eyed, 5-foot 7-inch man and contains markings that roughly correspond to the stigmata of Jesus. First historically recorded when put on display by Templar Knight Geoffroi de Charnay in 1389, it was contemporaneously denounced as fake by the Bishop of Troyes. In 1988 the origin of the cloth itself was finally determined by carbon-dating as between 1260 and 1390.

The taping of the door-lock at the museum and its subsequent discovery by Wesley may be a subtle reference to the way in which the 1972 Watergate break-in was discovered (see *All the President's Men* for further details).

Bitch!: Cordy jealously asks Wes if he's been to 'yet another glamourous celebrity-filled gala with Miss Virginia Bryce?' (see **28**, 'Guise Will Be Guise'). Plus her cry of 'back seat surfer!'

When Gunn sarcastically asks if he should knit while Angel tackles the case, Angel replies that he'd like a sweater ('something dark').

The Charisma Show: Cordelia, on sacrificing virgins: 'This has nothing to do with purity. [It's] all about dominance, buddy. You can bet if someone ordered a male body part for religious sacrifice, the world would be atheist like *that* [snaps fingers].'

And, on Angel: '*Au contraire*. His day is packed. Brood about Darla. Brood about Darla. Lunch. Followed by a little Darla-brooding.'

Vegas-Speak: Angel: 'You look sharp. That plastic surgeon, did he give you the big rebate?' And: 'Whoa, we need to talk, bro. Two things bringin' in the chicks, the dough and the ride.' And: 'Like the shirt. Where'd you get it, *Ed's Big and Spiny*?' And: 'Fellas. Cool your jets.'

Jay-Don: 'Nobody touches the glasses and the hair, doll.'

Lester: 'See how they do? They mess with your mind, man!' Gunn: 'Yo, spill it! We ain't got all night.'

Not Exactly A Haven For The Bruthas: Gunn, on vampires: 'Nothing but take, take, take. Take your blood, take your sister.'

Cigarettes and Alcohol: Bob smokes and drinks what looks like gin during the planning meeting.

'You May Remember Me From Such Films and TV Series As . . .': Dwayne L Barnes was in *Swimsuit: The Movie*, *Helicopter* and *Menace II Society*. R Emery Bright appears in *The Corner*. W Earl Brown played Kenny the Cameraman in *Scream*. His other movies include *Being John*

Malkovitch, Vanilla Sky, Vampire in Brooklyn and *Backdraft*. Robert Dolan was in *Bleach* while Tom Kiesche can be seen in *The Animal, Chicago Hope* and *18 Wheels of Justice*. Tony Todd played both Kurn, Worf's brother, and the older Jake Sisko in *Star Trek: Deep Space Nine*, Captain Darrow in *The Rock*, Ben in *Night of the Living Dead*, Cecrops in *Xena: Warrior Princess* and the title character in *Candyman* and its sequels. He was also in *Final Destination, Stir, Bird* and *Platoon*.

Don't Give Up The Day Job: Jim Hanna was a gag-writer for comedian Dennis Miller before acting in movies such as *North Beach* and *A Murder of Crows*.

Logic, Let Me Introduce You to This Window: When Jay-Don turns to look at Angel you can see his reflection in the bus he's standing next to. Similarly, when Angel walks into the vault, his full body reflection can be seen on the metal door. Nitroglycerine is so unstable that when it falls it should have exploded on Angel's foot. Since the reliability of Angel's sense of smell has been well-documented and he insisted that he would recognise Darla's scent, how could Angel mistake Kate for Darla in his hotel room? Why is Jay-Don on a downtown (i.e. local) bus in L.A. if he's arrived direct from Vegas? Menlo says that they need Angel to walk into the vault because any change in air temperature would trigger the alarm. But when the door opened, that would change the temperature anyway. The shroud is encased in consecrated wood, so why doesn't it burn Angel? Watch Kate's hair at the museum: two completely different styles that alternate depending on the shot. How does Angel, who never goes to the movies (according to himself), know who Chow Yun-Fat is? See, also, Angel's stated admiration for Denzel Washington and Charlton Heston.

I Just *Love* Your Accent: Wesley: 'I'm quite good with the ladies myself, you know.'

Quote/Unquote: Cordelia: 'Two words I don't like right off the bat. Tomb and unearthed.'

Wesley, on Angel: 'He helps people. When he's not in trouble himself.'

Angel, to Kate: 'Look at you rushing in here all by
yourself. You're the best cop ever.'
Notes: 'I'm not big on shrouds, they're an after-you-die
outfit.' Dramatically uncertain, bookended by the scenes of
Wesley being interrogated by the cops, this is one of the
weaker stories in a generally impressive run. The structure
is interesting but the characters are one-dimensional and
the Wesley/Cordelia subplot feels very artificial.

Angel notes that scared humans taste salty. Wesley
refers to Angel having recently taken human blood (see
Buffy: 'Graduation Day' Part 2). Cordelia searches the
website of the *Los Angeles Globe Register* (see **2**, 'Lonely
Heart'). Kate has two photos of her father on her desk.
The shroud was dyed with the blood of seven virgins
sacrificed on a full moon and then placed over the powerful
demon, Rahmon, preventing its resurrection. The box
containing it is lined with lead, which dampens the
shroud's effect. In 1803 the shroud was removed from its
casing and the entire population of El Incanto went insane,
mothers and children hacking one another to pieces, men
roaming the streets like rabid dogs. Detective Carlson (see
27, 'Dear Boy') is mentioned.

Did You Know?: Joss Whedon has a bone to pick with 20th
Century Fox, the studio behind *Angel*, as well as James
Cameron's flashy SF drama *Dark Angel*. Fox's decision to
put the Jessica Alba vehicle on Tuesday nights at 9 p.m.
resulted in a ratings decline for *Angel*. Whedon was out for
blood, as he told *TV Guide*: 'The fact that they put [*Dark
Angel*] on opposite a show that they produce, thereby
hurting it, shows that they really don't care. Their big
picture is clearly so big that whatever I'm doing doesn't
matter. I resent that. But I am not the "Big Picture Guy".
I'm just making my shows.' Marc Berman, TV analyst for
Mediaweek, agrees, calling Fox's scheduling of *Dark Angel*
'one of the less logical moves last fall'. In fact, by dividing
the young adult audience, he believes both shows are
suffering: 'Although *Dark Angel* has carved a niche for
itself, had *Angel* not been in the mix *Dark Angel*'s ratings
might be even stronger.' Despite his frustration, Whedon

insists that he hasn't asked Fox to move *Dark Angel*. 'I have no control over that,' he says. 'I am not someone that can say, 'Work your schedule'. As long as I get to make my shows, the people who want to watch them will.'

31
The Trial

US Transmission Date: 28 November 2000
UK Transmission Date: 2 March 2001 (Sky),
3 August 2002 (Channel 4)

Writer: Douglas Petrie & Tim Minear
Story: David Greenwalt
Director: Bruce Seth Green
Cast: Jim Piddock (Valet), Evan Arnold (Vampire)[20]

Angel must choose between watching Darla die from a terminal illness or giving her eternal life by turning her into a vampire again. He seeks The Host's advice and is told that he can submit to three deadly trials in order to win a new life for her. He accepts and survives but, because Darla has already had one 'second chance', her fate is sealed. As Angel and Darla decide to live out her remaining days together, Lindsey and his thugs burst in on them with Drusilla, who sires Darla by force.

Dudes and Babes: Darla is at her most toe-curlingly lovely here. And then just when you think it can't get any better, Drusilla turns up for a final twenty seconds of vampire lust.

Denial, Thy Name is Angel: Angel spends the episode denying what Darla is, putting himself through abject torture (the holy water bit is graphically *horrible*). And for what? There's no redemption for Darla, nor for Angel himself who ends up grovelling in the dirt watching Drusilla vampirise Darla again. 'How did you *think* this would end?' asks Linsdey, cynically. But the point of the

---

trial (and the valet perceptively spots this) is that Angel doesn't have time to consider consequences before acting and does so from his sense of obligation, rightly or (in this case) wrongly.

It's a Designer Label!: The Host's leopardskin shirt and Cordelia's large earrings.

References: *Survivor* ('after four hundred years of death and destruction, seems to me you get voted off the island'), *The Prisoner* ('*that* would be telling'), The Host quotes David Bowie's 'Space Oddity' ('Ground Control to Major Tom') and WB Yeats's 'The Second Coming' ('Things fall apart'). The vampire wears a Metallica T-shirt and mentions Anne Rice's novels. Angel calls the valet 'Jeeves' after the butler in PG Wodehouse's Bertie Wooster stories. The trials themselves seem influenced by *Indiana Jones and the Last Crusade*, not to mention *The Matrix* and a huge towering slab of Christ imagery.

Locations: The Royal Viking is a real motel on West 3rd Street ('conveniently located mere steps from scenic skid row').

Bitch!: Cordelia, to Angel: 'You lied to us.' Angel: 'I figured you'd nag.' Cordelia, to Darla: 'You're planning on sleeping over?' Darla: 'I'm dying.' Cordelia: 'So just for the one night then?'

Cordelia, to Darla: 'You're a prisoner.' Wesley: 'I'd have to concur with that.' Cordelia: 'You've got our friend all in knots.' Wesley: 'Can't say we like you much.' Cordelia: 'So, sorry about the dying, but if you try to escape we *will* hit you.' Wesley: 'On the head.' Cordelia: 'With very large and heavy objects. OK?'

L.A.-Speak: Angel: 'Something in a koi pond? They're very Zen.'

Gunn: 'Don't envy that particular talent. Not based on what I'm gettin' with just my standard issue human smeller. Man, not even for free cable.'

Angel: 'Where are you going?' Darla: 'Not back in there, everyone saw me leave with the mullet. Try something on the Westside, I guess.'

Darla: 'Is this how a guy like you gets his rocks off?'

Not Exactly A Haven For The Bruthas: Gunn proudly displays his wide ranging knowledge of L.A.'s low-rent hotels.

Cigarettes and Alcohol: The Host regrets his barman Ramone's betrayal of Angel in **28**, 'Guise Will Be Guise' and mentions what stunning Seabreezes he made (see **27**, 'Dear Boy'). He says, enigmatically, that Ramone is 'off the menu', which may imply he was killed for his treachery though personally I reckon The Host's far too nice for anything like that, and merely sacked him.

Darla drinks red wine with the vampire who is drinking beer. Lindsey, meanwhile is on the whisky while waiting in his apartment for Angel.

Sex and Drugs and Rock'n'Roll: Linsdey says that Darla was a working girl in the New World (see **29**, 'Darla') and was (and is again) dying from a syphilitic heart condition ('Today something like that could be cleared up with a few antibiotics, if you catch it in time. We're about a month and four hundred years too late.'). Cordelia, to Angel: 'You seem all calm and homey. Are you on drugs?'

Don't Give Up The Day Job: British actor Jim Priddock, best known as Hal Conway in *Mad About You*, and for roles in *Multiplicity*, *Independence Day*, *Lethal Weapon 2*, *Fame*, *Max Headroom* and *Coach*, is also a writer with credits on *One Good Turn* and *Traces of Red*.

Logic, Let Me Introduce You to This Window: How does Angel know where Lindsey lives? How did Angelus escape from the burning barn and the lynch mob in 1765? Gunn seems to have forgiven Angel remarkably quickly for attacking Kate. Angel tells Wes and Cordy that he's always had a connection to those he sired. So, why doesn't he realise Drusilla is in town? In the scene with Angel and The Host, notice The Host gets handed his drink twice. You can see a harness during the scene where Angel bisects the demon. Angel spits up blood while he's in chains but the blood is gone in the next shot. Drusilla cuts her chest with her fingernail, but the line of blood is above her finger.

I Just *Love* Your Accent: Cordy says that she thought Wesley was going to be a man and talk to Angel about his obsession with Darla. 'I was a man. I said . . . things,' notes Wesley, like: 'Did he prefer milk or sugar in his tea? It's how men talk about things in England.'

The valet uses cricketing euphemisms: 'You fielded our strokes from end to end. My hat's off to you, sir.'

Quote/Unquote: Darla, on Wolfram & Hart: 'I know a thing or two about mind games, we played them together for over a century.' Cordelia: 'But you were just soulless bloodsucking demons, they're lawyers.' Angel: 'She's right. We were amateurs.'

Angel: 'Do you love her Lindsey? Is that what this is? Look at you. A few months with her and you go all schoolboy. I was with her a hundred and fifty years.' Lindsey: 'But you never loved her.' Angel: 'I wasn't capable of it. And neither are you.'

Angelus: 'Don't these people know who we are?' Darla: 'I think they do, which would explain the lynch mob.'

Notes: 'Isn't the world a better place with you in it? You can save so many people. It seems she can barely save herself.' A cunning episode, though with a very shaky premise which turns out to be a huge MacGuffin designed purely to turn Darla bad again. Some lovely touches however (love Darla trying to get the really stupid vampire she meets in a bar to sire her, particularly his pride that he has been 'an eternal creature of the night' since 1992; full of sex metaphors and hints of impotence).

Angel does his own laundry, using a washer/dryer in the hotel basement. He mentions a vampire hunter named Holtz who chased him and Darla in France in 1765 and who Angel insists wasn't mortal. When Darla clobbered Angel and left him in the burning barn she said she hoped they would meet again in Vienna if he survived. Before France, Darla and Angelus were in Italy (they were planning to go to Naples when they left The Master five years previously, see **29**, 'Darla'). Angel, with a horribly prophetic edge, wanted to try his luck in Romania next. Darla recalls that Angel was 'made in an alley' (see *Buffy*: 'Becoming' Part 1). Angel and The Host discuss the events of **28**, 'Guise Will Be Guise' ('You sent me to that swami who was dead and his impostor tried to kill me? Why would I be testy about that?'). Angel is invited into Lindsey's home. Lindsey seems to collect cubist art. Wesley reads the business section of the *Los Angeles Times*.

Soundtrack: Julie Benz sings a glorious version of Arlan and Koehler's standard 'Ill Wind (You're Blowing Me No Good)', recorded by Ella Fitzgerald and Billie Holliday among others.

Did You Know?: In August 2000, it was widely reported that David Boreanaz was suing the driver of a car that crashed into his on 3 August 1999. According to the Los Angeles Superior Court lawsuit, Oren Kaniel's Mazda ran into the actor's Mercedes Benz on the Ventura Freeway. Boreanaz alleged that he was 'hurt and injured in his health, strength, and activity', and suffered 'injury to [his] nervous system'. The injuries 'have caused and will continue to cause [me] great physical, mental, and emotional pain, anguish, and suffering', Boreanaz claimed. Boreanaz does have a stunt double for the more serious on-set battles but he claims that his injuries prevent him 'from attending his usual occupation, thereby suffering a loss of earnings and profits, as well as a loss of earning capacity'.

Christian Kane's Comments: Christian, interviewed by *Entertainment Weekly Online*, was asked why his law firm doesn't have evil-paramedics on call to reattach Lindsey's severed hand. 'Exactly,' noted the actor. 'I'm rich as hell, I've raised someone from the dead and I've got a five dollar prosthetic hand. I complain about that rubber hand every day. But the producers have a reason for everything. The coolest thing about being on a show that deals with fantasy is, even if you die, that doesn't mean you're off the show. But my fantasy plotline is, Lindsey gets super powers. He ditches the rubber hand and gets a metal claw. And a leather jacket. And he's a badass.' (See **40**, 'Dead End'.)

32
Reunion

US Transmission Date: 19 December 2000
UK Transmission Date: 9 March 2001 (Sky),
10 August 2002 (Channel 4)

Writers: Tim Minear, Shawn Ryan
Director: James A Contner
Cast: Stephanie Manglaras (Landlord), Karen Tucker (Female Shopper),
Erik Liberman (Erik), Katherine Ann McGregor (Catherine Manners),
Michael Rotonoi (Burly Guy)

Angel searches for Darla's corpse, hoping to stake her
before she rises. But he's too late and Drusilla and Darla
go on a killing spree in L.A. Angel breaks into Wolfram &
Hart but Holland has him arrested. Kate frees him saying
she cannot stop the vampires alone. Angel learns that the
pair plan to massacre the attendees at Holland's wine-
tasting party. Angel arrives and decides that he isn't
interested in saving the lawyers from their own creations,
locking them in with Darla and Drusilla. Angel returns to
the hotel and reveals what he has done. Wesley, Cordelia
and Gunn are shocked; Angel tells them that they are fired.
Dudes and Babes: Darla and Dru, running amok in
downtown L.A.
It's a Designer Label!: Cordy's multicoloured dress with the
flower accessory. Gunn's orange anorak. Darla and Dru
go shopping (OK, ignore the floppy hats) and get themselves kitted out in fox furs and leather trousers.
References: Cordelia refers to General George Custer
(1839–76) who was killed by the Sioux at Little Bighorn.
Kellogg's Rice Krispies advertising slogan ('This kid's
ready to snap, crackle and pop'). Drusilla misquotes the
nursery rhyme *Mary Mary Quite Contrary* ('pretty lawyers
all in a row'). Also, *The Court Jester* ('Got it? Good.') and
Die Hard (Angel crashing through the window).
Locations: The magnificent view of downtown L.A.
from the nursery includes shots of the One Wilshire Blvd
building, the City National Bank on West 5th Street and a

sign for the Hotel Haywood Café on West 6th Street. Angel and co are seen driving along Hollywood Blvd past the Fox Theater.

Bitch!: Angel notes that the demon Morgog 'couldn't find his way to his hairy spine-hump without a road map'.

Angel, on Drusilla: 'She's a classicist.' Cordelia: 'She's a loony.'

'West Hollywood?': In the episode's best scene, Darla tenderly strokes Dru's hair to comfort her when she's upset. A bigot gets out of his car and shouts: 'Why don't you and your girlfriend take the make-out session on home? The rest of us have lives.' Followed, to the delight of anti-homophobes everywhere, by his very timely death.

L.A.-Speak: Gunn: 'Man, that weirds me out more than the whole blood-sucking thing.'

Cordelia: 'Way too many pronouns here.'

Cigarettes and Alcohol: Holland plans to uncork a case of 1928 Chateau Latour. Drusilla drank it once and thinks it tasted like lion's blood.

Sex and Drugs and Rock'n'Roll: A *slash*-fan's delight, particularly Darla asking Angel 'Come to punish us?' and Drusilla adding: 'Spank us till Tuesday. We promise to be bad if you do.' Drusilla then calls Angel 'daddy' . . . Let's not go there.

'You May Remember Me From Such Films, Playboy Videos and TV Series As . . .': Erik Liberman was 'Featured Male Talent' in *Playboy Video Centrefold*. Stephanie Manglaras was in *Love 101* and *Early Edition*.

Logic, Let Me Introduce You to This Window: It's implied that vampires first rise between sundown on the day they died and dawn the next day which flatly contradicts several *Buffy* episodes ('Welcome To The Hellmouth', 'Helpless' and 'The Freshman' spring to mind). Angel's invite into Holland's home is simply Mrs Manners saying 'Help us,' which seems rather vague. Darla is barefoot when she rises but acquires a pair of canvas shoes during the fight on the roof. Also her toenails were clear when she rose but later in the store where she and Dru were trying on clothes, they are painted red. Her hair changes dramatically between scenes. Julie Benz seems to breathe during at least one of the scenes where she's dead. When Drusilla is thrown over the car, her reflection can be seen in its finish. Similarly, when Angel is placed in the police car, the reflection of his head can be seen. Although Kate says the murders were at Panache on 5th & Hill, in Downtown, the location filming seems to be in the San Fernando Valley (possibly Sherman Oaks) judging by the telephone numbers glimpsed on several store fronts. When Angel sprawls on the couch, one angle has his hand in a fist on the arm of the chair. Another has it hanging over the edge. Angel's convertible has no rear view mirror. After Cordy's vision, Angel spins his car around. Skid marks from earlier takes can be seen on the street. When Drusilla attacks Angel, he had previously uncovered Darla's face. However in the subsequent shot she's shrouded again. Wesley calls Los Angeles 'a city of ten million people'. It's still closer to fifteen (see **29**, 'Darla'), but he's getting warmer.

I Just *Love* Your Accent: Lindsey's former landlord describes his 'cousin', Drusilla, as 'that sweet, but very odd English girl who was visiting him.'

Quote/Unquote: Angel: 'I'd be careful who you offer your hand to, Mr Manners. You might just lose it. Isn't that right, Lindsey?'

Lilah, seeing Darla's corpse, asks Lindsey: 'Think maybe *now* you've got a shot with her?'

Angel: 'You set things in motion, play your little games up here in your glass and chrome tower and people die. Innocent people.' Holland: 'And yet, I just can't seem to care.'

Wesley: 'The three of us are all that's standing between you and real darkness.' Angel: 'You're all fired.'

Notes: 'Angel, people are going to die.' 'And yet, somehow, I just can't seem to care.' Holy crud, what a *stunning* climax. It's a good episode up to that point, but the final three or four scenes are something else entirely. A majestic reformatting of the series and the start of a new story-arc that takes the series into some dark corners.

Cordelia refers to the vampire detectors in the Wolfram & Hart offices, seen in **21**, 'Blind Date'. Angel says Drusilla 'spent hours in my garden in Sunnydale, communing with the night sky', referring to the 'Angelus-arc' in *Buffy*'s second season. Drusilla previously sang the 'lamb is caught in the blackberry patch' song in *Buffy*: 'Lie to Me'. Angel abandons Holland to Drusilla and Darla in much the same way as he left Judy and the occupants of the Hyperion Hotel to the Thesulac in **24**, 'Are You Now or Have You Ever Been?' Angel previously threatened to fire Cordelia in **26**,'Untouched'. Drusilla has a mobile phone, though she sometimes forgets she has it and thinks she is ringing all by herself. Holland's job title is division head of the Special Projects department.

Soundtrack: Fear Factory's 'Shock'.

Critique: 'Relying for the most part on audience anticipation, 'Reunion' boasts the stunt quotient for an entire season of most shows,' *Xposé*'s Brian Barratt noted. 'There's a deal of ambiguity concerning the final massacre ... but that certainly works in the show's favour.'

Did You Know?: The location used for the arrest of Angel was a gas station close to Warner Brothers' studio in Burbank. Extra Dan Smiczek (see **17**, 'Eternity') played one of the police officers. 'In all it was two quick takes. For the second our timing was slightly adjusted but everything went as expected,' notes Dan. 'All in all an entertaining experience. I got to see some friends. But most of all, now I have visions of Julie Benz running around barefoot, grunting, and kicking ass. What more can you ask for?' What indeed?

33
Redefinition

US Transmission Date: 16 January 2001
UK Transmission Date: 16 March 2001 (Sky),
17 August 2002 (Channel 4)

Writer: Mere Smith
Director: Michael Grossman
Cast: Nicolas Surovy (Wolfram & Hart Executive),
Joel Stoffer (Vampire 1), Brad Kalas (EMT), Jamie McShane (Demon),
David Wolfson (Bartender)

Cordelia, Wesley and Gunn go their separate ways as Angel prepares himself for war with Darla and Drusilla. Lindsey and Lilah survive the bloodbath at Holland's home. Darla and Dru begin to recruit demon muscle while Cordelia, Wesley and Gunn all (independently) end up at Caritas. As Darla and Drusilla meet with their prospective recruits Angel has a surprise in store for them.

Denial, Thy Name is Darla: Notice how testy Darla gets when the subject of Angel is raised. 'Not everything is about Angel,' she notes.

Denial, Thy Name is Lindsey: Lindsey tells Lilah that, as the only survivors of a massacre, it's natural they're under suspicion. 'You know what I don't like about suspicion?' Lilah asks. 'The part where they find us two weeks from now, dead in some freak accident.' Lindsey insists that they did nothing wrong and that he was following orders. 'You *honestly* think that matters?' she continues, 'Indulge your denial. Don't doubt for a minute someone's gonna pay. And we're the only ones left.'

It's a Designer Label!: Darla's black dragon-design high-collared dress and Drusilla's pink sweater are obvious highlights. Also, Wesley's mustard jacket and The Host's blue suit. Sharp.

References: *Taxi Driver* (Angel training, and the voice-over). At the bar, Wesley considers singing something by 60s songwriter Cat Stevens ('I Love My Dog', 'Matthew and Son', 'The First Cut is the Deepest') while Cordelia is torn between Madonna and Shania Twain. Also, *Godzilla*, Drusilla alludes to the poem 'And Then There Were None', Wesley misquotes The Beatles' 'Let it Be' and there's a quote from Space's 'Neighbourhood'. Visual references to *Fight Club*. A tapestry map of the solar system adorns Caritas.

Locations mentioned include Beverly Hills (Cordelia asks whether there are any demon hideouts there; Wesley notes there are several) and San Pedro. La Cienega & Washington cross each other in Culver City. It appears Caritas may be in Chinatown. Cordelia lives fifteen miles from the club, in Silver Lake.

Bitch!: Cordelia's finest hour for some time, though, given the circumstances, that may be inevitable: 'One thing you can say about Angel, at least he's consistent. It's always some little blonde driving him over the edge.'

Darla: 'During my stint as Wolfram & Hart's puppet, something occurred to me. I loathe being used. If I recall, I sent you a fifteen-body memo to that effect.'

Gunn: 'If I had to listen to you two day in, day out. Snipe, snipe, snipe. Bitch, bitch, bitch. I figure y'all got off easy, cos I would've killed ya.'

'West Hollywood': Wesley: 'My arse is *not* pansy.'

The Charisma Show: She's *fabulous* in this episode, particularly her three-way sparring with Gunn and Wes at Caritas. 'Mr Big-Mojo-Guy, [you're] supposed to give us guidance.' Wesley: 'She's right. We came, we sang, we fought the urge to regurgitate.' Cordelia: 'So, spill already. [To Wesley] Not you!'

L.A.-Speak: Gunn: 'I have a rep to maintain, all right. I can't have you all seeing through my brusque and macho exterior.' And: 'This was just a side-gig for me.'

Lilah: 'As it is, I'm just pissed.'

Wesley: 'Angel has . . .' Cordelia: '. . . pulled a total wig?'

Merl: 'Is that how you get your rocks off, you sick . . .? I heard about your girls, Godzilla, Darcilla, whatever.'

Cigarettes and Alcohol: At Caritas, Wesley orders a Bloody Mary (without real blood). Cordy ruminates on the evil qualities of Tequila as she, Gunn and Wesley get *very* drunk. Angel smokes, and uses the cigarette to blazing effect.

Sex and Drugs and Tasty Mexican Food: Cordelia: 'What are we supposed to do now?' Gunn: 'I think I'll grab a burrito before I head home.'

'You May Remember Me From Such Films and TV Series As . . .': Brad Kalas was in *Wag the Dog*, *Martial Law* and *Party of Five*. David Wolfson can be seen in *Leather Jacket*, *Love Story* and *Island Prey*. Joel Stoffer was in *Kick of Death*. Jamie McShane played Michael Jacoby in *The Census Taker*. Nicolas Surovy featured in *The Man Who Captured Eichmann*, *Breaking Free*, *Forever Young*,

Stark, Bang the Drum Slowly, For Pete's Sake, The X-Files and *Murder One*.

Logic, Let Me Introduce You to This Window: All of Angel's swordwork is performed by Mike Massa; these shots are easy to spot as he's quite a bit leaner than Boreanaz. How did Darla and Drusilla enter Wolfram & Hart? Alarms should have gone off. Merl should not have a tongue, but it can be seen as he hangs upside down over the water. Where did Angel get his hooded sweatshirt? He left the sewers wearing only a black pullover. When the Wolfram & Hart executive talks to Lindsey and Lilah, make-up can be seen on his collar. As Cordelia leaves the hotel carrying a cardboard box there are clearly some clothes in it, so why the big hump with Angel in **39**, 'Disharmony'? It's not as if he gave away anything *decent* (see **34**, 'Blood Money'). Darla's got yet another new haircut. Does she have a stylist tied up in the basement?

I Just *Love* Your Accent: Gunn (delightfully) refers to Wesley as a 'pansy-ass British guy'.

Quote/Unquote: The Host: 'I can see the maudlin segment of tonight's binge is in full swing.'

Darla: 'In a perfect world, Angel would be here right now helping me burn this city to the ground . . . But, where is he? Probably flogging himself in a church somewhere.'

Wolfram & Hart Executive, to Lindsey and Lilah: 'Not to mention the fact that both of you have been extremely negligent about informing us of visits from certain ladies who, lest we forget, *ate* the majority of our contracts department.'

Notes: 'That wasn't Angel. It wasn't Angelus either. Who *was* that?' A gorgeous continuation of the series reformatting with Angel turning really dark and sinister. Lindsey waking up amid the bodies of Darla and Dru's massacre is one of the series' great moments.

Virginia suggests that Wesley, rather than being an unemployed demon hunter is actually 'a renowned specialist in supernatural Aid-And-Rescue.' Same difference, surely? She says that her father always used union conjurers ('the wizard community is very progressive'). Since he tried to sacrifice her to Yeska (see **28**, 'Guise Will Be Guise') she hasn't spoken to him, though she is healing, thanks to a lot of therapy and a gigantic trust fund. Wesley uses Doyle's stock phrase 'fight the good fight'. The office Apple Mac seems to belong to Cordy. Lilah refers to Lindsey protecting himself by stealing Wolfram & Hart secrets in **21**, 'Blind Date' and there's a reference to Bethany Chaulk (see **26**, 'Untouched'). Lindsey and Lilah are promoted to joint Acting Co-Vice Presidents of Special Projects.

Soundtrack: The instrumental tracks 'Call it Away' and 'Bleeder' by Paul Trudeau and 'Activity' by Mark Dold. Andy Hallett's epic rendition of LaBelle's bordello classic 'Lady Marmalade (Voulez-Vous Coucher Avec Moi, Ce Soir?)'. Cordelia, Gunn and Wesley's frightful massacre of Queen's turgid rocker, 'We Are the Champions'.

Did You Know?: Julie Benz's hobbies? As she told Paul Simpson and Ruth Thomas: 'I started learning golf. I have two border collies that I spend a lot of time with, and my husband, of course. We love going to the movies. The new obsession, and this is really cheesy, but I taught myself how to crochet this summer, and I've been making scarves and blankets and things like that. I'm working on a scarf for David, since he requested one. It's a great thing for me to do on set, with all the downtime we have. It keeps my energy up, keeps me focused. I think they put some sort of addictive chemical into the yarn.'

Mere Smith's Comments: 'Angel has moved away from his mission,' Mere told the *Posting Board*. 'His withdrawal from humanity makes him less human, more of a death machine. Same thing goes for all those soldiers that committed atrocities like My Lai [during the Vietnam War]. Angel is disconnecting at this point. Setting the girls on fire is a particularly distanced way of hurting/killing them.'

34
Blood Money

US Transmission Date: 23 January 2001
UK Transmission Date: 23 March 2001 (Sky),
24 August 2002 (Channel 4)

Writers: Shawn Ryan and Mere Smith
Director: RD Price
Cast: Mark Rolston (Boone), Jeffrey Patrick Dean (Dwight),
R Martin Klein (Husband), Jason Padgett (Holden),
Jennifer Roe (Serena), Deborah Carson (Liza)

Angel discovers that Wolfram & Hart are stealing large
contributions that were intended to go to a teen shelter run
by former Sunnydale resident Anne Steele. Rather than
resort to violence, Angel calls their bluff and exposes the
firm's criminal activities. Meanwhile, after their sacking,
Wesley, Gunn and Cordelia set up on their own.
Dudes and Babes: Boone is an eternal demon with blue
skin, enormous strength and resistance to pain. He has
steel coils that wrap around his hands. He is, in short,
pretty damn hard.
It's a Designer Label!: Angel gives away the clothes that
Cordelia left at the hotel to Anne's shelter (see **39**,
'Disharmony'), including the multicoloured top seen in **32**,
'Reunion'. Wes's crimson shirt, Cordy's bathrobe and fluffy
slippers, Anne's short skirt and extremely tight black jeans,
Cordelia's red dress and Lilah's slinky black evening gown.
References: On the videotape seen at the ball, Cordelia is
parodying a series of adverts for milk, which had celebri-
ties saying 'mmm … milk' or wearing a milk moustache.
Among those who took part were Sarah Michelle Gellar
and David Boreanaz. Wesley does a cute Sean Connery
impression. Wesley and Gunn play the board game Risk.
Also, the IRS, French dictator Napoléon Bonaparte
(1769–1821), *Dirty Harry* ('I got to know') and Emily Post
(1873–1960), the American authority on etiquette.
Bitch!: Boone tells Lindsey that, when Angel comes for
him, he will find Boone instead. Lindsey replies: 'I like it

and I'll tell you why. Because of the *finding you instead* part.'

'West Hollywood?': When actress, Serena, is asked 'this thing with making your character gay, is that like all about ratings?' it's a fairly obvious allusion to the controversy surrounding Willow's relationship with Tara on *Buffy*.

The Alexis and J August Show: Best bit of the episode is the little sequence of Wesley and Gunn telling Cordelia how they fought the fire-breathing demon (Wesley: 'Gunn hits him from behind, yelling, "Look at us when we kill you!" And both the heads turn . . .').

The Charisma Show: Cordelia as rap diva ('I've-got-a-gun-and-my-name-is-Gunn!')

L.A.-Speak: Gunn: 'Who's your ruler, baby? *What's my name?*'

Cigarettes and Alcohol: Cordelia, Wesley and Gunn drink cans of beer. There's a lot of champagne being drunk at the Highway Robbery Ball.

Sex and Drugs and Rock'n'Roll: One of the cast strips to their underwear. Unfortunately, it's Wesley.

'You May Remember Me From Such Films and TV Series As . . .': Julia Lee played the title role in *Ophelia Learns to Swim*. She was also in *Diablo* and *Charmed*. Gerry Becker was Stanley in *Man on the Moon*, Nixon on *Ally McBeal* and also appeared in *Stonewall*, *Hoffa*, *Mickey Blue Eyes* and *Donnie Brasco*. Mark Rolston played Gus Grissom in *From the Earth to the Moon* and Bogs Diamond in *The Shawshank Redemption* and was in *Rush Hour*, *Humanoids from the Deep* and *Aliens*. Jeffrey Patrick Dean's movies include *Snitch* and *.com for Murder*. Jason Padgett played Travis in *Dream Trap*. R Martin Klein provides the voice for Gomamon in *Digimon*.

Logic, Let Me Introduce You to This Window: Boone mentions an altercation he had with Angel in the 1920s over a señorita. This is probably a lie but it's surprising that Wolfram & Hart don't pick up on it, given the nature of Angel's curse. When Lilah introduces the stars of *Life Lessons*, she mentions four actors but the doors open behind her and six people emerge. Merl has an Apple Mac and several other bits of electronic equipment in his sewer lair. But has he got electricity?

I Just *Love* Your Accent: Gunn calls Wesley by the nickname 'English' for the first time.

Quote/Unquote: Lilah: 'What if this guy is as good as he says and actually kills Angel?' Lindsey: 'Boo-hoo. Let me wipe away the tears with my *plastic hand.*'

Merl, after Lilah becomes the third person in the episode to attack him in his lair: 'Jeez, does *everyone* know where I live?'

Angel: 'What did Lindsey say about me?' Anne: 'That you were a bad man. A psychotic vampire who cut off his hand, harassed his firm and is borderline schizophrenic. I was giving you the short version.'

Notes: 'The game. It's actually kind of fun when you know the rules. When you know that there aren't any. You screw with me . . . And now I get to screw with you.' A story about the ethics of revenge, 'Blood Money' is a bit like wading through a putrid swamp to find a couple of gold nuggets. Angel using everyone in sight to play his mind games with Lilah and Lindsey is rather disturbing, though this is counterbalanced by a beautiful, hard-edged little turn by Julia Lee, the debut of the excellent Gerry Becker and lots of cool TV industry jokes ('I'm not buying the make-up').

There's a reference to Cordelia having designed the business cards for the company (Gunn's opinion that the logo looks like 'a lobster with a growth' echoes Kate's in **2**, 'Lonely Heart'). Merl complains about Angel nearly drowning him in **33**, 'Redefinition'. When Anne finds out that Angel is a vampire she notes: 'A few years ago it would have been a big turn on. I thought vampires were the coolest . . . Then I met one.' This is a basic summation of the events of *Buffy*: 'Lie To Me' (the vampire she met being Spike). Anne (then known as Chanterelle), briefly met Angel when he, Xander and Willow visited Billy Fordham's vampire club, but they don't seem to recognise each other here. Serena notes that Wesley is the guy dating Virginia Bryce (see **28**, 'Guise Will Be Guise'). Merl likes Chinese takeaway food, but has bad taste in furniture. The

Wolfram & Hart vampire detector (see **21**, 'Blind Date') is called Zorn. Anne works for the East Hills Teen Centre on Crenshaw Street. According to Anne's driving licence, her address is 5632 Willoughby Ave, Los Angeles. The video played at the charity ball is captioned Holland Manners 1951–2000. The stars participating in the *Big Hold Up* are from the hit TV show *Life Lessons*: Serena Tate, Jordan Johns, Holden Raynes and CJ McCade. Nathan tells Lindsey and Lilah about Angel's true purpose. That he is to be a major player in the forthcoming Apocalypse. The only grey area is which side he'll be on.

During the first US broadcast of this episode there was a commercial for the movie *Valentine* starring David Boreanaz.

Soundtrack: Junkie XL's 'Legion' and 'Let 'er Rip' by Dixie Chicks.

Mere Smith's Comments: 'We talked about whether or not Anne would recognise Angel,' Mere told the *Posting Board*. 'We finally came down on the side of no. They had a brief exchange in 'Lie To Me' three years ago. To tell you the truth, I have a hard time remembering people I met three days ago.'

J August Richards's Comments: 'What's cool about the way they write my character is it's like an onion, like layers are constantly being peeled off him,' J August told *IGN Sci-Fi*. 'Then this whole firing thing whereas he [Gunn] was acting very nonchalant, he actually cares a lot. He's very passionate and very into it and he really cares about the people that he works with.'

35
Happy Anniversary

US Transmission Date: 6 February 2001
UK Transmission Date: 30 March 2001 (Sky),
7 September 2002 (Channel 4)

Writer: David Greenwalt
Story: Joss Whedon and David Greenwalt

Director: Bill Norton
Cast: Matt Champagne (Gene Rainey), Darby Stanchfield (Denise),
Mike Hagerty (Bartender), Victoria L Kelleher (Val),
Danny LaCava (Mike), Eric Lange (Lubber Demon 1),
Geremy Dingle (Student Clerk), Michael Faulkner (Guy on Stage),
Norma Michaels (Aunt Helen), Frank Noyak (Curdmudgeonly Father),
Al LeBrun (Man), Bob Jesser (Torto Demon)

Angel teams up with The Host to prevent a brilliant young scientist from causing the end of the world. Gene, desperate not to lose his girlfriend, has devised an ingenious way of making sure that they can be together forever. And, unknown to him, he has demonic help. Meanwhile, Cordelia, Gunn and Wesley take their first solo case. And are successful.

Dudes and Babes: The Host complains to Angel: 'I don't know why you fired those three plucky kids. They were good company. Not to mention, Cordelia, hooo, *hot-o-rama* in the "Oh my sizzlin' loins" sense of the word. And the British boy, he's gonna be playing a huge . . .' 'Are you gonna get to the world ending?' asks Angel. 'Or just chat until it does?'

Gene's girlfriend, Denise, studied physics, but switched to acting. This is their one-year anniversary.

Denial, Thy Name is Gene: Love can make you do strange things. Bringing the world to the brink of oblivion is a little excessive, however.

It's a Designer Label!: Angel sleeps in his vest. The Host wears an ugly red shirt. Nearly as bad is the barman's Hawaiian shirt and Wesley's white suit. Cordy's green blouse is nicer.

References: It's mostly aesthetic, but parts of this (dealing with the morality of time experimentation) echo David Greenwalt's *X-Files* episode 'Synchrony'. Some elements are reminiscent of *The Dead Zone* and there's an allusion to Orson Welles's 1939 radio broadcast of *The War of the Worlds* ('We interrupt this broadcast to inform you: World ending'). Also, the three most famous scientists in history: physicist and mathematician Sir Isaac Newton (1642–1727), nuclear physicist Albert Einstein (1879–1955) and theoretical quantum physicist Stephen Hawking (b. 1942). Black & Decker's DustBuster, *Star Trek*, *The Golden Child*, *Event Horizon*, manic depression, Goliath (the Philistine giant slain by David in 'I Samuel') and Lysol (a household disinfectant). The Host alludes to American novelist F Scott Fitzgerald (1896–1940) author of *This Side of Paradise*, *The Great Gatsby* and *Tender is the Night*. He hides behind a Russian–English dictionary while waiting for Angel in the library. Thomas Connor's novel 'Flesh and Blood' can be seen in the background.

The lengthy scenes of The Host and Angel driving features them on a number of roads in Burbank and Hollywood, including a stretch of Vine Street.

Bitch!: The Host: 'Is this because I sent you on a couple of missions that turned out to be a little . . .' Angel: 'Pointless and deadly?'

Mike: 'You know what you are?' Val: 'Yes. I do. And if you say it I'll put your face in liquid nitrogen.'

Val: 'Thank God you're here. Your boyfriend was just coming on to me with the old Einstein–Podolsky–Rosen correlation.'

'West Hollywood?': Angel: 'Why the hell is everyone so surprised that it's working? But, no, it's "Why are you cranky? You should lighten up. You should smile. You should wear a nice plaid."' The Host: 'Not this season, honey.'

The Charisma Show: The great bit where Wesley's on his Agatha Christie/Dorothy L Sayers riff and Cordelia's less interested in the identity of the murderer than whether she can pinch a few hors d'oeuvres. Plus the lovely scene at the end – Gunn, Wesley and Cordy strutting their funky stuff with their friends in their new office.

L.A.-Speak: The Host: 'We're all brothers under the skin, *mi amigo*. Although the garden hue and the horns have kept me out of some key public performances. Just once I'd love to sing in a Lakers game with our national anthem.' And: 'This whole *sourpussy* mode of yours, it's starting to grate.'

Val: 'I'm totally right here, aren't I?'

Virginia, on the Bointons: 'They invented, I don't know, like chairs or something.' And: 'That's so *sad.*'

Cigarettes and Alcohol: The new bartender at Caritas is called Elián. Unlike Ramone, he can't make a decent Seabreeze. Virginia brings a bottle of champagne to the opening of Angel Investigations' new offices. Angel, The Host and Gene share a beer in the aftermath of saving the world.

Sex and Drugs and Rock'n'Roll: Denise tells Val that she's going to break up with Gene on their anniversary. Val is horrified: 'You're going to give him the sympathy-bone, aren't you? It's going to be dinner, sympathy-bone and adios Gene . . .'

'You May Remember Me From Such Films and TV Series As . . .': The excellent Michael G Hagerty is best known as Davy in *Wayne's World* and Mr Treeger on *Friends*. He's also in *Inspector Gadget*, *Space Truckers*, *Dick Tracy*, *So I Married An Axe Murderer*, *Brewster's Millions*, *The Wonder Years*, *Murphy Brown* and *Cheers*. Matt Champagne can be seen as Mr Tippin in *The Specials* and *Crime and Punishment in Suburbia*. Michael Faulkner was in *Two Guys, a Girl and a Pizza Place*. Victoria Kelleher played Marjorie in *Code Blue* and also features in *What Women Want*, *Friends* and *Ally McBeal*. Norma Michaels was in *Big Shots* and *The Zodiac Killers*.

Don't Give Up The Day Job: Bob Jesser's appearance in *American Friends and Lovers* came in addition to his role on the visual effects team.

Logic, Let Me Introduce You to This Window: If Gene is a regular at Caritas, why is he so surprised by the existence of demons when Angel and The Host show up? But he isn't surprised to find a new mathematical formula on his whiteboard that wasn't there the previous evening? Charisma's hair gets more blonde streaks as the episode progresses. When The Host held that C note, why wasn't Angel affected?

I Just *Love* Your Accent: Wesley's finest hour, as he turns into a Christie/Sayers detective, even getting one of those hackneyed 'but here's what *really* happened' scenes straight out of *The Mirror Crack'd*. (Gunn: '*That* was cool.' Wesley: 'It wasn't that difficult. You just have to keep sifting the evidence until the truth finally hits you.')

Motors: The Host has never driven before. He learns whilst driving Angel's car.

Quote/Unquote: The Host: 'See if we can get a lead on him. That is, if you're not too busy killing lawyers and setting girls on fire?' And: 'Unless, of course, we don't get there on time, in which case you'll be frozen in this crappy mood forever.'

Mike, seeing The Host: 'What's that?' Angel: 'Don't worry. It's just the new school mascot.' Mike: 'For the Buccaneers?'

Client: 'Which one of you is Angel?' Wesley: 'It's just a name.'

Notes: 'I like the theory of freezing time as much as the next *Star Trek* nerd.' This is *fabulous*. Putting Andy Hallett and Boreanaz together is inspired, with The Host's pointed-yet-cheery barbs getting completely under Angel's skin (and turning him into a po-faced straight man, something Boreanaz is becoming very good at). Add to this Wesley, Cordy and Gunn's delightfully batty sub-Agatha Christie subplot, and some surprisingly serious issues about scientific responsibility and the pain of love and you've got a quite beautifully executed episode. One to watch with a pizza, some beer and a few mates.

Angel uses the alias Leonard Taubman. The Host says Angel's aura is beige. He can hold a note forever, and his pitch can shatter windows and be painful to sensitive hearing. Virginia supplies the new Agency with its first client, the Bointons (a filthy rich family). Kevin Bointon is impotent; an elder Bointon used to be a wizard; Derek, the eldest son, was killed by a Waikanay demon that his Aunt Helen summoned. Gunn says the office smells funky, similar sentiments to those he expressed about the Hyperion in **24**, 'Are You Now or Have You Ever Been?' The Host notes: 'Blood vengeance is a luxury of the lesser being,' – a reference to the Oracles and their term for demons and vampires (see **8**, 'I Will Remember You'). The

Lubber demons are a fanatical sect, awaiting a messiah who will usher in the end of human life – lot of demons don't talk about it in mixed company, but it is a popular theology in the underworld.

The Key To Time: The answer to the question that's baffled Newton, Einstein and Hawking (amongst others) is . . .

$$P = A \left(\frac{\Phi}{2} PX, 9^{17} \frac{C^2}{\Sigma^2}, \frac{V^3}{\Psi} - X \right)$$
$$E^2 = Mo^2C_4 + P^2C^2$$

While reading this book, therefore, you may slip into a different space–time continuum . . .

Soundtrack: Mocean Worker's 'Hey Baby'. At Caritas, there's a reasonable stab at Eric Carmen's 70s weepie 'All By Myself'. The Host sings a spirited rendition of 'The Star Spangled Banner'. In another karaoke bar we hear a fairly straight performance of the 16th century madrigal 'Green-sleeves'. (Often said to have been written by King Henry VIII for his second wife, Anne Boleyn, though this is almost certainly apocryphal. Recent research suggests it's actually a plagiarised version of a French folk song.) Also a Torto Demon and his parasite's awful version of The Everly Brothers' 'Bye Bye Love'. The barman sings a few lines of 'For He's a Jolly Good Fellow'.

Did You Know?: 'Once the make-up is on, it's fine,' Andy Hallett told *Horror Online*, 'but the contact lenses are irritating. I've never even worn regular contacts and these are much thicker. But I can't emphasise enough how extremely professional everybody is on the set, in every single department. Regarding the contacts, they have a lens technician who puts them in for me and takes them out. And he comes up to me, like, every two seconds and is asking if I need eye drops.'

36
The Thin Dead Line

US Transmission Date: 13 February 2001
UK Transmission Date: 6 April 2001 (Sky),
14 September 2002 (Channel 4)

Writers: Jim Kouf, Shawn Ryan
Director: Scott McGinnis
Cast: Mushond Lee (Jackson), Cory C Hardrict (Ray),
Kyle Davis (Kenny), Camille Mana (Les), Darin Cooper (Peter Harkes),
Brenda Price (Callie), Geoff Koch (Street Cop),
Jerry Giles (Desk Sergeant), Steven Barr (Captain Atkinson),
Suli McCullough (EMT)

Zombie-cops are on the street in Gunn's neighbourhood,
but Angel is too busy pursuing his vendetta against
Wolfram & Hart to care. So it's left to Wesley and
Cordelia to help their friend. Kate Lockley, meanwhile,
puts her job on the line for Angel.

It's a Designer Label!: Cordelia spots a girl wearing the
multicoloured top that Angel gave to Anne in **34**, 'Blood
Money'. 'I have a shirt just like that. The girl at the store
said it was one of a kind.' Also, her peach blouse and
Gunn's mustard sweatshirt.

References: The title is an allusion to 'The Thin Red Line',
the nickname for the 93rd Highlanders, from a phrase used
by *The Times* correspondent Dr WH Russell to describe
their formation during the Crimean War at the battle of
Balaclava (1854). It's also the title of James Jones's 1962
war novel subsequently filmed three times. Cordelia believes movie star Steven Seagal had some demonic assistance. Also, Rodney King (who became a symbol of
American racism and police brutality when an amateur
video showed L.A. policemen beating him in March 1991),
zombies (in voodoo belief, especially in Haiti, a body
without a soul that acts as the slave of a magician), the
theme song from the 1970s TV series *The Jeffersons*
('movin' on up, dawg ... De luxe apartment in the sky')
and the Miranda Rights. A can of Chock Full O'Nuts

coffee can be seen when Cordy and Wes are researching. The scene with the Zombie-cops trying to get into the shelter is a tribute to George Romero's *Night of the Living Dead*. Gunn reads *USA Today*.

Locations mentioned include Normandie and 5th, in the Wholesale District and Skid Row and St John's Hospital and Health Center in Santa Monica. The AMKO warehouse seen as the ambulance is speeding away is on East 9th Street in downtown L.A. Gunn's 'hood is near Anne's shelter on Crenshaw Street.

Bitch!: Cordelia's superb rant to Angel when he turns up at the hospital. 'You walked away. Do us a favour and just stay away.'

The Charisma Show: She notes that 'Gunn graduated with a major in Dumb Planning from Angel University and sat at the feet of the master, and learned well how to plan dumbly!'

L.A.-Speak: Paramedic: 'He's goin' south.'

Kenny: 'Cops. They've been hassling everybody lately. Which, hey, what else is new, right? Last night me and Les were hanging down on 39th.' Anne: 'Panhandling?'

Cordelia: 'Angel Investigations, home of the wicked high creep factor.'

Ray: 'Lookin' to put a cap in my ass, man!'

Not Exactly A Haven For The Bruthas: Gunn: 'I want you to roll the camcorder, wait for the cops to hassle us.' Anne: 'How do you know they will?' Gunn: 'Cos we'll be the ones "walkin'-while-black".' There's a clever juxtaposition between Gunn and Jackson as two sides of the same black coin. 'Why d'you think nobody cares they're clamping down on this neighbourhood?' asks Gunn. 'Cos they're a bunch of racist pigs?' suggests Jackson. 'There's that,' replies Gunn. 'And people like *you*.' Interestingly, there's an attempted justification by Kate of the Zombie-cop activities. She notes that three months ago the area had a terrible crime rate of murder, robbery and rape, and that, by stopping the Zombie-cops, Angel has re-established this for the people of the area.

Sex and Drugs and Rock'n'Roll: Wes is put on morphine

after being shot in the stomach. It is, he decides, 'bloody lovely'. Gunn says he has seen Ray dealing.

'You May Remember Me From Such Films and TV Series As . . .': Darin Cooper's CV includes *Roomies*, *The Setting Son*, *The Devil You Know* and *JAG*. Mushond Lee was Pam's boyfriend Slide in *The Cosby Show* and can also be seen in *Conspiracy Theory*. Jarrod Crawford was in *Belong* and *Felicity*. Steven Barr features in *Kazaam* and *Evasive Action*. Suli McCullough played Mouse in *The Jamie Foxx Show*, and also appeared in *The Cable Guy* and *Terminal Velocity*. Marie Chambers was in *The Next Big Thing*.

Don't Give Up The Day Job: Kyle Davis was a dolly grip on *Black and White* and *Gods and Monsters*, and an electrician on *The Killing Jar*. Geoff Koch was the writer/producer of the film *Prison Life*.

Logic, Let Me Introduce You to This Window: If Anne and Gunn hadn't seen each other in a long time, how did she find him at the new agency offices? At the beginning Angel walks into the hotel and the door isn't locked. Aren't there any thieves in L.A.? The shelter interior set is completely different from **34**, 'Blood Money', including the front staircase being missing completely. Kate has no scar from Angel's bite in **30**, 'The Shroud of Rahmon'. What happened to Gunn's jacket that he used to staunch the blood from Wesley's wound? The L.A. weather is certainly unpredictable: the rain stops and starts between camera angles. The head of the Zombie-cop that Angel kicks off is terribly fake.

I Just *Love* Your Accent: Merl tells Angel that 'at least that British guy understood what a working relationship was, had some respect.'

Motors: Kenny claims he spent last night washing his Mercedes.

Quote/Unquote: Anne: 'How are your laundry-folding skills?' Cordelia: 'I'm an actress, I can fake it.'

Cordelia: 'Nothing says "Aha, I'm on to you" like being on the receiving end of a vicious police beating.'

Angel: 'I need to talk to you.' Captain: 'About what?' Angel: 'Some of your more . . . dead cops?'

Notes: 'Screw the cops, they're the ones that did this.' A serious attempt at social comment that falls just the wrong side of soapboxing. Which is a shame as there's the potentially fascinating central question of whether you need to police a city full of demons *with* demons (both literal and metaphorical). The Wesley/Gunn relationship continues to impress, with Gunn feeling at first embarrassed by his white friend and then realising that someone who will take a bullet for him deserves a bit more.

Wesley wishes that a roving band of Prekian Demons would come by, though 'without the ritualistic slaying'. Merl tells Angel that Wolfram & Hart is having a meeting at Diaghilev (a very expensive restaurant on San Vicente Boulevard, West Hollywood), possibly over a new demon account. Angel kills a cop, badge number 4226. Kate identifies him as Peter Harkes (1965–2000) whose funeral she attended six months previously. The police caught the killer and he's on death row. At the cemetery, Angel can tell that Harkes's grave has been disturbed as has that of officer Kevin Helenbrook (1967–2000) who worked on vice. Kate's two open cases – two saleswomen murdered and thirteen Wolfram & Hart lawyers found slaughtered in a wine cellar – are references to **32**, 'Reunion'.

Soundtrack: Sucker Pump's 'On a Mission', OutKast's 'Ms Jackson' and 'Who's Got My Back?' by Seldom Seen.

Joss Whedon's Comments: 'If I could write for any show, it would be *The Simpsons* or *Twin Peaks*,' Joss told the *Buffy* magazine. 'I want to kill Aaron Sorkin, eat his brain and gain his knowledge because I love *The West Wing* so much. His stuff is just amazing.'

37
Reprise

US Transmission Date: 20 February 2001
UK Transmission Date: 13 April 2001 (Sky),
21 September 2002 (Channel 4)

Writer: Tim Minear
Director: James Whitmore Jr
Cast: Thomas Kopache (Denver), David Fury (First Worshipper),
Chris Horan (Second Worshipper), Jolene Hjerleid (Singing Lawyer 1),
Wayne Mitchell (Singing Lawyer 2), Eric Larson (Internal Affairs Guy),
Shirley Jordan (Internal Affairs Woman),
Carl Sundstrom (Lieutenant Lou)

Ritual evil is rife in L.A. Angel knows something big is coming and Wolfram & Hart are scared. A senior partner arrives on Friday for a 75-year review and, if it's anything like the last one, they're all in trouble. Meanwhile Cordelia, Wesley and Gunn have problems with a client who won't pay up.

Dudes and Babes: At least one senior partner of Wolfram & Hart is a Kleynak demon, which can travel between dimensions because of a ring, the Band of Blacknoll, that it wears. Legend says that the Kleynak demons rose from their demon world to rape and pillage the villages of man.

Denial, Thy Name is the Sharps: Steve Sharp says that, since it's impossible to be bitten by a demon and have a third eye in the back of one's head, obviously Angel Investigations are running some sort of scam. 'It's easier for the Sharps to cast us as con artists rather than to accept the grim reality that Skilosh spawn nearly hatched . . . out of their child's skull,' notes Wes sadly. 'While they're indulging their denial, we have bills to pay,' adds Cordelia.

It's a Designer Label!: Cordy's green top, Darla's red dress, Gunn's fleece jacket.

References: Angel's descent to the Home Office is reminiscent of the climax to the movie *Angel Heart*. Also, *New York Observer* film critic and star of *Myra Breckenridge* Rex Reed, (*Joseph and the Amazing Technicolor Dreamcoat*, *Jesus Christ Superstar* and *Evita* composer) Andrew Lloyd Webber, Roy Orbison's 'Running Scared', 'Zip-a-dee-doo-dah' from *Song of the South* and Pol Pot's Khmer Rouge, the Communist guerrilla organisation who overthrew the Cambodian government in 1975. Allusions to D:Ream's 'Things Can Only Get Better' and David Bowie's 'Scary Monsters (And Super Creeps)'. This is the first *Angel* episode to mention a black mass. A book on Italian Renaissance genius Michelangelo Buonarroti (1475–1564) can be seen behind Denver.

Hollywood Book City is again used as Denver's book shop (see **24**, 'Are You Now or Have You Ever Been?'). The store's real name can actually be seen on the window behind him when Angel enters. Locations mentioned include Covina, a town in the San Gabriel Valley (and the filming location for much of *Roswell*).

Bitch!: Lilah's delightfully dismissive 'stake the bitch' when Darla invades the summoning. Lilah gets most of the best lines, including: 'I dug up everything I could find on the last 75-year review . . . Makes the Christmas purge of '68 look like fun old times. Nearly half of mid-management was sacked. And, Lindsey, they used *real sacks*.' And 'I heard Henderson pulled her first born out of company daycare and offered it up . . . Brown-noser. My mother was right, I should've had children!'

'West Hollywood?': The Host calls Angel 'darlin''. Lindsey seems not to have a proper briefcase but rather a 'man-bag' with a shoulder strap (however, see **38**, 'Epiphany').

The Charisma Show: Her righteous anger when Mrs Sharp accused the gang of trying to pull a scam: 'The back of your kid's head was blinking!'

L.A.-Speak: Angel: 'So, sue me.'

Cordelia: 'What a jerk.'

Cigarettes and Alcohol: Kate drinks neat vodka and takes a potentially lethal cocktail of pills after being fired. The Host seems to be drinking vodka and lime when he refers to his Wolfram & Hart customers as 'the morally ambiguous crowd'.

Sex and Drugs and Rock'n'Roll: After Angel has pushed his weight around with his former friends, Cordelia is angry: 'If it was anybody else I'd just say, get laid already . . . But no, not him. One decent *boff* and he switches to Evil-Psycho-Vamp, which in a way would be better for everyone. Better for him, cos he'd get some, and better for us cos then we could stake him afterwards.'

Wesley uses Mandrake, a plant known to botanists as

Mandragora officinarum, a small perennial of the potato family, to help cure Stephanie.

'You May Remember Me From Such Films and TV Series As . . .': Wayne Mitchell was in *Attack of the Jungle Women*. Eric Larson appears in *'68* and *Billionaire Boys Club*. Shirley Jordan was Kate Wilkerson in *General Hospital* and also featured in *The West Wing*. Carl Sundstrom was in *Lost Highway* and *Nothing to Lose*. Kevin Fry's films include *A Civil Action*, *Femme Fontaine: Killer Babe for the C.I.A.* and *Clara*.

Don't Give Up The Day Job: One of the goat-sacrificing worshippers in the opening scene is writer/producer David Fury.

Logic, Let Me Introduce You to This Window: When Darla picks the glove off the floor, you can see her hand reflected on it. Similarly, as Angel falls from the Wolfram & Hart building, his reflection is seen in the windows just before he hits the ground. Denver looks pretty good for an 80-year-old. Darla is already in the room when security tells Nathan Reed that someone has let a vampire on to the floor. Denver says he has been using the knight's glove as an oven-mitt – rather dangerous if, as it appears, it's metal.

I Just *Love* Your Accent: Virginia's break up with Wesley. The viewer feels like they've just seen someone kicking a puppy to death.

Quote/Unquote: The Host: 'I think the general angst isn't so much about the review, more about the reviewer. Let's just say it ain't Rex Reed.' Angel: 'What is it?' The Host: 'It's evil. It's dark. It's merciless. Actually, now that I say it out loud it sounds an awful lot like Rex, doesn't it?'

Holland: 'I'm quite dead. Unfortunately, my contract with Wolfram & Hart extends well beyond that.'

The Host: 'I really can't divulge to you what I read in another being. But I can tell you what I overheard in the men's restroom.'

Notes: 'If there wasn't evil in every single one of them out there, they wouldn't be people, they'd all be angels.' So, Los Angeles *is* Hell after all. A literal end of the dark road that Angel has travelled and, from here, the series can (and does) only get lighter. What a great end to the episode: a triple cliffhanger with Cordy and Kate in mortal danger and Angel surrendering to Darla's bed. The opening tracking shot, through the L.A. gutters to a solitary Angel standing in the shadows, is one of the series' most memorable images.

Drusilla told Lindsey where Darla could be found after the events of 33, 'Redefinition', and then left L.A. for Sunnydale (see *Buffy*: 'Crush'). Lindsey found Darla in a sewer and she has been recovering in his apartment. Kate has a hearing with Internal Affairs as a result of complaints by Capt Anderson (see 36, 'The Thin Dead Line'). She is fired (her severance package includes psychological counselling). Denver (see 24, 'Are You Now or Have You Ever Been?') says that his meeting with Angel in 1952 changed his life. Wesley and Cordy took most of Wesley's books with them from the hotel. Virginia says she can handle the monsters but not Wesley being shot and breaks up with him. Wolfram & Hart are said to have been around since the time of cavemen in various forms, including the Spanish Inquisition and the Khmer Rouge (see 42, 'Over the Rainbow'). According to Holland, Wolfram & Hart have an apocalypse scheduled. The episode's end is an almost shot-for-shot recreation of the climax to *Buffy*: 'Surprise' in which Angel lost his soul (the title is also an obvious allusion to that episode).

Soundtrack: 'My Heart Doesn't Live Here Anymore' by Scott Nikoley and Jamie Dunlap and 'Poolside' by Daniel Stein. The lawyers sing 'Reunited', a 1978 hit for Peaches and Herb in Caritas. Love the horrible lift muzak played when Angel joins Holland in the elevator descending to Hell.

38
Epiphany

US Transmission Date: 27 February 2001
UK Transmission Date: 20 April 2001 (Sky),
28 September 2002 (Channel 4)

Writer: Tim Minear
Director: Thomas J Wright

Angel finds that, despite having sex, he *hasn't* lost his soul, much to Darla's disgust. He arrives in time to save Kate from suicide. The Host tells Angel that his crew are in danger and he determines to win back his friends . . . if he can get to them before they die.

Dudes and Babes: Wesley tells Angel that Cordelia has become a solitary girl far removed from the vain, carefree creature she was. Through the visions, she experiences the pain of those in need and is compelled to do something about it.

It's a Designer Label!: Lindsey wears what online fans subsequently described as 'Whup-Ass boots' when he fights Angel. The Host's yellow dressing gown, Gunn's red football shirt.

References: *Pulp Fiction* ('it's called a moment of clarity'), *It's a Wonderful Life* ('Zuzu's petals'), U2's 'With or Without You' and possibly *Sleepy Hollow* (Wesley splattered with goo in the face when he kills the demon). Locations mentioned include Topanga, west of Santa Monica. This was a fermenting ground for West Coast rock music in the 1960s when Neil Young, the Byrds and Joni Mitchell, among others, moved to the area.

'West Hollywood?': Lindsey turns up for a fight dressed as a lumberjack and driving a *man*'s truck. Some fans have suggested that he may be really struggling with his sexuality at this point. This is further evidenced when he's rummaging through his closet which is full of frilly female attire. Of course they *could* be Darla's, but I like the alternative.

The Charisma Show: Cordelia's hit by a vision of herself being attacked by the Skilosh just as they emerge from the shadows. '*That was helpful!*' she angrily tells The Powers That Be.

L.A.-Speak: The Host: 'Isn't this the sort of *'tude* that got you where you are now? I think I'm speaking for everyone when I say, if all you're gonna do is switch back to brood-mode, we'd rather have you evil.'

Cigarettes and Alcohol: The Host and Angel share whisky at Caritas.

Sex and Drugs and Rock'n'Roll: Angel has sex with Darla (three times) and emerges unscathed. 'You're not evil,' says an angry Darla. 'You cannot tell me that wasn't perfect. Not only have I been around for four hundred years but I used to do this professionally.' Angel is equally confused and seeks guidance from The Host, knocking loudly on his door. 'Jeez keep your pants on,' the demon shouts, then, seeing Angel, adds: 'I can see we're a little late with *that* advice.' 'You think you're the first guy who ever rolled over, saw what was lying next to him and went, "*Yeeeegh*!",' he adds. Angel thinks he should probably have killed Darla. The Host is dismissive: 'Kill her, give her cab fare. Whatever . . .'

Logic, Let Me Introduce You to This Window: How exactly *did* Angel manage to get into Kate's apartment without an invite? She calls it 'a matter of faith'. Woah, sister. *Quantum Leap* territory ahoy. Lindsey drives over Angel in a truck three times and then smashes him repeatedly in the face with a sledgehammer. This causes a bit of minor bruising and nothing else? An epiphany is a mental process, not a physical one. Where has Lindsey been hiding that old pickup? In the back of his closet along with his cowboy boots, maybe? In earlier episodes, it was stated that The Host could only read someone's aura when they opened themselves up by singing, yet he could 'read' Angel's carnal knowledge easily enough. Mind you, Angel can do *that* by smell (see **27**, 'Dear Boy'). The format of the Oklahoma licence plate is incorrect. It should be three letters then three numbers. The hand working the gears in Lindsey's car is a real one and not a prosthetic. When Lindsey drops the sledgehammer it's about four feet away from the truck. It's visible throughout the fight then suddenly moves to immediately behind the truck door. How does Gunn know that Cordy has three eyes when he can only see the front of her head through the window? There's some poor editing during the fight at the point where Lindsey screams 'Tell me'. Gunn had a switchblade in his boot – why didn't he use it to defend himself against the Skilosh? Why does Angel get up and stagger outside in pain after having sex with Darla? She and Angel stand on the balcony in the rain, yet neither is wet. After saving Kate by taking her into the shower, Angel's shirt and hair seem very dry.

I Just *Love* Your Accent: 'C'mon English, you know you're my man,' Gunn tells Wesley as they high-five. 'I see you guys have bonded,' notes a horrified Angel. 'This man took a bullet for me,' continues Gunn.

When the subject of Cordelia is raised Gunn asks if anyone has 'checked her pad'. Angel says he stopped by there earlier. 'You enjoyin' your visit to 1973?' asks Gunn. 'I meant her *message* pad.'

Motors: Lindsey drives a 1956 Ford F-100 pickup with an Oklahoma licence plate T-42633.

Quote/Unquote: Gunn: 'You had an epiphany? So what? You just wake up and *bang*?' Angel: 'It was sort of the other way around.'

Angel, on Cordelia: 'Does it make sense that she would go there in the middle of the night without calling either one of you?' Gunn and Wesley: 'They owe us money.'

Angel: 'I don't want you to come back and work for me. I wanna work for you.' Wesley: 'Why?' Angel: 'Because I think I can help.'

Notes: 'He had an epiphany.' Another remarkable, astute episode, 'Epiphany' starts as though it is going to be the darkest, nastiest, most depressing hour of TV ever and then, suddenly, becomes a comedy classic. *Fabulous.*

Kate lives in apartment 311. It appears The Host *lives* at Caritas. Angel has never visited Wesley's apartment (No. 105) before. A lady called Mrs Starns resides above Wesley. He owns a shotgun which he keeps in his closet. Angel Investigations' office hours are: Monday–Thursday 10–6, Friday 10–9, Saturday 9–9 and closed on Sunday (obviously the forces of darkness have a day off). Darla's accusation to Angel, 'you made me trust you', echoes the phone message Kate left in **37**, 'Reprise'. The Host tells Angel that The Powers That Be tried to stop the events of

32, 'Reunion' by sending Cordelia the vision of the young man about to commit suicide to distract Angel from his dark path. Wesley has Puzz-3D on his closet shelf, the game he tried to interest Cordy with in **12**, 'Expecting'. According to Wesley there are several ways to kill a Skilosh, but the most effective is 'hack it to pieces'. Lindsey's man-bag from the previous episode has been replaced by a more conventional briefcase.

The beginning of the episode mirrors the opening scene of *Buffy*: 'Innocence', when Angel reverted to Angelus. Similarly, Cordelia's arrival at the Sharp house and her discovery of the bodies parallels closely the opening of *Buffy*: 'The Body' (which broadcast immediately prior to this episode), in which Buffy finds Joyce Summers dead.

Critique: 'Scene by scene, "Epiphany" is a solid, pacy, wryly humorous way to lay the series' recent predicament – Angel, or Associates? – to rest,' noted Mark Wyman in *TV Zone*.

Did You Know?: During one of the scene breaks on the original US broadcast, a single frame features a clapper-board which says 'Angel K6/XS20/Take 1'. This is followed by another single frame, possibly an out-take, of David Boreanaz laughing.

Cast and Crew Comments: The cast and creators of *Angel* took part in a panel discussion at *The Museum of Television and Radio*'s 18th Annual William S Paley Festival on 3 March 2001. Joss Whedon, David Boreanaz, Charisma Carpenter, Alexis Denisof, J August Richards, Elisabeth Rohm, Christian Kane, Stephanie Romanov, David Greenwalt, Tim Minear and Marti Noxon all attended to answer fans' questions. 'It's been a great ride,' said Boreanaz, although Joss joked, 'he clearly wasn't working out [on *Buffy*]. No chemistry there.' Charisma added that being offered a spot on the new show came as a surprise. In fact, she thought she was about to be fired. 'Then [Joss] gave me a new job. I said "Hell, yeah!"' Charisma also revealed that we should look out for Cordelia in a bikini in a forthcoming episode. 'It even says in the script "Bend over more",' she noted (see **41**,

'Belonging'). Asked how he defined a soul and how Angel (a vampire with one) differed from the soulless vampires like Spike, Joss opined that soulless creatures can do good and souled creatures can do evil, but that the soul-free are instinctually drawn toward the latter. An audience member asked where Angel got all his money. Joss joked: 'He robs. We're not going to *show* that.' Asked why David Nabbit had suddenly disappeared, Joss said that they wanted him back but the actor was unavailable. 'We love him,' noted Joss. 'He was in *Office Space* so we thought he was the coolest thing in the world.' Greenwalt said that the show would be leaving Los Angeles for its last three episodes. 'Eventually the story starts telling us what's going to happen,' Whedon added, also agreeing that light storylines on *Buffy* balance out darker plots on *Angel* and vice versa. A key part of that was making sure Angel's redemption came on the same night that Joyce died in 'The Body', said Whedon, acknowledging that fans needed something positive after the *Buffy* episode. Several of the crew noted that they were becoming addicted to Internet postings. Tim Minear said it was impossible to stay away and that he can usually cite the number of hours since his last glimpse at the message boards. 'There's praise,' said Joss, 'then there's *more* praise. After a while it's like "I invented television!" It makes me say to my wife, "Why don't you think I'm cooler?" It does affect the way I think about the show. In moderation.'

Previously on *Buffy the Vampire Slayer* 'Forever': In the aftermath of Joyce Summers's untimely death, Angel returns to Sunnydale to comfort Buffy.

39
Disharmony

US Transmission Date: 17 April 2001
UK Transmission Date: 27 April 2001 (Sky),
5 October 2002 (Channel 4)

Writer: David Fury
Director: Fred Keller

Cast: Pat Healy (Doug Sanders), Adam Weiner (Caged Guy),
Rebecca Avery (Caged Girl)

While Angel tries to win back the trust of his friends,
Cordelia is delighted by the arrival in L.A. of her old pal
Harmony. And she isn't even going to let the small detail
of Harmony being a vampire get in the way of their
reunion.

Dudes and Babes: Doug Sanders is a motivational speaker,
a so-called *life-coach* who teaches 'Selective Slaughter' to
self-actualising vampires (his book is subtitled 'Turning a
Blood Bath into a Blood Bank'). Doug is the head of a
pyramid scheme that replaces money with human life.
Harmony was, of course, one of the Cordettes (see 5, 'Rm
W/a Vu').

Denial, Thy Name is Sexuality: The whole vampire/lesbian
mix-up. 'I thought I could resist these urges,' Harmony
tells her as Cordelia finds her friend standing over her in
the bedroom. 'You have no idea how hard it is to stay
away from you. Seeing you there looking so luscious.' A
concerned Cordelia rings Willow and asks why nobody
told her about Harmony. After a couple of moments at
cross purposes, Willow asks if Cordelia knows that Harmony is a vampire. Cordelia is actually *relieved*: 'I thought
she was a great big lesbo.' We don't hear Willow's reply
but an embarrassed Cordy says: 'Really? Well, that's *great*.
Good for you!'

Harmony's description of drinking blood to Angel is
disturbingly sexual: 'How can you deprive yourself of the
taste? The sensation of rich, warm, human blood flowing
into your mouth. Bathing your tongue. Caressing your
throat with its sweet, sticky . . .'

It's a Designer Label!: Harmony wears Cordy's pink fluffy
slippers and a cleavage-revealing white frilly nightdress
plus, later, red leather pants. Angel's grey shirt and
Cordy's very tight trousers and black top.

References: Big Bird from *Sesame Street*. Cordelia refers to
herself as 'the bird lady of Alcatraz' after the Burt
Lancaster movie *Birdman of Alcatraz*, the true-life story of

murderer Robert Stroud. Harmony's choice of songs at Caritas includes Elton John's 'Candle in the Wind' or 'Candle in the Wind (Princess Diana version)'. Doug Sanders's mantra of 'two vamps turn two humans, and they turn two humans, and so on, and so on' may be a reference to a TV advert for Breck Shampoo.

Locations: Lafayette Park in Westlake, four blocks from the more famous MacArthur Park. During the scene where the couple are abducted from the car the prominent sign for the former Regent Westlake Theater can be seen. Some scenes were shot on North Broadway in Chinatown.

Bitch!: Harmony doesn't drink pig's blood as it goes straight to her hips. She manages to piss off Wesley with just about everything she does: '*Someone* put a *stake* through that woman's heart if she persists in popping her bloody chewing gum.' ('Come on, Harm,' says Cordelia. 'Such a fitting nickname,' he replies.) The Host, on Harmony's singing: 'I think your friend should reconsider the name Harmony.' He later dubs her 'Cacophony'.

'West Hollywood?': When Angel buys Cordelia clothes to replace those he gave to Anne (see **34**, 'Blood Money') she notes 'you have, like, a gay man's taste.'

The Charisma and Mercedes Show: As a double act Cordy and Harmony take some beating. Love the scene of them reminiscing about Sunnydale, when they were 'powerful, rich and popular'.

L.A.-Speak: Wesley, on Cordelia: 'She won't listen to me.' Angel: 'Welcome to my world.'

Cordelia: 'I'm also jazzed.' And: '*Hate* that!' And: 'You *so* rule.'

Cordelia: 'I shot her down.' Willow: 'You wounded her?' Cordelia: 'She'll get over it. I never should have invited her to stay with me.' Willow: 'Say *what*?' Cordelia: 'I know. Awkward much?'

The Host: 'I picked up on the "betwixed-and-between, got-to-find-my-corner-of-the-sky" vibe loud and clear, kitten.'

Cigarettes and Alcohol: Cordy and Harmony share a bottle of red wine (in brandy glasses) while waiting for the pizza (pineapple and Tandoori chicken, thin crust, heavy on the sauce). At Caritas, Cordelia is drinking something blue (Bombay Sapphire gin, perhaps).

'You May Remember Me From Such Films and TV Series As . . .': Alyson Hannigan made her film debut aged eleven as Jessie Mills in *My Stepmother is an Alien*. She has guested on series as diverse as *Roseanne* and *Picket Fences* and her movies include several that explore the dark underbelly of the US education system: *Indecent Seduction*, *Dead Man on Campus*, *Boys and Girls* and the classic *American Pie* (as Michelle). Mercedes McNab, the daughter of former Huddersfield, Arsenal and England left-back Bob McNab, appeared in *Escape From Atlantis*, played the young Sue Storm in *The Fantastic Four* and was Amanda Buckman in *The Addams Family* and *Addams Family Values*. Pat Healy was Sir Edmund Godfrey in *Magnolia* and was also in *Big Canyon* and *Home Alone 3*.

Don't Give Up The Day Job: Adam Weiner was a production assistant on *Girls Town* and can be seen in *Voyeur.com*.

There's A Ghost In My House: Dennis slams the bedroom door to wake Cordelia when Harmony's 'urges' threaten to get the better of her. 'I don't wanna stay alone here with the ghost,' says a terrified Harmony as Cordy prepares to leave with Angel and Wesley.

Logic, Let Me Introduce You to This Window: When Harmony and Cordelia are singing, Harmony's head is reflected in the window behind her. The idea that spilling liquid on a computer keyboard would make the screen short out is absurd. There is only low power in the keyboard, and it's isolated from the display functions of the computer. As Angel walks in and out of Wesley's office at the end you can see his reflection on the door. Is Angel Investigations doing so well they can afford an espresso machine (and a fancy new computer)? Boreanaz can be seen chewing gum when the camera is behind him in Lafayette Park. When Cordelia is thrown to the ground by Harmony there's not a crossbow in sight, so how does she manage to produce not one but two? Harmony is wearing a light-grey jacket when she leaves Caritas, but in the car a scene later, it's burgundy. Vampires don't eat (at least until Spike developed his love for chicken wings and Weetabix in *Buffy*. See also **8**, 'I Will Remember You') but Harmony seems keen on the free potato skins at Caritas.

Quote/Unquote: Wesley, on Angel's new position: 'This is torture for you, isn't it?' Angel: 'Yes.' Wesley: 'Good.'

Wesley, bursting into Cordelia's apartment to find Harmony painting Cordy's toenails: 'Get away from her . . . foot.'

Harmony: 'We always said we were going to do something cool with our lives. Now look at us. You're an Office Manager and I'm dead.'

Gunn: 'Just so we're on the same page, when we find this vampire cult, we *are* gonna kill 'em this time, right?'

Notes: 'Atonement's a *bitch*.' Continuing the comedy theme of the previous episode, this delightfully silly story captures the right balance between action and humour. Best moments: the gang emerging from Caritas and walking, shoulder to shoulder, down the sidewalk – the camera pans across from a serious and focused Wesley, to Gunn, Angel, Cordelia . . . and on to a grinning Harmony; also, the ending with Cordelia's delight at her new clothes ('la-la-la!').

Wesley takes Angel's old office in the Hyperion. Cordelia and Harmony haven't seen each other 'since our high school blew up' (see *Buffy*: 'Graduation Day' Part 2). Harmony was turned into a vampire in that episode, but Cordelia (like Buffy and Willow in *Buffy*: 'The Harsh Light of Day') seems not to have noticed. Harmony says that she's coming off a bad relationship. She was, of course Spike's girlfriend off and on during the fourth and fifth *Buffy* seasons, finally leaving him in 'Crush'. Angel says some vampires can sense the presence of his soul (see **3**, 'In The Dark', **15**, 'The Prodigal'). Gunn likes mocha cappuccino. Cordelia takes her coffee with two sugars. Donnie Rae followed Cordelia around in 9th grade remedial Spanish, singing a song that went 'Oh, Cordelia/How I long to feel-ya!' Angel Investigations' new computer looks like an IBM NetVista X40, which retail for about $2,500.

Although is isn't specifically referred to, one would presume that between the end of the previous episode and this, Angel travelled to Sunnydale to attend Joyce's funeral, as seen in *Buffy*: 'Forever'. There's another clear shot of Charisma Carpenter's tattoo when Cordelia stands up from her couch (see **5**, 'Rm W/a Vu').

Soundtrack: 'Evening Comes' by Study of the Lifeless, Baba Googie and Rex's 'Don't Say It' and Mercedes McNab's *murder* of Barbara Streisand's 'The Way We Were'.

40
Dead End

US Transmission Date: 24 April 2001
UK Transmission Date: 4 May 2001 (Sky),
12 October 2002 (Channel 4)

Writer: David Greenwalt
Director: James A Contner
Cast: Michael Dempsey (Irv Kraigle), Mik Scriba (Parole Officer), Pete Gardner (Joseph Kramer), Stephanie Hash (Wife), Steven DeRelian (Bradley Scott), Robin Atkin Downes (Demon[21])

Lindsey McDonald is given a transplant by Wolfram & Hart, but to whom did the hand originally belong? Why is it constantly writing the word 'kill'? And does this have anything to do with Cordelia's horrifying vision of a man stabbing himself in the eye?

Evil Dudes and Dudes: Lindsey awakens and stops his radio alarm with the disfigured stump of his right arm. Using his left hand, he shaves, then he opens a dresser drawer and attaches his plastic hand. Next, we cut to the closet as he chooses one of several pre-knotted ties. His eyes fall sadly on his guitar leaning, neglected, against the wall. In one scene, without a word of dialogue, we learn so much about how awful Lindsey's life has become.

---

[21] Uncredited.

It's a Designer Label!: Lindsey uses a Gillette razor. Cordy's green top and extremely tight sky-blue hipsters, Angel's grey sweater, Lindsey's cool leather jacket, The Host's silver tuxedo, Gunn's baggy trousers.

References: 'You're in good hands' is a slogan for the Allstate Insurance Company. Angel offers to sing Led Zeppelin's hippy anthem 'Stairway to Heaven' at Caritas ('don't even joke about that,' says a horrified Wesley). Also, the enemies-work-together movie *48 Hours*, *Reservoir Dogs* ('Let's go to work'), screen cowboys John Wayne and Roy Rogers ('golly pilgrim, sure is good to have you back in the saddle') and *The Jetsons*. Henry Addison, the fictitious name Gunn uses when calling hospitals, was a British Army private who, during the Sepoy Rebellion (1803), heroically defended his injured officer against a large force. Elements of the story are an overt homage to HP Lovecraft's *Herbert West – Reanimator* and also, obliquely, to Luke Skywalker in *The Empire Strikes Back* and the movie *Coma*. For further 'evil hand' sources, see **4**, 'I Just Fall to Pieces'.

Bitch!: A sign in Caritas reads EATING THE CLIENTELE IS STRICTLY PROHIBITED.

Angel sticks a COPS SUCK sign on the back of Lindsey's truck as he drives away.

'West Hollywood?': Angel's jealousy when Lindsey turns out to be a talented musician ('Pick a style, pal!') could be a sign of his own latent insecurities.

The Charisma Show: Cordelia's little speech to Lindsey after his performance at Caritas: 'I know you're evil and everything. But that was just so amazing.' The strain of her continued visions is beginning to take its toll, and we get signs that she's finding it difficult to cope.

L.A.-Speak: The Host on Lindsey: 'He used to come all the time, before some caballero chopped off his strummin' hand.'

Cigarettes and Alcohol: Lindsey drinks TNT (tequila and tonic) at Caritas.

Sex and Drugs and Rock'n'Roll: Dr Melman gives Lindsey two milligrams of Versed (Midazolam HCl), a central nervous system depressant.

Lindsey uses his evil hand as an excuse when he pinches Lilah's bum.

'You May Remember Me From Such Films and TV Series As . . .': Michael Dempsey was in *The Schoolroom*, *Bowfinger* and *Random Shooting in L.A.* Mik Scriba's movies include *Wild Wild West*, *Gridlock'd*, *Sliver* and *Hefner: Unauthorized*. Robin Atkin Downes is best known as the poetry-spouting telepath Byron in *Babylon 5*.

Logic, Let Me Introduce You to This Window: How does Lindsey know Nathan's PC password? Weren't the secret Wolfram & Hart files kept in the sub-basement in **21**, 'Blind Date'? Boreanaz's stunt-double is clearly visible in the fight scene. What happened to the henchmen in the travel agency? If they came to, why didn't they rush downstairs and continue to fight? And if they were still out cold, where were they when Angel and Lindsey ran out before the explosion?

Motors: Lindsey's '56 Ford was from the first year they were made with wraparound windshields. Angel notes that in the 50s everyone thought life was going to be like *The Jetsons* by 2001. 'I'd *love* to have an air car. Wouldn't that be cool?'

I Just *Love* Your Accent: There's a poster for Scotland in the travel agency.

Quote/Unquote: Wesley tells Angel to check on Cordelia. Angel asks 'Me? You're the one in charge now.' Wesley: 'You're right. That's why I'm assigning this one to you.'

Angel: 'When I was in charge here, nobody questioned my methods. Or my singing.' Cordelia: 'You're half right.'

Lindsey, when Angel saves his life: 'Why aren't you trying to kill me?'

Notes: 'You do know you gave me an evil hand, right?' Christian Kane gets another chance to shine and does so, brilliantly, in an episode which includes fine comedy and really gruesome horror in equal doses. Lindsey's final scene at Wolfram & Hart, and his cries of 'EVIL HAND' are among the series' most wickedly funny moments.

After Angel explains that he hired a private detective with a friend in the police, Gunn notes '*We're* supposed to have a friend on the force.' 'We did. She got fired,' replies Angel, referring to Kate. Wesley makes the series' first reference to Doyle since the middle of Season One, when telling Gunn the origin of Cordelia's visions. Since Angel couldn't remember what Cordelia likes to eat, he bought roast beef, turkey, ham and vegetarian sandwiches, soup and salad. The Fairfield Clinic is Wolfram & Hart's main healthcare provider doing check-ups and the odd supernatural transplant; Dr Melman handles Lindsey's procedure. His new hand previously belonged to former Wolfram & Hart employee Brad Scott who served two years in Soledad for embezzlement of bearer bonds. He was paroled last month. Lindsey worked with him in the mailroom. Nathan Reed's password is 'ZEN'; he is married with a son. Southern California Travel (on West 1st Street) is the front for the body-part-harvesting organisation. Lilah steals Wolfram & Hart files for her own insurance (just as Lindsey did in **21**, 'Blind Faith'), including some detailing Nathan's offshore accounts and Ronnie's stock manipulations. She owns a handgun. Among Wolfram & Hart's current clients are Western Pacific Power (whom the Attorney General is investigating). Lilah and Lindsey meet Irv Kraigle, the CFO of Lycor, a company being sued for allowing carcinogens in their chocolate. Lindsey assures Kraigle that the Dryzon Company (an offshore firm) will be held responsible. The man who stabbed himself in the eye in Cordelia's vision was Joseph Kramer, married, with two children, Jesse and Hayley, who attend the Delancey school.

Lindsey accesses Nathan Reed's computer. The 'To Do' icon includes details on Blatt case deposition, L.A. office assignments, senior partner reports, special projects re-evaluation, Jackson case brief, vacation plans, partner compensation, feeder negotiation, New Associate recruiting, Shaman contracts and Europe fact-finding trip. Lindsey brings up the 'special projects re-evaluation' screen holding folders entitled: project history, personnel roster, Manners massacre, Bethany project, Darla, Drusilla (vampire), Angel, vampire detectors, Lilah Morgan,

Lindsey McDonald, youth center project, demon relations, terminated employees, and pending projects. Lilah's personal record notes that she was a graduate of Mortonson University School of Law in 1994 and was recruited to the L.A. office as a junior associate by Holland Manners. She became a senior associate in 1997 and a junior partner in 2000. Other members of the Wolfram & Hart board (who *don't* have an evil hand) include Charlie and Leon.

Soundtrack: Christian Kane performs the beautiful 'L.A. Song' (words by David Greenwalt) at Caritas.

Did You Know?: 'I love working on *Angel*,' Robin Atkin Downes told Paul Simpson and Ruth Thomas. 'But I couldn't go to the bathroom all day, because I had these gigantic fingers. I was also ridiculed all day because I was fifteen feet above the ground on a seesaw, to give me some elevation above the girls, and they were looking up my dress. It was very hard to be charming with these beautiful girls on the set.'

David Greenwalt's Comments: 'We accomplished what we wanted to this year,' David told *Zap2It.com*. 'To understand the history and background of our characters, particularly Angel. To bring him step by step into the world of humans. I think Cordelia's character has deepened enormously, her battle with how the visions affect and hurt her. I love Gunn, but we must do more with him next year.' Although Christian Kane rode off into the sunset in **40**, 'Dead End', Greenwalt hopes he'll be back. 'That was the completion of Lindsey's arc,' says Greenwalt, 'and I hope we're seeing a lot of him next year.' Greenwalt is also hoping for a guest appearance by Adrian Pasdar, who starred as a ruthless corporate shark in Greenwalt's Fox series *Profit*. 'We've been dying to bring him to *Angel*,' Greenwalt says. 'I would love him to appear in Wolfram & Hart.'

41
Belonging

US Transmission Date: 1 May 2001
UK Transmission Date: 11 May 2001 (Sky),
19 October 2002 (Channel 4)

Writer: Shawn Ryan
Director: Turi Meyer
Cast: Kevin Otto (Seth), Maureen Grier (Woman),
Lynne Maclean (Claire)

A disturbance at Caritas sends The Host to seek Angel's help. But when investigations lead to a library and a strange book, the problem turns out to be much closer to home than The Host wishes his friends to know.

Dudes and Demons: The Haklaar demon, which Gunn describes as bloated-looking, is killed off-screen by Angel, Gunn and Wesley. Descended from the Klensan order, the adult Haklaar demon can weigh as much as three tons. It wakes from hibernation during alternating full moons to feed and mate, often simultaneously. Incapable of speech the Haklaar demon has learned to communicate via a pattern of carefully timed facial ticks, not dissimilar to Morse code. Angel mentions a Voctar Witch, who wears a Brahanian Battle Shroud woven from the skin of dead children. Wesley refers to himself, Angel and Gunn as 'manly men'.

It's a Designer Label!: Cordy's beautiful new hairstyle in the restaurant scene. Divine. Also, Wesley's cream jacket, Gunn's orange sweatshirt and The Host's yellow suit and pink ruffle shirt. Highlight of the episode, if not the *series* (if not *all of television, ever*) is Charisma in that flimsy seashell swimsuit. She also wears the tightest jeans in history (see **42**, 'Over the Rainbow').

References: Fashion designer Laura Mina, Lorne Greene (the star of long-running TV show *Bonanza*), Elton John and his song 'Goodbye Yellowbrick Road'), the Munchkins from *The Wizard of Oz*, *To Die For*, Ophelia (Polonius's daughter in *Hamlet*), game show *Wheel of*

Fortune ('Pat, I'd like to buy a vowel') and JK Rowling's
Harry Potter novels (The Host seems to be a fan.). The
Deathwok, with their warrior culture and loud insistence
on honour over common sense, remind this author of the
Klingons in *Star Trek*.

The Angel Investigations team eat at the Monte Cito
Cafe to celebrate Cordelia being cast in a commercial.
Cordy subsequently gets food poisoning from a sashimi
couscous ($19 a plate). Other locations seen or mentioned
include Stage 6 at Paramount Studios (where the commercial is filmed), the L.A. Public Library on West 5th Street,
between Grand and Flower (opened in 1926 and modelled
by architect Bertram Goodhue on his previous creation,
the Nebraska State Capitol building), Lake Hollywood
(Mulholland Drive skirts the lake's north shore) and the
Acme Wiping Materials building at 1327 Palmetto St in
downtown L.A.

Bitch!: Director, on Angel: 'Let me guess. Wannabe rocker
or part-time male model? I could go either way on this
one.'

Hollywood Babylon: Angel is horrified by the world that
Cordelia wants to be part of: 'If you're not making it in
showbusiness, you're a step or ten down the food chain.
All *we* do is save the world, right?'

The Charisma Show: She's off-screen when it happens – the
silent contemplation of Wesley and Gunn after Angel
describes what Cordy was almost wearing in the commercial is hilarious.

L.A.-Speak: When the guys kill the Haklaar demon it was
about to eat a group of power walkers, one of whom hit
Wesley: 'Apparently she felt that I disrespected the Haklaar's culture by killing it.' 'This town sucks,' notes
Cordelia.

The Host: 'Guilt-trip leaving this station.' And: 'Hello.
Martyr-complex?'

Cigarettes and Alcohol: The gang drink expensive imported
white wine at the restaurant.

Sex and Drugs and Rock'n'Roll: The Host tells Landok,
'while the rest of you boys were out hunting, I was down

at the waterhole chatting up the señoritas, gathering a little *lurve.*'

'You May Remember Me From Such Films and TV Series As . . .': Amy Acker was Melissa in *To Protect and Serve* and appeared in *Groom Lake*. Brody Hutzler starred as Zachary Smith in *The Guiding Light* and Cody Dixon on *The Young and the Restless*.

Logic, Let Me Introduce You to This Window: How does Angel, whose lack of knowledge on TV has been mentioned before (see, for instance, **17**, 'Eternity'), know who Lorne Greene is or what *Bonanza* was? On two occasions actors appear distracted by what is happening off-camera: Cordelia during the scene in the lobby (she smiles at something); and then in the library, both Wesley and Angel almost stop their dialogue. How come no one notices Angel's lack of a reflection in the mirror at the restaurant? Or do they, and they're just too polite to mention it?

I Just *Love* Your Accent: Angel remembers when a few bob got you a good meal, a bottle and a tavern wench.

Wesley calls to wish his father a happy birthday, delightedly telling his parents that he's now in charge of the group. Mr Wyndam-Pryce ('English senior' as Gunn calls him; Wesley refers to him as 'Father' though he calls his mother 'Mum') seems rather dismissive of his son's ability, cruelly mentioning his sacking by the Watcher's Council (see **19**, 'Sanctuary'). We start to understand the reason behind Wesley's inferiority complex (see **14**, 'I've Got You Under My Skin').

Quote/Unquote: Librarian to The Host: 'The kids will flip over your costume. It looks so authentic . . . Except for the horns. But those are probably hard to fake.'

Angel, when The Host recognises Landok: 'You know him?' The Host: 'Just because I know his name doesn't mean you can't knock him unconscious, please continue.'

Landok: 'Your mother's burden is terrible.' The Host: 'Misses her little-green-boo does she?' Landok: 'She rips your image into tiny pieces, feeds them to the swine, butchers the pigs and has their remains scattered for the dogs.' The Host, nodding: 'Sounds like Ma.'

Notes: 'Oh crap!' A rather sedate and one-paced episode, which features nice background work on Wes, Cordelia and The Host but doesn't quite have the verve to catch viewer interest as often as it should. It's a pity – as much of the dialogue is excellent — but, as subsequently becomes apparent, it's chiefly a prologue to some major changes.

Winifred Burkle was a librarian who was sucked into a portal on 7 May 1996 in the Foreign Language Section of L.A. Public Library while reading a book called *SCRSQWRN*. She was studying to be a physicist.

The Host's name is Krevlorneswath of the Deathwok Clan and we meet his cousin, Landokmar, a fierce warrior. Lorne's vanishing was a great mystery to the clan, who hoped that he had sought atonement by forfeiting his life in the sacrificial canyons of Trelinsk. The Host's world knows 'only good and evil, black and white, no grey. No music, no art, just champions roaming the countryside, fighting for justice.' It has two suns. The portal between the worlds is opened by reading from the book. The easiest way to kill a Drakken is to stab it with a weapon dipped in thromide, an element that doesn't exist on Earth. The episode ends with Cordelia having been transported to The Host's dimension.
Soundtrack: The Host's searing version of Stevie Wonder's 'Superstition'.

42
Over the Rainbow

US Transmission Date: 8 May 2001
UK Transmission Date: 18 May 2001 (Sky),
19 October 2002 (Channel 4)

Writer: Mere Smith
Director: Fred Keller
Cast: Susan Blommaert (Vakma), Persia White (Aggie),
Daniel Dae Kim (Gavin Park), William Newman (Old Demon Man),
Drew Wicks (Blix)

With Cordelia in another dimension, Angel, Wesley, Gunn and The Host begin a frantic search for the means to follow her. Meanwhile, Cordy finds herself treated like a slave and meets another refugee from Los Angeles.

Dudes and Babes: Fred Burkle turns up alive and insane and wearing trampy rags in the other dimension.

It's a Designer Label!: Those incredibly tight jeans of Cordy's – particularly noticeable during a lengthy sequence of her running away from camera. Also, The Host's scarlet suit and two-tone brogues.

References: The title, and Cordelia clicking her heels together in an attempt to return home, refer to *The Wizard of Oz*. There's a very definite *Planet of the Apes* influence. Also, Polish astronomer Nicholas Copernicus (1473–1543) author of *De Revolutionibus Orbium Coelestium*, the queen of soul Aretha Franklin, *Cats*, *Titanic*, film noir (see **23**, 'Judgment'), the Hindu belief that cows are sacred animals, the Mafia, fashion magazine *Marie Claire*, *Happy Days* ('exactamundo'), Greek scholar Archimedes and his 'Eureka moment', 'Won't You Be My Neighbor?' a song from the TV show *Mister Rogers' Neighborhood*, the diner chain Eat at Joe's, *Star Trek* (Wesley uses Spock's catchphrase 'Fascinating') and the chic Sky Bar at the Mondrian Hotel in West Hollywood as frequented by Brad Pitt (*Kalifornia*, *Se7en*, *Interview With the Vampire*, *Twelve Monkeys*, *Fight Club*) and his wife Jennifer Aniston (*Friends*). And a priceless *Xena: Warrior Princess* pun. The third portal to Pylea (besides Caritas and the library, see **41**, 'Belonging') is at the entrance to Paramount Studios on Melrose Ave in Hollywood (where *Angel* is produced: 'Isn't this a movie studio?' asks Angel. 'It makes a certain kind of sense, no?' replies The Host). Visual references include *Back to the Future* (the car driving through the portal), *Return of the Jedi* (Cordy's Princess Leia-like costume), *Monty Python and the Holy Grail* and *The Masque of the Red Death*.

Bitch!: The Host: 'De-bunch your panties, Narwek.'

The Charisma Show: She gloriously steals the show with her indignation at being sold into slavery (and for such a cheap price!)

L.A.-Speak: Wesley: 'There's obviously not going to be any big swirly hole-jumping without a big swirly hole.'

The Host: 'I know it's Hollywood chic going incognito and all, but this hat's really chafing my horns!'

Gunn: 'Yo, that was *phat*.'

Not Exactly A Haven For The Humans: Pylea, The Host's dimension, is a feudal medieval society. It contains a variety of different races, but the lowest of the low are humans, who are treated as serfs and referred to as beasts of burden.

Sex and Drugs and Rock'n'Roll: Cordy fetches one pig and a pint of flib liquor when sold. The Host cannot get drunk ('ordinarily I handle bad news really well. I drown my sorrows in an ice-cold gin and tonic, little squeeze of lime, except they don't *have* them here.') Wesley owns a pair of handcuffs, the purpose of which we can only guess at.

'You May Remember Me From Such Films and TV Series As . . .': Susan Blommaert was Judge Steinman in *Law & Order* and appeared in *Clowns*, *The Jerky Boys*, *Pet Cemetary* and *Edward Scissorhands*. William Newman was in *The Postman Always Rings Twice*, *The Craft*, *Pie in the Sky*, *Mrs Doubtfire* and *Squirm*. Daniel Dae Kim played John Matheson in *Crusade* and Agent Tom Baker in *24* and can be seen in *The Jackal*, *Sun*, *Charmed* and *Addicted to Love*. Michael Phenicie was in *Evil Obsession*, *Carnival of Souls* and *9½ Ninjas!* Persia White appeared in *Operation Sandman*, *Red Letters* and *Breaker High*. Brian Tahash's movies include *Jane Austen's Mafia!* and *Tumbleweeds*.

Logic, Let Me Introduce You to This Window: When did The Host, Wesley and Angel find time to change their clothes? Where did the cut above Wesley's eye go? Why does Pylea have humans as cows but real horses? Gunn arrives at the Melrose Gate, but Angel left Gunn a phone message before The Host had told them the location of the portal. The watch Angel wears looks like the one he gave to the Oracles in **8**, 'I Will Remember You'. Cordelia's earrings seem different to those she was wearing at the end of **41**, 'Belonging'.

I Just *Love* Your Accent: Wesley says 'I was always horrified by those stories about the Tower of London,' referring to the ancient fortress on the north bank of the River Thames. Now a tourist attraction, it was a royal residence in the Middle Ages and a notorious jail for many illustrious prisoners who met some grizzly fates there. There's a suggestion that Angel may have spent time imprisoned there, but he's probably just joking.

Motors: Angel's car plays a major role in the boys making it through the portal together and in one piece.

Quote/Unquote: The Host, on his world: 'I was there. I came here. I *like* here. I don't wanna go there.' And, when Angel insists that he accompany them: 'Remember when I said . . . I'm never, never, never gonna leave? Exactly which 'never' did you not understand?'

The Host: 'Xenophobia, kind of a watchword where I'm from.' Gunn: 'I don't get it. Why're they afraid of Xena? I think she's kinda *fly*.'

The Host: 'Am I glad to see you? And so much less dead than I expected.'

Notes: 'Everyone just notice how much fire I'm not on?' An excellent and very unexpected reformatting of the series, turning it into a quasi-fairy tale (a theme that continues over the next two episodes) and, for once, giving everybody lots to do. Best bit: the boys fighting a huge gang of villagers, Wesley eagerly shouting 'I think we're winning' followed, the next shot, by the four of them bound, pissed off and on their knees.

Neither of Pylea's suns burn Angel. When Cordelia becomes princess, her Royal titles include: Venerable Monarch of Pylea, General of the Ravenous Legions, Eater of Our Enemies' Flesh, Prelate of the Sacrificial Bloodrites and Sovereign Proconsul of Death. The Host came through a portal five years ago (at the same time that Fred went in the opposite direction?) and landed in the abandoned building, where he established Caritas. He visits Aggie, a psychic friend, to help him find another hotspot. Blix used to be his best friend. Wolfram & Hart (represented by Mssrs Park and Hayes) want to buy the Hyperion when Angel's lease runs out. Vakma's shopping list includes viper's milk, sox packets of hefroot, four queeks, a bottle of flib liquor and a spatula. She buys Cordelia from Trensidoof of the Gathwok Clan. Gunn may have done some community service. Cordelia likes Thai food.

Did You Know?: J August Richards's first visit to Britain led up to the Nocturnal 3K convention in June 2001. As he told Paul Simpson and Ruth Thomas: 'I love how cities here have so much history and style. I've been thinking about Jimi Hendrix recently. He came over here and became a star. I realised why England is so inspiring to American artists. It's because everything is an exploration of an idea. Like in your architecture and your streets, the way you speak, the words you choose. It's all about the homogeny of an idea in the United States.' He also got the chance to do some sightseeing when 'Alexis rented us a bus and took us around. I haven't been inside the Tower of London yet but I'd like to. The British Museum I thought was just amazing.'

43
Through the Looking Glass

US Transmission Date: 15 May 2001
UK Transmission Date: 25 May 2001 (Sky),
26 October 2002 (Channel 4)

Writer: Tim Minear
Director: Tim Minear
Cast: Joss Whedon (Numfar)

Cordelia is now Pylea's sovereign, but court politics mean that she is soon split from her friends. And, for Angel and The Host in particular, things are looking rather grim.

Dudes and Babes: The Groosalugg is a handsome young Pylean who was reviled by his people because he is part-human. As a result, he was cast from his village but proved his worth by vanquishing every flame beast and destroying every Drokken, earning the title of 'Groosalugg, The Brave and Undefeated', along with the rite of com-shuk (ritual mating) with the Monarch of Pylea. He was called from the Scum Pits of Urr, where he had just defeated a Mogfan beast.

It's a Designer Label!: Among the proclamations that Cordy wants to make to improve the world is one outlawing polyester (even though it hasn't been invented yet). Angel likes the furs he is given by the Deathwok ('Nice!')

References: 'Off with their heads' is from Lewis Carroll's *Alice's Adventures In Wonderland*, the sequel to which provides the episode's title. Also, *Bambi*, author Hans Christian Andersen (1805–75) and director Quentin Tarantino (*Reservoir Dogs*, *Pulp Fiction*, *Jackie Brown*), *The Blair Witch Project* and *Mommy Dearest* ('No wire hangers'). The Host sings a few lines from the Supremes' 'Stop! In the Name of Love' (when he's about to be clubbed he changes the lyrics to 'think it o-o-oh shit!'). Numfar's dances may have been inspired by *Monty Python's Flying Circus* (though one is particularly reminiscent of the 'Frenchman' scene in *Holy Grail*).

The Charisma Show: Her delight at being made royalty knows few bounds ('it's not like my throne couldn't use a few extra cushions, but I'm really not gonna complain because, *throne*!'), and when trying to escape from the castle she wants to take the crown jewels with her ('A little something to remember my reign by. Is that so wrong?')

'West Hollywood': The Host calls Angel 'gorgeous' (see **25**, 'First Impressions').

L.A.-Speak: Gunn: 'No way!' And: 'Yo, priesty, what's the 411 on this Groosalugg?'

   Cordelia: '*Kidding.*'

Not Exactly A Haven For The Humans: The Covenant of Trombli is made up of priests, who have been the true rulers of Pylea for millennia. Led by Silas, they teach of a coming Messiah, a being with pure sight with a direct link to The Powers That Be, who will claim the throne and restore the monarchy. However, that is a fiction, as the monarch is merely a figurehead. They may be connected to Wolfram & Hart.

Sex and Drugs and Rock'n'Roll: Somehow Gunn guesses that the com-shuk is 'dirty'. 'It's been a really long time since I've had a good com-shuk,' notes a horrified Cordelia. 'If you ever find a way to get us out of here, I want you to find me a dimension where some demon *doesn't* want to impregnate me with its spawn . . . Do I put out some kind of com-shuk-me vibe?' When Constable Narwek suggests to Cordelia that the Most High may like to dine on the blood of her friends, she replies: '*You're* "most high" if you think *that*'s gonna happen.'

When she saves The Host from execution and asks 'Baby, are you okay?', The Host spots the Groosalugg. 'Not as good as you obviously. Should I call [the guards] back? You could borrow the cuffs.' Cordelia assumes that Gunn is accusing her of having a big butt when he suggests she'll struggle to get her 'booty' through the door.

'You May Remember Me From Such Films and TV Series As . . .': Tom McCleister played Red Wood in *Midnight Run*, Ike in *Married . . . with Children*, and was in *Fletch Lives*, *Twins*, *Cheers*, *Roswell* and *Grosse Pointe*. Mark Lutz appeared in *Interstate 60*, *Dick* and *Specimen*. Adoni Maropis was Paolo in *Sheer Passion*, Warren in *I'm Watching You* and Quan Chi in *Mortal Kombat: Conquest*. Andrew Parks appeared in *Donnie Brasco*, *The Mirror Has Two Faces*, *The Strawberry Statement*, *M*A*S*H*, *Hart to Hart*, *Cannon* and *The Virginian*.

Don't Give Up The Day Job: Joss Whedon confirmed his appearance on the *Posting Board*: 'I'll make my on-screen debut in *Angel*. I will not speak, and you won't see my face. But I'll make my presence known. Just remember my watchword: Dignity. Always dignity.'

Logic, Let Me Introduce You to This Window: Wesley carries a picture of himself, Cordelia and Angel with him? Not very likely, is it? When Cordy is trying to escape with her booty, Charisma catches her veil with her heel. When Angel is in the cave looking at his reflection in the water, he asks Fred 'Hurt you?' but his lips don't move. If you watch Fred when she's scrambling for cover as Angel fights the guardsman, you can see the bulge of a microphone pack on her back. Just like Jim Kirk in *Star Trek*, Angel's shirt seems to tear for no reason. Demon-Angel rips the guardsman's leg off, but when the camera switches to a distance shot, the guardsman has both legs intact. Cordelia has only been the monarch for one day, yet the rebels recognise her photo. Windows are reflected on Fred's glasses when she and Angel are supposed to be in a windowless cave. If the Groosalugg can *only* mate with a human and, according to the prophecy, is destined to mate with the princess, then why are the Covenant so surprised that their monarch is human? The dance of joy and the dance of honour seem to be, more or less, the same – though maybe that's the whole point.

Quote/Unquote: Angel seeing his hair in the mirror: 'This is because of going through the portal, right?' Cordelia: 'No, it always looks like that.'

Angel: 'Cordy? She's fine, they made her a princess.' Fred: 'Really? When I got here, they didn't do that.'

Lorne's Mother: 'Each morning before I feed, I go out into the hills where the ground is thorny and parched, beat my breast and curse the loins that gave birth to such a cretinous boy-child . . . Your father was right, we ate the wrong son.'

Notes: 'They jabbed me with hot pokers a while then made me a princess.' Even better, a second successive episode of *Cordelia: Warrior Princess* that takes a Brothers Grimm concept and subverts it in lots of neat and enjoyable ways. The dialogue sparkles, there are many memorable set-pieces and it includes *the* series highlight so far: Numfar's ridiculous dancing (made all the funnier when you know it's Joss Whedon doing it).

Angel describes his fight with Lindsey in **22**, 'To Shanshu in L.A.' to an enthralled audience of children: 'Whack! I chopped off the evil lawyer-beast's hand. And he screamed and he screamed. And then I left.' Landok pleads with Angel to 'tell the tale of the sorcerer who could remove his limbs and reassemble at will.' 'Cos *that*'s a good one,' notes The Host sarcastically, possibly referring to the production team's retrospective opinion of **4**, 'I Just Fall to Pieces'. The trionic books contain the prophecy of the cursed one and the Groosalugg and have a wolf, a ram and a hart etched on to the binding. The Host's brother, Numfar, danced the dance of joy for three moons when Lorne disappeared. His grandmother has a glass eye. Backnaal is a ritual killing performed with a crebbil (a ceremonial axe). Cordelia mentions that her parents were 'busted for tax-fraud and my trust fund dried up overnight' (see *Buffy*: 'The Prom').

Did You Know?: The highlight of the Nocturnal 3K convention at the Radisson hotel in Heathrow was Andy Hallett's performance of 'Lady Marmalade' and 'Superstition' (the latter in a stunning duet with J August Richards), while Joss Whedon found himself 'surrounded by a blanket of starry-eyed girlies who looked like all of their Christmases had come at once,' according to *SFX*. As James Marsters, ever the Bromley-contingent apostle, pogo'd to an assembled throng of 'swooning hearts and damp panties', Andy Hallett was heard to declare: 'This place is a *bomb*. We wanna live here!'

Joss Whedon's Comments: 'I kept saying, "There should be a guy in the background doing a stupid dance like this," ' Joss told *ign.com*. 'Finally Greenwalt and Minear said 'Why don't *you* do the stupid dance? You already look stupid, we've just gotta put make-up on. [It took] two and a half hours to make me look that good. I know what I am, I'm a *writer*. So I'd love to do more [cameos], but only if they're still funny.'

44
There's No Place Like Plrtz Glrb

US Transmission Date: 22 May 2001
UK Transmission Date: 2 June 2001 (Sky),
2 November 2002 (Channel 4)

Writer: David Greenwalt
Director: David Greenwalt
Cast: Lee Reherman (Captain), Jamie McShane (Rebel 2),
Alex Nesig (Slave 1), Whitney Dylan (Serving Wench)

Angel, with Fred's help, battles to regain his lost humanity. Wesley and Gunn become freedom fighters. Cordelia tries to assert her royal authority. And The Host has the difficult task of finding the body that goes with his head.

It's a Designer Label!: The Host's suit is French viscose.

References: The title (and some of the dialogue) allude to *The Wizard of Oz* while The Host sings a snatch from 'Somewhere Over the Rainbow'. Also, talkshow host Geraldo Rivera, *Mortal Kombat*, the Psychic Friends Network. Angel's 'I am not an animal' is the tagline from *The Elephant Man*. Cordelia's freedom speech is an amalgam of historical allusions such as the Declaration of Independence, the American Revolution and Civil War and the Emancipation Proclamation.

Bitch!: The Host, while Cordelia screams at him: 'I realise this is a bit of a shock, but I can explain. Take it easy. Okay, get it out of your system. You have to breathe sometime. Good Lord. Shut up, woman.'

The Charisma Show: Her scream when The Host's decapitated head starts to talk (which carries into the next scene) is wonderfully over the top. Plus, when she bangs The Host's head (which she is holding) into the wall while hugging the Groosalugg. Twice.

Not Exactly A Haven For The Bruthas (Fables of the Reconstruction Mix): Gunn explains freedom to Pylea: 'It means saying people are free don't make 'em free. You got races that hate each other. You got some folks getting work they don't want, others losing the little they had. You're looking at social confusion, economic depression and probably some *riots*. Good luck!'

Cigarettes and Alcohol: Pylean taverns are called at The Hall of Drink and Chance. It's here that The Host's mom suffers the nickname 'Mother of the Vile Excrement.'

When the gang arrive back at Caritas, The Host offers them all a nightcap.

Sex and Drugs and Rock'n'Roll: The Groosalugg says he may go to Tarkna for defying the priests but that it was worth it for one moment of Cordelia's intimate touch. Although he's merely talking about hugging, she gets

embarrassed and insists: 'That was an accident. It was kind
of dark . . .'

**'You May Remember Me From Such Films and TV Series
As . . .':** Lee Reherman was Hawk in *American Gladiators*
and appeared in *Champions* and *Crossfire*. Whitney Dylan
was in *Coyote Ugly* and *Scenes of the Crime*.

Logic, Let Me Introduce You to This Window: After five
years of slavery and degradation in Pylea, Fred has
managed to keep her spectacles intact. How does the
Groosalugg know that Landok is The Host's kinsman?
What's the power source of the device that triggers
detonation in the collars? During the fight scenes Angel's
shirt has no blood or dirt at various times. Due to poor
editing the combatants' positions are also reversed between
one frame and the next. Sasha appears to be watching the
fight between Angel and the Groosalugg (he's standing
behind Fred) then, several seconds later, he *arrives* with the
group that includes Wesley, Gunn and Cordelia to stop the
battle. How did Angel get his car out of Caritas?

I Just *Love* Your Accent: In Pylea, they give five cheers
when praising someone rather than the traditional three,
much to Wesley's delight.

Quote/Unquote: Gunn, about to be executed: 'I've got a
plan.' Wesley: 'Thank God. What is it?' Gunn: 'We die
horribly and painfully. You go to hell and I spend eternity
in the arms of baby Jesus.'

Wesley: 'Why do people keep putting me in charge of
things?' Gunn: 'I have *no idea*.'

Wesley, on leadership: 'You try not to get anybody
killed, you wind up getting *everybody* killed.' And, Wesley:
'Should people be bowing in a free society?' Cordelia:
'These things take time.'

Notes: 'You know where I belong? L.A. . . . Nobody
belongs there. It's the perfect place for guys like us.' What
a lovely finale. A fairy tale with a moral centre and cool
jokes, in which the hero rediscovers his humanity in the
face of overwhelming odds, the heroine sacrifices love and
an easy life for what is right and Wesley learns hard lessons
on leadership and emerges triumphant. Best bit (of many):

Angel, Wes and Gunn looking into the basket where The Host's head lies, giving him a somewhat half-hearted eulogy and then screaming like girls when his eyes open and he asks 'Is that *it*?!'

Angel explains to Wesley and Gunn that he fired them (in **32**, 'Reunion') because the darkness was rising in him and he wanted his friends protected from it. The Deathwok Clan has a unique physiology. They can live without their heads if their bodies are not mutilated. They don't have five toes and their hearts are in their buttocks. In Pylea, Angel is known as a vantal, a drinker of blood. Fred uses kalla berries to sweeten her oatmeal made of crug grains and thistles. She's been trying to make enchiladas from tree bark ('there's work to be done'). She likes tacos and is relieved when Angel tells her that they still exist on Earth. Fred explains that the words on the cave walls are 'consonant representations of a mathematical trans-figuration formula' and that to know precisely where a portal will open requires the 'trionic speechcraft formula-tion/modification' of the books ('Lutzbalm predicted it in Zurich in '89. Laughed him off the stage.') The Pylean version of hell is called Tarkna. Numfar performs, off-screen, the dance of shame. Angel, according to Fred, doesn't snore, though he does caterwaul.

At the end of the episode Willow appears at the Hyperion to give Angel and his friends the terrible news of Buffy's death in *Buffy*: 'The Gift'.

Angel: 'Ask me why I'm smiling.'
Cordy: 'I will, because it's scaring me.'

– 'Waiting in the Wings'

Angel – Season Three (2001–2002)

Mutant Enemy Inc/David Greenwalt Productions/Kuzui Enterprises/Sandollar Television/20th Century Fox

Created by Joss Whedon and David Greenwalt
Co-Executive Producer: Tim Minear
Consulting Producer: Marti Noxon
Producer: Kelly A Manners
Co-Producer: Skip Schoolnik, Jeffrey Bell, James A Contner (48, 59)
Executive Producers: Sandy Gallin, Gail Berman, Fran Rubel Kuzui, Kaz Kuzui, Joss Whedon, David Greenwalt

Regular Cast:
David Boreanaz (Angel/Angelus)
Charisma Carpenter (Cordelia Chase, 45–58, 62–66)
Alexis Denisof (Wesley Wyndam-Pryce)
Julie Benz (Darla, 45–46, 51–53)
Stephanie Romanov (Lilah Morgan, 46, 48, 50, 52–54, 59–61, 63–66)
J August Richards (Charles Gunn)
Andy Hallett (Lorne, 45–47, 49, 51, 53–58, 60–66)
Matthew James (Merl, 45, 47)
Jarrod Crawford (Rondell, 47)
Amy Acker (Winifred Burkle)
Mark Lutz (The Groosalugg, 57–58, 62–66)
Daniel Dae Kim (Gavin Park, 46, 48, 50, 52–54, 63, 66)
Keith Szarabajka (Daniel Holtz, 45, 51–53, 56, 60, 64–65)
David Denman (Skip, 46, 55, 66)
Justin Shilton (Billy Blim[22], 46, 50)
Heidi Marnhout (Fury #1, 47, 51)
An Le (Fury #2, 47, 51)
Madison Gray (Fury #3, 47, 51)
Jack Conley (Sahjhan[23], 51–54, 59–61)

---

[22] Credited as 'Young Man' in **46**, 'That Vision Thing'.
[23] Credited as 'Demon' in **51**, 'Offspring'.

Robert Peters (Arney, 51, 53)
John Rubenstein (Linwood Murrow, 52–54, 61, 66)
Bronwen Bonner-Davies (Caroline Holtz, 52–53)
Kasha Kropinski (Sarah Holtz, 52–53)
Laurel Holloman (Justine Cooper, 54, 56, 59–61, 65–66)
Kay Panabaker (Girl, 61)
Vincent Kartheiser (Connor[24], 63–66)

45
Heartthrob

US Transmission Date: 24 September 2001
UK Transmission Date: 17 January 2002 (Sky),
2 June 2003 (Channel 5)

Writer: David Greenwalt
Director: David Greenwalt
Cast: Ron Melendez (James), Kate Norby (Elizabeth),
Koji Kataoka (Pilgrim), Sam Littlefield (Young Man Hostage),
Dalila Brown-Geiger (Sandy), Christian Hasting (Vamp #1),
Bob Fimiani (Codger Demon), Robert Madrid (Rough Man),
Bob Morrisey (Dr Gregson)

Angel Investigations liquidate a group of vampires. One of
them, Elizabeth, was the eternal love of James, an ex-
protégé of Angelus. Swearing revenge on his former
mentor, James seeks out a demon doctor to obtain the
Cure, a medical procedure that renders a vampire temporarily indestructible. Meanwhile, in a seedy Nicaraguan bar,
a man is killed by a heavily pregnant Darla.
Dudes and Babes: James and Elizabeth were vampire lovers
who travelled with Angelus and Darla, circa 1767. A
proto-Spike and Drusilla, they spent the next 234 years in
a passionate relationship. When Angel kills Elizabeth,
James becomes invincible thanks to Dr Gregory's Cure
and seeks vengeance on Angel. Holtz, previously mentioned in **31**, 'The Trial', was a vampire hunter who
tracked Darla and Angelus halfway across Europe after
they murdered his family.

---

[24] Uncredited in **63**, 'The Price'.

There's A Ghost In My House: Phantom Dennis takes care of a nauseous and tired Cordelia, running her bath and sponging her back. She admits that she would be lost without him and confides to him that her visions are, literally, killing her (see **46**, 'That Vision Thing').

References: *Romeo and Juliet*, the Velvet Underground's 'I'm Sticking With You' and *Home Alone*. Fred's 'when it all comes together' speech is a probable allusion to *Field of Dreams*. The fight on the subway train is a visual tribute to *The French Connection*. There's a *de rigueur Crouching Tiger, Hidden Dragon*-inspired pre-title sequence.

Not Exactly A Haven For The Demons: Nester Demons live in the walls of people's homes, hatch several times a year, and will continue to infest until their queen is killed. Cordy remembers that the Angel Investigations team killed a Nester group in Hancock Park some months ago.

The Charisma Show: 'I'm Cordelia, I don't think, I *know*!' Cordy notes that her new necklace brings out her breasts. 'You were *all* thinkin' it,' she adds, quickly. When Angel bemoans that Buffy's death didn't affect him as deeply as he felt it should, Cordelia replies that if he were a sick, obsessed vampire he'd go to the extreme lengths that James did. Rather, Angel is a living, breathing – well, *living*, anyway – good guy who's trying to help people. That isn't betraying Buffy's memory, it's honouring her. Best bit: Cordy sticking out her tongue at James as the train pulls away from the platform.

Cigarettes and Alcohol: The happy hour at Caritas involves two drinks, a song and no waiting.

Sex and Drugs and Rock'n'Roll: Gunn believes the grieving Angel should have got hammered and gone to Vegas instead of Sri Lanka. Wesley replies that Angel doesn't need a lap dance; he needs peace and quiet. James says that Angel isn't the same man who 'screwed Darla' and couldn't care less about what happened to her. Angel, flustered, asks where James heard about this, before realising that James is referring to his time as Angelus and not the events of **37**, 'Reprise' and **38**, 'Epiphany'. Gunn describes Fred as an Angel groupie.

Darla notes that when Angelus caught up with her in Vienna, after her betrayal of him in 1765 (see **31**, 'The Trial'), she had to pay for her sins, painfully and repeatedly. **'You May Remember Me From Such Films and TV Series As . . .':** Ron Melendez played Jeremy Bradford in *Legacy*. He also appeared in *Voodoo*, *Children of the Corn II*, *Scorned* and *The Nanny*. Kate Norby's movies include *Manfest* and *Believe*. Keith Szarabajka was Charles Gracen in *Profit* and Mickey Kostmayer in *The Equalizer*. His CV also includes *We Were Soldiers*, *Spy Game*, *Golden Years*, *Unnatural Pursuits*, *Walker*, *Missing*, *Roswell*, *Law & Order* and *Babylon 5*. Bob Morrisey was in *Buffy*, *The Book of Stars* and *Total Reality*.

Don't Give Up The Day Job: Australian-born Director of Photography Ross Berryman had previously worked on *Timecop*, *Early Edition*, *Dead Calm*, *Strictly Ballroom*, *BMX Bandits* and *A Slice of Life*. Film Loader Karen Korn's CV also includes *I'm the One That I Want*, *Stuart Little*, *Happenstance*, *Lover Girl* and *Mocking the Cosmos*.

Logic, Let Me Introduce You to This Window: The Caritas, supposedly a secret, demon-only bar, seems to be developing a more diverse clientele judging by the normal-looking crowd seen in this episode. The bloodstains on Angel's white shirt change position a couple of times during the monastery fight. When Cordelia puts on the necklace that Angel bought her she lifts her arms, makes a saucy comment and then moves her arms down. In the next shot, her arms are back where they were previously. Cordy was wearing the necklace when she had her vision, but when she arrives home and undresses in the bathroom, it's missing. Why does Angel need an invitation to enter Fred's room? The Hyperion is a hotel – more specifically, it's *Angel's* hotel – so surely all the rooms are public domain, or belong to him? Either way, he shouldn't need an invite. Or is he simply being a gentleman? Then there's the question of Darla's pregnancy . . . A union between vampires is impossible; the series is quite clear about this.

Geographical error: Angel says the vampires are driving down 6th Street, heading east. There's then a shot of them driving past the Felix Chevrolet dealership on Figueroa Street, also in Downtown but a considerable distance from where they're supposed to be. On the subject of the dagger that Angel gives to Wes, there was *no* Murshan dynasty in the sixteenth century – the Ming accounted for the period from 1368 to 1644. Although Darla's gown appears correct for the period, some of the other clothing in the 1767 sequences seems anachronistic. Cordelia surely doesn't have the strength to lift a fire extinguisher of that size and hurl it across the lobby with such accuracy. Some fans have criticised James's accent, though, to be fair, there's nothing in the text to indicate that he *isn't* American. Holtz, on the other hand, is supposed to be English (established in **52**, 'Quickening'), yet *his* accent is clearly American. His clothes, similarly, also appear to be American colonial rather than Georgian English. There's also the vampires being photographed thing again (see **24**, 'Are You Now Or Have You Ever Been?')

Motors: The vampires escape in a 1958 Chevrolet convertible.

I Just *Love* Your Accent: Wesley uses the word 'rambunctious'.

Quote/Unquote: Elizabeth: 'You know neither poetry nor love, Angelus.' Darla: 'He knows other things. Marvellously vile and *ripping* things.'

Wesley: 'The only way some people can find a purpose in life is by becoming obsessed with demons ... Technically, that wasn't a Lurite Demon, it was a Murite, a subspecies ...' Gunn: 'Glad to know *we're* not the sad people obsessed with demons.'

James: '*You* loved someone, with all your heart? No you didn't. If you had you wouldn't be standing here playing games with me ... Because once some bastard killed her, it would have killed *everything* in you.'

Notes: 'You think you won just because you're still alive? I *lived*. You just *existed*.' *Angel*'s ability to be judged on its own merits was always going to be difficult whilst it remained in close proximity to *Buffy*. Now, through circumstances beyond its control, it was *forced* to stand alone. So, what does *Angel* have going for it? A lot, actually, and much of it's on display here. 'Heartthrob' is a story about love; in all its forms. Dark, unremitting love; unrequited love; brotherly love; and love that kills. We're given insight into deep philosophical questions on the nature of true love. When *Angel*'s on-song, it really is a *very* good series. I think it just needs to be reminded of that fact occasionally. 'Heartthrob' proves, if proof were needed, that *Angel* can survive – artistically and creatively – on its own terms.

Angel has spent the last three months at a spiritual retreat in Sri Lanka and appears to be fluent in the Sinhala language. During Angel's absence, Cordelia moved some of his weapons, including his axe, to the basement because they were collecting dust. Darla is currently living in Nicaragua. She's put on a bit of weight since we last saw her (see **38**, 'Epiphany'). Fred hasn't left her room since Angel went away (see **44**, 'There's No Place Like Plrtz Glrb'). Her love of tacos is again mentioned, as is her penchant for writing on walls (see **43**, 'Through the Looking Glass', **49**, 'Fredless'). Cordelia says she misses Pylea. Both Wes and Gunn dislike rats. There are references to the Ring of Amara (see **3**, 'In the Dark'). Merl has been living in Akron since he left L.A. (see **36**, 'The Thin Dead Line'). Before arriving in Marseilles in 1767, Angelus and Darla had killed a troubadour in Madrid, and Angelus's group attracted the attention of Holtz by burning down the villa of the Count de Leon. They were planning to go, next, to Morocco. *History and Life* and *World History* are two books briefly glimpsed in the college room where the vampires attacked. **Soundtrack:** Andy Hallett sings a gorgeous version of Douglass Cross and George Cory's 'I Left My Heart in San Francisco'. The song is best known from Tony Bennett's 1962 recording. Also 'Blackjack' by Morphic Field, The Crystal Method's 'The Winner' (the song playing in the vampires' car) and 'Travel Mexico #1' from the OGM Music Library.
Cast and Crew Comments: Holtz was a decent family man, David Greenwalt told *Zap2It.com*: 'He hunted Angel and

Darla across Europe in the 1700s. They reciprocated by eating his wife and children. So he has a *special* vendetta against them. He has something of the Wild West about him.'

Who's That Girl?: During the summer of 2001, J August Richards was regularly spotted around L.A. on the arm of *Felicity* star Tangi Miller. The couple met at a Hollywood Club the previous year. 'When she walked in I was completely taken by her,' Richards told *TV Guide*. 'She's my best friend but she also happens to be the hottest girl in the world. That's a deadly combination.' 'We love music, movies and travelling, especially if it involves an exotic locale,' Miller added.

Did You Know?: The biggest story surrounding *Angel* during spring 2001 had little to do with events on Pylea. Rather, it was about where the series would be broadcast next season. Tension erupted when *Angel*'s production company, Fox, asked the WB to pay $2 million per episode for *Buffy*, effectively doubling the previous cost. The resulting impasse sent shockwaves through the industry, with other networks itching to bid at any sign of a terminal break between parties. *Angel* became caught in the crossfire. David Boreanaz told *TV Guide* that he didn't have a preference whether his show stayed on the WB or followed *Buffy* to another network. 'If *Angel* ended up on, say, UPN I'd still go into work and do my thing,' he noted. 'That's what I get paid for.'

Eventually, after much haggling, the WB did renew *Angel* and moved it to a 9 p.m. Monday slot. '[*Angel*] has a slightly different audience than *Buffy*, and I believe it can stand alone,' Joss Whedon told *SciFi Wire*. Boreanaz conceded that having the two series on competing networks would make future crossovers difficult. 'If the storyline calls for a major crossover, we'll cross that bridge when we come to it,' he said. 'But I think the distance between the shows will enhance the storylines.' Whedon added, 'There will always be a lingering tie, but both have to move on . . . It's like other changes you face. If you lose a cast member, for instance like we did with Seth Green, you work through it.'

As for his title character, Boreanaz noted: 'Angel's going to be a bit more of an action hero, rather than a depressed person. He's gonna break out of that and his humour will come out more.' Joss confirmed that we could expect to see more of Angel's funny side. 'We'll always try humour because Boreanaz is truly funny. We have fun with the character when we lighten him up [and] show how cheap, vain or petty Angel can be. We're going to really pull him, emotionally. We're *not* going to turn him into an I-don't-speak-for-a-whole-episode killing machine, cos we already did that.'

A Change Of Channel: After Channel 4's shoddy and disgraceful treatment of *Angel* (see **3**, 'In the Dark'), which culminated in the broadcaster showing season two in a late-night slot to virtually no viewers, they declined to pick up their option to be the UK's terrestrial broadcaster for season three. The rights were subsequently picked up by Channel 5, who have developed a reputation for picking up interesting US shows and pitching them to a cult audience (*Charmed* and *CSI* are two of the network's best-rated shows, and they have also acquired *Alias*).

46
That Vision Thing

US Transmission Date: 1 October 2001
UK Transmission Date: 24 January 2002 (Sky),
9 June 2003 (Channel 5)

Writer: Jeffrey Bell
Director: Bill Norton
Cast: Frank Sotonoma Salsedo (The Shaman),
Ken Takemoto (Old Chinese Man), Alice Lo (Old Chinese Woman),
Mitchell Gibney (Innocuous Man), Bob Sattler (Masked Man),
Kal Penn (Young Man in Fez)

Cordelia begins to suffer physical consequences from the visions she receives. Angel, Wesley, Gunn and Fred find themselves in a race against time to gain a series of artefacts that will allow Angel to travel between dimensions, but, in doing so, they are caught in a sinister power struggle involving Wolfram & Hart.

Dudes and Babes: Fred has, at least, made it out of her room and downstairs since the last episode.

Denial, Thy Name is Cordelia: Cordy's visions are now leaving physical damage. Yet she keeps her stigmatic injuries from her colleagues until they become too noticeable to hide. These visions aren't being sent by The Powers That Be, however, but by Wolfram & Hart's fez-wearing psychic.

It's a Designer Label!: Gucci's tastefully expensive horse-bit loafers, as worn by Gavin here. Also, Cordy's delightful 'Cowboy' T-shirt. On the minus side, Lorne's purple and orange ensemble is distressing to the eye.

References: Lorne mentions *Star Trek* actor William Shatner, and his opinion that his singing is dreadful. Fred considers Cordy to be 'exactly like Lassie', as her visions are Angel's equivalent of knowing when Timmy's trapped down a well. Also, Sherlock Holmes, Julie Andrews and her performance in Rodgers and Hammerstein's *The Sound of Music*, *The Phantom of the Opera*, American Revolutionary leader John Hancock (1737–93) – the first signatory of the Declaration of Independence, the nursery rhyme *Pop Goes The Weasel*, *The Elephant Man* and the biblical Book of Job. 'Reach out and touch someone' was the advertising slogan for Bell Atlantic. Jeff Bell knows all about the Wan-Shang D'hole, a supposedly extinct Chinese dog with superhuman intelligence. One of his *X-Files* episodes, 'Alpha', featured the creature. There are dialogue allusions to *Indiana Jones and the Last Crusade*, *Star Wars*, *Magnum Force* and *Thunderball*, and visual nods to *The Usual Suspects*.

Locations include the Van Hoa Duong herbalist shop from which Angel, Wes and Gunn retrieved the coin, located at 823 N Broadway in Chinatown.

The Charisma Show: Poor girl, she really goes through the wringer in this – suffering a plague of boils and then third-degree burns. Charisma's acting has never been finer or more sympathetic, and she still gets two of the funniest lines in the episode.

Not Exactly A Haven For The Demons: The cheerful Skip guards a cell in what Lilah describes as a demon dimension. Although demonic-looking, however, Skip seems to work for The Powers That Be (see **55**, 'Birthday', **66**, 'Tomorrow', **83**, 'Inside Out'). He keeps the prisoner in a cube of eternal fire by the power of his will, which also prevents the prisoner's screams from being heard (see **50**, 'Billy'). Similarly, the Wan-Shang D'hole (or possibly Cantonese Fook Beasts, Wesley isn't certain), with their superhuman martial-arts skills, also appear to be on the side of The Powers, since they were guarding the coin, a vital part of the key that opens the dimensional walls. As Angel notes, it's hard to tell who the good guys are these days.

The fez-wearing psychic has the power to enter the celestial pipeline and transmit fearsome visions to others. He can also levitate, which he does when sending visions. He is hired by Wolfram & Hart to plague Cordelia, but Angel ultimately (and satisfyingly) kills him.

'You May Remember Me From Such Films and TV Series As . . .': David Denham was in *The X-Files*, *CSI: Miami* and *Out Cold*. Mitchell Gibney appeared in *JAG*. Alice Lo's CV includes *Suddenly*. Kal Penn was in *Malibu's Most Wanted*, *Buffy* and *Hector*, which he also produced. Frank Salsedo played Sam Lopez in *Centennial*. His CV also includes *Quantum Leap*, *Northern Exposure* and *Walker, Texas Ranger*. Bob Sattler's movies include *Anywhere But Here*, *Gone in Sixty Seconds* and *This Girl's Life*. Justin Shilton was in *Paper Cut*. Ken Takemoto appeared in *Dreamers* and *Moment Cafe*.

Don't Give Up The Day Job: Jeffrey Bell made his name as a writer/producer for several years on *The X-Files*. Production Designer Stuart Blatt's CV also includes *What's Cooking?*, *Susan's Plan*, *Serpent's Lair*, *Fear of a Black Hat* and *Munchie*.

There's A Ghost In My House: Dennis opens the door to show Fred out of Cordy's apartment just before Cordy has her boil-infested vision.

Logic, Let Me Introduce You to This Window: If vampires aren't welcome in the herbalist shop, shouldn't that have been a clue that the demons were working for The Powers That Be? Why doesn't Angel smell the blood from Cordy's wounds? Cordy takes an aspirin for her headache yet, as we subsequently discover in **55**, 'Birthday', she's been on much stronger medication than that for over a year. So what good is an aspirin going to do here? How did Cordy put on her blouse so quickly before opening the bathroom door? Does the concept of 'minutes' have any meaning in an eternal dimension like Skip's? Angel asks Fred to take Cordy home. That would seem to be the first time since returning from Pylea that Fred's been out of the Hyperion. Does she still know how to drive? Can she find her way to Cordy's place and then back to the hotel? If that was the Shaman's home, how could Darla enter uninvited?

Motors: Angel compares Cordelia to a 'very nice' car, but says that her visions are just an extra, like the Hurst shifter or Craiger wheels.[25]

Classic *Double Entendre*: Fred: 'I've been *forking* with Gunn.' Plus a hilarious conversation between Wesley and Gunn involving the words 'dick' and 'dong'.

I Just *Love* Your Accent: Wesley notes that, after Gavin's lovely reintroduction, he can 'piss off'.

Quote/Unquote: Gunn: 'She doesn't *choose* to have a vision. The Powers send them when they've got info to share.' Wesley: 'Think of them as gifts.' Cordelia: 'Yes. Having-my-head-torn-open-and-hot-lava-poured-into-my-skull gifts.'

Cordelia, on Gavin: 'OK, minion of darkness, Satan's toady, but that's a *nice* suit.' And to Fred: 'Wow. Next to you, I'm downright linear.'

Angel, on Lorne: 'He's fine. He's unconscious, but he's fine.'

Notes: 'Don't come at me through Cordelia again. You play that card a second time, I'll kill you.' Cordelia-centric

---

[25] Hurst has been the OEM supplier for the Pontiac GTO, Plymouth Barracuda and SuperBird, Ford Mustang and Oldsmobile. From Drag Racing to Street Rods, Hurst manufactures quality engineered shifters and transmission controls to fit the needs of the performance-minded driver. Craiger wheels were popular with hotrodders in the 50s and 60s.

episodes are a bit like Roger Moore's James Bond films. You know you shouldn't be enjoying them, because they're corny, derivative and juvenile. But even knowing that, you can't help yourself. 'That Vision Thing', however, is a contender for a Cordy episode that doesn't work – the *Angel* equivalent of *Octopussy*. The problem is, largely, in Jeff Bell's characterisation of Cordy herself, which misses the mark so badly, and in so many ways, that one wonders whether the author had *seen* this series before. That's a shame, because this episode depends on Cordy being *very* Cordy. So, whilst 'That Vision Thing' mostly works, there's something fundamentally wrong with it. The episode takes the form of a quest, full of sharp mythological references, clever jokes and watchable performances. But it could have been much better if time had been taken to explore the anguish that Cordelia is experiencing. The stigmata allusions, possible messianic overtones and the mention of Job all seem to be leading somewhere very specific but, ultimately, don't go there. Nevertheless, *Angel* episodes tend to disappoint only when they aren't being ambitious enough. It's therefore in 'That Vision Thing's favour that it merely fails to satisfy in areas of aesthetics rather than construction. Flawed, but interesting.

Wesley, Gunn and Fred all like Chinese food. Angel mentions the vampire alarms at Wolfram & Hart (see **21**, 'Blind Date'). Amongst the things that Fred finds fascinating are forks, peanut butter and the letter H. Strange girl. In 5th grade, she dreamed of going steady with Grayson Wells. It never happened. She is, however, very perceptive concerning levels of sincerity. Gunn has an aunt who used to get crusty stuff on her back each summer due to a shellfish allergy. The Hyperion is said to be violating 57 building codes, including lack of earthquake proofing, asbestos and termites ('Is that a lot?' asks Angel!). Gavin notes that Lilah has been given Lindsey McDonald's old office (see **40**, 'Dead End'). Lilah remembers Lindsey literally giving his blood for the company (see **22**, 'To Shanshu in L.A.'). Lilah has a golf simulation game on her office computer. Her printer is a very flashy Epson. The senior partners have moved Gavin into Special Projects from the Real Estate division. Darla is now in Honduras.

Did You Know?: J August Richards attended the University of Southern California with *Buffy* actors Danny Strong and George Hertzberg.

Cast And Crew Comments: When asked whose idea Darla's pregnancy had been, Tim Minear recalled that the discussion involved himself, David Greenwalt and Joss Whedon while the trio were walking near to the Santa Monica pier. 'We were saying, "It was great last year when we brought Darla back in a box." I said, "Let's bring something back in *Darla's* box!" Joss stopped and said, "You know, we *really* can." That's how *that* happened.'

David Greenwalt's Comments: *Angel's* somewhat static ratings frustrated its executive producer. 'We could do an all-nude episode, and we'd still get the same rating,' David told *zap2it.com*. Nonetheless, Greenwalt believed that *Angel* would make the most of its new time slot, which saw it airing after the WB's most popular series, *7th Heaven*. 'It's a weird lead-in, but a good one. *7th Heaven* is family fare and ours is a little harder hitting. The WB is supporting us.' (Later in the season Greenwalt was being somewhat less diplomatic about this bizarre scheduling, telling *TV Guide*, 'It was like following *Mary Poppins* with *Seven*. Nobody could imagine the people who like *7th Heaven* sticking around to watch our dark little show.') *Angel* would also be giving viewers some laughs, Greenwalt promised. 'I think we've stressed too much the darkness. It's escaped people that the show is a lot like *Die Hard*. We have a [protagonist] who does all the heroic things, but he's also funny and a little cheap and makes very human mistakes. That's one of my favourite things about him; he's capable of saving the wrong girl.'

47
That Old Gang of Mine

US Transmission Date: 8 October 2001
UK Transmission Date: 31 January 2002 (Sky),
16 June 2003 (Channel 5)

Writer: Tim Minear
Director: Fred Keller
Cast: Khalil Khan (Gio), Giancarlo Carimona (Gang Kid),
Steve Niel (Huge & Horrible), Josh Kayne (Cowering Demon),
Sam Ayers (Tough Guy Demon),
Candice Cook (Dead Masked Demon)[26]

Someone is killing Los Angeles's demons, seemingly at random. Gunn must choose sides when he discovers that his old gang are responsible for the wave of murders. During a lengthy stand-off at Caritas, Gunn saves Lorne and Angel, but at the cost of his friendship with Wesley.

Denial, Thy Name is Gunn: Discovering evidence that the demon killings were committed by someone on his old crew, he steals evidence from Wesley and is, initially, happy to let Rondell handle what he sees as a matter of internal discipline. It is only when he finds out that Gio had Rondell's full sanction that, too late, Gunn prepares to tell Wes what he knows.

It's a Designer Label!: Angel's leather pants and Cordy's hide vest and miniskirt.

References: The title was taken from the name of a song written by Ray Henderson, Billy Rose and Mort Dixon, which featured in the musical *Ziegfield Follies of 1923*. Visual references to *Psycho*.

Locations mentioned include Century City in West L.A., the Miracle Mile (a pedestrian shopping district on Pacific Avenue) and Venice Boulevard.

Awesome: Angel's insincere opening apology to Merl, and his subsequent baiting of the demon. And then, after Merl's death, his reaction to finding his own name at the top of Cordelia's list of Merl's enemies. (Cordy's rationale, that Angel begins with 'A', doesn't placate him.)

---

[26] Uncredited.

Not Exactly A Haven For The Bruthas: New blood, in the shape of the sinister Gio, is leading the vampire-killing crew – formerly under Gunn's leadership – to massacre any demons they can find, whether they're good, evil, or something in-between, at random and for sport. They have killed at least sixteen demons (including Merl) and, in this episode, wreck Caritas, threaten Lorne and expect Gunn to stake Angel as proof of his loyalty to them.

Caritas's possible location in Chinatown (see **33**, 'Redefinition') seems confirmed by the revelation that it is located near a restaurant called Pung Fat Lucy's.

Cigarettes and Alcohol: Merl tries to smash a bottle of Black Star beer into Angel's face at Caritas. Wesley is later seen drinking the same brand. Various Rolling Rock bottles are being used as candle-holders by Rondell's crew.

Sex and Drugs and Rock'n'Roll: We're introduced to three supernatural females, the Transuding Furies. They can float, cast protective spells, and seem to be linked mentally. They also know Angel. *Well.* Angel explains that Lorne hires them, monthly, to cast a Sanctorium spell on Caritas, preventing any demon violence within the bar. The Furies suggest that only Angel is equipped to repay the debt for lifting this spell and, thus, allowing him to help his friends. Cordelia thinks about this information for a moment then simply says, 'Ew!'

'You May Remember Me From Such Films and TV Series As . . .': Khalil Kain appeared in *Friends*, *Suddenly Susan*, *CSI*, *Girlfriends* and *The Tiger Woods Story*. Sam Ayers was in *24*, *The Pretender* and *Angels Don't Sleep Here*. Heidi Marnhout's movies include *Vice Girls*, *Roadkill* and *Mothers and Daughters*. Josh Kayne appeared in *The Discontents*. Candice Cook's CV includes *That '70s Show*, *The Drew Carey Show* and *Not Another Teen Movie*. She was also a Staff Assistant on *US Marshals* and Assistant Director on *Lycanthrope*. Madison Gray produced *Trois*.

Don't Give Up The Day Job: Assistant Production Co-ordinator Kimberley Bellanger also worked on *The X-Files*. Assistant Director Brenda Kalosh's CV includes *A Kiss So Deadly*, *The Hand That Rocks the Cradle*, *Steel*

Magnolias, *Mississippi Burning* and *Legal Eagles*. Leadman
Chris Carriveau previously worked on *Hyperion Bay*,
Boogie Nights and *From Dusk Till Dawn*. Key Grip Andre
Sobczak's movies include *Outside Ozona*, *Chameleon* and
Schindler's List.

Logic, Let Me Introduce You to This Window: How does
Merl, who seems to live underground (see **34**, 'Blood
Money'), get mail delivered to him? The Furies appear to
know Angel in the biblical sense. We must, therefore,
assume that it takes more than three celestial beings to
make him *truly* happy.

Quote/Unquote: Angel: 'That's Merl.' Gunn: 'Where's the
rest of him?' Angel: 'I stopped by this morning, thought I'd
give "sincere" one more shot. Even brought doughnuts . . .
So far, we've ruled out suicide.'

Furies: '*Mmmmm*, Angel!'

Lorne: 'This is a sanctuary.' Gio: 'Not any more.'

Wesley, to Gunn: 'It's never easy. The pull of divided
loyalties. Whatever choice we [make], we feel as though
we've betrayed someone.'

Notes: 'Charles Gunn? I know about you. That name's
part of the reason why I came out here.' **25**, 'First
Impressions' already gave the audience a look at the mean
streets from which Charles Gunn emerged to join Angel
Investigations. The death of his friend, George, in **42**,
'Over the Rainbow', emphasised that this wasn't Gunn's
world any more: he had bigger fish to fry with his new
white and green friends. 'That Old Gang of Mine' takes us
back to hard, black-and-white issues – and finds, instead,
only grey. Tim Minear is the emergent star of *Angel*'s
development from being a merely watchable show into a
truly *great* one. A keen observer of injustice and moral
uncertainty, Minear is equally interested in the life choices
that people have: whether to do the *right* thing or the *easy*
thing. **24**, 'Are You Now or Have You Ever Been?' and **29**,
'Darla' explored these issues, and this episode follows in
their footsteps by asking, in a city of monsters, who the
real monsters are. For an 'issue' episode, however, it's
surprisingly light on answers. There's lots of death and not

much resolution. In working with the contradiction of Gunn's life, it exposes a necessary truth within the *Angel* dynamic that's long overdue. When Gunn tells Rondell, 'It's about the mission. [Angel's] got it, you don't,' he's making a literal statement about the show's development into something far removed from what it was just a couple of years ago. Almost a critical summation of this development, 'That Old Gang of Mine' can be viewed as a dark, troubling allegory on racism and xenophobia cutting both ways and a crack in the assumption that the world can be reduced to monochrome realities. Or it can be watched as a simple morality tale which suggests that people who enjoy killing others are, generally, not very nice. Either way, Minear's story should be both enjoyed and thought about. In today's television of compromise that, in itself, is worthwhile. *Angel* is never finer than when it's angry. This is *raging*.

This episode takes place approximately three months after the events of **44**, 'There's No Place Like Plrtz Glrb'. Angel tells Gunn that Gunn will only prove his loyalty when the day comes that he has to kill Angel. This echoes similar conversations with Wesley (**14**, 'I've Got You Under My Skin') and Cordelia (**11**, 'Somnambulist'). Wesley tells Rondell that his bullet wounds sustained in **36**, 'The Thin Dead Line' took months to heal. Gunn still has nightmares about his sister's death (see **20**, 'War Zone'). He has a poster of a motorbike on his bedroom wall and, apparently, sleeps with the light on. One of Wesley's books is the Latin volume *Mastrii De Meldula*. Rondell placed George's remains in the river after the funeral (see **41**, 'Belonging'). Merl says that he spent three months in therapy after Angel left him hanging upside down in the sewer (**33**, 'Redefinition'). He owned a very expensive-looking stereo and a Rolodex. Gio suggests that Miami, like L.A., has a significant vampire problem. A Yarbnie is a balancing entity. They tend to nest in urban areas under roadways and are utterly non-violent. **Soundtrack:** Fred sings a beautiful version of Patsy Cline's torch ballad 'Crazy' at Caritas. Gio warbles a less impressive 'Wind Beneath My Wings'.

Critique: 'The best change,' noted *USA Today*'s Robert Bianco, 'may be the maturation of *Buffy*'s former spoiled brat Cordelia, played with increasing depth and dexterity by Charisma Carpenter. With Buffy out of the picture, Cordelia may even serve as a romantic interest for her vampire boss.'

Cast And Crew Comment: 'I'm *The Darla Guy*!' Tim Minear told *ign.com*'s Susan Kuhn. 'I used to be *The Kate Guy*. The reason I like writing Kate episodes or Darla episodes is because there's stuff to play.'

Did You Know?: One of the highlights of the *Angel* Season Three DVD box-set was Amy Acker's screen test, a mock-Shakespearean scene which also featured Alexis Denisof and J August Richards.

48
Carpe Noctem

US Transmission Date: 15 October 2001
UK Transmission Date: 7 February 2002 (Sky),
23 June 2003 (Channel 5)

Writer: Scott Murphy
Director: James A Contner
Cast: Rance Howard (Marcus Roscoe), Paul Benjamin (Fellow Resident),
Misty Louwagie (Christina), Paul Logan (Woody),
Lauren Reina (Escort #1), Magdalena Zielinska (Escort #2),
Steven W Bailey (Ryan)

An old man, Marcus, casts a body-swopping spell on Angel, and enjoys the pleasures of being eternally young, handsome and a vampire in Los Angeles. Meanwhile, a dying Angel tries desperately to get his real body back. Will his friends realise that something is wrong in time to save him?

Dudes and Babes: Marcus uses an Algurian spell, via a conjuring orb. This burns out the body of the victim, eventually killing them. Body-swopping has been seen before in the *Buffy* episodes 'The Witch' and 'This Year's Girl'.

Denial, Thy Name is Fred: Poor Fred suffers from unrequited love for Angel. It all ends, inevitably, in tears.

It's a Designer Label!: Fred glimpses Cordelia's fashion magazine and wonders why girls want to look like that. Fred notes that she spent five years in a cave, starving. 'What's their excuse?'

References: The title is Latin for 'seize the night', and alludes to *Dead Poets Society*. Fred believes that Angel's reading list may include Fyodor Dostoyevsky's *The Brothers Karamazov* and the works of James Joyce (1882–1941: *Ulysses, Finnegans Wake*) and Johann Wolfgang von Goethe (1749–1832: *Faust, Iphigenie auf Tauris*). She suggests that Angel's inability to experience love is worthy of F Scott Fiztzgerald (1896–1940: *Tender is the Night, The Great Gatsby, The Last Tycoon*). Angel describes a Charlton Heston double feature comprising two of Chuck's finest non-biblical movies: *Soylent Green* and *The Omega Man*. Cordy makes sarcastic references to Julia Roberts and *Pretty Woman*, a film with a risible, unrealistic presentation of prostitution. There are allusions to Florentine statesman and political philosopher Niccolò Machiavelli (1469–1527: *The Prince*), *Ski Slopes* magazine, the Pilates Method and Tae-bo (two fashionable exercise regimes), the sport of bungee jumping and the TV series *Kolchak: The Night Stalker*. (Or, possibly, the mid-80s serial killer and rapist Richard Ramirez, who was nicknamed 'the Night Stalker'.) One possible source for a story about a vampire being body-swopped is Anne Rice's 'Tale of the Body Thief'.

Locations mentioned include the NuArt Theater, located in Westside on Santa Monica Boulevard. The NuArt is one of California's most prestigious centres for independent and foreign-language cinema. It's also Los Angeles's home for *The Rocky Horror Picture Show*, which plays there every Saturday. All of Marcus's victims used prostitutes from First Class Escorts, located on La Brea and 6th Street, near Hancock Park. The club where Marcus goes cruising is the Hollywood Tropicana, on Western Ave.

Bitch!: Lilah calls Marcus a son of a bitch after he tries to bite her whilst inhabiting Angel's body.

'**West Hollywood?':** In the episode's best scene, Cordelia tells Marcus that he – Angel, that is – must speak to Fred and nip any blossoming relationship in the bud. Marcus assumes that Fred is a man and, therefore, that Angel must be gay. Marcus subsequently guesses that Wesley is Fred, and the pair have an awkward conversation which ends abruptly when Marcus realises who Fred really is.

L.A.-Speak: Phil: 'I heard he, like, died.' Angel: 'He, like, *did.*'

Sex and Drugs and Rock'n'Roll: The episode opens with a man having sex with two women in a hotel room, stopping only for them to catch their breath whilst he downs a Martini. Then he has a heart attack. He'd have *wanted* it that way.

Marcus, in Angel's body, shares a drink with Lilah, then they get down to business on the top of Wesley's desk, much to the watching Fred's distress. When Marcus goes clubbing, and tries to bite a woman he picks up, her boyfriend and two friends attack him. Marcus easily fends them off, causing the boyfriend to ask what he is on. 'I'd say I'm high on life,' notes Marcus, ironically.

'You May Remember Me From Such Films and TV Series As ...': The father of Ron and Clint Howard, Rance Howard's CV covers almost 50 years, and TV appearances in *Married ... With Children*, *Gentle Ben*, *Seinfeld*, *Dynasty*, *Happy Days*, *Battlestar Galactica*, *The Waltons*, *Kung Fu*, *The Virginian*, *The Thorn Birds*, *The Andy Griffith Show* and *Perry Mason*. His movies include *Spider-Man*, *Where Truth Lies*, *Apollo 13*, *Ed Wood*, *Parenthood*, *The Executioner's Song*, *Grand Theft Auto* (which he also wrote and produced), *Chinatown*, *Cool Hand Luke* and *The Music Man*. Paul Benjamin appeared in *Starsky and Hutch*, *Kojak*, *ER*, *Midnight Cowboy*, *Vanishing Point*, *Do the Right Thing* and *Last Rites*. Marc Brett was in *Ally McBeal* and *General Hospital*. Paul Logan's CV includes *Erotica Confessions*, *Savage Season* and *Days of Our Lives*. Steven Bailey was in *Phantasmagoria*. Lauren Reina played Marina in *Bare Witness*.

Don't Give Up The Day Job: Scott Murphy had previously written for *Strange Frequency*, *The Huntress*, *Nightmare*

Room and *Last Request*. Although he's acted in *Bandits* and *Practical Magic*, Rich Sickler is best known as an assistant director on movies like *The Scorpion King*, *What Lies Beneath*, *The Haunting*, *Batman & Robin* and *Heat*. Unit Production Manager Robert Nellans's CV includes *The X-Files*, *Beverly Hills 90210*, *The Abyss*, *Home Fires Burning* and *The Dukes of Hazzard*. Casting Associate Lonnie Hamerman's movies include *Jumbo Girl*, *Resurrection Mary* and *Big Time*.

Logic, Let Me Introduce You to This Window: As Angel reads the *Metro*, in several shots he's looking at the back page, with page one visible towards camera. Yet in others, when the camera is behind him, the newspaper is folded so that the middle is showing. When Angel is standing at the counter, his reflection can clearly be seen in the finish. Similarly, when he's destroying the answering-machine tape, a reflection shows on the table. There are also reflections seen on the desk as Angel shreds the files. The 213 area code (see **Notes**) is for Downtown; 323 is the code for Hollywood, which is the Hyperion's suggested location in several previous episodes (notably **24**, 'Are You Now or Have You Ever Been?').[27] There's such tight security at the retirement home that Angel can't get out. Yet visitors can, seemingly, come and go without incident – including some carrying weapons. Do Marcus's heart attacks cause his victims' bodies to die, or does the stress of body-swop trauma cause the heart attacks in the first place? Angel suggests that Marcus has 'finally found a body that won't burn out'. However, when Angel has a heart attack whilst in Marcus's body, we see no effects on Marcus in Angel's body.

Quote/Unquote: Angel: 'I'm *not* a eunuch.' Cordelia: 'Just a figure of speech.' Angel: 'Find a *better* one.'

Cordelia, on Angel: 'This is *totally* like him. Doing the mystery dance with some cheap blonde.' Fred: 'She was a cheap brunette.' Cordelia: 'You're right, this *isn't* like him.'

The location used for the Hyperion is the Los Altos Hotel and Apartments, built in 1925 and situated on Wilshire Boulevard.

Cordelia: 'You're Angel? With *that* cologne? I don't think so.'

Notes: 'I know who I am.' An obvious, by-the-numbers storyline which is, at least, enlivened by David Boreanaz's fine performance. Trouble is, we've seen this plot before. The body swop is such a staple of telefantasy shows (*The X-Files*' 'Dreamland', *Star Trek*'s 'Turnabout Intruder', *The Avengers*' 'Who's Who?', *Buffy*'s 'Who Are You?') that it's difficult to achieve anything new with it. And, sadly, nothing terrifically innovative appears here. Some good acting aside, the episode is highly forgettable.

Angel remains uncomfortable with the term 'eunuch' (see **28**, 'Guise Will Be Guise'). Angel Investigations still uses the business cards that Cordelia designed in **2**, 'Lonely Heart'. Cordy's describe her as 'Senior Associate'. Wesley and Gunn also have their own individualised cards. The Hyperion's address is 1481 Hyperion Avenue. Its phone number, 213-555-0162, had been partly revealed in **2**, 'Lonely Heart'. The answering-machine message has been changed from 'We help the hopeless' (see **4**, 'I Fall To Pieces'). Wesley is translating *Fassad's Guide* from the original Sumerian. He has a contact in the coroner's office and prefers loose tea to teabags. Gunn, seemingly, owns a Gameboy. Having accompanied Angel to the movies, Fred considers him to be chivalrous: he held the door open for her and bought her ticket, as well as popcorn, which they shared. Wolfram & Hart employs a graphic artist, Carter Williams, who is also an expert forger. As part of her ongoing power struggle with Gavin (**46**, 'That Vision Thing') Lilah gives Angel permits which mean the Hyperion satisfies various health and safety codes. The episode ends with Cordelia receiving a call from Willow to say that Buffy is alive – a summation of *Buffy*: 'The Gift' and 'Bargaining' Parts 1 and 2. These events, therefore, take place during *Buffy*: 'Flooded'.

The Comic: 'Reunion', a single-issue comic authored by Jane Espenson, tells the story of what happened during Buffy and Angel's off-screen meeting after this episode. Or, at least, what Xander, Anya and Dawn *speculate* may have happened.

Soundtrack: The Chemical Brothers' classic 'Galaxy Bounce' plays as Marcus cruises the Tropicana. Also, Limor's 'Jaded Heart'.

Critique: 'It's strange that a series based around one man's desperate need to make peace with himself should make you laugh out loud so often,' noted *Starburst*'s Jim Smith. 'But it does. This "try anything" approach can sometimes give *Angel* the appearance of near schizophrenia, but it's the series' unpredictability that has helped it sustain its appeal.'

Did You Know?: Constantly being voted one of the world's sexist women seems to have done wonders for Charisma Carpenter's self-confidence. Even a skin blemish, for so long neurotically covered up, has been allowed to blossom. 'It's not actually a mole,' Charisma told Ed Gross, 'it's a sun spot. When I was thirteen I went skiing and got severe sunburn on my face and it scabbed over. [Now I] embrace it, because it's too much work to hide it.'

49
Fredless

US Transmission Date: 22 October 2001
UK Transmission Date: 14 February 2002 (Sky),
30 June 2003 (Channel 5)

Writer: Mere Smith
Director: Maria Grabiak
Cast: Gary Grubbs (Roger Burkle), Jennifer Griffin (Trish Burkle)

Fred's parents unexpectedly arrive in L.A. However, far from being delighted to see them, Fred goes on the run rather than face them, leaving her friends to harbour some dark suspicions about Roger and Trish Burkle.

Denial, Thy Name is Fred: On her return from Pylea, Fred sent a letter to her parents asking them not to look for her. Lorne tells Fred that she has been running away from her fears and memories all her life, and that she doesn't seem to have run far enough yet. Ironically, Fred is the only member of the Angel Investigations team whose parents are subsequently revealed to be supportive of her chosen lifestyle and who still wish to be a part of her life.

References: When talking about the *Alien* movies, Mrs Burkle notes that her husband enjoyed them, except the last one, during which he fell asleep. That would be the one scripted by Joss Whedon. Angel alludes to novelist William Faulkner (1897–1962: *The Sound and the Fury*, *The Unvanquished*). Also *Judge Judy* (Lorne is a fan), *The Godfather Part III* (Lorne *isn't* a fan), *WWF Smackdown*, Jack Nicklaus's match with Gary Player at the 1963 Bob Hope Desert Classic, *Big* (Lorne telling Angel that he isn't a mystical vending machine), *Alice in Wonderland* ('I'm late'), naturalist Charles Darwin (1809–82) and disgraced former Vice President Spiro Agnew (1918–96). Fred describes Angel's team with imagery from the characters in *The Wizard of Oz*. Locations mentioned include the L.A. Public Library (see **41**, 'Belonging').

'West Hollywood?': Lorne admits to wearing eyeliner. Roger notes that men from Texas tend not to.

The Charisma Show: Why is such prominence given in the opening scene to Charisma's bottom? Not that I'm complaining, you understand . . .

L.A.-Speak: Cordy: 'We are so *immensely* dead.'

Sex and Drugs and Rock'n'Roll: There's a subtle allusion to Fred's parents being worried that she's involved in pornographic movies.

'You May Remember Me From Such Films and TV Series As . . .': Jennifer Griffin appeared in *Snoops*, *Six Feet Under*, *Born Into Exile*, *Vanilla Sky* and *Hotel Lobby*. Mississippi-born Gary Grubbs is one of those character actors who seems to have been in *everything*. His CV includes *The Astronaut's Wife*, *Will & Grace*, *The X-Files*, *JFK* (as Al Oser), *Foxfire*, *Silkwood*, *Caroline in the City*, *The A-Team*, *The Dukes of Hazzard*, *M*A*S*H*, *The Rockford Files* and *Charlie's Angels*.

Don't Give Up The Day Job: Marita Grabiak directed episodes of *ER* and *Firefly*. Previously, she had been a script supervisor on movies like *Bat*21*, *Young Guns* and *Mother's Boys*. Set Decorator Sandy Struth's CV also includes *Payback*, *Boogie Nights*, *Tracey Takes On . . .* and *S.F.W.* Camera Operator Eric Fletcher's previous work includes *Firestarter 2: Rekindled*, *18* and *Hail! Hail! Rock 'n' Roll*. *Angel*'s Stunt Co-ordinator Mike Massa was Ben Affleck's double on *Pearl Harbor*. His CV also includes *Miss Congeniality*, *Magnolia*, *Seven Days*, *America's Most Wanted*, *Roswell* and *Superboy*. When Mike himself isn't doubling for David Boreanaz, that job belongs to Chad Stahelski who has also worked on *Buffy*, *Kung Pow: Enter the Fist*, *Wild Wild West*, *The Matrix*, *8MM*, *Alien: Resurrection*, *Escape from L.A.*, *The Crow* and *Vampires*.

Logic, Let Me Introduce You to This Window: When the Durslar Beast's head starts to hatch we see arms appearing from it, but the creature that eventually emerges has completely different appendages. Angel reminds Fred that he only needs an invitation to her room once. However, see **45**, 'Heartthrob' concerning whether he should need an invitation *at all*. **41**, 'Belonging' established that Fred worked at the Los Angeles Public Library, and the impression given was that she had been there for some time. Yet her mother seemed to know nothing of her employment. When Angel holds the severed head and Roger says that his prop is dripping, a puddle can be glimpsed on the floor. In the next shot, when Angel throws the head away, the puddle has vanished. In **45**, 'Heartthrob' the walls of Fred's room were painted white, not green. A cellphone that works in the sewers?

I Just *Love* Your Accent: Gunn does a passable impression of Wesley at his most whiny. Cordelia's mimicry of Buffy is brilliant, although Wesley's take on Angel is only average.

Quote/Unquote: Lorne, on Caritas: 'I was kinda going for a Dresden-after-the-bombing feel.'

Wesley, to Roger: 'It's a long story. I'll tell you about it if we don't *die*.'

Roger: 'Spiro Agnew? I know he was . . .' Angel: 'A Grathnar Demon. I thought I was the only one that knew that.'

Notes: 'Fred's going through some changes.' An interesting little morality tale that brings a heartwarming ending to the dark and malevolent fairy tale of Fred's journey to Hell and back. Amy Acker's sweet performance helps to cover some of the less successful parts of the story. The clever subversion of her parents' characters, and their motivation, is also an unexpected bonus. The temptation, of course, is to see the Burkles initially as *The Clampets: The Next Generation*. By challenging such obvious stereotypes *Angel* proves, yet again, that it's a far deeper series than many people give it credit for. Best bit: Fred ranting away to herself in the bus station, and the crazy homeless guy sitting next to her looking concerned and moving away.

Cordy and Wesley's amusingly over-the-top summation of the Angel and Buffy story, for Fred's benefit, contains references to various *Buffy* episodes, notably 'Becoming' Parts 1 and 2. Even Angel, who arrives in the middle of the performance, seems impressed. Wesley remembers when he was a 'rogue demon hunter' (see **10**, 'Parting Gifts'). Cordelia speaks a little French. The team takes an inventory of the weapons cabinet: amongst the items in there are a Prothgarian Broadsword, a third-century Sancteus Dagger and a three-pronged Scythian Seath Spear. Wes once used the latter to attack a poodle, mistaking it for a Rodentius Demon. Gunn uses bleach when washing his hands after touching a decapitated demon head. Angel and Fred both like Häagen-Dazs ice cream. Fred has invented a catapult-like decapitation device. Or, possibly, a toaster. She has memorised the first 452 digits of pi and chants them as a way of staying calm. Fred's mother, Trish, drives a school bus; Fred's father, Roger, shares Angel's love of golf. Lorne wears a white terrycloth bathrobe, smokes, and has his heart in his left buttock (as vaguely alluded to in **43**, 'Through the Looking Glass'). Caritas is still a wreck after Gunn's old crew partied there in **47**, 'That Old Gang of Mine'. Lorne appears to harbour resentment towards Gunn over this. Wesley's prickly relationship with his parents (alluded to in

14, 'I've Got You Under My Skin', **28**, 'Guise Will Be Guise' and **41**, 'Belonging') is again mentioned: Wes speaks of a never-ending tirade of berating, debasement and scorn.

Soundtrack: Fred sings the traditional campfire song 'Row, Row, Row Your Boat' for Lorne's benefit.

Did You Know?: The fact that *Angel* blossomed away from *Buffy* was, David Greenwalt believes, only partly a coincidence. Greenwalt attributed the show's creative growth to the cast and writers becoming more comfortable with the characters. 'It takes time to find [the voice of] a show,' he told *zap2it.com*. He cited Cordelia as an example. She started off as the embodiment of the rich, pretty, popular girl everyone hated in high school, but is now saddled with debilitating visions that alert Angel to coming dangers. 'She's completely different from the vainglorious girl she was,' Greenwalt says. 'She's still very blunt, but now she's almost like a superhero. She *wants* the visions.'

50
Billy

US Transmission Date: 29 October 2001
UK Transmission Date: 21 February 2002 (Sky)

Writer: Tim Minear, Jeffrey Bell
Director: David Grossman
Cast: Richard Livingston (Congressman Blim), Jennifer Brooke (Clerk),
Cheri Rae Russell (Female Officer), Gwen McGee (Detective),
Kristoffer Polaka (Dylan), Rey Gallegos (Sanchez), Charlie Parker (Guy),
Joy Lang (Amber), Timothy McNeil (Cab Driver)

A terrible violence erupts within Angel Investigations when a demonic young man, Billy Blim, releases primal rage in his male victims. As a consequence, Wesley, Gunn and Angel must cope with murderously misogynistic urges that have Fred and Cordelia as their only outlet.

Dudes and Babes: Billy appears to have a demonic heritage, as part of an influential, rich political family. His touch brings out a primordial misogyny in men. Studying his blood, Wesley and Fred discover that his cells are super-charged, which may be the source of this power. Billy claims that he doesn't hate women and that he has never directly harmed one. He seems to have no greater respect for men, believing they are weakened by what is hidden under a woman's skirt. Subsequent to Angel releasing Billy from his demonic jail (see **46**, 'That Vision Thing'), Billy's touch causes a husband of 30 years to beat his wife to death, Gavin Park to assault Lilah, a male police officer to attack his female partner, a cab driver to beat a female fare and Wesley to stalk and injure Fred. Lilah stops Billy's reign of misery by shooting and killing him.

Denial, Thy Name is Wesley: Wes clearly has feelings for Fred (he calls her an extraordinary woman), though his natural shyness is getting in the way of any developing relationship. For instance, Cordelia suggests that the next time he plans to invite Fred to a candle-lit dinner for two at his place, he shouldn't invite the rest of the gang along with her.

It's a Designer Label!: Lilah, as she proudly notes, is wearing Boracci shoes. Also, Cordy's extremely tight stretchpants.

References: A photograph of former British Prime Minister Winston Churchill (1874–1965) decorates Wesley's office. Wesley's rant concerning Eve's fall from grace and her dragging Adam down with her alludes to Genesis 3. He notes, concerning information on the convenience-store murder, 'I got it the old-fashioned way,' which may be an oblique reference to a SmithBarney's advert starring John Houseman which featured a similar tag line. Fred attacks Wesley with a fire extinguisher, a homage to *Home Alone*. Wesley stalking Fred has visual references to *The Shining*. Cordelia refers to the THX audio system pioneered by George Lucas and named after *THX-1138*. Lilah says that the Blim family are the closest thing America has to royalty, a probable allusion to the Kennedys. Also, *The Terminator* and the Talking Heads' 'Psycho Killer'. Locations: Fred mentions Santa Monica,[28] Beverly Hills[29] and Malibu.[30] Sanchez asks his partner why she's taking Pico Boulevard, which starts in Santa Monica. As the police car crashes, in the background a sign is visible for Megatoys, an internationally renowned toy company whose head-quarters are on East 2nd Street in Downtown.

The building used for Billy's home is owned in real life by former Los Angeles Mayor Richard Riordon. Many of the Hyperion interiors were actually filmed in the abandoned Ambassador Hotel. This location was also used heavily in **63**, 'The Price'.

Bitch!: Having been called a vicious bitch, Lilah asks if Cordelia believes she knows her that well. Cordy replies that she *was* Lilah, only 'with better shoes', and notes that when it comes to male aggression towards women it's not the pain that makes it so bad for the victim but the helplessness. No woman, Cordy continues, should ever have to go through that. And no woman strong enough to wear the mantle of 'vicious bitch' should *ever* put up with it.

The Charisma Show: This is very much Cordelia's episode, a beautiful feminist parable about male aggression and the terrors of being trapped in a cycle of abuse. Charisma gets most of the best scenes, particularly her confrontations first with Lilah and then Billy. In the latter, she gets to taser him in the gonads. You *go*, girl. Her reply when Fred asks

---

[28] One of the most desirable places to live in L.A., Santa Monica is most famous for its pier, the luxurious state beach and Third Street Promenade; not forgetting the numerous bars on Santa Monica Boulevard itself, immortalised in Sheryl Crow's 'All I Wanna Do'. It's also home to the Mutant Enemy production lot where *Buffy* and some of *Angel* are filmed. Santa Monica has certainly changed since Raymond Chandler used it as the setting for *Farewell My Lovely* and described it as resembling a giant funfair.

[29] A small town for the very wealthy, Beverly Hills occupies less than six square miles of land and is situated in a gap in the Santa Monica Mountains overlooking the L.A. basin. Like the even more upmarket neighbouring Bel Air it's an insular community that defines its elite subdivision from the rest of the world, with imposing black gates fronting Sunset Boulevard and discouraging visitors. *Beware*, they appear to scream, *rich people live here*.

[30] Malibu is a closely knit ocean-side residential community characterised by its carefully preserved rural atmosphere.

her how she can contemplate facing Billy alone, 'How can I not?', is this episode's message in a nutshell.

L.A.-Speak: Cordy: 'No, asswipe!'

Cigarettes and Alcohol: In the aftermath of her vicious beating at Gavin's hands, Lilah sits alone in her darkened apartment drinking whisky.

'You May Remember Me From Such Films and TV Series As . . .': Richard Livingstone was in *3rd Rock From the Sun*, *Scrubs*, *Cocktail*, *Entropy*, *Bel Air* and *Poor White Trash*. Gwen McGee's CV includes *Babylon 5*, *Eddie Murphy Raw* (as Eddie's mum), *Frailty*, *Bulletproof*, *Charmed* and *Mercury Rising*. Cheri Rae Russell played Jody in *Motorcycle Cheerleading Moms* and appeared in *Little Witches*. Joy Lang played Liza in *. . . Or Forever Hold Your Peace*. Timothy McNeil was in *Speedway Junkies* and *Starship Troopers*.

Don't Give Up The Day Job: Daniel Dae Kim's stand-in, Dino Juico, also worked on *Bubble Boy*, *Artificial Intelligence: AI*, *Blade* and *Ally McBeal*. Editor Casey O Rohrs' CV includes *Boys and Girls*, *She's All That*, *Millennium*, *Chasing the Dragon* and *Doogie Howser, M.D.* Costumer Carrie Grace's movies include *The One*, *Cold Heart* and *The Bookie's Lament*.

Logic, Let Me Introduce You to This Window: When Fred leaves Wesley's apartment, Amy Acker bumps into the wall outside. How did Gunn know that Wes and Fred were in the abandoned section of the hotel, or what was going on between them? Angel looks at surveillance photos and states that one picture was taken at 11.22, twenty minutes before the crime. But when we next see the photo it is clearly time-coded 10.52. How does Wesley get so much information from the police concerning Officer Sanchez and his partner? Why do neither Wesley nor Gunn suffer any lasting brain damage after the severe cranial trauma that both undergo? How does Fred build her somewhat elaborate booby-trap for Wesley in the short time she has available before he smashes down the door?

Quote/Unquote: Cordy, to Billy: 'I'm feeling superior because I have an arrow pointed at your jugular. And the irony of using a phallic-shaped weapon is *not* lost on me.'

Wesley: 'What do you tell a woman who has two black eyes? Nothing you haven't already told her twice.'

Notes: 'Angel feels responsible for this guy because he brought him back from Hell. I feel responsible because he did it to save me. You, who *are*, actually, responsible . . . feel nothing.' What a thoroughly dark and disturbing episode and how well handled it is. Like **26**, 'Untouched', this is *Angel* stepping into some on-the-edge areas of dramatic concern and emerging with both dignity and (more importantly) conscience intact. A story shaded by what are at times uncomfortably pointed observations on the male/female dynamic, 'Billy' is tough viewing, but is ultimately worth sitting through because its message is important. Also, amid a bunch of terrific performances, a special word about Alexis Denisof: for the last two years, this fine actor had been the hidden gem at *Angel*'s heart. Alexis does so much, in little glances, body language and odd, pithy one-liners, to make an audience (many of whom once loudly complained when he replaced fan-favourite Glenn Quinn) care deeply about his character. It's something of a game amongst fans of Joss Whedon's shows to name the character who has developed the furthest over the seven years since *Buffy* began. It's true that the journeys made by Willow, Xander, Cordelia, Spike and Angel have been long and emotional ones. But let's not forget Wes, a character who in many ways embodies all that is central to *Buffy* and *Angel* – morality, honesty, nobleness and redemption for past mistakes. Wesley Wyndam-Pryce, one of the *truest* champions in a universe full of them.

Cordelia notes that she spent three years on the varsity cheerleading squad at Sunnydale High (see various *Buffy* episodes from 'The Witch' to 'Earshot'). Lilah tells Gavin that, unlike Lindsey McDonald, she doesn't switch sides when it gets rough (see **21**, 'Blind Date', **40**, 'Dead End'). Angel and Gunn play a video game in which Angel keeps getting killed. Wesley has a contact who obtains crime-scene photos for tabloid newspapers. Angel doesn't seem to need an invitation to enter Billy's house. As Billy had his own private room in Hell in **46**, 'That Vision Thing', this seems in line with previous revelations concerning the invitation rule. We see Angel Investigations' police scanner for the first time since Wesley used it in **11**, 'Somnambulist'.

Soundtrack: Gorillaz's 'Clint Eastwood' is heard as Dylan and his friends play pool. Also, 'Slow' by Elwood.

Did You Know?: Two of the most impressive scenes in the episode – Angel and, subsequently, Cordelia's visits to Lilah's apartment – were written by Joss Whedon specifically so that Tim Minear, who was trying to co-write the episode in just five days, could attend a reading at Whedon's house. This was the episode of *Angel* that was being written on 11 September 2001, and Tim Minear recalls that he was in the middle of a particularly heavy writing session when a friend called to tell him to turn on his TV to watch events unfolding in New York.

Cast and Crew Comments: 'One of the things I love about this show is that they always take the unexpected,' noted Jeff Bell. 'Each of the women characters is responsible for their own salvation,' he added, refuting suggestions that the episode was anti-woman. It's a theme that Tim Minear echoes. 'Fred says that [the male violence] is not something *in* Wesley but something that was *done* to him. Therein, to me, lies the theme of the episode. Is man primarily not a misogynist, but a barbarian? Is it a choice that we have to make to civilise ourselves, or does a spark of civilisation already exist?'

51
Offspring

US Transmission Date: 5 November 2001
UK Transmission Date: 28 February 2002 (Sky)

Writer: David Greenwalt
Director: Turi Meyer
Cast: Steve Tom (Stephen Mills), Sergio Premoli (Monseigneur),
Van Epperson (Bus Driver), Peyton Miller (Johnny),
Christian Miller (Johnny), Kathleen McMartin (Mom),
Theresa Arrison (Johnny's Mom)

Angel comes face to face with the consequences of his night of passion with Darla last year. She arrives at the Hyperion, inexplicably pregnant. Whilst Angel must decide whether to destroy his unborn child, his friends discover a prophecy that predicts the arrival of a powerful entity.

Dreaming (As *Buffy* Often Proves) is Free: Cordy has a dream/vision concerning Darla's child having a heartbeat and a soul. This, both she and Angel realise, explains why Darla has been craving the pure blood of children to satisfy her insatiable hunger.

Denial, Thy Name is Angel: His less than truthful comments to Cordelia in **39**, 'Disharmony' concerning his not having had sex with Darla in **37**, 'Reprise' come back to haunt Angel in the shape of a heavily pregnant vampire. Cordelia initially empathises with Darla, having herself experienced a supernatural pregnancy in **12**, 'Expecting'. It's only when Darla tries to make a meal of Cordy that she becomes a bit more sympathetic towards the father.

It's a Designer Label!: Cordy's red T-shirt. Darla's shawl. Lorne's electric-blue shirt.

References: Darla, according to Angelus, loved the Sistine Chapel. Built in the Vatican City during the reign of Pope Sixtus IV (1475–83), the chapel has the exact dimensions of the Temple of Solomon. Holtz wonders if her fascination was due to the ceiling artwork of Florentine Renaissance genius Michelangelo Buonarroti (1475–1564). Angelus replies that she favoured the frescos of Sandro Botticelli (1444–1510). *The Temptation of Christ* was her favourite, he continues, probably because of the leper. Cordelia mentions the NASDAQ, the world's premier electronic stock market. The references to the Spanish Inquisition are historically accurate but were still, probably, inspired by *Monty Python's Flying Circus*. Their chief weapon is, after all, surprise ... Also, Ken and Barbie dolls, Simple Minds' 'Alive and Kicking' and *The Hunger*. Possible allusions to *The Omen* and *Demon Seed*. Darla arrives in L.A. on a no. 108 bus on the Downtown to Hollywood 5-8 line.

The Charisma Show: Lorne senses that Cordy has been

hurt by Angel's deception. Not that you need to be a mystic to work *that* out.

Not Exactly A Haven For Prophecies: The Nyasian Prophecy foretells the coming of the Tro-Clon, 'born out of darkness to bring darkness', a being slated either to ruin or purify humanity. Sahjhan, when releasing Holtz from being encased in stone for 200 years, quotes the *Kalada* by Kadshi, which states that in the first year of the final century one who had lived before shall arise.

Cigarettes and Alcohol: In the beautiful scene where Angel is trying to tell Cordelia of his feelings, she completely misunderstands him and asks if someone has been putting vodka in his blood.

Sex and Drugs and Rock'n'Roll: Wesley mentions the anabolic sedative GBH (Gamma Hydroxybutyrate, also known as 'liquid ecstasy') and the notorious date-rape drug Rohypnol, the trademark used for flunitrazepam.

'You May Remember Me From Such Films and TV Series As . . .': Steven Tom was in *Silk Stalkings*, *Gilmore Girls*, *Action* and *The West Wing*. Jack Conley often gets meaty detective-type roles in movies like *Payback*, *Mercury Rising*, *L.A. Confidential* and *Get Shorty*. He played Cain in *Buffy* and also appeared in *Collateral Damage*, *Traffic*, *Apollo 11* and *Apollo 13*, *NYPD Blue*, *Dark Skies* and *Kindred: The Embraced*. Robert Peters was in *Catch Me If You Can*, *Ocean's Eleven*, *Everwood*, *Go*, *The Red Shoe Diaries*, *Mulholland Falls*, *Coach* and *In the Line of Fire*. He also produced and directed the movies *Project Redlight* and *The Bus Stops Here*, and was Ted Danson's assistant on *Three Men and a Little Lady*. Sergio Premoli appeared in *The Doors* and *Leaving Las Vegas*. Van Epperson's CV includes *Enterprise*, *Manic*, *The Green Mile*, *Eight Days a Week*, *Thick as Thieves*, *Grounded for Life*, *Murphy Brown* and *Star Trek: The Next Generation*. Kathleen McMartin was in *Candyman: Day of the Dead* and *Ellen*.

Logic, Let Me Introduce You to This Window: Why were Wesley and Gunn looking for this particular scroll? Did Cordelia have a vision about it off-screen? When Darla leaves the bus, the surroundings don't look much like a street in Downtown L.A. Were there such things as sunglasses in 1771? Darla's costume also seems a bit anachronistic for that period. Holtz was trying his best to eviscerate Angelus with a hooked trident, yet there's no blood evident on Angelus's body. We later discover that Sahjhan is noncorporeal in this dimension, yet he touches objects (handfuls of sand, for instance) here. There's only one copy of *The Blue Boy*, which is in the Huntington collection in San Marino, California. Unless *that*'s a fake, the owner should be doubting the authenticity of his collection.

I Just *Love* Your Accent: Wesley refers to Gunn having a snitch, instead of several more British terms for informers such as grass or nark. He's clearly been in California for too long.

Quote/Unquote: Cordelia: 'What are friends for?' Darla: 'Knocking you up and leaving you high and dry?'

Fred: 'Who's Darla?' Gunn: 'Angel's old flame.' Fred: 'The one who died?' Gunn: 'The *other* one that died. And came back to life.' Fred: 'Y'all have a chart or something?'

Cordelia, on the Furies: 'Three more of Angel's *chippies*. You girls are on the pill, I hope?'

Cordelia, on Darla: 'Angel boned her.' Angel: 'Just once, the one night. Uh, just the two–three–one times that one night.'

Notes: 'Screw destiny. If this evil thing comes, we'll fight it ... Destiny is just another word for inevitable, and nothing's inevitable as long as you look it in the eye and say, "You're *evitable*."' A story about responsibility, 'Offspring' fluffs a couple of good opportunities to make telling points (particularly the Angel/Cordelia awkwardness), but redeems itself beautifully when it comes to twists. The plot has holes and, as part of a much larger ongoing storyline, possibly takes too long to deliver what it has to say, but the set pieces are highly effective and the dialogue is terrific. An important part of a much bigger jigsaw.

Angel and Cordelia continue their fight training, first seen in **50**, 'Billy'. Cordelia asking what friends are for echoes similar sentiments in **11**, 'Somnambulist', when she assured Angel that she would kill him if she had to. Angel *still* doesn't know how to use the voice mail on his cellphone (see **13**, 'She'). Wesley refers to his translation of the Aberjian prophecies in **22**, 'To Shanshu in L.A.' Daniel Holtz's wife was named Caroline. She and the rest of Holtz's family were killed by Angelus and Darla in 1765 (see **52**, 'Quickening'). After Holtz had chased the couple through France (see **31**, 'The Trial'), they evaded him in North Africa (see **45**, 'Heartthrob') before he captured Angelus in Rome in 1771 and Darla came to his rescue. Angel has seen three prophecies in his lifetime, none of which came true. (This may refer to the events of *Buffy*: 'Prophecy Girl' and 'Graduation Day', and to **22**, 'To Shanshu in L.A.'.) Gunn and Wesley steal the remnants of the Nyasian Scroll. The current owner has many priceless exhibits, including a Muselok Trancing Amalgam, Cyopian Conjuring Spheres and *The Blue Boy* by Thomas Gainsborough (1727–88). Fred loves fake flowers. She uses the office's Apple Mac laptop. Darla says that she has visited every shaman and seer in the western hemisphere to try and discover the nature of the creature she carries. 'Kyerumption' is a Pylean term which describes two great heroes meeting on the field of battle and recognising their mutual fates. (In its archaic form, it means a grog made of ox-dung.) 'Moira' is another Pylean term meaning the physical attraction between two larger-than-life souls. Lorne has hired a demon builder named Arney to remodel Caritas. Arney is charging $1,200 more than his original estimate. Lorne brings the Furies to the club to cast an anti-violence spell which will protect against human violence in addition to demon attacks.

Soundtrack: Nigel Ogden's 'Art Deco Suite'. Darla sings a brief snatch of 'Danny Boy', Frederick Weatherly's lyrical adaptation of Rory Dall O'Cahan's 'The Londonderry Air'.

Did You Know?: On Channel 4's *T4* interview with David Boreanaz in January 2002, there was confirmation of a dreadful rumour that had been doing the rounds. Yes, David is, indeed, a Manchester United supporter. Well, *that* figures. He only lives 5,000 miles away from Old Trafford, which makes him a local boy compared to most of their fans.

Cast And Crew Comments: 'I moved to London when I was a teenager,' Alexis Denisof told Rob Francis. 'I had thought that I'd probably be there for a year or two, but I fell in love with England and stayed. Many years went by and finally I came back to L.A., but I still have a house in London, and lots of good friends. And lots of funny accents as a result.'

52
Quickening

US Transmission Date: 12 November 2001
UK Transmission Date: 7 March 2002 (Sky)

Writer: Jeffrey Bell
Director: Skip Schoolnik
Cast: José Yenque (Tarfall), Matt Casper (Cyril),
Michael Robert Brandon (Psychic), William Ostrander (Commander),
John Durbin (Dr Petraovich), Angelo Surmelis (Tech Guy),
Christopher Leps (The Assassin)

Angel must do all that he can to protect Darla and their unborn baby when Wolfram & Hart launches an attack to capture the pregnant vampire. In addition, the Angel Investigation team cope with the sinister attentions of a vampire cult who believe that Angel's offspring is *The Miracle Child*.

Dudes and Babes: The demon Sahjhan is able to travel through dimensions, including time, and this ability has kept him young (in Holtz's eyes, at least). Sahjhan can hide his demon face behind a human one. In demon guise, he has marks etched into the grey skin of his face, is noncorporeal, and turns into a column of black smoke if threatened. Doctor Fetvanovich, late of the Balkans, is the world's pre-eminent expert in paranormal obstetrics. Clearly not of human origin, the doctor appears to have chicken feet. Cyril, the officious young Wolfram & Hart mailroom staffer, is really a minion of Master Tarfall, the Underlord of Pain. Tarfall may be the leader of a cult of vampires who are awaiting the coming of Darla and Angel's child.

Denial, Thy Name is Darla: Seeing their baby's image on an ultrasound machine appears to have a significant effect on Darla (as it does on Angel).

It's a Designer Label!: Darla's unflattering maternity top. Bet Cordy bought that for her in revenge for the biting incident in **51**, 'Offspring'.

References: The title refers to the first movement of an unborn child felt by the mother. It was also used as a subtitle for the second, dreadful, *Highlander* movie. There are several further pregnancy references, such as Braxton Hicks contractions, random spasms named after John Braxton Hicks, who first described them in 1872. Fred paraphrases some of Honeybunny's dialogue from *Pulp Fiction*. Linwood misquotes Harry Truman's maxim 'the buck stops here'. Gunn alludes to the obscure horror movie *C.H.U.D.*, which features cannibalistic humanoid underground dwellers. Darla refers to Switzerland's traditional position of neutrality. Also, *Gunsmoke* ('get out of Dodge'), Band-Aid and Health Bar Crunch, one of Ben & Jerry's most popular ice-cream flavours. Images on the TV screens that Holtz is watching include a shuttle launch, Mao Tse-tung (1893–1976), one of the lunar landings, the Statue of Liberty, Mahatma Gandhi (1869–1948), Martin Luther King (1929–68), an assembly line, a Hula-Hoop and an atomic bomb detonation. Visual references to *Toy Story*, *The Drunken Master*, *Twins of Evil* and *Raiders of the Lost Ark*.

Bitch!: Cordy punches Darla in the face. Gavin suggests that, her brief interlude in **48**, 'Carpe Noctem' aside, Lilah hasn't had a meaningful relationship in years.

The Good Grub Guide: Sahjhan says that in Los Angeles, one can get really good Thai food at two in the morning.

'You May Remember Me From Such Films and TV Series As . . .': John Rubinstein played Harrison Fox Jr in *Crazy Like a Fox* and appeared in *The Boys from Brazil*, *The West Wing*, *Cannon*, *Red Dragon*, *Roots: The Next Gener-*

ation and *The Car*. The son of piano virtuoso Arthur Rubinstein, John was a composer on series like *China Beach* and *Harry O*. He also won a Tony in 1980 for his performance in *Children Of A Lesser God* and was the original lead in the Broadway production of Bob Fosse's *Pippin*. Matt Casper was in *Pearl Harbor*. Michael Robert Brandon appeared in *Hatred of a Minute*. Jose Yenque's CV includes *The X-Files*, *The Division*, *Traffic* and *Innocent*. William Ostrander's movies include *Mulholland Drive*, *Red Heat* and *Christine*. John Durbin appeared in *The A-Team*, *Star Trek: The Next Generation*, *Kansas City*, *Tapeheads*, *Dead Man Walking* and *The Breed*. Christopher Leps was in *CSI* and *Sorority Boys*. He was also a stuntman on *Clutch*, *Alias* and *Birds of Prey*.

Don't Give Up The Day Job: Visual Effects Creator Randy Goux's talents can also be seen on *The Rage: Carrie 2*, *X-Men* and *The Lord of the Rings*. Musical Editor Tim Isle worked on *Bring It On*, *Whatever It Takes* and *Watching Ellie*.

Logic, Let Me Introduce You to This Window: The transcripts that Gavin gets are, it's claimed, complete to last week. Lilah then reads about Darla's arrival within the transcript. However, the dialogue that the technician is *currently* transcribing onto computer is from the beginning of **51**, 'Offspring', which was *before* Darla arrived. Nobody in York in 1764 has any semblance of an English accent, much less a Yorkshire one. In 1773, Holtz thinks about how Angelus and Darla killed his family. This matches exactly what did happen despite the fact that Holtz wasn't a witness to the atrocities. How, exactly, do Gunn and Fred 'acquire' an ultrasound machine in a busy inner-city hospital?

I Just *Love* Your Accent: Sahjhan tells Holtz that in the 227 years since their agreement, empires have risen and fallen, mankind has harnessed the power of the sun,[31] walked on

---

[31] A probable reference to the science surrounding the splitting of the atom pioneered by Ernest Rutherford (1871–1937), which led to subsequent developments in atomic and nuclear research and, ultimately, the creation of the atomic bomb. However, some commentators suggest this may allude to the first production, in 1954, of solar electricity.

the moon[32] and turned arid deserts into green fields. When asked about Holtz's beloved England, Sahjhan notes that the country went through a rough patch 60 years ago, but that it's mostly unchanged: warm beer, boiled meat, bad teeth.[33] This is, he notes, why he moved to L.A. 'Have you followed this part of the history?' Sahjhan asks, mentioning the American Revolution, Manifest Destiny,[34] Westward expansion and the Beach Boys.[35]

Quote/Unquote: Angel: 'I'd had a bad day.' Darla: 'So, you . . . pushed me onto the bed and took what you wanted?' Angel: 'Seemed like the thing to do.'

Angel: 'How you feeling?' Darla: 'I haven't had blood in almost a day and your devil's spawn is trying to rip its way outta my body.'

Wesley: 'We'll wait for it to be born, then chop its head off.' Fred: 'What if it doesn't have a head?' Cordy: 'We're gonna need a *really* big mallet.'

Notes: 'You want me to protect the vampire bitch who bit me, and her evil love child? OK, I'm in.' A disappointingly fragmented episode, very much the filling in a big sandwich. 'Quickening' sees the introduction of numerous characters on the periphery of the action, much of which diverts attention from the really interesting stuff surrounding the Angel Investigations team and Darla. Some good stuff, and lots of funny dialogue, but the ending is very weak indeed.

---

[32] On 20 July 1969, Neil Armstrong and Buzz Aldrin were the first men to set foot on another world. Unless you believe various fruitcake theories that the entire Apollo programme was an elaborate hoax pulled by NASA, the Nixon administration, the CIA and the military/industrial complex.

[33] A rather typical, uncharitable American view of various British stereotypes, two of which are mostly inaccurate. At least we've got a National Health Service. And cool bands. And a sense of humour.

[34] A political view held by many Americans in the 1840s that the United States was destined to expand across the continent, using force if necessary against the indigenous races. The controversy over slavery further fuelled expansionism, as the North and South each wanted the nation to admit new states that supported their own economic and political policies. After the subsequent civil war, by the end of the nineteenth century Manifest Destiny was used to support further US expansion in the Caribbean and the Pacific.

[35] Classic surf-pop band formed in 1961 by brothers Brian, Dennis and Carl Wilson, with Mike Love and Alan Jardine. Produced *Pet Sounds* in 1966, one of the most influential LPs of all time.

Gunn wants the A.I. team to get a flame-thrower that he can be in charge of (see **54**, 'Dad'). Cyril delivers a CD-ROM to Lilah from Gavin. This contains scenes of her and Angel getting close to copulating in the Hyperion in **48**, 'Carpe Noctem'. Lilah uses her own blood to sign certain documents. Blood oaths seem to be a big part of Wolfram & Hart's operating policy – Lilah's smarmy boss Linwood also mentions that the company has a Demon Resources Department where someone named Pendihook works, and branches in Berlin, Singapore, the Balkans and an apparently significant one in Muncie, Delaware. Wolfram & Hart's mind-readers were last seen in **21**, 'Blind Date'. The 'exterminators' whom Gunn discovered in the Hyperion in **46**, 'That Vision Thing' weren't sent to kill bugs but rather to *plant* them, on Gavin's instructions. When Darla is about to bite Holtz's daughter, Sarah, she uses the phrase 'close your eyes', exactly the same phrase she used to Liam when she sired him (see *Buffy*: 'Becoming' Part 1). Holtz made his bargain with Sahjhan nine years later (presumably in 1773). Master Tarfall, the Underlord of Pain, amusingly shares an answering machine with a cheerful-sounding couple named Christine and Bentley Tittle. Further to the Tro-Clon mentioned in the last episode, Fred speculates that it may not necessarily be a single person but, rather, a confluence of events.

Soundtrack: Ministry's 'Corrosion'.

Did You Know?: One of the 'flash'-style scene breaks in this episode features a series of one-frame shots from various points in L.A., including an unidentified Hollywood nightclub and the Osaka Sushi restaurant on West 3rd Street.

Joss Whedon's Comments: 'I'm probably less involved with *Angel* [than] I am with *Buffy*,' Joss told Ian Spelling. 'But I'm still there helping to break the stories. I can't really let that part of it go.'

53
Lullaby

US Transmission Date: 19 November 2001
UK Transmission Date: 14 March 2002 (Sky)

Writer: Tim Minear
Director: Tim Minear
Cast: Jim Ortlieb (Vampire Hunter)

As the birth of Darla's child approaches, Angel finally comes face to face with Holtz, a man on a mission of revenge. Angel must face the responsibility of becoming a father and the possibilities of the destruction his son may bring to the world.

Denial, Thy Name is Darla: Having been incapable of caring about anything other than herself since she became a vampire in 1609, Darla discovers what it is to love. Sadly, this is an artificial emotion produced as a by-product of the soul of the child she carries (see **83**, 'Inside Out'). She knows that when the baby is born, or dies in her womb, she will lose these feelings. It's for this reason, chiefly, that she sacrifices herself to do what any mother would, and gives her baby the most precious gift of all – life.

It's a Designer Label!: Lorne's fashion sense is at its ugliest, a bright orange shirt clashing alarmingly with his powder-blue suit.

References: Namechecks for Attila the Hun, Buddha (Siddhartha Gautama, c. 563–483 BC) and Vaseline Petroleum Jelly (as invented by Robert Augustus Cheesebrough in Pennsylvania in 1859). The entire episode is an overt allusion to the birth of Christ. Darla turning Sarah into a vampire parallels Lestat's siring of Claudia in *Interview With the Vampire*. Several publications state that Angel finds Darla on the roof of the legendary Hollywood Roosevelt Hotel (the site of the initial Academy Awards presentation in 1929). He doesn't – the hotel in question is, in fact, the Rosslyn Hotel on Main Street in the Skid Row area of L.A. This location was also used in *Blade Runner*. Tim Minear has noted the influence of a particular sequence in Philip Kaufman's *Invasion of the Body Snatchers* on Darla's death.

Bitch!: Lilah, when the translator drones on at length about the complexities of decoding Ga'Shundi tenses, notes that she has a gun.

Cigarettes and Alcohol: When the team sit in Caritas getting maudlin about the probability of Angel's son dying, Lorne offers to get everyone a drink. Sadly, he never gets around to it as Holtz chooses this moment to throw an explosive into the club.

'You May Remember Me From Such Films and TV Series As . . .': Jim Ortlieb played Nasedo in *Roswell*. His CV also includes a memorable role in *Magnolia*, *Chain Reaction*, *Home Alone*, *Flatliners*, *Running Scared*, *Spin City*, *The West Wing*, *Felicity* and *Early Edition*.

Don't Give Up The Day Job: *Angel*'s Casting Directors, Anya Collof, Jennifer Fishman and Amy McIntyre Britt, worked together on *Bones*, *The Hollywood Sign*, *Buffy*, *Rats in the Can* and *Class Warfare*.

Logic, Let Me Introduce You to This Window: In the first flashback, Holtz's wife moves her legs even though she's dead. Where does the body of the Grappler Demon that Darla ran over go? Considering that the final scenes are taking place in what seems like a monsoon, there are several close-up shots in which Julie Benz and David Boreanaz don't seem to be getting rained on much. We know Angel's son is a remarkable baby but he's apparently born without an umbilical chord, yet *with* a navel. Lilah tells Gavin, 'They don't crucify here. It's too Christian.' Whilst it's an important part of Christian iconography, the actual practice of crucifixion wasn't Christian at all; it was a Roman method of execution used *on* Christians – and anybody else they didn't like, of various faiths.

Quote/Unquote: Holtz: 'You said you work for the law.' Lilah: 'No, I said I'm a lawyer. I don't *care* about the law.'

Darla: 'I promise I won't throw anyone out of the car. Not while it's moving.'

Sahjhan, on Angel: 'His hair's a little spikier. He's using product. But it's the same guy.'

Notes: 'What do I have to offer a *human* child, besides ugly death?' Lots of Christlike imagery peppers this excellent episode. Once again, it's the sum of disparate parts enlivened by great dialogue and the terrific book-ending Holtz/Angel scenes. Best bit: The amusing running joke of people hitting Gunn to test if the Caritas anti-violence spell is working.

Darla reminds Angel that *he* died in an alley (see *Buffy*: 'Becoming' Part 1, **15**, 'The Prodigal'). Sahjhan appears to share Spike's disgust of Angel's use of hair gel (see **3**, 'In the Dark'). A one-eyed translator named Forsche works for Wolfram & Hart in Ancient Symbols and Icons.

Soundtrack: The hymn that Holtz sings to his daughter is 'All Through the Night', an 1880s adaptation, by Harold Boulton, of the Welsh folk song 'Ar Hyd y Nos'.

Did You Know?: Tim Minear christened the dirty thoroughfare in which the opening scenes were filmed as 'Piss Alley'. 'It reeked of urine,' he noted, adding that huge rats lived there. During one take a rat ran over Alexis Denisof's foot, causing Charisma Carpenter to shriek loudly. The idea of having Holtz kill one of his children who had been sired by Darla was Mere Smith's.

Critique: In *Word*, acclaimed rock critic Charles Shaar Murray describes Connor's birth as 'one of the weirdest and most haunting nativity scenes ever committed to film . . .' Genre TV, Murray continued, simply had no right to be as good as *Buffy* and *Angel*, which have 'taken long-running episodic fantasy television to its highest artistic peak whilst avoiding the Scylla of triviality and the Charybdis of pomposity.'

Tim Minear's Comments: 'Ross Berryman, our director of photography, really brought something to the show,' notes Minear. 'It got darker.' Concerning the destruction of Lorne's club, Tim commented, 'It took hours to set up. We shot at 3.30 in the morning, had four or five cameras going and blew the shit out of Caritas.'

54
Dad

US Transmission Date: 10 December 2001
UK Transmission Date: 21 March 2002 (Sky)

Writer: David H Goodman
Director: Fred Keller
Cast: Kira Tirimacco (Doctor), Stephanie Courtney (Gwen)

Angel discovers the meaning of fatherhood as the demon underworld makes a collective assault on his newborn son. Holtz kills his demon henchmen and begins recruiting individuals who have lost their family to vampires. As it appears that the Hyperion will be overrun with Angel's enemies he takes the baby and goes on the run, leaving the various factions to fight each other.

Dudes and Babes: An attractive, if rather stern-looking, woman named Gwen works in Wolfram & Hart's Files and Records division. Although human in appearance she has a literally photographic memory and her eyes do a weird spooky thing when she accesses her memories.

Denial, Thy Name is Angel: His reaction when Wesley talks about s-e-x in front of the baby is *very* revealing.

References: When Angel and Lorne sing to Connor, it's reminiscent of a sequence in *Three Men and a Baby*. Lilah refers to Connor being untimely ripped from his mother's womb, an allusion to Macduff in *Macbeth*. Justine describes Holtz's 'Mr Miyagi groove thing', a reference to *The Karate Kid* – she also quotes from the movie ('Wax on, wax off'). During the siege, Wesley tries to imagine himself as John Wayne in *Rio Bravo*. Gunn's role model is Austin Stoker in *Assault on Precinct 13*. Justine lives at 7221 Spalding – probably a reference to Spalding Drive in Century City.

'West Hollywood?': Cordy notes that Angel doesn't have a woman's touch, whatever his taste in clothes may indicate to the contrary. Wesley observes that diapers are lined with a material originally designed for NASA astronauts. He find this interesting, though rather disturbing, as he then gets a mental picture of grown men wearing nappies.

L.A.-Speak: Cordelia: 'You guys *rock*, way to go!'

Cigarettes and Alcohol: Justine smokes and drinks, both helping to numb the pain of her sister's murder by vampires.

'You May Remember Me From Such Films and TV Series As ...': Laurel Holloman appeared in *Blossom Time*, *Boogie Nights*, *Popcorn Shrimp* and *The Incredibly True Adventures of Two Girls in Love*. Stephanie Courtney played Kate in *Sweet Bird of You*.

Don't Give Up The Day Job: David Goodman began his career as a transportation manager on *Evil Dead* and *Crimewave*. He was subsequently studio manager on *Evil Dead II* and a producer on *Stark Raving Dad*.

Logic, Let Me Introduce You to This Window: Starting immediately after the end of the previous episode – or, at least, after as long as it takes to drive from Caritas to the Hyperion – all of the cast are wearing exactly the same clothes as they were in **53**, 'Lullaby'. Except for Lorne, who's changed both his shirt and his suit. Also, considering that they've all been in the rain, they seem remarkably dry. This is the first occasion that the two neon Los Altos Hotel signs have been seen above the Hyperion. There is no China Palace takeaway in Los Angeles; the closest is seven miles away in Montebello. Cordelia tells Wes and Gunn, 'If we live through this, trade in your DVD players and *get a life*,' but *Assault on Precinct 13* hadn't been released on DVD when this episode was first broadcast. Angel knows how to change nappies. How? When has he ever had the need to learn (unless it concerned the child that he saved from Darla in 1900? See **29**, 'Darla'). Does Angel spend enough time in the Mojave that he knows how to lead a large group of chasing enemies into a mine? Where did he get the bomb from? Did he assemble it in the janitor's closet? Speaking of the closet, did Angel and his friends do *all* of their planning in there? This would seem the only plausible explanation, since it's the sole part of the hotel not covered by Wolfram & Hart's surveillance. But wouldn't it look strange to observers to see a steady stream of employees going in and out of the closet? Angel climbs out of a square sewer that has a round cover. When the Lilliad Demons attack, one shot shows both rooftop neon signs illuminated. In the next shot only one is. Watch out for the scratch on the baby's cheek which keeps appearing and disappearing throughout the episode. Where did Holtz get the poison he uses to kill the Grapplers from?

Quote/Unquote: Wesley: 'As you once nearly had sex on my desk, I shouldn't be surprised that now there's a baby on it.'

Cordelia: 'Are you gonna circumcise?' Gunn, as the baby cries: 'I think he heard you.'

Lorne: 'Is that bacon I smell or did somebody fall asleep with the curtains open?'

Gavin: 'Is Lilah worried we're gonna hurt the itty-biddy baby?' Lilah: 'No. I'm afraid you'll kill him before we have a chance to cut him open and find out how the hell he's alive in the first place.'

Notes: 'He's not even a day old and he's got an enemies list. How would you feel?' A rather frantic end to an interesting – if overstretched – arc. Once again, the story is carried by dialogue and characterisation, as much of the plot is one-dimensional and, occasionally, illogical (the dénouement, especially). However, there's the introduction of one excellent new character, the proto-Slayer Justine, and much good work on the regulars. Best bits: *Everything* involving Lorne; Angel playing with Connor's teddy bear; Wesley's comments that some bastard blew up the elevator doors and Angel replying, 'My bastard!'

Angel uses the alias Geraldo Angel for Connor's medical records. Fred also states that Geraldo is a pet psychiatrist with a small practice in Pacoima. Angel's room at the Hyperion is 312. Angel hopes to send his son to Notre Dame University, and insists that Wolfram & Hart, and specifically Linwood, aid in Connor's protection. Wesley makes a list of everyone who is, or may be, seeking the baby. Amongst these are the Order of Phillius, Beltar the Cremator, Piper Beast, The Scourge (see **9**, 'Hero') and

Frank, a local mobster who's big on kidnapping. Angel
Investigations now *does* own a flame-thrower (see **52**,
'Quickening', **78**, 'Calvary') although, interestingly, it's
Wes and not Gunn who uses it here. Gunn has a cousin
whom he helped raise since she was a week old.

After the second destruction of Caritas (see **53**, 'Lullaby'), Lorne is now in residence at the Hyperion. His other
offer was to stay with a Mulix Demon. He hires the Furies
(see **47**, 'This Old Gang of Mine') to put a protection spell
on the hotel. He is able to sense the surveillance cameras
that Wolfram & Hart installed. Daniel Holtz has an entry
in the Larson/McMillian *Vampiricus Conquestus* (p. 412).
He killed 378 vampires on his quest to find Angelus and
Darla. Holtz's infant son, killed by Angel and Darla in
May 1764, was also named Daniel. Lilah's clearance
number is 0112773. Wolfram & Hart has 35 cabinets full
of files on Angel. From these Lilah discovers, for instance,
that Angel's human name was Liam (see **15**, 'The Prodigal'). Linwood likes children and notes that the Senior
Partners took his before he really got to know them.
Sahjahn knows the Heimlich Manoeuvre, but cannot
perform it in this dimension because he can't physically
touch people. Three websites have been set up by groups
hunting the baby. These seem to include the already
established *Demons Demons Demons* (see **16**, 'The Ring').
Cordelia accesses the webpage of the *Los Angeles Globe
Register* (see **2**, 'Lonely Heart'). Justine's twin sister, Julia
Cooper, was killed by vampires in June 2001. Lilliad
Demons make broth from the bones of children. Their
powers are influenced by the lunar cycle. The Pylean word
for hedgehog has a very different, and amusing, meaning
in English.
Soundtrack: Angel's lullaby is 'Too-Rah-Loo-Rah-Loo-
Rah' by James Royce Shannon. The song is most often
associated with Bing Crosby, who sang it in *Going My
Way* (1944). After this, Lorne attempts to put an unhappy
Connor to sleep with Smokey Robinson and the Miracles'
'Ooh, Baby Baby'. It doesn't work, prompting Lorne to
ask if Angel is *certain* this child has a soul.

Did You Know?: Three different baby Connors were used for the required scenes, each was only able to work for twenty minutes at a time and all of the actors required to handle any of them had to wear hand-sanitiser. In the scenes that do not feature a close-up of the baby's face, a doll was used. Andy Hallett told *Starburst* that, 'Alexis used to smack [the doll] around and throw it across the set. When the *real* baby came in, the assistant director would shout, "Real baby on the set. No tossing!"'

Cast and Crew Comments: The birth of David Boreanaz's son, Jaden, has interesting parallels to Angel's sudden discovery of the joys of fatherhood. 'Looking at my child, I know that *this* is what life is all about,' he told *Cult Times*. 'It can be very stressful, but I have a very loving wife who supports me immeasurably.' Quite a successful one too. Whilst David has become an international star, his actress wife Jaime Bergman has recently starred in the comedy series *Son of the Beach*.

55
Birthday

US Transmission Date: 14 January 2002
UK Transmission Date: 28 March 2003 (Sky)

Writer: Mere Smith
Director: Michael Grossman
Cast: Patrick Breen (Nev), Max Baker (Hyperion Clerk),
Heather Weeks (Tammy), Aimee Garcia (Cynthia)

On her birthday, Cordelia has a vision so powerful that she leaves her body. As the Angel Investigations team struggle to bring her back, Cordelia is visited by Skip, who tells her that she was never meant to have the visions and offers her the opportunity to change her past. Reluctantly, Cordelia chooses to become a successful sitcom actress with a strange feeling that her destiny belongs elsewhere.

Dreaming (As *Buffy* Often Proves) is Free: The Powers That Be never intended for Cordelia, or any human for that matter, to receive the visions. The last human to have the gift was an English girl named Tammy in the 1630s. As a result, within a year the back of her skull was blown out. In her vision, Cordelia sees a demon with three mouths terrorising a teenager called Cynthia who accidentally summoned it using a pentagram. She was attempting to cast a retrieval spell for her absent father, but the book she used got stained with Diet Coke.

Dudes and Babes: Skip's new job for The Powers (possibly as a result of his allowing Angel to rescue Billy, see **46**, 'That Vision Thing') is as a guide to the astral plane. It's unclear if this is demotion or promotion (**83**, 'Inside Out' suggests that it's neither). He offers Cordelia a different life but, when she ultimately turns him down, he has the power to 'demonise' her.

Denial, Thy Name is Cordelia: The only way a human can safely maintain the visions is to become half-demon. Thus, half-demon Cordelia has pain-free visions and can levitate.

Denial, Thy Name is Sunnydale: What is it with Sunnydale folk? Gunn asks, describing Cordy, Wes and Angel as the three most 'denying-est' people he's ever met.

It's a Designer Label!: Gunn's red sweatshirt, Lorne's gold lamé shirt, Cordy's cleavage-revealing dress and incredibly tight jeans.

References: The classic *It's a Wonderful Life/A Christmas Carol* 'what if' concept has become a staple on long-running TV shows. 'Birthday' also takes elements from *This is Your Life*. There are visual allusions to one of the Sistine Chapel frescos, *The Creation of Adam*. The title sequence of *Cordy* is reminiscent of *The Mary Tyler Moore Show* and *Friends*. Skip finds time, despite his responsibilities, to watch the latest Hollywood blockbusters, mentioning *The Matrix* (he's a fan) and Russell Crowe's performance in *Gladiator* ('didn't love it'). Also, a misquote from 'Gonna Make You a Star' by David Essex, the board game *CandyLand*, Jude Law (*Gattaca, eXistenZ, Midnight in the Garden of Good and Evil, The Talented Mr Ripley*) and the ninth circle of Hell from Dante's *Inferno* (see **64**, 'A New World'). Cynthia lives at 171 Oak Street in Reseda. Other locations mentioned include Glendale and Ojai (see **28**, 'Guise Will be Guise').

The Charisma Show: Yes, it *literally* is. And it's about time everybody realised that.

Cigarettes and Alcohol: Lorne's love of a Sea Breeze is again mentioned.

Sex and Drugs and Rock'n'Roll: Cordelia has been taking large doses of Sentrax, a powerful migraine medication. At Cordy's house, Gunn asks Fred if she has ever hidden anything in her underwear drawer. Fred begins to reply that for five years she didn't have one, then asks him if they can avoid talking about her underwear. Wes and Cordelia refer to their awkward kiss in *Buffy*: 'Graduation Day' Part 2.

'You May Remember Me From Such Films and TV Series As . . .': Patrick Breen appeared in *Oz*, *Will & Grace*, *The West Wing*, *Get Shorty*, *Men in Black*, *Galaxy Quest* and *Just a Kiss*, which he also wrote. Max Baker was in *Felicity* and *The Time Machine*. Heather Weeks played Carol in *The Man With Rain in His Shoes*. Aimee Garcia's CV includes *The Good Girl*, *American Family* and *Resurrection Blvd*.

Don't Give Up The Day Job: Second Unit Script Supervisor Bridgette Kelley also worked on *Woman on Top*, *Sensation*, *The X-Files*, *Sweet Poison* and *Private Benjamin*. Costume Designer Jessica Pazdernik's CV also includes *The Next Tenant*. Set Dresser Kimberley Rosenberg's movies include *Confidence*, *American Pie 2* and *Kingdom Come*.

There's A Ghost In My House: Phantom Dennis has planned a surprise party for Cordelia, complete with a banner and a party hat. Having been introduced to the ghost, Gunn and Fred, with his help, locate Cordelia's stash of medication under her bed.

Logic, Let Me Introduce You to This Window: When Angel falls asleep he snores – but he doesn't breathe. How did Phantom Dennis either make or purchase the 'Happy Birthday' banner, the hat and the glitter? Cordelia's first vision after she becomes half-demon causes no pain. Yet Doyle, who was also a half-demon, experienced blinding pain when *he* had them. Angel makes Cordy wash her hands before he lets her hold Connor, yet her clothing, against which she cuddles the baby, is *filthy*. Cordy learns how to possess Angel's body by reading Wesley's book. However, from the brief glimpse we're given, it's written in Latin. Since when was she able to read that? Tammy's accent fluctuates between West Country, Midlands and broad Cockney. How does the 171 Oak writing appear on the wall of the Hyperion in the alternate reality?

Another Girl, Another Planet: The scenario focuses on what could have happened to Cordelia if she hadn't encountered Angel at the party in **1**, 'City Of' but had, instead, met a powerful talent agent (possibly Oliver, see **17**, 'Eternity'). From this she becomes a star in her own, two-time Emmy-winning sitcom. The credits to *Cordy* note that, besides Cordelia Chase, the show stars Gregory Dunne, Elliott Simms and Carol Wright, and was created by Phlegmont and Mendoza. In this, Cordy, 'the girl with the million-dollar smile', plays the eponymous title character, who owns a design firm. In this alternate universe, it was Angel who received the visions from Doyle in **9**, 'Hero'. (One has to wonder if they were passed to him in the same way that they were passed to Cordy.) Coupled with the loneliness and isolation he was already feeling, these visions subsequently sent Angel mad. Both Wesley and Gunn still joined Angel's cause, though the former lost his left arm to a Kungai Demon (presumably in **10**, 'Parting Gifts'). All of this suggests that the dividing point for this reality was the events of **1**, 'City Of'. *However*, here the Hyperion is still a hotel, and a pretty swanky one at that. Yet in **24**, 'Are You Now or Have You Ever Been?', it's stated that the Hyperion closed as a hotel in 1979.

Quote/Unquote: Cordy: 'You've seen *The Matrix*?' Skip: 'Loved that flick! When Trinity's all "Dodge this!" . . . I'm not really instilling awe any more, am I?'

Angel: 'I'm more afraid of dying than she is.'

Cordy, to Wesley: 'Angel gets the visions of people who are gonna die and you go out and slay? This is how you make your living? That has got to be the suckiest job in the world.'

Notes: 'It was an honour being your guide, Cordelia Chase.' A *gorgeous* script by Mere Smith, and quite beautifully played, 'Birthday' enters an age-old debate, questioning whether free will is an illusion. A militantly downbeat parable follows, which is almost a deliberate mirror image of the metaphor in the *Buffy* episode 'The Wish'. In *that* story, Cordelia was given a literal example of the truism 'be careful what you wish for, it might come true'. The idea is subverted to incorporate questions of identity, denial, fate and redemption. An important, deeply introspective building-block in *Angel*'s continuing observations on the true nature of heroism, and an episode touched with not inconsiderable magnificence.

The events of this episode indicate that Cordelia's birthday falls around the second week of January (see **15**, 'The Prodigal'). Lorne almost loses one of his horns in a scuffle with a demon. It will, he notes, take three days to grow back. The Powers (or, perhaps, the Conduit) cast a spell that literally prevents Lorne from telling Angel how to contact them. People who exist on astral planes typically have an altered appearance, one that makes them more attractive than in their normal existence. The wallpaper in the alternate-universe Hyperion was designed by Jacques Latour.

Soundtrack: 'Drumroll', 'Tension' and 'Game Show' from the Opus 1 Music Library, and 'Tears Down My Cheek' from First Come Music Library, all feature. Also, the gorgeous 'Baby Stay Awhile (Theme from *Cordy*)' sung by Marti Noxon, written by David Greenwalt. Angel, Wesley, Gunn and Fred sing 'Happy Birthday' to Cordelia.

Did You Know?: The girl with whom Cordelia is sharing a coffee in the *Cordy* opening credits is Marti Noxon. A five-minute scene from an episode of the *Cordy* sitcom was filmed but was cut from 'Birthday'. This was both due to timing reasons and also, according to Tim Minear, 'because it felt like a parody of a bad sitcom, which we didn't want it to be'. This sequence *was* subsequently added as an extra to the Season Three *Angel* DVD box-set, together with a different version of the *Cordy* title sequence. The scene was shot on the *Dharma & Greg* set.

Critique: 'In the midst of Season One this [episode] would have been stunning,' noted David Darlington. 'Now such quality is anticipated, even expected. Perhaps this shows how far *Angel* has come in two years.'

Cast and Crew Comments: 'When I first started playing Cordelia, she wasn't nice,' Charisma Carpenter told *DreamWatch*. Yet the actress noted how far her character had come in the seven years since she first appeared in *Buffy*. 'She has really deepened and has a stronger sense of responsibility. She now understands what the mission is.' In another interview with Rob Francis, Charisma noted that, 'The road Cordelia had travelled has been such a joy to play as an actress. There have been so many chances to do different emotions; heroic, vulnerable, angry, possessed, funny. I get to be all those different things.'

56
Provider

US Transmission Date: 21 January 2002
UK Transmission Date: 4 April 2002 (Sky)

Writer: Scott Murphy
Director: Bill Norton
Cast: Jeffrey Dean Morgan (Sam Ryan), Eric Bruskotter (Brian),
Sunny Mabrey (Allie), Tony Pasqualini (Harlan Elster),
Alan Henry Brown (Lead Nahdrah), David Ramirez (Pizza Chef),
Brett Wagner (Nahdrah Prince), Benjamin Benitez (Tattoo Vamp #2)

Angel becomes obsessed with making money for Connor's future. As a consequence Angel Investigations starts an aggressive advertising campaign, and the team are swamped with business from human and demon clients. Angel is employed by a businessman to destroy a nest of vampires. Wesley and Gunn help a woman being stalked by her dead ex-boyfriend. And Fred and Lorne are hired to solve a puzzle for a group of demons. But can any of these jobs be taken at face value?

Denial, Thy Names are Wesley and Gunn: Both have clear feelings for Fred, and a minor argument here concerning to which of them she had aimed a compliment suggests a rocky road ahead for the trio.

It's a Designer Label!: Fred's canary-yellow jumper is a highlight. On the other hand, Lorne's vile purple dressing-gown, scarlet jacket and Technicolor shirt can surely qualify as war crimes?

References: Angel's increasing list of priorities is an obvious allusion to the Spanish Inquisition sketch from *Monty Python's Flying Circus* (see **51**, 'Offspring'). Also, *Yellow Pages*, futurist novelist Jules Verne (1828–1905, *Journey to the Centre of the Earth* and *Twenty Thousand Leagues Under the Sea*), billionaire New York real-estate personality Leona Helmsley, Kahlua (a Mexican coffee liqueur with herbs and vanilla), *Ghostbusters*, Rolex and Timex. Cordelia refers to 'snap, crackle and pop', the logo for Kellogg's Rice Krispies. There are oblique dialogue allusions to *Always* and David Bowie's 'The Man Who Sold the World', and a possible conceptual debt to the *Doctor Who* story 'The Brain of Morbius'. Fred quotes from *If* by Rudyard Kipling (1865–1936). Locations mentioned include Malibu and the exclusive ski resort of Aspen, Colorado. The vampire nest that Angel attacks is at 83rd and Vermont in Morningside Park. Harlan Elster runs Elster Printing & Graphics, on Ocean Avenue in Santa Monica. The Nahdrah Demons reside on a barge in Marina del Rey.

L.A.-Speak: Angel: 'Aren't we just the *scary* serial vamps? With the spooky lair and the taking of the trophies of our victims? *Lame*.'

Cigarettes and Alcohol: Lorne says that he can hold his liquor.

Sex and Drugs and Rock'n'Roll: Lorne uses a special fire-water to loosen the tongue of his Garwok snitch. This seemingly involves setting water on fire, much chanting and a bong. When Allie fondly remembers the sex she used to have with her zombie boyfriend, Brian, both Gunn and Wesley give mumbled replies which suggest that neither of them have had it, or anything resembling it, in months. Wesley mentions an Internet article he's writing. Lorne adds that it will be downloadable from i'llneverknow-theloveofawoman.com.

'You May Remember Me From Such Films and TV Series As . . .': Jeffrey Dean Morgan was in *JAG* and *Roadkill*. Eric Bruskotter's CV includes *Cheers, Quantum Leap, Six Feet Under, The Wonder Years, Crimson Tide, Tour of Duty* and *The Fan*. Brett Wagner appeared in *Finding Kelly, Nikki, Bicentennial Man, Sliders* and *Dark Skies*. Sunny Mabrey played Mia in *A Midsummer Night's Rave*. David Ramirez played Wilson in *Eco Moda*.

Logic, Let Me Introduce You to This Window: When Angel leaves Connor with Cordelia it's sunny outside, he says that Connor should get his next feeding at 3.00. This suggests it's early afternoon. But when Angel arrives at Elster's company, it's dark. When Gunn attacks Brian with the stake, it's a painfully obvious rubber one. The Apple Mac laptop that Fred takes with her to help solve the Nahdrah puzzle is not the office PC. That's black, this one is white.

Quote/Unquote: Holtz, to Justine: 'I want you to find others like you. People who have suffered as we have. People with the same rage.'

Lorne: 'I yield the floor to the person not tied up on it.'

Gunn: 'You cut off the snake's head . . .' Wesley: 'You piss the other snakes off.'

Cordy, on the $50,000: 'They tried to cut Fred's head off. We earned *every penny*.'

Notes: 'Whoever heard of a vampire out to make a buck?' In some ways 'Provider' is a rather heartless episode with a central message that seems to regard greed as, in some cases, good. That appallingly 80s attitude leaves a bitter taste even though, ultimately, there's a happy ending. The woman that Wes and Gunn are protecting, for instance, seems to have effectively got away with murder and been rewarded for it. Nevertheless, the episode contains a couple of great fight scenes and some good jokes. It's just a pity it doesn't have a bit more *soul*.

Cordelia's dedication to the true mission of Angel Investigations, as stated repeatedly throughout this episode, dates from her exposure to the suffering of others in **22**, 'To Shanshu In L.A.' Angel finds $1.83 in loose change among the couch cushions in the Hyperion, which he puts in a piggy bank in the office safe. Wesley and Gunn post 6,000 flyers around town advertising the services of Angel Investigations. However, these mistakenly contain the phone number of Fabrizio's Pizza (213-555-0126). Angel Investigations now has its own 'bold, but tasteful' website, apparently designed by Fred, which describes the company as PARANORMAL SPECIALISTS. It contains the slogan WE HELP THE HELPLESS. NO CASE IS TOO SMALL. There are several subsections: ABOUT US, AGENCY SERVICES, DEMON DIRECTORY, LINKS and CONTACT US. (Note it's the 'helpless' and not the 'hopeless' that they now aid (see **4**, 'I Fall to Pieces'). Also, one has to wonder to whom they have LINKS? Presumably the webpage for *The Magic Box* in Sunnydale, designed by Anya, would be an obvious one (see *Buffy*: 'I Was Made To Love You'). Lastly, how accurate *is* the ABOUT US section without getting, you know, scary?) Wesley apparently has two articles on the website. One pertains to DNA fusion comparisons, the other to triped demon populations. He's working on another about gene-mapping for demons with no genes. He tells Gunn that, contrary to popular belief, zombies rarely eat flesh. Lorne speaks the language of the Nahdrahs. Well, sort of. The Nahdrahs are not so much born as disgorged. Holtz stabs a spike through Justine's hand to see how much pain she can withstand and to teach her a lesson for her disobedience. He says that she can remove it any time, as a test of her loyalty. The cheque that Sam Ryan writes for Angel dates the episode as taking place on 17 April 2002. **Did You Know?:** The triplets who took it in turns to play baby Connor were Jake, Trent and Connor Tupen. In one of the flash scenes (whilst Wes and Gunn are in Ally's apartment) a white-haired stagehand can be seen setting up a shot. An amusing outtake from this episode appeared on the Season Three DVD box-set: when Fred completes the puzzle the Nahdrahs perform the Macarena.

Cast and Crew Comments: 'I had a passion for the classical theatre,' Alexis Denisof told *DreamWatch*, relating to his initial move to England. 'I was lucky and joined the RSC [Royal Shakespeare Company] and worked with them for ten years. Then I moved [back to Los Angeles]. In two weeks I got a job and haven't stopped working since.'

57
Waiting in the Wings

US Transmission Date: 4 February 2002
UK Transmission Date: 11 April 2002 (Sky)

Writer: Joss Whedon
Director: Joss Whedon
Cast: Mark Harelik (Count Kurskov), Summer Glau (Prima Ballerina),
Thomas Crawford (Manager), Don Tiffany (Security Guard)

Angel's suggestion of a pleasant evening at the ballet has unexpected consequences for the team. Angel initially becomes suspicious when he realises that the company's dancers are the same ones that he saw more than a century ago. When Angel and Cordelia go backstage to investigate, they find themselves consumed with an overwhelming passion as the spirits of unrequited lovers possess them.

Dudes and Babes: Count Kurskov is a wizard who was obsessed with a ballerina. When she fell in love with another dancer, Kurskov flew into a jealous rage. He pulled her out of reality and doomed her to dance the same performance of *Giselle* for eternity. The Count has the ability to create a time flux and control demon minions. His source of power is an amulet with a jewelled centre.

Denial, Thy Name is Wesley: The convergence on the mythic hot spot which draws Angel and Cordy and Gunn and Fred closer together leaves Wesley a rather haunted, sad and lonely figure, excluded from the fun and games that his friends get to experience. 'Your heart automatically goes out to the guy who doesn't get the girl,' notes Joss Whedon. 'At least, mine does, through years of experience.'

It's a Designer Label!: Fred asks if Cordelia is certain that the upmarket store they're shopping in is the place for them. Cordy replies that they *could* always get their outfits at Cavegirl's House of Burlap, but that's *so* last season. Cordelia admits that she saves money by buying dresses and then returning them after she has worn them once. Lorne uses soda water to clean a stain on Angel's tuxedo.

References: A caustic variant on Michael Powell and Emeric Pressburger's *The Red Shoes*. The ballet that the Blinnikov perform is Adolphe Adam's *Giselle*. Fred's family used to see Tchaikovsky's *The Nutcracker* every Christmas, and she confesses that she had her first ever sexual dream about the Mouse King. The demons are living embodiments of comedy/tragedy masks, the international symbols of the theatre from Greek and Roman drama onwards, and also associated with mime and Japanese kabuki theatre. Visual influences include several associated with Joss Whedon's *Buffy* creations The Gentlemen, as well as *Batman*'s The Joker. Also, Charles Schultz's comic-strip character Snoopy, *The Usual Suspects* ('man with a plan') and the German airship the zeppelin. Gunn describes his favourite band, Mahta Hari, as the tightest in L.A. He once saw them perform at legendary West Hollywood concert hall the Troubadour.[36] Cordelia asks if Angel wishes to wander backstage like Spinal Tap, a reference to the 'rockumentary' *This is Spinal Tap*, about Britain's loudest band, whose inability to find their way on stage in Cleveland is almost as long-lasting as the average lifespan of their drummers. Elements also seem to have been inspired by the Sorcerer's Apprentice sequence in *Fantasia*. Much of the episode was filmed at the Orpheum Theater on South Broadway in Downtown (see **3**, 'In the Dark').

The Charisma Show: Cordelia spends the episode delivering some devastating *double entendres* (see, for instance, her line about Wesley's 'hot iron'). Her hair is gorgeous. And then there's the dress.

---

[36] Mahta Hari is, coincidentally, the name of a band featuring Joss Whedon's brother.

L.A.-Speak: Cordelia, on Angel: 'Up to his ass in demon gore, fine. But ask him *to mack on a hottie* and he *wigs*. My champion, ladies and gentlemen.'

Sex and Drugs and Rock'n'Roll: Cordelia remembers a time when Wesley thought she was the loveliest thing in the world, referring to their relationship in the later episodes of *Buffy*'s Season Three.

'You May Remember Me From Such Films and TV Series As …': A noted ballerina, Summer Glau's magnificent performance in this, her first acting role, resulted in her being cast as River in Joss Whedon's next project, *Firefly*. Mark Harelik's CV includes *Wings*, *Veronica's Closet*, *Election* and *Jurassic Park III*. Thomas Crawford appeared in *Charmed*, *40*, *The West Wing*, *7th Heaven*, *Apollo 13*, *Catch Me If You Can* and *Live From Baghdad*.

Don't Give Up The Day Job: Stuntman and sword-master Tim Weske also worked on *The X-Files*, *Blossom*, *Gilmore Girls* and *Sabrina, The Teenage Witch*. Assistant Director Ian Foster Woolf's CV also includes *Clockstoppers*, *Detroit Rock City*, *Addams Family Values*, *Indecent Proposal*, *Noises Off*, *Backdraft*, *Blue Velvet* and *Cat's Eye*. Special Effects Co-ordinator Mike Gasper also worked on *The Italian Job*, *Roswell*, *Pleasantville*, *Con Air*, *Courage Under Fire* and *Waterworld*. Visual Effects Supervisor Loni Peristere, in addition to legendary work on *Buffy* and *Angel*, also provided the effects for *Volcano*.

'West Hollywood?': 'Joss is a very large-brained person,' David Greenwalt told reporters at the WB's winter press tour. 'Apparently he's in love with the ballet. I guess he felt the show wasn't quite gay enough yet.' To which David Boreanaz quickly replied, 'Angel is *not* gay.' 'Have you *seen* the outfits? You tell me,' Greenwalt replied. During an online interview, Tim Minear added, 'I hear it's been said that *Angel* is queerer than *Queer As Folk*!'

There's A Ghost In My House: Cordelia notes that she was the ditsiest bitch in Sunnydale and that she could have had any man she wanted. Now, however, despite her super-heroine status, the best action she can get is an invisible ghost who's good with a loofah (see **45**, 'Heartthrob'). At

the ballet, Cordelia is possessed by the ballerina's spirit, Angel by her lover, Stefan, and Wesley by Count Kurskov.
Logic, Let Me Introduce You to This Window: What happened to Cordelia's fight and sword training? Is all that forgotten if you're coiffed and dressed in evening wear? In the ballerina's dressing-room, Angel's tie is crooked in one shot and straight in the next. There's a clear suggestion that Angel gets an erection at one point. How is this possible for a vampire whose heart doesn't beat?
I Just *Love* Your Accent: Cordelia considers Wesley to be a gentleman.
Quote/Unquote: Lorne: 'Can't fight *Kyrumption*, cinnamon buns. It's fate.' Angel: 'Stop saying that. And stop calling me pastries.'

Fred: 'We're watching the exact same troupe you saw in 1990?' Gunn: 'I think he said *1890*.' Fred: 'OK, that's *much more* impossible.'

Gunn: 'I was *cool* before I met you all.'

Ballerina: 'I don't dance. I echo.'

Kurskov: 'She danced only for *me*.' Angel: 'You love her *that* much, start a website.'

Notes: 'It will be the performance of a lifetime.' An astonishing piece of dramatic self-indulgence, 'Waiting in the Wings' is a series of interlocking elements of conceptual art that, together, create an epic. It's not quite the best episode of *Angel*, but it's a thing of intricate beauty which deserves, and indeed requires, repeated viewing. A story about obsession, the difference between being a lover and being a fan and the wounding nature of desire, Whedon's script accurately captures the confusion and betrayal inherent in unrequited relationships. As darkly amusing as you'd expect, but with subtle layers of characterisation as a bonus; it's a 24-carat gem.

Angel saw the Blinnikov production of *Giselle* in 1890. He notes that he cried like a baby, even though he was *evil* in those days. It seems he regularly used to attend the ballet. He would always get box seats. Or simply *eat* the people who had them. Angel mentions that he's been possessed by the spirit of a star-crossed lover before. This

happened in *Buffy*: 'I Only Have Eyes For You'. Lorne
comments on Angel's record of being attracted to ex-
cheerleaders. Cordelia, of course, was a cheerleader
throughout her appearances in *Buffy* (see **50**, 'Billy'). Buffy
herself was in the squad, briefly, in 'The Witch'. Lorne also
notes that Angel is a man of many contradictions. Fred is,
apparently, a big eater. Wesley's fencing skills had previously been seen in *Buffy*: 'Graduation Day' Part 1. Sorialus
the Ravager is a six-breasted demon who will rise to kill
the humans who destroyed her mate sometime next month.
At the climax, the Groosalugg appears at the Hyperion.
Lorne says that once everyone on Pylea got their freedom
following the toppling of the Covenant of Tromboli (see
44, 'There's No Place Like Plrtz Glrb'), the Groosalugg
was deposed and replaced with a people's republic (see **58**,
'Couplet'). So he came looking for his true love, Cordelia.
Soundtrack: 'Menuetto: Allegretto String Quartet Op. 17,
in F Major'. Lorne sings an amusing, if rather wordy,
lullaby to Connor which includes references to Lorne
selling the baby to the first vampire cult that makes him a
decent offer.
Did You Know?: According to Joss Whedon, the genesis for
this episode was a chance remark by Amy Acker that she
had studied ballet as a teenager. Intended to showcase
Amy's skills, the episode was constructed around a fantasy
sequence which featured Fred and Wesley dancing on
stage. Though filmed, this scene was cut from the final
episode as Joss felt that it interfered with the narrative.
Thankfully it *was* added to the Season Three DVD box-set.
Critique: 'An extremely entertaining diversion,' according
to *Shivers*; the episode 'leads unsuspecting viewers up a
wish-fulfilment *cul-de-sac*'.
Cast and Crew Comments: 'He's one of the funniest men in
America,' Joss Whedon says of Alexis Denisof. 'He can go
from James Bond to Peter Sellers in the blink of an eye.'
Joss Whedon's Comments: Describing the shooting of this
episode as 'the best time I ever had in my life', Joss notes
that he wrote it in the immediate aftermath of his musical
Buffy episode, 'Once More, With Feeling', when he was

becoming interested in musical experimentation. 'I am ruled by the last thing I see,' he continued. 'I had no idea how much I was trying to make *Moulin Rouge* when I shot this.'

58
Couplet

US Transmission Date: 18 February 2002
UK Transmission Date: 18 April 2002 (Sky)

Writer: Tim Minear, Jeffrey Bell
Director: Tim Minear
Cast: Bernard K Addison (Monster), Fanshen Cox (Anita),
Steven Hack (Lionel), Marisa Matarazzo (Susan), Scott Donovan (Jerry),
Bob Rumnock (Business Man), Vanie Poyey (Pillow Fight Woman),
Michael Otis (Pillow Fight Man)

Fred and Gunn try to balance their romantic and work lives as Cordelia and the Groosalugg search for a method of having sex that won't result in Cordy losing her visions. Meanwhile, Angel feels emasculated as the Groosalugg can do everything that he can, and more.

Dreaming (As *Buffy* Often Proves) is Free: Just as she and the Groosalugg are about to get to know each other well, Cordelia has a sudden vision of the Sineh'D Demon. Is this, perhaps, The Powers' way of warning Cordy not to have sex and lose her gift of vision? In a later conversation with Wes and Angel, Cordy appears to suggest that her visions come with a sense of smell.

Revolution, Thy Name is Pylea: The Groosalugg describes the political upheaval on Pylea in the aftermath of Cordelia's departure. Endless committees were formed, he notes. These splintered into factions and the factions into coalitions, until finally the more radical elements, spurred by a charismatic leader, did *The Dance of Revolution*. All of which suggests that Numfar (see **43**, 'Through the Looking Glass') now leads Pylea. Groo also notes that the tedium of government was too much for him after life on the battlefield. This is something many great generals down the years have discovered – war is easier than politics.

Denial, Thy Name is Cordelia: Cordy cuts Groo's hair and re-dresses him. This, effectively, turns him into a clone of Angel. Overwhelming subtext: Cordelia subconsciously loves Angel, but fears that she cannot have him because of his curse. So she is, in essence, building a *safe* version of Angel in the Groosalugg.

It's a Designer Label!: Cordy's red sweater and short black skirt. Also, Angel's purple shirt which looks so good on Groo but which gets ruined in the fight with the demon-tree thing. Cordelia notes that she would have been ripping it off Groo shortly, anyway.

References: Greta Garbo (1905–90), 'Hansel and Gretel', the biblical story of Samson losing his strength when his hair is cut by Delilah (Judges 14), L Ron Hubbard's *Battlefield Earth* and, obliquely, the thirteenth-century Danish historian Saxo Grammaticus, author of *Gesta Danorum*. Supernatural trees occur in numerous sources. See, for instance, *The Wizard of Oz* and *The Lord of the Rings*. Angel notes that Connor's birth was foretold and that not many other people can claim that. Well, there was Jesus, for a start ... There are dialogue allusions to *Roadhouse*, *Macbeth* and *Apocalypse Now*, and visual references to *Almost Famous*. The only Sorensen Park in California is on Rosehedge Drive in Santa Fe Springs. The tree demon is located in Plummer Park on North Vista Street, in West Hollywood.

'West Hollywood?': Anita, the brothel keeper, asks if Angel and Groo are together. Not *together*, Angel says, quickly. They're just here for the paranormal prophylactic potion. So that Groo can com-shuk his princess, Groo adds happily. 'Just to reiterate, *not* the princess,' says Angel, pointing to himself. It's a good job the Pyleans never made Cordy queen, otherwise Angel would *really* have some explaining to do.

Cordy thinks that Groo is a hunk and, dreamily, asks Wes and Angel if they agree. The pair simply cough, mutter unintelligible replies and look uncomfortable.

L.A.-Speak: Gunn: 'We lost the dude 'cause we were macking on the job.'

Not Exactly A Haven For The Demons: The Senih'D is a spine-covered monster who takes physical form only to feed. The Groosalugg says it resembles the Pylean Bleaucha, which nests in the Scum Pits of Urr.

Sex and Drugs and Rock'n'Roll: Gunn notes that there are numerous different kinds of magic including demonic love spells, mojo sex chants and voodoo booty rituals. Dialogue about sex marbles the entire episode: Wesley asks Cordelia why she can't have any, to which she brilliantly replies, 'I could lose my vision-ity.' (First revealed in **44**, 'There's No Place Like Plrtz Glrb'.) Wesley, apparently, has difficulty in believing that Cordelia is still a virgin. Cordy also notes that at least she isn't upsetting the Hyperion average, as none of her friends ever gets any sex either. She ultimately sends Angel to a demon brothel to get a paranormal love potion which will allow her and Groo to, in her own words, 'com-shuk like bunnies'. In the brothel, Groo and Angel find a businessman chained up in Anita's room. Groo is prepared to free him from slavery, but the man objects, angrily telling Groo not to judge him!

'You May Remember Me From Such Films and TV Series As . . .': Bernard Addison's CV includes *Celebrity* and *Frasier*. Steven Hack appeared in *Sirens*, *Minority Report* and *Scrubs*. Bob Rumnock's movies include *Wild Wild West* and *Anacardium*. Michael Otis was in *Aurora*.

Logic, Let Me Introduce You to This Window: How many leather coats does Angel have? Where was Dennis when Cordy and Groo were getting friendly at Cordy's place, and wasn't he the least bit jealous? Fred states that the tree demon is made of flesh, not wood. How does she know that? (She seems to know an awful lot about the creature, noting that it doesn't appear to have any vital organs, and that it uses humans as its energy source like batteries.) There seem to be three different types of handwriting on Wesley's pad at the episode's end.

Quote/Unquote: Angel: 'Life's short. OK, not mine but, you know, most people.'

   Groo: 'I shall present this beast's head to my princess as a token.' Angel: 'Right, 'cause she'd *love* that.'

Gunn, on Fred: 'What are you, her brother?' Wesley: 'Apparently.'

Notes: 'You're the reason we've all come together. It's your mission which animates us. We each contribute, it's true, but you're unique.' An episode chock-full of positively *filthy* innuendo and lots of good jokes, 'Couplet' walks a tightrope in dramatic terms. The crushing nature of unrequited love has an apparently positive initial effect on both Wes and Angel, who form a bruised yet curiously un-cynical double act. Yet the episode is at its best in showing just how mean and petty an individual Angel can be, and Boreanaz is simply wonderful at pulling this off. Complete with Robert Kral's excellent music, 'Couplet' avoids most of the pitfalls of the radical juxtaposition of emotions that it's striving for. One of the best episodes of the season.

Angel has been solo through most of his vampire life, he tells Wesley. When he wasn't, it never turned out well (references to his relationships with first Darla and then Buffy). Cordelia has a cousin, Timmy, whose hair she used to cut when they were children. At the climax, Angel gives Cordelia some money and tells her to take Groo somewhere sunny for a couple of weeks. Wesley has ordered a copy of *Grammaticus's Third Century Greek Commentaries*. He translates a prophecy from the Nyasian Scrolls which, he believes, relates to Connor, as 'The father will kill the son'. Gunn and Fred have been having breakfast together for several weeks (see **57**, 'Waiting in the Wings'). They usually split the bill. The Groosalugg is impressed with Angel's weapon collection, particularly his favourite broadsword. The team's newest client is Ms Frakes, who suspects that her boyfriend, Jerry, has fallen victim to witchcraft. The tree demon is equipped with computers and a DSL line. It uses the Internet to entice lonely young men to feed from.

Soundtrack: Afterlife's 'Dub in Ya Mind' and David Greenwalt's 'Back in the Blue'.

Did You Know?: On first broadcast, this episode was prefixed by a commercial for Verizon Wireless which featured an actor superimposed on scenes from *Angel* and with the *Angel* theme playing in the background. The advert also appeared during **59**, 'Loyalty' and other subsequent episodes.

David Greenwalt's Comment: Angel cannot spend every episode stuck with unsolvable problems and pain, Greenwalt told *Shivers*. 'You need to tell a good story, have a good plot and a cool monster. You need to have fun too. The show is wickedly funny if we've done our jobs right. I can't do something without humour.'

59
Loyalty

US Transmission Date: 25 February 2002
UK Transmission Date: 25 April 2002 (Sky)

Writer: Mere Smith
Director: James A Contner
Cast: Wendy Davis (Aubrey Jenkins), Enrique Castillo (Doctor),
Susan Martino (Mother #1), Annie Talbot (Mother #2),
Marci Hill (Nurse), Chris Devlin (Holtzian Man),
Thom Scott II (Holtzian Man #2)

Angel is becoming concerned about Wesley's increasingly erratic behaviour. But Wesley's own worst fears are secretly confirmed – the prophecy he has interpreted is true. He is given the three signs to look for before Angel murders his own son, the first of which arrives in the shape of an earthquake.

Dreaming (As *Buffy* Often Proves) is Free: Wesley's nightmare has Angel killing Connor whilst Wes himself has literal blood on his hands. As Gunn perceptively notes, Wesley is running out of time.

Dudes and Babes: There are loads of great-looking, and scantily clad, boys and girls at the pier. One of the mothers attending the baby clinic that Angel uses steals a flask of Connor's blood for, we subsequently discover, Wolfram & Hart.

Denial, Thy Name is Fred: Fred attempts a bit of match-making for Wesley with the apparently lonely single mum

Aubrey, much to Wes's annoyance. The fact that he probably suspects, even at this stage, that Aubrey is one of Holtz's rabble army proves that, depressed as he is, Wes still has *his* mind on the job at hand. Wish the same could be said for Fred and Gunn.

References: 'The road to Hell is paved with good intentions' was first attributed to St Bernard of Clairvaux (1090–1153) by St Francis of Sales (1567–1622). Variations have been used by, amongst others, George Herbert in *Jacula Pruentum*, John Ray in *English Proverbs*, Samuel Johnson and George Bernard Shaw in *Maxims for Revolutionists*. Sahjhan refers to the Moonies, the common term for disciples of the Unification Church, a borderline Christian cult originally founded in Korea by the Reverend Sun Myung Moon. The three portents that the Loa mentions are clear allusions to various portents of Armageddon prophesied in Revelation 8. Also, *Candid Camera*, KC and the Sunshine Band's 'Boogie Shoes', the Who's 'Behind Blue Eyes', *Mr Mom*, *The Hitchhikers Guide to the Galaxy* ('he already knows the answer, he's just looking for the question') and *Twilight Zone: The Movie*. The nest of vampires close to an amusement pier was probably inspired by *The Lost Boys*. This location is the Santa Monica pier, which includes Pacific Park arcade, UCLA Ocean Discovery Center and the 75-year-old Carousel. The geographic co-ordinates where Wes finds the Loa (34.12°N 118.21°W) place this somewhere in the San Fernando Valley. One of the popular hand-drawn Unique Media maps of Los Angeles decorates Wesley's office wall.

'West Hollywood?': Don't Wesley and Angel look just like a gay couple when they take Connor to the clinic?

Tehcnophobia: Gunn observes that Angel has no last name or bank account, and wonders how he's able to order goods from the web. Fred replies that all one has to do is to hack into the shipping database, find a customer who has ordered what you want, then substitute your address. Except, of course, that would be high-tech robbery. Angel merely memorised Cordelia's credit-card number. Fred notes that *this* is, actually, low-tech robbery.

L.A.-Speak: Lilah: 'My company *rocks*.'

Not Exactly A Haven For The Prophecies: Wesley calls an unnamed wizard for information on the baby prophecy. He is directed to a giant hamburger, the icon of a local fast-food chain. This is actually the Loa – a powerful entity which can foretell the future. According to the Loa, the three signs that the prophecy is about to be realised are an earthquake, fire and blood.

Holtz mentions an object called a Resikhian Urn, which can trap the essence of certain demons, including Sahjhan.

Cigarettes and Alcohol: Lilah orders a 30-year-old Scotch with two ice cubes at a bar.

Sex and Drugs and Rock'n'Roll: Given the choice, Gunn would place his relationship with Fred over his job of fighting demons.

'You May Remember Me From Such Films and TV Series As . . .': Wendy Davis appeared in *Mother Ghost* and *High Incident*. Enrique Castillo's CV includes *The Incredible Hulk*, *The Waltons*, *Nixon* and *Mars Attacks!* Susan Martino was in *Charmed* and *The Shield*. Anne Talbot's movies include *Down Periscope*. Chris Devlin played Louis in *Picture Perfect*.

Logic, Let Me Introduce You to This Window: Angel tells Wesley that Connor makes him happy. But not *perfectly* happy, apparently. Unless it really, genuinely, *is* only sex that gets Angel to *that* state. Convenient, isn't it, that Holtz has found a deserted mansion in which to train his army? Why is it that bad guys always get the coolest pads? How does Aubrey come to the conclusion that Fred is a science expert? Aubrey didn't spend enough time in the hotel to make that kind of deduction, and Fred certainly doesn't say or do anything remotely scientific whilst she was there. After the railing gives way in the carousel fight sequence, the slats – except for the one that Fred throws to Gunn – are all missing.

Quote/Unquote: Angel: 'How cute is this?' Gunn: 'Seriously? I'd say you got *way* too much time on your hands.'

Lilah: 'You don't have an appointment.' Sahjhan: 'That's it? No "Wow, how'd he do that?" You twenty-first-century-types are *so* jaded.'

Loa: 'Your insolence is displeasing.' Wesley: '*You* try chatting with a cranky hamburger.'

Wesley, to Holtz: 'If it's a sacrifice you require, then take me. Angel's no more responsible for the crimes of Angelus than I am.'

Notes: 'Holtz is one of the good guys. He has every right to hate me. And if he ever comes close to any of my people again, I'll kill him.' A grim and shocking tale of wrestling consciences, 'Loyalty' paints Wesley as a haunted figure, the sole possessor of dangerous knowledge. Certain key phrases remind us that what we're watching is a metaphorical summation of the entire series – 'things aren't always black and white', 'love can be a terrible thing', references to something being 'the right thing to do'. All of the best scenes involve Wes. His soulful conversations with Angel veer from touching to painful. The confrontation with Holtz, Justine and their gang is a season highlight, a chilling game of moral absolutes. Betrayal and agony lie ahead for Wesley, the Loa tells him. After Wesley has come to the conclusion that life is 'funny and beautiful' and that he's worrying about things that will never happen, the episode climaxes with a sinister foretaste of the horrors to come. A brilliant, anguished tale of broken loyalty in extreme circumstances.

Angel mentions that Cordelia is on vacation with the Groosalugg (see **58**, 'Couplet'). Angel uses a tape recording of a vacuum cleaner to send Connor to sleep. He has really good hearing and cold hands. Angel likes ice hockey (as does Gunn, despite the sport's 'whiteness'), and dreams of his son playing centre one day. For breakfast Gunn has an orange juice, pancakes, sausage and egg. Fred goes for coffee, a burger and fries. Lilah talks to her mother, rather callously, on the phone. Her mother seems to be in some sort of hospital. Sahjhan travels 133 years through time to meet Lilah at the bar. He is aware of Wolfram & Hart existing in other dimensions (see **43**, 'Through the Looking Glass'). Sajhjan seeks Connor's blood and is surprised that Lilah has access to some. Lilah mentions that Wolfram & Hart have a girl who knows everything in their files, a reference to Gwen (see **54**, 'Dad'). She also refers to Wolfram & Hart's official policy on Angel, which is to keep him alive until he becomes useful. Sahjhan claims to have invented Daylight Saving Time.

Although Charisma Carpenter is credited in the title sequence of this and the next two episodes, she doesn't appear in any of them except during the 'Previously on Angel' segment.

Did You Know?: 'I'm not a method actor, but my cruel behaviour caused Daniel [Dae Kim] to doubt whether it was Lilah or me talking to him,' Stephanie Romanov told *DreamWatch*. 'I genuinely think he was afraid of me. Of course, after the scene I apologised.'

Critique: '*Angel* is stronger now than it's ever been,' wrote Jim Smith in *Starburst*. 'The current general approach of producing a quip-laden, action-packed, characterful soap opera is one of the series' most effective yet.'

Cast and Crew Comments: One of the highlights of Alexis Denisof's career was the chance, whilst with the Royal Shakespeare Company, to appear in Sir Ian McKellen's 1992 production of *Hamlet*. 'There are few actors that I've worked with in my life where I've been so impressed,' Alexis told *Cult Times*. 'In rehearsals, I saw him find a hundred different ways to play a scene and all of them were fantastic.'

60
Sleep Tight

US Transmission Date: 4 March 2002
UK Transmission Date: 2 May 2002 (Sky)

Writer: David Greenwalt
Director: Terrence O'Hara
Cast: Marina Benedict (Kim), Jeff Denton (Lead Guitar),
Jhaemi Willems (Drummer), J Scott Shonka (Commando #1),
Robert Forrest (Warrior #2)

Angel's erratic behaviour and sudden cravings for human blood frighten Wesley into kidnapping Connor to keep the baby from his father. Unfortunately, Wesley's plan to protect Connor fails to take into account Holtz's thirst for revenge against Angel.

Dudes and Babes: Two rather skanky, and barely dressed, teenage girls are dancing provocatively to the demon metal band.

Lilah notes that she has started to sense Angel's presence when he's around. Angel asks if she ever gets tired of her *femme fatale* act. Lilah replies that she's had to be better, smarter and quicker than every man in Wolfram & Hart. It's not a feminist thing, it's a survival thing. She has, she continues, made lots of devil's bargains and stuck to them. As a result, she lives somewhat dangerously, but quite comfortably. Every morning she puts on her game face and does what she has to to survive. However, she *became* the game face years ago. She admits that she occasionally gets moments of doubt as to what she is involved in, but a few minutes spent with Angel normally reminds her what her true mission is – making the rest of his eternal life miserable.

References: Inhabitants of the worst dimensions of Hell, according to Angel, include disgraced former US President Richard Nixon (1919–94) and Britney Spears. Dialogue allusions to *The Great Rock and Roll Swindle*, *Julius Caesar* and *Almost Famous* ('musicians get the chicks'), Rodin's *Gates of Hell*, the poem 'Wreck of the Hesperus' by Henry Longfellow (1807–92) and the 60s Sally Fields sitcom *The Flying Nun* (Angel seems to have been a big fan). Also, Genesis 2–3 (Holtz offering Wesley an apple), the Rat Pack (see **30**, 'The Shroud of Rahmon', **69**, 'The House Always Wins') – specifically Sammy Davis Jnr singing a version of Frank Sinatra's 'My Way' – Shirley McLaine and boxer Mike Tyson. A possible biblical allusion is the parallel between Wesley and Judas Iscariot in Matthew 26. The demon metal band's rehearsal room is located in a loading dock behind a Shop & Go in Echo Park. Lilah's men track Holtz to Spring Street near the 6th-Street Bridge in Downtown. Other locations mentioned include The Flamingo Casino in Las Vegas.

Bitch!: Sahjhan describes Lilah as a back-stabbing, traitorous bitch.

State of Confusion: Fred and Gunn have an amusingly convoluted telephone conversation about whether Texas or California is best. To briefly sum up: Texas may, or may not, hate the black man. California, alternatively, has a good climate, an ocean, the L.A. Lakers and excellent music, but also the earth that opens and swallows you whole, traffic congestion and dangerous levels of smog.

Not Exactly A Haven For The Demons: The Quor-toth is described as the darkest of the dark dimensions. Sahjhan has the ability to open portals to this place (but only once: see **61**, 'Forgiving').

Cigarettes and Alcohol: Angel orders a straight whisky in the bar.

Sex and Drugs and Rock'n'Roll: Kim, a talented girl guitarist who is a friend of Lorne's, recently joined a rock band with three mellow, organic types who, she notes, never touched drugs or played a diminished chord. Shortly thereafter, her fellow members began exhibiting demon characteristics and their music turned into what she describes as beyond industrial trash-noise funk. They are, in fact, Wraithers – demons who can assume the form of humans for short times and contaminate those around them. Kim's infection can be cured with Cylenthium powder, a mystical antibiotic. The disease was most likely transmitted by the Penloxia in saliva.

'You May Remember Me From Such Films and TV Series As . . .': Marina Benedict played Luna in *Nikki*. Jeff Denton appeared in *Art House*. Bryan Friday was in *The Cape*, *Alias*, *Cherry Falls* and *The Time Machine*.

Don't Give Up The Day Job: Terrence O'Hara directed the movie *Darkroom* and episodes of *Smallville*, *Dark Angel*, *Brimstone*, *The Pretender*, *Star Trek: Voyager* and *The X-Files*.

Logic, Let Me Introduce You to This Window: Angel admits that for the last couple of days Connor has smelled like food to him. Yet he never said a thing to anyone, choosing, instead, to endanger his son? Angel is, apparently, happy to let Wesley not only take Connor to the park or the beach, but also away from the hotel for the night. Compare this with how protective Angel was in the episodes immediately after his son's birth – not even letting Cordelia *hold* Connor in **54**, 'Dad', for instance. In the scenes filmed under the 6th-Street Bridge, some shots appear to be composites. The timing of Angel and Holtz running towards the portal is very confused. Angel is initially already running with Holtz, but the following shot shows him standing still. Also, Lilah alternates between covering her head and ducking away from the portal and standing straight. In one overhead shot of the Hyperion's lobby, Angel is quite a distance from the weapons cabinet, but in the next shot he is close to it.

I Just *Love* Your Accent: Angel tells Connor that Uncle Wes loves him very much but doesn't show it very well as he's English. Wes notes that Angel is 'awfully chipper' today.

Motors: Wesley drives a Jeep (licence 3QTI895), which Justine steals after slitting his throat.

Quote/Unquote: Wesley: 'You're a soldier, you work for a man who you think is noble and good. I respect that. Trouble is, he's not.' Justine: 'You work with a vampire.' Wesley: 'Who, in fact, *is* noble and good. Quirky, but there it is.'

Angel: 'You look like hell. Not the fun one where they burn you with hot pokers for all eternity, but the hardcore one. You know, Nixon and Britney Spears?'

Lilah: 'How'd you find me?' Angel: 'Your assistant.' Lilah: 'I'll have his arms broken.' Angel: 'Already taken care of.'

Notes: 'I will take good care of him, as though he were my own son. He'll never even know you existed. Don't come after me. You will, though, won't you?' One of the most depressingly downbeat 45 minutes of television ever made. A thorough negation of every rule of series TV that exists, without a happy ending, or even a positive sign for the future, anywhere. And it's *brilliant* – a wonderfully well-acted piece of cod-Shakespearean revenge tragedy that takes the viewer into some dark places. Highlights of the episode include the Wesley/Holtz/Justine stand-off, and the later scenes of Angel and Lilah in the bar.

Angel has no earthquake insurance on the hotel (as alluded to in **42**, 'Over the Rainbow'). Wesley lives across the street from a park and mere minutes away from the Drew Medical Center, which has a noted paediatric care unit. His house number appears to be 2337. Fred has an Aunt Viola who drank lots of Southern Comfort. Lilah's mother (see **59**, 'Loyalty') no longer recognises her. Holtz is not fond of Styrofoam cups. The house where Holtz's army is hiding is at 2239 Santa Elena in Silver Lake. Holtz renames the baby Steven Franklin Thomas, and he and Justine plan to take the baby to Utah.

Soundtrack: There are brief snatches of songs performed by Marina Benedict and the demon metal band.

Did You Know?: One of the flash sequences in this episode features a red Metro Rapid bus passing in front of the Hyperion location.

Cast And Crew Comments: 'In American television, the writer is king,' David Greenwalt told Rob Francis. 'You have a lot of control over your work, particularly if you become a producer at the same time.'

61
Forgiving

US Transmission Date: 15 April 2002
UK Transmission Date: 9 May 2002 (Sky)

Writer: Jeffrey Bell
Director: Turi Meyer
Cast: Kenneth Dolin (Bum), Tripp Pickell (Holtzian),
Sean Mahon (Truck Driver)

Angel seeks revenge against Wesley who, he believes, kidnapped his son and gave him to his enemy, Holtz. While Fred and Gunn try to reason with him, Angel conjures dark magic and risks ripping right through the fabric of reality in an effort to find Connor.

Denial, Thy Name is Everyone: An episode full of extreme examples: Angel's inability to see that revenge will not get his son back; Fred's disbelief that Wesley could possibly have taken Connor; Justine's blind devotion to Holtz's flaws (as Fred notes, there *is* no happy ending for Justine).

The White Room: This is accessed through the elevator at Wolfram & Hart (the floor sequence is 18-23-20-28-27). The room itself is home to an entity who appears as a small girl. It likes violence but hates chaos and, apparently, has access to much valuable knowledge, which it will reveal, for a price (see **74**, 'Habeas Corpses').

References: The White Room concept has conceptual links to *Twin Peaks*, *Star Trek: Deep Space Nine*, *Roswell* (which had an episode thus entitled), *The Matrix* and *The Man Who Fell To Earth*. It was also the name of a best-selling and hugely influential LP by maverick trance-house collective the KLF, and a song by Cream. Also, Tonka Toys and misquotes from *Hamlet* ('this mortal coil'), and The Beatles' 'Strawberry Fields Forever' ('*everything* is real'). A copy of the Jehovah's Witness magazine *The Watchtower* can be seen on the hospital table.

'West Hollywood?': Sahjhan notes that he has flitted back and forth in time, but flitted in a *manly* way.

Not Exactly A Haven For The Demons: Sahjhan's kind were once corporeal, but they brought about chaos due to their love of torture. Therefore, certain Powers That Be intervened and made them insubstantial, forcing them into the role of watcher instead of participant. Only a dark ritual, involving a pentagram, blood and the incantation *Corpus granok Sahjhan demonicus*, can make Sahjhan solid again. The Nyasian prophecy, which Sahjhan read 1,100 years ago, stated that the son of the vampire with a soul would kill him. Sahjhan, therefore, travelled back in time and rewrote the prophecy. His plan would have worked, too, had Holtz killed Darla before Connor was born. But Holtz only wanted to take the boy as replacement for his own lost son, thus delivering the ultimate punishment to Angel. Holtz takes Connor into Quor-toth, which is described as a Hell dimension created by a rip in the fabric of reality. A portal to Quor-toth cannot be opened more than once without endangering the universe.

Cigarettes and Alcohol: Linwood drinks whisky in Lilah's office.

Sex and Drugs and Rock'n'Roll: Angel tells a severely beaten Justine that, as he isn't her boyfriend, she should find somebody else to smack her around.

'You May Remember Me From Such Films and TV Series As . . .': Kay Panabaker was in *Dead Heat* and provided voice work on *Monsters, Inc.* Kenneth Dolin appeared in *Malcolm in the Middle*. Sean Mahon's movies include *Screenland Drive* and *Predators From Beyond Neptune*. He was also the producer and writer of the 1996 movie *Macabre Pair of Shorts*, which was David Boreanaz's acting debut. Tripp Pickell was in *Chinde*.

Logic, Let Me Introduce You to This Window: If Angel wanted to kill Wesley so badly, why choose suffocation instead of simply breaking his neck? Why did Wesley discard his diaries, thus leaving a trail of evidence behind? If Sahjhan is noncorporeal, how could he rewrite the prophecy? A close-up of one of Sahjhan's fellow demons shows his make-up stopping at his ears. When Justine walks into the mansion she has nothing in her hand. Seconds later, the angle switches and she's carrying a stake. In the final scene, the X-rays on the wall are, initially, of a chest and a skull. In close-up, however, they change to an upside-down chest X-ray and an abdominal X-ray. Sahjahn is said to have materialised at the corner of Taber and National. However, the location used for this sequence was actually Melrose Avenue – note the Newspace art gallery in the background of several shots.

Motors: The truck that hits Sahjhan has the number plate 3Q49985.

Quote/Unquote: Girl, to Angel: 'You have a taste for red too. And revenge. It's so much more fun than forgiveness.'

Linwood: 'And you are . . .?' Lorne: 'Deeply troubled.' Linwood: 'Then you and Angel have a lot in common.'

Angel: 'Help me find my son, we'll call it even.' Sahjhan: 'Really? You and me, buddy cops, summer release? We iron out our wacky differences and bond? Don't think so.'

Notes: 'You thought I was going to turn evil and kill my son ... this isn't Angelus talking, it's *me*. You know that, right? You son of a bitch, you're gonna pay for what you did.' A glorious meditation on how hard the concept of forgiveness can be, the episode sees various characters searching, in vain, for someone on whom to blame their misfortunes. Cunningly, 'Forgiving' avoids obvious dramatic exposition and, instead, creates a maelstrom of confusion and despair, apparently ending with a conclusion of hope, only for this to be smashed to pieces in the final, astonishing scene.

Cordelia is in Mexico (see **58**, 'Couplet'). Wesley keeps a Mossberg 12-gauge shotgun in his closet (see **38**, 'Epiphany'). *Phisto's Dictionary of Demons and Dimensional Spirits* is written in Ga-Shundi. Which, unfortunately, Fred doesn't speak. Lilah worked for Wolfram & Hart for three years before she knew of the existence of The White Room. The last employee to enter it is now in an asylum. Linwood's job title is Division President of Special Projects. The truck driver who hits Sahjahn is named Al Stokely.

Soundtrack: Ken Nelson's 'Poolside' plays in the Wolfram & Hart lift.

Did You Know?: 'The third season is like the first season of the show,' David Boreanaz told *Teen Hollywood*. 'Everything just fell into place.' The fact that *Angel* had successfully separated itself, in tone and style, from *Buffy*, was something that was clearly important to both Boreanaz and David Greenwalt. 'It is its own show,' noted Greenwalt. '*Frasier* clearly grew out of *Cheers*. To me, they're two entirely different shows.'

62
Double or Nothing

US Transmission Date: 22 April 2002
UK Transmission Date: 16 May 2002 (Sky)

Writer: David H Goodman
Director: David Grossman
Cast: Jason Carter (Repo Man), Patrick St Espirit (Jenoff),
John David Conti (Male Eldery Demon),
PB Hutton (Female Elderly Demon), Nigel D Gibbs (Doctor)

Angel puts his soul on the line when a supernatural repo man comes to collect on Gunn's past deal to sell his soul. Cordelia is back from her vacation and tries to console Angel over the loss of Connor. Meanwhile, Fred tells Wesley that the prophecy was fake and that his efforts were all for nothing.

Dudes and Babes: Angel seems to be notorious in the demon underworld (as previously alluded to in several episodes).

It's a Designer Label!: What on *earth* is Cordelia wearing in the opening scene? It looks like it's made out of string. Check out, also, Lorne's sickly yellow shirt.

References: Bargaining a soul is a theme common to Marlowe's *Dr Faustus*, Goethe's *Faust* and two versions of *Bedazzled*, amongst countless others. The episode also shares elements with *King Lear*, *Robin and the Seven Hoods*, *Ocean's 11* and Stephen King's *Needful Things*. There are visual references to *The Godfather* (Cordy staking Jenoff in the hand) and *Alien*. The scenario that Fred describes ('young and in love, then someone dies of leukaemia') is a probable reference to Erich Segal's *Love Story*. Jenoff's 'Feeling lucky?' misquotes *Dirty Harry*. Also, possible oblique references to Soft Cell's 'Where the Heart Is' and Val Doonican's 'The Jarvie Was a Leprechaun'.

Dodger Stadium, the ball park of the Los Angeles Dodgers, is situated on a hill overlooking Downtown L.A. It's known for its hot dogs, ushers in straw boaters and the great views of the San Gabriel Mountains and the city skyline. Three poker variations, Omaha, Texas Hold'em and 7-Card Stud, are referenced. Locations mentioned include Topanga Canyon.[37]

---

[37] About 25 miles from central L.A. in the Santa Monica Mountains, Topanga is located on Highway 27, five miles north of the Pacific Coast Highway.

The Charisma Show: Thank goodness Charisma's back. Cordelia is now a blonde (though no one seems to have noticed). Her scenes with Angel, discussing loss and recovery, are some of the best of the season.

L.A.-Speak: Repo man: 'You got a name, or just a 'tude?'

Not Exactly A Haven For The Bruthas: The impish Skench Demon squats in the lairs of other demons, and chases them out by shrieking at night and shooting projectile phlegm. Jenoff is a demon who owns a casino. Commonly known as the Soul Sucker, he collects souls by inserting his fingers into his victims' eyes.

'You May Remember Me From Such Films and TV Series As . . .': British-born Jason Carter is best known as Marcus Cole in *Babylon 5*. His CV also includes *She-Wolf of London*, *Charmed* and *Behind the Red Door*. John David Conti appeared in *Roseanne*, *The West Wing*, *The Rain Killer* and *Flashfire*. Patrick St Esprit was in *Police Squad!*, *Walker, Texas Ranger*, *Knight Rider*, *Black Dawn*, *The Wild Pair* and *We Were Soldiers*. Nigel Gibbs appeared in *Models Inc.*, *Melrose Place*, *Pump Up the Volume*, *Up Close and Personal* and *Dragonfly*. PB Hutton's movies include *Lost World: Jurassic Park*.

Logic, Let Me Introduce You to This Window: Seven years ago would appear to be either late 1994 or early 1995. 'Gangsta's Paradise' wasn't a hit until September 1995. How can a casino owned and patronised by demons exist in Downtown and *not* be discovered by ordinary people? When Gunn first went to Caritas in **28**, 'Guise Will Be Guise', he wondered how he'd lived in L.A. all his life and not noticed 'weird-ass stuff' going on. Yet he was, apparently, aware of a demon casino from an early age. Angel attempted to murder Wesley before several witnesses and yet no one called the police? When Cordelia says 'this place can use a little happiness', the line is obviously an overdub as her lips don't match the words. Before Cordy sits down to talk to Gunn, her sandwich is sticking a few inches out of the bag, but a moment later the sandwich is inside the bag. Why is Angel in room 208 when he's been in room 312 the rest of the season? It's clearly meant to be the same room he was in during the earthquake in **59**, 'Loyalty'. The only intersection of Alvarado and Clark in California is in Pomona, about 31 miles from L.A. Gunn's attitude towards Wesley has mysteriously hardened between the final scenes of the previous episode and this. Gunn signed his blood oath with Jenoff seven years ago, yet when Jenoff sends the repo man out to find Gunn he gives him an Angel Investigations card. Where did he get it and how did he discover that this was where Gunn now worked?

Motors: Seven years ago, when Gunn was seventeen, he offered to trade his soul to Jenoff for the truck that he still drives.

Quote/Unquote: Groosalugg, on Gunn: 'He is very fortunate to have such a woman looking after his weapon.' Lorne: 'I'm not touching that one.'

Cordelia: 'Life will just keep happening. There'll be people who need us so we'll help them. 'Cause that's what we do.'

Notes: 'It's not like we have to cram the rest of our lives into one single day.' Alexis Denisof continues to do a quite wonderful job. If any one actor can be said to stand out in this brilliant ensemble cast, it's Denisof. There's such power in Wesley's silence throughout this episode. In particular, the scene where he comes home, alone and betrayed, with his rather pathetic box of belongings, is astonishingly poignant. As, indeed, is the quiet but devastating sequence in which Angel dismantles Connor's crib. The main problem with 'Double or Nothing' is the Gunn subplot which, despite J August giving it some real anger, is a bit inconsequential and is dealt with in a *faux-naïf* fashion which undercuts the episode's dramatic tension.

Angel believes that Connor would have been left-handed. He was unaware that Gunn and Fred were dating. Cordelia mentions having lived on the Hellmouth (see *Buffy* Season One). Gunn serves Fred breakfast in bed – pancakes and waffles from her favourite diner (see **58**, 'Couplet'). Angel Investigation's latest customers are a Gurfong Demon couple, Syd and Monica Fryzylka, who have been married for over 300 years and whose home is infested by a Skench Demon. Shiv-roth is the Pylean term for the vigil of the bereaved. Jenoff's casino phone number is 213-555-2928.

Soundtrack: Coolio's 'Gangsta's Paradise' and 'Geist' from Kid Gloves Music Library.

Did You Know?: The shooting location for Jenoff's establishment was Larry Flynt's Hustler Casino outside Los Angeles. 'I thought there were gonna be strippers or, at least, scantily clad cocktail waitresses,' Charisma Carpenter told *TV Guide*. J August Richards added, 'Our location department sent out a memo saying, "There will be armored-car deliveries while we're here, so the security officers will likely be a little wary of any masked demons".'

Cast And Crew Comments: Going on location (about 60 per cent of the show is filmed outside the studio) isn't a problem for David Boreanaz. He prefers it. He told Ellen Gray, 'It gives you an opportunity to deal with the elements, the surprises and the challenges. Because you can really lock it down pretty hard on the set. On location, there's always something happening that's exciting and spontaneous.'

63
The Price

US Transmission Date: 29 April 2002
UK Transmission Date: 23 May 2002 (Sky)

Writer: David H Goodman
Director: David Grossman
Cast: John Short (Phillip J Spivey), Wayne Ford (Kid),
Waleed Moursi (Manager)

Angel pays the price for using dark magic in a failed attempt to find his son, as the Hyperion becomes infected with supernatural creatures. One of these possesses Fred, leaving Wesley as Gunn's only hope of saving her. Meanwhile, Cordelia experiences a shocking new power and the team learn of the coming of the Destroyer.

References: Robert Heinlein's *The Puppet Masters* concerns parasite slugs. Also, the classic Jules Dassin movie *Never on Sunday*, Neil Gaiman's horror comic *The Sandman* and Walter Williams' vicious Mr Sluggo, who constantly killed Mr Bill (see **26**, 'Untouched'). 'Ring around the lobby' refers to a Lever Brothers ad for Wisk. 'Live, drink and be merry' is a variant on a biblical phrase found in Ecclesiastes, Isaiah, 1 Corinthians and Luke. Similarly, 'reap what he's sown' misquotes Galatians 6:7. And Lou Reed's 'Perfect Day'. There are several allusions to the Dark Side from the *Star Wars* movies. Cordelia alludes to Hitchcock's *The Birds* and Angel to Albert Hammond's 'It Never Rains in Southern California'. Lilah and Gavin's bitching session, whilst walking through the corridors of Wolfram & Hart, may have been influenced by *The West Wing*. There are visual references to *The Terminator* and *Jurassic Park*. Locations mentioned include the popular tourist region of Baja California in Northern Mexico. Also, Inglewood, an area in South Central close to L.A. Airport, famous as home to the Hollywood Park Racetrack, Randy's Donuts on Manchester Boulevard and as Jules Winnfield's home-boy turf in *Pulp Fiction*. The opening shot is of Santa Monica pier (see **8**, 'I Will Remember You', **59**, 'Loyalty').

Not Exactly A Haven For The Demons: Jellyfish-like in appearance, the translucent slugs have limited intelligence. Violating humans through the mouth, the slugs draw all the moisture from their hosts until the humans, literally, turn to dust. The slugs are difficult to kill, but fear bright light and the coming of the Destroyer.

Cigarettes and Alcohol: Wesley gives Gunn a bottle of Smirnoff Vodka to help Fred get rid of the slug that has infested her.

Sex and Drugs and Rock'n'Roll: Cordy describes Groo as a puppy dog, albeit a sexy, well-built, go-all-night puppy dog. There are several bits of *double entendre* concerning how well-endowed the Groosalugg is.

'You May Remember Me From Such Films and TV Series As ...': Born in Minneapolis in May 1979, Vincent

Kartheiser's movies include *Dandelion*, *The Unsaid*, *Crime + Punishment in Suburbia*, *Another Day in Paradise* and *Heaven Sent*. John Short's CV includes *How the Grinch Stole Christmas*, *Welcome to Hollywood*, *Apollo 13*, *Brenda Starr* and *Maximum Overdrive*. He also wrote and produced *The Pickets*. Wayne Ford was the writer and director of *Into the Darkness*.

Logic, Let Me Introduce You to This Window: Last episode Fred told Wesley to stay away from the hotel and never come back. Here, she's keen on a reconciliation. Although such occurrences are rare it does, occasionally, snow in Southern California (see **Notes**). The last time it happened in L.A. was in 1949. Since when did Groo become an expert on interior design? When the Hyperion lights come back on at the end of the episode Gunn, Fred, Lorne and Groo are all standing in the hotel's lobby and, seconds later, Angel and Cordelia come through a side door from the kitchens where they have successfully vanquished the slugs. So, who was down in the basement turning on the power?

Quote/Unquote: Groo: 'This ebola is a weapon forged in magic?' Lorne: 'Nah, forged in monkey poo.'

Angel: 'What are you fleeing from?' Fred: 'The Destroyer.' Cordelia: 'That is just *not* the name you wanna hear.'

Cordelia: 'You can avoid talking about this, but you know as well as I do, stuff we do usually comes back to bite us in our respective *assi*.'

Notes: 'There's a cosmic price for using primordial powers. There could be repercussions.' What a disappointment. After the pointedly hostile menace of the previous episodes, carefully built to a sinister climax in each case, here we have a clumsy *Aliens* variant featuring, wait for it, the Shrimps from Hell. That's just *not* scary in the least. Not only that, but the normally reliable David Fury's script seems over-heavy and lacking in the writer's usual quick-fire humour and solid characterisation. Worst episode of the season by some distance.

Angel once bought a musical snow globe for Connor. The south wing of the Hyperion has remained unused since

Angel took up residency. Angel says it never snows in Southern California. Cordelia replies that it did once (a reference to the snow sent by The Powers That Be in *Buffy*: 'Amends'). Cordelia also refers to Angel having lived in a dirty old mansion before (see *Buffy*: 'I Only Have Eyes For You'). Wesley tells Gunn that when he thought he was dying, he fought to live to see his friends again and explain to them his side of what happened with Connor. Fred notes that everything she reads on thaumogenesis (see *Buffy*: 'After Life') is cryptic and full of words that she's never heard, like emolutives. She has to keep cross-referencing *Chauldon* with *Arcadian Magics*. She suggests that if asked to research wave particle dualities or the Shrödinger Equation she'd be in her element. Lilah keeps a magic tarantula in a hidden compartment behind her desk, and uses it to open secret emails. Linwood is currently on vacation. He left a cellphone number with Gavin. Lilah and Gavin discuss last year's massacre (see **32**, 'Reunion'). Wolfram & Hart employ a shaman exterminator. Groo's mother was named Pomegranate. The slugs are, he says, like the glass eels of the Kraag Swamps in UxenBlarg. It's been over a week since Angel Investigations had its last customer. There is a juice bar across the street from the Hyperion, which doesn't accept credit cards. Connor returns to this dimension in a very similar fashion to his father's return from Hell in *Buffy*: 'Faith, Hope and Trick'.

Did You Know?: When Joss Whedon asked Andy Hallett to accompany him to a screening of Baz Luhrmann's *Moulin Rouge* on Cape Cod (Hallett's home, and Whedon's vacation home), he could hardly say no – even though he wanted to. 'I never watch movies,' Hallett told *zap2it.com*'s Kate O'Hare. 'I can't sit still for that long. My girlfriend gets so mad at me. That was the last movie I saw. I enjoyed it, but it's only because it was a dark, rainy night on Cape Cod, nothing to do. Joss and I have been talking about doing a Host CD. I'm all for it, make it kind of Las Vegas, lounge songs. We're in talks about it right now. Hopefully it will materialise.'

Cast and Crew Comments: 'My friend Andy Hallett emailed me some fan comment about my character being some Fabio and Keanu Reeves love child,' Mark Lutz says, referring to Groo's flowing locks. 'He's such an interesting character. He's got a dichotomy to him where he's all brave and noble on one hand, and so naive and brainwashed on the other,' Lutz told *zap2it.com*. 'A lot of the fans say, "Oh, he's not the sharpest knife in the drawer", but I think there's more to him than that.'

64
A New World

US Transmission Date: 5 May 2002
UK Transmission Date: 30 May 2002 (Sky)

Writer: Jeffrey Bell
Director: Tim Minear
Cast: Erika Thormahlen (Sunny), Anthony Starke (Tyke),
Deborah Zoe (Mistress Myrna)

Connor returns from Quor-toth as a feral teenage warrior. He is also, seemingly, bent on extracting a manic vengeance against his blood father for the evil deeds of his past. His attempt to kill Angel fails and he finds himself alone in a bewildering new world.

Dudes and Junkie Babes: One of the first people Connor meets in L.A. is a cute if completely helpless teenage kleptomaniac smack addict, Sunny. After he helps her by violently beating up her abusive dealer, Tyke, and cutting his ear off as a trophy, Sunny takes Connor back to her squat. There she clothes him and feeds him and they start to get friendly but, before any relationship can develop, she overdoses in the toilet.

References: The episode title refers to Aldous Huxley's *Brave New World*. Lilah gives Wesley a copy of Dante Alighieri's *Inferno* (1314), part of *The Divine Comedy*. It's not a first edition, being published around 1500, but it *is* in the original Tuscan. Wesley says he's read it several times. In this, the ninth circle of Hell contains Judas Iscariot, frozen and damned for eternity for his betrayal of Christ. Also, references to JM Barrie's *Peter Pan*, Robin Hood, Krazy Glue, Robert Heinlein's *Stranger in a Strange Land* and the Oscars. Connor obliquely alludes to the TV movie *I Know My First Name is Steven*, based on the true story of Steven Stayner, who was kidnapped by a transient stranger as a child. The bus Connor leaps onto is no. 17, which stops at Union Station. There are visual references to *The Matrix*.

The Charisma Show: Love Cordelia's miserable attempt to close the portal. Gunn notes that the last time they saw Connor he was in diapers, so how come he's now a teenager? Cordelia asks someone to assure her they don't live in a soap opera.

Sex and Drugs and Rock'n'Roll: When Sunny hits Tyke he throws her into the back of his car and clearly intends to rape her. Sunny tells Connor that lots of people squat in the abandoned condo. Most are friendly, but if a fat guy wearing furry slippers asks Connor to play 'Teddy Bear in the Hole', Connor should be wary. Connor finds someone's bra in the squat, but Sunny tells him that it doesn't look like his size.

'You May Remember Me From Such Films and TV Series As . . .': Erika Thormahlen played Ashley Gordon in *Just Deal*. Anthony Starke appeared in *Suddenly Susan*, *Charmed*, *Cold Feet*, *Licence to Kill* and *Return of the Killer Tomatoes*! Deborah Zoe was Megan Ryan in *Pensacola: Wings of Gold* and appeared in *Road Trip* and *Going Back*.

Logic, Let Me Introduce You to This Window: Padding is visible around Boreanaz's torso during the fight with Connor. Watch, specifically, the upward kick at Connor's chin. Connor was raised in the Quor-toth, so Los Angeles should be a completely alien environment. Yet he makes his way to a rendezvous with Holtz with very little geographical trouble. Observe closely the axe that Groo throws towards Connor. It's clearly CGI, leaving his hand while his fingers are open. Actually there's a bit too much CGI in this episode, particularly the scenes of Connor on top of the bus, which all look dreadfully fake. How does Gunn manage to get information from the police about what appears to have been a drug deal gone wrong without himself being arrested? When, in Quor-toth, did Connor learn to kiss with tongues? It's dark outside when Connor and Sunny are at the squat. However, the next scene shows Fred and Gunn arriving back at the Hyperion and it's still light outside.

Quote/Unquote: Lilah: 'When she slit your throat, she nicked your sense of humour.' Wesley: 'Not at all. I find you being here *extremely* funny.'

Gunn: 'Folks not used to seeing a kid in animal skins riding on top a bus. Well, not south of Santa Monica Boulevard, anyway.'

Myrna: 'I hope this pentagram wasn't some dark attempt to close the fissure.' Gunn: 'No, that was a dark attempt to open one. Long story.'

Angel: 'What do you know about vampires?' Connor: 'Decapitation, stake in the heart, daylight, fire. I forget anything?'

Notes: 'The worst spot in Hell is reserved for those who betray.' Conceptually, 'A New World' is something of a damp squib; virtually nothing happens plot-wise in the episode. However, it's magnificently played and, a couple of stabs of social-comment realism (which fall flat on their face) aside, is pulled off very well. Some of the lengthy fight scenes work (the opening in the Hyperion, especially). Some don't (the stagy and logically baffling shoot-out at the squat). But there are enough moments of clever or dangerous set pieces to keep the whole thing ticking along.

Lilah offers Wesley a job with Wolfram & Hart, complete with medical and dental benefits and a 401k tax plan. The company, she notes, is home to the largest library on mystical, occult and supernatural references in the world (see **88**, 'Home'). Pylean warriors are trained for endurance. Wesley owns an Apple Mac laptop. Connor says he is called Steven, the name Holtz gave him in **60**, 'Sleep Tight'. One of Lorne's demon acquaintances has 50 hands. Groo once came upon a herd of Burrbeasts who will, apparently, couple with anything that moves. He was, therefore, forced to stand perfectly still for eleven days and nights. Mistress Myrna specialises in dimensional magic. She's a friend of a guy who knows a guy who knows Lorne. She has the ability to slip in and out of our dimension, and also to close tears in reality.

Did You Know?: In Shakespeare's *King Lear* the monarch's youngest daughter, Cordelia, refuses to court favour with her father and thus be awarded dominion over part of his realm. Her honesty ultimately costs Cordelia her life. It's probably no coincidence, therefore, that the brutally honest character on *Angel* played by Charisma Carpenter is also named Cordelia. 'She's really the best friend you could ask for,' Carpenter told *zap2it.com*. 'She always tells the truth.'

The chance to expand Cordelia's character was a big part of what drew Carpenter to *Angel*. She says that she was flattered by the offer from Joss Whedon and Greenwalt, but wondered whether any of the people who made *Buffy* what it was would be moving over to the new series. 'I just trusted – which is not my nature, actually – because I believed so truly in [Whedon's] ability as a writer and as a visionary, that it would be fine,' she continued. Charisma's expanded role has also allowed her to take part in the demon-fighting action that makes up a chunk of each episode. Which is ironic, since she didn't get to kill a vampire on *Buffy* until her final episode. 'That was the final thing I asked for Cordelia to be able to do,' she remembers. 'She lived on a Hellmouth but didn't stake a vampire until the third-season finale. She was always the damsel in distress, and I was constantly frustrated by that.' Now, Charisma regularly works with the stunt team, learning how to handle an array of fearsome weaponry. She's even considering doing some training on her own. 'If we [continue to] go in that direction, I'd possibly have an interest in pursuing martial arts. Also, I've gained a bit of weight and I'd like to work on that.'

Cast And Crew Comments: One of David Boreanaz's heroes as an aspiring actor was Yul Brynner. 'His conviction, his strength, his stature was very powerful when I saw him on stage in a production of *The King & I* in Philadelphia when I was a kid,' David told Rob Francis. 'He was someone who had passion coming out of his eyes and his heart. That gave me inspiration.'

65
Benediction

US Transmission Date: 13 May 2002
UK Transmission Date: 6 June 2002 (Sky)

Writer: Tim Minear
Director: Tim Minear

After an interestingly violent reunion, Angel finds himself battling vampires with Connor in a nightclub. Discovering that Holtz is back in this dimension, Angel, with Fred and Gunn's help, confronts the man who stole his son.

Dudes and Babes: The nightclub sequence gave the production team their first opportunity for some time to feature lots of scantily clad (and, seemingly, off-their-face) ravers. Lots of short skirts, leather pants and sweating can be seen.

It's a Designer Label!: It's nice to see that Fred's discarded the vile orange T-shirt she's been wearing for the last couple of episodes in favour of a much nicer fluffy pink thing. Also, kudos for Lorne's tasteful crimson suit. *Sharp*.

References: *Batman* ('who's the Boy Wonder?'), Oreo cookies, *Wild Wild West* and *that thing you do!* Holtz reads *USA Today*. Gunn alludes to David Bowie's *Scary Monsters* and there are dialogue nods to *The Terminator*.

Awesome: Groo's little heart-to-heart with Lorne, sneaky with a subtext and metaphor-heavy, as Groo realises he is losing his princess to Angel long before she does. A season highlight. Also, Lorne referring to Cordy as 'Miss Demony Britches' and noting that she gave Connor the equivalent of a soul colonic to cure him of the rage that he had carried with him from Quor-toth.

Cigarettes and Alcohol: Wesley is drinking red wine in his apartment whilst eating a rather sad microwave dinner. At the nightclub, Lilah has what appears to be a Martini, whilst Justine is drinking a glass of beer. Later, Lorne mixes himself a Seabreeze.

Logic, Let Me Introduce You to This Window: There is no Palm Terrace in Los Angeles.

Quote/Unquote: Lilah, on Justine: 'She has been pissing off a lot of undead Americans lately.'

Connor: 'Filthy demon.' Lorne: 'Actually, that's *Uncle* Filthy Demon to you.'

Angel, on Holtz: 'I'm not gonna kill him.' Cordelia: 'I don't care if you kill him. He stole Connor's childhood . . . But don't lie to your son.'

Angel: 'Taking Connor from me was never justice. It was vengeance.' Holtz: 'But every time you look upon his face . . . you'll be reminded of that which you took and can never give back.'

Notes: 'Walk in his world, learn all you can . . . But be on your guard. Remember what I've taught you. The devil will show you bright things, many colours.' One of the best episodes of the season, 'Benediction' is, once again, a deliberate restating of many of *Angel*'s core values, centred on the inability of several of the main characters to express remorse properly. There are several outstanding sequences between Boreanaz and firstly Vincent Kartheiser then Keith Szarabajka, which demonstrate how much *Angel*'s focus has changed. Tim Minear's script is witty and clever and has a climax that promises mayhem to follow. Excellent.

The long-running joke that Angel doesn't know how to use his cellphone, last discussed in **56**, 'Provider', is mentioned again. Angel appears to have moved his punching bag (seen in the basement in several episodes) upstairs to his room. Cordelia is able to return to her visions and see as much of the scene as she wants. She stops Connor's attack with her new glowy power, first seen in **63**, 'The Price'. Wesley gets an online invitation to be at 782 W Palm Terrace at 8.30. This turns out to be a dance club where Justine is attacked by a group of enraged vampires who object to her proto-Slayer activities. The invitation was from Lilah so that she could observe Wesley's reaction. Lorne comments on the gang's continued scrubbing of the lobby floor, referring to the pentagram used by Angel during the ritual he performed in **61**, 'Forgiving'. Holtz and Connor stay at the French Cottage Motel, on W Sunset Boulevard. Like his father, Connor has extraordinary hearing. Cedrian Crystals aren't normally enchanted but, when properly prepared, they're capable of searching out mystical energy. Lorne acquired them from a six-horned Laxnie Hag. Fred uses the crystal in a Geiger counter to locate any being that might have come through the reality rift. There aren't many people in Quor-toth, and nor do there seem to be any oceans.

Soundtrack: An unidentified, and rather anonymous, techno instrumental accompanies the scenes in the nightclub.

Did You Know?: Another highlight of the *Angel* Season Three DVD box-set is Vincent Kartheiser's amusingly convoluted screen test, in which he plays a sullen and angry youth left in Angel's care. Although the dialogue is trite and ordinary, the charisma between Vincent and David Boreanaz is electric and it's easy to see why the lad got cast.

Cast and Crew Comments: Alex Denisof's father is not able to watch *Angel* episodes when they air as he lives in a rural area on the East Coast. Denisof told Jean Cummings, 'He [gives] blank tapes to a friend who lives fifty miles away. He watches it usually three or four days later, so I always get a call after that. He'll give me a long review over the phone. Often, I have no idea which episode he's talking about!'

Joss Whedon's Comments: Joss told the *SciFi Wire* website that Wesley would be rejoining the group in Season Four, but that it would take time for the character to rebuild trust with Angel. 'It's a complex issue,' he noted. 'It's not going to be simple. Wesley's learned a lot about trust in the last year, and he's going to be dealing with that.' Alexis

Denisof told the site that he was looking forward to continuing the exploration of Wesley's exclusion. 'Emotions are running high and I think it will be a good few episodes before it's resolved. I know they have some exciting plans for next year, and it's an interesting turn for the character to be isolated and have to find his own way.'

66
Tomorrow

US Transmission Date: 20 May 2002
UK Transmission Date: 13 June 2002 (Sky)

Writer: David Greenwalt
Director: David Greenwalt
Cast: Doug Wax (C&G Techie)

The joyful reunion between Angel and Connor is short-lived when the enraged teenager seeks revenge against Angel for the murder of Holtz. Just at the moment when Cordelia and Angel are finally ready to face their feelings for each other, Cordy is sent a message from The Powers That Be concerning her future.

References: Skip alludes to a famous quotation by Baron Acton (1834–1902): 'Power corrupts, absolute power corrupts absolutely.' Connor refers to Angel as 'the Prince of lies', a biblical description of Lucifer. Lilah seducing Wes seems to have been inspired by Samson and Delilah. Also, *The Vampire Lestat*, in which Claudia and Louis send Lestat to a watery grave and, subsequently, Louis is condemned to spend eternity in a box; the musical *Cats*, Bill Forsyth's *That Sinking Feeling*, Russian dictator Joseph Stalin (1879–1953), the White Cliffs of Dover, Gladys Night and the Pips' 'Midnight Train to Georgia', Oasis's 'Live Forever' and The Three Degrees' 'When Will I See You Again?' Cordy misquotes from *Alice's Adventures in Wonderland* ('I'm late and it's not a date'). There's an allusion to Martin Scorsese's *Alice Doesn't Live Here Anymore*. Fifty cents is a good allowance, notes Cordelia, if you're Tom Sawyer. Cordelia instructs Angel to meet her at Point Dume, which is located at the first turn off North Kanan. Lilah asks if Connor isn't something without precedent in human history. Wesley notes that, on the contrary, Greek, Mesopotamian, Hindu and Celtic myth, the bible, and even Charles Darwin's theory of evolution, all support the coming of something that wasn't possible before.

The Charisma Show: Cordelia discovers that when she needs to give herself a good talking to, she can astrally project a facsimile of herself. She ends the episode by becoming a higher being and ascending to heaven like an, ahem, angel . . .

Cigarettes and Alcohol: Wesley drinks beer, enlivened by a whisky chaser, in the bar when he meets Lilah.

Sex and Drugs and Rock'n'Roll: Waking up after a night of passion with Lilah, Wesley asks her to leave. Lilah suggests that Wes knows how to channel his rage, frustration and hate, which, to her, is always a bigger turn-on than love. His former boss may have a soul but she believes Wesley is losing his. Groo says that it is always an honour to have sex with Cordelia. Lorne has, seemingly, ventured into the music industry. He gives Angel a CD of his, called *Songs For the Love, Lorne*. The groan-inducing title was, Lorne says, suggested by his publicist.

'You May Remember Me From Such Films and TV Series As . . .': Doug Wax appeared in *Firefly* and *Star Trek: Nemesis*. He was also Kevin Bacon's stand-in on *Stir of Echoes*.

Logic, Let Me Introduce You to This Window: Could Justine and Connor get all the materials that they needed to send Angel to his watery grave (a boat, a metal coffin, welding equipment) in such a short space of time? It takes some believing that they could arrange everything in the hour since Connor learned Angel would be meeting Cordy near the ocean. Helicopters and men flood into a crowded drive-in theatre and there's no panic? No one gets out of their car except Angel and Gunn. Angel gives Connor a bookcase containing all of his old favourite books from when he was Connor's age. So, presumably not much published after 1744, the year in which Angel was sixteen. The movie that Angel takes Connor to see appears to be *Courage Under Fire*, an excellent drama but hardly what you'd call an action movie. The hand of the frozen motorist during the scene in which Skip tells Cordelia of her destiny moves position at least twice between shots. Where did Cordy get that dreadful yellow Meccano-kit car from? Why doesn't Connor's taser weapon get wet when he and Angel fight in the Pacific surf? Where did Connor learn how to use a power tool so effectively? Come to that, Justine's sudden acquisition of impressive welding skills is also a bit suspicious.

Quote/Unquote: Lilah: 'Mind if I join you?' Wesley: 'On many levels of great intensity.'

Angel: 'I found Holtz. I didn't kill him.' Cordelia: 'Maybe you're growing as a person.'

Angel: 'Someday you'll learn the truth and you'll hate yourself. Don't. I don't blame you.' Connor: 'Liar.'

Notes: 'I will do as you taught me. I will cling to the good and I will lay waste to the evil. Sleep now, Father. And forgive me.' The metaphor of the season – Cordy ascending/Angel descending – is taken to a literal end in the finale. A pointed study of betrayal and trust, and of missed opportunities, 'Tomorrow' features many fabulous set pieces. These include Lilah and Wesley charming each other amid veiled threats, first in the bar, then in bed; Connor playing on Angel's vanity and fatherly pride to learn his weaknesses; and beautiful leaving scenes for Groo and Lorne (the latter temporarily).

Angel *still* doesn't own a TV (see **17**, 'Eternity'). Cordy suggests that Angel has a rather cheap streak. She admits that she once used her glowy powers as a night-light after a particularly bad nightmare. Angel tries to persuade Cordy to give Connor the 'facts of life' speech. Lorne is leaving for Vegas. A friend there offered him a nightclub job (see **67**, 'Deep Down', **69**, 'The House Always Wins'). He speaks some Italian. 'Shlug-tee' is Plyean for a tense neck. And not sex, as Cordelia thinks. Groo gives Cordelia a Mockk-na, a drink to relieve tension, made from mud, creeping fig and sourgrass from the garden. Groo's favourite foods are tuna and ice cream. Linwood refers to Angel kidnapping and torturing him in **61**, 'Forgiving'.

Did You Know?: Asked about the visual influences on *Angel*, David Greenwalt came up with a surprising answer. 'Animé. Angel looks like a graphic comic-book character – David has a sort of sculptured, square profile. We try to catch that cool sense of movement, the big sweeping action. It's more of a subliminal influence than a direct one.' However, the series is very popular in Japan.

Cast and Crew Comments: 'David Boreanaz is great as Angelus. He's wonderful as Angel, but there's a glint in his eye and a spring in his step when he's evil,' Jeffrey Bell told the *Ventura County Star*. So did this mean that we could expect a return appearance from the wicked Angelus again in Season Four? 'We'll have to find out,' Bell noted, enigmatically. 'We won't take any shortcuts.'

No Charisma?: The period immediately following Season Three brought a flurry of speculation in the media concerning the future of Charisma Carpenter. *E! Online* columnist Wanda noted that 'a WB source told me it had not been decided whether Charisma would return to *Angel*, as she's been struggling with a personal problem that affected production. Charisma was allegedly told to take a month off to take care of it. If she didn't, she'd be out.' *TV Zone* stated that the actress had been in 'quite a bit of trouble' with the producers concerning this personal problem. Carpenter's agent, however, hotly denied such allegations, suggesting that perhaps Wanda was confusing Charisma with [*Witchblade* star] Yancy Butler.

'Magic again. You people rely way too much on that junk.'

— 'Salvage'

'From the depths of solitude, Angel returns . . .'

Angel – Season Four (2002–2003)

Mutant Enemy Inc/Kuzui Enterprises/Sandollar Television/20th Century Fox Television

Created by Joss Whedon and David Greenwalt
Consulting Producer: David Fury, David Greenwalt, Tim Minear[38]
Co-Executive Producer: Jeffrey Bell
Producer: Kelly A Manners, Ben Edlund (82–88)
Co-Producer: Skip Schoolnik, Steven S DeKnight,
James A Contner (76, 80)
Executive Producers: Sandy Gallin, Gail Berman, Fran Rubel Kuzui,
Kaz Kuzui, Joss Whedon

Regular Cast:
David Boreanaz (Angel/Angelus)
Charisma Carpenter (Cordelia Chase)
Alexis Denisof (Wesley Wyndam-Pryce)
Julie Benz (Darla, 83)
Stephanie Romanov (Lilah Morgan, 67–68, 70–71, 73–74, 78–79, 88)
Eliza Dushku (Faith, 79–81)
J August Richards (Charles Gunn)
Andy Hallett (Lorne, 67, 69–88)
Alyson Hannigan (Willow Rosenberg, 81)
Amy Acker (Winifred Burkle)
Daniel Dae Kim (Gavin Park, 67, 73–74)
David Denman (Skip, 83)
John Rubenstein (Linwood, 67)
Kay Panabaker (Girl, 74)
Laurel Holloman (Justine Cooper, 67)
Vincent Kartheiser (Connor)
Rod Tate (Bruiser, 67, 69)

---

[38] David Simpkins was an uncredited member of the production team on episodes **67–68**.

Alexa Davalos (Gwen Raiden, 68, 75, 82)
Sven Holmberg (Delivery Guy, 69, 72)
Vladimir Kulich (The Beast, 72–79)
Roger Yuan (Wo-Pang, 76, 78)
Peter Renaday (Master's Voice, 80–81)
Gina Torres (Jasmine, 83–88)

67
Deep Down

US Transmission Date: 6 October 2002
UK Transmission Date: 23 January 2003 (Sky)

Writer: Steven S DeKnight
Director: Terrence O'Hara
Cast: Noel Guglielmi (Driver Vamp), Ingrid Sonray (Marissa),
Jeff Chase (Gang Vampire)[39]

With Angel trapped on the ocean floor and Cordelia stuck on a mystical plane, Fred and Gunn are frustrated at the lack of clues regarding their friends' whereabouts. Especially when the only eyewitness to Angel's disappearance is murdered by Connor. However, Angel's salvation comes from an unlikely alliance.

Dreaming (As *Buffy* Often Proves) is Free: Suffering from starvation, Angel hallucinates a series of strange scenarios. These include wish fulfilment (a dinner with all of his friends during which Angel is unable to get any food), a romantic setting with Cordelia (which ends with Angel siring her), and a shared battle with Connor (which culminates in Angel, shockingly, killing his son).

Dudes And Babes: Fred makes an *extremely* convincing bully when she tasers Connor.

It's a Designer Label!: Little on offer, except for Lorne's extraordinary fluffy coat.

References: Gunn mentions *Vampirella*, the comic heroine made famous by Jose Gonzalez's artwork (a 1996 movie adaptation starred Talisa Soto) and Robert E Howard's pulp hero *Conan* (which also became a film, starring

---

[39] Uncredited.

Arnold Schwarzenegger). Linwood tells Lilah that Wolfram & Hart is his corner of the sky – John Rubinstein was the original Pippin on Broadway and sang 'Corner of the Sky'. *Justine* was the heroine of the eponymous novel by the Marquis de Sade (1740–1814), so the BDSM references concerning her character are particularly apposite.

There's an allusion to Bert Kaempfert's 'Danke Schoen' (best known from Wayne Newton's 1963 hit version, and Matthew Broderick singing it in *Ferris Bueller's Day Off*). Also, *The Evil Dead*, *Life Is Beautiful* (*La Vita e Bella*), Take That's 'Everything Changes', hearing-aid manufacturers Miracle-Ear, Captain Ahab from *Moby Dick* and Dutch surrealist lithographer Maurits Cornelis Escher (1898–1972), whose best known works include *Tower of Babel*, *Cycle*, *Ascending and Descending*, *Relativity*, *Metamorphosis*, *Castrovalva* and *Belvedere*. Marissa lived in a condemned tenement on Figueroa.

Bitch!: Gunn refers to Lilah as the evil bitch queen.

L.A.-Speak: Fred: '*Word.*'

Lorne: 'You wanna *bitch-slap* sourpuss over there for practice?'

Cigarettes and Alcohol: During Angel's first hallucination, Wesley proposes a toast with red wine.

Sex and Drugs and Rock'n'Roll: Wesley is still involved in his tawdry (yet apparently enjoyable) sexual liaison with Lilah. This involves much neck licking. Justine notes that Wesley was once considered a beacon of purity. That was before he started banging the enemy and keeping a slave girl in his closet, however. Wes's complex relationship with Justine is full of pointed BDSM and humiliation metaphors; she is, apparently, a willing partner (see **Quote/Unquote**). Consider, also, Lilah's extremely suggestive and erotic fingering of a leather chair after her latest session with Wes.

'You May Remember Me From Such Films and TV Series As …': Noel Gugliemi appeared in *Training Day*, *The X-Files*, *24* and *CSI: Crime Scene Investigation*. Rod Tate's movies include *Edtv* and *Jerry Maguire*. Jeff Chase was in *Alias* and *Dunsmore*. He also worked as a stuntman on *Signs* and *She Spies*.

Logic, Let Me Introduce You to This Window: Wesley
states that a vampire can exist indefinitely without feeding,
though the brain damage from prolonged starvation can be
catastrophic. If *he* knew that, why didn't Giles in *Buffy*:
'Pangs'? Wesley also directly contradicts information given
by Spike in the same episode. Why does Gunn tell Fred to
let the phone ring? Shouldn't both of them be following up
any leads concerning Angel and Cordelia? The scars on
Angel's left cheek, clearly visible during his rescue and still
there when Wesley brings him to The Hyperion, vanish
moments later when he confronts Connor.

Quote/Unquote: Gunn, to Connor: 'That's right, Sparky,
Daddy's coming home. And I'm guessing there's gonna be
a spankin'.'

Wes, as Justine prepares to attack him: 'I'll take away
your bucket.'

Angel: 'Nothing in the world is the way it ought to be.
It's harsh and cruel, but that's why there's us. *Champions*.'

Notes: 'How was your summer? Mine was fun. Saw some
fish. Went mad with hunger.' Though filming was supposedly beset by various backstage crises, *Angel*'s fourth
season opens in a satisfyingly intense way. An episode that
uses hallucinations as a dramatic tool, 'Deep Down'
successfully continues many of the previous season's
themes. Some elements work better than others: Gunn and
Fred cast as surrogate parents to Connor, frankly, takes
some believing. Much better is Wesley's story – a complex
riddle in which he plays dangerous, sexually provocative
games with both Justine and Lilah whilst, simultaneously,
searching for Angel. Because it's the right thing to do.
Dark, funny and inventive.

Gunn and Fred have spent three months searching for
Angel and Cordelia without any success. Angel mentions
having been sent to Hell for a hundred years by his
girlfriend (see *Buffy*: 'Becoming' Part 2). Angel Investigations has received at least one eviction notice in the three
months since **66**, 'Tomorrow'. Lorne is now working in
Las Vegas. Despite repeated attempts by Fred and Gunn
to contact him, he seems reluctant to speak to them (see

69, 'The House Always Wins'). Lorne's family nickname on Pylea translates as 'fragrant tuber'. Gunn's self-styled nickname is Big Dog. Connor likes bologna sausage sandwiches without tomato. One of the senior partners at Wolfram & Hart is named Mr Suvata. He's an accomplice to Lilah's stunning coup as she murders Linwood and takes over the Special Projects Division. The senior partners have been working on the Apocalypse since the beginning of time, according to Lilah (though she may be exaggerating). Gavin learns of the Wesley/Lilah affair from psychics whom he hired to locate Angel.

Soundtrack: Lorne sings the traditional lullaby 'Mockingbird'.

Did You Know?: New *Angel* showrunner David Simkins, who had previously worked as a writer/producer on *Lois & Clark*, *Roswell*, *Charmed* and *Dark Angel*, had certainly been doing his homework as he prepared to take charge. 'He sat down this summer, with his wife, and watched [all] 66 episodes,' Alexis Denisof told reporters at a press event. 'That's more than many hardcore fans would do.'

Critique: 'Once again, the spin-off fires on more cylinders than *Buffy*, with an hour of surprises, humor and sharp dialogue,' noted the *Pittsburgh Post-Gazette*'s Rob Owen. Trouble in the production offices might catch up with *Angel* at some point, Owen suggested, 'but so far it's off to an excellent start'.

Cast and Crew Comments: When we last saw Wesley he was kicking Lilah out of his apartment after a little 'angry revenge sex', as Alexis Denisof described it. 'The first show [of Season Four] is nuts,' Alexis told *zap2it.com*. 'There are so many twists and turns, and every scene where you think you know what's going to happen, you get an uppercut. We're really stoked for this season.' Of course Alexis, speaking at the WB's critics party in July, wouldn't reveal any specific plot elements, but he noted, concerning his character, 'He's flirting with, and investigating, the dark side of himself. There are going to be some things that really surprise the audience.'

Joss Whedon's Comments: David Greenwalt's departure from *Angel* to create *Miracles* for ABC had, his co-creator confessed, surprised him. '[It] was a shock, because he's such a central part of *Angel*,' Whedon told reporters at the WB's fall preview event. 'The process is more difficult without David, but the show isn't going to suffer. I won't let it.' Joss went on to describe newcomer David Simkins as 'someone that we could really get into the story with, who can work with the actors and do all the things we need a producer to do. He's done a lot of shows, and he understands the dynamic. He's a really gracious guy, and he really fits with our sensibility.' Just days later, Simkins left the production.

68
Ground State

US Transmission Date: 13 October 2002
UK Transmission Date: 30 January 2003 (Sky)

Writer: Mere Smith
Director: Michael Grossman
Cast: Rena Owen (Dinza), Tom Irwin (Elliot),
Belinda Waymouth (Ms Thorpe), Heidi Fecht (Mrs Raiden),
Michael Medico (Mr Raiden), Jessica M Kiper (Nick),
Easton Gage (Young Boy), Megan Corletto (Young Gwen)

As the search for Cordelia continues, Wesley advises Angel to visit Dinza, a dark goddess of the lost, who has important information. Angel is told that a mystical antiquity, the Axis Of Pythia, can locate souls trapped in other dimensions. Angel, Fred and Gunn break into an auction house to retrieve the Axis, only to discover that a glamorous cat burglar with extraordinary powers has the same intention.

Flashbacks (As *Buffy* Often Proves) are Free: One of the finest openings to an *Angel* episode, 'Ground State' starts with a flashback to 28 October 1985 in Gills Rock, Wisconsin. The anxious Mr and Mrs Raiden leave their daughter, Gwen (dressed in a heavy coat and gloves), at Thorpe's Academy. The Raidens have donated a large sum to the school for Gwen's special needs. Gwen is told that she isn't allowed to touch other students. Later, Gwen befriends a young boy, who gives her a toy. The brief contact between them violently knocks the boy to the ground and melts the toy.

Dudes and Babes: 'I'm a freak,' says Gwen, concerning her partial control of powers over electricity. She claims to have been hit by lightning fourteen times (see **82**, 'Players') and can kill people with a touch, fry electrical systems and bend lasers by exciting the subatomic particles. She's also a highly competent thief. Dinza is one of the Eleusian Mysteries, a dark demigoddess. Only the dead can approach her. She is incredibly fast and knows the location of all lost things. Lilah mentions that Wesley allowed Justine her freedom following the events of **67**, 'Deep Down'. Gunn is, briefly, killed by a huge electrical shock delivered by Gwen. She uses the same power to revive him.

It's a Designer Label!: Gwen's skin-tight red leather pants (also a black pair, seen later), revealing matching top and black satin gloves.

References: The title refers to the state of least possible energy in a physical system, as of elementary particles. Lilah alludes to Simon and Garfunkel's 'Mrs Robinson' and the character of the same name, played by Anne Bancroft, in Mike Nicholl's *The Graduate*. Angel's list of lost things includes the City of Atlantis, the Holy Grail and Teamsters Union leader Jimmy Hoffa (allegedly murdered by the Mafia in 1975, though his body has never been found). Gunn mentions the online auction facility *eBay* (which, judging from Anya's comments in *Buffy*: 'Bargaining' Part 1, is a hotbed of trading in demon artefacts). Also, *Batman*, Superman's nemesis Lex Luthor, the slogan for the popular children's toy Slinky ('it's fun for a boy and a girl'), Denzel Washington (see **25**, 'First Impressions'), Shirley MacLaine, *Flash Gordon*, and Electro Girl, a comic heroine who first appeared in *G-Boy* (1947). There's also an oblique reference to Sid and Marty Kofft's *Electra Woman and Dynagirl*.

Allusions to *All Quiet On The Western Front* and K-Mart's *Blue Light Special* campaign. Lilah not doing errands unless they're *evil* errands is a probable reference to Dr Evil's *raison d'être* in *Austin Powers: International Man of Mystery*. Gwen's surname may have been inspired by the character Rayden in *Mortal Kombat*, who controls the power of lighting and electricity. Or it could refer to a Japanese lightning god, Raydan.

Cigarettes and Alcohol: Gwen orders a Redcoat, a cocktail made from rum, vodka, apricot brandy and lime.

Sex and Drugs and Rock'n'Roll: When Angel meets Lilah, he tells her that he can smell Wesley all over her. Lilah notes that Wesley likes bad girls and challenges him to *make* her shut up when he wants her to (see the S&M metaphors in **67**, 'Deep Down'). There's also a tiny bit of strangulation involving a leather belt.

Gwen and Angel have a brief attachment in the lift that, apparently, involves tongues. Fred feels that Connor needs some corporal punishment with a large, heavy mallet.

'You May Remember Me From Such Films and TV Series As . . .': Alexa Davalos played Bess in *The Ghost of F Scott Fitzgerald*. Jessica Kiper was Shane in *Gilmore Girls*. She also appeared in *2001 Maniacs* and *Sorority Boys*. Belinda Weymouth's CV includes *Murder One*, *Hard Drive* and *Stargate SG-1*. Heidi Fecht's movies include *American Icarus* and *Three Days*. Rena Owen appeared in *Once Were Warriors*, *Artificial Intelligence: AI* and *Star Wars: Episode 2 – Attack of the Clones*. Tom Irwin was in *The Outer Limits*, *Midnight Run*, *My So-Called Life* and *The Haunting*. Michael Medico's CV includes *Life's Too Good*, *Roswell* and *Frasier*. Easton Gage appeared in *Malcolm in the Middle* and *That '70s Show*. Megan Corletto was in *Days of Our Lives* and played the young Phoebe in *Charmed*.

There's A Ghost In My House: Phantom Dennis (in what may be his final lack of appearance) is said to be angry that Cordelia's friends haven't found her yet. His mood probably isn't improved by Fred shouting at him that Cordelia isn't coming back.

Logic, Let Me Introduce You to This Window: Why hasn't anyone mentioned Groo's disappearance? He left the very same night that Cordy and Angel went missing. It seems odd that Angel is immune to Gwen's electrical powers, as he's been attacked, painfully, with electrical tasers previously. Angel's reflection is glimpsed on the shiny walls during the fight in Elliot's office. Shouldn't ripping out the wires from the junction box set off the security alarms? How do Fred and Angel get the badly injured Gunn out of a sealed vault once Gwen has climbed up the rope and, presumably, shut off the only escape route?

Quote/Unquote: Wesley: 'Angel is necessary.' Lilah: 'For what?' Wesley: 'Fighting people like *you*.'

Fred: 'I'm working on a plan. So far, it involves being sent to prison and becoming somebody's bitch.'

Gunn, on Fred's diagram: 'I liked your little ghost guy.' Fred: 'I haven't slept, Charles!'

Gwen: 'I'm *fibbing*. It's lying, only classier.'

Notes: 'This is that "guilt is its own punishment" thing, isn't it?' A bizarrely addictive mixture of *Firestarter* and *Entrapment*, 'Ground State' is another example of *Angel*'s ability to effortlessly sample exterior texts; and to do so without suffering from any obvious lack of originality in how it handles the stolen merchandise. Angel and Lilah charming each other on the 6th Street bridge amongst dire threats is one of *Angel*'s finest moments, and the fight sequences are excellent. Plus, of course, a *sexy superhuman chick*. What more can the viewer ask? Well, possibly a bit more of Charisma Carpenter, who appears in this episode for all of five seconds.

There are continuity references to Angel having engaged in breaking and entering on two previous occasions. See *Buffy*: 'Choices', when Angel helped Buffy to steal the Box of Gavrok, and **28**, 'The Shroud of Rahmon'. Gunn refers to the latter as the time they stole the 'crazy-making death shroud' that nearly killed them. Cordelia had a surround-sound hi-fi system in her apartment. Gunn and Fred called the police at least eight times in their efforts to find the missing Cordelia. Wesley now has his own team, amongst them an agent named Hawkins and a secretary called Diana. Their current assignment is to rescue a Mr O'Leary, who is being held prisoner in a motel room. Wesley has a file based on his extensive investigation of Cordelia's disappearance. The walls of Wesley's apartment are soundproofed – for reasons probably best left to the viewer's imagination.

Connor is currently sleeping rough, though Angel continues to keep a fatherly eye on him. The Axis of Pythia allows the user to locate souls across dimensions. It was forged from the tripod of the Dephic Oracle and is worth $33 million. The Axis was to be auctioned at Chandler's, known for its dealings with the black market. Angel got the building plans from a snitch who thought he was dead. Gwen steals the Axis but subsequently loans it to Angel, who uses the device to see Cordelia in the higher dimension.

Did You Know?: David Simkins only lasted a short time as the showrunner on *Angel*. But Joss Whedon noted that the split shouldn't be seen as a slight against the writer. 'We tried to put him in a job that was nearly impossible to do,' Whedon told *SciFi Wire*. 'It's hard to come in and be in a leadership position on a show where everyone's been doing it for years. The chances of succeeding are [minimal] at best.'

Cast and Crew Comments: 'This character is not stereotypical,' J August Richards told the BBC on Gunn. 'How he speaks is original, it's in his vernacular. One minute he'll be answering *Jeopardy* questions, the next he'll be using street slang, it's very authentic.' In the same interview the actor confessed that his nickname with his friends is Julie, after the cruise director on *The Love Boat*.

69
The House Always Wins

US Transmission Date: 20 October 2002
UK Transmission Date: 6 February 2003 (Sky)

Writer: David Fury
Director: Marita Grabiak

Cast: Clayton Rohner (Lee DeMarco), Morroco Omari (Spencer), Jennifer Autry (Lornette #2), Matt Bushell (Security Guard #2), Tom Scmid (Well-Dressed Man), Brittany Ishibashi (Vivian), Diana Saunders (Bejeweled Woman), John Colelle (Croupier), Beyondka Fields, Tara Archuleta , Jill Landess, Olga Shalyganov, Kristin L Lenmark, Marina Vantskous, Natalya Filatova, Suzanne Basington, Nicole Covacevich, Krisanne Malloy, Kristin Hillier, Tiffany Deal (Featured Dancers)

Angel, Gunn and Fred travel to Las Vegas to visit Lorne, who is performing at the Tropicana. They discover that their friend has been kidnapped by the casino owner, Lee DeMarco, and is being used to steal the destinies of members of the audience to sell on the black market.

References: The plot draws inspiration from *Diamonds Are Forever*. Wesley telling Lilah to take off her underwear during a telephone conversation may have been inspired by a famous sequence in *Get Carter*. Angel has acquired a penchant for name-dropping. This includes references to meeting Sammy Davis Jnr, Frank Sinatra and Dean Martin at the Copa Room in Jackie Entratter's Sands Hotel and attending Elvis and Priscilla Presley's wedding reception. He was, he remembers, drunk and somewhat surly and was mistaken for one of Elvis's band members. Also, mimic Danny Gans, the Las Vegas hotels The Dunes and The Golden Nugget, mobster Bugsy Siegel (1906–47), the Blue Man Group (two of whom are said to be demons), the Pulitzer Prize literary award, Tony Bennett and an allusion to the Tickle Me Elmo doll.

'West Hollywood?': Lorne's ghastly (overproduced, in Angel's opinion) Vegas show, a garish juxtaposition of dry ice, mullet haircuts and rhinestone.

Sex and Drugs and Rock'n'Roll: Fred, when dressed as one of the Lornettes, is asked if she is Lorne's nightly 'diddle'. After some hesitation, she realises what's being alluded to and flusters dreadfully.

'You May Remember Me From Such Films and TV Series As . . .': Clayton Rohner's CV includes *Star Trek: The Next Generation*, *Charmed*, *Jack & Jill*, *Murder One*, *G vs E* and *I, Madman*. Jennifer Autry played Silvia in *Transamerican Killer*. Morocco Omari appeared in *A Song for*

Jade and *Girlfriends*. Brittany Ishibashi was in *Charmed* and *Felicity*. Matt Bushell's movies include *Way Cool?*, which he also produced. John Colella played Vito Stellini in *The Untouchables*.

Logic, Let Me Introduce You to This Window: Gunn refers to the monastery that Angel went to in **45**, 'Heartthrob'. But it was in Sri Lanka, not Tibet. When Gunn, Fred and Lorne leave the casino they end up on Glitter Gulch, which is approximately eight miles from The Tropicana, on the opposite end of The Strip. Although never stated specifically, the episode implies that the entire adventure takes place during one night. Given that it's at least a five-hour drive from L.A. to Vegas, that's stretching credulity somewhat. Note, also, that Fred, Gunn and Lorne have all changed clothing between leaving The Tropicana and arriving back at the Hyperion. How did Fred get into the Lornettes' dressing-room? It's in plain view of the men guarding Lorne's door. Why didn't Lorne see Cordelia when he entered the Hyperion shortly before Angel? It's surprising to hear Angel bragging about having had a life before he met Fred and Gunn, playing tennis with Bugsy Siegel (presumably at night?), having drinks with the Rat Pack and gatecrashing Elvis's wedding. It was pretty much established in *Buffy*: 'Becoming' Part 1 and **24**, 'Are You Now or Have You Ever Been?' (and, again, in **81**, 'Orpheus') that Angel had limited contact with humans between 1900 and 1996. The implication is that nobody has *ever* won at the casino since DeMarco's scheme began. *No one*? Surely *somebody* would have noticed such an outrageously fixed establishment? Elvis and Priscilla's reception, in 1967, took place at Milton Prell's Aladdin Hotel, not at The Tropicana.

Quote/Unquote: A very cheesed-off Cordelia: 'Ah, for crap's sake . . .'

Gunn: 'Something's starting to feel a lot not-right about this.' Fred: 'That's what I've been saying. Only with better grammar.'

Lorne: 'I have more insightful bon mots like that. But I've been stuck in a car for five and a half hours and I gotta pee.'

Notes: 'This is Vegas. Generally speaking, you lose here, you don't get it back.' 'The House Always Wins' serves a similar purpose in *Angel* to the *Roswell* episode 'Viva Las Vegas'. That is, to shoehorn some fun back into an increasingly dark mix. There's something about the sleazy and neon plastic-fantastic false glamour of Vegas that screams 'Entertainment!'. A story about deliberately tampering with the delicious ironies of fate, the episode is a light comedy with some decidedly shady undertones. Boreanaz is on top form, yet again proving that his true value lies in his abilities as a comedy straight man. Fred gets into a very skimpy costume (and overacts in it wonderfully), Gunn has a few excellent fights and Lorne cracks a bunch of pithy one-liners. Fabulous stuff.

Angel considers that Vegas was much nicer when the Mob ran it. Fred thinks Gunn has a nice singing voice. With Cordelia's help, Angel wins $300,000 and a car on a slot machine. Cordy is, seemingly, watching Angel's every move whilst stuck in 'Misty Magicland', in the hope that he will help her escape. According to Lorne, asking about a non-existent dog, Fluffy, is a universally accepted code to alert the listener that someone is being held prisoner (he mentioned Fluffy when Fred spoke to him in **67**, 'Deep Down'). Lee DeMarco was a second-rate magician who recently acquired an artefact that allowed him to liberate people from their destinies. DeMarco kept Lorne prisoner and used the Pylean's ability to foretell people's destiny when they sing (see **23**, 'Judgment'). Those chosen were given a token to play a *Spin To Win* game, rigged so that they would lose their futures. These were then offered on the black market. DeMarco convinced Lorne to be part of this scheme by killing one of the Lornettes and then threatening to kill more should he refuse again. Wesley takes Angel's clients while he's out of town.

Soundtrack: Andy Hallett belts out fantastic renditions of Kermit the Frog's theme song 'Bein' Green' and 'Lady Marmalade' (see **33**, 'Redefinition').

Did You Know?: J August Richards has ambitions to become involved in the creative department of *Angel*. He confirmed during an interview with *TV Zone* that he had plans to write an episode which would involve the actors 'playing our real selves on the *Angel* set. Angel would be David, Cordy would be Charisma . . . We'd go home and be living these lives that aren't really ours . . . I think it would make a cool story. Now I just have to sit down and write it.'

Critique: 'Perhaps the only disappointment lies in the resolution of the plot,' noted David Darlington in *Shivers*. 'Rather than echoing the themes of the main story by turning the gambling aspect back on the baddies, it basically all wound up with a big explosion.'

Cast And Crew Comments: 'We knew we had an unrequited love. Cordelia finds out she loves Angel. She rushes to a place to see him, and we knew we had to get them as far away from each other as possible,' Jeff Bell noted. Originally, plans had called for Angel to be buried under a mall, until his trip to the bottom of the ocean was chosen instead.

70
Slouching Towards Bethlehem

US Transmission Date: 27 October 2002
UK Transmission Date: 13 February 2003 (Sky)

Writer: Jeffrey Bell
Director: Skip Schoolnik
Cast: David Grant Wright (Minivan Dad), Carol Avery (Minivan Mom),
Steven Mayhew (Minivan Teen), Nynno Ahil (Carlo),
Thomas Crawford (Eater Demon)

Cordelia is back. However, she is *sans* memory. Angel and his friends decide it's probably not a good idea to confront her with the true reality of her former status as a conduit to The Powers That Be. And the fact that she numbers vampires and demons amongst her closest friends. A suspicious Cordy, therefore, finds herself in a hotel full of strange people hiding secrets from her.

It's a Designer Label!: Angel tries to jog Cordelia's memory by showing her the shoes that she wore to the ballet in **57**,

'Waiting in the Wings'. Lorne's sharp electric-blue shirt
(see **51**, 'Offspring') puts in another appearance. Also,
Wesley's tasteful suede jacket.

'West Hollywood?': Lorne tells Cordelia that she may find
some of her lingerie missing. But that it was for 'a friend'.

References: The title is a misquotation from *The Second
Coming*, by Irish existentialist WB Yeats (1865–1939).
Lilah refers to Angel and company as 'good and plenties',
alluding to a candy produced by the Quaker City Confec-
tionery Co. 'Clobbering time!' was Ben Grimm's battle cry
in *The Fantastic Four*. Also, *The Godfather* ('sleeping with
the fishes'), Wayne Wang's *Slamdance* and *Enter The
Dragon* (an allusion to Angel's righteous fury). Angel again
mentions his admiration for Barry Manilow (see **23**,
'Judgment', **81** 'Orpheus').

Post-Modernism: There are a few examples of the production poking fun at some of the more bizarre moments from
its own past. In particular, there's a great scene in which a
bemused Cordy looks through photographs of her past
hairstyles. She gets to the dreadful Courtney Cox/Dudley
Moore one from mid-Season Two and lets out a startled
yelp.

The Charisma Show: At least her time on screen is counted
in minutes rather than seconds this episode.

Cigarettes and Alcohol: Cordelia refers to Gunn as a Black
Russian, alluding to a cocktail made with vodka and
kahlua.

Sex and Drugs and Rock'n'Roll: Lilah and Wesley enjoy
another night of sordid passion. They had an ongoing $1
bet concerning which of them would use the word 'relationship' first. Wesley lost. Angel is said to have caffeinated
his blood on at least one previous occasion.

**'You May Remember Me From Such Films and TV Series
As . . .':** David Wright's CV includes *Silk Stalkings* and
Blowback. Carol Avery was in *Titus*. Nynno Ahli appeared
in *JAG*, *Days of Our Lives* and *24*.

Logic, Let Me Introduce You to This Window: Lorne makes
a common mistake, referring to the last book of the Bible
as Revelations – it's actually Revelation. Didn't the team

literally just get home at the beginning of this episode? Yet Lorne has a client within minutes. And would Lorne really let a human-hungry demon loose in the hotel with Cordelia and Fred about? With regard to where Connor is living, why can Angel enter uninvited? Does this suggest that Connor is non-human? When Lilah goes to answer her cellphone, how does Wesley get from the bedroom door back into bed in such a minuscule space of time?

Quote/Unquote: Cordelia: 'Your friends were talking about murdering children. There's singing, blood and pointy things ... What the hell's going on here, Angie?' Angel: 'Angel.' Cordelia: '*Whatever.*'

Gunn: 'How horrible is this thing?' Lorne: 'I haven't read the Book of Revelations lately, but if I was searching for adjectives, I'd probably start there.'

Notes: 'Tell me this is Halloween and he isn't what I think he is.' Like a pocket symphony, 'Slouching Towards Bethlehem' builds on solid, undramatic foundations. A story about how telling the truth is almost always preferable to the alternatives, it yet again sees *Angel* handling its core material skilfully, and with real imagination. The main bonus here, obviously, is the return of Charisma Carpenter, who proves that she still knows her way around a witty quip better than anyone else on the show. There's some delightful silliness as the gang attempt to keep Cordelia from discovering all of those awkward parts of her past. Boreanaz, especially, sneaking around the hotel trying to conceal jars of blood, is a good laugh. There's also a clever final act, and some more beautifully woven characterisation.

Angel considers himself a ballad man when it comes to music. Gunn dislikes being called anyone's sidekick. Whilst recapping her life, Cordelia refers to herself as having been, amongst other things, a princess (see **42**, 'Over the Rainbow'). Cordelia owns a blue soft toy of some description. Several of the signatures in Cordelia's *Sunnydale High School Yearbook* mention the events of the episode in which it was last seen, *Buffy*: 'Graduation Day' Part 2. (Photos of Cordy as a cheerleader come from 'Earshot'.)

Amongst the things that Cordelia cannot remember, much
to her distress, are whether she has any brothers or sisters,
and who her first kiss was with. Connor is able to fill in a
few of the blanks, telling her, helpfully, that she likes shoes
and doughnuts, and that she is very brave. Lilah tells
Wesley that her firm knows about them (which she learned
in **67**, 'Deep Down'), and that Angel is also aware of their
tryst (see **68**, 'Ground State'). One of Lilah's operatives is
named Carlo. Connor has moved into a dingy squat above
what appears to be a warehouse. The entire plot of the
episode is a gigantic diversionary ruse on behalf of
Wolfram & Hart, to allow them to brain-suck the images
that Lorne extracted when he read Cordelia.

Soundtrack: The Eater Demon is requested to sing for
Lorne, and responds with a shaky rendition of The
Archies' 'Sugar Sugar'. Similarly, Cordelia sings Michael
Masser and Linda Creed's 'The Greatest Love Of All' (a
hit for George Benson and, more famously, Whitney
Houston). That this song has personal meaning for her is
obvious – it's the same one she sang (equally badly!) in
Buffy: 'The Puppet Show'.

Cast and Crew Comments: 'At the end of last season there
was a realization that this year is like a rebirth,' David
Boreanaz told Jean Cummings. 'Now, I think we all know
how the show works best. We've gone from learning in the
beginning to finally understanding where it's going.'

71
Supersymmetry

US Transmission Date: 3 November 2002
UK Transmission Date: 20 February 2003 (Sky)

Writer: Elizabeth Craft, Sarah Fain
Director: Bill Norton
Cast: Randy Oglesby (Dr Oliver Seidel), Jerry Trainor (Jared),
Jennifer Hipp (Laurie)

After Fred has a physics article published, she is invited to
speak at a high-profile symposium. During her speech a

dimensional portal opens but her friends save her from being dragged into it. Angel and Gunn discover that other students have disappeared mysteriously and when Fred learns that her old professor has been banishing his brightest students, she plans an intricate revenge. Connor begins training Cordelia to fight vampires, but an awkward attraction between the pair compels Cordelia to ask Angel whether they were once in love.

Denial, Thy Name is Wesley: His continued attraction to Lilah, despite the fact that she used him so badly in the previous episode, hints at a growing addiction. Lilah buys Wes a very expensive medieval armour helmet. It will, she notes, take him *hours* to thank her properly.

It's a Designer Label!: Lorne's silk dressing-gown and Lilah's glossy brown top (and red underwear).

Physics References: The magazine that publishes Fred's article ('Supersymmetry and P-Dimensional Subspace') is *Modern Physics Review*. Supersymmetry is a field theory that attempts to unify the fundamental forces by postulating a symmetry relating the known fermions to hypothetical bosons and vice versa. Apparently. String Theory is a description of elementary particles based on one-dimensional curves, or strings, instead of point particles. Superstring Theory attempts to unify the four fundamental forces of nature. The strings are embedded in a space-time having as many as ten dimensions – the three ordinary ones, plus time and several as yet unnamed. Kaluza-Klein Theory is a model which unifies gravity and electromagnetism. The episode also refers to the mechanism, proposed in 1964 by Peter Higgs, that provides an explanation for how fundamental particles could have mass, which is known as the Higgs Scalar.

References: The comic that Angel browses is *The Ghost* (issue 13). Gunn refers to *Daredevil* 181 (in which Bullseye kills Elektra). There's a reference to Dark Horse, the publishers of the *Angel* comic series. Also, an oblique allusion to *Monty Python's Holy Grail* ('Come on, I'm holding your *head*'). Sturm und Drang was a movement in German literature that flourished during the 1770s. The name was derived from a play by FM von Klinger, and the ideas of Jean-Jacques Rousseau (1712–78) were a major stimulus of the movement, whose key figure was Johann Wolfgang von Goethe (1749–1832: *Götz von Berlichingen*, *The Sorrows of Young Werther*). Other important writers include Friedrich Klopstock and Friedrich Müller.

Also, *peau de soie*, an extremely beautiful fabric, baseball stars Sammy Sosa and Nomar Garciaparra, and California's Pelican Bay State Prison. There's an oblique reference to the Jolly Green Giant, the trademark of the company which specialises in canned vegetables. Lilah calls Fred Gidget, referring to the popular character who first appeared in Frederick Kohner's 1957 novel. This was the basis for a movie starring Sandra Dee and, subsequently, a TV sitcom featuring Sally Fields. Lilah uses the Incredible Hulk's catchphrase, 'Hulk smash'. One of the books visible in Seidel's office is *Einstein: His Life and Times*.

Bitch!: Fred asks if a flail-whipping would kill Seidel slowly. Angel absent-mindedly remembers from his Angelus days that it takes *hours* 'if you do it right'.

Cigarettes and Alcohol: Wesley shares a beer with Fred when she visits him.

Sex and Drugs and Rock'n'Roll: There is something disturbing about the opening scene, in which Fred, wearing the shortest skirt you've ever seen, climbs on top of Gunn and starts fondling him whilst he reads her physics paper aloud. Cordelia and Connor kiss after Cordy kills a vampire, much to Connor's enjoyment and Cordelia's bewilderment. The episode ends on a massive emotional cliffhanger as Cordy, still suffering from amnesia, returns to Angel and asks if they were lovers.

'You May Remember Me From Such Films and TV Series As …': Randy Oglesby's CV includes *Star Trek: Deep Space Nine*, *Picket Fences*, *The X-Files*, *Ally McBeal*, *The West Wing*, *Pearl Harbor* and *Independence Day*. Jerry Trainor played Tommy in *Evolution*. Jennifer Hipp was Christina in *Out of Sync*.

Logic, Let Me Introduce You to This Window: One exterior shot of the Hyperion clearly shows the 'Los Altos Hotel & Apts' sign on the roof. Angel's reflection is briefly visible on the Hyperion's glass doors as he descends the stairs. If the portal was strong enough to suck the professor and some furniture into it, why don't Fred and Gunn also get sucked in? Where did the symbol on the lobby floor go? Just a few episodes ago, Fred was on the verge of a breakdown trying to hold Angel Investigations together. Yet she's apparently had the time to write a very impressive scientific paper. Fred tells Gunn and Angel that she is due to speak between two eminent professors, Ed Witten and Brian Green. But she is the first speaker introduced once inside the auditorium. Jared tells Angel that three students went missing prior to Fred and one after. However, when a list of names of the missing students is shown on the university website (presumably in chronological order) Winifred is positioned third, after Naomi Hara and Sadie Atkins but before Nashad Taki and Marvin Eick.

Quote/Unquote: Gunn: 'I'm gonna need simultaneous translating on this. Like the President with the Russians, but just give me the highlights.'

Jared: 'You know how it is. You hear things, like from a friend of a friend's room-mate.' Gunn: 'Like the story about the girl, the cat and the peanut butter?' Angel: 'That one's true . . . Long story.'

Notes: 'You know what they say about payback? Well, I'm the bitch!' Three words, sadly, sum up 'Supersymmetry'. Out of character. *Everybody* is at it here. Sweet, lovely Fred turns into a hardened cold-eyed killer. Hot-headed Gunn becomes a fluffy 'hey, let's talk' TV liberal in the Fox Mulder/Daniel Jackson mould. Wesley stands around and broods a lot whilst Lilah sexually stalks him. As for Angel and Cordelia, I'm genuinely not sure that they *have* characters in this episode – merely cardboard cut-outs of the real thing. The script, by former *Glory Days* duo Craft and Fain, is competent enough – it's even amusing in places (Angel's discovery that his activities have produced an Internet following, for example). But there's a sense of important ongoing plotlines being pushed to one side simply to make the episode function. That's a lot of work for, sad to say, little reward.

Angel is a popular subject of discussion on various Internet forums and online chatrooms. The Voynok Demon that Angel fights is spiny and has nine lives (plus the ability to regenerate its own head). Although they've been mentioned several times (in both *Buffy* and *Angel*), we've never actually seen Cordelia's parents until they're briefly glimpsed in a photograph in this episode. Fred was a history major before studying physics. After her attack in the auditorium, she reverts to writing equations on the wall, which she did whilst in her cave on Pylea and for some time in the hotel. Professor Oliver Seidel, a former teacher of Fred's, arranged to have his most talented students sucked into alternate dimensions to avoid competition. To stop Fred from killing Seidel, Gunn kills him instead.

Did You Know?: For the first time in its history, during this period *Angel* was getting slightly higher ratings than *Buffy*. Aided by a new Sunday-night slot and the popular series *Charmed* as its lead-in show, *Angel* had WB spokesmen expressing their delight for how well the show was performing. They were so pleased, in fact, that after seven episodes they took the show off air for almost two months and, when it returned, placed it in the seemingly doomed slot of 9 p.m. on Wednesday, replacing the cancelled *Birds of Prey*.

72
Spin the Bottle

US Transmission Date: 11 November 2002
UK Transmission Date: 27 February 2003 (Sky)

Writer: Joss Whedon
Director: Joss Whedon
Cast: Kam Heskin (Loca)

Lorne casts a spell to restore Cordelia's missing memory. An unexpected side effect is the regression of all the Angel Investigations team to their teenage personas. Once the spell is broken, however, Cordelia's memory is restored.

Dreaming (As *Buffy* Often Proves) Can Go Disastrously Wrong: The entire episode is told in flashback by Lorne. He obtains a spell to restore Cordelia's memory from a wraith who deals in such charms professionally. It involves six people seated in a circle around a supernatural bottle. Unfortunately, the spell causes everyone's memories to revert to their teen years.

Denial, Thy Names are Gunn and Fred: This episode takes place just hours after the events of *71*, 'Supersymmetry'. Fred and Gunn's relationship is very strained following Gunn's killing of Seidel.

It's a Designer Label!: Lorne's white suit, Cordelia's purple, cleavage-revealing dress.

References: 'My parade is rainproof' alludes to the song 'Don't Rain On My Parade' from *Funny Girl*. Cordelia, amusingly, notes that she can remember who the President is (and she sort of wishes she couldn't). Also, Scarlett O'Hara from *Gone With The Wind*, *Motel Hell*, Marie Antoinette (1755–93), death-metal band Slayer (see also *Buffy*: 'Doomed'), *The Simpsons*, Grateful Dead's 'Dark Star' ('a little trip through the transitive nightfall of diamonds') and Roman Polanski's *The Fearless Vampire Killers* (aka *Dance Of The Vampires*). There's an allusion to one of the series' favourite sources, *The Wizard of Oz*. Gunn says he must be the muscle of the group, since he isn't the leader and doesn't have brains like Wes and Fred, or a champion's heart like Cordelia. Lorne's narration (and his breaking of the fourth wall when commenting on various characters' stupidity) was possibly inspired by similar techniques used in Thornton Wilder's *Our Town* – although addressing the audience directly from inside a play is a trick that even Shakespeare used (cf. *Macbeth*'s ten-line soliloquy, *Hamlet*'s many musings on life and death, etc.). One of Wesley's theories about what's happening is that they are all strangers brought together by a mysterious evil which is, in fact, one of them – the basic premise of Agatha Christie's novel, *And Then There Were None*. Locations mentioned include the Beverly Center (California's premier trendsetting mall, located between La Cienega and San Vicente Boulevards) and Malibu. The Mondrian is a luxury hotel on Sunset Boulevard.

Bitch!: Some of the insults that the memory-transgressed team throw around are fantastic. There is *no* finer sight on television than Cordelia, in full-on *uber*-bitch mode, calling Gunn 'Hair Club for Men' or Wesley 'Head Cheese'.

'West Hollywood?': Liam's father said he was a sinner and would come to a bad end. But Liam always considered his father to be a self-righteous bastard (see **15**, 'The Prodigal'). He confirms that he was never much for fighting, preferring instead to satisfy his sinful urges. He then asks Cordy if she considers him womanish. Oh, *dead* giveaway.

When Wesley and Gunn wrestle in their battle to become the alpha male of the situation, Cordelia tells them she isn't impressed by their homoerotic buddy-cop session.

The Charisma Show: Cordelia, though still amnesiac, knows all of the shoe stores in L.A. (see *Buffy*: 'Welcome to the Hellmouth').

Awesome: Best moment, in an episode full of such gems, is Wesley's discovery of his retractable arm weapon, and his *terrified* reaction to it. Note, also, that when Fred tells her alien abduction and anal-probing story, Wesley's weapon suddenly shoots out. One doesn't need to be a psychologist to work out what *that*'s a metaphor for.

L.A.-Speak: Lorne: 'Oh, *balls*!'

Not Exactly A Haven For The Bruthas: When Wesley and Gunn are fighting, Liam says that he hopes that 'the slave' wins.

Sex and Drugs and Rock'n'Roll: Fred, seemingly, smoked weed as a teenager. It's always the quiet ones, isn't it? Connor saves the life of a slutty hooker, who wishes to reward him. But only for $50. Poor kid, engine running and stuck in park, as Lorne notes. It gets worse when Cordelia offers Connor more or less the same deal if he kills Angel.

Angel tells Cordelia that she was his dearest friend and that he had feelings for her, but he's uncertain if they were reciprocated. At the climax, having had her memory restored, Cordy confirms that she was in love with Angel before The Powers That Be took her.

'You May Remember Me From Such Films and TV Series As . . .': Kam Heskin appeared in *Sunset Beach*, *Tomcats*, *Blackjack* and *This Girl's Life*. Vladimir Kulich began his career in his native Czechoslovakia. Fluent in several languages, he worked widely in Canada, played Buliwyf in *The 13th Warrior* and appeared in *Seven Days*, *Necronomicon*, *Crash* and *MacGyver*.

Logic, Let Me Introduce You to This Window: The teenage Gunn doesn't mention his sister, Alonna. Given the close relationship established in **20**, 'War Zone', this seems rather unlikely. Why didn't Lorne revert to a seventeen-year-old version of himself? Liam is fascinated by the radio but not by electric lighting. The fight between Connor and Angel is obviously between two stuntmen who look nothing like Kartheiser and Boreanaz. Given what we subsequently discover about what happened to Cordelia at the climax of this episode, it's worth asking when, where and to whom Lorne is telling his story. It must be after **87**, 'Peace Out', if not later. Cordelia says that Connor is eighteen. Wasn't he supposed to be sixteen last season? The spell *did* work, as Lorne subsequently confirms, so was it something else that caused the reversion-to-teenagers side effect? Cordelia smashing the bottle, for instance? This is implied, but not specifically stated within the episode. And was it the reversal of this that led to the entity that occupies Cordelia gaining control? Again, this is subsequently implied (indirectly, by Skip in **83**, 'Inside Out').

I Just *Love* Your Accent: Cordelia refers to Wesley as Princess Charles. The teenage Liam hated the British (he calls Wesley an English pig), taking the attitude all good Irish lads of the 1750s would have had towards the foreign invaders.

Motors: Hurrying outside to escape the madness in the hotel, a terrified Liam assumes that the passing cars are shiny demons.

Quote/Unquote: Gunn: 'What happened to you, man?'
Wesley: 'I had my throat cut and all my friends abandoned
me.'

Wesley: 'I happen to be head boy.' Cordelia: 'Gee, I
wonder how you earned *that* nickname?'

Wesley: 'The cross obviously doesn't affect me, or our
friend the pugilist.' Gunn: 'Your ass better pray I don't
look that word up.'

Notes: 'No pain, no side effects. I'm telling you, swingers,
there is no way this can fail. So I'm an idiot. What are you?
Perfect?' An episode that concentrates on characterisation
and is the funniest and most scary episode of *Angel* since
Joss Whedon last wrote for his most underrated creation.
It's also, ironically, Whedon's most traditional TV script in
ages. In a very literal way 'Spin the Bottle' is a step back
in time; a look at roads not taken. It's a bottle-show in
more ways than one, confined totally to the Hyperion and
featuring almost no additional cast. The return of characters we used to know – the bitchy Cordelia from *Buffy*
Season One; the nervous, bumbling Wesley of *Buffy*
Season Three; the angry young Gunn of *Angel* Season One
– is welcome. The teenage characterisations of Liam and,
especially, of Fred, are equally revealing. 'Spin the Bottle'
deals, as the best *Buffy* and *Angel* episodes usually do, with
secrets and hidden laughter. As an example of Whedon's
work, it's virtually flawless; as a piece of *Angel*'s ongoing
story, it's exemplary.

Under the spell, Angel refers to himself as Liam and
talks of his domineering father. We learned of Angel's
human name and his awkward relationship with his father
in **15**, 'The Prodigal'. When seeing Angel for the first time
after the spell, Cordelia says, '*Hello*, salty goodness,'
exactly what she said on first seeing him in *Buffy*: 'Never
Kill A Boy On The First Date'.

Wesley was head boy at the Watchers Academy in South
Hampshire (see *Buffy*: 'Bad Girls'). He knew karate (or, at
least, he *thought* he did) and was, frankly, a bit useless –
we knew that anyway (see various *Buffy* Season Three
episodes). Wesley mentions a test that Watchers give to

Slayers, in which they are trapped in a house with a vampire and must fight to the death. This test, *Cruciamentum*, was central to *Buffy*: 'Helpless'. In **69**, 'The House Always Wins', Wesley told a visitor to get Emil to obtain a package for him. We learn here that this included Wesley's arm weapons (similar to those used by Angel in **1**, 'City Of').

Fred attended high school in San Antonio and once took a personality disorder test (one of the questions, concerning the participant wanting to be a florist, had been the subject of a discussion between Buffy and Willow in *Buffy*: 'Dopplegängland'). Fred had a schoolfriend named Levon, who believed in government conspiracies.

Gunn remarks sarcastically that symbols on the floor are always a good sign (see **61**, 'Forgiving'). He mentions that he has been killing vampires since he was twelve (see **20**, 'War Zone').

Lorne refers to the time when he was attacked by Wolfram & Hart (**70**, 'Slouching Towards Bethlehem') and makes a spiteful comment about his mother (see **43**, 'Through the Looking Glass').

Soundtrack: Lorne sings Marvin Hamlisch's easy-listening standard 'The Way We Were'. Also, Robert Kral's trippy sitar-based incidental music that accompanies the scene after the spell has been cast.

Did You Know?: 'Joss gives a lot of [helpful] notes when he directs,' J August Richards told *TV Zone*. 'The same is true of David Greenwalt. They have very specific ideas about these characters. However, they're totally open to your thoughts and suggestions on how you would like to approach a scene. It's a great way to work.'

Critique: 'The framing device of having Lorne narrate the story seems a bit sub-*Trek*, although with a lightness of touch rare to that franchise,' wrote David Darlington. 'However, it's nice to see the gang more or less interacting as a team for the first time in about a year.'

Joss Whedon's Comments: 'It started with Alexis,' Whedon said in an online interview. 'We talked about how cool his character had become. But we liked the blithering bumpkin he was when he arrived. I got the idea of doing the show where everybody [was as they] used to be. Cordelia has become wonderful and fascinating, [but] wasn't it fun when she was the biggest bitch in the universe?'

73
Apocalypse Nowish (aka: Rain of Fire)

US Transmission Date: 17 November 2002
UK Transmission Date: 6 March 2003 (Sky)

Writer: Steven S DeKnight
Director: Vern Gillum
Cast: Tina Morasco (Mrs Pritchard), Molly Weber (Waitress)

The Angel Investigations team struggle to deal with a sudden spate of biblical plagues. Meanwhile, Cordelia reveals to Connor that she had a vision concerning something arising from beyond her worst nightmares. Having gained Lilah's reluctant help, Angel, Wesley, Gunn and Lorne go searching for their new nemesis. And find . . . The Beast.

Dreaming (As *Buffy* Often Proves) is Free: Cordelia says that she hasn't slept since the events of the previous episode, but we subsequently find out that this is part of a dream.

Dudes and Babes: The Beast is a horned demon with cloven feet and skin that looks like molten lava (it's actually, as we subsequently discover, made largely of rock). It's remarkably strong and easily defeats Angel, Wesley, Gunn, Lorne and Connor. Cordelia's eyes turn white during her vision and she tells Connor that she can taste the blood of all the people that the coming evil is going to kill.

Denial, Thy Names are Gunn and Fred: They still haven't touched each other (sexually or otherwise) since the events of **71**, 'Supersymmetry'.

It's a Designer Label!: Lorne's colour scheme just gets worse – dark purple and pale yellow. On the brighter side, Cordy's mauve top and Fred's red sweater.

References: The title refers to Francis Ford Coppola's 1979 Vietnam war epic *Apocalypse Now*. Also, *Saved By The Bell*, *Pod People*, *The Exorcist* ('maybe we should have brought a priest'), *Casper The Friendly Ghost*, Brainiac from *Superman*, Drano Liquid Clog Remover, *Jaws* ('I'm gonna need a bigger arrow'), Johnny Cash's 'Ring Of Fire', Niagara Falls, *Ghostbusters*, Wonder Girl, Chanel perfume and 409 All-Purpose Cleaner. 'Chuck Heston plague-athon' alludes to the film *The Ten Commandments*. The attack of the sparrows on the Hyperion is influenced by Hitchcock's *The Birds* (1963). The sequence with the rats in Mrs Pritchard's bathroom contains visual links to *The X-Files* episode 'Teso Dos Bichos'. The Beast's physical appearance is reminiscent of the creature in *Legend*. Also, visual references to *The Matrix*, *An American Werewolf In London* (a dream within a dream) and the films of John Woo (Wesley firing two guns in slow motion).

Awesome: Some of the telephone conversations that Lorne and Gunn are involved in – all, seemingly, concerning biblical plagues, apocalyptic scenarios, evil cats and mucus – are hilarious.

Cigarettes and Alcohol: Lorne drinks what looks like a glass of rosé.

Sex and Drugs and Rock'n'Roll: Lilah's somewhat desperate attempts to get Wesley's attention culminate in a rather cruel impersonation of a Fredlike schoolgirl with pigtails, spectacles and a very short miniskirt. Wesley is disdainful but, significantly, when the pair subsequently have sex, he tells Lilah to keep her glasses on.

Cordelia, believing that the world is about to end, regrets the fact that Connor has missed out on so many things in his life. So she lies back, thinks of . . . shoes and, ahem, gives herself to him. *Ewww*. Anyone else as disturbed about this as the author? Angel sees them at it and looks as though he's not very happy about the developing situation vis-à-vis the love of his life sleeping with his son.

'You May Remember Me From Such Films and TV Series As . . .': Tina Morasco played Janet in *Just Ask My Children*. Molly Weber appeared in *Stark Raving Mad*.

Logic, Let Me Introduce You to This Window: Cordelia should *not* be sleeping with Connor. It's the *law*! OK, not really, but this conceptual incest is ... *really* tacky (something the series itself subsequently acknowledges: see **77**, 'Soulless'). In several shots, The Beast's cloven feet aren't cloven. When The Beast picks up Connor and throws him aside, it's obvious that the stuntman pretending to be Connor is on some sort of harness.

Quote/Unquote: Angel, on the contents of his weapons cabinet: 'You think I should keep these alphabetical or rearrange them by how much damage they inflict?'

Gunn: 'Woman in Hancock Park's hearing spookies in her pipes. Don't know whether to bring my axe or a plunger.' Angel: 'See, worst thing we got going on is a haunted toilet.'

Angel: 'The enemy of my enemy ...' Lilah: '... can kiss my ass.'

Notes: 'It's not like the world's going to end right now.' Starting with some of the most scary imagery that *Angel* has ever attempted, 'Apocalypse Nowish' contains just about every dramatic trick in the book: dream sequences, fractured and soured personal relationships, sexually provocative elements and a not inconsiderable dose of ultra-violence. Touching, torrid and very angry, this is another example of Angel at its very best.

Angel always wanted to be a prince of some description. Cordelia has moved back in with Connor since recovering her memory (see **72**, 'Spin the Bottle'). When she was a higher being, Cordy was able to relive the horror of all of Angelus's victims and sense how much he enjoyed those grisly deeds. Gunn's fear of rats (see **45**, 'Heartthrob') is mentioned again. The diner that Fred goes to is the same one that she and Gunn visited in **58**, 'Couplet' and **59**, 'Loyalty'. Connor now has a TV in his home. He suffers broken ribs after his battle with the demon (it's implied that this is the first time he's broken any bones, even on Quor-toth). Wolfram & Hart are using psychics to attempt to decipher Lorne's recent psychic reading of Cordelia. Any who come close to the extracted material, however, have died rather messily. Angel tortures Gavin to obtain information (Lilah asks if Angel couldn't have tortured Gavin more than he did. Angel *really* wanted to, but Gavin wouldn't stop talking so Angel couldn't concentrate). The notes that Angel gets from Wolfram & Hart form the Eye of Fire, an ancient alchemical symbol representing fire and destruction. Lilah makes a sarcastic reference to the highly ineffective vampire detectors at Wolfram & Hart (see **21**, 'Blind Date', **32**, 'Reunion', **54**, 'Dad'). The team locate The Beast at the Kimble Building, in a club known as The Sky Temple. The Beast rises at the exact spot where Darla sacrificed her life in allowing Connor to be born in **53**, 'Lullaby'. Glurg Demons are 90 per cent pus.

Did You Know?: 'Having someone in your life does offer the support one needs when working the time and hours we do,' Alexis Denisof noted concerning his relationship with fiancée Alyson Hannigan. 'I think it gives you a centre away from work that's important. Alyson has the same schedule, more or less, that I do, so we understand what we're going through together.'

Cast and Crew Comments: 'We've tried to get Angel to the place where he can make peace with what he's done. He's doing the right thing *because* it's the right thing and not to atone for what he's done in the past,' Jeffrey Bell told Dave Mason. However, as Angel approaches a point of contentment, it's important to take some peace away from him. That's the philosophy of mixing pain and joy in *Angel* and *Buffy*. 'On our show, anyone can die at any moment. You never know,' Bell notes.

Time For A Break: Jeff Bell told *SciFi Wire* that he wasn't worried about *Angel*'s latest time-slot change. 'They've moved us each year. Every time they move us the same people show up. We were terrified of Sundays at 9, which I think is the hardest hour in TV. [But] we were doing fine. For whatever reason, we're now going to be Wednesdays at 9.' The move meant that, after two steady years on Tuesdays following *Buffy*, *Angel* had been moved three times in a year and a half. The move put the series up against UPN's *The Twilight Zone* and NBC's *The West*

Wing. But Bell believed that the biggest competition would come from ABC. 'The one that could really kill us is *The Bachelor*.'

74
Habeas Corpses

US Transmission Date: 15 January 2003
UK Transmission Date: 13 March 2003 (Sky)

Writer: Jeffrey Bell
Director: Skip Schoolnik

Another day dawns for Angel Investigations; The Beast leaves a deadly trail across L.A. The team gathers at the Hyperion after a night of facing the rain of fire. There, they learn that Connor is trapped within Wolfram & Hart. Angel and his friends prepare to rescue his son. But first they must face the firm's employees, who have all undergone a transformation.

Zombie Dudes and Zombie Babes: All the dead employees of Wolfram & Hart are turned into zombies. It's unclear if The Beast was responsible for this or if, as Wesley suspects, it was one of the security measures that Wolfram & Hart had within the building itself. The only way to kill a zombie, Angel notes, is to stop its brain activity.

It's a Designer Label!: Cordelia's flowery blouse and short black skirt. Lilah's chunky white sweater.

References: The title is a pun on the legal term habeas corpus meaning, literally, 'produce the person'. Lorne's Cirque de Flambé refers to Cirque du Soleil, formed in 1984 by a troupe of street performers. There are allusions to *Mommie Dearest*, the Rice Krispies slogan 'snap, crackle and pop' (see **56**, 'Provider'), the LoJack Corporation (the world's leading stolen-vehicle recovery organisation), 'Keep The Home Fires Burning', Sherlock Holmes, *Star Wars* ('the evil empire'), *Dead Man Walking*, *The Terminator* and *Little Red Riding Hood*. The zombie theme is an obvious homage to *Night of the Living Dead*, *Dawn* *of the Dead*, *Day of the Dead*, etc. Also, visual references to *Resident Evil*.

Cigarettes and Alcohol: When the team suddenly appear in the lobby of the Hyperion, having been transported from The White Room, Lorne looks at them, and then, suspiciously, at his drink.

Sex and Drugs and Rock'n'Roll: Last time, most of the gang were dealing with the apocalypse, whilst Cordy and Connor were busy com-shucking like there was going to be no tomorrow. Which, at the time, it looked like there might not have been. Thankfully, the latter disgrace is swiftly put to bed – excuse the pun – with Cordelia apparently finding herself as disgusted with this situation as everyone else (see **77**, 'Soulless'). Connor is less than happy at being rejected. As for the apocalypse ... *that's* still a work in progress.

   Wesley breaks up with Lilah, opting to remain on the side of good. Lilah is bitter and angry, but this doesn't stop Wes from, subsequently, saving her life.

Logic, Let Me Introduce You to This Window: It has to be asked: at what point is Jasmine in control of Cordelia's actions? **83**, 'Inside Out' suggests that it's from the moment that Lorne gave her the reversal spell in **72**, 'Spin the Bottle'. However, her actions in this and several subsequent episodes simply don't support this reading. Why did the lawyers at Wolfram & Hart only bleed on their papers (as well as, admittedly, the walls) and not on the floor? Connor is thrown against a concrete pillar with such force that it shatters. Why doesn't this bring the roof down? And why isn't his spine turned to dust by such trauma? Why didn't Lilah pass out, considering the serious wound that she had received? How can Fred make an elevator that has no electricity work? Rewiring it wouldn't change anything because there was no power. How does The Beast get into and out of The White Room? Once again, in distance shots of The Beast, its cloven hooves disappear, to be replaced by feet.

Quote/Unquote: Lilah: 'Funny thing about black and white. You mix it together, you get *grey*.'

Connor: 'What's a zombie?' Angel: 'An undead thing.' Connor: 'Like you?' Angel: 'No. Zombies are slow, dim-witted things that crave human flesh.' Connor: 'Like you?'

Notes: 'Now take your new boyfriend and get out.' Jeff Bell's cunningly layered script moves events along at a considerable pace. A particular highlight is a carnage-ridden set piece involving Wesley, Lilah and The Beast within Wolfram & Hart, that's straight out of 'The *24* Book of Blowing Things Up'. The episode ends with yet another melange of explosions, zombie attacks, daredevil escapes, mystical plot devices and one-liners. A critical summation of the entire series, you might say. Except for the zombies, *they're* new. *Angel* is at its very best when the material is at its darkest. 'Habeas Corpses' is about as dark as they come.

Angel has a photographic memory. He remembers the elevator combination to access The White Room (**61**, 'Forgiving'). Wesley says that he has a man on the inside at Wolfram & Hart (though he's probably referring to Lilah). The little girl in The White Room transports the team back to the Hyperion using the last of her strength before dying (see **75**, 'Long Day's Journey'). She also tells them that 'the answer is among you'. Fred mentions that Wesley now has his own team (see **68**, 'Ground State' – interestingly, from this point onwards, they're never mentioned again and Wes is, effectively, back in the Angel Investigations fold). The senior partners of Wolfram & Hart want to make a deal with The Beast to facilitate their already-planned apocalypse. Lilah doesn't believe The Beast has a specific agenda, but she's wrong. She keeps a loaded handgun in her desk. The Wolfram & Hart building is designed to lock down in case of an internal attack. There's a secret exit to the sewer tunnels, located in a third-floor utility closet. According to the radio, the authorities are describing the rain of fire as meteorite showers.

Did You Know?: When The Beast impaled Lilah, this was not a new experience for Stephanie Romanov. 'Coinciden-tally, I guest-starred on *Seven Days* with Vladimir Kulich, and he stabbed my character on that programme,' she told

TV Zone. Stephanie also revealed that her father had become friendly with his fellow Czech, Kulich. 'I couldn't believe it when I discovered that Vladimir was playing The Beast.'

75
Long Day's Journey

US Transmission Date: 22 January 2003
UK Transmission Date: 20 March 2003 (Sky)

Writer: Mere Smith
Director: Terrence O'Hara
Cast: Jack Kehler (Manny), Michael Chinyamurindi (Ashet)

The Beast is systematically exterminating all five members of the Ra-Tet, an ancient mystical order. Their destruction will enable The Beast to cloak the sun and plunge Los Angeles into an eternity of darkness. The Angel Investigations team are determined to stop him, but they discover a shocking secret about one of the team's own past.

Dudes and Babes: The girl entity in The White Room (see **61**, 'Forgiving', **74**, 'Habeas Corpses') was Mesektet, a totem of the Ra-Tet, a mystical order associated with the sun god Ra. The Beast needed to collect each totem – five in all – to perform a ritual to blot out the sun. The other totems were Ashet, Ma'at, Semkhet and Manjet. Ashet was killed during a meeting with Gwen, and Lorne's contact confirms that Ma'at is also dead. Angel and Gwen travel to Death Valley, only to find Semkhet's body. Manjet (or Manny) is killed in a panic room in Gwen's home, whilst Cordelia and Angel are guarding him (see **83**, 'Inside Out').

It's a Designer Label!: There's some cracking stuff on display: Lorne's orange shirt, mustard slacks and silver cravat, Cordy's tasteful trouser suit and Gwen's Catwoman-style black leather outfit. Manny mentions Italian designer Giorgio Armani.

References: The title refers to Eugene O'Neill's 1940 play *Long Day's Journey Into Night*. Also, allusions to the book of Revelation, Michael Powell's *Peeping Tom*, *Voyage to the Bottom of the Sea*, author Stephen King, the munchkins from *The Wizard of Oz*, *Sports Illustrated Swimsuit Edition*, the snack food Cracker Jack (which has a surprise toy in every box), Albert Einstein, Denzel Washington (see **25**, 'First Impressions'), the bands Supertramp and Dr Feelgood, the cable TV channel Cinemax and *Goldilocks*. The names of the totems come from Egyptian mythology, a source for many of the place and character names in *Stargate SG-1*. The reference to Achilles' heel comes from Greek myth. Mary Janes is an American term for strap shoes.

Bitch!: Angel deliberately uses Gwen – and a long drive to Death Valley – in an attempt to make Cordelia jealous.

'West Hollywood?': Gwen notes that The Beast wasn't wearing lamé. Lorne replies that evil demons can't pull that off – it looks camp.

Sex and Drugs and Rock'n'Roll: Manny twice asks if Gwen would be prepared to give him a lap dance.

'You May Remember Me From Such Films and TV Series As …': Jack Kehler's CV includes *Babylon 5*, *Grand Canyon*, *Waterworld*, *Murder One*, *Austin Powers: The Spy Who Shagged Me* and *Dirt*. Michael Chinyamurindi played Isaac in *The Young and the Restless*. He also appeared in *The West Wing*, *The X-Files* and *Congo*.

Logic, Let Me Introduce You to This Window: The fight between Connor and The Beast is worthy of considerable praise, except for a painfully obvious bit where Connor is swung about by the arm. Though no wires are visible, Connor almost stops in mid-air. And *not* in a cool, *The Matrix*-style way, either. Why does The Beast knock on Connor's door? Do demons with the strength of an army have *manners*? Where did Gwen get fresh blood from? Is what Cordelia tells Angel about her vision disinformation designed to provoke the rising of Angelus? Cordelia's hair is considerably darker than it was in the last episode, which is said to have taken place just two days previously.

Where's the John?: This episode reveals something many fans had long wondered: where, exactly, are the Hyperion staff toilets situated? Apparently, they're next to Angel's office.

Motors: Angel drives quite often and it's reasonable to deduce that sometime within the last hundred years he'd have learned the basics. However, assuming that his car is within the specifications of California State law, and given that he's had a *certain* amount of contact with the police, if he were ever asked to produce a valid driving licence, could he? After all, driving tests are normally conducted during the day when there's all that pesky sunlight about.

Quote/Unquote: Cordy, to Angel: 'I swear, like father, like son. The two of you have cornered the market on teenage snits.'

Gwen: 'Jeez, where were you when they taught stealth in superpower school?'

Notes: 'Things are going to Hell,' says Gunn early in this handsome episode. Quite literally. Elsewhere, in Mere Smith's piece, Gwen is back (see **68**, 'Ground State'), and Angel uses her in a cynical game of one-upmanship with Cordelia. Overall, the episode concerns facing up to insurmountable odds and does so very nicely. On a more literal level, however, it's about malevolent darkness, this season's recurring theme.

Angel and Gwen are referred to as 'Superhunk' and 'Spandexia' by Manny. Cordelia again mentions that she experienced Angel's life as Angelus when she was a higher being (she also watched, although seemingly didn't particularly enjoy, his adventure with Gwen). Fred hates cryptic messages. Wesley uses *Rhinehart's Compendium* for his research (see **78**, 'Calvary'). Gunn is uncomfortable at the mention of the word 'portal' (see **71**, 'Supersymmetry'). Lorne brings Angel a glass of O-positive blood. Connor mentions his super-hearing ability, first witnessed in **65**, 'Benediction'. Angel gave the Axis Of Pythia back to Gwen after using it to locate Cordelia (see **68**, 'Ground State'). Gwen apparently used the money she got from selling it to build herself a palace in a nondescript Downtown tenement. She has a butler who is currently in Tahiti. Gwen's apartment is monitored by numerous security cameras, which were cut off ten minutes prior to the attack on Manny. She tells Gunn something about her life before being sent to the Thorpe Academy (see **68**, 'Ground State'), which seems to have involved unfortunate incidents with two gardeners and at least four nannies. The episode ends with the revelation that, at some time in the past, Angelus knew The Beast, a relationship that Angel can't remember.

Did You Know?: One of the locations used for this episode was an oil refinery situated close to Jefferson Boulevard, south of Downtown L.A. The same site was also used for a particularly memorable sequence in the first season of *24*.

Cast And Crew's Comments: J August Richards notes that his character has to deal with lots of personal issues as well as various global ones. 'The way he handles himself will show audiences that he's not the same guy he used to be . . .' Richards told Steven Eramo. He continued that he beleived Gunn needs a woman in his life to watch over because of the way in which he failed his sister. 'Not that he doesn't love Fred, but that's where their relationship stems from.'

In Loving Memory Of Glenn Quinn: A dreadful moment of reality hit the fantasy world of *Angel* with the announcement, on 2 December 2002, that Glenn Quinn, one of the series' original co-stars, had died aged 32. Glenn was found at a friend's home in North Hollywood and was believed to have overdosed on drugs. This, the first episode completed after Quinn's death, was dedicated to him on screen.

76
Awakening

US Transmission Date: 29 January 2003
UK Transmission Date: 27 March 2003 (Sky)

Writer: David Fury, Steven S DeKnight
Director: James A Contner
Cast: Larry McCormick (Newsreader)

As L.A. stews in its own darkness, Wesley searches for a way to unleash Angelus upon The Beast. A dark mystic shaman is summoned who appears to have his own sinister agenda. But what is truth and what is reality where Angel's soul is concerned?

Dreaming (As *Buffy* Often Proves) is Free: The entire episode turns out to be an elaborate fantasy in which Angel seeks and finds reconciliation with all of his friends and, specifically, Connor, gets the girl, finds the Sword of Bosh M'ad, and kills The Beast.

Denial, Thy Name is Angel: His fantasy is psychologically revealing. Angel sees himself as battling not only inner demons but the mistrust of his friends. He needs Cordelia's acceptance of his past and, most importantly, craves Connor's affection and respect.

References: The entire set-up of Angel's fantasy is drawn from a combination of *Raiders of the Lost Ark* and *Indiana Jones and the Last Crusade*. Which at least proves that Angel knows his Spielberg – a definite point in his favour. The title was also a 1980 film starring series favourite Charlton Heston. Lorne mentions Angel singing Vicki Lawrence's 1973 hit 'The Night the Lights Went Out in Georgia'. Also, the Thomas Guide (the publishers of US street maps), Orange Zinger tea, CliffsNotes study books, the nine antediluvian patriarchs in Genesis (the line that includes Adam, Seth, Enos, Cainan, Mehalaleel, Jared, Enoch, Methuselah, Lamech and Noah) and Rashi (one of the most important Jewish sages of the Middle Ages. His commentaries on the Bible and the Talmud are still regarded as essential for understanding the texts). There are allusions to *Kolchak: The Night Stalker*, Hallmark greetings cards (or possibly the Hallmark channel), Creedence Clearwater Revival's 'Bad Moon Rising' and Muddy Waters' 'Got My Mojo Working'. Visually, *Crouching Tiger, Hidden Dragon*.

'West Hollywood?': In Angel's fantasy he's *very* touchy-feely with Wesley.

The Charisma Show: Her finest moment of the season. Cordelia is much more smart-alecky in Angel's fantasy than she has been since she returned from the Higher Powers. Plus, of course, Charisma is given the opportunity for a love scene with Angel at long last.

Sex and Drugs and Rock'n'Roll: Cordelia tells Angel that his past doesn't matter to her, because when she is with him she feels all of the good that he has done. Then they have sex. What a pity it all turns out to be part of Angel's fantasy. Earlier, Cordelia says that the elaborate entrance to the place where the mystical sword is held is like something left over from an S&M bondage party.

'You May Remember Me From Such Films and TV Series As . . .': Roger Yuan was in *Lethal Weapon 4* and *Shanghai Noon*. He is also a stuntman, and worked as such on *Blade* and *Spawn*. The brother of musician Charles McCormick, Larry McCormick is a well-known newscaster on KTLA-TV (Los Angeles's WB affiliate). His CV also includes *Barnaby Jones*, *Throw Momma From a Train* and *Fly Away Home*.

Logic, Let Me Introduce You to This Window: One of *Angel*'s few overt continuity errors: Wesley *has* met Angelus before, three years ago, in *17*, 'Eternity'.

Quote/Unquote: Angel: 'Grow up! You think you're the only one who ever wished his father were dead?' Connor: 'Yeah, but mine *already is*.'

Angel: 'Was that an apology?' Wesley: 'I was careless, made a mistake that almost cost you your life. Would have made pulling you out of the ocean a big waste of my time.'

Angel: 'We've done things we're sure can never be forgiven, but . . . we've never let the darkness win . . . It's because we believe in each other, not just as friends or lovers, but as champions.'

Notes: 'Nothing in this world is the way it ought to be, right. It's harsh and cruel, because of you.' A beautifully structured story in which, as Gunn notes, the only victory that the team can claim is that they're not dead yet. The whole episode focuses on teamwork and on the true nature of being a champion. Yet the final scene, in the best tradition of *The Usual Suspects*, renders the entire second half of the episode a complete fiction. That's a disappointment, but only a slight one.

Cordelia recounts the details of Angel's gypsy curse, and the 'perfect happiness' clause (see *Buffy*: 'Angel' and 'Innocence'). With hindsight, Cordelia's conversation with Angel about him not allowing his soul to be removed is clearly designed to get him to do *just that*, thus fitting in with Jasmine's plans (see **84**, 'Shiny Happy People'). Wesley hired a shaman, Wo-Pang, who is a member of a group called the Kun-Sun-Dai and an expert in extracting and restoring souls, to bring forth Angelus. The receptacle that stores Angel's soul is called the Muo-Ping. The Sword of Bosh M'ad is accessible from 100 points on earth, including one under Los Angeles. Of course, all of this is part of Angel's fantasy. Having said that, it's stated that The Beast can be killed by stabbing and that this will restore the sun, both of which subsequently turn out to be true (see **79**, 'Salvage'). Gwen has skipped town since the last episode. A television report states that the strange phenomenon of the sun being blocked out is localised to the immediate L.A. area.

Did You Know?: The original US trailer for this episode somewhat gave away the fantasy nature of the plot by including the final shot (Angelus laughing). When, two minutes from the end, this sequence still hadn't featured, most fans began to suspect that *something* was amiss.

77
Soulless

US Transmission Date: 5 February 2003
UK Transmission Date: 3 April 2003 (Sky)

Writer: Elizabeth Craft, Sarah Fain
Director: Sean Astin

Connor valiantly struggles to contain the rampant crime wave that is currently exploding across a permanently dark L.A. Meanwhile, Angel is gone – his soul trapped in a jar. In his place is Angelus.

Dudes and Babes: In 1789 The Beast attempted to recruit Angelus to kill a trio of women called the Svear Priestesses.

They had the power to banish The Beast from this dimension. The modern-day Svear family, part of a mystical order and descendants of a powerful Nordic priestess, were located in Pacoima until someone killed them a few days previously.

As they are Angel's main link to humanity, it's clear that Angelus hates the team and his intelligent sowing of the seeds of discord amongst them is designed to weaken their resolve.

Denial, Thy Name is Everyone: Angelus mocks Wes, Gunn, Connor and Fred with vicious barbs and innuendoes, dividing and manipulating them into fighting amongst themselves. Cordelia makes him a deal, offering to sacrifice herself to him in exchange for information. Intrigued, Angelus agrees.

It's a Designer Label!: Cordelia gives Connor one of Angel's black shirts, much to Angelus's chagrin.

References: Visually and conceptually Wesley's confrontation with the caged Angelus comes from *The Silence of the Lambs* and the dazzling mind games played by Hannibal Lecter on his alleged interrogator, Clarice Starling. Angelus describes Angel's perfect-day fantasy in the previous episode (**76**, 'Awakening') with specific reference to *Raiders of the Lost Ark*. 'Foul rag and bone shop of a heart' is the final line of WB Yeats's *The Circus Animals' Desertion* (see **70**, 'Slouching Towards Bethlehem'). Angelus calls Gunn and Fred Othello and Desdemona, and alludes to their quasi-*ménage à trois* involving Wesley (presumably cast as the villainous Iago) in terms of Shakespeare's *Othello*.

Showing what a well-read vampire he was, Angelus's comments to Connor (see **Quote/Unquote**) allude to Sophocles's tragedy *Oedipus Rex*. Also, the Sex Pistols' bassist Sid Vicious (1957–79), Jerry Stahl's exposé of the drug-addled L.A. television industry in *Permanent Midnight*, Billy Sherrill and Tammy Wynette's 'Stand By Your Man', the *Los Angeles Chronicle* (headline: CRIME WAVE SHUTS DOWN CITY), *Diff'rent Strokes*, Mike Tyson and R.E.M's *Out Of Time*. There's a misquote from *The Rime of the Ancient Mariner* by Samuel Taylor Coleridge (1772–1834). Cordelia refers to Morse code.

Sex and Drugs and Rock'n'Roll: The caged Angelus cunningly sneers lewd suggestions at Wesley when the latter is trying to interrogate him. He plays on Wesley's affection for Fred by constantly alluding to what Fred and Gunn get up to in the bedroom. He also asks Wes which is the worst crime: kidnapping Connor, as Wesley did, or 'banging him' as Cordelia is still doing? Angelus tells Fred that when he hears her and Gunn at night in their room, it sexually excites him. Subsequently, Wesley and Fred kiss.

Angelus tells Cordelia that, once free of his cage, he will do horrible things to her before killing her, noting that he loves a woman with nice ripe thighs. He describes Buffy as 'a pistol', and mentions the phallic sword in Angel's fantasy in **76**, 'Awakening'.

Don't Give Up The Day Job: The son of Patty Duke and stepson of John Astin, Sean Astin is best known as an actor for his performance as Sam in *The Lord of the Rings* trilogy. His other movies include *Please Don't Hit Me Mom*, *The Goonies*, *Memphis Belle*, *Teresa's Tattoo*, *Courage Under Fire* and *Bulworth*. As a director, he's worked on *The Long and the Short of it* (which he also wrote) and *Kangaroo Court*.

Logic, Let Me Introduce You to This Window: Angel was strapped down on a table in the cage at the end of the previous episode. This one starts with him free to walk around. So, which brave soul went in there to take off the straps and remove the table? Pacoima is said to be about 25 minutes' drive from the Hyperion. By *helicopter*, possibly. More like an hour, even if the traffic is relatively light – this Los Angeles is clearly the same one seen in *24*, where people can get from one side of the city to the other in just minutes. Wesley notes he's done years of research on Angelus. Odd, then, that he didn't seem to know who Angel was when they first met in *Buffy*: 'Bad Girls'. Everyone automatically assumed that The Beast killed the Svear. Why? If he couldn't do so in the past, then how could he now? Of course, when we find out who actually *did* kill them (see **83**, 'Inside Out'), it *all* makes sense.

When Wesley, Cordy and Connor arrive at the Svear's home, Wesley leaves his SUV parked in front of the house. Connor rushes out to be sick and the car is still there. When the vampires subsequently attack, the vehicle has vanished, only for Wesley to rescue Connor and Cordy with it a few moments later. Some of the clothes in the 1789 flashbacks are anachronistic. Connor is violently sick outside the Svear home. Seconds later, he and Cordy sit to talk mere inches away from where a mound of vomit should be but isn't.

Motors: Cordelia offers to make Angelus a deal. He notes that he wouldn't mind a car, saying that he's heard the 2003 Mustang is nice.

Quote/Unquote: Wesley, on Angelus: 'I've spent my whole life training for this and I'm still not ready. He's smarter than I am.'

Angelus: 'Let's talk about Cordy. Now *there's* a rack to write home about. Too bad about the personality, though.'

Angelus, to Connor: 'The first woman you boned is the closet thing you've ever had to a mother. Doin' your mom, and trying to kill your dad? There should be a play!'

Notes: 'Anything you want to know. How sweet that virgin gypsy tasted? Special smell of a newborn's neck? My first nun? *That's* a great story.' After not seeing him for a while the viewer can forget how good David Boreanaz's Angelus *really* is. It puts his sometimes wooden and one-dimensional Angel into caustic perspective too, and shows that much of this is also characterisation. As Angelus, Boreanaz is charismatic and viciously sarcastic. His *Manhunter*-style verbal battle with Wesley, which takes up much of the first half of this episode, is a series highlight – *brilliantly* played by Denisof and Boreanaz. The literate script, so much better than Fain and Craft's disappointing previous effort, includes allusions to the bizarre love triangle that is Fred, Gunn and Wesley. And to the Oedipal origins of Connor, who happily slept with his surrogate mother and wants to kill his father. Yet in this episode Connor – literally, as well as metaphorically – wears his father's clothes.

Angelus first encountered The Beast in Prussia in 1789, while en route to Vienna (this was, presumably, during one

of the periods when Angelus was operating independently of Darla). He mentions the suicides of Holtz and Darla (see **65**, 'Benediction' and **54**, 'Lullaby' respectively). Angelus taunts Wesley about his lack of a relationship with his father (see **14**, 'I've Got You Under My Skin', **41**, 'Belonging') and about having been a lousy Watcher to Faith (see *Buffy*: 'Bad Girls', 'Consequences' and 'Enemies'). Wesley puts Angel's soul in the office safe (see **56**, 'Provider'), though by the end of the episode it has vanished. The vampires that Connor kills in the teaser are from Tucson. Lorne mentions that Cordelia told him about Angelus having once nailed a puppy to a tree (Giles alluded to this event in *Buffy*: 'Bewitched, Bothered and Bewildered'). Wesley translates some of the Svear's runes to confirm that they banished The Beast in 1789, noting that a literal translation of the creature's name is 'big hard thing'.
Soundtrack: Angelus sings 'The Teddy Bear's Picnic' (lyrics by James Kennedy).
Did You Know?: Introduced by a mutual friend to David Greenwalt, Sean Astin mentioned that he would love the chance to direct an *Angel* episode. 'He arranged for me to observe Tim Minear working on a couple of stories,' Astin told *Xposé*. 'The job was a lot harder than I thought it was going to be. The learning curve of the first few days was very steep.'
Critique: 'There are some excellent and mainly subtextual moments,' noted *Shivers*. 'And David Boreanaz enjoys himself enormously as the bad guy. But, on the whole, it's something of a waste of time.'

78
Calvary

US Transmission Date: 12 February 2003
UK Transmission Date: 10 April 2003 (Sky)

Writer: Jeffrey Bell, Mere Smith, Steven S DeKnight
Director: Bill Norton

Angel's soul is missing. Without it, his friends are, as the shaman notes, well and truly screwed. Then Lilah Morgan turns up at Angel Investigations carrying a crowbar and seeking revenge.

Denial, Thy Name is Everyone: Angelus continues to mock the team, manipulating them into fighting amongst themselves. When Cordelia has a vision revealing how to restore Angel's soul, a ritual is performed and, it seems, Angel has returned. Even Lorne's reading of Angel's aura detects nothing of Angelus. Angel feels that he should stay in the cage but Cordelia is determined to let him out. But Angelus is still in control, and is free to wreak havoc.

References: *Star Wars*, *Little Bo Peep*, Sax Rohmer's oriental master-fiend Fu Manchu, the Jehovah's Witness magazine *The Watchtower*, Wladziu Valentino Liberace (1919–87), popular juice drink Capri Sun and Eleanor Hodgman Porter's *Pollyanna*. Allusions to *The Bone Collector* and *Macbeth* ('done is done'). The title was the name of the hill outside the walls of Jerusalem where Christ was crucified in Luke 23.

Bitch!: The episode includes a spectacular, long-awaited bitch session between Cordy and Lilah, which has to be seen to be believed.

'West Hollywood?': Angelus notes, with regard to Wesley, that if he were *that way inclined* himself, Fred would have some serious competition.

The Charisma Show: The final scene, as Cordelia kills Lilah: 'Why do you think I let him out, you stupid bitch?'

L.A.-Speak: Gunn, on Lilah: 'What kind of brain fart made that witch try and let Angelus out?'

Sex and Drugs and Rock'n'Roll: Angelus plays further sexually provocative games, telling Fred that Wesley is rugged and handsome and has brains. The only problem with Wes, he continues, is that he's been banging Lilah for the past six months.

Logic, Let Me Introduce You to This Window: If an Orb of Thesulah only restores souls that have gone to the afterlife, then why was Willow using one to restore Angel's soul *before* he went to Hell (in *Buffy*: 'Becoming' Part 2)? For that matter, why did Jenny Calendar bother to translate the gypsy curse and obtain an Orb of Thesulah for the same task in *Buffy*: 'Passion'? When did Lilah and Fred find time to get cleaned up and do their hair? If Lilah has been living in the sewers, then how did she obtain a book on the pan-dimensional black market? On one occasion Wesley refers to *Rhinehart's Companion* as opposed to *Compendium*. Why, apart from plot-based convenience, does nobody look at the monitor and notice Cordelia lying unconscious in the cage after Angelus has escaped?

I Just *Love* Your Accent: Angelus notes that Wesley is proper and English. 'Chicks just *love* a good accent. Makes 'em all buttery in their nether regions.' He adds that he had a bit of an Irish brogue himself and that he'd be happy to use it on Fred when he rapes her to death.

Quote/Unquote: Angelus: 'Look at yourself, Lilah. All these years wanting to meet me, you couldn't run a comb through your hair, maybe slap on a little lipstick? Evil doesn't have to mean sloppy.'

Lilah: 'It's just like being at work, except *Suits by Liberace*.' Lorne: '. . . please warn this walking infection that I haven't forgotten how she poked my head open, and . . . if need be I will smack her down!'

Lilah: 'It's my inner megalomaniac. I rebel at serving coffee.'

Notes: 'Look at you. Heroes so tangled up in your own crap you can't even find the world to save it.' After the sexually charged, character-heavy density of the previous two episodes comes, well, more of the same, basically. A complex and multi-layered script, lacking some of the intricate subtleties of recent weeks, but just as exciting and challenging. And with – as ever – excellent performances at its heart. A story about often selfish and cruel desires, and how wishful thinking can blind one to necessary truths, 'Calvary' continues what is easily the best season of *Angel* with considerable swagger. And it concludes with one of the finest closing scenes in television. Ever. One that will leave viewers staring blankly at their TV screens for several moments after it has faded into history, such is the impact.

Angelus, like Angel, is a damn good actor (see *Buffy*: 'Enemies'). Gunn and Fred are officially no longer a couple. The Soul Eater was buried by Chumash Indians (see *Buffy*: 'Pangs') 200 years ago. Gunn and Connor dig up the creature to obtain its skull, necessary for the spell to restore Angel's soul. When guarding Angelus, Gunn menacingly plays with the office flame-thrower (see **54**, 'Dad'). The Beast killed everyone associated with Wolfram & Hart, not just those present in the building when he attacked (see **74**, 'Habeas Corpses'). Lilah, apparently, the sole survivor, has been living underground since the carnage. She obtained her copy of *Rhinehart's Compendium* via the pan-dimensional black market. It contains information on The Beast that Wesley's copy does not. All knowledge of The Beast seems to have been erased from this dimension. Angelus was an exception to this, as he was trapped within Angel when the spell took place.

Soundtrack: Angelus sings 'Raindrops Keep Falling On My Head', most often associated with BJ Thomas and the movie *Butch Cassidy & The Sundance Kid*.

Did You Know?: One of the flash sequences briefly glimpsed in this episode is a shot of Santa Monica pier at night from a helicopter. This cost, according to Tim Minear, 'more than three or four scenes put together'.

Critique: According to Matt Roush in *TV Guide*, *Angel* is 'one of the six best shows you may not be watching' (an accolade he also bestowed on the highly rated *Alias*).

Cast And Crew Comments: 'I thoroughly enjoyed working on "Calvary",' Stephanie Romanov told *TV Zone*. 'The range of emotions I got to play was, in many ways, a culmination of Lilah from the beginning of her time on the show right to the end.'

79
Salvage

US Transmission Date: 5 March 2003
UK Transmission Date: 17 April 2003 (Sky)

Writer: David Fury
Director: Jefferson Kibbee
Cast: Kara Holden (Young Woman), Billy Rieck (Paco),
Joel David Moore (Karl), Alonzo Bodden (Prison Guard),
Joshua Grenrock (Demon in Bar), Addie Daddio (Rosaria),
Brett Wagner (Borg'dar Demon), Spice Williams (Debbie)

Angelus learns that the rain of fire, the blocking of the sun
and the stealing of Angel's soul aren't key parts of The
Beast's masterplan to create chaos and disorder, as everyone had thought. They are, rather, elements of something
far more complicated. Meanwhile, Wesley releases a rogue
Vampire Slayer from prison to recapture Angelus.

Dreaming (As *Buffy* Often Proves) is Free: Wesley has a
hallucination of Lilah telling him some harsh truths, as he
prepares to decapitate her dead body.

Dudes and Babes: Angelus's reaction, when he discovers
that his next opponent *isn't* Buffy, is one of disappointment. 'The *other one*,' he snarls, after a telephone conversation with Dawn Summers has established that her sister
is still in Sunnydale. Everyone else (except, possibly,
Cordelia) seems happy to see Faith. This is especially true
of Connor, who finally shows an interest in something
other than killing things. 'A weakness for Slayers. You're
definitely *his* son,' notes a disgusted Cordy.

Denial, Thy Name Is Wesley: In one of the year's most
touching scenes, Wesley holds a conversation with the dead
Lilah that gets into some deep philosophical areas. Wesley
admits he had hoped he could help Lilah to find redemption, but that he couldn't save her from her own darkness.

References: Wesley's conversation with the dead Lilah may
have been inspired by *Six Feet Under* or *Randall and
Hopkirk (Deceased)*, or other examples of this style of
narrative. Allusions include *ftd.com* (an Internet and
telephone marketer of flowers and speciality gifts), The
Stooges' 'No Fun', *That's The Way It Is* ('Angel has left
the building'), *The Simpsons*, *Rocky*, *The Hunting Party*,
Marvin Gaye's 'Let's Get It On', the megalithic monument
Stonehenge, *Speed* ('what do you do, hotshot?') and *The
Wizard of Oz* ('ding dong, The Beast is dead'). There's a

possible oblique reference to Somerset Maugham's *The Razor's Edge*. Angelus pinning the demon's hand to the bar echoes a scene in *The Godfather*.

Bitch!: Angelus kills The Beast using the knife that the demon fashioned from its own bone as an offering to its master.

Sex and Drugs and Rock'n'Roll: Cordelia tells Connor that she is expecting his child, presumably as a consequence of their night of passion in **73**, 'Apocalypse Nowish'.

'You May Remember Me From Such Films and TV Series As . . .': Kara Holden was in *Gilmore Girls*. Billy Rieck's movies include *Freedom Park* and *Shadow Fury*. Joel Moore appeared in *Boston Public* and *Deep Cover*. Alonzo Bodden was in *Grounded For Life*. Joshua Grenrock's CV includes *Eight is Enough* and *Nightmares*. Spice Williams appeared in *From Dusk Till Dawn*, *Star Trek V: The Final Frontier* and *Beyond Chance*. She was also a stuntwoman on *The Lost Boys*, *Natural Born Killers*, *Liar Liar* and *Galaxy Quest*.

Logic, Let Me Introduce You to This Window: Fred uses a belt as a tourniquet on Cordy's leg. Moments later, when Cordelia stands in the hall looking at Lilah, the belt has gone. When Angelus has his hand around the demon's throat, it's obvious that he's not squeezing very hard. Stunt doubles who look nothing like Eliza Dushku and Alexis Denisof fall from the prison window. Connor says that he doesn't give 'a flying sluck' about what Wesley thinks. Eh? There's not much blood on Wesley's axe considering that he's just cut Lilah's head off with it. Why has the knife-wielding prisoner that Faith fights got a mullet haircut? How long has *she* been inside? Doesn't she realise that the 80s are over? Faith's prisoner number in **23**, 'Judgment' was 43001. Here, it's 431009.

Quote/Unquote: Lilah, to Wesley: 'We both knew sooner or later it would come to a messy end. For one of us, anyway.'

Faith: 'You OK?' Wesley: 'Five by five.'

Angelus: 'Aw, *crap*! You mean killing The Beast really *does* bring back the sun? I thought that was Angel's retarded fantasy.'

Notes: 'Well, that's not fun . . .' is the opening line of 'Salvage'. Seldom can a piece of dialogue have been *less* appropriate as a critical summation of the episode that it's a part of. David Fury's story sees the team caught in the middle of a violent maelstrom and desperately needing their champion back. Unfortunately he's off on a mayhem and misery trip. This is one of Wesley's finest, if most tortured hours – a dignified reaction to the heartbreak of loss. His solution is, appropriately, redemption, which brings us to Faith. Complete with a double whammy of surprise endings, 'Salvage' maintains the quality of this extraordinary season.

Angelus was once acquainted with a vampire named Rosaria, whom he met in 1845 near Tuscany. Lorne needs bloodroot to perform his anti-violence spell. Having called the Furies for advice (see **47**, 'That Old Gang of Mine'), he discovers that cloves are an acceptable replacement. Faith is imprisoned at the Northern California Women's Facility in Stockton. She was given a 25-years-to-life sentence for second-degree murder.

Did You Know?: A Boston native of Albanian and Danish parents (both are college professors), Eliza Dushku grew up in a strict Mormon household and, consequently, suffered at school from bullies. 'I don't care who you are, everyone has been through it – the feeling where you'd like to be somewhere else,' she told *Shivers*. 'High school, with all those girls trying to be cool – they compare it to prison and I'm with them all the way.'

Critique: 'When Angel is bad, *Angel* is sensational,' wrote Matt Roush in *TV Guide*. '[It] has lately eclipsed *Buffy* with an apocalyptic storyline of stunning twists. The return of bad-girl Slayer Faith adds a new level of sexy intrigue to this powerfully entertaining supernatural adventure.'

Cast And Crew Comments: Andy Hallett told *SciFi Wire* of his delight at becoming a regular cast member. 'You'll be seeing more of Lorne, which I never expected. I was originally signed on for, like, two episodes at the very beginning.'

80
Release

US Transmission Date: 12 March 2003
UK Transmission Date: 24 April 2003 (Sky)

Writer: Steven S DeKnight, Elizabeth Craft, Sarah Fain
Director: James A Contner
Cast: Christopher Neiman (Demon), Darren Laverty (Lackey Vamp #1),
Sam Stefanski (Lackey Vamp #2), Catalina Larranaga (Vamp Waitress),
Becka Linder (Drugged Girl), Chris Huse (Drugged Vamp #2),
Ian Anthony Dale (Drugged Vamp #3), Randall Rapstine (Reg),
Andrew McGinnis (Mullet-Head Vamp)

In the aftermath of The Beast's vanquishing, Angelus finds himself being guided by voices. Meanwhile, Faith trashes Wesley's bathroom and a hugely pregnant Cordelia begins to exhibit strange new powers.

Dreaming (As *Buffy* Often Proves) is Free: Cordelia telepathically communicates with Angelus, using a *big scary voice*. She also causes him to hallucinate briefly.

Dudes and Babes: Wesley caring for Faith's wounds is reminiscent of Giles doing the same for Buffy in 'Helpless'. Like the former example, this episode relies on an old fan-fiction standby, setting a character up to be hurt so they can then be comforted. This is obviously a necessary Watcher thing – observing their charges getting severely beaten, then hovering around with hot towels and soothing words. Poet Sylvia Plath (1932–63) was a great exponent of the Electra complex (the female equivalent of the Oedipus complex, again proposed by Freud and based on the Greek myth of Agamemnon's daughter). In such poems as *Full Fathom Five*, *Electra on Azalea Path* and *Daddy* she explored her relationship with her father and her search for a replacement figure. Faith, whose father has never been mentioned, would seem an unlikely candidate for such deep-rooted emotions, but her relationships with Mayor Wilkins, Wesley and Angel all suggest something along these lines. Note, for instance, Faith's insistence that she intends to save Angel because he was the only person who ever saw the chance of redemption for her.

It's a Designer Label!: Evil Cordy's black dress.

References: The fight between Angelus and Faith is in the style of Hong Kong action movies. Also, Tourette's Syndrome, Minnie Mouse, Supergirl, *The Brady Bunch*, *Beastmaster* and *Dark Shadows*. Allusions to the *Stargate SG-1* episode 'Smoke and Mirrors', *Hamlet* ('Goodnight, not-so-sweet prince'), *The Dark Knight Returns* ('the boy hostage'), Sherlock Holmes's nemesis Moriarty, *Futurama* ('you can kiss my vampire ass'), *Scooby Doo* and *GQ* magazine. Locations mentioned include Olive Street in Downtown L.A.

'West Hollywood?': The junkie girl considers Faith pretty and asks if she wants to make out.

Cigarettes and Alcohol: Lorne mentions his love of tequila.

Sex and Drugs and Rock'n'Roll: The vampire equivalent of a crack den had previously been seen in *Buffy*: 'Crush'. Wesley explains that junkies shot up before vampires fed on them, using the human as a filter. The effects, he notes, could be intoxicating for both parties. 'Release' contains a series of corporal punishment references. Faith hits the junkie girl to get information. When none is forthcoming, Wesley brutally stabs the girl in the shoulder and she tells them what they want to know. Wesley subsequently notes that the girl probably enjoyed Faith hitting her. Angelus tells Faith that she's still looking for someone to beat the badness out of her. (See Faith's acts of self-flagellation in this episode, her punching Wesley's bathroom wall, and *Buffy*: 'Who Are You?' Note, also, her knowledge of BDSM terminology in *Buffy*: 'Consequences' and her conversation with Spike in *Buffy*: 'Dirty Girls' concerning dressing like a schoolgirl for one ex-lover. Compare this to Buffy's miserable self-loathing when she believes that she has abused her Slayer powers in *Buffy*: 'Dead Things'.)

'You May Remember Me From Such Films and TV Series As . . .': Christopher Neiman appeared in *The West Wing*, *3rd Rock from the Sun* and *Auto Focus*. Darren Laverty played Rae in *My Dark Days* and Tommy in *Shame, Shame, Shame*. Catalina Larranaga appeared in *Voyeur Confessions*, *Bare Witness*, *Radius* and *Corporate Fantasy*, which she also wrote. Becka Linder played Jennifer in *Exit 9*. Chris Huse appeared in *Port Charles*. Randall Rapstine was in *Grosse Pointe* and *Roswell*. Pete Renaday appeared in *The Cat from Outta Space*, wrote and directed *Cellar Doors* and was the voice of Master Splinter in *Teenage Mutant Ninja Turtles*.

Logic, Let Me Introduce You to This Window: Is Connor really so unobservant that he can walk into Cordelia's room and *not* see her sitting there with the orb? Seemingly. There's more blood on Faith's face in the shower scene than there was previously, but most of the wounds are dry, suggesting that she's stopped bleeding. Fred has yet another new haircut (the second in three episodes). Where does she find the time?

Quote/Unquote: Angelus: 'You're preaching to the guy who ate the choir.'

Faith: 'Screw you.' Angelus: 'Maybe after. I like my girls to lie still.'

Notes: 'It's all about choices, Faith. The ones we make, the ones we don't and the consequences. Those are always fun.' From a disturbingly voyeuristic opening shower sequence all the way to its shocking cliffhanger, 'Release' is an episode about rage in all its forms. It's also about facing up to the harshness of consequences. Aided by James Contner's consistently assured direction, the episode features another fine performance by Boreanaz. The finale, a brilliantly staged Angelus/Faith fight, is a pocket action movie within itself. 'Release' proves, yet again, that the depth of *Angel*'s dramatic well is deeper than most of us ever believed possible. Television's best-kept secret continues to surprise, to entertain and, occasionally, to astonish.

The books that Angelus stole to research The Beast are written in various demon languages that he can't read. Angelus then breaks into an occult shop and tortures the owner, Reg, for information. One of the volumes in Angel's office is a runic translation guide (presumably the one Wesley used in *77*, 'Soulless'). The phoney talisman that Angelus carries, supposedly to counteract the

Hyperion's anti-violence spell, was made in China. The creature that Wesley shoots in the bar is a Strom Demon. Its face will grow back, eventually. Both Wesley and Angelus refer to the events of **18**, 'Five By Five', when Faith tortured Wesley and begged Angel to kill her as punishment. Connor is revealed to be at least partly demon. Cordelia comforts him, noting that she's also part-demon (see **56**, 'Birthday').

Soundtrack: 'Here' by Vast.

Critique: 'The focus stays on Wesley and Faith,' noted David Richardson. 'Their scenes together are the episode's highlight . . . This pair really is the only natural choice for the next *Buffy* spin-off series.'

Did You Know?: Charisma Carpenter has some interesting TV-related ambitions. 'I'd love to get a sitcom and have that run,' she told *DreamWatch*. 'I think that half-hour television would be the ideal thing for me because I also want to have a family.'

Cast And Crew Comments: Both Alexis Denisof and Amy Acker have nothing but praise for Eliza Dushku. 'She's great,' Acker told *scifi.com*. Denisof added, 'I love her character, and she's great to work with. She gives you so much, and she's spontaneous, fun and dangerous. I'm always happy when they put our characters together.'

81
Orpheus

US Transmission Date: 19 March 2003
UK Transmission Date: 1 May 2003 (Sky)

Writer: Mere Smith
Director: Terrence O'Hara
Cast: EJ Callahan (Old Craps Man), Jeremy Guskin (Cashier),
Nate Dushku (Armed Robber), Adrienne Wilkinson (Flapper Girl)

Spiked by Faith's drug-tainted blood, Angelus spirals back into the private hell of the last century of Angel's past. In this dose of severe psychic psychedelia, however, he has a

Slayer for company. Meanwhile, Fred seeks help in restoring Angel's soul. She finds it in Sunnydale.

Dreaming (As *Buffy* Often Proves) is Free: Faith and Angelus spend the episode stuck in Angel's flashback/dream sequence.

Dudes and Babes: Willow describes Wesley as the Marlboro Man's extra-stubbly, mentally unstable, insomniac first cousin. Which, this author supposes, is *sort of* a compliment from Alyson Hannigan to her future husband.

Denial, Thy Name is Wesley: He tells Willow that he's seen a darkness in himself which he isn't sure that she'd understand. Willow replies that she flayed someone alive and tried to destroy the world (see *Buffy*: 'Villains', 'Grave'). Wesley, rather taken aback, mutters that he had a woman chained in his closet (see **67**, 'Deep Down'), but that that doesn't really compare.

It's a Designer Label!: 'I looked like David Cassidy with the wig,' David Boreanaz told *Entertainment Weekly Online* concerning the scenes of Medallion Angel in the 70s. No, David, you *really* didn't. Also, Fred's gypsy skirt.

References: In Greek myth, Orpheus was the son of Calliope and Apollo (some sources give Oeagrus as the father). In Neil Gaiman's *The Sandman* he was the son of Morpheus, the master of dreams. Also, Peter, Paul and Mary's 'Puff The Magic Dragon', *This Is Your Life*, Marley's Ghost from *A Christmas Carol*, *Star Wars*, 'Dust In The Wind' by Kansas, Elton John's 'Candle In The Wind', Hecate – the Greek goddess of the crossroads, Glinda – the Good Witch of the South (from *The Wizard of Oz*), Dylan Thomas's 'Do Not Go Gentle Into That Good Night' and E!-Entertainment's *True Hollywood Stories*. There are possible allusions to The Jam's 'Private Hell' and *Dracula: Prince of Darkness*.

Bitch!: Cordelia, revealing her true colours to Connor: 'What the hell is it with you and Faith? She cracked her whip and you *liked* it. You were practically in her leather-clad lap.'

'West Hollywood?': Willow notes that Connor must be Angel's handsome yet androgynous son. She adds that the sneer seems to be genetic. Fred and Willow get on really well. Perhaps too well for Willow's liking as, before leaving, she tells Fred that she's seeing someone (Kennedy – see *Buffy*: 'Get It Done').

The Charisma Show: Is it just this author's opinion, or does it seem like Charisma is on autopilot throughout this episode, and indeed several others during this period? Nevertheless, despite being for so long the best single reason to watch *Angel*, her character's presence in the series now seems to be an awkward compromise, clashing madly with other storylines. (Having Cordy hardly appear at all in the season's first three episodes, and in a coma during its last five, suggests two lots of hasty rewriting to fit in with various real-world events like Charisma's pregnancy.) It's a real shame that the actress whom, for many, defines why this show is so good, should have been sidelined to such an extent.

Sex and Drugs and Rock'n'Roll: The drug that Faith and Angelus were injected with is called Orpheus, a mystical opiate. The only customers whom Lorne ever turned away from Caritas were dealing the drug. After their ordeal, Angel asks Faith how she feels. 'Like I did mushrooms and got eaten by a bear,' is the reply.

Fred asks Wes if he thinks that Connor and Cordelia's relationships is *icky*.

'You May Remember Me From Such Films and TV Series As . . .': EJ Callahan appeared in *Friends*, *Even Stevens*, *The Tick*, *Paris* and *Romy and Michele's High School Reunion*. The older brother of Eliza Dushku, Nate Dushku's CV includes *Felicity*, *Wolf Girl* and *Reality Check*. Adrienne Wilkinson played the duel role of Livia/Eve in *Xena: Warrior Princess*, Lois in *Undressed* and Nikki in *As If*.

Don't Give Up The Day Job: Production Co-ordinator David Eck's CV also includes *Roswell*, *Once and Again*, *Office Space*, *Eden* and *Dante's Peak*. Hair Stylist Gloria Ponce previously worked on *Orange County*, *Bowfinger*, *Ally McBeal*, and *Star Trek: Voyager*. Script Supervisor Jain Sekuler was an actress in *The Enforcers*, and worked

on *Firefly*, *Sand*, *Brimstone* and *They Come at Night*.
Digital Effects Supervisor Rocco Passionino's CV includes
Point of Origin, *Swordfish*, *Little Nicky*, *The Faculty*,
Titanic and *Apollo 13*.

Logic, Let Me Introduce You to This Window: General
question: just how gullible is Connor? No, don't answer
that ... How exactly did a stinking, lice-infested Angel,
with no identity papers, get through immigration at Ellis
Island in 1902? We've all seen *The Godfather Part II* –
shouldn't he have been required to go into quarantine
(and, thus, risk exposure to sunlight) before being allowed
into the Land of the Free? Why didn't Wesley think of
calling Willow, the only living person to have previously
restored Angel's soul, in the first place? When Angel saves
the puppy, two different dogs are used in successive shots.
How could Faith beat Angelus so vigorously at the climax
of the previous episode if she was already pumped full of
junk? Those look like rather ineffective little padlocks on
Angelus's leg-irons. Cordelia throwing a knife that narrowly misses Willow's head is a *really* dumb contrivance. How
would she have explained *that* to the others? Or does The
Beast's master simply not care about such trivialities by
this stage? If Angelus and Faith were insubstantial during
their reliving of Angel's life, then how were they able to sit
on the diner's plastic chairs?

I Just *Love* Your Accent: After Wesley avoids physical
contact as they part, Faith notes that Brits know how to
say goodbye. Angel, by contrast, wanted to hug her.

Quote/Unquote: Faith: 'Do you know what the definition
of insanity is? Performing the same task over and over and
expecting different results. Learned that in murder rehab!'

Wesley: 'I think my sense of humour's trapped in a jar
somewhere.' Willow: 'Does seem like you've given in to the
grumpy side of the force.'

Willow: 'How've you been?' Cordelia: 'Higher Being.
You?' Willow: 'Ultimate Evil. I got *better*!'

Notes: 'I love this episode.' Mere Smith's script takes the
form of an allegory of fighting one's inner demons – one
of *Angel*'s core concerns. The look of disgust on Angelus's

face as his alter-ego enters a sleazy 70s diner wearing a dodgy haircut and enormous flares and cues up 'Mandy' on the jukebox is *truly* priceless. The episode's big selling point, of course, is the appearance of Alyson Hannigan. Willow dominates much of the viewer's attention from the moment she arrives, mid-episode. The much-anticipated scenes with Alexis Denisof are pretty good and there's an obvious charisma between the couple when discussing who's been further to the dark side. 'Orpheus's central metaphor lies in the remarkable scenes in which Angel must, literally, fight himself for the possession of his soul. Wrapped up in pyrotechnics and flashy, eye-catching visuals, *Angel* continues to get it right.

Angel first arrived in America in New York in 1902 (see *Buffy*: 'Angel'), having avoided human contact during the voyage from Europe by hiding in the hold. He was in Chicago in the mid-20s, where he once saved a puppy from being hit by a car. In the 70s, Angel attended numerous Barry Manilow concerts, much to Angelus's disquiet (and, on this occasion, it's hard not to agree). During this period he also fed from a dying doughnut-shop clerk, who was shot in a botched hold-up. This was probably Angel's first taste of human blood since he left Darla's company in 1901. The guilt led to him spending the next two decades living in the sewers of New York (see *Buffy*: 'Becoming' Part 1). Angelus reminds Faith that he ate his own mother (**15**, 'The Prodigal'). Wesley mentions that The Beast's master contacted Angelus (**80**, 'Release') after the same thing happened to Willow. Fred called Willow for suggestions on restoring Angel's soul (see *Buffy*: 'Lies My Parents Told Me'). Willow plans to use something called Delothrian's Arrow to shatter the jar housing Angel's soul, despite the location being unknown. Once the soul is released, she uses an Orb of Thesulah for the restoration, as she previously did in *Buffy*: 'Becoming' Part 2. Willow notes that good things come in jars and mentions peanut butter, jelly and two-headed foetal pigs in the Natural History Museum. Faith has been comatose before (see

Buffy: 'Graduation Day', 'This Year's Girl'). Faith accompanies Willow back to Sunnydale at the end of this episode (see *Buffy*: 'Dirty Girls', 'Empty Spaces', 'Touched', 'End of Days', 'Chosen').

Soundtrack: Lorne sings a couplet from Jimmy Webb's 'MacArthur Park' (a hit for Richard Harris) to Faith. Strange choice for a bedside ballad although, given Faith's drug-addled state, not wholly inappropriate. During the 70s diner sequence, Donna Summer's disco version of the same song is heard before Barry Manilow's 'Mandy' comes on the jukebox (see **23**, 'Judgment').

Did You Know?: The initial US broadcast of this episode was interrupted in many areas by news coverage of the outbreak of the US invasion of Iraq, meaning that fans missed up to ten minutes. 'Orpheus' was subsequently repeated by the WB on Sunday 23 March.

82
Players

US Transmission Date: 26 March 2003
UK Transmission Date: 8 May 2003 (Sky)

Writer: Jeffery Bell, Elizabeth Craft, Sarah Fain
Director: Michael Grossman
Cast: Dana Lee (Takeshi Morimoto), David Monahan (Garrett),
Hope Shin (Little Asian Girl), Wendy Harris (Over-Jewelled Woman),
Michael Patrick McGill (Checkpoint Guard),
John Fremont (Security Guy)

Whilst the Angel Investigations team are digesting the ramifications of Cordelia's sudden pregnancy, there is still work to do. Gwen arrives seeking Gunn's help on a mission of mercy to free a kidnapped child. Then there's the identity of The Beast's master to be established.

Dudes and Babes: Wesley and Fred have an interesting conversation when Fred wonders how Connor and Cordelia began their relationship. Wesley notes that they were probably as surprised as everyone else, and that both were probably lonely. Fred still can't grasp the concept, so

Wesley uses his own relationship with Lilah as a further example.

It's a Designer Label!: Cordelia's black-widow maternity dress. Also, the clothes that Gwen and Gunn wear to the swanky party. Gunn gets to keep the suit.

References: Allusions to *Picnic At Hanging Rock* ('everything happens for a reason'), the comic *The Prez* and *Pulp Fiction* ('The Big Kahuna'). Also, *Clueless*, the Easy-Bake Oven, *Clash of the Titans*, James Bond, Dungeons & Dragons and the games console Xbox. Allusions to Lollapalooza, Superman's Fortress of Solitude, *A Clockwork Orange* (the eye-clamping discussion), Al Jolson's 'Me And My Shadow' and *Invasion of the Body Snatchers*. A Magic 8-Ball toy features in the last scene.

Bitch!: Wesley, Gunn, Fred and Lorne have a lengthy discussion about Angel and Cordelia sulking in neutral corners, Connor's relationship with Cordelia and the fact that he is part-demon. Lorne asks whether Angel shouldn't be part of this discussion just as Angel emerges from the office and summarises their conversation in eight words, then adds, 'And I *don't* sulk.'

The Charisma Show: Her hypothetical 'I'm The Beast's master' conversation with Angel is the best bit of dramatic tension involving Cordelia this season. Also, she observes that no one is more shocked by her pregnancy than herself, then turns to Connor and notes, 'OK, maybe him.'

Not Exactly A Haven For The Bruthas: Gunn learned all he knows about Japanese customs from watching samurai movies.

Cigarettes And Alcohol: Gunn drinks white wine at the party.

Sex and Drugs and Rock'n'Roll: Due to her very touch being deadly, it's implied that Gwen is a virgin. At least, until Gunn uses the L.I.S.A device they steal to, literally, turn her off.

'You May Remember Me From Such Films and TV Series As . . .': Dana Lee's CV includes *Kung Fu*, *Tales of the Gold Monkey*, *Futureworld*, *Married . . . With Children* and *Beethoven's 3rd*. David Monahan played Toby Barrett in

Dawson's Creek. Michael Patrick McGill was in *ER* and *Fourteen*.

Logic, Let Me Introduce You to This Window: It's been several weeks since the unleashing of Angelus, completely contradicting implications given during the previous four episodes that they all took place over the course of about two days. When did Gwen have the opportunity to steal back the jade tiger? At least fifteen million people live in greater L.A., not eight million as Gwen suggests. When Gwen shoots lightning at Morimoto and his men, note that she does so with both hands, including the one that is gloved and holding the L.I.S.A. device. Even if she can do this without scorching her glove, shouldn't the gadget be damaged by being in contact with high doses of electricity?

Quote/Unquote: Wesley: 'When you're alienated from the people . . . You start to look other places.' Fred: 'But you hated her.' Wesley: 'It's not always about holding hands.'

Morimoto: 'You realise who you are up against.' Gunn: 'If it's those two girls, I already kicked their ass once.'

Wesley's translation of the sentence that Angel writes in demon language: 'I am not a buckethead.'

Notes: 'Has Cordy been a bad, bad girl?' If, as Gunn suggests, much of the last year of *Angel* has been a turgid supernatural soap opera, then this episode is akin to one of those sudden lurches into stand-alone drama that soaps occasionally attempt. Such experiments are usually interesting failures. This, on the other hand, is a flawed *masterpiece*. A story about the bitter alienation and harsh realities of love, 'Players' avoids being constrained by limited ambitions. Basically, it sees Gunn in a buddy-cop adventure with Gwen which turns into a kung-fu movie.

Angel reveals that Angelus did not kill Lilah, as everyone believed (see **78**, 'Calvary'). Angel is able to visualise the text from Lilah's book on The Beast. What Angel remembers is written in a Fellorian code system, a tricky language for Wesley to translate. Angel sent Lorne to a demon named Wanda, to help him regain his psychic abilities. Wesley remembers that Cordelia has been pregnant before and came to term overnight (**12**, 'Expecting').

Cordelia mentions the recent visits by Faith and Willow (**81**, 'Orpheus'). Cordelia says that she is still creeped out by Angel's ability to know when she is standing outside his door. Gunn has various scars from fighting vampires in places like Boyle Heights, Alhambra and Encino. He reminds Gwen that she has already killed him once (**68**, 'Ground State'). Gwen collects jade figurines on her travels – the latest being a dolphin she bought in Tahiti (see **75**, 'Long Day's Journey'). The businessman whose home Gwen and Gunn go to is named Takeshi Morimoto. He holds several honorary degrees and is involved in charity work involving animals. Nevertheless, Morimoto has also been involved in fraud, smuggling and money laundering. His daughter is named Aiko. Morimoto's company has invented a covert device called L.I.S.A., an acronym for Localised Ionic Sensory Activator, for use in Black Ops. Morimoto intends to sell this to the highest bidder (either China or North Korea). Amongst L.I.S.A.'s functions are regulating body temperature and heartbeat. A Gathbar Demon's spikes grow to full size in the womb before it is born.

Did You Know?: On 24 March 2003, at Cedar Sinai hospital in Beverly Hills, Charisma gave birth to her and partner Damien Hardy's first child, a boy named Donavan.

Critique: '*Angel* uses both its supernatural elements and its guest characters to plunge the regulars into deeper and more testing situations,' noted John Binns. 'A dalliance with the highly charged Gwen gave Gunn an excellent chance to show what he could do.'

83
Inside Out

US Transmission Date: 2 April 2003
UK Transmission Date: 15 May 2003 (Sky)

Writer: Steven S DeKnight
Director: Steven S DeKnight
Cast: Stephi Lineburg (Girl Sacrifice)

As Cordelia appears not to be in control of her own actions, Angel concludes that something took her over whilst she was on the higher plane. In an effort to find out what, he goes to see Skip for some answers.

Dudes and Evil Babes: Having told Connor in **82**, 'Players' that she might ask him to do things for her to protect their baby, Evil Cordy convinces Connor that they don't have to live by the same rules as others. And that, with Angel seemingly intent on destroying their unborn child, they must induce the birth. To do this, they must apparently kill a virgin. Connor provides one, a teenage girl whom he saves from a vampire attack. But he is then haunted by visions of his mother. It's never made clear whether these are real or figmentary, although Cordy certainly feels another presence in the room, suggesting that Darla is indeed a real ghost, sent by The Powers That Be. (There is, of course, another delicious possibility: that Darla is, in fact, The First – see *Buffy*: 'Amends', 'Lessons' et al. – who can't be too chuffed at the idea of Jasmine taking over the world just as it is about to try the same thing in *Buffy*.) Darla tries to persuade Connor not to kill the girl but is unsuccessful and, in one of the most disturbing moments in *Angel*, Cordelia slits the innocent girl's throat. Cordy then prompts Connor to leave a bloodied palm-print on her belly. Once he does this, Cordy goes into labour.

Does the Evil-Cordelia Back Story Make Sense?: A necessary gathering together of the plots from about two and a half seasons, the revelation that Cordelia is evil provokes a giant example of exposition drama, with a sequence nearly five minutes long full of reshot flashbacks and intense, earnest voice-over explanations. But does it all make sense? Angel speculates that whatever controls Cordelia returned with her from the higher dimension (**70**, 'Slouching Towards Bethlehem'). Gunn wonders if her amnesia was fake, but Wesley concludes that it was more likely a side effect of the return to this dimension. Angel speculates that the evil probably lay dormant within her until Lorne's spell in **72**, 'Spin the Bottle' woke it up. Lorne realises that this is the information Wolfram & Hart were so desperate to suck from his head. Angel notes that it was Cordelia who spiked his blood at Gwen's and killed Manny (**75**, 'Long Day's Journey'). She seems to have done so naked to avoid being covered in blood. Angel surmises that taking out the Svear Priestesses (**77**, 'Soulless') was much easier for her. Cordelia simply slipped away from the hotel and slaughtered them while everyone was reeling from the shock of losing Angel's soul. The spell to re-ensoul Angel was pure misdirection, which actually clouded Lorne's ability to read anyone. Wesley then realises that it was Cordelia who murdered Lilah (see **78**, 'Calvary'). Actually, yes, that *does* all make sense. How unusual is *that* in television these days?

References: Allusions to the aphorism 'all good things come to an end', the Gap Band's 'Oops Upside Your Head', William Cowper's *Olney Hymns* ('mysterious ways'), *Spider-Man*, The Rolling Stones' 'Monkey Man', Lizzie Borden (1860–1927), The Legion of Doom, *Monty Python's Holy Grail* ('or what, you'll bleed on me?'), Tarzan and Hoss Cartwright from *Bonanza*. Also, *Skippy*, *Mother Love*, Sid Vicious (see **77**, 'Soulless'), James Brown's 'Papa's Got A Brand New Bag', Johnny Cash's 'Ring of Fire' (see **73**, 'Apocalypse Nowish') and the Dustbuster. The concept of a woman being born fully grown comes from the Greek myth of Athena. There's a discussion between Fred and Gunn on the existence of free will that echoes a famous sequence in the *Doctor Who* story 'Inferno'. Also, a visual allusion to *Batman*.

Bitch!: Lorne refers to Evil Cordy as 'Queen Bee-atch.'

Cigarettes and Alcohol: On discovering that Cordelia is evil, Gunn shares Lorne's whisky.

Sex and Drugs and Rock'n'Roll: Gunn indicates that being close to Gwen can screw up your equipment. As it happens, he's talking about his cellphone, but it's fair to assume, since he's still alive, that the L.I.S.A. device worked and that Gwen is no longer a virgin.

'You May Remember Me From Such Films and TV Series As . . .': Stephi Lineburg was in *Zoe* and *City by the Sea*. Gina Torres played Cas in *The Matrix Reloaded*, Zoë

Warren in *Firefly*, Anna Espinosa in *Alias* and Nebula in *Hercules: The Legendary Journeys*.

Quote/Unquote: Angel: 'Lilah and I weren't exactly friends.' Wesley: 'You were mortal enemies. Why would you care what happened to her?' Angel: 'Because *you* did.'

Skip: 'Cordelia was chosen to become a higher being because she's such a pure, radiant saint. *Please!*'

Wesley, to Angel: 'What do you want to do?' Skip: 'The only thing he can do. Kill the woman he loves and save the world. Times like this, really gotta suck being you.'

Notes: 'Guy steps out for a few hours, half the place goes supervillain.' A story with incredible scope, if not a huge amount of subtlety, the episode is driven by a kind of adrenaline-fuelled emotional fascism. Steven De Knight's wordy but interesting script gives Charisma Carpenter the chance, for once, to play a *real* Queen Bee-atch. There's also one of the finest scenes of the season, a genuinely touching moment of restated friendship between Angel and Wesley. Robert Kral's sinister Erik Satie-influenced piano score, some of the series' most disturbing imagery and a final revelation are added bonuses. A vital linking strand between the previous Faith arc and the Jasmine-induced horrors to come, 'Inside Out' is tough, dangerous and unexpected. *Angel* in a nutshell.

Angel sensed Cordelia's evilness when she used the words 'my sweet', which she also used repeatedly when talking in Angelus's head. Wesley mentions the time Angel pleaded with The Powers That Be to cure Darla (**31**, 'The Trial'). Cordelia expects her baby to be born in less than two weeks, unless the blood ritual is performed to make it sooner. Cordelia's baby, it transpires, will be the manifestation of the evil former higher power that has been possessing her since the events of **72**, 'Spin the Bottle'. The team use a Bishundi ritual to track down Cordelia. They need a sacred Hutamin paw for this and, as luck would have it, Cordelia kept one in her desk, using it as a backscratcher. Skip (**46**, 'That Vision Thing') smokes and likes buffalo wings and watching football on TV. He notes that nobody comes back from paradise. Except a Slayer, once (see *Buffy*: 'The Gift', 'Bargaining'). He also reveals, eventually, that the plot to turn Cordelia evil has been ongoing for a long time in human terms, noting that all the events in Cordelia's life since she came to L.A. have led to it, including her getting the visions from Doyle (**9**, 'Hero'), being turned half-demon (**56**, 'Birthday') and her ascension (**66**, 'Tomorrow'). But it doesn't end with Cordelia. Skip asks if the team have any idea how many timelines had to intersect in order for something of this scope to work. He gives examples: Angel and Darla sleeping together to produce Connor, Lorne leaving Pylea, the death of Gunn's sister, Fred opening the wrong book and Wesley sleeping with the enemy. Skip suggests that he took a dive when Angel fought him and released Billy from his box of fire (**46**, 'That Vision Thing'). Skip is bound in place with the Sands of the Red Palm. Angel and Fred threaten to trap him in the Sphere of Infinite Agonies unless he co-operates. Fred can conjure up a sphere in twenty minutes.

Did You Know?: When the WB gave early renewal notices to six of their top shows, *Angel* was, to the surprise of many commentators, not amongst them. However, fans quickly leapt into action, with hundreds mailing postcards to the network, demanding that executives renew their favourite series. 'We're being proactive,' Vanessa Calvin, co-founder of renewangel.com, told Paul S Katz at *TV Guide*. Their efforts were certainly appreciated by the production team. 'The fans' reaction means we're doing our job right,' noted Joss Whedon.

84
Shiny Happy People

US Transmission Date: 9 April 2003
UK Transmission Date: 22 May 2003 (Sky)

Writers: Elizabeth Craft & Sarah Fain
Director: Marita Grabiak
Cast: Sam Witwer (Young Man), David Figlioli (Vamp Leader), Suzette Craft (Teacherly Woman), Annie Wersching (Awed Woman),

Steven Bean (Middle-aged Man), Lynette Romero (News Anchor),
Lyle Kanouse (Diner Counter Guy),
Tawny Rene Hamilton (Host of *Good Morning L.A.*),
Chane't Johnson (Martha Jane), Jackie Tohn (Woman #1)

The messianic Jasmine has come to save the world from
itself. In her presence the team become her disciples, as
they welcome their saviour with open arms. But one of the
gang has reservations – and they could get her killed.

Dudes and Babes: Jasmine appears to exude peace and
happiness to everyone around her. She says that she has been
on earth before and tells a story of a time before man that is
consistent with Giles's comments in *Buffy*: 'The Harvest'. In
the beginning great beings walked the earth and untold
power emanated the seeds of what would become good and
evil. Then the earth became a demon realm. Those of the
higher powers who had the will to resist left but remained
watchful. However, Fred sees another face of Jasmine.

Angel's guilt at having intended to kill Cordelia and,
thus, deprive the world of Jasmine's love overwhelms him
and he cries like a girl.

Denial, Thy Names are Wesley and Charles: Jasmine notes
that both Wes and Gunn have the same love for Fred.
That should, she continues, bring them closer together, not
force them apart.

It's a Designer Label!: Angel's white shirt and Lorne's
mustard-coloured suit.

Awesome: The sequence in the bowling alley with Fred and
Jasmine casually strolling through the carnage that the
guys are creating (love Wesley's balletic fighting style).

References: The title is a 1990 song by R.E.M. Lorne notes
that when Jasmine went out for a walk it resembled a scene
from *A Hard Day's Night*. The Powers That Be, notes
Jasmine, merely observe humanity and refuse to interfere,
similar to the attitude of the Time Lords in *Doctor Who*.
Also, the concept of ego death via Carl Jung's conceptual
'oceanic consciousness', Aldous Huxley's visions of Zen
utopianism and Timothy Leary and Richard Alpert's *The
Psychedelic Experience* ('we are all one'), Paul Leder's 1972
trash classic *I Dismember Mama*, The Beatles' 'Here

Comes The Sun' and Clorox liquid bleach. There are allusions to *Yellow Submarine* ('Are you still evil-ish?'), Ecclesiastes 3 ('everything has its season'), John 14 ('in my name'), *Star Wars: Episode 1 – The Phantom Menace* ('fear breeds hatred') and the death speech of Madame Roland (1754–93). Jasmine appears on the television talk-show *Good Morning L.A.* Visually, there are references to *They Live* and *Fright Night 2*.

'You May Remember Me From Such Films and TV Series As . . .': Sam Witwer was in *Dark Angel*. David Figlioli played Billy Bucklin in *Hard Ground*. Chane't Johnson appeared in *Sticky Fingers*. Jackie Tohn was in *Bad Boy*.

Logic, Let Me Introduce You to This Window: When does John Stoller come into contact with Jasmine's blood to enable him to see her true face?

Quote/Unquote: Fred: 'There's been an awful lot of dismembering going on in that basement lately if you ask me.' Lorne: 'Well, it's been a busy month . . .'

Nurse: 'Are you a family member?' Fred: 'Yes, I have a family, I am a member.'

Notes: 'Nothing like a homicidal maniac to put a damper on an impromptu spiritual gathering.' In an episode full of quasi-biblical allusions, *Angel* speaks to its disciples, telling the parable of false gods. And does so *beautifully* and with some righteous anger. In lesser hands, this sort of thing could've been an unqualified disaster, full of preachy moral certainties and random sermonising. That this *doesn't* happen is largely down to the complete sincerity with which the cast treat Gina Torres's Christlike Jasmine. The episode's undertones – a caustic fear of change; what dreadful secrets lie behind hidden faces; the dangers of blind fanaticism – are handled with just the right degree of cynicism. 'Shiny Happy People's ultimate message – that nothing should ever be taken at face value, no matter how much we'd like it to be – is as valid as anything that's ever been said on this show.

Gunn and Wesley use a buzz-saw to dismember Skip (see **83**, 'Inside Out'). Gunn's grandmother was named Helen. Fred's diner breakfast consists of bacon, hash browns, two eggs (sunny side up) and black coffee. Lorne mentions that his species is immune to decapitation (**44**, 'There's No Place Like Plrtz Glrb'). Jasmine reminds Angel of the trials he endured to save Darla (**31**, 'The Trial'). She tells Connor that she specifically chose Angel and Darla to be his parents and that he was created to father Jasmine herself, who, she says, has returned to rid the world of evil. Jasmine needs to be named by those who love her (there are some rules of the world that even she must follow, she tells Fred). Jasmine's touch seemingly decays the skin. The decrease in L.A.'s crime rate since Jasmine's arrival is attributed to the city's 'tough on crime' policy, which was instituted the previous month.

Did You Know?: WB trailers for this and subsequent episodes used *US Weekly*'s quote that *Angel* was 'TV's hippest show' prominently.

Cast And Crew Comments: 'Because *Firefly* was shorter lived than any of us wanted, I believe that my being cast as Jasmine was born from [Joss Whedon's] desire to see more of what I could bring to the table,' Gina Torres told *Cult Times*.

85
The Magic Bullet

US Transmission Date: 16 April 2003
UK Transmission Date: 29 May 2003 (Sky)

Writer: Jeffrey Bell
Director: Jeffrey Bell
Cast: Danny Woodburn (Executive Demon), Patrick Fischler (Ted),
Terrylene (Deaf Woman), Mia Kelley (Woman),
Andre Hotchko (Man in Lobby), Ajgie Kirkland (Black Man),
Michael McElroy (Young Boy), Chad Williams (Rock Dude),
Phyllis Flax (Very Old Woman), Amy Raymond (Weeping Woman),
Steve Forbess (Mexican Man), Zakk Wylde (Himself)[40]

Fred is on the run in an L.A. that is rapidly becoming a utopian wonderland, fleeing from Jasmine's growing army

---

[40] Uncredited.

of fanatical followers, which includes her friends at Angel Investigations. In an effort to find some answers, she visits a shop specialising in books on mind-control techniques.

The Conspiracy Starts At Closing Time: Fred visits a bookstore looking for literature on mass hypnosis. Amongst the items for sale are volumes on astral projection, *Satan's Dictionary* and *Making Mind Control Work For You*. The store's owner believes that he has implants in his head that allow the CIA access to his thoughts. (There's a reference to MK-ULTRA, the CIA's programme of mind control.) The store is named The Magic Bullet, which takes viewers to a whole sub-genre of conspiracy theory via *JFK*, *The X-Files* and its spin-off *The Lone Gunmen*. Jasmine subsequently rewards the owner's loyalty by assuring him, in all sincerity, that in Dallas, on 22 November 1963, Lee Oswald acted alone. With a manual bolt-action Mannlicher-Carcano rifle. Hitting a moving target at 90 yards, through dense foliage. In exactly 5.6 seconds (as established by Abraham Zapruder's 8mm film of the event). Well, *that* sounds reasonable.

References: A 'demon jihad' refers to the Arabic word for struggle which has become associated with a holy war, especially in defence of Islam. Allusions to Bette Midler's *The Divine Miss M*, Slim Jim beef jerky, Eddie Izzard (an *executive* demon), *Blackadder II* ('stranger things have happened'), Christ's betrayer Judas Iscariot (see **60**, 'Sleep Tight', **64**, 'A New World'), Harry Houdini (1874–1926), Nevada talk-radio host and arch-conspiracy theorist Art Bell, the story of George Washington chopping down a cherry tree, mind-reader George Kreskin, Martha and the Vandellas' 'Nowhere To Run' and the Edwin Hawkins Singers' 'Oh Happy Day'.

Also, Barbara Streisand's 'People' (see **4**, 'I Fall To Pieces'), the Greek myth of the Sirens, *The Lord of the Rings* ('a movie about magical dwarves'), George Stevens' *The Greatest Story Ever Told*, *Quest For Fire* and Regis Philbin (the host of *Live with Regis and Kelly*). Jujube is the name for the fruit of two species of a thorny evergreen tree of the genus Ziziphus. 'Count the ways' alludes to Elizabeth Barrett Browning's *Sonnets from the Portuguese*.

Fred mentions 'Shiny Happy People', the title of the previous episode.

Not Exactly A Haven For The Bruthas: The hotel is overbooked with customers wanting to meet Jasmine. One follower offers Lorne his house (complete with pool) in exchange for a room.

Sex and Drugs and Rock'n'Roll: Whilst pursued by Jasmine's followers, Fred snogs Angel as a diversionary tactic.

'You May Remember Me From Such Films and TV Series As ...': Danny Woodburn played Carl the Gnome in *Special Unit 2* and was in *Charmed*. Patrick Fischler was Pepe in *Nash Bridges* and appeared in *Mulholland Drive* and *Speed*. Terrylene played Julie in *Natural Born Killers*. Mia Kelley was in *Resin*. Andre Hotchko appeared in *Hard as Nails*. Ajgie Kirkland played James Trout in *Blow*. Michael McElroy's CV includes *The Young and the Restless*. Chad Williams was in *Gorge*. Phyllis Flax's movies include *Loved*. Amy Raymond appeared in *Radio Free Steve*, which she also produced.

Don't Give Up The Day Job: Stuntman Thom Williams also worked on *Birds of Prey* and *Highway*. His colleague Erik Betts's CV includes *Alias* and *Bringing Down the House*. Zakk Wylde is the guitarist with Ozzy Osbourne's band.

Logic, Let Me Introduce You to This Window: For Fred's plan to work, Angel needed to be standing directly behind Jasmine when Fred fired the gun. A few inches to either side and the bullet wouldn't have hit Angel and, thus, 'cured' him. That bullet looks remarkably intact after going through Jasmine's dense skin and tough bone, before emerging and hitting Angel. Where have we heard *that* before? Why does Wesley leave the door open whilst the team capture Connor and mix his blood with Cordelia's? How did Jasmine, Angel and Connor get to the bookshop in such a short space of time?

Quote/Unquote: Old Woman: 'I have thirty-seven cats, and I've just changed all their names to Jasmine.'

Notes: 'Not a huge demand for serial-killer autopsies when you're living in a utopian wonderland.' Jeff Bell's script is a perfect allegory for Los Angeles; the sinister, edgy, paranoid shade behind the bright, sunny faces. In Jasmine's case, that's meant literally, as well as metaphorically. Full of false-religion iconography and biblical references, 'The Magic Bullet' sees *Angel* playing witty intertextual games. Once again Amy Acker is centre stage for the bulk of the episode, and the final act is a beauty, with the spectre of betrayal all around and, just when the audience prematurely feel that they've got a handle on where the story is heading, another twist of the knife.

Angel notes that gunshot wounds feel like bee stings to vampires (see *Buffy*: 'Angel'). Wesley is developing a website for Jasmine. Connor first learned to track people in Quor-toth at around five years of age. Holtz would tie him to a tree and Connor had to free himself and track Holtz down. His personal best was five days. Connor has the ability to scalp people. Jasmine speaks Mandarin and Spanish and says that she loves movies. She has begun taking a selected few of her followers for private audiences, during which she eats them. Jasmine's blood is the key to seeing her true identity. Mixed with a person's own blood, it allows them to see her real face, which is disgusting. Cordelia's blood also carries this feature, the process working on everyone except Connor, presumably through his own blood link to Jasmine. Lorne declares an open-mic night at the hotel. Amongst the speakers are a young boy named Linford Detweiler, a woman who can't stop crying, a deaf woman and an elderly lady with 37 cats.

Some of the filming for this episode took place on Mulholland Drive bordering Griffith Park.[41]

---

[41] One of the most famous roads in the world, named after pioneering hydrologist William Mulholland. From its starting point near the 101 Freeway to its terminus at L.A. County's Pacific boundary, Mulholland twists for 21 miles through mountain passes and canyons, offering extraordinary views of Los Angeles to the south and the Valley to the north. The road passes through the Hollywood Hills and is famous for the numerous celebrities who've had homes on or near it. (These include Elvis Presley who, in August 1965, had his only meeting with The Beatles there.) Mulholland has also been immortalised in songs (R.E.M's 'Electrolyte') and movies (David Lynch's *Mulholland Drive*).

Soundtrack: The episode opens with The Beach Boys' 1966 classic 'Wouldn't It Be Nice?' Lorne, backed by Zakk Wylde, sings a version of Curtis Mayfield's 'Freddie's Dead'. Angel and Connor then croon a Jasmine-inspired variant of 'Mandy' (see **23**, 'Judgment', **81**, 'Orpheus').

Did You Know?: Although professing himself not to be a particularly rabid fan of Barry Manilow, the first concert that the teenage David Boreanaz attended in Philadelphia was, he admitted to Rob Francis, one featuring the large-nosed 'Mandy' singer/songwriter.

86
Sacrifice

US Transmission Date: 23 April 2003
UK Transmission Date: 5 June 2003 (Sky)

Writer: Ben Edlund
Director: David Straiton
Cast: Avery Kidd Waddell (Randall Golden), Micah Henson (Matthew), Jeff Ricketts (Creature), Tristine Skylar (Holly), Bradley Stryker (Vamp), Taylor Lundeen (Little Girl)

Fleeing from the wrath of Jasmine's followers, the Angel Investigations gang find themselves going underground. There, they endure a long diversion.

Dudes and Babes: The demon who captures Wesley says that he is from another, older world, where humans could not exist (Wesley's lungs would burn, should he ever visit). The demon's kind loved Jasmine before humans even existed, although they knew her as 'the devourer, the song, the peace'. Her true name was only known to a high priest. Speaking this name appears to be the secret to destroying her. After Angel kills the demon, he and Wesley find a blue orb which, when activated by blood, opens a portal to the creature's home dimension.

Denial, Thy Name is Everyone: Jasmine's sphere of influence continues to grow and now encompasses all of California (as Wesley notes, the Angel Investigation team are the only non-worshippers left).

References: The Archdiocese of Los Angeles comprises three counties: Los Angeles, Ventura and Santa Barbara. Allusions to *The Stepford Wives*, another reference to *Invasion of the Body Snatchers*, the Great Pyramid of Giza, Dr Pepper, Led Zeppelin's 'Whole Lotta Love' and Data, the android on *Star Trek: The Next Generation*. Also, *Dracula*, the Jewish dietary laws kashrut ('keeping kosher'), *Captain Clegg* (the sequence in which the demon pulls out the vampire's tongue), *Almost Famous* ('it's happening'), Percy Shelley's *The Mask of Anarchy* ('we are many') and James Tilton's *Lost Horizon* ('Shangri-La-La-Land'). Finding out Jasmine's true name in order to destroy her alludes to the dénouement of the fairytale 'Rumplestiltskin'. Locations mentioned include LaBrea (near Wilshire Boulevard in Downtown L.A.).

Not Exactly A Haven For The Bruthas: In the sewer, the gang run into a group led by Randall, whose brother, Tommy Golden, is a former acquaintance of Gunn. Randall stole Gunn's truck at the age of twelve. Tommy was killed by the sewer demon whilst setting traps. The street kids have been living underground since the sun disappeared (see **75**, 'Long Day's Journey').

Lorne gives Golden's crew a little life lesson on racism against green-skinned demons.

Sex and Drugs and Rock'n'Roll: Jasmine is, says Gunn, a tough drug to kick – cold turkey.

'You May Remember Me From Such Films and TV Series As . . .': Avery Kidd Waddell was in *Road Trip*. Tristine Skylar's CV includes *The Intern* and *Cadillac Man*. Bradley Stryker appeared in *Bruce Almighty*.

Don't Give Up The Day Job: Ben Edlund wrote and illustrated the comic book *The Tick*.

Logic, Let Me Introduce You to This Window: During the brief fight scene between Angel and Matthew, it's obvious that the stuntman playing Matthew is an adult and not a small boy. Jasmine's followers, rushing to Connor's aid, take an age to get from one end of a hotel corridor to the other (enough time for Wes, Lorne, Gunn and Fred to escape from the fourth floor to the ground via a fire escape). Jasmine eats people whilst they are apparently still wearing their underwear. How does Matthew come into contact with Jasmine in the short time that he is on the surface? Golden says that his group have been hiding in the sewers for two weeks. When they went down the sun was still blocked, placing those events pre-**79**, 'Salvage'. Which means that everything from then onwards has taken place in a fortnight, making further nonsense of the dating of Cordelia's pregnancy mentioned in **82**, 'Players'.

Quote/Unquote: Fred: 'They're all so happy.' Gunn: 'They'll be happier when they're gouging out our eyes and stomping us till their shoes get sticky.'

Fred: 'We're professional monster-killers.'

Notes: 'Love is sacrifice.' What a crushing disappointment – after so much careful build-up and multi-layered characterisation over the previous dozen stories, suddenly we find ourselves in a typical *Doctor Who* episode three. In other words, an episode full of escape-capture-escape with lots of running up and down corridors. Or, in this case, sewer tunnels. It's almost as though the production team had the entire season plotted out but, at the last moment realised that they'd miscalculated and only had 21 episodes' worth of plot. 'Sacrifice' is the resulting hole where the rain got in. It's a dreadful fudge of an episode, all talk, talk, talk and no action. The only scene with any real heart is a sinister little confrontation between Wesley and the demon. That's also, ironically, the only scene that actually moves the overall plot forwards. Elsewhere the dialogue is frequently trite, particularly during a painful-to-watch scene between Gunn and Fred. The odd good line crops up every now and then, just to remind the viewer that, yes, this *is* actually *Angel* they're watching. Running on the spot? That fact that the spot in question is a sewer is a suitable metaphor for 45 minutes of his life that this author will never get back.

Fred mentions her conversation with Jasmine in the bowling alley in which Jasmine said that she needed to be named (**84**, 'Shiny Happy People'). Lorne suggests Belize as a hideout for the gang. He tells Angel that he always sucked at sports. The mayor of L.A. is now referring to the town as The First Citadel of Jasmine. The L.A. Archdiocese has instructed that all churches remove any false idols and replace them with images of Jasmine. The Governor of California has agreed to dissolve his administration. Jasmine has the ability to heal wounds with her hands.

Did You Know?: Where does David Boreanaz see Angel going in the future? 'I just let the writers do their thing and enjoy the ride,' he told *Starburst*. 'I don't have a mental wish list.' However, if there's one thing that the actor would like to see happen, it's being behind the camera. 'I'd love to be able to direct,' he noted. 'I understand the show, the way it's shot, the fight sequences, the special effects. I'd really enjoy that.'

87
Peace Out

US Transmission Date: 30 April 2003
UK Transmission Date: 12 June 2003 (Sky)

Writer: David Fury
Director: Jefferson Kibbee

Cast: Robert Towers (High Priest), Bonita Friedericy (Patience),
Eliza Pryor Nagel (Susan), Bob Pescovitz (News Producer),
Gerry Katzman (Technician), Audrey Kearns (Young Woman),
Kristin Richardson (Female Reporter), Kyle Ingleman (Jeremy),
Jeff Scott Bass (Brent), Kimble Jemison (Cop #1),
Blair Hickey (Male News Reporter),
Angelica Castro (Telemundo Reporter),
Brian Bradley (Frizzled Reporter)

In the dimension that Jasmine, the people-eating Power That Was, last subjugated, Angel's quest for answers involves him climbing a mountain and fighting the Keeper of the Sacred Word. Meanwhile, back in Los Angeles, things look bleak for Angel's friends.

Dudes and Babes: Jasmine's reign of peace and happiness (fuelled by some people-eating, admittedly) comes to an end when Angel brings back the head of the Keeper of the

Word. When Angel cuts the stitching that holds its mouth
shut, the Keeper says Jasmine's name and the spell is
broken, revealing Jasmine's true features to everyone. The
result is chaos on the streets of L.A. Seeking vengeance,
Jasmine intends to destroy humanity, but is killed by
Connor before she can.

Denial, Thy Name is ... Unknown: A race of blue-skinned
arachnitaurs in a different dimension suffered many wars
amongst themselves until the coming of the Blessed
Devourer, who united them. Jasmine claims to have altered
the creatures' evolution as well as their society, but
considered them merely a trial run prior to conquering a
more worthy dimension, one with technologies that would
make her conquest easier.

References: The title is a slang term for goodbye. *The
Twilight Zone* episode 'To Serve Man' shares many plot
similarities with this storyline and is alluded to by Gunn.
The concept of demonic/alien enslavement of mankind via
television broadcasts is something of a running theme in
British telefantasy (*Quatermass*, the *Doctor Who* story
'Ambassadors of Death', *The Changes*, etc.). Wesley refers
to the insect creatures as zealots, a term for religious
fanatics named after an extremist Jewish fundamentalist
sect who violently resisted the Roman occupation of
Palestine during the first century AD. Connor's conversation with the comatose Cordelia may have been visually
influenced by the scene in which Livia justifies her murder
of her husband, Augustus, to his dead body in *I, Claudius*.
Seen on the noticeboard of the church in which Connor
finds Cordelia is GOD IS NOWHERE. This was a catchphrase
from David Greenwalt's 2003 series *Miracles*. Also, *Sunset
Boulevard*, Bugsy Siegel (see **69**, 'The House Always
Wins'), the Shamen's 'Possible Worlds', the L.A. Lakers,
Kato – the valet and chauffeur of the Green Hornet, John
Donne's *Devotions*, *Galaxy Quest* ('never give up, never
surrender'), John 14 ('She is the Light, she is the Way'),
The Wizard of Oz, the 1984 apocalypse/zombie movie
Night of the Comet and Porky the Pig's catchphrase 'that's
all folks'.

'You May Remember Me From Such Films and TV Series As ...': Robert Towers was in *Einstein's Playground*. Bonita Friedericy appeared in *The Stepdaughter* and *Scrubs*. Eliza Pryor Nagel was in *Weeki Wachee Girls*. Bob Pescovitz's CV includes *Breaking Hard*. Gerry Katzman was in *Ordinary Madness*. Kristin Richardson played Samantha in *Rock Star* and appeared in *Charmed*. Kyle Ingleman was in *Trancers 6*. Kimble Jemison appeared in *Bowfinger*. Blair Hickey played Michael in *Standing By*. Angelica Castro played the Harlot in *The Scorpion King*. Brian Bradley appeared in *Parker Lewis Can't Lose*.

Logic, Let Me Introduce You to This Window: It's difficult to believe that Gunn could bust out of a cage that Angelus was unable to break out of. Why, exactly, does Connor kill Jasmine? Further timescale questions: Jasmine says she made the insect world peaceful and gained control millennia ago, but the high priest speaks of her occupation being just centuries in the past. How can the priest speak when Angel is holding him by the neck several feet off the ground? Why, other than dramatic licence, does the car that Jasmine picks up and throws at Angel explode in mid-air? There's another example of the weak cement that they seem to use in L.A. (see **73**, 'Apocalypse Nowish'). A concrete lamppost disintegrates when Jasmine throws Angel at it. Between the sequence when they encounter Lilah and Angel's return to the hotel, Wes, Gunn, Fred and Lorne have all changed clothes and cleaned themselves up. Presumably they did so one at a time so as not to leave Lilah, whom they trust about as far as they can comfortably spit, alone?

The Free Will Versus Happiness Debate: Her plans for global domination in ruins, Jasmine asks Angel if he learned nothing from his time working for The Powers. There are, she continues, no absolutes of right or wrong in life, only choices. The choice *she* offered was paradise. Angel says *he* chose not to accept this because he *could*, adding that Jasmine tried to take from everyone the *right* to choose. Jasmine looks around the burning city and suggests he observe the devastation that free will has caused mankind.

Angel notes that thousands died because of Jasmine: directly, through her eating them, and indirectly, via the rain of fire and the vampires that overran the city when she obscured the sun. Jasmine suggests that she could have stopped wars, disease and poverty. Given a chance, she could have saved *billions*. She adds that now 'this world is doomed to drown in its own blood'. Angel says the price was too high, that humanity's fate must be its own or they are nothing. Jasmine says she loved this world and sacrificed everything she was to be part of it. She suggests Angel knows that the other Powers That Be don't care about the fate of the world.
Quote/Unquote: Jasmine: 'Where's Angel?' Wesley: 'You're omniscient. You tell us!'

Fred: 'Weird, Connor walking out like that, leaving us unguarded.' Lorne: 'Yeah. If he's not careful, we might move about freely in our impervious steel cage.'

Angel: 'I didn't say we were smart. I said it's our right. It's what makes us human.' Jasmine: 'You're *not* human.' Angel: 'Workin' on it.'

Notes: 'I know she's a lie. My whole life's been built on them. I guess I thought this one was better than the others.' Forget the CGI overload of the first scene and the occasional laboured parody of religious bureaucracy. *This is better* than **86**, 'Sacrifice'! A David Fury script which contains several interesting discussions about appearances not being, ultimately, important, 'Peace Out' benefits from much arresting visual imagery, and the message that in life there *are* no absolutes, only choices. It includes key confirmations of several of *Angel*'s core elements – like Gunn's stubborn refusal to give in to the inevitable, and Wesley's trust in Angel's abilities. It also features dozens of funny one-liners. Everyone's on top form, but a special word of praise for Vincent Kartheiser, whose character suddenly flowers – with little warning – into a solid three-dimensional *person* via his best scene of the season: a beautifully delivered soliloquy of passion and betrayal to his unconscious love, Cordelia. 'Peace Out' is *Angel* recovering from what is hopefully a one-off aberration with much dignity. All this, *and* a bit of mild nudity.

Jasmine mentions the prophecy which says that Angel will play a major part in the apocalypse (see **34**, 'Blood Money'). Angel repels the Arachnitaur Demons using the blue orb. Connor has been able to see Jasmine's true face since she first arrived. He grew up in Quor-toth, he notes, meaning that he has a different concept of what is beautiful and what isn't. He tells Gunn that Jasmine eats people (see **85**, 'The Magic Bullet'). The cage that Connor locks the gang in is the same one they built for Angelus in **76**, 'Awakening'. Jasmine says that she was forged in the inferno of creation. The TV crew in the hotel lobby is preparing to broadcast Jasmine's message to Paris, Moscow and Nairobi. One of the TV reporters is named Tracy Bellows, and works for KTLA. Yet again, a prophecy the audience thought had been disproved turns out to have been true (see **22**, 'To Shanshu in L.A.'). Maybe Wesley was too preoccupied with the relevance to Angel and Connor to notice an incorrect gender. Could 'The Father Will Kill The Son' actually have said 'The Father Will Kill The Daughter'? (see **58**, 'Couplet'). Although, technically, of course, Angel *does* kill Connor, in a way, to give him a new life (see **88**, 'Home').

Critique: Scott Pierce noted that *Angel* hadn't been done any favours by its network. 'The show has showed signs of life in the ratings recently. The WB ought to give it some stability, give it all the promotion it can muster and give it a fifth season . . . *Angel* is [one of] the best the WB has.'

Did You Know?: Prior to the WB's decision to renew *Angel* for a fifth season, *USA Today* ran its sixth annual *Save Our Shows* survey on 5 May 2003. *Angel* topped the poll with 49 per cent of all votes registered (almost 60,000).

88
Home

US Transmission Date: 7 May 2003
UK Transmission Date: 19 June 2003 (Sky)

Writer: Tim Minear
Director: Tim Minear
Cast: Jim Abele (Connor's Father), Jason Winer (Preston),
Michael Halsey (Sirk), Jonathan Woodward (Knox),
Merle Dandridge (Lacey), Jason Padgett (Suicidal Cop),
James Calvert (Surgery Patient), Anthony Diaz-Perez (Hostage Father),
Adrienne Brett Evans (Connor's Mother),
Stacy Solookin (Connor's Aunt), Emma Hunton (Connor's Kid Sister),
Ariel Baker (Angel Greeter #1), Michael Ness (Angel Greeter #2),
Alex Craig Mann (Angel Greeter #3),
Nichole Pelerine (Angel Greeter #4),
Joshua Grenrock (Angel Greeter #5)

The Angel Investigations team have, much to their disappointment, ended world peace. Now all of their dreams may be about to come true, whether they like it or not, when they are made the offer of a lifetime: to become the new owners of Wolfram & Hart (L.A. branch). Meanwhile, a disillusioned Connor seeks his own form of redemption.
Dreaming (As *Buffy* Often Proves) is Free: Gunn and Lacey (see Notes) are in the elevator when the button for The White Room appears. Gunn protests, but Lacey tells him that the answers he seeks lie there. Gunn finds himself in The White Room with a black panther. Subsequently, when he returns to the lobby, Gunn seems changed by the experience. Was the panther a member of the new Ra-Tet (see **75**, 'Long Day's Journey') and, if so, has Gunn also become a quasi-god? Answers, hopefully, next season . . .
Dudes and Babes: Wolfram & Hart are, according to Lilah, ceding the L.A. territory to Angel Investigations as a reward for ending world peace. Wesley argues that Jasmine was creating a slave state and Angel reminds Lilah that Jasmine was eating people. Lilah notes that those people knew what they were getting into (Lorne: 'Her stomach?'). Lilah reminds the gang that peace comes at a price and that Jasmine understood that. She consumed perhaps a dozen souls a day to end the suffering of millions.

Lilah confirms that Cordelia is safe, albeit still in a coma. She will get the best medical and metaphysical care available, and if there's a way to bring her back, the company will find it.

It's a Designer Label!: Lorne's purple suit and peach shirt, Fred's burgundy top, Wesley's Ralph Lauren polo shirt, Lilah's svelte purple dress.

The Conspiracy Starts At Closing Time: Lilah tells Angel that taking over Wolfram & Hart is an opportunity and reminds him of the things he could do with such resources at his fingertips. She explains that nothing in the world is how it should be. That's why he's there. She says the people need a man who knows how to compromise and beat the system from within the belly of the beast. Lilah then gives Angel an amulet and a folder. The latter, she notes, contains information about Sunnydale. The amulet is said to be crucial to the battle about to take place there (see *Buffy*: 'End of Days', 'Chosen').

The deal that Angel eventually strikes is that the senior partners will bend time so that Connor has a second chance at a normal life. After this has been achieved, Angel tells Lilah that he needs to see Connor one final time. As Angel heads off to a waiting limo, Fred asks, 'Who's Connor?' Angel finds the answer, looking through the window of a suburban house. Connor is sitting at the dinner table with his new family, happily discussing his plans for college.

References: Allusions include Roald Dahl's *Charlie and the Chocolate Factory*, Dungeons & Dragons, the Richard Dean Anderson vehicle *MacGyver*, *Macbeth* ('we three'), *Star Wars*, *Let's Make a Deal*, Cecil Frances Alexander's 'All Things Bright And Beautiful', *Die Hard*, the Taj Mahal, Pop Tarts, Adolf Hitler, Las Vegas masters of illusion Siegfried and Roy and the nursery rhyme 'Little Miss Muffet'.

Bitch!: Lilah returns from Hell with her head back on her shoulders and her bitchiness intact.

'You May Remember Me From Such Films and TV Series As . . .': Jim Abele played Ralph Burton in *24*. Jason Winer appeared in *The Sum of All Fears*. Michael Halsey was in *Sabotage!* Jonathan Woodward appeared in *Pipe Dream*. Jason Padgett was in *Spider-Man*. James Calvert was in *Remembrance*. Anthony Diaz-Perez played Randy in *Boomtown*. Stacy Solookin appeared in *CSI*. Michael Ness

was in *Judging Amy*. Alex Craig Mann appeared in *Fear
and Loathing in Las Vegas*. Nichole Pelerine was in *Rockin'
Good Times*.

Logic, Let Me Introduce You to This Window: Connor, the
poster child for instability and teenage dysfunction, is
somehow able to persuade a suicidal policeman back to
rationality. **48**, 'Carpe Noctem' established the Hyperion's
address as 1481 Hyperion; however, this episode suggests
that the number is 4121. The sudden transformation of
L.A. from riot central is a bit *too* sudden. When Connor
and Lorne were in the city it was chaos, with rampant
looting and suicide. But by the time Connor tried to blow
up a store full of hostages a few hours later, it was open
for business, emergency services responded to the crisis and
the TV news service was able to cover the event.

Quote/Unquote: Gunn: 'You want to give us your evil law
firm. We ain't lawyers.' Fred: 'Or *evil*. Currently.'

Wes: 'You decapitate a loved one, you don't expect them
to come visiting.'

Notes: 'This is the offer of a lifetime. Just not, you know,
mine.' So *Angel* moves into another reality – and becomes
L.A. Law in the process. Tim Minear's challenging,
perceptive script is one of the funniest (and most intrigu-
ing) in the series' history, full of sociopolitical observations
and startling imagery (Gunn's little sojourn in The White
Room, for instance). Chief amongst the surprises is the
further development of Wesley into an action hero willing
to go to extraordinary and dangerous lengths to save a
lady's soul. 'Home' is a fabulous end to what has been,
quite simply, one of the best seasons of popular television
in *years*; a critical summation of the many strengths that
this multifaceted show has at its disposal. The episode
reminds us that *Angel* is a show about hope – just as *Buffy*
always was. The future's bright and seemingly *spiky* as fire
and skill combine to produce an underrated, under-
appreciated, overlooked gem.

Wesley mentions that the Watchers Council no longer
exists – its headquarters were destroyed by The First Evil
in *Buffy*: 'Never Leave Me'. Fred has a friend named

Matthew Partney, who lives at 6200 Crestwood Blvd in Lubbock. Lilah's perpetuity contract with Wolfram & Hart extends beyond her death (the company seems to do this regularly; see also Holland Manners' comments in **37**, 'Reprise'). The contract is written on indestructible paper, despite Wesley's attempts to burn it and save her soul. Lilah mentions Angelus having fed off her and Wesley's cutting off her head (see **79**, 'Salvage'). Wolfram & Hart has been completely restaffed since The Beast's attack (see **74**, 'Habeas Corpses'). Each of the team is assigned a guide for their tour of Wolfram & Hart. Lorne's is a slick young man called Preston from the Entertainment Department, Wesley's is Rutherford Sirk, an English former member of the Watcher's Council. Gunn's guide is named Lacey Shepard, and Fred's is Knox, temporary manager of the Science Division. The Wolfram & Hart building has an actual dungeon. They also have the most comprehensive collection of prophecy archives anywhere (Wesley requests a book called the *Devandire Sibylline Codex*). Angel's new office has a private elevator, a big-screen high-definition TV and necro-tempered glass that shields him from the sun's rays, and is 30 per cent more energy-efficient.

Soundtrack: The song that Lorne sings is Leonard Bernstein's 'Something's Coming' from *West Side Story*.

Did You Know?: In June 2003 *Angel* came an astonishing fourth in *TV Zone*'s readers' poll for Top Cult TV Show of all time. In beating such legends as the various *Star Trek* series, *The X-Files* and *Babylon 5*, it was only outplaced by *Stargate SG-1*, *Buffy* and *Doctor Who*.

Critique: Concerning Charisma Carpenter's likely departure, *Cult Times*'s Paul Spragg felt that 'frankly, she's not likely to be missed. The *Angel* cast's growth over the last few years has meant some of the characters have lost out, and cutting the regulars makes a lot of sense.'

Cast And Crew Comments: According to Tim Minear, *Angel* is 'the best place ever to work'. As he told Rob Francis, 'directing is heaven. I find it unbelievably easy. You have all these incredibly talented people helping you. It's not the isolated trauma that writing is.'

Subsequently, on *Buffy the Vampire Slayer*: 'End of Days'/ 'Chosen': With the information that Lilah provided, Angel travels to Sunnydale and gives Buffy the amulet to help the Slayer and her friends in their battle against The First. Aided by this powerful device, which Spike uses at the cost of his own destruction, and Willow's spell to turn the potential Slayers into warriors, the Hellmouth is closed for good.

The Angel Novels

Eager to match the worldwide success of their *Buffy* series, Pocket Pulse quickly began to publish *Angel* novels. As with *Buffy*, these actually arrived in the UK some months ahead of the show via specialist shops like Forbidden Planet. All of the novels published thus far take place prior to **9**, 'Hero', and therefore feature Doyle rather than Wesley.

not forgotten

Writer: Nancy Holder
Published: April 2000
Tagline: The price for immortality is steep . . .

When Angel rescues workers from a sweatshop factory, he is bitten by a snake-demon who warns him that 'this world does not want you'. He, Cordelia and Doyle become involved with a group of Indonesians who are trying to raise Latura, a god of the Dead. This is linked to a demon, Golgothla, whom Angel encountered before he was sired.

It's a Designer Label: Cordelia is shopping in an unfashionable market when she encounters Jusef Rais and becomes caught up in the plot.

References: Angel tells Kate he is living 'la vida loca' like Ricky Martin. *Batman*, *The Bone Collector*, *Charmed*, *Jeopardy*, *Big Trouble in Little China*, *How to Marry a Millionaire*, *The Wizard of Oz*, *Indiana Jones*, *Star Wars*, *Rolling Stone* Magazine, *Die Hard*, Monopoly.

The Charisma Show: A classic Cordelia line: 'No! My dates only die in Sunnydale, OK? Not here too!'

A Haven for the Bruthas: Focuses on the Indonesian population and makes the point that over half the children in L.A. are non-Caucasian.

Cigarettes and Alcohol: Angel and Doyle end up in an Irish bar. It's noted that Cordelia is too young to drink.

'West Hollywood?': An emergency driver overtly comes on to Angel.

Logic, Let Me Introduce You to This Window: The author realises that cellphones shouldn't work underground, but never explains how they do; the flashback to Galway is set in 1752, but is said to be only a fortnight before Angel was sired. Alice's journal is misdated to 1920, rather than 1930.

I Just *Love* your Accent: Cordelia asks Doyle if he has a green card.

Notes: Angel has visited Thailand/Siam at some point in the past. This is set two months or so after *Buffy*: 'Graduation Day' (although this contradicts the impression from **1**, 'City Of' that it has been some time since Angel and Cordelia last saw each other). Doyle can't drive a manual (stick-shift) car.

redemption

Writer: Mel Odom
Published: June 2000
Tagline: History can repeat itself . . .

Whitney Tyler plays Honor Blaze in *Dark Midnight* – a TV show about a vampire DJ – but people are trying to kill her because they think she's a real vampire. When Angel meets her, she is the double of Moira, someone who was trying to kill Angel and Darla in Galway in 1758. In fact Whitney *is* Moira – when Angel killed her she became possessed by a banshee – now hunted by her own former co-hunters, the Jesuit Blood Cadre.

Dudes and Babes: A couple of rich leather-clad L.A. kids slum it in an alley and are set upon by vampires.

Denial, Thy Name is Kate: Kate is recommending Angel and helping him, although she tells him that she wants to know a lot more about why he's doing what he does.

References: *Charlie's Angels, Salem's Lot, Forever Knight, A Current Affair, Winnie the Pooh, Pollyanna, Little House on the Prairie, Snow White.*

The Charisma Show: Cordelia deduces that Whitney hasn't had a childhood – a vital clue to her real nature.

Not Exactly A Haven For The Bruthas: A cabbie is given dialogue that even Ian Fleming would have found racist.

Cigarettes and Alcohol: We open in a bar where Angel and Doyle are drinking.

Logic, Let Me Introduce You to This Window: There was supposed to be a 'Scottish rebellion' in 1758. Angel is still making references in mortal terms in 1758, five years after he was sired. Whistler is alleged to have taught Angel how to hide after he regained his soul, yet according to *Buffy*: 'Becoming' Part 1 Angel didn't meet Whistler until 1996.

Notes: *Dark Midnight* allows a lot of riffs on a vampire TV series, although its central conceit – a vampire DJ – echoes LaCroix in *Forever Knight*. Wolfram & Hart are mentioned in passing. Filming takes place outside a bar called 'Hannigan's'. Doyle calls on Mama Ntombi, a wise-woman and Angel seeks help from occult investigator Bascomb, whom he knew about before coming to L.A.

close to the ground

Writer: Jeff Mariotte
Published: August 2000
Tagline: Fortune and glory don't always come *naturally* . . .

An ancient sorcerer, Mordractus, needs Angel as bait in order to complete a spell that will summon the demon Balor. Angel is hired by film producer, Jack Willitts, to look after his daughter, Karinna, but this is to distract him from Mordractus's schemes.

There's A Ghost in My House: Phantom Dennis helps Cordy choose clothes before she goes for her first day at Monument Pictures.

It's a Designer Label!: Gucci and Mark Clark are name-checked.

References: *Police Woman*, *Batman*, Warren Beatty, Julia Roberts, Kevin Costner, James Cameron, Barbie, *People* magazine, Richard Gere, Tom Cruise, *The Ed Sullivan*

Show, *Seinfeld*, *Friends*, Philip Marlowe, Sam Spade, The Three Stooges.

The Charisma Show: Cordy's dreams of becoming a starlet turn out to be a job as a tour guide at the studio.

Sex and Drugs and House: Karinna takes Angel clubbing (the techno beat hurts his ears).

Logic, Let Me Introduce You to This Window: Angel needs to be invited twice into Karinna's house. He says that he's making eighteenth-century judgements about the twenty-first, but since this is set before Doyle's death, it has to be 1999. No one notices, in a nightclub filled with mirrors, that Angel has no reflection.

Notes: The pacing feels a bit off at times, but otherwise this could have made a good episode. According to this, Angel made the decision to help people in 1898 after seeing another vampire kill (which is contradicted by **29**, 'Darla' and *Buffy*: 'Becoming' Part 1). We see Angel getting obsessed with a case – but this time, unlike with Darla, he listens. Doyle doesn't know who Willow is. Trevor Lockley remembers Angel from **6**, 'Sense and Sensitivity'. Wolfram & Hart take over Wilitts's responsibilities at Monument after his fall from grace.

shakedown

Writer: Don DeBrandt
Published: November 2000
Tagline: A natural disaster with supernatural causes . . .

Doyle has a vision of L.A. suffering the Big Earthquake. He, Angel and Cordelia are caught between the demon Serpentene and the Earth-core dwelling Tremblors – but how do Wolfram & Hart fit into the picture?

It's a Designer Label!: Versace, and Cordy gets help from a Serpentene demon who works at Neiman-Marcus.

References: *Armageddon*, Hulk Hogan, Mr Potato Head, The Mole Men (from *Superman*), *Vogue*, Wendy's burger chain, *Dracula*, *Batman*, *The Twilight Zone*, Marvel Comics, *Wonder Woman*, Smashing Pumpkins, *Ally*

McBeal, Barney the dinosaur, Hannibal Lecter, *Baywatch*, *The Flintstones*, *Xena: Warrior Princess*, The Marlboro Man, Monopoly, baseball star Roger Clemens, Wile E. Coyote, The Boulder Brothers, *Miami Vice*, *The Great Escape* and *The Wizard of Oz*.

L.A.-Speak: 'I know this bitchin' dress. It'll look great on you!' Angel is told . . .

Cigarettes and Alcohol: Cordy gets drunk with the Serpentene. Doyle and Angel hit the bars.

Logic, Let Me Introduce You to This Window: Cordy casually drinks with demons. This is the same Cordelia who was nearly sacrificed to a serpent god in *Buffy*: 'Reptile Boy'?

Notes: Angel was in Madrid and Lisbon in 1755 with Darla (it's possible, though **29**, 'Darla' suggests they came directly to England after leaving Ireland). Angel knows the words to 'Old Hundredth' (Psalm 100). He saw Mozart and Beethoven perform when they were children.

hollywood noir

Writer: Jeff Mariotte
Published: January 2001
Tagline: All that glitters is sometimes *evil* . . .

Angel Investigations and the LAPD get caught up in Private Detective Mike Slade's vendetta against the man who killed him. In 1961 . . .

It's a Designer Label!: Cordy sports DKNY drawstring pants.

References: *The Untouchables*, Leonardo DiCaprio, *Friends* actor Giovanni Ribisi, Freddie Prinze Jr, The Dave Clark Five, The Rat Pack, *Flash Gordon*, *Casper*, Humphrey Bogart, Elvis, *Family Fortunes*, *77 Sunset Strip*, Greta Garbo, *Cagney & Lacey*, *This is Your Life*, *Nancy Drew*, *Who Wants to be a Millionaire?*, Audrey Hepburn, George Hamilton, Dr Seuss.

Cigarettes and Alcohol: Betty was a cigarette girl at the Rialto Lounge.

Logic, Let Me Introduce You to This Window: Would Betty McCoy have been able to afford luxury items like a TV and a hi-fi in 1961?

Notes: A weird mixture of private detective schlock and an *Angel* story that doesn't quite gel. Which is a shame because a lot of the elements and the writing style are genuinely excellent.

avatar

Writers: John Passarella
Published: March 2001
Tagline: Evil has a new domain . . .

Eliot Grundy is using the demon Yunk'sh to achieve fortune and glory, ignoring the fact that Yunk'sh is killing the people he meets in web chatrooms. Angel, Kate and the cult of the Omni are all on the demon's path.

Denial, Thy Name is Kate: Kate believes that the demonic strength used on the victim meant the perpetrator was using PCP (Phencyclidine).

It's a Designer Label!: Louis Vuitton, Prada, Docker, Rockpants.

References: *South Park*, WWF, Jay Leno, David Letterman, *The Today Show*, *The Fly*, *Superman*, *Marvin the Martian*, Brad Pitt, Jean-Claude Van Damme, Jude Law.

Sex and Drugs and Rock'n'Roll: Like the demon in **2**, 'Lonely Heart', Yunk'sh can assume any form. He entices his victims, then devours them.

Logic, Let Me Introduce You to This Window: For someone who knows nothing about computers, Angel is amazingly *au fait* with chatrooms when talking to Kate. But, later, he has to ask Cordelia about them. Cordy is said to have become part of the Scooby Gang because of her relationship with Xander.

Notes: When Yunk'sh assumes the visage of the person each of the detectives wants, Doyle sees Cordy, Angel sees Buffy – and Cordy sees Doyle.

soul trade

Writers: Thomas E Sniegoski
Published: May 2001
Tagline: The black market is trading on humanity . . .

Uforia is a new drug formed from human souls, specially for the demons of L.A. Angel has a vested interest in getting to the bottom of the trade – particularly when he is haunted by the ghost of his sister.

It's a Designer Label!: Veronique Boutique for hair and nails and a Versace dress.

References: *Pokémon*, Barney (Doyle hates him), *Love Story*, *Steel Magnolias*, *Beaches*, *ER*, Brad Pitt, Gwyneth Paltrow, *Doogie Howser MD*, *Cats*, *Starlight Express*, *Phantom of the Opera*, *Evita*, *There's Something About Mary*, *Jaws*, Jeeves, *Batman*, Bram Stoker, Indiana Jones.

The Charisma Show: Cordy assumes the alias Vicky Vale to fool the demons. She also acts as *Distract-O-Girl* and has a great scene in which she decides what weapons to take with her when she goes to the rescue.

Logic, Let Me Introduce You to This Window: Angel has been in L.A. for over a year at this stage, which cannot possibly be right.

Notes: Angel hates the music of Andrew Lloyd Webber. Doyle tries to catch the older audience by claiming he works for Angelo, *The Saint*! Harry, Doyle's ex-wife, has dumped Richard, the demon who needed Doyle's death in 7, 'The Bachelor Party'.

Angel and the Internet

To a series such as *Angel*, the Internet is the only fan forum that actually matters. *Buffy* has been called 'the first *true* child of the Internet age'. If this is accurate (and it pretty much is), then *Angel* is the medium's first grandchild – a series not only born *on*, but also (due to the instantaneous nature of fan reaction) *by* the Net. Within weeks of *Angel*'s debut a flourishing Net community had spawned newsgroups, mailing lists and websites, often as annexes to already existing *Buffy* domains. As with most fandoms much of what has emerged is great, but there's also some downright scary stuff out there. This is a rough guide to it.

Newsgroups: The *Buffy* usenet group alt.tv.buffy-v-slayer also includes posts about *Angel*, debating the merits of new and old episodes. It's often a stimulating forum with debate encouraged. However, it also, at times, attracts a distinctly aggressive and vocal contingent who are unhappy with the current direction of both shows and want the whole world to know it. The group also, sadly, features that curse of usenet: 'trolling' (people who send offensive messages specifically to stir up trouble). Hell hath no fury like overgrown schoolchildren with access to a computer. A case in point: when the last edition of *Slayer* was published, it was criticised by some posters because they regarded the above one-line description of trolling as a personal insult to them. This generated a heated thread with over 150 postings. All of which proves that, as with many fandoms, some of the users of *a.t.b-v-s* like talking about *Buffy* and *Angel* but mostly they prefer talking about themselves. Still, on a good day, it's worth popping in to see what everybody thinks of the latest episode. The *Angel* newsgroup, alt.tv.angel, began before the series and had somewhat humble origins (many initial posts were from fans of *Touched By An Angel* wondering why everyone was talking about vampires). It's growing steadily and has yet to acquire much of the cynicism and self-aggrandisement of the *Buffy* group. There's also some official input as Tim Minear drops in occasionally.

alt.fan.buffy-v-slayer.creative is a fan-fiction forum and carries a wide range of missing adventures, character vignettes, 'shipper' (relationship-based erotica) and 'slash' (same-sex erotica), some of it of a very high standard. uk.media.tv.buffy-v-slayer and uk.media.tv.angel both feature gossip from the States. There are also lively newsgroups in Europe (alt.buffy.europe) and Australia (aus.tv.buffy) where *Buffy* and *Angel* have big followings.

Mailing Lists: More relaxed than usenet, at http://groups.yahoo.com/ you'll find numerous *Buffy* groups listed. Many are 'members only', like the impressive *JossBtVS* discussion list which also features daily updates on the activities of the cast and crew. Other lists include *angelseries*, a large general *Angel* group with over 600 members, *YesWesNews* (a pro-Wesley group) and *BuffyWatchers* (basically, a group of friends, including this author, who allow visitors to join us for after-dinner chats. A *Buffy* and *Angel* version of the Algonquin club, if you will).

Posting Boards: www.thewb.com/angel/ is the official posting board site, which includes regular contributions from Joss Whedon and other members of the production team and cast (including writers like David Fury and Mere Smith). This is an excellent forum (particularly as it features a direct line to the production office). The only problem is the sheer size of it. Asked about his Internet usage, Joss told *DreamWatch*, 'I came to it late. I'm still: "What's download?"'

Websites: There are thousands of sites relating to both *Buffy* and *Angel*. What follows is a (by no means definitive) list of some of the author's favourites. Many of these are also part of webrings that link to other related sites. An hour's surfing can get you to some interesting places. Joss Whedon confirmed in an online interview that he often surfs the Net specifically looking for comments and to see which subjects fans are discussing. 'What they're liking, not liking, all of that stuff. I'm fascinated by it.'

Disclaimer: websites are transitory at the best of times and this information, though accurate when written, may be woefully out of date by publication.

UK Sites: The BBC's *Buffy Online* (www.bbc.co.uk/cult/buffy/index.shtml) has become a resource of considerable depth and scope, with one of the most up-to-date *Buffy* and *Angel* news services on the Net. It also features numerous exclusive interviews, video clips and a plethora of other goodies.

US Sites: http://slayground.net (*Little Willow's Slayground*) is a delightful treasure-trove of photos, articles and reviews, plus all of the latest news. Includes 'Who Says?', the VIP archive of the *BtVS* Posting Board, fun sections like 'The Xander Dance Club', filmographies and official webpages for *Buffy* regulars Danny Strong (Jonathan) and Amber Benson (Tara). There's also a useful link to the *Keeper Sites* (www.stakeaclaim.net/), a webring with numerous pages. Again it's possible to find something new on each visit. www.buffymusic.net/ (*Buffy and Angel Music Pages*), Leslie Remencus's frequently updated site, is devoted to the music on the two shows plus has lots of interviews, musical allusions, tour dates, etc. An absolute gem.

http://rhiannon.dreamhost.com/angel/ (*The Angel Annex Presented by The Sunnydale Slayers*) is part of the 'Suns' group and was, according to the authors, set up by 'a gang of people ... who wanted to talk about, lust after and discuss in depth *Buffy*'. It includes fiction, well-written reviews and biographies.

http://www.geocities.com/angelsecrets (*Angel's Secrets*), Chrystal's long-running site, is devoted to all things Boreanaz and is always worth a visit. Includes a regularly updated news section with numerous links to obscure interviews.

http://sanctuary.digitalspace.net/ (*The Sanctuary Devoted to David Boreanaz and Angel*) prides itself on being 'the most comprehensive site on *Angel* on the Net'. It's certainly very impressive, with extensive fan fiction, a very interesting rumours page ('The Runes') and a section containing detailed episode summaries.

http://angel.fcpages.com/ (*Two Demons, A Girl & A Bat-Cave*). A domain that shares many qualities with the equally impressive *Complete Buffy Episode Guide* (www.buffyguide.com). Full episode synopses, reviews and character studies are the hallmark of this intelligent site. It does take a while to load, however, so be patient.

http://www.ayelle.net/thecityofangel/ (*The City of Angel*) is another highly entertaining and enthusiastic site with a big section on 'creative fandom' (fiction and artwork).

www.angelicslayer.com/angelsoul/main.html (*An Angel's Soul*) is a spin-off from the legendary *Buffy Cross and Stake* (www.angelicslayer.com/tbcs/main.html) and has a very impressive media section (an invaluable research tool) containing interviews and lots of good links.

http://cityofangel.com/ (*City of Angel*). The design of this domain is first rate and it has lots of unique content, with production staff and comics interviews, a 'behind the scenes' section and excellent news coverage.

http://slayerfanfic.com/ (*The Slayer Fanfic Archive*) is, as the name suggests, a site dedicated to *Buffy* and *Angel* fan fiction with links to related pages offering all sorts of amateur writing.

www.buffysmut.com (*Bad Girls*) is designed for those adults yet to discover the joys of shipper and slash fanfic.

www.tdsos.com/ (*The Darker Side of Sunnydale*) is another excellent fanfic site. 'I love fanfic,' Jane Espenson noted on the Posting Board. 'I'm not really allowed to read *Buffy* [stories] but I do read other fandoms. There's some great stuff out there. Also some crappy stuff, but people should feel free to read/write that as well.' On the same forum, Joss Whedon has commented, 'On the subject of fanfic, I *am* aware that a good deal of it is naughty. My reaction to that is mixed; on the one hand, these are characters played by friends of mine, and the idea that someone is describing them in *full naughtitude* is a little creepy. On the other hand, eroticising the lives of fictional characters you care about is something we all do, if only in our heads, and it certainly shows that people care. So, I'm not really against erotic-fic and I certainly don't mind the other kind. I wish I'd had this kind of forum when I was a kid.' Marti Noxon, meanwhile, is full of praise for amateur writers. 'We're in a weird position,' she told the *Washington Post*. 'It's flattering because a universe you're a part of has inspired people to continue imagining.' The writers, however, have to be careful. A TV story covering similar ground to previously published fanfic could result in accusations of plagiarism. 'Because of legalities, we have to be judicious about how much we read,' notes Marti.

Both Charisma and David have numerous unofficial websites: www.charisma-carpenter.com (*Charisma-Carpenter. com*) and www.david-boreanaz.com [*David-Boreanaz.com*] are amongst the best. There are also several nice Alexis Denisof pages like *Go Wes Go* (http://naturalblues.org/ gowesgo/) and *AD Unofficial* (http://ad.elusio.net/). Christian Kane also has a terrific unofficial website *Christian-Kane.net* (http://christiankane.cjb.net/) which includes details on his musical activities. Curiously, one of the best general *Angel* sites is dedicated to a former cast member. Tara O'Shea's *Doyle – Glenn Quinn* (http://ljconstantine. com/doyle/) is a beautiful celebration of both the series and the late actor. Widespread coverage of all aspects of the show and a huge archive section make this a must-see for all *Angel* fans. As Suzanne Campagna notes in *Intergalactic Enquirer*, 'It's a wonderful site, easy to navigate [with] lots to look at.'

Miscellaneous: Space prevents a thoroughly detailed study of the vast array of *Angel* websites from around the world, but a few deserve to be highlighted. For European readers, French site *Black Angel* (www.ifrance.com/blackangelfan/), Germany's *Angel Investigations* (www.angelinvestigations. de/) and *The Italian Angel Page* (www.buffysweetslayer. com/italianangelpage/) offer impressive coverage, whilst readers down-under need to check out the Australian site *Angel's Southern Cross* (www.angelfire.com/wa2/ angelthorn/).

Danny Sag's *Buffy and Angel Episode Title Explanations* (www.geocities.com/glpoj/buffy/) is also well worth a visit. http://angelsredemption.mainpage.net/ (*Countdown to Re-*

demption) has several unique features. Finally, www.
buffysearch.com ('your portal to the *Buffy* and *Angel*
community') is an invaluable search engine that includes
links to most of the above sites and hundreds more.

Redeeming Qualities

> Marcus: 'You did terrible things when you were bad,
> didn't you? And now you are trying so hard to do
> good ... What do you want, Angel?'
> Angel: 'I want forgiveness.'
> – 'In the Dark'

Redemption is one of the key elements in epic storytelling. In hundreds of literary styles from the Greek and Roman myths and the Bible onwards the quest for atonement to transcend past unworthy deeds remains a beguiling and fascinating one for most audiences. Because, like the man said, 'we've *all* got *something* to atone for'.

In *Angel*, the central character has more to purge than most. A killer without compassion or feeling ('the meanest vampire in all the land,' according to Doyle's fairytale version of Angelus's origins), he spent over a century engaged in deranged acts of torture, mayhem and ultraviolence. And he did it with a song in his heart. Angelus killed not through fear, or madness, or a need to survive. He killed because he *enjoyed* it, and it's the realisation of this (via a gypsy curse, admittedly) that allows him to understand what he has to put right. When Doyle tells him that the Ring of Amara is 'your redemption. It's what you've been waiting for,' in 3, 'In the Dark', Angel replies: 'I did a lot of damage in my day.' Doyle asks: 'You don't get the ring because your period of self-flagellation is over. Think of all the people you could help between nine and five.' Angel isn't satisfied: 'The whole world is designed for them, so much that they have no idea what goes on around them after dark. They don't see the weak ones lost in the night, or the things that prey on them. If I join them, maybe I'd stop seeing too ...'

It's a theme that is repeated throughout *Angel*. All of the regular characters have their own dark places and a need to shine some light on them. Like alcoholics giving up the drink (a metaphor that the series intended to take very literally at one time) they have to realise themselves that they *need* to change before the process of redemption can begin.

For Cordelia, in **5**, 'Rm W/a Vu', a new home offers her a fresh beginning. 'Working for redemption,' as Angel puts it. 'I'm still getting punished' she laments. 'For everything I said in high school just because I could get away with it. Then it all ended and I had to pay. But [with] this apartment, I could be me again. Like I couldn't be *that* awful if I get to have a place like that?' It's when she comes to terms with her past that she receives her reward.

In **12**, 'Expecting', that process continues. She admits to Wilson that: 'In high school I knew my place and, OK, it was a haughty place and maybe I was a *tad* shallow.' As the season progresses, Cordy also accepts the gift of vision from Doyle and The Powers That Be and, by **22**, 'To Shanshu in L.A.', has come to realise, through being exposed to *everyone*'s pain and suffering, that she and her friends have the chance to do real good: 'I know what's out there. We have a lot of people to help.' In the second season, the visions begin to take their toll. As Wesley tells Angel in **38**, 'Epiphany', they have changed Cordelia radically. But they are now a part of what she is and she even passes up the chance to be rid of them in **44**, 'There's No Place Like Plrtz Glrb'. Her decision not to have sex with the Groosalugg and lose the visions is the flip side of Angel's inability to experience perfect happiness through copulation. They don't because, if they did, the world would be a worse place because of it. And they *know* that.

Doyle discovers in **9**, 'Hero' that 'you never know your strength until you're tested,' is not an empty slogan, but a necessary step to wiping out the past. Doyle thinks that Angel's actions in **8**, 'I Will Remember You' qualify him for special treatment: 'I would have chosen the pleasures of the flesh over duty and honour . . . I just don't have that

strength.' But Doyle, who in **7**, 'The Bachelor Party', tells
Angel that his marriage failed because *he*, rather than
Harriet, could not accept his demon heritage, finally
confronts his darkest secret – his betrayal of his kin – in **9**,
'Hero'. This, it transpires, is why he was cursed. 'The idea
of having family obligations with guys that looked like big
blue pin cushions was . . . too much to take.'

Even when Doyle has made the ultimate sacrifice, the
theme of redemption (his and others) is weightily present
in the immediate aftermath with both Cordelia and Angel
(in **10**, 'Parting Gifts' and **14**, 'I've Got You Under My
Skin' respectively) struggling to cope with their personal
grief and also facing their guilt. In the midst of this, Angel
is further disturbed by 'killing dreams' and the discovery
that one of the unfortunate souls he murdered during his
Angelus days is still active (**11**, 'Somnambulist'): 'I'm
sorry,' he tells Penn, 'for what I turned you into.' He
genuinely means it.

The gap in Cordelia and Angel's lives is partly filled by
the welcome return of Wesley, whose stereotypical stiff
upper lip hides (poorly at times) a decent and emotional
man who cares deeply about his friends. But Wesley, too,
has secrets. An unhappy childhood (**14**, 'I've Got You
Under My Skin', **41**, 'Belonging', something he shares in
common with Angel in **15**, 'The Prodigal'), and an
inferiority complex (**17**, 'Eternity'), almost certainly a
consequence of the emotional burdens placed upon him. 'A
father doesn't have to be possessed to terrorise his
children,' he tells Angel. Perhaps it's for this reason that he
understands Bethany Chaulk's psychosis before anyone
else in **26**, 'Untouched'. 'I'm a fool' he says in **10**, 'Parting
Gifts'. 'I had two Slayers in my care . . . Fire me? I'm
surprised [the Council] didn't cut my head off.' If Angel's
salvation is the knowledge that he has the ability to make
amends; Cordelia's comes from the (lengthy) process that
opens up her world-view to the pain in others; Wesley,
ultimately, is redeemed as a character and a person by the
loyalty he shows to Angel (particularly in **19**, 'Sanctuary'
where he refuses to sell his friend out to the Watcher's

Council even with the promise of reinstatement and forgiveness), Cordy and Gunn (literally taking a bullet for his new friend in **36**, 'The Thin Dead Line'). By **44**, 'There's No Place Like Plrtz Glrb', he's discovering the complex nature of leadership. How, if you try to protect everyone, you end up protecting no one. It's a defining moment at the end of an emotional learning curve.

Redemption is key, also, to the ongoing story of Faith. In **18**, 'Five By Five', we see an anguished and world-weary figure; a girl sick of all the horror in her life and of the taint of evil within her. More even than her two-part appearance in *Buffy*, here we see Faith reaching, literally, the end of the line; sadistically torturing her former Watcher, Wesley, for the simple reason that it will make Angel interested enough to kill her. That she chooses the path of redemption in **19**, 'Sanctuary' is almost entirely down to Angel's refusal to play the vengeance game, however much Buffy may want him to. By refusing to fight her, Angel forces Faith to face herself, and come to terms with what she is, a process that continues in **23**, 'Judgment'. In his argument with Buffy at the end of **19**, 'Sanctuary', Angel realises that *he* has changed, and that, while Buffy has her own life to lead in Sunnydale, his priorities have been altered.

Redemption is there for other characters too. Gunn (in **20**, 'War Zone') survives the loss of the sister he has protected since childhood and emerges a willing convert to Angel's crusade – albeit one who will find the journey, at times, brings him into conflict with demons of his own (**25**, 'First Impressions', **42**, 'Over the Rainbow'). Redemption occurs also, briefly (and then more permanently), for Lindsey McDonald (**21**, 'Blind Faith', **40**, 'Dead End') and equally temporarily for Trevor Lockley (**15**, 'The Prodigal'). The former is seduced back to the dark side after a crisis of conscience much to Angel's regret, only to find that he is ultimately (and beautifully) redeemed through love ... and unrequited love at that. The latter dies with a halo, protecting the daughter he loved but never shared his feelings with. That such tragedy can be found amid the life-affirming qualities of *Angel* gives the series a poetic, almost Shakespearean touch – especially in its ruminations of how being redeemed actually works: 'There's no simple answer,' Angel tells Faith in **19**, 'Sanctuary'. 'I won't lie to you and tell you that it'll be easy because it won't. Just because you've decided to change doesn't mean that the world is ready for you to. The truth is, no matter how much you suffer, no matter how many good deeds you do to try to make up for the past, you may never balance out the cosmic scale.'

For some, the price isn't worth paying. Kate Lockley won't be redeemed until she has learned to accept greater truths than those found in monochrome. The only things in life that are wholly black and white are Laurel and Hardy films and police officers' attitudes. Kate's disbelief in **15**, 'The Prodigal' that 'There are *not-evil* "evil things"?' is a step away from a reality that she is fully aware of. Angel has saved her life on three occasions (**2**, 'Lonely Heart', **6**, 'Sense and Sensitivity', **11**, 'Somnambulist'), yet Kate is, for a long time, unable to accept him as anything other than a monster of the kind that killed her father. That part of Angel's epiphany is no longer to view Kate as the lost cause she seemed to be in **22**, 'To Shanshu in L.A.', is cause for some hope. There is also the case of The Host. Introduced in the second season as – literally – a guardian angel for Angel himself, Lorne also has a redemption to face; that of his relationship with his family and his origins. Again, it's an interesting mirror image of Angel. One killed his family in the search for acceptance, the other left home and never wants to return. But Lorne must, if only to find that his search for a place to truly belong continues in Los Angeles rather than Pylea.

When Wesley tells Angel in **19**, 'Sanctuary', that, 'I hope [Faith] is strong enough to make it. Peace is not an easy thing to find,' Angel's reply isn't a glib or unrealistic one. He, and the audience, are intelligent enough to know that working for redemption doesn't come without a price – philosophical *and* metaphorical. 'She has a chance,' says Angel, which is, ultimately, what the series is all about. It's the – literal – Hope In Hell – the dreams of someone down in the gutter looking up at the stars. It's Cordelia's sudden realisation that the world doesn't end at her garden gate ('that was the *old* me,' she notes in **22**, 'To Shanshu in L.A.', aware that being taken to the edge of insanity has cleansed her of some worthless baggage). There's the maturing of Wesley from a hollow caricature into a man of great promise ('I've confronted more evil . . . done more good while working with Angel than I *ever* did while in the Council's employ,' he tells Collins in **19**, 'Sanctuary'). The selflessness with which Doyle gave his own life to save not only a city but also two friends is mirrored in Angel's rejection of a life-altering gift and, later, the chance of true happiness with Buffy because it wasn't how the story was meant to end. Yet, ironically in Angel's case, the price of redemption may be worth paying after all, when he regains the humanity he lost 240 years ago.

The storylines of Seasons Three and Four concern this endless search of several of the characters to either forget, come to terms with or cancel out elements of their past. It's a central prop in **46**, 'That Vision Thing', **49**, 'Fredless', **55**, 'Birthday', **57**, 'Waiting in the Wings' and **63**, 'The Price', and, also, during the arcs involving Darla's pregnancy, Connor's birth, Wesley's conflict of loyalty, Gunn's murder of Professor Seidel and the returns of both Angelus and Faith. Each of the characters is given, for various reasons, more to atone for and must fight, not only to redeem themselves, but to do so in the sight of their friends as well. 'We've done things we're sure can never be forgiven, but we're always there for each other when it counts,' says Angel in **76**, 'Awakening'. 'We've never let the darkness win . . . because we believe in each other.'

'The road to redemption is a rocky path.'

– 'Judgment'

Select Bibliography

Abery, James, 'Where Angel Fears to Tread', *Shivers*, issue 71, November 1999.

Abery, James, 'Fallen Angel?', *Shivers*, issue 102, January 2003.

Acker, Amy, and Denisof, Alexis, 'Angel's Angels', interview by Jenny Cooney Carrillo, *DreamWatch*, issue 103, March 2003.

'Angel Restores Faith', *DreamWatch*, issue 68, April 2000.

'Angel's Darkest Day', *DreamWatch*, issue 103, March 2003.

Anthony, Ted, '12 Weeks After Columbine, Delayed "Buffy" airs', *Associated Press*, 12 July 1999.

Appelo, Tim and Williams, Stephanie, 'Get Buffed Up – A Definitive Episode Guide', *TV Guide*, July 1999.

Ausiello, Michael, '*Angel* Mystery: Will Cordy Wake Up?', *TV Guide*, 26 May 2003.

Atherton, Tony, 'Fantasy TV: The New Reality', *The Ottawa Citizen*, 27 January 2000.

Atkins, Ian, 'Fallen Angel', *Cult Times*, issue 47, August 1999.

Atkins, Ian, 'I Will Remember You' review, *Shivers*, issue 77, May 2000.

Baldwin, Kristen, Fretts, Bruce, Schilling, Mary Kaye, and Tucker, Ken, 'Slay Ride', *Entertainment Weekly*, issue 505, 1 October 1999.

Barratt, Brian, 'Rm W/A Vu', 'Sense and Sensitivity', 'The Bachelor Party' and 'I Will Remember You' reviews, *Xposé*, issue 42, January 2000.

Barratt, Brian, 'First Impressions', 'Untouched', 'Dear Boy' and 'Guise Will Be Guise' reviews, *Xposé*, issue 52, January 2001.

Barratt, Brian, 'Darla', 'The Shroud of Rahmon', 'Trial', 'Reunion' reviews, *Xposé*, issue 53, February 2001.

Barrett, Brian, 'Waiting in the Wings' to 'Sleep Tight', *Xposé*, issue 67, May 2002.

Benz, Julie, 'Little Miss Understood', interview by Ed Gross, *SFX Unofficial Buffy Collection*, 2000.

Benz, Julie, 'Princess of the Night', interview by Ian Spelling, *Starlog*, issue 14, June 2001.

Binns, John, 'Times Past', *Cult TV*, issue 93, June 2003.

Boreanaz, David, Landau, Juliet, and Marsters, James, 'Interview with the Vampires', interview by Tim Appelo, *TV Guide*, September 1998.

Boreanaz, David, 'Leaders of the Pack', interview (with Kerri Russell) by Janet Weeks, *TV Guide*, November 1998.

Boreanaz, David, 'City of Angel', interview by David Richardson, *Xposé*, issue 35, June 1999.

Boreanaz, David, 'Aurora Boreanaz', interview by Sue Schneider, *DreamWatch*, issue 69, May 2000.

Boreanaz, David, 'Good or Bad Angel?', interview by David Richardson, *Shivers*, issue 77, May 2000.

Boreanaz, David, 'Moving On Up', interview by Christina Radish, *DreamWatch*, issue 80, May 2001.

Boreanaz, David, 'Dead Man Talking', interview by Jenny Cooney Carrillo, *Dreamwatch*, issue 96, September 2002.

Boreanaz, David, 'Voice of an Angel', interview by Jean Cummings, *Cult Times*, issue 86, November 2002.

Boreanaz, 'Reflections of the Undead', interview by Joe Nazzaro, *Starburst*, Special 57, March 2003.

Bunson, Matthew, *Vampire: The Encyclopaedia*, Thames and Hudson, 1993.

Campagna, Suze, 'Website of the Month', *Intergalactic Enquirer*, March 2000.

Campagna, Suze, 'Bite Me: The History of Vampires on Television', *Intergalactic Enquirer*, October 2000.

Campagna, Suze, 'The World of Joss Whedon', *Intergalactic Enquirer*, February 2001.

Campagna, Suze, 'TV Tid Bits', *Intergalactic Enquirer*, March 2001.

Carpenter, Charisma, 'Charismatic', interview by Jim Boulter, *SFX*, issue 40, July 1998.

Carpenter, Charisma, 'Femme Fatale', interview by Mike Peake, *FHM*, issue 117, October 1999.

Carpenter, Charisma, 'Charisma Personified', interview by Jennifer Graham, *TV Guide*, 1 January 2000.

Carpenter, Charisma, 'In Step With ...' interview by James Brady, *Parade*, 5 March 2000.

Carpenter, Charisma, 'Charisma!', interview by Ed Gross, *SFX*, issue 75, March 2001.

Carpenter, Charisma, 'Heaven Sent', interview by Jenny Cooney Carrillo, *DreamWatch*, issue 103, March 2003.

Carter, Bill, '*Dawson's Clones*: Tapping into the youth market for all it is, or isn't, worth', *New York Times*, 19 September 1999.

'Chase is On, The', *Cult Times*, issue 82, July 2002.

'Cheers and Jeers', *TV Guide*, 2 December 2000.

Collins, Scott, '*Buffy* star goes to the woodshed over remark about sticking with the WB', *Los Angeles Times*, 30 January 2001.

Cornell, Paul, Day, Martin, and Topping, Keith, *The Guinness Book of Classic British TV*, 2nd edition, Guinness Publishing, 1996.

Cornell, Paul, Day, Martin, and Topping, Keith, *X-Treme Possibilities: A Comprehensively Expanded Rummage Through the X-Files*, Virgin Publishing, 1998.

Cornell, Paul, '20th Century Fox-Hunting', *SFX*, issue 63, April 2000.

Darlington, David, 'Heartthrob' to 'Fredless', *Shivers*, issue 94, December 2001.

Darlington, David, 'Billy' to 'Dad', *Shivers*, issue 95, February 2002.

Darlington, David, 'Waiting in the Wings' to 'Sleep Tight', *Shivers*, issue 97, May 2002.

Darlington, David, 'Deep Down' to 'Slouching Toward Bethlehem', *Shivers*, issue 101, November 2002.

Darlington, David, 'Supersymmetry', to 'Spin the Bottle', *Shivers*, issue 102, January 2003.

Darlington, David, 'Soulless' to 'Salvage', *Shivers*, issue 104, May 2003.

DeKnight, Steven, 'DeKnight in Shining Armour', interview by Joe Nazzaro, *DreamWatch*, issue 103, March 2003.

Denisof, Alexis, 'Vogue Demon Hunter', interview by Matt Springer, *Buffy the Vampire Slayer*, issue 7, Spring 2000.

Denisof, Alexis, 'Half Price', interview by Paul Spragg, *Xposé*, issue 65, March 2002.

Denisof, Alexis, 'The Right Pryce', interview by Steven Eramo, *TV Zone*, issue 150, April 2002.

Denisof, Alexis, 'Denisof On One', interview by Jean Cummings, *Cult Times*, issue 86, November 2002.

Dougherty, Diana, 'Angel – Season One', *Intergalactic Enquirer*, July 2000.

Dushku, Eliza, 'Keeping Faith', interview by Ed Gross, *SFX Unofficial Buffy Collection*, 2000.

Ellis, Martin, 'Bad Girl Does Good', *Shivers*, issue 104, May 2003.

Espenson, Jane, 'Superstar Scribe', interview by Joe Nazzaro, *DreamWatch*, issue 74, November 2000.

Espenson, Jane, 'The Write Stuff', interview by Joe Nazzaro, *DreamWatch*, issue 103, March 2003.

Ferguson, Everett, *Backgrounds of Early Christianity* [second edition], William B. Eerdmans Publishing, 1993.

Francis, Rob, 'Buffy the Vampire Slayer Season 4', *DreamWatch*, issue 71, August 2000.

Francis, Rob, 'TV Heroes', *TV Zone*, Special 45, April 2002.

Fretts, Bruce, 'City of Angel', *Entertainment Weekly*, April 1999.

Gabriel, Jan, *Meet the Stars of Buffy the Vampire Slayer: An Unauthorized Biography*, Scholastic Inc., 1998.

Gammage, Jeff, 'Guardian Angel', *Inquirer*, September 2000.

Gellar, Sarah Michelle, 'Staking the Future', interview by John Mosby, *DreamWatch* issue 61, Sept 1999.

Giglione, Joan, 'Some Shows Aren't Big on TV', *Los Angeles Times*, 25 November 2000.

Gray, Ellen, 'There's nowhere that *Angel* star fears to tread', *Knight Ridder Newspapers*, 24 February 2002.

Green, Michelle Erica, 'Darla and Topolsky Are More Than Bad Girls', *Fandom Inc*, September 2000.

Greenwalt, David, '*Angel* delivers a devil of a time', interview by Charlie Mason, *TV Guide*, 14 August 2001.

Greenwalt, David, 'Angel's Guardian', interview by James Abery, *Shivers*, issue 98, July 2002.

Greenwalt, David, 'Miracles Do happen', interview by Davids Richardson, *Xposé*, issue 76, January 2003.

Gross, Ed, 'The Trial', 'Reunion' reviews, *SFX*, issue 75, March 2001.

Hallett, Andy, 'Angelic Host,' interview by Pat Jankiewicz, *Starburst*, issue 272, April 2001.

Hallett, Andy, 'Smells Like Green Spirit', interview by Tom Mayo, *SFX*, issue 81, August 2001.

Hallett, Andy and Lutz, Mark, 'The two gentlemen of Pylea', interview by Nick Joy, *Starburst*, issue 289, July 2002.

Hannigan, Alyson, 'Willow Pattern', interview by Kate O'Hare, *Sydney Herald News*, 1 February 2003.

Head, Anthony Stewart, 'Heads or Tails', interview by Paul Simpson and Ruth Thomas, *DreamWatch*, issue 69, May 2000.

'Hell is for Heroes', *Entertainment Weekly*, issue 505, 1 October 1999.

Holder, Nancy, *Angel: city of – a novelisation of the series premiere*, Pocket Pulse, December 1999.

Huff, Richard. 'WB Net Returns to Gender-Build on Initial Appeal Among Young Women', *New York Daily News*, 14 September 1999.

Johnson, Allan, 'Willow's Soulful Visit Illuminates *Angel*', *Chicago Tribune*, 19 March 2003.

Katz, Paul S, 'Fans rally for their favorite vampire', *TV Guide*, 12 April 2003.

Katner, Ben with Michael Ausiello, 'Is *Angel* Livin' On A Prayer?', *TV Guide*, 5 May 2003.

Littlefield, Kinney, 'Avenging Angel', *The Orange County Register*, October 1999.

Lowry, Brian, 'WB Covers A Trend Too Well', *Los Angeles Times*, 29 June 2000.

Malcolm, Shawna, 'Angel Bites', *TV Guide*, 4 May 2002.

Marsters, James and Caulfield, Emma, 'Vamping It Up', *Alloy*, Summer 2000.

Marster, James, 'I, Spike', interview by Ed Gross, *SFX Unofficial Buffy Collection*, 2000.

Martino, John, 'Dead, Sexy', *Shivers*, issue 96, March 2002.

Mason, Dave, 'When Bad Things Happen To Good Vampires', Scripps Howard News Service, 22 October 2002.

Mauger, Anne-Marie, 'Staking their Claims', *Sky Customer Magazine*, January 2001.

May, Dominic, '*Angel* co-creator says show's future is secure', *TV Zone*, issue 150, May 2002.

May, Dominic, and Spilsbury, Tom, 'Return to Sunnydale High for Buffy Season 7', *TV Zone*, issue 153, July 2002.

May, Dominic, *Angel* 'I Quit', *TV Zone*, issue 154, August 2002.

May, Dominic, '*Angel* Gains An Extra Soul', *TV Zone*, issue 164, June 2003.

McIntee, David, *Delta Quadrant: The Unofficial Guide to Voyager*, Virgin Publishing, 2000.

Middendorf, Tracy, *Insider: The Next Guest Thing*, interview by Shawn Malcom, *TV Guide*, 15 January 2000.

Minear, Tim, '*Angel*: Year One', interview by Ed Gross, *SFX Unofficial Buffy Collection*, 2000.

Mosby, John, 'UK-TV', *DreamWatch*, issue 71, September 2000.

Mosby, John, 'Last Writes', *Impact*, issue 127, July 2002.

Nelson, Resa, 'Angel makes us ask: why do bad boys make us feel so good?', *Realms of Fantasy*, Feb 2000.

Nelson, Resa, 'To Live and Die in L.A.', *Science Fiction World*, issue 1, June 2000.

Noxon, Marti, 'Soul Survivor', *DreamWatch*, issue 63, November 1999.

O'Hare, Kate, 'WB's Core Series *Buffy* and *Angel* Cross Time and Space', *TV Weekly*, 12 November 2000.

O'Hare, Kate, 'While *Buffy* Rages, *Angel* Still Flies', *St Paul Pioneer Press*, 15 April 2001.

Pearce, Scott, 'Spike is in, Cordelia is out', *Deseret News*, 26 May 2003.

Queenan, Joe, 'Cross-Checked By An Angel', *TV Guide*, 15 April 2000.

Richards, J August, 'Gunn Fighting', interview by Mark Wyman, *Cult Times*, Special 16, 2000.

Richards, J August, 'Smoking Gunn', interview by Steve Eramo, *TV Zone*, issue 136, February 2001.

Richards, J August, 'Real Gunn Kid', interview by Paul Simpson and Ruth Thomas, *SFX*, issue 81, August 2001.

Richards, J August, 'Gunn Fighter', interview by Jennifer Dudley, *Sydney Herald Sun*, 29 January 2003.

Richards, J August, 'Charles in Charge', interview by Steven Eramo, *TV Zone*, issue 2003, February 2003.

Richards, J August, and Kartheiser, Vincent, 'Younger Guns', interview by Jenny Cooney Carrillo, *DreamWatch*, issue 102, March 2003.

Richardson, David, 'The House Always Wins' to 'Spin the Bottle', *Xposé*, issue 76, January 2003.

Robins, Max J, 'To Be Or WB? It's No Longer A Question', *TV Guide*, 1 January 2003.

Robson, Ian, 'Action Reply: Buffy's Show'll Slay You' ('City Of' review), *Sunday Sun*, 9 January 2000.

Romanov, Stephanie, 'The Rise of the Romanov Empire', interview by Nick Joy, *DreamWatch*, issue 96, September 2002.

Romanov, Stephanie, 'Naughty, But Nice', interview by Steven Eramo, *TV Zone*, issue 162, April 2003.

Roush, Matt, 'The Roush Review', *TV Guide*, 11 December 1999.

Roush, Matt, 'The Roush Review: Alluring *Angel* Stingless Scorpion', *TV Guide*, 17 February 2001.

Roush, Matt, 'The Roush Review: Great Performances – Andy Hallett', *TV Guide*, 21 April 2001.

Roush, Matt, 'Daddy Darkest', *TV Guide*, 13 April 2002.

Roush, Matt, 'Roush Rave', *TV Guide*, 8 March 2003.

Sangster, Jim and Bailey, David, *Friends Like Us: The Unofficial Guide to Friends* [revised edition], Virgin Publishing, 2000.

'Sarah gets a spanking: *Buffy* star forced to eat humble-pie after "Quit" gaff', *Daily News*, 31 January 2001.

Sepinwall, Alan, '*Buffy* Network Switch Could Slay TV Industry Practices,' *St Paul Pioneer Press*, 29 April 2001.

Shaar Murray, Chalres, 'A passionately perverse sexiness', *The Word*, issue 4, June 2003.

Simpson, Paul and Thomas, Ruth, 'Interview With The Vampire', *DreamWatch*, issue 62, October 1999.

Simpson, Paul and Thomas, Ruth, 'The Lizard King', *SFX*, issue 80, July 2001.

Smith, Jim, 'This Hollywood Life', *Starburst*, issue 283, February 2002.

Spelling, Ian, 'Biting Talent – An Interview With Charisma Carpenter', *Starlog*, May 2000.

Stanley, TL, 'Is It the End of the Road for *Buffy–Angel* Connection?, *Los Angeles Times*, 21 May 2001.

Streisand, Betsy, 'Young, hip and no-longer-watching-Fox', *US News & World Report*, 15 November 1999.

Topping, Keith, *Slayer: The Revised and Updated Unofficial Guide to Buffy the Vampire Slayer*, Virgin Books, 2000.

Topping, Keith, *High Times: The Unofficial & Unauthorised Guide to Roswell*, Virgin Books, 2001.

Topping, Keith, *Inside Bartlet's White House: An Unofficial and Unauthorised Guide to The West West*, Virgin Books, 2002.

Topping, Keith, *Beyond the Gate: The Unofficial and Unauthorised Guide to Stargate SG-1*, Telos Publishing, 2002.

Topping Keith, *Slayer: The Next Generation: An Unofficial and Unauthorised Guide to Season Six of Buffy the Vampire Slayer*, Virgin Books, 2003.

Topping, Keith, *A Day in the Life: The Unofficial and Unauthorised Guide to 24*, Telos Publishing, 2003.

Topping, Keith, 'Angel Delight', *DreamWatch*, issue 65, January 2000.

Topping, Keith, '*Sed Quis Custodiet Ipsos Custodes?*', *Intergalactic Enquirer*, May 2001.

Topping, Keith, 'Has *Buffy* Jumped the Shark?', *Shivers*, issue 97, May 2002.

Topping, Keith, '*Le Cirque des Vampires*', *Shivers*, issue 100, September 2001.

Topping, Keith, 'Reviews 2002: *Angel*', *TV Zone*, Special 45, October 2002.

Topping, Keith, *Angel* Season Four reviews, *TV Zone*, issues 157–164, November 2002–June 2003.

Topping, Keith, 'So Let Me Rest in Peace', *TV Zone*, issue 158, December 2002.

Topping, Keith, 'Do You Know This Man?', *TV Zone*, issue 160, February 2003.

Topping, Keith, 'This town ain't big enough . . .', *Shivers*, issue 107, September 2003.

Topping, Keith, 'Soul to Soul', *Shivers*, issue 108, October 2003.

Torres, Gina, 'Heaven Scent?', interview by Paul Spragg, *Cult Times*, issue 93, June 2003.

Tucker, Ken, 'Angel Baby', *Entertainment Weekly*, 3 December 1999.

Udovitch, Mim, 'What Makes Buffy Slay?', *Rolling Stone*, issue 840, 11 May 2000.

Weir, William, 'Wesleyan Mafia Racks Up Credits: New Center For Film Studies Is Evidence Of A College Program Building On Success', The Hartford Courant, 30 December 2002.

Whedon, Joss, 'How I Got To Do What I Do', interview by Wolf Schneider, *teen movieline*, issue 1, March 2000.

Whedon, Joss, 'Whedon, Writing and Arithmetic', interview by Joe Mauceri, *Shivers*, issue 77, May 2000.

Whedon, Joss, 'Blood Lust', interview by Rob Francis, *Dream-Watch*, issues 71–72, August/September, 2000.

Whedon, Joss, 'Prophecy Boy', interview by Matt Springer with Mike Stokes, *Buffy the Vampire Slayer*, issue 20, May 2001.

Whedon, Joss, 'Buffy, R.I.P?', interview by John Mosby, *Dream-Watch*, issue 84, September 2001.

Whedon, Joss, 'The Wonderful World of Whedon', interview by Ian Spelling, *Cult Times*, issue 79, April 2002.

Wigmore, Gareth, 'Powers That Be Wanted Us Here', *TV Zone*, issue 154, August 2002.

Wilde, MJ, 'The TV Queen', *Albuquerque Tribune*, 1 October 2002.

Wright, Matthew, 'Endings and New Beginnings', *Science Fiction World*, issue 2, July 2000.

Wyman, Mark, 'Buffy Joins The Banned – A Fable for the Internet Age', *Shivers*, issue 68, August 1999.

Wyman, Mark, 'The Thin Dead Line', 'Reprise', 'Epiphany' reviews, *TV Zone*, issue 140, July 2001.

Wyman, Mark, 'Who's The Daddy?', *TV Zone*, issue 150, April 2002.

Wyman, Mark, 'The Price' to 'Tomorrow', *TV Zone*, issue 152, June 2002.

Grr! Arrrgh!

For a while, as Season Four careered towards its dramatic conclusion, it looked as though this may have been our final glimpse of the activities of Angel Investigations. The perilous nature of US network television is such that even if a show is highly regarded critically (and *Angel* undoubtedly is), if the ratings aren't up to scratch then the series is unlikely to last. *Angel*'s ratings have always been in that awkward borderline region – never so bad that it was an *obvious* candidate for cancellation but, conversely, never so high as to be free of the threat. With *Buffy* about to end, there was a real danger during early 2003 that Mutant Enemy's entire production would be closing for good. Following several months of speculation, however, the revamp proposed by the production team in **88**, 'Home' paid off and the series was picked up in May by the WB for a fifth year.

The network had delayed the decision whilst it looked at its other drama pilots and negotiated a new licensing deal with 20th Century Fox which also, happily, includes options for years six and seven of *Angel*. Whilst there was a lot of behind-the-scenes manoeuvring over the renewal, Jordan Levin, the WB's Entertainment President, said it was a relatively easy choice and that it 'felt like the right thing to do'. Additionally, '*Dawson's Creek* taught us the value of being able to provide closure for a show that's been important to it's audience. With *Angel*, it felt like it would've been extremely abrupt to have brought the whole mythology of *Buffy* to an end,' Levin told *Deseret News*. Levin also noted that the WB would pay Fox more for episodes next year – meaning the network won't actually make a profit on *Angel*.

It will be something of a homecoming for Joss Whedon, who is likely to be working close to full time on *Angel* next year. 'Part of the appeal was getting the team back together,' Levin noted in another interview with *scifi.com*. 'We still feel a strong, proprietary interest in *Buffy*. The finale was emotionally a big deal for all of us at the network.' *Angel* will remain in its 9 p.m. Wednesday slot on the network, again being broadcast opposite big-hitting rivals like NBC's *The West Wing* and ABC's *The Bachelor*. However, *Angel*'s lead-in show, at least, couldn't be much better – one of the WB's best-rated series, *Smallville*. It was also confirmed that James Marsters would be joining the regular cast, reprising his popular role as Spike, the (second) vampire with a soul. 'We think Spike could add something to the show,' Tim Minear told *Cult TV*. 'He's a great character and a great actor.' David Boreanaz was equally delighted. 'The addition of someone like [James] will be fantastic. He's been stuck in a small town for too long. He needs to get out in a big city and see where the big dogs play.' So, how would Spike be returned after the very public death he suffered in the *Buffy* finale? 'Joss is obviously a very creative person,' noted Levin. 'He hasn't let us down in the past and I'm sure that he will figure out a way.' Fans immediately began to speculate on the prophecy of Shanshu (see **22**, 'To Shanshu in L.A.'), which states that the vampire with a soul, once he fulfills his destiny, will become human. It didn't, of course, say *which* vampire with a soul. 'That's *an* interpretation,' Joss told *TV Guide*. 'It may become *the* interpretation if we decide to go that way.'

However, as one door opens, another closes, and the news that Charisma Carpenter would not be returning for Season Five was greeted with disappointment and surprise by many fans. Her departure 'makes way for characters like Spike and others', said Levin. Sensing a potential scandal, *TV Guide* asked Whedon specifically about the circumstances of Carpenter's departure. 'We felt like we had taken that story about as far as it could go,' Joss said, noting that the Angel/Cordelia romance had not been popular with fans, a claim that has been disputed by many within the *Angel* fan community. Additionally, it does seem rather contradictory for Whedon to suggest that this move was designed to appease fans when, just a year earlier, he had told many of those same fans, outraged at the death of Tara in *Buffy*, that it was his job to give them what they needed, *not* what they wanted. 'I'm hoping that we'll get Charisma to do some episodes sometime during the year,' continued Joss. 'She's a new mother, so I'm waiting to hear what her schedule is like.' Asked if the parting had been on good terms, Whedon's reply was enigmatic: 'That's stuff between us and not stuff that I would talk about in an interview.' Amy Acker was somewhat caught off guard with questions concerning Carpenter during an interview with *Sci-fi Wire*. 'She's been doing it for a long time and now she has the baby, so she has two jobs now,' Acker replied. As for Charisma herself, according to the *Watch With Kirsten* website, the actress had stated during early 2003 that David Greenwalt was always the biggest supporter of Cordelia. 'He really *was* her champion,' Charisma was quoted as saying. 'He suggested that I was the perfect nemesis for Angel. Seeing him go, I was worried personally because Cordelia has always been his baby.' Immediately after leaving *Angel*, Charisma flew to Montreal to begin working on a TV movie, *See Jane Date*, with Zachary Levi and *Charmed* star Holly Marie Combs. Marsters was also due to be spending the summer expanding his CV, appearing in *Italian Heat* with Sean Bean and Derek Jacobi. Sadly this was postponed.

Running *Angel*'s fifth season will be Jeff Bell, who made such a good job of the previous year, and in such difficult circumstances. Tim Minear's involvement is likely to diminish as his work on Fox's mid-season show *Wonderfalls* increases. Having, in effect, provided the pilot for the future of *Angel* with **88**, 'Home', Minear feels that the new direction 'allows [*Angel*] to break out of its cannibalising soap opera-ness. It's not feeding on itself,' he told *zap2it.com*. 'There are more opportunities to tell stand-alone stories. It gives all of the characters something new to do.' David Greenwalt, who will continue to act as a consulting producer, believes that *Angel* could match *Buffy* and run for seven years, but notes that the new set-up will enable characters to face new dilemmas. 'Obviously [Wolfram & Hart] wish to corrupt our people and some of them will be corrupted,' he noted in an Internet interview. 'Gunn is going to be the coolest ... Lorne is in heaven because he gets to talk to Michael Jackson. Meanwhile they can use Wolfram & Hart to help people.' Greenwalt also says that he hopes Sarah Michelle Gellar may find the time in her expanding movie career to make an appearance. 'I bet you'll see her,' he noted. 'David's done a lot for her. When we launched the show, she showed up on the set in Downtown L.A. in the middle of the night with a cake. She's quite capable of the big, lovely gesture.' Another returning actor will be Vincent Kartheiser, who has been contracted for one episode suggesting that Connor's story is far from over.

Angel's fifth season began on 1 October 2003 with a Jos Whedon episode, 'Conviction', which sees the team some weeks into their running of Wolfram & Hart. Angel *loves* his fleet of cars, though he feels the Special Ops team who follow him everywhere cramp his style somewhat. Fred's having fun in the Practical Science department, Gunn acquires knowledge that the team put to good use and Lorne enjoys hanging out with the celebrities that the company has as clients. Only Wesley, it seems, sees a downside to their new position. There's a new face in the office: Eve, the team's liaison to the senior partners, played by *Boston Public*'s Sarah Thompson. And familiar faces, too, with the reappearance of Harmony, whom Wesley hires as Angel's secretary and, at the episode's climax, a ghostly Spike.

The ramifications of Spike's return from the afterlife are central to David Fury's 'Just Rewards'. 'I must be in hell,' Spike notes. No, confirms Lorne, it's Los Angeles. 'A lot of people make that mistake.' These, then, are two effective pilots for the parallel paths that *Angel* will hope to travel: the cynical view of monsters as a metaphor for corporate America and the sitcom buddy-cop shenanigans of Angel and Spike, bound together by destiny. They're both TV series that would have a lot going for them individually. If the dichotomy of the two strands can mesh together, then this coming season could well be a sight to see. Future episode titles include 'Unleashed', 'Hellbound', 'Night of the Luchadors' and an, as yet untitled, episode featuring an appearance by Wesley's father, Roger.

Summing up *Angel*'s new direction, Greenwalt noted that it mixed in elements of *The West Wing* and *L.A. Law*. 'It's not going to be dreary and dark. To me it's like a brand new show.' Yet it's a show with a devoted fanbase that has followed various characters through the twists and turns of 144 *Buffy* episodes and 88 on *Angel*. Just in case you're as *sad* as me, that's approximately 10,000 minutes of our lives that we've spent watching these people over the last seven years. In becoming emotionally involved in *their* lives as they try to do what's right in the face of overwhelming odds. *Angel*, like *Buffy* before it, knows the value of creating characters with whom the audience empathise and identify. What the future has in store, we'll find out in a few short months.